Happily Ever After

Also edited by John Klima

Logorrhea: Good Words Make Good Stories

Electric Velocipede

HAPPILY EVER AFTER

EDITED BY

JOHN KLIMA

NIGHT SHADE BOOKS

SAN FRANCISCO

Cover design by Amy Popovich
Interior layout and design by Amy Popovich

An extension of this copyright page appears on pages 476-477

First Edition

Printed in Canada

ISBN: 978-1-59780-220-8

Night Shade Books
Please visit us on the web at
http://www.nightshadebooks.com

 *For Froggy*

Contents

Contents

INTRODUCTION

Bill Willingham

I have to confess I'm no good at writing a proper introduction, because, I'm in the storytelling business, which means I get to lie for a living, and I've become well practiced at it. But introductions are supposed to be true. After so many years, I despair if I have much unvarnished truth still in me.

I probably shouldn't bother telling you how good these stories are, because nobody reads a boring introduction in the process of making up one's mind on whether or not to buy the book. Since you've already committed yourself to reading the stories in the pages that follow, you'll discover on your own how delightful they are.

Truth is (and now we discover there seems to be some truth left in me, after all), what I'd really prefer to do is to tell you a story of my own (and thereby sneak my way in through the back door, into the august company that John Klima has gathered here).

So that's what I'll do. I'll tell you a story. And since this is the introduction, I guess I'll have to tell you a true one that actually happened to me. . .

A Night in the Lonesome November

Bill Willingham

The intruder was slim, of indeterminate age, and composed of ordinary parts. And he wasn't human.

It took me a moment to realize why. He moved too deliberately. He didn't fidget or shift about, even in the most minuscule ways that only register unconsciously. He sat motionless in my favorite chair, until he had a specific purpose for moving—to lift his (my) wineglass, for instance—at which point he acted with preternatural grace and deliberation. Even the most relaxed human can't do that.

"You have a lovely home," he said.

He'd opened my prized bottle of 1989 Château Pétrus. I was saving it for a special celebration—when I won a Hugo, or turned in my 200th issue of… Well, for some damned moment important enough to mark the occasion. Certainly not for a common home intrusion.

Or even an uncommon one.

"I'd be denounced for saying this," he continued, "but just between us, gentlemen of discretion that we are, our vines in the Fair Realm can't come close to what you can produce here in the Bright World. Perpetual twilight isn't conducive to the abundant growth of anything. Truth is we've been masking our deficiencies from the beginning, with powerful glamours, to preserve the myth of uncanny Faerie wines. But it's a losing game. Every year it takes more to achieve less."

He had a scabbarded rapier leaning against the side table, within easy reach. It had an elaborate silver basket hilt resembling the thorned twines of a rosebush, much scratched by what I feared was frequent use.

I mentally ran through the short list of weapons I owned for home protection, all of which were hopelessly out of reach, in my car, in the garage, or locked away in my bedroom.

"Believe me," he said, "if the Two Courts ever unite again, for one last martial extravagance, it will be an invasion of the Bright World, for the express purpose of capturing your vineyards. Won't happen though. Too much cold iron.

"More's the pity."

He finished the last sip of wine from his glass and rose from his seat, in a ridiculously fluid motion.

"I could happily go on all night about your truly splendid Earthly vintages, but I've got promises to keep and miles to go, and so on. Shall we be about our business then?"

"What business is that?" I said. I was trying for calm and reasonable, but I couldn't keep the obvious fear out of my voice.

"I'm Timon Aedre Aefentid, landed Knight of the Evening Stream, currently in service extant to Her Glorious Majesty, Queen Mab." He didn't bow, but it was included in the tone of his voice. "And I'm here to execute you for crimes against her Court."

"Why?" I backed up a step, and then another, and then ran out of room to retreat further. We were in my library-slash-writing room. My back was pressed against a wall of books. The only doorway out was at least three steps farther than I could expect to survive. I thought about screaming for help, but dismissed the idea. I'd picked this place to build my dream house because of its solitude. Woods, river and a barrier wall of limestone cliffs separated me from my closest neighbor.

"You write about us," he said.

"Excuse me?"

"You write fairy tales, Mr. Willingham, and you've gotten lamentably prolific at it in recent years."

"What's wrong with that?" I said. "I never knew you folks were real, and I think I've been pretty favorable, if not outright flattering."

"Doesn't matter," he said. "Writing about us at all is the crime. Every word diminishes us."

"How?"

He'd made no move to retrieve his sword yet. The thought of a length of steel piercing me, or cutting me open, was among the most horrifying things I could imagine. If talk failed, I wondered if I could at least talk him into using my handgun, for an instant flip-the-switch sort of ending.

"It wasn't always the case. In earlier ages, when mortals wrote about the Fair Realm, it strengthened us. Belief magic can be powerful, when generated by so many readers. What is it they call it now? Consensus Reality?"

"Then what's the problem?" I said. "If writing about you creates belief..."

"And there's the rub. You let your world get too modern. You educated your readership. Back in the days, pretty much anything in print was believed. But now readers are more sophisticated. Every one of them is acutely aware of the difference between fiction and non-fiction, and has been indoctrinated that fairy tales steadfastly belong in the realm of fiction. Now it's disbelief that is encouraged with each and every jot written and read. Like an organ turned malignant, what used to sustain us is killing us."

"Seriously?"

"You aren't convinced this is a serious matter yet? Better adapt soon. You've only seconds left to at least get your mind in order. I'm sorry to say there won't be time to order your affairs."

He turned his hand and there was a small glint of light. I noticed for the first time that a dagger had appeared there, sometime after he'd finished with my wine.

"Wait!" I cried. "Let's think this through!"

"We already have. The thinking and judging has been done. Explaining why I'm going to kill you is only a courtesy on my part. I believe a man should know why he's doomed to die, when practicable. But it's a personal philosophy only, not strictly required by courtly precedent."

"But now that I know the damage it's causing, I can stop writing about your world. I'll go back to superheroes and ray guns and rocket ships!"

"Too late."

"Or murder mysteries! I've been thinking about switching to mysteries!"

"I've scant faith in promises. This way ensures that you never write about us again."

He raised the dagger. I pressed myself back into the books, trying to disappear into them.

"But if you let me live, I can also spread the word! I'll get others to stop. I know most of those working in the field!"

"So do I," he said. "They're on the list. I'll get to each one of them eventually. Another reason to cut short the time I spend here."

He sounded impatient now. I realized my next argument would be my last. Better make it a good one.

"I'll help then!" I was practically whimpering by now. "What if, in return for letting me go, I were to get everyone else together? Wouldn't that be better—save you from traveling from one person to another, all the while they're still producing the work that's harming you?"

He'd been advancing on me, but now stepped back a half step.

"Oh? Tell me what you have in mind," he said.

"Everyone's going to be there. All the big guns, like Gaiman and Yolen and Maguire and de Lint." I started rattling off every name in the fairy tale business I could think of. "Nancy Kress. Peter Straub. Holly Black and Garth Nix, for God's sake! All the giants in the field, where I'm such small potatoes."

"You'd sell out dozens of your colleagues to save your own skin?" I swear I could hear both contempt and admiration in his voice.

"In a second," I said, with perhaps more enthusiasm than I care to admit today, but I did promise a true account of the evening. "Writers never really like each other anyway. Our insecurities get in the way."

"And you can get them all in one place?"

"It's already done. Klima did all the heavy lifting. I just need to find a way to weasel myself onto the guest list. But I've no shame about using my credentials to strong arm the fellow. One phone call and you save months of effort."

"Let's have one more glass of this very good wine, and discuss this a bit further." And so we did.

Which brings us to here and now. I'm not happy about it, Mr. Aefentid, and far from proud of myself, but I kept my promise. Thirty-three of the Bright World's best fairy tale writers, all in one place, and none suspects a thing. I trust you'll keep your promise too, and we won't have to see each other again.

The Seven Stage a Comeback

Gregory Maguire

Gregory Maguire is loved by millions of readers for his novel *Wicked*, a retelling of the characters from *The Wizard of Oz*, and its sequels—*Son of a Witch*, *A Lion Among Men*, and the forthcoming *Out of Oz*—as well as his novels *Confessions of an Ugly Stepsister*, *Lost*, and *Mirror, Mirror*. In addition to his excellent books for adults, Maguire has written more than a dozen books for children including *The Good Liar* and *Leaping Beauty*. Like the central theme of this anthology, Maguire often takes children's stories or fairy tales and provides his readers with a different take on the story. His interest in children's stories is not just an idle fancy as Maguire co-founded Children's Literature New England and serves as a board member for the National Children's Book and Literary Alliance.

His novel *Wicked* was made into a very successful Broadway musical. This is important to note as readers of the original version of "The Seven Stage a Comeback" may be surprised to find themselves reading a play. In early 2010, Maguire revised the story to be performed on stage for Company One, a resident company at the Boston Center for the Arts. Company One performed "The Seven Stage a Comeback" and six other retellings of Grimm Brothers' fairytales in the summer of 2010. As a testament to Maguire's writing skill, the story works as well as a play as it did as a story.

A one-act play in six scenes.

Setting. some nameless north European forest

Dramatis Personae

Line numbers assigned to characters, below, don't represent printed lines of text but approximate number of times the character speaks.

Seven dwarves:
1. The Leader (storyteller; kindly oldest one). 40 lines.
2. The Poet (maybe has half-specs to appear smart). 26 lines.
3. The Singer (token dwarf out of folklore). 19 lines.
4. The Gourmande (food, beer, cupcakes). 20 lines.
5. The Curmudgeon (antagonist). 39 lines.6. The Sergeant (sees the job gets done). 27 lines.
7. The Lamenter (blinded by grief, becomes sighted with joy). Few lines, a whole lot of moans.

Snow White: A young married woman, newly mature.
1 monologue

Props

an apple with a bite taken out of it;
1 glass coffin (this could be mimed: It is made of glass, after all! Thus invisible.)
1 rush-basket, about a foot high, with some soft cloth hanging over the side, as if a basket of laundry
various dwarfish things: a pick-axe, boots, hats, mittens, scarves, a lantern or two, a pike or staff or two, beer steins, etc.
1 silver guitar (small spray-painted child's guitar would do)
1 bundle of cloths or baby doll, to simulate SW's infant
a pipe or two

SCENE ONE:

Lights up, but dimly; it is nighttime.
In a small, cozy but disorganized room or a cave, seven dwarves are snoring. In unison, in sequence? Perhaps there is a candle in a lantern. Number 7 cries out in his sleep, a wordless utterance of sudden fear, evidence of a nightmare.

7. ——— (*wordless cry*)
1. (*Sits up.*)

What? What is it?

Others. What what what what what what what?

7. — *(Whimpers in a wordless complaint, a small voice.)*

6. *(Pushes aside the others, who are useless, crosses to 7, puts his ear next to 7's mouth, listens, nods, turns to the others, shrugs, makes air quotes as he speaks to indicate he is communicating 7's message; he speaks in a mocking voice.)*
"Where can she be?"

5. Are you for real? Can you remember nothing?

1. *(To 7)*
Calm down. You suffer the amnesia of sleep, nothing more. You're okay. We're right here.

5. All except *her.*
(7 wails briefly again at the thought.)

2. "Where can she be?" you ask? *(thinks.)* Good question for a midnight colloquy. Whatever has happened, she's passed to glory like nothing *we'll* ever know.

3. Tell us again, tell us, do tell.

1. Ahh, go on with you. You know the tale.

3. *(wheedingly)* But you tell it *so* well.

1. It's spilt milk, brothers. It's yesterday's rainbow. Why fasten on the empty caterpillar chrysalis when the butterfly has flown away?
(They put their heads together, mumbling incoherently and loudly, in questioning upstrokes of tone, in argument, all talking at once except 7, who moans, for ten seconds.)

1. *(Insistently.)* STOP. Whatever our history, there's no changing it now. *(incredulous).* You really don't remember?
(The others assume attitudes of rapt attention, except for 5, who fiddles with a pipe, his back mostly turned.)
(Ploddingly.) The man with the crazed expression claws open her coffin, kiss her awake, and, *foof* (*after he says this, he exhales in the manner of a French farmer, emphasizing action of the lips and up-ticking of his head*)...carries her off.

2. So much for our lovely daughter. *(Wipes his glasses on his beard.)* Here yesterday, gone yesterday.

5. *(turning to face his comrades.)* We're better off without her. Pathologically fickle.
(To 1.) I always told you that.
(To 2, 3, and then 4 and 6) And you, and you, and you two too.
(pointing to 7). You, I hardly bother. Mop up your nose.
(Gestures wildly at his own nose to make his point.)

2. How can you talk like that about her? She gave us meaning. She gave us purpose.

4. She gave us cupcakes.

5. She gave us orders. Wasn't she always on us about something?
"Can't you tidy the woodpile some?" "Hasn't anyone heard of a thing called

soap?" I don't trust little men who grow beards; they're trying to compensate." And then with the sighs. The expressive eyes. Followed by floods of agitated song—

3. Frankly, I liked the singing. *(Beat. They all look at him like he's nuts. Perhaps 6 makes the loco sign, forefinger twirling near his temple.)*

5. When she ate that poisoned apple? Oh, yes, I was sad, I cried—
But you want to know what else? I thought: *At last. A little peace and quiet around here.*

1. *(kindly; puts his hand on 5's shoulder.)*
So why are your eyes always rimmed with red? You loved her as we all did.

2. *(in transports, rhapsodic, clasping hands together at breast-height)*
Her with her lips like October apples, her hair like the wind on April nights.

5. (*pointing at 2*) You've been nipping at elvish brandy while we were asleep?

4. Oh, is brandy on the menu? Don't mind if I do.

2. (*in a more normal voice, to 5*) Ahh, you mutter about her because you like having someone to complain about. Makes you feel lofty.

5. Hey, haven't you noticed? Dwarves *don't get to feel lofty*. And anyway, don't name me my motivations. I don't have any.

2. You kept your vigil as I did.

1. *(placatingly)* As we all did.
So, frankly, and not to put too fine a point on it…

5. (*muttering, in 1's tone of voice, finishing his thought*)…what? *shut up?*

2. *(interrupting an old quarrel)*
And all that's left is the apple that fell from her lips and that glass crate we laid her in.

1. And if the occasional nightmare is proof of anything, our troubled hearts.

6. *(swaggeringly)* A plan, a plan. Dwarves like a plan. A scheme, a campaign…
We could—but what? Find out where she went ?

2. Pay her a social call? Show up as a big surprise? A reunion of the fraternity!

6. In her case, soldier, the term *fraternity* doesn't quite spread the mustard.

4. The old gang! Why not? I suppose there'd be refreshments?

3. *(musically, rhythmically)*
We're dwarves, not trolls. Let's face the facts.
We should be grabbing the pick and the axe
And wandering o'er the mountain tracks.
Sing ho! for the life of a dwarf.
(The other look at him. A beat.)

6. Let's junk the jaunty, singy bits this time, shall we? *(To 2)* But you: you're right. We need to move! On the count of seven. Out in the world, wreaking mayhem and mess…

5. Lining our pockets…*(rubbing his hands)*

4. Filling our bellies…*(rubbing his belly)*

3. Raising our voices and cheering the nation! *(raising his arms and punching the air, victory style)*

5. Cheating the gentry and souring the milk! *(mimes milking a cow.)*
6. A little exercise will serve us well. *(He stands.)*
(4 and 5 pick up beer steins, clink them)
On the count of seven, I said. One, two—
(sees the steins)—Beer. Well, men, that's not a bad idea, either. *(Sits again.)*
7. Oh, oh…
They all take a sip except 7. Pause, wipe their mouths, belch, sigh in contentment of a sort.)
2. (*Ruminatively.*) How did we get from there to here?
1. Now listen, guys. Though life hasn't been kind to us, we can muddle through. What's so odd about what we've done? We find an orphan girl, we take her in. Locate some moldy blankets to keep her warm. Porridge in the morning, porridge in the evening.
3. *(striking a pose, a little caper)*
A little dwarf folk music to cheer her up.
1. It was a humble life, but it was ours. And we shared it with her.
2. Every mildewy bit of it. No wonder we're still upset. We can't focus.
1. Well, we have to shape up. We're falling to pieces here.
5. *(shrugs)* Easy come, easy go.
2. You trade the sharpest insults, but you're the one who moans her name in your sleep. Face it. We all miss her.
(pause) When's the last time any one of us laughed out loud?
5. When she left our lives, she stole our laughter.
She's a thief. You know it. End of story.
4. But what can we do?
5. I say let's find out where she went. Let's drop in. We got the right. We earned the right.
4. Guess who's coming to dinner! But she better have high chairs.
1. We'll need a present. What could we bring her?
4. Cupcakes?
1. *She* made the cupcakes.
4. Porridge?
1. I think it was porridge that killed the marriage.
5. The poison apple?
(A beat) It's good as new. Don't you remember? We tucked the part she didn't eat into the casket with her. Though she scarpered, the apple is there still, fresh as sin. Why not return it to her? She's been out in the world a few months. She'll likely have come across a good use for that poison apple by now.
3. Our satchels and axes upon our backs
We'll wander o'er the mountain tracks.
Sing ho! For the life of a dwarf.
6. Please, would you stop your singing, please?
(indicating 7.) It's hard enough to think around Mister Weepy.
1. I still fear she might not want to see her old buddies.

5. We know too much? Is that it? *So what.* Face it. She left us high and dry when she married that traveling prince. She'll be regretting it, no doubt. She'll be thrilled to pieces to see us again.
2. They could be nine kingdoms away by now. It's been months already.
1. And we might never be able to find her.
6. I'm all for it. You know me—I'm one for putting on boots…
2. And marching impressively right off a cliff?
6. Better than sitting around with tears in our beards! Let me hunt for a map, a compass. *(Counts on his fingers)* We need gall and gumption, grit and nerve, stout hearts, resolve, and—*(pauses, not able to think of a seventh thing)*
4. Cupcakes?
(2,5,6). *She made the cupcakes*!
4. Well, then. Um. Mittens.
6. Up from your sloth, you miserable slugs. Pocket your bread and cork your ale! Tighten your belts and lace your boots.
Somebody grab the iron-head hammer. Somebody bring the silver guitar. Lord, it'll be good to get out for a stretch! The moment is here. We're off and away to pay a visit.
3. At least can we sing a marching song?
6. What are you putting in your mitten, you?
4. *(sheepishly)* Porridge?
6. (*to 7*) And you, are you weeping again, you fool? What is it? Early onset homesickness? We haven't even left yet.
7. Oh, oh, oh…

(Lights down as they begin arranging their things to travel)

SCENE TWO:

Lights up.
Outside the cave or house. It is autumn: red and gold, leaves on the ground, bare limbs, perhaps a pumpkin or two to indicate autumn. The dwarves appear one by one, prepared for a long trek.
1 and 4 emerge first.

1. Goodbye to the house in the autumn woods.
4. So long to our bachelor hideaway.
1. I hope our seeking her out isn't a lapse in etiquette.
2. There's no life left for us here. Our little house? It's nothing but a moldy old tomb. Not our tomb, but the grave and marker of what we lost when she went away.
(As 2 is speaking, 5 and 6 enter, either carrying or miming carrying a glass coffin at waist level, like pall bearers.)
1. What the hell are you doing with *that*?

5. We've put the bit of apple in the glass casket and closed it up again.
6. The coffin keeps things quick with life. And for a good long time, it seems.
1. I still think that as a house gift that a poison apple is a little—well—iffy. But wrapped in a *coffin*?
5. A poison apple could come in handy. You never know. Be ready, I say. Listen. We're not leaving home without it.
(1 pauses, puts out his hand, but is overruled by action.)
1. Well (*dubiously*) we cleave as seven, through muck and mayhem. We always have and we always will. So, if we must, hoist that casket upon your backs, and off we go, to live another tale I'll be able to tell the next time someone wakes up with a nightmare. But the coffin is ornamental only, fellows. Remember that.
6. Keep the pace, steady she goes.
Hup, one, two, and so on.
1. Now I name you the world as it dawns today, to collect it in my noggin for telling later. The air is cold, the light is wet. The clouds come in. The wind is…*(he licks his finger, holds it up around his head, turning it to judge, shrugs)*… the wind is high.
2. *(to 1).* Do you feel a sadness in your bones? This seems a shaky step to take. We're going to give her the glass coffin as—a souvenir of her early years? A housewarming gift? Sends the wrong message, don't you think? Dwarves don't give trinkets. Dwarves don't send cards. *Big* mistake.
4. I still think a pocket of porridge would have brought back happy memories, but does anyone listen to me? No.
1. *(Consolingly, to 2)* Don't worry. We won't step out of line. Remember, we did take her in when she was lost….
5. We lost her in our turn, when she betrayed our hospitality.
1. (*to 2*) She'll be overjoyed and surprised as hell.
2. (*to 1*) But are we losing ourselves as well?
5. (*mockingly*) "The sky is high, I'd like some rum
Because my freakin' bum is numb."
This isn't some nursery roundelay. We'll find our beauty where she rests, and invite her to return with us.
(The others stop in their tracks for two or three beats)
5. *(continuing, arrogantly, aggressively?)* What? What's wrong with that? Surely she can entertain the thought? The least she owes us is a little loyalty. She never should have eaten the apple, one, nor, two, gone off with the first available prince.
1. (*again, placatingly*) Beauty is as beauty does.
5. What kind of beauty abandons her friends? She'd be (damn) lucky to find us unlocking the door for her a second time.
2. But why would she want to come back? Whatever did she see in us?
5. She thought us small because we are short. She thought us needy. She thought us oafish. Well, you guys are small and oafish. I—*(lowers his eyes modestly)*—

I—am magnificent.

1. We were small, and needy. No shame in that.

3. *(with false jollity, trying to shift the mood)*
A casket is just some bric-a-brac
We're carrying o'er the mountain track.
Sing ho! for the life of a dwarf.

1. You're not talking coercion, I hope.

6. Course not. It's more like persuasion.

1. I hope so. I don't endorse any cruel idea.

5. We work as one. You know that. We're seven. We separate at our peril. As you always remind us. So sit and dither and imperil yourself if you like. I'm forging ahead.
(They start up again, 1 shaking his head.)

6. *(the drill sergeant now, in a sing-song army base voice)*
(maybe the dwarves repeat each line after him, except 7, who wails without words instead?)
I don't know but I've been told

All (but 7). I don't know but I've been told

6. She looked sweet but what a scold.

All (but 7). She looked sweet but what a scold.

6. Anyone leaves her friends behind

All (but 7). Anyone leaves her friends behind

6. Gotta be outa her friggin' mind.

All (but 7). Gotta be outa her friggin' mind.

6. Steady boys; don't lock the knees.
Minds on your business, if you please.
Hey ho!

All (but 7). Hey ho!

6. Hey ho!

All (but 7). Hey ho!

3. *(a little desperately)*
Sing ho! For the life of a dwarf.
(They're starting to march offstage.)

1. *(almost to himself)* I *did* like her company. *I* was grateful for a little variety in my social circle. Things can get a little predictable around here with this lot. (*in singsong, echoing the rhythm of "hey ho," above.*) Ho hum, ho hum.
(Lights down.)

SCENE THREE:

(Lights up.
Mountains; perhaps leaves scatter from above in the wind.
This is a quick scene, begins when the first dwarf processes on from stage left or right, the others in single file behind him, two of them hoisting the coffin, and ends as the last one

leaves the stage in procession.)

4. On top of her sudden evacuation from our midst, this: she's dragging us to kingdom come for our reunion. She better have one fine banquet on hand to restore us. I'm in the mood for some bacon and beans.

5. Have I mentioned that we're better off without her? Her debts are mounting. She owes us. Big time.

1. *(almost to himself)* The wind on the mountain chills my heart. I fear the clouds are seeded with snow.

2. The snow will be white as her death-pale skin.

3. Sing ho! for the life of a dwarf. Not much rhymes with dwarf, does it? I can't make it work.

1. Does our merry band make a touch of menace as we go? Ho hey, make way.

2. If we cling to the affection we learned from her, we make good.

3. Song has no opinion about goodness. Make music.

4. *I* have no opinion about goodness. Make cupcakes.

5. We're dwarfs, not stunted angels. Make mischief.

6. Make sense, make time, make tracks. Look sharp.
(to 7)
I'll smash your head with the iron-head hammer if you don't stop your infernal racket.

7. Oh, oh, oh…

Others: *(mocking him, joining in, even 1 this time)*
Ohhhh, ohhh, ohhhh!
(They move off. Lights down.)

SCENE FOUR:

(Lights up. Icy ravine; deep snow. Dwarves in caps and mittens and scarves.

1. Just ahead, a precipice to cross. If we dropped the coffin in the snow, that's the end of it. It's clear as light and it would become invisible. Better to turn back. No? It's not too late. Look, this was a smart effort, but no use throwing good money after bad. I say, who's for heading home, and a nice round or two of ale to seal the memory?

4. Would there be onion rings back home, I wonder?

5. *(who by now is gunning to rival 1 for leadership.)* Sure, we're better off without her. That's my motto and I stick to it. But by now, I'd rather have our say with her. I'll be the one to ask her how she could leave us high and dry.

4. Well, hardly high. We're dwarves, after all.

2. We're only friends who come a-calling. What's wrong with that? The coffin's handy. We can give her a ride. We'll ask her to rejoin us. We'll give her the choice.

5. Or not.

(*beat. 1 approaches 5 and stares him in the eye, from very close up.*)
The coffin's just her size.

1. What? Abduct our own daughter? Are you mad?
2. He's crazed with travel weariness. It's called leg lag.
5. Hey, I'm not one for kidnapping old friends. But *I* didn't run off with the first prince to offer me a kiss.
3. I suspect that offer has yet to be tendered. You're hardly the glass of fashion and the mold of form.
1. Her youth and innocence is no excuse for monstrous behavior. I'll have no part in this campaign.
5. We separate at our peril, remember?
(*5 has 1 here. Tentatively they begin to move again, 1 shaking his head.*)
3. *(nervously, interrupting abruptly, to change the subject, lift the mood)*
The coffin weighs upon our backs
And makes too steep these snowy tracks.
Sing oy— for the life of a dwarf.
5. and 6: Cut out that noise! *(and)* For the last time, stow it!
3. *(nervously, in a wobbly voice)* Jingle bells?
1. I see that the ice that prickles in the nose and crusts the eyes over is invading our dwarfish hearts. Against my higher hopes, we grow ready to make trouble.
2. I fear what we're about, but I can't stop. We're bewitched; no more, no less.
6. Snow drifts are no friend to a three-foot dwarf.
4. Her beauty calls us; we can't escape. Is that our fault, or hers?
7. Oh, oh, oh, oh, oh.
(6 reaches forward and ties the scarf around 7's mouth, muffling his moans.)
(Lights down.)

SCENE FIVE.

(Lights up.
Outside an inn. Dwarves 1 through 6 have shucked their winter gear. 1 hurries in.)

3. *(To 1)* You're back! Well done.
5. I half believed you'd scarper.
1. Seven days don't make a week if Wednesday takes a holiday. We're seven together, for good, for ill. My penance is my protection.
3. Tell us what you saw when you hurried ahead.
2. Yeah, tell us.
1. *(In storyteller mode, trying to create a spell, to change minds even at this stage.)* Here in the inn-yard, huddled about a fire, a tankard of watered beer, we take our rest. The winter months have given us dark thoughts, but time brings us a hopeful spring. No? Today I learn that the girl we seek lives just beyond the ridge, in a noble home. No dragons to guard the moat, no spells to break. No annoying brambles a hundred feet high. No demons to lurk upon the several

roofs. Nothing to offend a dwarf. We could wave from a distance, leave the apple somewhere for her to find as a surprise, and hightail it home in seven winks. The better weather will secure us a quicker return.

4. You noticed a healthy kitchen fire ablaze, I trust? Could you smell anything cooking on the hob that seemed a little divine? Nothing short of irresistible?

6. *(Ignoring 4, in a tense, bitten off voice, Iago-like)*
Nothing to stop us from going the final steps. Here we'll commit what crime we may, and live to rue, or praise, the day.

7. Oh, oh.... *(he moans softly through the rest of the scene, drawing little attention to himself.)*

5. Let's give her the poisoned sleep and lock her within her windows. We're better off without her. What's dead can't live to leave us again. We love her too much to allow her to live.

1. If we proceed, gentlemen, we obscure all our earlier charity.

6. Why measure a troll against a god? Face it. We're smaller than human men, with smaller hearts. Our strength is in mighty arms, for smashing rocks. We aren't built to know what's right or wrong. We're hardly more than pagan animals.

1. *(a last ditch effort)* We met her when she was young, we took her in—

5. —as much to serve us at our filthy home as out of any wish to tend the poor. Don't revise our cunning into compassion.

6. Let's finish the job we started, and shed no tears for being smaller creatures than we'd like. Up to the mansion, then, to take her home. Let those who want to cherish her incorruptible form.

5. I'm in for the action, but as to worshiping a corpse, I've got better things to do.

6. The glassy walls of the coffin are polished clear, and the apple awaits to do its lethal job. Now we to our work, and she, our beauty—she to *her* work, again, at last, forever.

3. Let's lift the coffin from our backs
And see what sleeper it attracts.
Sing ho! for the life of a dwarf.

1. *(despondently, almost to himself)*
Choose a minor key, friend; the time is approaching for a dirge.

2. *(to 1)* Steady. Together in right, together in wrong.

6. We're decided then; the deed is clear. The time is now.
We leave to claim our prize.
(7 buries his face in his hands. 1 consoles him but doesn't protest further. They rise to leave. Lights down.)

SCENE SIX:

Lights up. An orchard. The young woman sits on a stool, sewing or doing needlework; a basket about a foot high, with some soft cloth draping out one side, is at her feet. She hums a little as the dwarves come on in a wide circle from stage right and left.

1. There she sits, in an orchard soft with blossom. Who could have thought she'd be more beautiful than memory could picture?

5. We're better off—we're better off—we're better—

4. You stutter out of shock. And me—I've lost my appetite. Was she always this splendid?

6. Hush, lest she hear us before we make our approach. Stealth, brothers, stealth.

2. Her hair is longer, see how the wind enjoys it! See how her smile blossoms. She looks aside, shyly, at mending collected inside the basket that rests in the fragrant grass near her pretty feet.

1. She always favored the household task. She sang when she worked. Who can forget her voice? But once I wondered, bringing the silver guitar, if she sang to keep her spirits high.
As if we were not the world she truly wanted, however sweet our accompaniment, fierce our protection, rewarding our everlasting porridge.

6. Now let us creep up closer to observe. Softly, gentlemen, if you please.

3. Sing ho, sing ho, sing ho, sing ho.
Off with the girl and away we go.

1. She smiles upon the laundry with a certain radiance.

4. I always thought she preferred baking to laundry.

1. She stirs the cloth as if something lies gently within,

2. A bruisable apple, a blossom? A porcelain toy?

6. Now is the time. There's nobody else around. At the count of three, we leap from these thickets, see. Surround her—

5. Confound her—

2. Astound her—

5. Accuse her—

6. One—two—

7. *(not softly, but the woman never looks up; she can't hear them. A rising volume throughout the opening utterance.)*
Three is the number we never expected. Yes, you will listen, all of you! Hear me out. It isn't just the prince and his beauty we come to disturb. That basket of washing is laughing at its mother. Are you wholly blind? *There's a child within.* One step more, and I'll swing this iron-head hammer at your skulls. I'll smash the coffin seven directions to heaven. Peril to come, or no.
(softer now)
Dwarfish mischief we make, and dwarfish music, but mischief and music never draw closer together than in the laugh of an infant adoring its mother.
(The dwarves close in around her. We can't see her now, since they are the same height as she is. Perhaps she has bowed her head toward the basket. Perhaps the other six dwarfs drone softly as each speaker in his turn declaims his couplet. Whatever music we devise, it should last ten, fifteen seconds, to allow for the appreciation that a change of heart, or hearts, has occurred. The end should be

stately, ceremonial, almost liturgical, like a baptism, a sacrament.)

1. We come from distant regions, cold and wild,
To bring you dwarfish music for your child.
2. We come to see what loneliness is worth;
It risks new life upon the ancient earth.
4. We smash the casket of your former life
Seeing you grown to woman, mother, wife.
3. The dwarf is ancient, and his song is sung
To demonstrate the glee in being young.
Sing ho! for the life of a child.
5. And if you can't perceive a thing about us,
It may be that you're better off without us.
6. Standing as near we dare, given our station,
We sing you blessings, thanks, and consolation.
7. All of us loved you as much as we could grieve.
As hard as we could do, each in our way.
Now hand me the silver guitar, and I will play
The final notes before we take our leave.

(The woman picks up the baby and stands, looking out, beyond and over the heads of the dwarves. She doesn't see them. Then she looks down at her baby, cradling it in her arms.)

Mother: *(not in a singsong, but in prose rhythms.)*
What do you say? Shall we make some cupcakes today?
But it's almost too nice to go inside.
After this horrible winter, how sweet the spring! It's as if the wind is strumming invisible harps.
Mmmmmm. I'm being silly, full of fancy. Like a child. But the light is such a welcome visitor. Pinkish, rosy, slanting through the blossoms of the orchard. How I love the blossoms of apples.
The morning light reminds me of a dream I must have had. As if I had lived somewhere else, once upon a time. I never did of course. I was always here; awake; and in my life. With my beloved within the sound of my voice, and my baby at my breast, smiling as if at some mysterious joke, some secret only babies know.

(She lifts the baby to her bosom. The dwarves begin to inch backward into the shadows.)

Smiling—how babies smile!—as if the *happily ever after* of stories begins right now, at the very start of life.

(She begins to sing a song, a string of nonsense syllables, maybe even oh-oh-oh-oh-oh's, in harmony with and beginning a fourth above the drone of the dwarves, as the lights fade.)

The music begins to fade. The dwarves to back away. Lights begin to come down. The mother lifts the baby closer to her face.)

And in Their Clad Rags

Genevieve Valentine

Genevieve Valentine's fiction has appeared or is forthcoming in *Clarkesworld*, *Strange Horizons*, *Journal of Mythic Arts*, *Fantasy Magazine*, *Electric Velocipede*, and *Apex*, and in the anthologies *Federations*, *The Way of the Wizard*, *Running with the Pack*, *Teeth*, and more. Her nonfiction has appeared in *Lightspeed Magazine*, Tor.com, and *Fantasy Magazine*. Her first novel, *Mechanique: A Tale of the Circus Tresaulti*, is forthcoming from Prime Books in 2011.

Valentine is a writer that I've recently discovered and every piece I read from her is stronger than the last. This is the first of several retellings of Little Red Riding Hood in this anthology. Valentine has set her version in the 1920s which gives it a rather *Great Gatsby* feel in my opinion.

Amelia Howard, it was later agreed, had done very well for herself after that first fellow. That sharp-faced singer had stood in for the lead and done it badly; he couldn't be heard above the violin and slicked back his fox-red hair with shaking hands between verses. The night Amelia came she watched him padding about in the circle of gaslight, never looked away, never applauded.

Two weeks later, when the show moved north to Boston, Amelia went with it.

"Poor thing," declared Margaret Cavendish, and most of New York agreed with her. Amelia was broad-faced and thick-armed, the daughter of inauspicious parents, and after admitting a certain determination in her character, there was nothing more to be said about her.

Ten years later, Amelia returned as the wife of a banker, some middle-of-the-road man who'd come into money in Boston. Without so much as renting on the Upper East Side they settled into a house on the Island near Blue Point, surrounded by a gate and a large, dark wood.

"Ambitious," muttered Margaret Cavendish.

New York was even more surprised a year later when the banker passed away, and Amelia moved into the city with a daughter in tow.

If the daughter was a little tall for a child of eight, she'd had the good luck to inherit her mother's chestnut hair, which quieted the gossip about her parentage. Amelia did away with the remaining rumormongers by opening her dining room for three parties that winter, each more exclusive than the last. New York changed its mind about Amelia's suitability, and even if Margaret Cavendish wanted to cast aspersions about the child, Amelia's short guest lists kept her silent.

With each passing year the parties became smaller until only a select few ever set foot within the townhouse, and the Island property, which no one had ever seen, became legend. Gradually New York accepted that the estate was unattainable, and as the townhouse opened its doors regularly, most of New York was appeased.

Twenty years after Amelia had eloped with the opera singer, she had a fortune, a widowhood, and the most powerful invitations in New York.

"Ridiculous," whispered Margaret Cavendish when she was sure she was alone.

Amelia's daughter Anna married at eighteen; a promising young architect stepped forward for her, and Anna went into marriage as quietly as she'd sulked around the dinner parties. Amelia retired to the Island House and gave her daughter the apartment as a wedding present.

Almost immediately, the family legend sank. It was impossible to remember what Mrs. Graves looked like, she was so unremarkable. One or two families hired Mr. Graves to modernize their summerhouses, just to get a look at him; they said he had been leonine, with wide pale eyes and a serious air, but he was as quiet as his wife and no one ever found out another thing about him.

When their daughter was born, she was to be the only child; a family takes after itself, everyone knew. Mr. and Mrs. Graves found an early end of influenza five years afterwards, and there was little sadness and no surprise. There was nothing else to expect from the Howards.

It was that spring's dullest chore to pay respects to Amelia Howard and the fidgety little girl who sat at the far end of the parlor, swinging her legs and looking out the window like a simpleton.

Alice Graves was sent away to boarding school, and was written off as the final failure of a promising dynasty.

After that, no one in New York gave Amelia Howard a thought for ten years, and would have gone on not thinking of her if the invitations hadn't arrived.

It was 1925, and Amelia Howard was holding a weekend party beginning the Fourth of September, in the Island House, to close out the summer.

The typesetting and the paper were the same as they had always been, and stirred the same vicious politeness as ever, and all other plans for that weekend were cancelled. The first look inside the Island House was not to be missed. New York pitied the poor souls who had the abysmal timing to be on the Continent and were unable to catch a boat in time. Margaret Cavendish had the unique honor of canceling her own planned event and RSVPing for Mrs. Howard, with pleasure.

The interest generated by the invitations verged on the obscene; dressmakers and tailors as far as Boston were overrun, and car sales boomed. (Unthinkable to pull up to the Island House in a cab.) Two or three seamstresses took early retirement from the strain of beading twenty calf-length dresses on two months' notice.

In between fittings, New York muttered how it was abominably rude for Amelia to have decamped all those years back without a word about her tastes. When hosting she had been always politely and unremarkably dressed, and no one recalled seeing her in anything less formal. The last thing anyone remembered were the calls of condolence, and two or three women who had ordered dresses in black wondered if they were making a mistake.

Through the primping and the pandering and the preparations, no one ever thought to ask what had driven Amelia Howard to open the doors of the big glass house in the center of the dark wood.

Alice Graves was the only girl in her class who hadn't adopted the Marcel, and the man stepping off the train behind her caught her long hair in his pocket watch.

"I'm so sorry!" he said, pulled four long dark hairs out of the hinge. "You must think—"

She pinched the hairs in two fingers before he could throw them away. "These are mine."

He looked at her sidelong and disappeared into the crowd. Probably looking for his girl, Alice thought. Guys with pocket watches always had a girl on their arms; Ethel and Clara both had men like that who picked them up on the weekends from right in front of school, in front of the parents. Those girls were dumb as dirt.

She slid the four hairs into her purse. Never throw anything like that away, Grandmother Amelia had told her when she was three or four.

"Your grandfather," she'd said, "could do amazing things with one strand of hair."

In the cab, Alice opened her handbag (too big for the fashion, but she made do with last year's things) and pulled Amelia's last letter from between the pages of *A History of Paris*.

It was four months old, and threatening to fall apart at the creases where she had folded it too carefully.

Dearest Alice,

I received your grades; not bad, though I wish you'd try harder in math. How do you think you're going to make it studying in university without being able to add?

Can't wait to see you at last when you come for the party. I've arranged for you to drive over something a little particular—I know you can handle it, it's only a trunk with some refreshments, a little something just to see the last night through.

Amelia Howard.

"Miss Alice," Thomas greeted from the front desk of the apartment building, "welcome back. Your grandmother sent a parcel, and a box arrived from Bloomingdale's. There are also two trunks that arrived; from school, I presume."

Thomas presumed a lot of convenient things. It was why her grandmother liked him so much.

Alice folded her arms on the counter and slid a flat amber bottle across it, label up. "Would you mind having those trunks loaded into my car, Thomas? I'll be an hour."

Thomas glanced at the French lettering and tucked the bottle into his jacket.

"Of course, Miss."

In the apartment, Alice sliced off the box strings. Her grandmother had sent a dress of gray chiffon, long and studded with sequins.

A note was attached to the top of the box. "Careful with the hem in the car. See you Saturday."

Alice smiled, set the box aside, and opened the parcel from Bloomingdale's. The velvet burnoose was lipstick-red ("Exotic Intrigue from the Orient!" the catalog claimed, "Topped with Tassels of Finest Silk!"). It was machine-made, but Alice hoped Grandmother wouldn't object. Red was red.

The cape made her look older than fifteen, made her look like her mother and her grandmother, and she turned in the mirror, watching the moon of her face turn into the mountain range of her profile, the strong brow and wide thin lips that belonged to some other age. She didn't know how to make the Cupid's bow with her lipstick, and her mouth looked like a fresh cut in her face.

In the lobby, Thomas took in the red cape, her red lips, her silver shoes.

"Have a lovely evening, Miss."

The car was always unfamiliar her first few days back from a term, and she was grateful she'd always had sharp eyes in the dark. It was at least three hours to the summerhouse, and she didn't want to risk getting lost; the woods were dark, and the road narrow.

She glanced at the backseat, where the two trunks were propped like passengers.

One trunk had her clothes in it; the other had two grand in contraband with the labels all in French.

A little something just to see the last night through.

The benefit of being a day late to a party was that there weren't a lot of cars full of nosies on the way across the Island.

The engine roared and the car sputtered into the traffic, headed through the woods to Grandmother's house.

The little house in the center of the wood was built by a man who made his fortune in glass, and what he lacked in imagination he'd made up for in passion for his livelihood; the house stood three stories high, with glass windows nearly floor-to-ceiling in every wall. It sat at the edge of the water, with the front door bravely facing the woods and the back doors leading down to the dock, and when the house was freshly washed Amelia Howard could stand in her third-floor gallery and see only water stretching out before her.

To a woman of imagination, this view would have been a glass ship on a quiet sea, a floating palace, a bird's nest. Amelia Howard, utterly unburdened with imagination, saw only that the sun was setting behind the water line, and that her back lawn was covered in picnickers.

She sighed down at the lawn, where she was certain one of the dogs was going to choke on a stray chicken bone before the weekend was over.

Mrs. Howard kept four Irish hounds on the property; Margaret Cavendish had seen them yesterday on her arrival and cooed over them.

"Oh, aren't they darling! Such an English-country-house air, Amelia, how quaint of you."

Those who thought more kindly of Amelia Howard dismissed the idea she was putting on airs, and suggested the four beasts served as guards for the extensive and lonely property. Mrs. Howard kept a small household; if there was no gatekeeper, at least there were four sentries.

Out on the lawn, people had started to pack up their baskets; it was the hour between afternoon and dinner, and the race was on to be fashionably late. Margaret Cavendish, on her way inside, knelt to pick up a stray chicken bone.

Amelia looked at her feet, where the four hounds lay curled.

"Time to get dressed, boys. Only an hour till dinner, and you can finally meet Alice."

The biggest of the hounds, so pale his fur was nearly white, thumped his tail twice on the ground.

The dress she'd had made for the evening was a deep blue Japonaise that bordered on the matronly, but she couldn't be bothered to girdle, and she approved of the simple lines of the dress, the fall of the kimono sleeves. There were no rosettes, no pleats, no sparkle—she left beads to the young and flashy. Her only adornment was a draped diamond necklace and two sapphire earrings.

"Good enough," she told the mirror, and behind her the hounds rose together in a knot of sleek movement, swam around her as she made for the stairs.

Night was coming, and they were all expecting Alice.

Alice's eyes were better than her headlights, which was why saw the man in the tuxedo just before she hit him.

The car squealed as she yanked the brake, pulled on the wheel, and the thing scudded to a halt perpendicular to the road. The trunks slid across the backseat and banged into the door frame, and there was the tinkle of broken glass. Under the hood, the engine shuddered and died.

"Yipes," she breathed. Her heart pounded in her ears.

When she looked out her window to see how dead he was, he was standing right where he had been, looking at the hood of the car like he'd been timing something.

Then he laughed.

Alice frowned. "Hey! What's wrong with you? You lit or something?"

He was tall and thin, and beneath his open coat he was wearing a tuxedo. On his way to Grandmother Amelia's; there was no other reason to be dressed like that out here at night.

When he looked at her he smiled, and the hair on the back of her neck stood up.

"No," he said (low voice, easy voice, like he hadn't almost been killed a second ago). "Everything's fine."

She was baffled. "I almost ran you over."

"Sorry about that. I was on my way to the Howard party and my car broke down, but I'm so late that nobody else was coming by. They all showed up yesterday. So, figured I would walk."

"Can't be that great a party."

He grinned, white teeth gleaming in the headlamps. "It's supposed to be. In any case, the walk there is better than the walk back to the city, if you've got to walk."

The crickets filled in the silence where she was supposed to offer up the passenger seat.

"Or," he said finally, "you could give me a ride and we'll be there in an hour, and we can find out for ourselves."

"I don't think that's a very sharp idea," she said, knowing as she spoke that it was a lost cause; she'd have to crank the car to get it going again, and if she got out of the car that would be it for her.

He must have known it too, because he smiled and said, "Let me get us started," held out his hand for the crank.

After a long moment she handed it over. He winked and walked to the front of the car.

The engine roared to life, and in the time it took Alice to throw the car into reverse he was sliding into the passenger seat. This close she could see his sharp face, dark eyes, his wide smiling mouth.

"I don't think my grandmother is going to like this," she said.

He grinned. "She might surprise you," he said, pulled a silver cigarette case from his jacket. "Smoke?"

She turned the car silently, and they were a mile down the road before she said, "I don't know your name."

"James," he said. "You smoke?"

"Do I look old enough to smoke?" Clara told her she looked younger than her age ("You'd be perfect for a friend of Tom's", Clara always said), but in the cape she might look older. She felt older. The question came out like a challenge.

"Well, you don't look old enough to be driving that liquor around in your backseat, but I've been fooled before." He held up the cigarettes.

She'd smoked before—it was what you did when you turned fourteen, and no matter how much the chaperones searched the cigarettes constantly blossomed in people's hands like magic. Smoking wasn't a problem. And for sure she didn't want him to think she was a kid (God knew what he'd do with all that liquor in the back if he thought there was nothing she could do to stop him). But he said it like he was offering her more than a smoke, and she licked her waxy lips, shook her head no.

James grinned and popped the case open, slid out a lighter and two cigarettes. "You sure, kiddo?"

Kiddo. Damn.

"Yeah," she said, "I'd love one."

He smiled, put both cigarettes in his mouth, and lit them from a single flare.

"Nice trick," she said.

"You've seen it before?"

"Ethel's guy can light four. He tries to impress us all the time, hands them out like party favors."

"Did you take them? Or were you waiting for a guy of your own to light one for you?"

"If I were waiting for a guy of my own," she said, then stopped, frowned out at the dark. He wasn't the person to tell about this kind of thing.

She pulled her long hair from behind her ear so it fell in a curtain over her face, so that when she glanced at him she was shielded from his look.

"One smoke, coming up." He slid closer to her and lifted the cigarette to her pressed red lips.

Alice's knuckles went white against the steering wheel. This close she could smell soap, could smell the tang of tobacco on his breath, and she thought for a long time about opening her mouth for it (for him) before she unwrapped one hand from the wheel and pinched the cigarette out of his hand.

"Nice try," she said, voice shaking.

He sat back (closer than he had been before) and smiled. "Just trying to be helpful."

She leaned back like it was nothing, but under the red burnoose her heart pounded, and she could smell cap and bark and leaves on his tuxedo. Ahead of them the woods shone in a sharp circle of light, the wide encroaching dark.

Amelia had based her dinner menu on the meal the Waldorf Hotel served to Coolidge. It was not an inspired selection, but it was impressive: the anchovy canapés, the fresh asparagus, the lamb medallions, the rose-petal-wrapped chicken breasts. By the time the waiters brought out Venetian ice cream and champagne even Margaret Cavendish could find nothing to say, though she did leave her chicken untouched as a matter of principle. "Roses on the outside and matching pink on the inside," she said to her neighbor. "One really must hire a cook one can trust. I don't believe in the once-hires."

Her neighbor raised his fluted glass for champagne.

Margaret raised her glass as well; it was one thing to be dissatisfied with the main course, and quite another to refuse good champagne.

After the first glasses were empty Amelia stood up from the head of the table. The four dogs stood, too, pulling themselves up out of nowhere, and Margaret shuddered; the way they moved worried her.

"Ladies and gentlemen," Amelia said, "it's good to see your faces again; thank you all so much for coming. However, I've never liked long speeches on a full stomach; the ballroom is open, with dance music, dessert, and other…refreshments."

"I hear she has everything," someone near Margaret whispered.

"I want bourbon," someone else whispered. "It's been ten years. I'd kill for a bourbon."

In the next room, the band struck up "Just Like a Melody Out of the Sky", and those who had anticipated dancing slid off their chairs and moved for the ballroom.

The ballroom was the crowning glory of the house; it took up one whole wall of windows, and from it one could look out the back of the house to the water, or out the front to the herd of cars that, in the candlelight, seemed to be nudging each other to get a closer look. The floor was inlaid in the Roman style—the glassmaker had studied the Classics—and at one end the ten-piece band was playing.

The ballroom's floor-to-ceiling windows would soon be shut tight with velvet drapes against the cold, but for one last summer evening the room was alive with light, and the reflections of the couples danced like ghosts on the lawn.

The first cigarette burned down to the filter without Alice taking a single drag. She clenched it between damp fingers and wished she could do something about this guy; wished she could know exactly what she wanted to do.

James sat quietly and smoked his cigarette, looking at her and the road, watching her drive without really looking where they were going. He kept one leg propped against the doorjamb, and once in a while he tried awkwardly to stretch, and then his long legs filled the passenger side until he curled back in on himself.

She kept one hand on the gearshift and one hand on the wheel, because when he shifted on the seat his tux whispered, and she didn't want to be tempted to touch it.

It was the first time she'd been so alone with a man—Miller, the headmaster, was the only man in the school and he was sixty-five, and even he kept his office door open when he had to call her in.

James had a sweet voice, a low voice, and she was afraid of what she might answer if he asked.

"You must be the life of the party," he said. "Watch it; you'll burn your fingers."

She pinched the butt in her fingers and pushed it awkwardly out the crack in the window. "I wouldn't know," she said.

"You don't like parties?" He snorted a laugh. "You picked the wrong night to visit your grandmother."

"When Grandmother invites, you go," she said. That was obvious; Headmaster Miller had let her leave just four days before the start of term, and just as he was dismissing her from his office he'd angled for an invitation to the Friday afternoon lawn-tennis tournament.

James pulled out two new cigarettes and tapped them idly against the box. "Darling girl, don't sound so burdened. Worse things could happen to a girl than being invited to a party."

The statement had the undertone of someone who desperately wanted to always be at a party, but Alice shrugged. She liked the talkies, which Grandmother allowed, but the parties on the screen looked staged and uncomfortable, stiff glad rags scraping the ground. Alice preferred a good mystery, or an adventure.

"I want to go to university," she said. "Work in a museum. I want to study."

"And what does Grandmother say?"

"She said we'll discuss what to do during the Christmas holidays, that we'd make a plan for my future." She smiled at the dark road ahead, happy to think of university, remembering Grandmother like a talisman. "I'm sure I'll go to university for my studies."

He rested his hand on her knee (how had he gotten so close?) and his voice was soft and low when he asked, "Are you going to fly away, clever little bird?"

She flushed, felt her pulse under her skin like the fluttering of wings.

"Light me a cig," she said, so he'd do something else with his hands.

"Happy to." He held up a new cigarette and lit it off the cherry of his old one, never lifted his left hand from her knee.

He handed it over and she took a drag off it, let the smoke curl through her. Under his gaze a crackle of electricity slid up her back, and she inhaled the next three drags faster than she should have.

He couldn't be much older than twenty. It wouldn't be so bad; not like Clara's man who was nearly thirty. James was young enough, maybe, to be a beau.

Too young for this party, anyway.

"How do you know my grandmother?"

"I don't. Got the invite through my family—no one else was able, so they suited me up and sent me out."

He'd pulled his bow tie undone, and his collar was drooping.

"And you borrowed your grandfather's tux," she said.

"Couldn't find a tailor."

Grandmother's last letter had mentioned all the tailors were booked. Alice's silver sequins had been ordered months back, before the invitations had gone out, just to be sure it would be ready.

At least it's comfortable enough to move in."

"You know how to dance?"

He grinned. "You'll find out when we get there."

So it was yes. She'd known already. You just knew when a guy could dance. Clara's guy could really dance; from the moment he stepped out of his car everyone could see that he knew how to move. The first time he'd brought Clara back from a weekend they'd danced in the parking lot at four in the morning on a Monday, and Alice had put out the candle in her window and watched them swaying back and forth in silence, his face bent to her hair.

"I like foxtrot," she said. She imagined James's right arm sliding around her, the smell of his neck under his open collar, the sound of his voice in her ear.

He looked at her with hunter's eyes. "My favorite."

The cigarette tasted sweeter this time, and when she breathed in the smoke mixed with the forest smell of his neck. It was as though he were kissing her, and she let the smoke linger in her mouth.

It was less than half an hour to the house; the smell of the sea was already rolling in over the road, little hints of salt air. Only half an hour. All she needed was the shelter of Grandmother's house.

"You look like you're dreaming, darling girl."

Alice looked over at James, blinked as if she was coming out of a dream.

"You have a hair on your suit," she said.

The champagne ran out at ten o'clock, but the band launched into a Charleston just in time, and after "Happy Feet" everyone was so desperate for a drink that they didn't think to complain about the tumblers of Coca-Cola mixed in with the champagne flutes. Amelia declined a dance with a shipping magnate and excused herself into the front hall, where the grandfather clock (a too-old throwback to younger days) ticked steadily forward, and still no sign of Alice.

One of the dogs pushed its snout under her hand, trying for comfort. She scratched his ear.

They had another half hour to reach the party before Amelia sent the dogs out looking for them. Maybe a little longer; it was difficult to balance the timing of the party with her own curiosity. It had been a long time since she had seen Alice.

It was a pity, but it had been necessary to bide her time and regroup after Anna's spectacular failure as a Howard—or as a Graves, for that matter.

Perhaps Anna would have rallied herself if she had lived to see her daughter easing into the world; if Anna had realized how important it was to present a mystery to people who were bored enough to need one. But one could only judge by the evidence, and Anna had been quiet as a mouse, the little dullard, right through the day sickness swallowed her up.

The dogs sprawled at her feet, and she looked out onto the dark shells of the cars packed across her lawn, waiting for one last pair of headlights.

Amelia wondered, not for the first time, if she should have stayed with the fox-singer long enough to have a little redhead, a girl with some fire in her. It had been a mistake to stop at one.

But there was nothing to be done for it; one could hardly go backwards, and Amelia was making up for it now. She had shaken a city off the ground with only a hundred hand-lettered invitations, and with Alice she had planned better than with Alice's mother. No more watery banker-fathers to coddle a girl into docility. Alice had gotten a taste for loneliness in that little school; she would be ready for some adventure now she was out. Alice would do what was needed to keep her Grandmother happy.

At ten-thirty, a car turned off the main road, and the dogs lifted their heads, and Amelia smiled at her reflection in a hundred windows.

Alice was coming.

Alice parked at the edge of the lawn and stood on the stepboard to look across the herd of cars.

"I hope we reach the house before dawn," she said.

James laughed and buttoned his tux jacket. "If I'd known, I'd have brought extra cigarettes for the trip."

He turned and offered his arm.

Alice smoothed her hair with her hands, picked up her clutch purse, and shook out the red cloak so it fell in even folds across her shoulders.

"How do I look?" she said.

"Like you're stalling," he said. "But red's your color."

She headed for the house without saying anything, and when he caught up and rested his hand on her back she let him. His skin was warm even through the cape.

"We have to stop this before we get to the house," she said. "My grandmother won't like it."

"We'll see," he said, and they set off picking their way through the cars.

Halfway across the lawn the ballroom came into view, and Alice gaped at the bleeding lights and the crowd.

It was grander than any party she'd ever seen even in movies, and she watched the bright flares of satin and beads, listened in silent delight to the horns carrying the melody of "Remarkable Girl" past the glowing ballroom and across the dark lawn.

Behind her James said, "A hundred people here and only three good dancers. You'd think they'd be able to take lessons; they've got nothing else to do."

Alice smoothed her hands over the grey spangled dress. "I've never taken lessons."

"Don't worry, darling girl," James said, and there were hollows under his eyes.

"I've got you. Come on."

Alice pulled the red cloak tighter around her and approached the front door, a giant thing carved of dark wood that didn't suit the delicate pale-green windows on either side. Alice guessed the door was Amelia's addition to the house, and no sooner had she thought of her grandmother than a stately figure moved into sight in the hallway, surrounded by a knee-high knot of fur that Alice realized were a pack of dogs.

Amelia opened the door and smiled, and Alice was overwhelmed; Amelia had sent a picture of herself six years ago with her Christmas present, and she seemed no different—it was the same solid face, sturdy frame, sensible expression that Alice had memorized from the little photograph. The diamond necklace looked as if it were too heavy, somehow, but otherwise it was her Grandmother, through and through.

"Welcome home, Alice," she said.

Alice blushed and didn't move until Amelia prompted her, "Well, come say hello."

The dogs parted as Alice wrapped her arms around Amelia. "Hello, Grandmother," she said into the shoulder of the dark blue dress.

"Well, now, that's enough," Amelia said after a moment, stepping back. "You've certainly gotten strong at school, that's for sure. You weren't playing sports?"

"No."

"Good." Amelia turned and took in James. "And your friend?"

"This is James," Alice said, and then realized she didn't know his last name.

Amelia nodded. "Fenris. I know his family. And you've been getting to know each other?"

"My car broke down in the woods. Alice was kind enough to give me a ride." James stepped forward with his hand out and was stopped when the dogs closed in against him, growling.

"Heel," hissed Amelia, and they sat back trembling, ears pressed to their heads, as James bared his teeth at them.

"Come into the party," Amelia said, moving down the hallway towards the ballroom. "It's just time for sorbet and soda, and you'll need it after that long ride."

Alice fell into step behind Grandmother and felt her fear fading like a bruise; Amelia knew James's family, Amelia was happy to see her, Amelia would take care of it all.

Around them the dogs moved as sentinels, and safely behind was James, hands in his pockets, keeping his distance from the hounds.

Just before they reached the ballroom, Amelia held out her hand.

"Let's have the cape," she said. "It's smart for travel, but it will hardly do for the party."

"Oh, but I liked it," Alice said, and Amelia cut in, "Of course you did, but really, a face as round as yours and the long hair and a cape on top of it all—this is a party, not a play."

Alice frowned, handed over the cape. "It looks like a play from outside," she said under her breath.

"Don't be smart in front of company," Amelia said, tossed the cape on a chair.

"James, would you take Alice in?"

"A pleasure," James said, and slid his arm around Alice's, and as soon as Amelia's back was turned he pressed his lips to the top of her ear.

Alice shivered and flushed as the room seemed to open up and swallow her, and the next minutes were a blur of music, greetings, the press of strangers' hands, the sheen of marble floors, and Alice smiled and said polite nothings and leaned into James's warm side.

When she was able to focus again, she was holding a glass of champagne ("She brought the best," James was saying to some woman across the room, his voice carrying to Alice somehow), sitting at a small table amid a cluster of tables that were set up on the conservatory. Down a short hallway the band still played in the ballroom, and groups of people came and went, always smiling, shaking her hand, paying their respects, nodding to each other that she looked remarkably like Amelia, just like.

It all felt unreal, too much for her to understand, and Alice said, in a voice that didn't sound like hers, "I don't like this."

"That's to be expected, you've never really been to parties. I wish your grandfather could be here. He would have been so proud of you."

Alice beamed.

Amelia greeted someone in a green dress, and then leaned on the armrest close to Alice. "As soon as I saw your grandfather I knew he had what I wanted to give to my daughter, and her daughter. I think it's always like that; I think somehow you know right from the first what's best."

Alice imagined herself at Oberlin. "I agree."

Amelia sat back. "Excellent."

"It's why I've been trying to tell you in my letters," said Alice, "how much I want to go abroad and study."

"Yes, and when you were nine years old you wrote me how much you wanted to be a mermaid, two things of about equal sense." Amelia waved down a waiter. "Want a sorbet? It's warm for September."

Alice set her jaw, sat up straighter. "What I want is to continue school."

Her voice was different, and Amelia looked over her glass in the middle of a sip of champagne.

A thin, pinched woman in a purple dress hung with beads stopped by the table.

"This must be Alice," she said to Amelia. "At last, you've brought her out of hiding! We were beginning to wonder if you'd smuggled her away for good."

Amelia raised an eyebrow. "Alice, this is Margaret Cavendish."

Alice held out her hand, and Margaret Cavendish looked right at her, narrowed her eyes as she shook hands.

"And will we be seeing you?" she asked.

"Oh," said Alice, "well, there are my studies. I mean, it would be my pleasure I'm sure, but school is—"

"School is under discussion," Amelia said.

Margaret Cavendish frowned, pressed Alice's hand a little harder.

"Pity," she said to neither one of them, and then she was gone.

The music in Margaret's wake seemed falsely cheerful, and Alice flinched.

Amelia sighed. "Don't look at me like that, Alice. Dreams are well and good, but the next three generations are going to rest on you, and I wanted to make sure you had a good start. Your mother was worthless about it all. Better to begin again from nothing and have everyone start wanting to suck up at once."

Once last year Alice had studied Mesopotamia for an exam that turned out to be on Byzantium, and she had that same knot in her stomach as she'd had a year ago. All Amelia's plans had been made without her; Alice safely out of the way until Amelia decided it was time to talk about the next three generations, and how Alice would have to be mother to them all.

"But you kept me in that school for ten years?" she said. "What else did I have but studying?"

"Do you think I would really leave you alone?" Amelia rested her hand on Alice's arm. "I've worked for a decade to make sure our family line scraped itself out of the dark your mother left it in. You'll find your way much easier than you think."

"And university?"

"College is for smart girls with no money and no family," Amelia said, smiled, rested a hand on Alice's arm. "And you have money and family, now."

Amelia took a sorbet off the arriving tray and said, not without some satisfaction, "I've taken care of everything. Wouldn't I take care of my darling girl?"

Alice watched as the dancers paired up for the waltz, sequins swinging heavily, patent shoes gleaming, and felt as though the floor had turned to sand under her feet.

Ten years of sitting in her room, drawing and reading and waiting for the day her grandmother would pull up outside to take her away and take care of her. And here was the glass palace where Alice would live quietly and do what she was told, and Amelia would bring her up to be a terrible matron with children and guest lists and a house in the center of the wood around which New York would gather every year like butterflies in glad rags.

Across the room, James was talking with a blonde girl, his dark head bent towards her, his champagne glass casting shadows over his fingers.

"And his car broke down on the road?" she asked.

Amelia 'hmm'ed. "It's amazing how those things can happen."

Yes, Alice thought, it certainly was.

"How do you know his family?"

"You could say they ran in the same circles as your grandfather," Amelia said. "He'll surprise you, Alice, if you let him. You could do much worse."

Alice didn't bother to point out that he was the least of the evening's surprises. At least she'd had the sense to be wary of him.

She felt suddenly older, as if her skeleton had stretched her skin to breaking, as if the bones of her hands were going to spread longer and frailer than birds' wings.

Absently she made fists of her hands, closed her eyes against the bright light of the lamps. Behind her eyelids, Amelia and James were taking tea in the back parlor, James's long legs bunched up under the little chairs. James tucked Alice's school picture inside his shabby coat. Amelia counted out stacks of cool green bills. Both of them laughed a little about poor Alice, so lonely and willing in that far-off school.

"He must be very special," Alice said.

"You had no idea what I went through to find him," Amelia agreed, and dropped her hand to the dogs knotted at her feet. They lifted their eyes, licked their teeth with their pink tongues. "There are some desperate beasts in this world, you know."

The room was suddenly cold, and Alice shivered. "What did Grandfather teach you?"

"I'll show you," Amelia said with a real grin, and Alice saw that Amelia could look remarkable after all. "I'll show you everything, Alice, I promise you. No school in the world can show you what I will."

Alice stared at the dogs. "So they were—"

"Don't worry," Amelia said. "The world's better off with the four dogs in it."

Before Alice could reach down to the dogs, James's arm was around her, pressing her forward into the crowd of dancers.

"It's foxtrot."

"I don't know how to dance," she said.

He flexed his hand on her waist. "I'll teach you."

"I hope she's paid you enough," said Alice casually. Smart people with no family or money could be made to do almost anything.

"Enough to buy a suit every week of the year," he said. "Not bad for my kind."

They were already on the dance floor, Alice's silver sequins weighing down her knees, and as he stepped into her Alice saw in his profile for a moment the sleek, dark shape of the wolf.

"And now that you've met me?"

"A pleasant surprise," he said softly.

Even as he said it she wanted to kiss him.

She leaned into him, and he grinned down, swayed gently as the first notes sounded, triumphant to have her in his arms.

Since her bones had stretched past the limits of her skin she was taller, and her hands were wings. Her silver shoes tapped against the marble when he turned her.

The night sky pressed on the windows, the sleeping cars jostling for a look at the glitter inside, and around them all was the safety and the silence of the dark wood.

"And they say that the one I admire isn't even remotely concerned," James sang softly against her temple. He had a sweet low voice, and he didn't notice when she plucked a single dark hair off his white collar and held it carefully between her fingers.

Amelia would teach her, and then, well, you could do amazing things with one strand of hair.

The Sawing Boys

Howard Waldrop

There was a place in the woods where three paths came together and turned into one big path heading south.

A bearded man in a large straw hat and patched bib overalls came down one. Over his shoulder was a tow sack, and out of it stuck the handle of a saw. The man had a long wide face and large thin ears.

Down the path to his left came a short man in butternut pants and a red checkerboard shirt that said Ralston-Purina Net Wt. 20 lbs. on it. He had on a bright red cloth cap that stood up on the top of his head. Slung over his back was a leather strap; hanging from it was a big ripsaw.

On the third path were two people, one of whom wore a yellow-and black-striped shirt, and had a mustache that stood straight out from the sides of his nose. The other man was dressed in a dark brown barn coat. He had a wrinkled face, and wore a brown Mackenzie cap down from which the earflaps hung, even though it was a warm morning. The man with the mustache carried a narrow folding ladder; the other carried a two-man bucksaw.

The first man stopped.

"Hi yew!" he said in the general direction of the other two paths.

"Howdee!" said the short man in the red cap.

"Well, well, well!" said the man with the floppy-eared hat, putting down his big saw.

"Weow!" said the man with the wiry mustache.

They looked each other over, keeping their distance, eyeing each others' clothing and saws. "Well, I guess we know where we're all headed," said the man with the brown Mackenzie cap.

"I reckon," said the man in the straw hat. "I'm Luke Apuleus, from over Cornfield County way. I play the crosscut."

"I'm Rooster Joe Banty," said the second. "I'm a ripsaw bender myself."

"I'm Felix Horbliss," said the man in stripes with the ladder. "That thar's Cave Canem. We play this here big bucksaw."

They looked at each other some more.

"I'm to wonderin'," said Luke, bringing his toe sack around in front of him. "I'm wonderin' if 'n we know the same tunes. Seems to me it'd be a shame to have to play agin' each other if 'n we could help it."

"You-all know 'Trottin' Gertie Home'?" asked Felix.

Luke and Rooster Joe nodded.

"How about 'When the Shine comes Out'n the Dripper'?" asked Rooster Joe.

The others nodded.

"How are you on 'Snake Handler's Two-Step'?" asked Luke Apuleus.

More nods.

"Well, that's a start on it," said Cave Canem. "We can talk about it on the way there. I bet we'd sound right purty together."

So side by side by bucksaw and ladder, they set out down the big path south.

What we are doing is, we are walking down this unpaved road. How we have come to be walking down this unpaved road is a very long and tiresome story that I should not bore you with.

We are being Chris the Shoemaker, who is the brains of this operation, and a very known guy back where we come from, which is south of Long Island, and Large Jake and Little Willie, who are being the brawn, and Miss Millie Dee Chantpie, who is Chris the Shoemaker's doll, and who is always dressed to the nines, and myself, Charlie Perro, whose job it is to remind everyone what their job is being.

"I am astounded as all get-out," says Little Willie, "that there are so many places with no persons in them nowise," looking around at the trees and bushes and such. "We have seen two toolsheds which looked as if they once housed families of fourteen, but of real-for-true homes, I am not seeing any."

"Use your glims for something besides keeping your nose from sliding into your eyebrows," says Chris the Shoemaker. "You will have seen the sign that said one of the toolcribs is the town of Podunk, and the other shed is the burg of Shtetl. I am believing the next one we will encounter is called Pratt Falls. I am assuming it contains some sort of trickle of fluid, a stunning and precipitous descent in elevation, established by someone with the aforementioned surname."

He is called Chris the Shoemaker because that is now his moniker, and he once hung around shoestores. At that time the cobbler shops was the place where the policy action was hot, and before you can be saying Hey Presto! there is Chris the Shoemaker in a new loud suit looking like a comet, and he is the middle guy between the shoemakers and the elves that rig the policy.

"Who would have thought it?" asked Little Willie, "both balonies on the rear blowing at the same time, and bending up the frammus, and all the push and pull running out? I mean, what are the chances?"

Little Willie is called that because he is the smaller of the two brothers. Large Jake is called that because, oh my goodness, is he large. He is so large that people have confused him for nightfall—they are standing on the corner shooting the breeze with some guys, and suddenly all the light goes away, and so do the other guys. There are all these cigarettes dropping to the pavement where guys used to be, and the person looks around and Whoa! it is not night at all, it is only Large Jake.

For two brothers they do not look a thing alike. Little Willie looks, you should excuse the expression, like something from the family Rodentia, whereas Large Jake is a very pleasant-looking individual, only the pleasant is spread across about three feet of mook.

Miss Millie Dee Chantpie is hubba-hubba stuff (only Chris the Shoemaker best not see you give her more than one Long Island peek) and the talk is she used to be a roving debutante. Chris has the goo-goo eyes for her, and she is just about a whiz at the new crossword puzzles, which always give Little Willie a headache when he tries to do one.

Where we are is somewhere in the state of Kentucky, which I had not been able to imagine had I not seen it yesterday from the train. Why we were here was for a meet with this known guy who runs a used furniture business on South Wabash Street in Chi City. The meet was to involve lots of known guys, and to be at some hunting lodge in these hills outside Frankfort, where we should not be bothered by prying eyes. Only first the train is late, and the jalopy we bought stalled on us in the dark, and there must have been this wrong turn somewhere, and the next thing you are knowing the balonies blow and we are playing in the ditch and gunk and goo are all over the place.

So here we are walking down this (pardon the expression) road, and we are looking for a phone and a mechanically inclined individual, and we are not having such a hot time of it.

"You will notice the absence of wires," said Chris the Shoemaker, "which leads me to believe we will not find no blower at this watery paradise of Pratt Falls."

"Christ Almighty, I'm gettin' hungry!" says Miss Millie Dee Chantpie of a sudden. She is in this real flapper outfit, with a bandeau top and fringes, and is wearing pearls that must have come out of oysters the size of freight trucks.

"If we do not soon find the object of our quest," says Chris the Shoemaker, "I shall have Large Jake blow you the head off a moose, or whatever they have in place of cows out here."

It being a meet, we are pretty well rodded up, all except for Chris, who had to put on his Fall Togs last year on Bargain Day at the courthouse and do a minute standing on his head, so of course he can no longer have an oscar anywhere within a block of his person, so Miss Millie Dee Chantpie carries his cannon in one of her enchanting little reticules.

Large Jake is under an even more stringent set of behavioral codes, but he just plain does not care, and I do not personally know any cops or even the Sammys who are so gauche as to try to frisk him without first calling out the militia. Large Jake usually carries a powder wagon—it is the kind of thing they use on mad elephants or to stop runaway locomotives only it is sawed off on both ends to be only about a foot long.

Little Willie usually carries a sissy rod, only it is a dumb gat so there is not much commotion when he uses it—just the sound of air coming out of it, and then the sound of air coming out of whomsoever he uses it on. Little Willie has had a date to Ride Old Sparky before, only he was let out on a technical. The technical was that the judge had not noticed the big shoe box full of geetas on the corner of his desk before he brought the gavel down.

I am packing my usual complement of calibers which (I am prouder than anything to say) I have never used. They are only there for the bulges for people to ogle at while Chris the Shoemaker is speaking.

Pratt Falls is another couple of broken boards and a sign saying Feed and Seed. There was this dry ditch with a hole with a couple of rocks in it.

"It was sure no Niagara," says Little Willie, "that's for certain."

At the end of the place was a sign, all weathered out except for the part that said 2 MILES.

We are making this two miles in something less than three-quarters of an hour because it is mostly uphill and our dogs are barking, and Miss Millie Dee Chantpie, who has left her high heels in the flivver, is falling off the sides of her flats very often. We are looking down into what passes for a real live town in these parts.

"This is the kind of place," says Little Willie, "where when you are in the paper business, and you mess up your double sawbuck plates, and print a twenty-one-dollar bill, you bring it here and ask for change. And the guy at the store will look in the drawer and ask you if two nines and a three will do."

"Ah, but look, gentlemen and lady," says Chris the Shoemaker, "there are at least two wires coming down over the mountain into this metropolis, and my guess is that they are attached to civilization at the other end."

"I do not spy no filling station," I says. "But there does seem to be great activity for so early of a morning." I am counting houses. "More people are already in town than live here."

"Perhaps the large gaudy sign up ahead will explain it," says Little Willie. The sign is being at an angle where another larger dirt path comes into town. From all around on the mountains I can see people coming in in wagons and on horses and on foot.

We get to the sign. This is what it says, I kid you not:

BIG HARMONY CONTEST!
BRIMMYTOWN SQUARE SAT MAY 16
$50 FIRST PRIZE
Brought to you by Watkins Products and
CARDUI, Makers of BLACK DRAUGHT
Extra! Sacred Harp Singing
Rev. Shapenote and the Mt. Sinai Choir.

"Well, well," says Chris. "Looks like there'll be plenty of e'trangers in this burg. We get in there, make the call on the meet, get someone to fix the jalopy, and be on our way. We should fit right in."

While Chris the Shoemaker is saying this, he is adjusting his orange-and-pink tie and shooting the cuffs on his purple-and-white pinstripe suit. Little Willie is straightening his pumpkin-colored, double-breasted suit and brushing the dust off his yellow spats. Large Jake is dressed in a pure white suit with a black shirt and white tie, and has on a white fedora with a thin black band. Miss Millie Dee Chantpie swirls her fringes and rearranges the ostrich feather in her cloche. I feel pretty much like a sparrow among peacocks.

"Yeah," I says, looking over the town, "they'll probably never notice we been here."

They made their way into town and went into a store. They bought themselves some items, and went out onto the long, columned verandah of the place, and sat down on some nail kegs, resting their saws and ladders against the porch railings.

Cave Canem had a big five-cent RC Cola and a bag of Tom's Nickel Peanuts. He took a long drink of the cola, tore the top off the celluloid bag, and poured the salted peanuts into the neck of the bottle. The liquid instantly turned to foam and overflowed the top, which Canem put into his mouth. When it settled down, he drank from the bottle and chewed on the peanuts that came up the neck.

Rooster Joe took off his red cap. He had a five-cent Moon Pie the size of a dinner plate and took bites off that.

Horbliss had a ten-cent can of King Oscar Sardines. The key attached to the bottom broke off at the wrong place. Rather than tearing his thumb up, he took out his pocketknife and cut the top of the can off and peeled the ragged edge back. He drank off the oil, smacking his lips, then took out the sardines between his thumb and the knife blade and ate them.

Luke had bought a two-foot length of sugarcane and was sucking on it, spitting out the fine slivers which came away in his mouth.

They ate in silence and watched the crowds go by, clumps of people breaking away and eddying into the stores and shops. At one end of town, farmers stopped their wagons and began selling the produce. From the other end, at the big open place where the courthouse would be if Brimmytown were the county seat, music started up.

They had rarely seen so many men in white shirts, even on Sunday, and women and kids in their finest clothes, even if they were only patched and faded coveralls, they were starched and clean.

Then a bunch of city flatlanders came by—the men all had on hats and bright suits and ties, and the woman—a goddess—was the first flapper they had ever seen—the eyes of the flatlanders were moving everywhere. Heads turned to watch them all along their route. They were moving toward the general mercantile, and they looked tired and dusty for all their fancy duds.

"Well, boys," said Luke. "That were a right smart breakfast. I reckon us-all better be gettin' on down towards the musical place and see what the otherns look like."

They gathered up their saws and ladders and walked toward the sweetest sounds this side of Big Bone Lick.

"So," says Little Willie to a citizen, "tell us where we can score a couple of motor-man's gloves?"

The man is looking at him like he has just stepped off one of the outermost colder planets. This is fitting, for the citizen looks to us vice versa.

"What my friend of limited vocabulary means," says Chris the Shoemaker to the astounding and astounded individual, "is where might we purchase a mess of fried pork chops?"

The man keeps looking at us with his wide eyes the size of doorknobs.

"Eats?" I volunteers.

Nothing is happening.

Large Jake makes eating motions with his mitt and goozle.

Still nothing.

"Say, fellers," says this other resident, "you won't be gettin' nothing useful out'n him. He's one of the simpler folks hereabouts, what them Victorian painter fellers used to call 'naturals.' What you want's Ma Gooser's place, straight down this yere street."

"Much obliged," says Chris.

"It's about time, too," says Miss Millie Dee Chantpie. "I'm so hungry I could eat the ass off a pigeon through a park bench!"

I am still staring at the individual who has given us directions, who is knocking the ashes out of his corncob pipe against a rain barrel.

"Such a collection of spungs and feebs I personally have never seen," says Chris the Shoemaker, who is all the time looking at the wire that comes down the hill into town.

"I must admit you are right," says Little Willie. And indeed it seems every living thing for three counties is here—there are nags and wagons, preggo dolls with stair-step children born nine months and fifteen minutes apart, guys wearing only a hat and one blue garment, a couple of men with what's left of Great War uniforms with the dago dazzlers still pinned to the chests—yes indeedy, a motley and hilarity-making group.

The streets are being full of wagons with melons and the lesser legumes and things which for a fact I know grow in the ground. The indigenous peoples are selling everything what moves. And from far away you can hear the beginnings of music.

"I spy," says Chris the Shoemaker.

"Whazzat?" asks Little Willie.

"I spy the blacksmith shop, and I spy the general mercantile establishment to which the blower wire runs. Here is what we are doing. William and I will saunter over to the smithy and forge, where we will inquire of aid for the vehicle. Charlie Perro, you will go make the call which will tender our apologies as being late for the meet, and get some further instructions. Jacob, you will take the love of my life, Miss Millie, to this venerable Ma Gooser's eatatorium where we will soon join you in a prodigious repast."

The general mercantile is in the way of selling everything on god's green earth, and the aroma is very mouth-watering—it is a mixture of apple candy and nag tack, coal oil and licorice and flour, roasted coffee and big burlap sacks of nothing in particular. There is ladies' dresses and guy hats and weapons of all kinds.

There is one phone; it is on the back wall; it is the kind Alexander Graham Bell made himself.

"Good person," I says to the man behind the counter, who is wearing specs and a vest and has a tape measure draped over his shoulder, "might I use your telephonic equipment to make a collect long-distance call?"

"Everthin's long-distance from here," he opines. "Collect, you say?"

"That is being correct."

He goes to the wall and twists a crank and makes bell sounds. "Hello, Gertie. This is Spoon. How's things in Grinder Switch?...You don't say? Well, there's a city feller here needs to make a co-llect call. Right. You fix him up." He hands me the long earpiece, and puts me in the fishwife care of this Gertie, and parks himself nearby and begins to count some bright glittery objects.

I tells Gertie the number I want. There are these sounds like the towers are falling. "And what's your name," asks this Gertie.

I gives her the name of this known newspaper guy who hangs out at Chases' and who writes about life in the Roaring Forties back in the Big City. The party on the other end will be wise that that is not who it is, but will know I know he knows.

I hear this voice and Gertie gives them my name and they say okay.

"Go ahead," says Gertie.

"We are missing the meet," I says.

"Bleaso!" says the voice. "Eetmay alledoffcay. Ammysays Iseway! Izzyoway and Oemay erehay."

Itshay I am thinking to myself. To him I says:

"Elltay usoway atwhay otay ooday?"

"Ogay Omehay!"

He gets off the blower.

"I used to have a cousin that could talk Mex," says Spoon at the counter. I thank him for the use of the phone. "Proud as a peach of it," he says, wiping at it with a cloth.

"Well, you should be," I tell him. Then I buy two cents worth of candy and put it in a couple of pockets, and then I ease on down this town's Great White Way.

This Ma Gooser's is some hopping joint. I don't think the griddle here's been allowed to cool off since the McKinley Administration. Large Jake and Miss Millie Dee Chantpie are already tucking in. The place is as busy as a chophouse on Chinese New Year.

There are these indistinguishable shapes on the platters.

A woman the size of Large Jake comes by with six full plates along each arm, headed towards a table of what looks like two oxdrivers in flannel shirts. These two oxdrivers are as alike as all get-out. The woman puts three plates in front of each guy and they fall into them mouth first.

The woman comes back. She has wild hair, and it does not look like she has breasts; it looks like she has a solid shelf across her chest under her work shirt. "Yeah?" she says, wiping sweat from her brow.

"I'd like a steak and some eggs," I says, "over easy on the eggs, steak well-done, some juice on the side."

"You'll get the breakfast, if 'n you get anything," she says. "Same's everybody else." She follows my eyes back to the two giants at the next table. Large Jake can put away the groceries, but he is a piker next to these two. A couple of the plates in front of them are already shining clean and they are reaching for a pile of biscuits on the next table as they work on their third plates.

"Them's the Famous Singin' Eesup Twins, Bert and Mert," says Ma Gooser. "If 'n everybody could pile it in like them, I'd be a rich woman." She turns to the kitchen.

"Hey, Jughead," she yells, "where's them six dozen biscuits?"

"Comin', Ma Gooser!" yells a voice from back in the hell there.

"More blackstrap 'lasses over here, Ma!" yells a corncob from another table.

"Hold your water!" yells Ma. "I only got six hands!" She runs back towards the kitchen.

Chris the Shoemaker and Little Willie comes in and settles down.

"Well, we are set in some departments. The blacksmith is gathering up the tools of his trade and Little William will accompany him in his wagon to the site of the vehicular happenstance. I will swear to you, he picks up his anvil and puts it into his wagon, just like that. The thing must have dropped the wagon bed two foot. What is it they are feeding the locals around here?" He looks down at the plates in front of Large Jake and Miss Millie. "What is dat?"

"I got no idea, sweetie," says Miss Millie, putting another forkful in, "but it sure is good!"

"And what's the news from our friends across the ways?"

"Zex," I says.

He looks at me. "You are telling me zex in this oomray full of oobrays?"

"No, Chris," I says, "the word is zex."

"Oh," he says, "and for why?"

"Izzy and Moe," I says.

"Izzy and Moe?! How did Izzy and Moe get wise to this deal?"

"How do Izzy and Moe get wise to anything," I says, keeping my voice low and not moving my goozle. "Hell, if someone could get them to come over, this umray unningray biz would be a snap. If they can dress like women shipwrecks and get picked up by runners' ships, they can get wind of a meet somewhere."

"So what are our options being?" asks Chris the Shoemaker.

"That is why we have all these round-trip tickets," I says.

He is quiet. Ma Gooser slaps down these plates in front of us, and coffee all round, and takes two more piles of biscuits over to the Famous Singing Eesup Twins.

"Well, that puts the damper on my portion of the Era of Coolidge Prosperity," says Chris the Shoemaker. "I am beginning to think this decade is going to be a more problematical thing than first imagined. In fact, I am getting in one rotten mood." He takes a drink of coffee. His beezer lights up. "Say, the flit in the Knowledge Box got nothing on this." He drains the cup dry. He digs at his plate, then wolfs it all down. "Suddenly my mood is changing. Suddenlike, I am in a working mood."

I drops my fork.

"Nix?" I asks nice, looking at him like I am a tired halibut.

"No, not no nix at all. It is of a sudden very clear why we have come to be in this place through these unlikely circumstances. I had just not realized it till now."

Large Jake has finished his second plate. He pushes it away and looks at Chris the Shoemaker.

"Later," says Chris. "Outside."

Jake nods.

Of a sudden-like, I am not enjoying Ma Gooser's groaning board as much as I should wish.

For when Chris is in a working mood, things happen.

They had drawn spot #24 down at the judging stand. Each contestant could sing three songs, and the Black Draught people had a big gong they could ring if anyone was too bad.

"I don't know 'bout the ones from 'round here," said Cave Canem, "but they won't need that there gong for the people we know about. We came in third to some of 'em last year in Sweet Tater City."

"Me neither," said Rooster Joe. "The folks I seen can sure play and sing. Why even the Famous Eesup Twins, Bert and Mert, is here. You ever hear them do 'Land Where No Cabins Fall'?"

"Nope," said Luke, "but I have heard of 'em. It seems we'll just have to outplay them all."

They were under a tree pretty far away from the rest of the crowd, who were waiting for the contest to begin.

"Let's rosin up, boys," said Luke, taking his crosscut saw out of his tow sack.

Felix unfolded the ladder and climbed up. Cave pulled out a big willow bow strung with braided muletail hair.

Rooster Joe took out an eight-ounce ball peen hammer and sat back against a tree root.

Luke rosined up his fiddle bow.

"Okay, let's give 'er about two pounds o' press and bend."

He nodded his head. They bowed, Felix pressing down on the big bucksaw handle from above, Rooster Joe striking his ripsaw, Luke pulling at the back of his crosscut.

The same note, three octaves apart, floated on the air.

"Well, that's enough rehearsin'," said Luke. "Now all we got to do is stay in this shady spot and wait till our turn."

They put their instruments and ladder against the tree, and took naps.

When Chris the Shoemaker starts to working, usually someone ends up with cackle fruit on their mug.

When Little Willie and Chris first teamed up when they were oh so very young, they did all the usual grifts. They worked the cherry-colored cat and the old hydrophoby lay, and once or twice even pulled off the glim drop, which is a wonder since neither of them has a glass peeper. They quit the grift when it turns out that Little Willie is always off nugging when Chris needs him, or is piping some doll's stems when he should be laying zex. So they went into various other forms of getting the mazuma.

The ramadoola Chris has come up with is a simple one. We are to get the lizzie going, or barring that are to Hooverize another one; then we cut the lines of communication; immobilize the town clown, glom the loot, and give them the old razoo.

"But Chris," says I, "it is so simple and easy there must be something wrong with your brainstorm. And besides, it is what? Maybe a hundred simoleons in all? I have seen you lose that betting on which raindrop will run down a windowpane first."

"We have been placed here to do this thing," says Chris the Shoemaker. We are all standing on the porch of Ma Gooser's. "We cut the phone," says Chris, "no one can call out. Any other jalopies, Large Jake makes inoperable. That leaves horses, which even we can go faster than. We make the local yokel do a Brodie so there is no Cicero lightning or Illinois thunder. We are gone, and the news takes till next week to get over the ridge yonder."

Miss Millie Dee Chantpie has one of her shoes off and is rubbing her well-turned foot. "My corns is killing me," she says, "and Chris, I think this is the dumbest thing you have ever thought about!"

"I will note and file that," says Chris. "Meantimes, that is the plan. Little William here will start a rumor that will make our presence acceptable before he goes off with the man with the thews of iron. We will only bleaso this caper should the flivver not be fixable or we cannot kipe another one. So it is written. So it shall be done."

Ten minutes later, just before Little Willie leaves in the wagon, I hear two people talking close by, pointing to Miss Millie Dee Chantpie and swearing she is a famous chanteuse, and that Chris the Shoemaker is a talent scout from Okeh Records.

"The town clown," says Chris to me in a while, "will be no problem. He is that gent you see over there sucking on the yamsicle, with the tin star pinned to his long johns with the Civil War cannon tucked in his belt."

I nod.

"Charlie Perro," he says to me, "now let us make like we are mesmerized by this screeching and hollering that is beginning."

The contest is under way. It was like this carnival freak show had of a sudden gone into a production of No, No Nanette while you were trying to get a good peek at the India Rubber Woman.

I am not sure whether to be laughing or crying, so I just puts on the look a steer gets just after the hammer comes down, and pretends to watch. What I am really thinking, even I don't know.

There had been sister harmony groups, and guitar and mandolin ensembles, three guys on one big harmonica, a couple of twelve-year-olds playing ocarinas and washboards, a woman on gutbucket broom bass, a handbell choir from a church, three one-man bands, and a guy who could tear newspapers to the tune of "Hold That Tiger!"

Every eight acts or so, Reverend Shapenote and the Mt. Sinai Choir got up and sang sacred harp music, singing the notes only, with no words because their church believed you went straight to Hell if you sang words to a hymn; you could only lift your voice in song.

Luke lay with his hat over his eyes through two more acts. It was well into the afternoon. People were getting hot and cranky all over the town.

As the next act started, Luke sat up. He looked toward the stage. Two giants in coveralls and flannel shirts got up. Even from this far away, their voices carried clear and loud, not strained: deep bass and baritone.

The words of "Eight More Miles To Home" and then "You Are My Sunshine" came back, and for their last song, they went into the old hymn, "Absalom, Absalom":

Day-Vid The—He-Wept—and Wept Saying—Oh My Son—Oh my son …

and a chill went up Luke's back.

"That's them," said Rooster Joe, seeing Luke awake.

"Well," said Luke Apuleus, pulling his hat back down over his eyes as the crowd went crazy, "them is the ones we really have to beat. Call me when they gets to the Cowbell Quintet so we can be moseying up there."

I am being very relieved when Little Willie comes driving into town in the flivver; it is looking much the worse for wear but seems to be running fine. He parks it on Main Street at the far edge of the crowd and comes walking over to me and Chris the Shoemaker.

"How are you standing this?" he asks.

"Why do you not get up there, William," asks Chris. "I know for a fact you warbled for the cheese up at the River Academy, before they let you out on the technical."

"It was just to keep from driving an Irish buggy," says Little Willie. "The Lizzie will go wherever you want it to. Tires patched. Gassed and lubered up. Say the syllable."

Chris nods to Large Jake over at the edge of the crowd. Jake saunters back towards the only two trucks in town, besides the Cardui vehicle, which, being too gaudy even for us, Jake has already fixed while it is parked right in front of the stage, for Jake is a very clever fellow for someone with such big mitts.

"Charlie Perro," says Chris, reaching in Miss Millie Dee Chantpie's purse, "how's about taking these nippers here," handing me a pair of wire cutters, "and go see if that blower wire back of the general mercantile isn't too long by about six feet when I give you the nod. Then you should come back and help us." He also takes his howitzer out of Miss Millie's bag.

"Little William," he says, turning. "Take Miss Millie Dee Chantpie to the car and start it up. I shall go see what the Cardui Black Draught people are doing."

So it was we sets out to pull the biggest caper in the history of Brimmytown.

"That's them," said Rooster Joe. "The cowbells afore us."

"Well, boys," said Luke, "it's do-or-die time."

They gathered up their saws and sacks and ladder, and started for the stage.

Miss Millie Dee Chantpie is in the car, looking cool as a cucumber. Little Willie is at one side of the crowd, standing out like a sore thumb; he has his hand under his jacket on The Old Crowd Pleaser.

Large Jake is back, shading three or four people from the hot afternoon sun. I am at the corner of the general mercantile, one eye on Chris the Shoemaker and one on the wire coming down the back of the store.

The prize moolah is in this big glass cracker jar on the table with the judges so everybody can see it. It is in greenbacks.

I am seeing Large Jake move up behind the John Law figure, who is sucking at a jug of corn liquor—you would not think the Prohib was the rule of the land here.

I am seeing these guys climb onto the stage, and I cannot believe my peepers, because they are pulling saws and ladders out of their backs. Are these carpenters or what? There is a guy in a straw hat, and one with a bristle mustache, and one with a redchecked shirt and red hat, and one with a cap with big floppy earflaps. One is climbing on a ladder. They are having tools everywhere. What the dingdong is going on?

And they begin to play, a corny song, but it is high and sweet, and then I am thinking of birds and rivers and running water and so forth. So I shakes myself, and keeps my glims on Chris the Shoemaker.

The guys with the saws are finishing their song, and people are going ga-ga over them.

And then I see that Chris is in position.

"Thank yew, thank yew," said Luke. "We-all is the Sawing Boys and we are pleased as butter to be here. I got a cousin over to Cornfield County what has one uh them new cat-whisker crystal raddio devices, and you should hear the things that comes right over the air from it. Well, I learned a few of them, and me and the boys talked about them, and now we'll do a couple for yew. Here we're gonna do one by the Molokoi Hotel Royal Hawaiian Serenaders called 'Ule Uhi Umekoi Hwa Hwa.'

Take it away, Sawing Boys!" He tapped his foot.

He bent his saw and bowed the first high, swelling notes, then Rooster Joe came down on the harmony rhythm on the ripsaw. Felix bent down on the ladder on the handle of the bucksaw, and Cave pulled the big willow bow and they were off into a fast, swinging song that was about lagoons and fish and food. People were jumping and yelling all over town, and Luke, whose voice was nothing special, started singing:

"Ume hoi uli koi hwa hwa Wa haweaee omi oi lui lui..."

And the applause began before Rooster Joe finished alone with a dying struck high note that held for ten or fifteen seconds. People were yelling and screaming and the Cardui people didn't know what to do with themselves.

"Thank yew, thank yew!" said Luke Apuleus, wiping his brow with his arm while holding his big straw hat in his hand. "Now, here's another one I heerd. We hope you-all like it. It's from the Abe Schwartz Orchestra and it's called 'Beym Rebn in Palestine.' Take it away, Sawing Boys."

They hit halting, fluttering notes, punctuated by Rooster Joe's hammered ripsaw, and then the bucksaw went rolling behind it, Felix pumping up and down on the handle, Cave Canem bowing away. It sounded like flutes and violins and clarinets and mandolins. It sounded a thousand years old, but not like moonshine mountain music; it was from another time and another land.

Something is wrong, for Chris is standing very still, like he is already in the old oak kimono, and I can see he is not going to be giving me the High Sign.

I see that Little Willie, who never does anything on his own, is motioning to me and Large Jake to come over. So over I trot, and the music really washes over me. I know it in my bones, for it is the music of the old neighborhood where all of us but Miss Millie grew up.

I am coming up on Chris the Shoemaker and I see he has turned on the waterworks. He is transfixed, for here, one thousand miles from home he is being caught up in the mighty coils of memory and transfiguration.

I am hearing with his ears, and what the saws are making is not the Abe Schwartz Orchestra but Itzikel Kramtweiss of Philadelphia, or perhaps Naftalie Brandwein, who used to play bar mitzvahs and weddings with his back to the audience so rival clarinet players couldn't see his hands and how he made those notes.

There is maybe ten thousand years behind that noise, and it is calling all the way across the Kentucky hills from the Land of Gaza.

And while they are still playing, we walk with Chris the Shoemaker back to the jalopy, and pile in around Miss Millie Dee Chantpie, who, when she sees Chris crying, begins herself, and I confess I, too, am a little blurry-eyed at the poignance of the moment.

And we pull out of Brimmytown, the saws still whining and screeching their jazzy ancient tune, and as it is fading and we are going up the hill, Chris the Shoemaker speaks for us all, and what he says is:

"God Damn. You cannot be going anywhere these days without you run into a bunch of half-assed klezmorim."

For Arthur Hunnicutt and the late Sheldon Leonard.

Glossary to "The Sawing Boys"

Balonies—tires Bargain Day—court time set aside for sentencing plea-bargain cases
Beezer—the face, sometimes especially the nose
Bleaso!—1. an interjection—Careful! You are being overheard! Some chump is wise to the deal! 2. verb—to forgo something, change plans, etc.
The Cherry-colored Cat—an old con game
Cicero Lightning and Illinois Thunder—the muzzle flashes from machine guns and the sound of hand grenades going off
Do a minute—thirty days
Dogs are barking—feet are hurting
Fall Togs—the suit you wear going into, and coming out of, jail
Flit—prison coffee, from its resemblance to the popular fly spray of the time
Flivver—a jalopy
Frammus—a thingamajig or doohickey
Geetas—money, of any kind or amount
Glim Drop—con game involving leaving a glass eye as security for an amount of money; at least one of the con men should have a glass eye …
Glims—eyes
Goozle—mouth
Hooverize—(pre-Depression)—Hoover had been Allied Food Commissioner during the Great War, and was responsible for people getting the most use out of whatever foods they had; the standard command from parents was "Hooverize that plate!"; possibly a secondary reference to vacuum cleaners of the time.
Irish buggy (also Irish surrey)—a wheelbarrow
Jalopy—a flivver
Lizzie—a flivver
Mazuma—money, of any kind or amount
Mook—face
Motorman's gloves—any especially large cut of meat
Nugging—porking
The Old Hydrophoby Lay—con game involving pretending to be bitten by someone's (possibly mad) dog
Piping Some Doll's Stems—looking at some woman's legs
Pull—gas and oil
Sammys—the Feds
Zex—Quiet (as in bleaso), cut it out, jiggies! Beat it!
Laying zex—keeping lookout

Rules of pig Latin: initial consonants are moved to the end of the word and -ay is added to the consonant; initial vowels are moved to the end of the word and -way is added to the vowel

Bear it Away

After "Goldilocks and the Three Bears"

Michael Cadnum

Michael Cadnum is an American poet and novelist. He has written more than thirty books for adults, teens and children. He is best known for his adult suspense fiction, and young adult fiction based on myths, legends, and historical figures. Cadnum is the recipient of a National Endowment for the Arts fellowship for poetry.

I always thought Goldilocks got off a little too easily in the original fairytale. It always made me mad that she ate their food, broke their furniture, and then slept in their beds only to get away without any consequences. In reading this story, I suspect Cadnum must share my opinion.

I never liked the woodland, even in my youth, but the forest here has never been one of your lowly hoar-wilds, all crag and moss. It was really very pleasant, a happy mix of pine cones and little red ants, dock and nettles. You wouldn't want to muss your skirt, going on a picnic in the cockle burrs. But it was nice wood, little yellow flowers when the snow melted, and mushrooms shaped like willies. Some of our more prominent watercolorists traveled here to set up their easels, and botanists collected herbs along the streams.

A maiden could go berry picking with the silversmith's son, or slip off to meet the young professor from down-valley, and if she ran across a bear it would be one of the old traditional bears, little eyes, big rumps, snuffling the air, trying to see if you were trouble or something to eat. If a bear said anything at all it was in antique bear-tongue, not much to it, really, just good-bye or go away, all a bear needed to know.

From time to time a typical bear fracas broke out. A sow bear killed a miller down by the well, for example, when he stepped on a cub, it being night and the miller having lost his spectacles in the inn. The she-bear threw him over her shoulder and left him by the quarrymen's privy quite a boneless puddle. But what did we expect? It was reassuring, in a way, having bears to worry about. Kids afraid of the dark were easier to quiet down. A sudden gust or a scuttling acorn on the roof and Mom and Dad would roll their eyes and whisper, "A bear looking for children who won't eat their cabbage!"

Gentlemen of rude humor would disguise a burp by muttering, "Must've been a bear, growling in the glade," and if things got boring on a long summer's day, the villagers would unpen the hounds, run down a granddad bruin, and pen the bear in a sand pit. It was sport, all fair-play, joy under a summer's eve. Bets would flow hand to hand on the question which would expire first, bear or dog. Life was simple. Mosquitoes and holidays, ale and bear skins.

But it changed.

Some people say it was better nutrition, trout multiplying as the rivers ran clear.

The weather changed, the magnetic poles shifted—we all had our theories. I don't know how, but it happened. One day we had dumb bears rolling logs to gobble worms, and the next we had bears in the vicarage library. They were wood-bears, still, and kept off to themselves, when they weren't stocking up on rhyming dictionaries. But a revolution was underway.

It could be overlooked for a while. Bears still slept half the year and they still had trouble seeing. But when a boar-bear lumbered into the fletcher's wife one afternoon and offered effusive apologies for treading on her toe, we all knew something profound had happened to bear nature. The bears rushed her to the surgeon, stood around waiting for news of her recovery. Mrs. Fletcher regained her health and sanity, until she stepped out a week later to take some medicinal sun. A bear made-way from the midden, dainty-like, a she-bear, and said, "I hope I see you well."

Which killed the fletcher's dame. She died of the shock. Many of us understood exactly. I didn't mind a bit of sass from a blue jay or the tinsmith's mutt, but I did think that this was more than mortal humans need endure, a curtsy from a bear wearing a bonnet.

Myself, I was blonde, and if the glazier liked the look of me as well as the joiner, why, let them all have an eyeful, was how I always felt. I was charitable with my smiles, but when a bear asked how I was on this finest of mornings, and held the post office door open for me, I hurried right past and never said a word.

A long era of tranquillity was underway, bears writing essays, offering opinions on the likelihood of rain, bears making excellent neighbors. And most humans liked this, an age of peace. But I never got use to bears reading haiku, bears laughing at our human jokes. Months went by, entire seasons, and a bear never ate a single human. Not one.

There was bear laughter and bear song, noon and night.

I had a plan.

I wanted a hunter, one of those always just in time to drill a musket shot through a wolf's lights. And if he was fine of leg and loin, I wouldn't mind parting the bracken a bit with such a man, not being quite so young as I had been, and looking for the right sort to share my winter nights. Although this was not the point-entire. I wanted to teach the bears why they shouldn't weave rugs and write plays, and give them a lesson they'd never forget.

I wanted to teach them to keep their bear-talk to themselves. And if the cottage-dwelling men were too weak kneed to educate the bears, I'd find myself a red-jacketed crack shot and make him mine.

And so I did. He was a square-jawed elk-hunter from the vale to the east. His red jacket was sappy-brown along the sleeves, and he smelled of brandy, but he showed me how he double-powdered both barrels and blew twin holes in my mum's quilt hanging out to dry—and he paid gold florins for a new one.

He was perfect.

I recall that early morning well, how I tickled him awake. I tugged him from the bed, red-cheeked, unshaven. I remember the dawn as if it were a week ago, although these days I'm the only one alive who can sing the words to a single bear madrigal. I led my hunter to the woods, mist in the tulips, wood smoke in the thatch. I filled him with my scheme, and before I let him yea-or-nay, I kissed him wide awake, and said, "Follow me."

Bears are fond of walking—or they were, our wise bears used to be. They walked, they slept. Peripatetic brethren, as the priest would say, they were always cooking their oats, howling when the porridge scalded, and using the excuse for another ramble, up one trail and down the next. My hunter and I spied a family, dad, mam and wee one. They ambled off, blinking in the sunlight, happy as cows to be out in the grass, the little one hopping, rabbit-like. "Stay here," I whispered to my gunner.

I hid behind a berry bush. I waited, and when the family vanished up the trail, I scurried into the cottage. I violated their breakfast bowls, hot and cold, and made sure they would see the mess when they returned to table. Spoon and finger, I tasted, scooped, and splattered. (It was delicious—just the right amount of honey.) I did what I could with the furniture, the chairs and settles too stout for the likes of me to break. All I could manage was a high chair in the corner, one the bear-lad must have just outgrown.

I broke that into kindling, and left it sowed around the nook. I took myself upstairs. I flung wide the shutters so Redcoat would hear me shriek when the time came, and I settled myself in the largest of the three beds. This mattress was packed with straw so coarse it was like sprawling in a thicket. So I tried the middle bed, just my size, but it was so cratered by the weight of Mistress Griz that I climbed up and down the bedding, clinging to the edges.

Finally I escaped the bed and found the laddie's bunk, and slept. Why did you fall asleep, moon-calf, I would demand of myself in years to come. And I have no retort. No clever answer to myself. I lay, I slept. Not one to stoop to excuses, but mayhap the hunter's nip, that brandy wine he said was courage, over-did my wakefulness. "Just a taste," he had said, tasting some himself.

I never heard them on their way. When the three rambled back into the cottage, I had no inkling they were home, peering at their porridge, aghast at the broken highchair, nosing the air. Or perhaps I had a hint of what was happening, in one part of my mind.

Step by step, they ascended to the bedroom. The oak door creaked. Their heavy steps were slow, the floorboards groaning. Only then did I hear them, words as clear as any tinker's. "What's this—my pillow all mussed," said the father.

"And here, my mattress half-in, half-out," said Mum-bear, near-sighted, nose to her bed. "And me, and me!" cried the pup-bruin. "My bed too!" he cried.

I am now the only one in the land who knows, how like to our own speech it was, this language, this Bear tongue. "Mine too," he stammered, "and she is still—still here!"

I didn't have to feign my horror, yelling from the window, tangled in a sheet, screaming, bellowing. I called out, "What are you waiting for?" But my huntsman was lying in plain sight, sound asleep, sunlight in the green grass gleaming off his gun.

"She's here, she's here!," cried the cub. Both parents trying to make me out, blinking in the bright morning light through the open window.

I ran home.

In my haste, I soaked my skirts in the ford, dragged them in the thistles, muddied them and tore them, all the way to hearth and safety. I was scolded by my Mum, and I sobbed into the shot-rent quilt, swearing virtue, good deeds, and chastity to God.

I kept my visit secret. And a perfect secret it was, too.

Except that the silence fell.

No ursine gardeners peddled roots from door to door. No kindly bear held the pasture gate to let a goodwife pass. No bear song drifted from the meadow. Nine days later a pigeon-hunter accidentally uncovered the powder horn, one weather-glazed hunter's boot, and one sap-stained quarter of a jacket.

"A mishap," said the magistrate, eyeing the tooth marks in the shoulder of the scrap. "A lamentable misadventure," he said, with sadness. "A mystery." Anyone could see the nature of the hunter's sudden end, but the sheriff said it was beyond us all, what might have taken place. Because the bears were loved, and loved in return, in their bluff, like-human way.

But all the bears had vanished. Their cottages stood dark. No one knew what caused this blight, or where the speaking grizzlies repaired to, why they left our woods.

No one except myself.

The last time I saw a bear beside a creek, not a fortnight past, she stood on her two hind paws and listened while I bid her a good evening. "And good health to you," I said.

She turned away, and left me alone, the stream beside me running like a song.

Only I know, and I keep it to myself. But I see too clearly what happened. I know exactly how the huntsman leaped to his feet, face red with sleep and drink. I see too well in the eye of my mind how the Redcoat brandished his double-shotted gun.

I see him drawing aim upon the cub, and in my waking dream I see what a bear can eat for breakfast, when she has to on a sunny morn.

Mr Simonelli or the Fairy Widower

Susanna Clarke

Susanna Mary Clarke is a British author best known for her debut novel *Jonathan Strange & Mr Norrell* (2004), a Hugo Award-winning alternate history. Clarke began *Jonathan Strange* in 1993 and worked on it during her spare time while she was an editor at Simon and Schuster's Cambridge office, where she worked on their cookery list. In 2003 Bloomsbury bought her manuscript and began work on its publication.

Like much of Clarke's writing, this story doesn't retell one single fairytale, but rather it evokes the feelings and stories from many fairytales. I can't even begin to imagine how to keep all this information sorted in order to write like this, but thankfully I don't have to. I can just sit back and be amazed with her skill.

Allhope Rectory, Derbyshire
Dec. 20th., 1811.

To Mrs Gathercole

Madam, I shall not try your patience by a repetition of those arguments with which I earlier tried to convince you of my innocence. When I left you this afternoon I told you that it was in my power to place in your hands *writ-*

ten evidence that would absolve me from every charge which you have seen fit to heap upon my head and in fulfilment of that promise I enclose my journal. And should you discover, madam, in perusing these pages, that I have been so bold as to attempt a sketch of *your own character*, and should that portrayal prove *not entirely flattering*, then I beg you to remember that it was written as a private account and never intended for another's eyes.

You will hear no entreaties from me, madam. Write to the Bishop by all means. I would not stay your hand from any course of action which you felt proper. But one accusation I must answer: that I have acted without due respect for members of your family. It is, madam, my all too lively regard for your family that has brought me to my present curious situation.

I remain, madam, yr. most obedient & very humble Sert.
The Reverend Alessandro Simonelli

From the Journals of Alessandro Simonelli

Aug. 10th., 1811. Corpus Christi College, Cambridge.

I am beginning to think that I must marry. I have no money, no prospects of advancement and no friends to help me. This queer face of mine is my only capital now and must, I fear, be made to pay; John Windle has told me privately that the bookseller's widow in Jesus-lane is quite desperately in love with me and it is common knowledge that her husband left her nearly £15 thousand. As for the lady herself, I never heard any thing but praise of her. Her youth, virtue, beauty and charity make her universally loved. But still I cannot quite make up my mind to it. I have been too long accustomed to the rigours of scholarly debate to feel much enthusiasm for *female* conversation—no more to refresh my soul in the company of Aquinas, Aristophanes, Euclid, and Avicenna, but instead to pass my hours attending to a discourse upon the merits of a bonnet trimmed with coquelicot ribbons.

Aug. 11th., 1811.

Dr Prothero came smiling to my rooms this morning. "You are surprized to see me, Mr Simonelli," he said. "We have not been such good friends lately as to wait upon each other in our rooms."

True, but whose fault is that? Prothero is the very worst sort of Cambridge scholar: loves horses and hunting more than books and scholarship; has never once given a lecture since he was made Professor though obliged to do so by the deed of foundation every other week in term; once ate 5 roast mackerel at a sitting (which very nearly killed him); is drunk most mornings and every evening; dribbles upon his waistcoat as he nods in his chair. I believe I have made my opinion of him pretty widely known and, though I have done myself no good by my honesty, I am pleased to say that I have done him some harm.

He continued, "I bring you good news, Mr Simonelli! You should offer me a glass of wine—indeed you should! When you hear what excellent news I have got for you, I am sure you will wish to offer me a glass of wine!" And he swung his head around like an ugly old tortoise, to see if he could catch sight of a bottle. But I have no wine and so he went on, "I have been asked by a family in Derbyshire—friends of mine, you understand—to find them some learned gentleman to be Rector of their village. Immediately I thought of you, Mr Simonelli! The duties of a country parson in that part of the world are not onerous. And you may judge for yourself of the health of the place, what fine air it is blessed with, when I tell you that Mr Whitmore, the last clergyman, was ninety-three when he died. A good, kind soul, much loved by his parish, but not a scholar. Come, Mr Simonelli! If it is agreeable to you to have a house of your own—with garden, orchard and farm all complete—then I shall write tonight to the Gathercoles and relieve them of all their anxiety by telling them of your acceptance!"

But, though he pressed me very hard, I would not give him my answer immediately. I believe I know what he is about. He has a nephew whom he hopes to steer into my place if I leave Corpus Christi. Yet it would be wrong, I think, to refuse such an opportunity merely for the sake of spiting him.

I believe it must be either the parish or matrimony.

Sept. 9th., 1811.

I was this day ordained as a priest of the Church of England. I have no doubts that my modest behaviour, studiousness and extraordinary mildness of temper make me peculiarly fitted for the life.

Sept. 15th., 1811.The George, Derby.

Today I travelled by stage coach as far as Derby. I sat outside—which cost me ten shillings and sixpence—but since it rained steadily I was at some trouble to keep my books and papers dry. My room at The George is better aired than rooms in inns generally are. I dined upon some roast woodcocks, a fricassee of turnips and apple dumplings. All excellent but not cheap and so I complained.

Sept. 16th., 1811.

My first impressions were not encouraging. It continued to rain and the country surrounding Allhope appeared very wild and almost uninhabited. There were steep, wooded valleys, rivers of white spurting water, outcrops of barren rock surmounted by withered oaks, bleak windswept moorland. It was, I dare say, remarkably picturesque, and might have provided an excellent model for a descriptive passage in a novel, but to me who must now live here it spoke very eloquently of extreme seclusion and scarce society characterized by ignorant minds and uncouth manners. In two hours' walking I saw only one human habitation—a grim farmhouse with rain-darkened walls set among dark, dripping trees.

I had begun to think I must be very near to the village when I turned a corner and saw, a little way ahead of me in the rain, two figures on horseback. They had stopped by a poor cottage to speak to someone who stood just within the bounds of the garden. Now I am no judge of horses but these were quite remarkable; tall, well-formed and shining. They tossed their heads and stamped their hooves upon the ground as if they scorned to be stood upon so base an element. One was black and one was chestnut. The chestnut, in particular, appeared to be the only bright thing in the whole of Derbyshire; it glowed like a bonfire in the grey, rainy air.

The person whom the riders addressed was an old bent man. As I drew near I heard shouts and a curse, and I saw one of the riders reach up and make a sign with his hand above the old man's head. This gesture was entirely new to me and must, I suppose, be peculiar to the natives of Derbyshire. I do not think that I ever before saw any thing so expressive of contempt and as it may be of some interest to study the customs and quaint beliefs of the people here I append a sort of diagram or drawing to shew precisely the gesture the man made.

I concluded that the riders were going away dissatisfied from their interview with the old cottager. It further occurred to me that, since I was now so close to the village, this ancient person was certainly one of my parishioners. I determined to lose no time in bringing peace where there was strife, harmony where there was discord. I quickened my steps, hailed the old man, informed him that I was the new Rector and asked him his name, which was Jemmy.

"Well, Jemmy," said I, assuming a cordial manner and accommodating my language to his uneducated condition, "what has happened here? What have you done to make the gentlemen so angry?"

He told me that the rider of the chestnut horse had a wife who had that morning been brought to bed. He and his servant had come to inquire for Jemmy's wife, Joan, who for many years had attended all the women in the neighbourhood.

"Indeed?" said I in accents of mild reproof. "Then why do you keep the gentleman waiting? Where is your wife?"

He pointed to where the lane wound up the opposite hillside, to where I could just discern through the rain an ancient church and a graveyard.

"Who takes care of the women in their childbeds now?" I asked.

There were, it seemed, two executors of that office: Mr Stubb, the apothecary in Bakewell, or Mr Horrocks, the physician in Buxton. But both these places were two, three hours' hard ride away on bad roads and the lady was already, in Jemmy's words, "proper poorly."

To own the truth I was a little annoyed with the gentleman on the chestnut horse who had not troubled until today to provide an attendant for his wife: an obligation which, presumably, he might have discharged at any time within the last nine months. Nevertheless I hurried after the two men and, addressing the rider of the chestnut horse, said, "Sir, my name is Simonelli. I have studied a great variety of subjects—law, divinity, medicine—at the University at Cambridge and I have for many years maintained a correspondence with one of the most eminent physicians of the age, Mr Matthew Baillie of Great Windmill-street in London. If it is not disagreeable to you, I shall be happy to attend your wife."

He bent upon me a countenance thin, dark, eager. His eyes were exceptionally fine and bright and their expression unusually intelligent. His black hair was his own, quite long, and tied with a black ribbon in a pigtail, rather in the manner of an old-fashioned queue wig. His age, I thought, might be between forty and fifty.

"And are you an adherent of Galenus or Paracelsus?" he said.

"Sir?" I said (for I thought he must intend the question as a joke). But then, since he continued to look at me, I said, "The ancient medical authorities whom you mention, sir, are quite outdated. All that Galen knew of anatomy he got from observing the dissections of pigs, goats and apes. Paracelsus believed in the efficacy of magic spells and all sorts of nonsense. Indeed, sir," I said with a burst of laughter, "you might as well inquire whose cause I espoused in the Trojan War as ask me to chuse between those illustrious, but thoroughly discredited, gentlemen!"

Perhaps it was wrong to laugh at him. I felt it was wrong immediately. I remembered how many enemies my superior abilities had won me at Cambridge, and I recalled my resolution to do things differently in Allhope and to bear patiently with ignorance and misinformation wherever I found it. But the gentleman only said, "Well, Dando, we have had better fortune than we looked for. A scholar, an eminent physician to attend my lady." He smiled a long thin smile which went up just one side of his dark face. "She will be full of gratitude, I have no doubt."

While he spoke I made some discoveries: to wit that both he and his servant were amazingly dirty—I had not observed it at first because the rain had washed their faces clean. His coat, which I had taken to be of brown drugget or some such material, was revealed upon closer inspection to be of red velvet, much discoloured, worn and matted with dirt and grease.

"I had intended to hoist the old woman up behind Dando," he said, "but that will scarcely do for you." He was silent a moment and then suddenly cried, "Well, what do you wait for, you sour-faced rogue?" (This startled me, but a moment later I understood that he addressed Dando.) "Dismount! Help the learned doctor to the horse."

I was about to protest that I knew nothing of horses or riding but Dando had already jumped down and had somehow tipped me on to the horse's back; my feet were in the stirrups and the reins were in my hands before I knew where I was.

Now a great deal is talked in Cambridge of horses and the riding of horses and the managing of horses. A great number of the more ignorant undergraduates pride themselves upon their understanding of the subject. But I find there is nothing to it. One has merely to hold on as tight as one can: the horse, I find, does all.

Immense speed! Godlike speed! We turned from the highway immediately and raced through ancient woods of oak and ash and holly; dead leaves flew up, rain flew down, and the gentleman and I—like spirits of the sad, grey air—flew between! Then up, up we climbed to where the ragged grey clouds tore themselves apart like great doors opening in Heaven to let us through! By moorland pools of slate-grey water, by lonely windshaped hawthorn trees, by broken walls of grey stones—a ruined chapel—a stream—over the hills, to a house that stood quite alone in a rain-misted valley.

It was a very ancient-looking place, the different parts of which had been built at many different times and of a great variety of materials. There were flints and stones, old silverygrey timbers, and rose-red brick that glowed very cheerfully in the gloom. But as we drew nearer I saw that it was in a state of the utmost neglect. Doors had lost their hinges and were propped into place with stones and stuffed round with faded brown rags; windows were cracked and broken and pasted over with old paper; the roof, which was of stone tiles, shewed many gaping black holes; dry, dead grasses poked up between the paving stones. It gave the house a melancholy air, particularly since it was surrounded by a moat of dark, still water that reproduced all this desolation as faithfully as any mirror.

We jumped off our horses, entered the house and passed rapidly through a great number of rooms. I observed that the gentleman's servants (of which he appeared to have a most extraordinary number) did not come forward to welcome their master or give him news of his wife but lurked about in the shadows in the most stupid fashion imaginable.

The gentleman conducted me to the chamber where his wife lay, her only attendant a tiny old woman. This person was remarkable for several things, but chiefly for a great number of long, coarse hairs that grew upon her cheeks and resembled nothing so much in the world as porcupine quills.

The room had been darkened and the fire stoked up in accordance with the old-fashioned belief that women in childbirth require to be heated. It was abominably hot. My first action upon entering the room was to pull back the curtains and throw open the windows but when I looked around I rather regretted having done any such thing, for the squalor of that room is not to be described.

The sheets, upon which the gentleman's wife lay, were crawling with vermin of all sorts. Pewter plates lay scattered about with rotting food upon them. And yet it was not the wretchedness of poverty. There was a most extraordinary muddle everywhere one looked. Over here a greasy apron embraced a volume of Diderot's Encyclopeadie; over there a jewelled red velvet slipper was trapped by the lid of a warming-pan; under the bed a silver diadem was caught on the prongs of a gardenfork; on the window-ledge the dried-out corpse of some animal (I think a cat) rested its powdery head against a china-jug. A bronze-coloured velvet garment (which rather resembled the robe of a Coptic pope) had been cast down on the floor in lieu of a carpet. It was embroidered all over with gold and pearls, but the threads had broken and the pearls lay scattered in the dirt. It was altogether such an extraordinary blending of magnificence and filth as I could never have conceived of, and left me entirely astonished that any one should tolerate such slothfulness and neglect on the part of their servants.

As for the lady, poor thing, she was very young—perhaps no more than fifteen—and very thin. Her bones shewed through an almost translucent skin which was stretched, tight as a drum, over her swollen belly. Although I have read a great deal upon the subject, I found it more difficult than I had imagined to make the lady attend to what I was saying. My instructions were exceptionally clear and precise, but she was weak and in pain and I could not persuade her to listen to me.

I soon discovered that the baby was lodged in a most unfortunate position. Having no forceps I tried several times to turn it with my hand and at the fourth attempt

I succeeded. Between the hours of four and five a male child was born. I did not at first like his colour. Mr Baillie told me that newborn children are generally the colour of claret; sometimes, he said, they may be as dark as port-wine but this child was, to all intents and purposes, black. He was, however, quite remarkably strong. He gave me a great kick as I passed him to the old woman. A bruise upon my arm marks the place.

But I could not save the mother. At the end she was like a house through which a great wind rushes making all the doors bang at their frames: death was rushing through her and her wits came loose and banged about inside her head. She appeared to believe that she had been taken by force to a place where she was watched night and day by a hideous jailoress.

"Hush," said I, "these are very wild imaginings. Look about you. Here is good, kind…" I indicated the old woman with the porcupine face, ". . . who takes such excellent care of you. You are surrounded by friends. Be comforted." But she would not listen to me and called out wildly for her mother to come and take her home.

I would have given a great deal to save her. For what in the end was the result of all my exertions? One person came into this world and another left it—it seemed no very great achievement.

I began a prayer of commendation, but had not said above a dozen words when I heard a sort of squeal. Opening one eye, I saw the old woman snatch up the baby and run from the room as fast as her legs could carry her.

I finished my prayer and, with a sigh, went to find the lady's husband. I discovered him in his library where, with an admirable shew of masculine unconcern, he was reading a book. It was then about seven or eight o'clock.

I thought that it became me as a clergyman to offer some comfort and to say something of the wife he had lost, but I was prevented by my complete ignorance of everything that concerned her. Of her virtue I could say nothing at all. Of her beauty I knew little enough; I had only ever seen her with features contorted in the agonies of childbirth and of death. So I told him in plain words what had happened and finished with a short speech that sounded, even to my own ears, uncommonly like an apology for having killed his wife.

"Oh!" he said. "I dare say you did what you could."

I admired his philosophy though I confess it surprized me a little. Then I recalled that, in speaking to me, she had made several errors of grammar and had employed some dialect words and expressions. I concluded that perhaps, like many gentlemen before him, he had been enticed into an unequal marriage by blue eyes and fair hair, and that he had later come to regret it.

"A son, you say?" he said in perfect good humour. "Excellent!" And he stuck his head out of the door and called for the baby to be brought to him. A moment later Dando and the porcupine-faced nurse appeared with the child. The gentleman examined his son very minutely and declared himself delighted. Then he held the baby up and said the following words to it: "On to the shovel you must go, sir!" He gave the child a hearty shake; "And into the fire you must go, sir!" Another shake; "And under the burning coals you must go, sir!" And another shake.

I found his humour a little odd.

Then the nurse brought out a cloath and seemed to be about to wrap the baby in it.

"Oh, but I must protest, sir!" I cried, "Indeed I must! Have you nothing cleaner to wrap the child in?"

They all looked at me in some amazement. Then the gentleman smiled and said, "What excellent eyesight you must have, Mr Simonelli! Does not this cloath appear to you to be made of the finest, whitest linen imaginable?"

"No," said I in some irritation, "it appears to me to be a dirty rag that I would scarcely use to clean my boots!"

"Indeed?" said the gentleman in some surprize. "And Dando? Tell me, how does he strike you? Do you see the ruby buckles on his shoes? No? What of his yellow velvet coat and shining sword?"

I shook my head. (Dando, I may say, was dressed in the same quaint, old-fashioned style as his master, and looked every inch what he no doubt was—a tattered, swaggering scoundrel. He wore jack-boots up to his thighs, a bunch of ragged dirty lace at his throat and an ancient tricorne hat on his head.)

The gentleman gazed thoughtfully at me for a minute or two. "Mr Simonelli," he said at last, "I am quite struck by your face! Those lustrous eyes! Those fine dark eye-lashes! Those noble eye-brows! Every feature proclaims your close connexion with my own family! Do me the kindness, if you will, of stepping before this mirror and standing at my side."

I did as he asked and, leaving aside some difference in our complexions (his as brown as beechmast, mine as white as hotpressed paper), the resemblance was, I confess, remarkable. Everything which is odd or unsettling in my own face, I saw repeated in his: the same long eye-brows like black pen-strokes terminating in an upward flourish; the same curious slant to the eye-lid which bestows upon the face an expression of sleepy arrogance; the same little black mole just below the right eye.

"Oh!" he cried. "There can be no doubt about it! What was your father's name?"

"Simonelli," I said with a smile, "evidently."

"And his place of birth?"

I hesitated. "Genoa," I said.

"What was your mother's name?"

"Frances Simon."

"And her place of birth?"

"York."

He took a scrap of paper from the table and wrote it all down. "Simon and Simonelli," he said, "that is odd." He seemed to wait for some further illumination upon the matter of my parentage. He was disappointed. "Well, no matter," he said. "Whatever the connexion between us, Mr Simonelli, I shall discover it. You have done me a great service and I had intended to pay you liberally for it, but I have no notion of relations paying for services that ought to be given freely as part of the duty that family members owe one another." He smiled his long, knowing smile, "And so I must examine the question further," he said.

So all his much-vaunted interest in my face and family came to this: he would not pay me! It made me very angry to think I could have been so taken in by him! I informed him briefly that I was the new Rector of Allhope and said that I hoped to see him in church on Sunday.

But he only smiled and said, "We are not in your parish here. This house is Allhope House and according to ancient agreement I am the Lord of Allhope Manor, but over the years the house and village have become separated and now stand, as you see, at some distance from each other."

I had not the least idea what he was talking about. I turned to go with Dando who was to accompany me back to the village, but at the library door I looked back and said, "It is a curious thing, sir, but you never told me your name."

"I am John Hollyshoes," said he with a smile.

Just as the door closed I could have sworn I heard the sound of a shovel being pushed into the fire and the sound of coals being raked over.

The ride back to the village was considerably less pleasant than the ride to Allhope House had been. The moonlight was all shut out by the clouds and it continued to rain, yet Dando rode as swiftly as his master and at every moment I expected our headlong rush to end in broken necks.

A few lights appeared—the lights of a village. I got down from the black horse and turned to say something to Dando, whereupon I discovered that in that same instant of my dismounting he had caught up the reins of the black horse and was gone. I took one step and immediately fell over my trunk and parcels of books—which I presume had been left for me by Dando and which I had entirely forgot until that moment.

There seemed to be nothing close at hand but a few miserable cottages. Some distance off to the right, half a dozen windows blazed with light and their large size and regular appearance impressed me with ideas of warm rooms, supper tables and comfortable sofas. In short they suggested the abode of a *gentleman.*

My knock was answered by a neat maidservant. I inquired whether this was Mr Gathercole's house. She replied that *Admiral* Gathercole had drowned six years ago. Was I the new Rector?

The neat maidservant left me in the hall to go and announce me to someone or other and I had time to look about me. The floor was of ancient stone flags, very well swept, and the bright gleam upon every oak cabinet, every walnut chest of drawers, every little table, plainly spoke of the plentiful application of beeswax and of pleasant female industry. All was cleanliness, delicacy, elegance—which was more, I discovered, than could be said for me. I was well provided with all the various stains, smears and general dishevelments that may be acquired by walking for hours through heavy rain, galloping through thickly wooded countryside and then toiling long and hard at a childbed and a deathbed; and in addition I had acquired a sort of veneer of black grease—the inevitable result, I fancy, of a sojourn in John Hollyshoes's house.

The neat maidservant led me to a drawing-room where two ladies waited to see what sort of clergyman they had got. One rose with ponderous majesty and announced herself to be Mrs Gathercole, the Admiral's relict. The other lady was Mrs

Edmond, the Admiral's sister.

An old-fashioned Pembroke-table had been spread with a white linen cloath for supper. And the supper was a good one. There was a dish of fricasseed chicken and another of scalloped oysters, there was apple tart, Wensleydale cheese, and a decanter of wine and glasses.

Mrs Gathercole had my own letter and another upon which I discerned the unappetising scrawl of Dr Prothero. "Simonelli is an Italian name, is it not?" asked Mrs Gathercole.

"It is, madam, but the bearer of the name whom you see before you is an Englishman." She pressed me no further upon this point and I was glad not to be obliged to repeat the one or two falsehoods I had already uttered that day.

She took up Dr Prothero's letter, read aloud one or two compliments upon my learning in a somewhat doubting tone and began to speak of the house where I was to live. She said that when a house was for many years in the care of an ancient gentleman—as was the case here—it was liable to fall into a state of some dilapidation—she feared I would have a good many repairs to make and the expense would be very great, but as I was a gentleman of independent property, she supposed I would not mind it. She ran on in this manner and I stared into the fire. I was tired to death. But as I sat there I became conscious of something having been said which was not quite right, which it was my duty to correct as soon as possible. I stirred myself to speak. "Madam," I said, "you labour under a misapprehension. I have no property."

"Money, then," she said, "Government bonds."

"No, madam. Nothing."

There was a short silence.

"Mr Simonelli," said Mrs Gathercole, "this is a small parish and, for the most part, poor. The living yields no more than £50 a year. It is very far from providing an income to support a gentleman. You will not have enough money to live on."

Too late I saw the perfidious Prothero's design to immure me in poverty and obscurity. But what could I do? I had no money and no illusions that my numerous enemies at Cambridge, having once got rid of me, would ever allow me to return. I sighed and said something of my modest needs.

Mrs Gathercole gave a short, uncheerful laugh. "You may think so, Mr Simonelli, but your wife will think very differently when she understands how little she is to have for her housekeeping expences.

"My wife, madam?" said I in some astonishment.

"You are a married man, are not you, Mr Simonelli?"

"I, madam? No, madam!"

A silence of much longer duration.

"Well!" she said at last. "I do not know what to say. My instructions were clear enough, I think! A respectable, married man of private fortune. I cannot imagine what Prothero is thinking of. I have already refused the living of Allhope to one young man on the grounds of his unmarried state, but he at least has six hundred pounds a year."

The other lady, Mrs Edmond, now spoke for the first time. "What troubles me rather more," she said, "is that Dr Prothero appears to have sent us a scholar. Upperstone House is the only gentleman's house in the parish. With the exception of Mrs Gathercole's own family your parishioners will all be hill-farmers, shepherds and tradesmen of the meanest sort. Your learning, Mr Simonelli, will all be wasted here."

I had nothing to say and some of the despair I felt must have shewed in my face for both ladies became a little kinder. They told me that a room had been got ready for me at the Rectory and Mrs Edmond asked how long it had been since I had eaten.

I confessed that I had had nothing since the night before. They invited me to share their supper and then watched as everything I touched—dainty china, white linen napkins—became covered with dark, greasy marks.

As the door closed behind me I heard Mrs Edmond say, "Well, well. So that is Italian beauty! Quite remarkable. I do not think I ever saw an example of it before."

10 o'clock, Sept. 17th., 1811.

Last night complete despair! This morning perfect hope and cheerfulness! New plans constantly bubbling up in my brain! What could be more calculated to raise the spirits than a bright autumn morning with a heavy dew? Everything is rich colour, intoxicating freshness, and sparkle!

I am excessively pleased with the Rectory—and hope that I may be allowed to keep it. It is an old stone house. The ceilings are low, the floor of every room is either higher or lower than the floors of neighbouring rooms and there are more gables than chimneys. It has fourteen rooms! What in the world will I do with fourteen rooms?

I discovered Mr Whitmore's clothes in a cupboard. I had not, I confess, spared many thoughts for this old gentleman, but his clothes brought him vividly before me. Every bump and bulge of his ancient shoes betray their firm conviction that they still enclose his feet. His half-unravelled wig has not yet noticed that his poor old head is gone. The cloath of his long, pale coat is stretched and bagged, *here* to accomodate his sharp elbows, *there* to take account of the stoop of his shoulders. It was almost as if I had opened the cupboard and discovered Mr Whitmore.

Someone calls me from the garden…

4 o'clock, the same day.

Jemmy—the old man I spoke to yesterday—is dead. He was found this morning outside his cottage, struck clean in two from the crown of his head to his groin. Is it possible to conceive of any thing more horrible? Curiously, in all the rain we had yesterday, no one remembers seeing any lightning. The funeral will be tomorrow. He was the first person I spoke to in Allhope and my first duty will be to bury him.

The second, and to my mind *lesser*, misfortune to have befallen the parish is that a young woman has disappeared. Dido Puddifer has not been seen since early this morning when her mother, Mrs Glossop, went to a neighbour's house to borrow a nutmeg grater. Mrs Glossop left Dido walking up and down in the orchard with her baby at her breast, but when she returned the baby was lying in the wet grass and Dido was gone.

I accompanied Mrs Edmond to the cottage to pay a visit of sympathy to the family and as we were coming back Mrs Edmond said, "The worst of it is that she is a very pretty girl, all golden curls and soft blue eyes. I cannot help but suppose some passing scoundrel has taken a fancy to her and made her go along with him."

"But does it not seem more likely," said I, "that she went with him of her own accord? She is uneducated, illiterate, and probably never thought seriously upon ethical questions in her life."

"I do not think you quite understand," said Mrs Edmond. "No girl ever loved home and husband more than Dido. No girl was more delighted to have a baby of her own. Dido Puddifer is a silly, giddy sort of girl, but she is also as good as gold."

"Oh!" said I, with a smile. "I dare say she was very good until today, but then, you know, temptation might never have come her way before."

But Mrs Edmond proved quite immoveable in her prejudice in favour of Dido Puddifer and so I said no more. Besides she soon began to speak of a much more interesting subject—my own future.

"My sister-in-law's wealth, Mr Simonelli, causes her to overrate the needs of other people. She imagines that no one can exist upon less than seven hundred pounds a year, but you will do well enough. The living is 50 pounds a year, but the farm could be made to yield twice, thrice that amount. The first four or five years you must be frugal. I will see to it that you are supplied with milk and butter from Upperstone-farm, but by midsummer, Mr Simonelli, you must buy a milch-cow of your own." She thought a moment. "I dare say Marjory Hollinsclough will let me have a hen or two for you."

Sept. 20th., 1811.

This morning Rectory-lane was knee-deep in yellow and brown leaves. A silver rain like smoke blew across the churchyard. A dozen crows in their clerical dress of decent black were idling among the graves. They rose up to flap about me as I came down the lane like a host of winged curates all ready to do my bidding.

There was a whisper of sounds at my back, stifled laughter, a genteel cough, and then: "Oh! Mr Simonelli!" spoken very sweetly and rather low.

I turned.

Five young ladies; on each face I saw the same laughing eyes, the same knowing smiles, the same rain-speckled brown curls, like a strain of music taken up and repeated many different ways.

There were even to my befuddled senses the same bonnets, umbrellas, muslins, ribbons, repeated in a bewildering variety of colours but all sweetly blending together, all harmonious. All that I could have asserted with any assurance at that moment was that they were all as beautiful as angels. They were grouped most fetchingly, sheltering each other from the rain with their umbrellas, and the composure and dignity of the two eldest were in no way compromised by the giggles of the two youngest.

The tallest—she who had called my name—begged my pardon. To call out to someone in the lane was very shocking, she hoped I would forgive her but, ". . . Mama has entirely neglected to introduce us and Aunt Edmond is so taken up with the business about poor Dido that. . .well, in short, Mr Simonelli, we thought it best to lay ceremony aside and introduce ourselves. We are made bold to do it by the thought that you are to be our clergyman. The lambs ought not to fear the shepherd, ought they, Mr Simonelli? Oh, but I have no patience with that stupid Dr Prothero! Why did he not send you to us earlier? I hope, Mr Simonelli, that you will not judge Allhope by this dull season!" And she dismissed with a wave of her hand the sweetest, most tranquil prospect imaginable; woods, hills, moors and streams were all deemed entirely unworthy of my attention. "If only you had come in July or August then we might have shewn you all the beauties of Derbyshire, but now I fear you will find it very dull." But her smile defied me to find any place dull where *she* was to be found. "Yet," she said, brightening, "perhaps I shall persuade mama to give a ball. Do you like dancing, Mr Simonelli?"

"But Aunt Edmond says that Mr Simonelli is a scholar," said one of her sisters with the same sly smile. "Perhaps he only cares for books."

"Which books do you like best, Mr Simonelli?" demanded a Miss Gathercole of the middle size.

"Do you sing, Mr Simonelli?" asked the tallest Miss Gathercole.

"Do you shoot, Mr Simonelli?" asked the smallest Miss Gathercole, only to be silenced by an older sister. "Be quiet, Kitty, or he may shoot *you*."

Then the two eldest Miss Gathercoles each took one of my arms and walked with me and introduced me to my parish. And every remark they uttered upon the village and its inhabitants betrayed their happy conviction that it contained nothing half so interesting or delightful as *themselves*.

Sept. 27th., 1811.

I dined this evening at Upperstone House. Two courses. Eighteen dishes in each. Brown Soup. Mackerel. Haricot of mutton. Boiled chicken particularly good. Some excellent apple tarts. I was the only gentleman present.

Mrs Edmond was advising me upon my farm. ". . . and when you go to buy your sheep, Mr Simonelli, I shall accompany you. I am generally allowed to be an excellent judge of livestock."

"Indeed, madam," said I, "that is most kind, but in the meantime I have been thinking that there is no doctor nearer than Buxton and it seems to me that I could not do better than advertise my services as a physician. I dare say you have heard reports that I attended Mrs Hollyshoes."

"Who is Mrs Hollyshoes?" asked Mrs Edmond.

"The wife of the gentleman who owns Allhope House."

"I do not understand you, Mr Simonelli. There is no Allhope House here."

"Whom do you mean, Mr Simonelli?" asked the eldest Miss Gathercole.

I was vexed at their extraordinary ignorance but, with great patience, I gave them an account of my meeting with John Hollyshoes and my visit to Allhope House. But the more particulars I gave, the more obstinately they declared that no such person and no such house existed.

"Perhaps I have mistaken the name," I said—though I knew that I had not.

"Oh! You have certainly done that, Mr Simonelli!" said Mrs Gathercole.

"Perhaps it is Mr Shaw he means," said the eldest Miss Gathercole, doubtfully.

"Or John Wheston," said Miss Marianne.

They began to discuss whom I might mean, but one by one every candidate was rejected. This one was too old, that one too young. Every gentleman for miles around was pronounced entirely incapable of fathering a child and each suggestion only provided further dismal proofs of the general decay of the male sex in this particular part of Derbyshire.

Sept. 29th., 1811.

I have discovered why Mrs Gathercole was so anxious to have a rich, married clergyman. She fears that a poor, unmarried one would soon discover that the quickest way to improve his fortune is to marry one of the Miss Gathercoles. Robert Yorke (the clergyman whom Mrs Gathercole mentioned on my first evening in Allhope as having £600 a year) was refused the living because he had already shewn signs of being in love with the eldest Miss Gathercole. It must therefore be particularly galling to Mrs Gathercole that I am such a favourite with all her daughters. Each has something she is dying to learn and naturally I am to tutor all of them: French conversation for the eldest Miss Gathercole, advanced Italian grammar for Miss Marianne, the romantic parts of British History for Henrietta, the bloodthirsty parts for Kitty, Mathematics and Poetry for Jane.

Oct. 9th., 1811.

On my return from Upperstone House this morning I found Dando at the Rectory door with the two horses. He told me that his master had something of great importance and urgency to communicate to me.

John Hollyshoes was in his library as before, reading a book. Upon a dirty little table at his side there was wine in a dirty glass. "Ah! Mr Simonelli!" he cried, jumping up. "I am very glad to see you! It seems, sir, that you have the family failing as well as the family face!"

"And what would that be?" said I.

"Why! Lying, of course! Oh, come, Mr Simonelli! Do not look so shocked. You are found out, sir. Your father's name was not Simonelli—and, to my certain knowledge, he was never at Genoa!"

A silence of some moments' duration.

"Did you know my father, sir?" said I, in some confusion.

"Oh, yes! He was my cousin."

"That is entirely impossible," said I.

"Upon the contrary," said he. "If you will take a moment to peruse this letter you will see that it is exactly as I say." And he handed me some yellowing sheets of paper.

"What your aim may be in insulting me," I cried, "I cannot pretend to guess, but I hope, sir, that you will take back those words or we shall be obliged to settle the matter some other way." With the utmost impatience I thrust his letter back at him, when my eye was caught by the words, "the third daughter of a York linen-draper." "Wait!" I cried and snatched it back again. "My mother was the third daughter of a York linen-draper!"

"Indeed, Mr Simonelli," said John Hollyshoes, with his long sideways smile.

The letter was addressed to John Hollyshoes and had been written at The Old Starre Inn in Stonegate, York. The writer of the letter mentioned that he was in the middle of a hasty breakfast and there were some stains as of preserves and butter. It seemed that the writer had been on his way to Allhope House to pay John Hollyshoes a visit when he had been delayed in York by a sudden passion for the third daughter of a York linen-draper. His charmer was most minutely described. I read of "a slight plumpness", "light silvery-gold curls", "eyes of a forget-me-not blue."

By all that I have ever been told by my friends, by all that I have ever seen in sketches and watercolour portraits, this was my mother! But if nothing else proved the truth of John Hollyshoes's assertion, there was the date—January 19th., 1778—nine months to the day before my own birth. The writer signed himself, "Your loving cousin, Thomas Fairwood."

"So much love," I said, reading the letter, "and yet he deserted her the very next day!"

"Oh! You must not blame him," said John Hollyshoes. "A person cannot help his disposition, you know."

"And yet," said I, "one thing puzzles me still. My mother was extremely vague upon all points concerning her seducer—she did not even know his name—yet one thing she was quite clear about. He was a foreign gentleman."

"Oh! That is easily explained," he said. "For though we have lived in this island a very long time—many thousands of years longer than its other inhabitants—yet still we hold ourselves apart and pride ourselves on being of quite other blood."

"You are Jews perhaps, sir?" said I.

"Jews?" said he. "No, indeed!"

I thought a moment. "You say my father is dead?"

"Alas, yes. After he parted from your mother, he did not in fact come to Allhope House, but was drawn away by horse races at this place and cock-fighting at that place. But some years later he wrote to me again telling me to expect him at midsummer and promising to stay with me for a good long while. This time he got no further than a village near Carlisle where he fell in love with two young women..."

"Two young women!" I cried in astonishment.

"Well," said John Hollyshoes. "Each was as beautiful as the other. He did not know how to chuse between them. One was the daughter of a miller and the other was the daughter of a baker. He hoped to persuade them to go with him to his house in the Eildon Hills where he intended that both should live for ever and have all their hearts' desire. But, alas, it did not suit these ungrateful young women to go and the next news I had of him was that he was dead. I discovered later that the miller's daughter had sent him a message which led him to believe that she at least was on the point of relenting, and so he went to her father's mill, where the fast-running water was shaded by a rowan tree—and I pause here merely to observe that of all the trees in the greenwood the rowan is the most detestable. Both young women were waiting for him. The miller's daughter jangled a bunch of horrid rowan-berries in his face. The baker's daughter was then able to tumble him into the stream whereupon both women rolled the millstone on top of him, pinning him to the floor of the stream. He was exceedingly strong. All my family—our family I should say—are exceedingly strong, exceedingly hard to kill, but the millstone lay on his chest. He was unable to rise and so, in time, he drowned."

"Good God!" I cried. "But this is dreadful! As a clergyman I cannot approve his habit of seducing young women, but as a son I must observe that in this particular instance the revenge extracted by the young women seems out of all proportion to his offence. And were these bloodthirsty young women never brought to justice?"

"Alas, no," said John Hollyshoes. "And now I must beg that we cease to speak of a subject so very unpleasant to my family feelings. Tell me instead why you fixed upon this odd notion of being Italian."

I told him how it had been my grandfather's idea. From my own dark looks and what his daughter had told him he thought I might be Italian or Spanish. A fondness for Italian music caused him to prefer that country. Then he had taken his own name, George Alexander Simon, and fashioned out of it a name for me, Giorgio Alessandro Simonelli. I told how that excellent old gentleman had not cast off his daughter when she fell but had taken good care of her, provided money for attendants and a place for her to live and how, when she died of sorrow and shame shortly after my birth, he had brought me up and had me educated.

"But what is most remarkable," said John Hollyshoes, "is that you fixed upon that city which—had Thomas Fairwood ever gone to Italy—was precisely the place to have pleased him most.

Not gaudy Venice, not trumpeting Rome, not haughty Florence, but Genoa, all dark shadows and sinister echoes tumbling down to the shining sea!"

"Oh! But I chose it quite at random, I assure you."

"That," said John Hollyshoes, "has nothing to do with it. In choosing Genoa you exhibited the extraordinary penetration which has always distinguished our family. But it was your eyesight that betrayed you. Really, I was never so astonished in my life as I was when you remarked upon the one or two specks of dust which clung to the baby's wrapper."

I asked after the health of his son.

"Oh! He is well. Thank you. We have got an excellent wetnurse—from your own parish—whose milk agrees wonderfully well with the child."

Oct. 20th., 1811.

In the stable-yard at Upperstone House this morning the Miss Gathercoles were preparing for their ride. Naturally I was invited to accompany them.

"But, my dear," said Mrs Edmond to the eldest Miss Gathercole, "you must consider that Mr Simonelli may not ride. Not everyone rides." And she gave me a questioning look as if she would help me out of a difficulty.

"Oh!" said I. "I can ride a horse. It is of all kinds of exercise the most pleasing to me." I approached a conceited-looking grey mare but instead of standing submissively for me to mount, this ill-mannered beast shuffled off a pace or two. I followed it—it moved away. This continued for some three or four minutes, while all the ladies of Upperstone silently observed us. Then the horse stopt suddenly and I tried to mount it, but its sides were of the most curious construction and instead of finding myself upon its back in a twinkling—as invariably happens with John Hollyshoes's horses—I got stuck halfway up.

Of course the Upperstone ladies chose to find fault with me instead of their own malformed beast and I do not know what was more mortifying, the surprized looks of Miss Gathercole and Miss Marianne, or the undisguised merriment of Kitty.

I have considered the matter carefully and am forced to conclude that it will be a great advantage to me in such a retired spot to be able to ride whatever horses come to hand. Perhaps I can prevail upon Joseph, Mrs Gathercole's groom, to teach me.

Nov. 4th., 1811.

Today I went for a long walk in company with the five Miss Gathercoles. Sky as blue as paint, russet woods, fat white clouds like cushions—and that is the sum of all that I discovered of the landscape, for my attention was constantly being called away to the ladies themselves. "Oh! Mr Simonelli! Would you be so kind as to do this?"; or "Mr Simonelli, might I trouble you to do that?"; or "Mr Simonelli! What is your opinion of such and such?" I was required to carry picnic-baskets, discipline unruly sketching easels, advise upon perspective, give an opinion on Mr Coleridge's poetry, eat sweet-cake and dispense wine.

I have been reading over what I have written since my arrival here and one thing I find quite astonishing—that I ever could have supposed that there was a strong likeness between the Miss Gathercoles. There never were five sisters so different in tastes, characters, persons and countenances. Isabella, the eldest, is also the prettiest, the tallest and the most elegant. Henrietta is the most romantic, Kitty the most light-hearted and Jane is the quietest; she will sit hour after hour, dreaming over a book. Sisters come and go, battles are fought, she that is victorious sweeps from the room with a smile, she that is defeated sighs and takes up her embroidery. But Jane knows nothing of any of this—and then, quite suddenly, she will look up at me with a slow mysterious smile and I will smile back at her until I quite believe that I have joined with her in unfathomable secrets.

Marianne, the second eldest, has copper-coloured hair, the exact shade of dry beech leaves, and is certainly the most exasperating of the sisters. She and I can never be in the same room for more than a quarter of an hour without beginning to quarrel about something or other.

Nov. 16th., 1811.

John Windle has written me a letter to say that at High Table at Corpus Christi College on Thursday last Dr Prothero told Dr Considine that he pictured me in ten years' time with a wornout slip of a wife and a long train of broken-shoed, dribblenosed children, and that Dr Considine had laughed so much at this that he had swallowed a great mouthful of scalding-hot giblet soup, and returned it through his nose.

Nov. 26th., 1811.

No paths or roads go down to John Hollyshoes' house. His servants do not go out to farm his lands; there *is* no farm that I know of. How they all live I do not know. Today I saw a small creature—I think it was a rat—roasting over the fire in one of the rooms. Several of the servants bent over it eagerly, with pewter plates and ancient knives in their hands. Their faces were all in shadow. (It is an odd thing but, apart from Dando and the porcupine-faced nurse, I have yet to observe any of John Hollyshoes's servants at close quarters: they all scuttle away when ever I approach.)

John Hollyshoes is excellent company, his conversation instructive, his learning quite remarkable. He told me today that Judas Iscariot was a most skilful beekeeper and his honey superior to any that had been produced in all the last two thousand years. I was much interested by this information, having never read or heard of it before and I questioned him closely about it. He said that he believed he had a jar of Judas Iscariot's honey somewhere and if he could lay his hand upon it he would give it to me.

Then he began to speak of how my father's affairs had been left in great confusion at his death and how, since that time, the various rival claimants to his estate had been constantly fighting and quarrelling among themselves.

"Two duels have been fought to my certain knowledge," he said, "and as a natural consequence of this two claimants are dead. Another—whose passion to possess your father's estate was exceeded only by his passion for string quartets—was found three years ago hanging from a tree by his long silver hair, his body pierced through and through with the bows of violins, violoncellos, and violas like a musical Saint Sebastian. And only last winter an entire houseful of people was poisoned. The claimant had already run out of the house into the blizzard in her nightgown and it was only her servants that died. Since I have made no claim upon the estate, I have escaped most of their malice—though, to own the truth, I have a better right to the property than any of them. But naturally the person with the best claim of all would be Thomas Fairwood's son. All dissension would be at an end, should a *son* arise to claim the estate." And he looked at me.

"Oh!" said I, much surprized. "But might not the fact of my illegitimacy...?"

"We pay no attention to such things. Indeed with us it is more common than not. Your father's lands, both in England and elsewhere, are scarcely less extensive than my own and it would cost you very little trouble to procure them. Once it was known that you had my support, then I dare say we would have you settled at Rattle-heart House by next Quarter-day."

Such a stroke of good fortune, as I never dreamt of! Yet I dare not depend upon it. But I cannot help thinking of it *constantly*! No one would enjoy vast wealth more than I; and my feelings are not entirely selfish, for I honestly believe that I am exactly the sort of person who *ought* to have the direction of large estates. If I inherit then I shall improve my lands scientifically and increase its yields three or fourfold (as I have read of other gentlemen doing). I shall observe closely the lives of my tenants and servants and teach them to be happy. Or perhaps I shall sell my father's estates and purchase land in Derbyshire and marry Marianne or Isabella so that I may ride over every week to Allhope for the purpose of inquiring most minutely into Mrs Gathercole's affairs, and advising her and Mrs Edmond upon every point.

Seven o'clock in the morning, Dec. 8th., 1811.

We have had no news of Dido Puddifer. I begin to think that Mrs Edmond and I were mistaken in fancying that she had run off with a tinker or gypsy. We have closely questioned farm-labourers, shepherds and innkeepers, but no gypsies have been seen in the neighbourhood since midsummer. I intend this morning to pay a visit to Mrs Glossop, Dido's mother.

Eight o'clock in the evening, the same day.

What a revolution in all my hopes! From perfect happiness to perfect misery in scarcely twelve hours. What a fool I was to dream of inheriting my father's estate!—I might as well have contemplated taking a leasehold of a property in Hell! And I wish that I might go to Hell now, for it would be no more than I deserve. I have failed in my duty! I have imperilled the lives and souls of my parishioners. My parishioners!—the very people whose preservation from all harm ought to have been my first concern.

I paid my visit to Mrs Glossop. I found her, poor woman, with her head in her apron, weeping for Dido. I told her of the plan Mrs Edmond and I had devised to advertise in the Derby and Sheffield papers to see if we could discover any one who had seen or spoken to Dido.

"Oh!" said she, with a sigh. " 'Twill do no good, sir, for I know very well where she is."

"Indeed?" said I in some confusion. "Then why do you not fetch her home?"

"And so I would this instant," cried the woman, "did I not know that John Hollyshoes has got her!"

"John Hollyshoes?" I cried in amazement.

"Yes, sir," said she, "I dare say you will not have heard of John Hollyshoes for Mrs Edmond does not like such things to be spoken of and scolds us for our ignorant, superstitious ways. But we country people know John Hollyshoes very well. He is a very powerful fairy that has lived hereabouts—oh! since the world began, for all I know—and claims all sorts of rights over us. It is my belief that he has got some little fairy baby at End-Of-All-Hope House—which is where he lives—and that he needs a strong lass with plenty of good human milk to suckle it."

I cannot say that I believed her. Nor can I say that I did not. I do know that I sat in a state of the utmost shock for some time without speaking, until the poor woman forgot her own distress and grew concerned about me, shaking me by the shoulder and hurrying out to fetch brandy from Mrs Edmond. When she came back with the brandy I drank it down at one gulp and then went straight to Mrs Gathercole's stable and asked Joseph to saddle Quaker for me. Just as I was leaving, Mrs Edmond came out of the house to see what was the matter with me.

"No time, Mrs Edmond! No time!" I cried and rode away.

At John Hollyshoes' house Dando answered my knock and told me that his master was away from home.

"No matter," said I, with a confident smile, "for it is not John Hollyshoes that I have come to see, but my little cousin, the dear little sprite..."—I used the word "sprite" and Dando did not contradict me— "... whom I delivered seven weeks ago." Dando told me that I would find the child in a room at the end of a long hallway.

It was a great bare room that smelt of rotting wood and plaster. The walls were stained with damp and full of holes that the rats had made. In the middle of the floor was a queer-shaped wooden chair where sat a young woman. A bar of iron was fixed before her so that she could not rise and her legs and feet were confined by manacles and rusty chains. She was holding John Hollyshoes's infant son to her breast.

"Dido?" I said.

How my heart fell when she answered me with a broad smile.

"Yes, sir?"

"I am the new Rector of Allhope, Dido."

"Oh, sir! I am very glad to see you. I wish that I could rise and make you a curtsey, but you will excuse me, I am sure. The little gentleman has such an appetite this morning!"

She kissed the horrid creature and called it her angel, her doodle and her dearie-darling-pet.

"How did you come here, Dido?" I asked.

"Oh! Mr Hollyshoes' servants came and fetched me away one morning. And weren't they set upon my coming?"—she laughed merrily— "All that a-pulling of me uphill and a-putting of me in carts! And I told them plainly that there was no need for any such nonsense. As soon as I heard of the poor little gentleman's plight,"—here she shook the baby and kissed it again— "I was more than willing to give him suck. No, my only misfortune, sir, in this heavenly place, is that Mr Hollyshoes declares I must keep apart from my own sweet babe while I nurse his, and if all the angels in Heaven went down upon their shining knees and begged him he would not think any differently. Which is a pity, sir, for you know I might very easily feed two."

In proof of this point she, without the slightest embarrassment, uncovered her breasts which to my inexperienced eye did indeed appear astonishingly replete.

She was anxious to learn who suckled her own baby. Anne Hargreaves, I told her. She was pleased at this and remarked approvingly that Nan had always had a good appetite. "Indeed, sir, I never knew a lass who loved a pudding better. Her milk is sure to be sweet and strong, do not you think so, sir?"

"Well, certainly Mrs Edmond says that little Horatio Arthur thrives upon it. Dido, how do they treat you here?"

"Oh! sir. How can you ask such a question? Do you not see this golden chair set with diamonds and pearls? And this room with pillars of crystal and rose-coloured velvet curtains? At night—you will not believe it, sir, for I did not believe it myself—I sleep on a bed with six feather mattress one atop the other and six silken pillows to my head."

I said it sounded most pleasant. And was she given enough to eat and drink?

Roast pork, plum pudding, toasted cheese, bread and dripping: there was, according to Dido Puddifer, no end to the good things to be had at End-Of-All-Hope House—and I dare say each and every one of them was in truth nothing more than the mouldy crusts of bread that I saw set upon a cracked dish at her feet.

She also believed that they had given her a gown of sky-blue velvet with diamond buttons to wear and she asked me, with a conscious smile, how I liked it.

"You look very pretty, Dido," I said and she looked pleased.

But what I really saw was the same russet-coloured gown she had been wearing when they took her. It was all torn and dirty.

Her hair was matted with the fairy-child's puke and her left eye was crusted with blood from a gash in her forehead. She was altogether such a sorry sight that my heart was filled with pity for her and, without thinking what I did, I licked my fingertips and cleaned her eye with my spittle.

I opened my mouth to ask if she were ever allowed out of the golden chair encrusted with diamonds and pearls, but I was prevented by the sound of a door opening behind me. I turned and saw John Hollyshoes walk in. I quite expected him to ask me what I did there, but he seemed to suspect no mischief and instead bent down to test the chains and the shackles. These were, like everything else in the house, somewhat decayed and he was right to doubt their strength. When he had finished he rose and smiled at me.

"Will you stay and take a glass of wine with me?" he said. "I have something of a rather particular nature to ask you."

We went to the library where he poured two glasses of wine.

He said, "Cousin, I have been meaning to ask you about that family of women who live upon my English estates and make themselves so important at my expense. I have forgot their name."

"Gathercole?" said I.

"Gathercole. Exactly," said he and fell silent for a moment with a kind of thoughtful half-smile upon his dark face. "I have been a widower seven weeks now," he said, "and I do not believe I was ever so long without a wife before—not since there were women in England to be made wives of. To speak plainly, the sweets of courtship grew stale with me a long time ago and I wondered if you would be so kind as to spare me the trouble and advise me which of these women would suit me best."

"Oh!" said I. "I am quite certain that you would heartily dislike all of them!"

He laughed and put his arm around my shoulders. "Cousin," he said, "I am not so hard to please as you suppose."

"But really," said I, "I cannot advise you in the way you suggest. You must excuse me—indeed I cannot!"

"Oh? And why is that?"

"Because...Because I intend to marry one of them myself!" I cried.

"I congratulate you, cousin. Which?"

I stared at him. `What?" I said.

"Tell me which you intend to marry and I will take another."

"Marianne!" I said, "No, wait! Isabella! That is..." It struck me very forcibly at that moment that I could not chuse one without endangering all the others.

He laughed at that and affectionately patted my arm. "Your enthusiasm to possess Englishwomen is no more than I should have expected of Thomas Fairwood's son. But my own appetites are more moderate. One will suffice for me. I shall ride over to Allhope in a day or two and chuse one young lady, which will leave four for you."

The thought of Isabella or Marianne or any of them doomed to live for ever in the degradation of End-Of-All-Hope House! Oh! it is too horrible to be borne.

I have been staring in the mirror for an hour or more. I was always amazed at Cambridge how quickly people appeared to take offence at everything I said, but now I see plainly that it was not my words they hated—it was this fairy face. The dark alchemy of this face turns all my gentle human emotions into fierce fairy vices. Inside I am all despair but this face shews only fairy scorn. My remorse becomes fairy fury and my pensiveness is turned to fairy cunning.

Dec. 9th., 1811.

This morning at half past ten I made my proposals to Isabella Gathercole. She—sweet, compliant creature!—assured me that I had made her the happiest of women. But she could not at first be made to agree to a secret engagement.

"Oh!" she said. "Certainly mama and Aunt Edmond will make all sorts of difficulties, but what will secrecy achieve? You do not know them as I do. Alas, they cannot be reasoned into an understanding of your excellent qualities. But they can be worn down. An unending stream of arguments and pleas must be employed and the sooner it is begun, the sooner it will bring forth the happy resolution we wish for. I must be tearful; you must be heartbroken. I must get up a little illness—which will take time as I am just now in the most excellent good looks and health."

What could the mean-spirited scholars of Cambridge not learn from such a charming instructress? She argued so sweetly that I almost forgot what I was about and agreed to all her most reasonable demands. In the end I was obliged to tell her a little truth. I said that I had recently discovered that I was related to someone very rich who lived nearby and who had taken a great liking to me. I said that I hoped to inherit a great property very soon; surely it was not unreasonable to suppose that Mrs Gathercole would look with more favour upon my suit when I was as wealthy as she?

Isabella saw the sense of this immediately and would, I think, have begun to speak again of love and so forth, only I was obliged to hurry away as I had just observed Marianne going into the breakfast-room.

Marianne was inclined to be quarrelsome at first. It was not, she said, that she did not wish to marry me. After all, she said, she must marry someone and she believed that she and I might do very well together. But why must our engagement be a secret? That, she said, seemed almost dishonourable.

"As you wish," said I. "I had thought that your affection for me might make you glad to indulge me in this one point. And besides, you know, a secret engagement will oblige us to speak Italian to each other constantly."

Marianne is passionately fond of Italian, particularly since none of her sisters understand a word. "Oh! Very well," she said.

In the garden at half past eleven Jane accepted my proposals by leaning up to whisper in my ear: "His face is fair as heav'n when springing buds unfold." She looked up at me with her soft secret smile and took both my hands in hers.

In the morning-room a little before midday I encountered a problem of a different sort. Henrietta assured me that a secret engagement was the very thing to please her most, but begged to be allowed to write of it to her cousin in Aberdeen. It seems that this cousin, Miss Mary Macdonald, is Henrietta's dearest friend and most regular correspondent, their ages—fifteen and a half—being exactly the same.

It was the most curious thing, she said, but the very week she had first beheld me (and instantly fallen in love with me) she had had a letter from Mary Macdonald full of her love for a sandy-haired Minister of the Kirk, the Reverend John McKenzie, who appeared from Mary Macdonald's many detailed descriptions of him to be almost as handsome as myself! Did I not agree with her that it was the strangest thing in the world, this curious resemblance in their situations? Her eagerness to inform Mary Macdonald immediately on all points concerning our engagement was not, I fear, unmixed with a certain rivalry, for I suspected that she was not quite sincere in hoping that Mary Macdonald's love for Mr McKenzie might enjoy the same happy resolution as her own for me. But since I could not prevent her writing, I was obliged to agree.

In the drawing-room at three o'clock I finally came upon Kitty who would not at first listen to any thing that I had to say, but whirled around the room full of a plan to astound all the village by putting on a play in the barn at Christmas.

"You are not attending to me," said I. "Did not you hear me ask you to marry me?"

"Yes," said she, "and I have already said that I would. It is you who are not attending to me. You must advise us upon a play. Isabella wishes to be someone very beautiful who is vindicated in the last act, Marianne will not act unless she can say something in Italian, Jane cannot be made to understand any thing about it so it will be best if she does not have to speak at all, Henrietta will do whatever I tell her, and, oh! I long to be a bear! The dearest, wisest old talking bear! Who must dance—like this! And you may be either a sailor or a coachman—it does not matter which, as we have the hat for one and the boots for the other. Now tell me, Mr Simonelli, what plays would suit us?"

Two o'clock, Dec. 10th., 1811.

In the woods between End-Of-All-Hope House and the village of Allhope.

I take out my pen, my inkpot and this book.

"What are you doing?" whimpers Dido, all afraid.

"Writing my journal," I say.

"Now?" says she in amazement. Poor Dido! As I write she keeps up a continual lament that it will soon be dark and that the snow falls more heavily—which is I admit a great nuisance for the flakes fall upon the page and spoil the letters.

This morning my vigilant watch upon the village was rewarded. As I stood in the church-porch, hidden from all eyes by the thick growth of ivy, I saw Isabella coming down Upperstone-lane. A bitter wind passed over the village, loosening the last leaves from the trees and bringing with it a few light flakes of snow. Suddenly a spinning storm of leaves and snowflakes seemed to take possession of Upperstone-lane and John Hollyshoes was there, bowing low and smiling.

It is a measure of my firm resolution that I was able to leave her then, to leave all of them. Everything about John Hollyshoes struck fear into my heart, from the insinuating tilt of his head to the enigmatic gesture of his hands, but I had urgent business to attend to elsewhere and must trust that the Miss Gathercoles' regard for me will be strong enough to protect them.

I went straight to End-Of-All-Hope House and the moment I appeared in the bare room at the end of the corridor, Dido cried out, "Oh, sir! Have you come to release me from this horrid place?"

"Why, Dido!" said I, much surprized. "What has happened? I thought you were quite contented."

"And so I was, sir, until you licked your finger and touched my eye. When you did that the sight of my eye was changed. Now if I look through this eye,"—she closed her left eye and looked through her right— "I am wearing a golden dress in a wonderful palace and cradling the sweetest babe that ever I beheld. But if I look through this eye,"—she closed the right and opened her left— "I seem to be chained up in a dirty, nasty room with an ugly goblin child to nurse. But," she said hurriedly (for I was about to speak), "whichever it is I no longer care, for I am very unhappy here and should very much like to go home."

"I am pleased to hear you say so, Dido," said I. Then, warning her not to express any surprize at any thing I said or did, I put my head out of the door and called for Dando.

He was with me in an instant, bowing low.

"I have a message from your master," I said, "whom I met just now in the woods with his new bride. But, like most Englishwomen, the lady is of a somewhat nervous disposition and she has taken it into her head that End-Of-All-Hope House is a dreadful place full of horrors. So your master and I have put our heads together and concluded that the quickest way to soothe her fears is to fetch this woman… "—I indicated Dido— "…whom she knows well, to meet her. A familiar face is sure to put her at her ease."

I stopped and gazed, as though in expectation of something, at Dando's dark, twisted face. And he gazed back at me, perplexed.

"Well?" I cried. "What are you waiting for, blockhead? Do as I bid you! Loose the nurse's bonds so that I may quickly convey her to your master!" And then, in a fine counterfeit of one of John Hollyshoes' own fits of temper, I threatened him with everything I could think of: beatings, incarcerations and enchantments! I swore to tell his master of his surliness. I promised that he should be put to work to untangle all the twigs in the woods and comb smooth all the grass in the meadows for insulting me and setting my authority at nought.

Dando is a clever sprite, but I am a cleverer. My story was so convincing that he soon went and fetched the key to unlock Dido's fetters, but not before he had quite worn me out with apologies and explanations and pleas for forgiveness.

When the other servants heard the news that their master's English cousin was taking the English nurse away, it seemed to stir something in their strange clouded minds and they all came out of their hiding places to crowd around us. For the first time I saw them clearly. This was most unpleasant for me, but for Dido it was far worse. She told me afterwards that through her right eye she had seen a company of ladies and gentlemen who bent upon her looks of such kindness that it made her wretched to think she was deceiving them, while through her other eye she had seen the goblin forms and faces of John Hollyshoes' servants.

There were horned heads, antlered heads, heads carapaced like insects' heads, heads as puckered and soft as a mouldy orange; there were mouths pulled wide by tusks, mouths stretched out into trumpets, mouths that grinned, mouths that gaped, mouths that dribbled; there were bats' ears, cats' ears, rats' whiskers; there were ancient eyes in young faces, large, dewy eyes in old worn faces, there were eyes that winked and blinked in parts of anatomy where I had never before expected to see any eyes at all. The goblins were lodged in every part of the house: there was scarcely a crack in the wainscotting which did not harbour a staring eye, scarcely a gap in the banisters without a nose or snout poking through it. They prodded us with their horny fingers, they pulled our hair and they pinched us black and blue. Dido and I ran out of End-Of-All-Hope House, jumped up upon Quaker's back and rode away into the winter woods.

Snow fell thick and fast from a sea-green sky. The only sounds were Quaker's hooves and the jingle of Quaker's harness as he shook himself.

At first we made good progress, but then a thin mist came up and the path through the woods no longer led where it was supposed to. We rode so long and so far that—unless the woods had grown to be the size of Derbyshire and Nottinghamshire together—we must have come to the end of them, but we never did. And whichever path I chose we were for ever riding past a white gate with a smooth, dry lane beyond it—a remarkably dry lane considering the amount of snow which had fallen—and Dido asked me several times why we did not go down it. But I did not care for it. It was the most commonplace lane in the world, but a wind blew along it—a hot wind like the breath of an oven, and there was a smell as of burning flesh mixed with sulphur.

When it became clear that riding did no more than wear out ourselves and our horse I told Dido that we must tie Quaker to a tree—which we did. Then we climbed up into the branches to await the arrival of John Hollyshoes.

Seven o'clock, the same day.

Dido told me how she had always heard from her mother that red berries, such as rowan-berries, are excellent protection against fairy magic.

"There are some over there in that thicket," she said.

But she must have been looking with her enchanted eye for I saw, not red berries at all, but the chestnut-coloured flanks of Pandemonium, John Hollyshoes' horse.

Then the two fairies on their fairy-horses were standing before us with the white snow tumbling across them.

"Ah, cousin!" cried John Hollyshoes. "How do you do? I would shake hands with you, but you are a little out of reach up there." He looked highly delighted and as full of malice as a pudding is of plums. "I have had a very exasperating morning. It seems that the young gentlewomen have all contracted themselves to someone else—yet none will say to whom. Is that not a most extraordinary thing?"

"Most," said I.

"And now the nurse has run away." He eyed Dido sourly. "I never was so thwarted, and were I to discover the author of all my misfortunes—well, cousin, what do you suppose that I would do?"

"I have not the least idea," said I.

"I would kill him," said he. "No matter how dearly I loved him."

The ivy that grew about our tree began to shake itself and to ripple like water. At first I thought that something was trying to escape from beneath it, but then I saw that the ivy itself was moving. Strands of ivy like questing snakes rose up and wrapped themselves around my ancles and legs.

"Oh!" cried Dido in a fright and tried to pull them off me.

The ivy did not only move; it grew. Soon my legs were lashed to the tree by fresh, young strands; they coiled around my chest and wound around the upper part of my right arm. They threatened to engulf my journal but I was careful to keep that out of harm's way. They did not stop until they caressed my neck, leaving me uncertain as to whether John Hollyshoes intended to strangle me or merely to pin me to the tree until I froze to death.

John Hollyshoes turned to Dando. "Are you deaf, Ironbrains? Did you never hear me say that he is as accomplished a liar as you and I?" He paused to box Dando's ear. "Are you blind? Look at him! Can you not perceive the fierce fairy heart that might commit murder with indifference? Come here, Unseelie elf! Let me poke some new holes in your face! Perhaps you will see better out of those!"

I waited patiently until my cousin had stopped jabbing at his servant's face with the blunt end of his whip and until Dando had ceased howling. "I am not sure," I said, "whether I could commit murder with indifference, but I am perfectly willing to try." With my free arm I turned to the page in my journal where I have described my arrival in Allhope. I leant out of the tree as far as I could (this was very easily accomplished as the ivy held me snug against the trunk) and above John Hollyshoes' head I made the curious gesture that I had seen him make over the old man's head.

We were all as still as the frozen trees, as silent as the birds in the thickets and the beasts in their holes. Suddenly John Hollyshoes burst out, "Cousin…!"

It was the last word he ever spoke. Pandemonium, who appeared to know very well what was about to happen, reared up and shook his master from his back, as though terrified that he too might be caught up in my spell. There was a horrible rending sound; trees shook; birds sprang, cawing, into the air. Any one would have supposed that it was the whole world, and not merely some worthless fairy, that was being torn apart. I looked down and John Hollyshoes lay in two neat halves upon the snow.

"Ha!" said I.

"Oh!" cried Dido.

Dando gave a scream which if I were to try to reproduce it by means of the English alphabet would possess more syllables than any word hitherto seen. Then he caught up Pandemonium's reins and rode off with that extraordinary speed of which I know him to be capable.

The death of John Hollyshoes had weakened the spell he had cast on the ivy and Dido and I were able quite easily to tear it away. We rode back to Allhope where I restored her to joyful parent, loving husband, and hungry child. My parishioners came to the cottage to load me with praises, grateful thanks, promises of future aid, etc., etc. I however was tired to death and, after making a short speech advising them to benefit from the example I had given them of courage and selflessness, I pleaded the excuse of a headache to come home.

One thing, however, has vexed me very much and that is there was no time to conduct a proper examination of John Hollyshoes' body. For it occurs to me that just as Reason is seated in the brain of Man, so we Fairies may contain within ourselves some organ of Magic. Certainly the fairy's bisected corpse had some curious features. I append here a rough sketch and a few notes describing the ways in which Fairy anatomy appears to depart from Human anatomy. I intend to be in the woods at first light to examine the corpse more closely.

Dec. 11th., 1811.

The body is gone. Dando, I suppose, has spirited it away. This is most vexatious as I had hoped to have it sent to Mr Baillie's anatomy school in Great Windmill-street in London. I suppose that the baby in the bare room at the end of the corridor will inherit End-Of-All-Hope House and all John Hollyshoes' estates, but perhaps the loss of Dido's milk at this significant period in its life will prevent its growing up as strong in wickedness as its parent.

I have not abandoned my own hopes of inheriting my father's estate and may very well pursue my claim when I have the time. I have never heard that the possession of an extensive property in Faerie was incompatible with the duties of a priest of the Church of England—indeed I do not believe that I ever heard the subject mentioned.

Dec. 17th., 1811.

I have been most villainously betrayed by the Reverend John McKenzie! I take it particularly hard since he is the person from whom—as a fellow clergyman—I might most reasonably have expected support. It appears that he is to marry the heiress to a castle and several hundred miles of bleak Scottish wilderness in Caithness. I hope there may be bogs and that John McKenzie may drown in them. Disappointed love has, I regret to say, screwed Miss Mary Macdonald up to such a pitch of anger that she has turned upon Henrietta and me. She writes to Henrietta that she is certain I am not be trusted and she threatens to write to Mrs Gathercole and Mrs Edmond. Henrietta is not afraid; rather she exults in the coming storm.

"You will protect me!" she cried, her eyes flashing with strange brilliance and her face flushed with excitement.

"My dear girl," said I, "I will be *dead*."

Dec. 20th., 1811.

George Hollinsclough was here a moment ago with a message that I am to wait upon Mrs Gathercole and Mrs Edmond *immediately*. I take one last fond look around this room…

The Black Fairy's Curse

Karen Joy Fowler

Karen Joy Fowler is the author of six novels and five short story collections. Her novel *The Jane Austen Book Club* spent thirteen weeks on the *New York Times* bestsellers list and was a *New York Times* Notable Book. Fowler's writing has won the Nebula and World Fantasy awards.

In Fowler's version of Sleeping Beauty, not everything is as we've always been told. The story is short, so perhaps it's best if you begin reading than spend more time with me in the introduction.

She was being chased. She kicked off her shoes, which were slowing her down. At the same time her heavy skirts vanished and she found herself in her usual work clothes. Relieved of the weight and constriction, she was able to run faster. She looked back. She was much faster than he was. Her heart was strong. Her strides were long and easy. He was never going to catch her now.

She was riding the huntsman's horse and she couldn't remember why. It was an autumn red with a tangled mane. She was riding fast. A deer leapt in the meadow ahead of her. She saw the white blink of its tail.

She'd never ridden well, never had the insane fearlessness it took, but now she was able to enjoy the easiness of the horse's motion. She encouraged it to run faster.

It was night. The countryside was softened with patches of moonlight. She could go anywhere she liked, ride to the end of the world and back again. What she would find there was a castle with a toothed tower. Around the castle was a girdle of trees, too narrow to be called a forest, and yet so thick they admitted no light at all. She knew this. Even farther away were the stars. She looked up and saw three of them fall, one right after the other. She made a wish to ride until she reached them.

She herself was in farmland. She crossed a field and jumped a low, stone fence. She avoided the cottages, homey though they seemed, with smoke rising from the roofs, and a glow the color of butter pats at the windows. The horse ran and did not seem to tire.

She wore a cloak which, when she wrapped it tightly around her, rode up and left her legs bare. Her feet were cold. She turned around to look. No one was coming after her.

She reached a river. Its edges were green with algae and furry with silt. Toward the middle she could see the darkness of deep water. The horse made its own decisions. It ran along the shallow edge, but didn't cross. Many yards later it ducked back away from the water and into a grove of trees. She lay along its neck and the silver-backed leaves of aspens brushed over her hair.

She climbed into one of the trees. She regretted every tree she had never climbed. The only hard part was the first branch. After that it was easy, or else she was stronger than she'd ever been. Stronger than she needed to be. This excess of strength gave her a moment of joy as pure as any she could remember. The climbing seemed quite as natural as stair steps, and she went as high as she could, standing finally on a limb so thin it dipped under her weight, like a boat. She retreated downward, sat with her back against the trunk and one leg dangling. No one would ever think to look for her here.

Her hair had come loose and she let it all down. It was warm on her shoulders. "Mother," she said, softly enough to blend with the wind in the leaves. "Help me."

She meant her real mother. Her real mother was not there, had not been there since she was a little girl. It didn't mean there would be no help.

Above her were the stars. Below her, looking up, was a man. He was no one to be afraid of. Her dangling foot was bare. She did not cover it. Maybe she didn't need help. That would be the biggest help of all.

"Did you want me?" he said. She might have known him from somewhere. They might have been children together. "Or did you want me to go away?"

"Go away. Find your own tree."

They went swimming together, and she swam better than he did. She watched his arms, his shoulders rising darkly from the green water. He turned and saw that she was watching. "Do you know my name?" he asked her.

"Yes," she said, although she couldn't remember it. She knew she was supposed to know it, although she could also see that he didn't expect her to. But she did feel that she knew who he was—his name was such a small part of that. "Does it start with a W?" she asked.

The sun was out. The surface of the water was a rough gold.

"What will you give me if I guess it?"

"What do you want?"

She looked past him. On the bank was a group of smiling women, her grandmother, her mother, and her stepmother, too, her sisters and stepsisters, all of them smiling at her. They waved. No one said, "Put your clothes on." No one said. "Don't go in too deep now, dear." She was a good swimmer, and there was no reason to be afraid. She couldn't think of a single thing she wanted. She flipped away, breaking the skin of the water with her legs.

She surfaced in a place where the lake held still to mirror the sky. When it settled, she looked down into it. She expected to see that she was beautiful, but she was not. A mirror only answers one question, and it can't lie. She had completely lost her looks. She wondered what she had gotten in return.

There was a mirror in the bedroom. It was dusty, so her reflection was vague. But she was not beautiful. She wasn't upset about this, and she noticed the fact, a little wonderingly. It didn't matter at all to her. Most people were taken in by appearances, but others weren't. She was healthy, she was strong. If she could manage to be kind and patient and witty and brave, then there would be men who loved her for it. There would be men who found it exciting.

He lay among the blankets, looking up at her. "Your eyes," he said. "Your incredible eyes."

His own face was in shadwo, but there was no reason to be afraid. She removed her dress. It was red. She laid it over the back of the chair. "Move over."

She had never been in bed with this man before, but she wanted to be. It was late, and no one knew where she was. In fact, her mother had told her explicitly not to come here, but there was no reason to be afraid. "I'll tell you what to do," she said. "You must use your hand and your mouth. The other—it doesn't work for me. And I want to be the first. You'll have to wait."

"I'll love waiting," he said. He covered her breast with his mouth, his hand moved between her legs. He knew how to touch her already. He kissed her other breast.

"Like that," she said. "Just like that." Her body began to tighten in anticipation.

He kissed her mouth. He kissed her mouth.

He kissed her mouth. It was not a hard kiss, but it opened her eyes. This was not the right face. She had never seen this man before, and the look he gave her—she wasn't sure she liked it. Why was he kissing her, when she was asleep and had never seen him before? What was he doing in her bedroom? She was so frightened, she stopped breathing for a moment. She closed her eyes and wished him away.

He was still there. And there was pain. Her finger dripped with blood, and when she tried to sit up, she was weak and encumbered by a heavy dress, a heavy coil of her own hair, a corset, tight and pointed shoes.

"Oh," she said. "Oh." She was about to cry, and she didn't know this man to cry before him. Her tone was accusing. She pushed him and his face showed the surprise of this. He allowed himself to be pushed. If he hadn't, she was not strong enough to force it.

He was probably a very nice man. He was giving her a concerned look. She could see that he was tired. His clothes were ripped; his own• hands were scratched. He had just done something hard, maybe dangerous. So maybe that was why he hadn't stopped to think how it might frighten her to wake up with a stranger kissing her as she lay on her back. Maybe that was why he hadn't noticed how her finger was bleeding. Because he hadn't, no matter how much she came to love him, there would always be a part of her afraid of him.

"I was having the most lovely dream," she said. She was careful not to make her tone as angry as she felt.

My Life As A Bird

Charles de Lint

Charles de Lint, along with writers like Terri Windling and John Crowley, popularized the genres of urban fantasy and mythic fiction. While most of de Lint's fiction has been written for adults, he's also penned several books for young people. His latest young adult novel, *The Painted Boy*, was released by Viking Books as their lead title in November 2010. Two books for middle-grade readers (as yet unscheduled) will be published by Little, Brown and Company. He is currently writing a young adult novel for Penguin Canada.

Fans of de Lint know him for his tales set in Newford, a fictional town very similar to Toronto, but with a stronger influx of magical creatures and events. This story features Jilly, one of my favorite Newford residents. If you haven't experienced Newford before, you're in for a treat.

From the August, 1996 issue of the Spar Distributions catalogue:

THE GIRL ZONE, No. 10. Written & illustrated by Mona Morgan. Latest issue features new chapters of *The True Life Adventures of Rockit Grrl, Jupiter Jewel & My Life as a Bird.* Includes a one-page jam with Charles Vess.
My Own Comix Co., $2.75
Back issues available.

"My Life as a Bird"
Mona's monologue from chapter three:

The thing is, we spend too much time looking outside ourselves for what we should really be trying to find inside. But we can't seem to trust what we find in ourselves—maybe because that's where we find it. I suppose it's all a part of how we ignore who we really are. We're so quick to cut away pieces of ourselves to suit a particular relationship, a job, a circle of friends, incessantly editing who we are until we fit in. Or we do it to someone else. We try to edit the people around us.

I don't know which is worse.

Most people would say it's when we do it to someone else, but I don't think either one's a very healthy option.

Why do we love ourselves so little? Why are we suspect for trying to love ourselves, for being true to who and what we are rather than what someone else thinks we should be? We're so ready to betray ourselves, but we never call it that. We have all these other terms to describe it: Fitting in. Doing the right thing. Getting along.

I'm not proposing a world solely ruled by rank self-interest; I know that there have to be some limits of politeness and compromise or all we'll have left is anarchy. And anyone who expects the entire world to adjust to them is obviously a little too full of their own self-importance.

But how can we expect others to respect or care for us, if we don't respect and care for ourselves? And how come no one asks, "If you're so ready to betray yourself, why should I believe that you won't betray me as well?"

"And then he dumped you—just like that?"

Mona nodded. "I suppose I should've seen it coming. All it seems we've been doing lately is arguing. But I've been so busy trying to get the new issue out and dealing with the people at Spar who are still being such pricks...."

She let her voice trail off. Tonight the plan had been to get away from her problems, not focus on them. She often thought that too many people used Jilly as a combination den mother/emotional junkyard and she'd promised herself a long time ago that she wouldn't be one of them. But here she was anyway, dumping her problems all over the table between them.

The trouble was, Jilly drew confidences from you as easily as she did a smile. You couldn't not open up to her.

"I guess what it boils down to," she said, "is I wish I was more like Rockit Grrl than Mona."

Jilly smiled. "Which Mona?"

"Good point."

The real-life Mona wrote and drew three ongoing strips for her own bi-monthly comic book, *The Girl Zone*. Rockit Grrl was featured in "The True Life Adventures of Rockit Grrl," the pen & ink-Mona in a semi-autobiographical strip called "My Life as a Bird." Rounding out each issue was "Jupiter Jewel."

Rockit Grrl, AKA "The Menace from Venice"—Venice Avenue, Crowsea, that is, not the Italian city or the California beach—was an in-your-face punkette with an athletic body and excellent fashion sense, strong and unafraid; a little too opinionated for her own good, perhaps, but that only allowed the plots to pretty much write themselves. She spent her time righting wrongs and combating heinous villains like "Didn't-Phone-When-He-Said-He-Would Man" and "Honest-My-Wife-and-I-Are-As-Good-As-Separated Man."

The Mona in "My Life as a Bird" had spiky blonde hair and jean overalls just as her creator did, though the real life Mona wore a T-shirt under her overalls and she usually had an inch or so of dark roots showing. They both had a quirky sense of humour and tended to expound at length on what they considered the mainstays of interesting conversation—love and death, sex and art—though the strip's monologues were far more coherent. The stories invariably took place in the character's apartment, or the local English-styled pub down the street from it, which was based on the same pub where she and Jilly were currently sharing a pitcher of draught.

Jupiter Jewel had yet to make an appearance in her own strip, but the readers all felt as though they already knew her since her friends—who did appear—were always talking about her.

"The Mona in the strip, I guess," Mona said. "Maybe life's not a smooth ride for her either, but at least she's usually got some snappy come-back line."

"That's only because you have the time to think them out for her."

"This is true."

"But then," Jilly added, "that must be half the fun. Everybody thinks of what they should have said after the fact, but you actually get to use those lines."

"Even more true."

Jilly refilled their glasses. When she set the pitcher back down on the table there was only froth left in the bottom.

"So did you come back with a good line?" she asked.

Mona shook her head. "What could I say? I was so stunned to find out that he'd never taken what I do seriously that all I could do was look at him and try to figure out how I ever thought we really knew each other."

She'd tried to put it out of her mind, but the phrase "that pathetic little comic book of yours" still stung in her memory.

"He used to like the fact that I was so different from the people where he works," she said, "but I guess he just got tired of parading his cute little Bohemian girlfriend around to office parties and the like."

Jilly gave a vigorous nod which made her curls fall down into her eyes. She pushed them back from her face with a hand that still had the inevitable paint lodged under the nails. Ultramarine blue. A vibrant coral.

"See," she said. "That's what infuriates me about the corporate world. The whole idea that if you're doing something creative that doesn't earn big bucks, you should consider it a hobby and put your real time and effort into something serious. Like your art isn't serious enough."

Mona took a swallow of beer. "Don't get me started on that."

Spar Distributions had recently decided to cut back on the non-superhero titles they carried and *The Girl Zone* had been one of the casualties. That was bad enough, but then they also wouldn't cough up her back issues or the money they owed her from what they had sold.

"You got a lousy break," Jilly told her. "They've got no right to let things drag on the way they have."

Mona shrugged. "You'd think I'd have had some clue before this," she said, more willing to talk about Pete. At least she could deal with him. "But he always seemed to like the strips. He'd laugh in all the right places and he even cried when Jamaica almost died."

"Well, who didn't?"

"I guess. There sure was enough mail on that story."

Jamaica was the pet cat in "My Life as a Bird"—Mona's one concession to fantasy in the strip since Pete was allergic to cats. She'd thought that she was only in between cats when Crumb ran away and she first met Pete, but once their relationship began to get serious she gave up on the idea of getting another one.

"Maybe he didn't like being in the strip," she said.

"What wasn't to like?" Jilly asked. "I loved the time you put me in it, even though you made me look like I was having the bad hair day from hell."

Mona smiled. "See, that's what happens when you drop out of art school."

"You have bad hair days?"

"No, I mean—"

"Besides, I didn't drop out. You did."

"My point exactly," Mona said. "I can't draw hair for the life of me. It always looks all raggedy."

"Or like a helmet, when you were drawing Pete."

Mona couldn't suppress a giggle. "It wasn't very flattering, was it?"

"But you made up for it by giving him a much better butt," Jilly said.

That seemed uproariously funny to Mona. The beer, she decided, was making her giddy. At least she hoped it was the beer. She wondered if Jilly could hear the same hysterical edge in her laugh that she did. That made the momentary good humour she'd been feeling scurry off as quickly as Pete had left their apartment earlier in the day.

"I wonder when I stopped loving him," Mona said. "Because I did, you know, before we finally had it out today. Stop loving him, I mean."

Jilly leaned forward. "Are you going to be okay? You can stay with me tonight if you like. You know, just so you don't have to be alone your first night."

Mona shook her head. "Thanks, but I'll be fine. I'm actually a little relieved, if you want to know the truth. The past few months I've been wandering through a bit of a fog, but I couldn't quite figure out what it was. Now I know."

Jilly raised her eyebrows.

"Knowing's better," Mona said.

"Well, if you change your mind…."

"I'll be scratching at your window the way those stray cats you keep feeding do."

When they called it a night, an hour and another half pitcher of draught later, Mona took a longer route home than she normally would. She wanted to clear her head of the decided buzz that was making her stride less than steady, though considering the empty apartment she was going home to, maybe that wasn't the best idea, never mind her brave words to Jilly. Maybe, instead, she should go back to the pub and down a couple of whiskeys so that she'd really be too tipsy to mope.

"Oh damn him anyway," she muttered and kicked at a tangle of crumpled newspapers that were spilling out of the mouth of an alleyway she was passing.

"Hey, watch it!"

Mona stopped at the sound of the odd gruff voice, then backed away as the smallest man she'd ever seen crawled out of the nest of papers to glare at her. He couldn't have stood more than two feet high, a disagreeable and ugly little troll of a man with a face that seemed roughly carved and then left unfinished. His clothes were ragged and shabby, his face bristly with stubble. What hair she could see coming out from under his cloth cap was tangled and greasy.

Oh my, she thought. She was drunker than she'd realized.

She stood there swaying for a long moment, staring down at him and half-expecting him to simply drift apart like smoke, or vanish. But he did neither and she finally managed to find her voice.

"I'm sorry," she said. "I just didn't see you down…there." This was coming out all wrong. "I mean…."

His glare deepened. "I suppose you think I'm too small to be noticed?"

"No. It's not that. I…."

She knew that his size was only some quirk of genetics, an unusual enough trait to find in someone out and about on a Crowsea street at midnight, but at the same time her imagination or, more likely, all the beer she'd had, was telling her that the little man scowling up at her had a more exotic origin.

"Are you a leprechaun?" she found herself asking.

"If I had a pot of gold, do you think I'd be sleeping on the street?"

She shrugged. "No, of course not. It's just...."

He put a finger to the side of his nose and blew a stream of snot onto the pavement. Mona's stomach did a flip and a sour taste rose up in her throat. Trust her that, when she finally did have some curious encounter like the kind Jilly had so often, it had to be with a grotty little dwarf such as this.

The little man wiped his nose on the sleeve of his jacket and grinned at her.

"What's the matter, princess?" he asked. "If I can't afford a bed for the night, what makes you think I'd go out and buy a handkerchief just to avoid offending your sensibilities?"

It took her a moment to digest that. Then digging in the bib pocket of her overalls, she found a couple of crumpled dollar bills and offered them to him. He regarded the money with suspicion and made no move to take it from her.

"What's this?" he said.

"I just...I thought maybe you could use a couple of dollars."

"Freely given?" he asked. "No strings, no ties?"

"Well, it's not a loan," she told him. Like she was ever going to see him again.

He took the money with obvious reluctance and a muttered "Damn."

Mona couldn't help herself. "Most people would say thank you," she said.

"Most people wouldn't be beholden to you because of it," he replied.

"I'm sorry?"

"What for?"

Mona blinked. "I meant, I don't understand why you're indebted to me now. It was just a couple of dollars."

"Then why apologize?"

"I didn't. Or I suppose I did, but—" This was getting far too confusing. "What I'm trying to say is that I don't want anything in return."

"Too late for that." He stuffed the money in his pocket. "Because your gift was freely given, it means I owe you now." He offered her his hand. "Nacky Wilde, at your service."

Seeing it was the same one he'd used to blow his nose, Mona decided to forgo the social amenities. She stuck her own hands in the side pockets of her overalls.

"Mona Morgan," she told him.

"Alliterative parents?"

"What?"

"You really should see a doctor about your hearing problem."

"I don't have a hearing problem," she said.

"It's nothing to be ashamed of. Well, lead on. Where are we going?"

"We're not going anywhere. I'm going home and you can go back to doing whatever it was you were doing before we started this conversation."

He shook his head. "Doesn't work that way. I have to stick with you until I can repay my debt."

"I don't think so."

"Oh, it's very much so. What's the matter? Ashamed to be seen in my company?

I'm too short for you? Too grubby? I can be invisible, if you like, but I get the feeling that'd only upset you more."

She had to be way more drunk than she thought she was. This wasn't even remotely a normal conversation.

"Invisible," she repeated.

He gave her an irritated look. "As in, not perceptible by the human eye. You do understand the concept, don't you?"

"You can't be serious."

"No, of course not. I'm making it up just to appear more interesting to you. Great big, semi-deaf women like you feature prominently in my daydreams, so naturally I'll say anything to try to win you over."

Working all day at her drawing desk didn't give Mona as much chance to exercise as she'd like, so she was a bit touchy about the few extra pounds she was carrying.

"I'm not big."

He craned his neck. "Depends on the perspective, sweetheart."

"And I'm not deaf."

"I was being polite. I thought it was kinder than saying you were mentally disadvantaged."

"And you're certainly not coming home with me."

"Whatever you say," he said.

And then he vanished.

One moment he was there, two feet of unsavoury rudeness, and the next she was alone on the street. The abruptness of his disappearance, the very weirdness of it, made her legs go all watery and she had to put a hand against the wall until the weak feeling went away.

I am way too drunk, she thought as she pushed off from the wall.

She peered into the alleyway, then looked up and down the street. Nothing. Gave the nest of newspapers a poke with her foot. Still nothing. Finally she started walking again, but nervously now, listening for footsteps, unable to shake the feeling that someone was watching her. She was almost back at her apartment when she remembered what he'd said about how he could be invisible.

Impossible.

But what if…?

In the end she found a phonebooth and gave Jilly a call.

"Is it too late to change my mind?" she asked.

"Not at all. Come on over."

Mona leaned against the glass of the booth and watched the street all around her. Occasional cabs went by. She saw a couple at the far end of the block and followed them with her gaze until they turned a corner. So far as she could tell, there was no little man, grotty or otherwise, anywhere in view.

"Is it okay if I bring my invisible friend?" she said.

Jilly laughed. "Sure. I'll put the kettle on. Does your invisible friend drink coffee?"

"I haven't asked him."

"Well," Jilly said, "if either of you are feeling as woozy as I am, I'm sure you could use a mug."

"I could use something," Mona said after she'd hung up.

"My Life as a Bird"

Mona's monologue from chapter eight:

Sometimes I think of God as this little man sitting on a café patio somewhere, bewildered at how it's all gotten so out of his control. He had such good intentions, but everything he made had a mind of its own and, right from the first, he found himself unable to contain their conflicting impulses. He tried to create paradise, but he soon discovered that free will and paradise were incompatible because everybody has a different idea as to what paradise should be like.

But usually when I think of him, I think of a cat: a little mysterious, a little aloof, never coming when he's called. And in my mind, God's always a he. The Bible makes it pretty clear that men are the doers; women can only be virgins or whores. In God's eyes, we can only exist somewhere in between the two Marys, the Mother of Jesus and the Magdalene.

What kind of a religion is that? What kind of religion ignores the rights of half the world's population just because they're supposed to have envy instead of a penis? One run by men. The strong, the brave, the true. The old boys' club that wrote the book and made the laws.

I'd like to find him and ask him, "Is that it, God? Did we really get cloned from a rib and because we're hand-me-downs, you don't think we've got what it takes to be strong and brave and true?"

But that's only part of what's wrong with the world. You also have to ask, what's the rationale behind wars and sickness and suffering?

Or is there no point? Is God just as bewildered as the rest of the us? Has he finally given up, spending his days now on that café patio, sipping strong espresso, and watching the world go by, none of it his concern anymore? Has he washed his hands of it all?

I've got a thousand questions for God, but he never answers any of them. Maybe he's still trying to figure out where I fit on the scale between the two Marys and he can't reply until he does. Maybe he doesn't hear me, doesn't see me, doesn't think of me at all. Maybe in his version of what the world is, I don't even exist.

Or if he's cat, then I'm a bird, and he's just waiting to pounce.

"You actually believe me, don't you?" Mona said.

The two of them were sitting in the windowseat of Jilly's studio loft, sipping coffee from fat china mugs, piano music playing softly in the background, courtesy of a recording by Mitsuko Uchida. The studio was tidier than Mona had ever seen it. All the canvases that weren't hanging up had been neatly stacked against one wall. Books were in their shelves, paint brushes cleaned and lying out in rows on the worktable, tubes of paint organized by colour in wooden and cardboard boxes. The drop cloth under the easel even looked as though it had recently gone through a wash.

"Spring clean up and tidying," Jilly had said by way of explanation.

"Hello? It's September."

"So I'm late."

The coffee had been waiting for Mona when she arrived, as had been a willing ear as she related her curious encounter after leaving the pub. Jilly, of course, was enchanted with the story. Mona didn't know why she was surprised.

"Let's say I don't disbelieve you," Jilly said.

"I don't know if I believe me. It's easier to put it down to those two pitchers of beer we had."

Jilly touched a hand to her head. "Don't remind me."

"Besides," Mona went on. "Why doesn't he show himself now?" She looked around Jilly's disconcertingly tidy studio. "Well?" she said, aiming her question at the room in general. "What's the big secret, Mr. Nacky Wilde?"

"Well, it stands to reason," Jilly said. "He knows that I could just give him something as well, and then he'd indebted to me, too."

"I don't want him indebted to me."

"It's kind of late for that."

"That's what he said."

"He'd probably know."

"Okay. I'll just get him to do my dishes for me or something."

Jilly shook her head. "I doubt it works that way. It probably has to be something that no one else can do for you except him."

"This is ridiculous. All I did was give him a couple of dollars. I didn't mean anything by it."

"Money doesn't mean anything to you?"

"Jilly. It was only two dollars."

"It doesn't matter. It's still money and no matter how much we'd like things to be different, the world revolves around our being able to pay the rent and buy art supplies and the like, so money's important in our lives. You freely gave him something that means something to you and now he has to return that in kind."

"But anybody could have given him the money."

Jilly nodded. "Anybody could have, but they didn't. You did."

"How do I get myself into these things?"

"More to the point, how do you get yourself out?"

"You're the expert. You tell me."

"Let me think about it."

Nacky Wilde didn't show himself again until Mona got back to her own apartment the next morning. She had just enough time to realize that Pete had been back to collect his things—there were gaps in the bookshelves and the stack of CDs on top of the stereo was only half the size it had been the previous night—when the little man reappeared. He was slouched on her sofa, even more disreputable looking in the daylight, his glower softened by what could only be the pleasure he took from her gasp at his sudden appearance.

She sat down on the stuffed chair across the table from him. There used to be two, but Pete had obviously taken one.

"So," she said. "I'm sober and you're here, so I guess you must be real."

"Does it always take you this long to accept the obvious?"

"Grubby little men who can appear out of thin air and then disappear back into it again aren't exactly a part of my everyday life."

"Ever been to Japan?" he asked.

"No. What's that got to—"

"But you believe it exists, don't you?"

"Oh, please. It's not at all the same thing. Next thing you'll be wanting me to believe in alien abductions and little green men from Mars."

He gave her a wicked grin. "They're not green and they don't come from—"

"I don't want to hear it," she told him, blocking her ears. When she saw he wasn't going to continue, she went on, "So was Jilly right? I'm stuck with you?"

"It doesn't make me any happier than it does you."

"Okay. Then we have to have some ground rules."

"You're taking this rather well," he said.

"I'm a practical person. Now listen up. No bothering me when I'm working. No sneaking around being invisible when I'm in the bathroom or having a shower. No watching me sleep—or getting into bed with me."

He looked disgusted at the idea. Yeah, me too, Mona thought.

"And you clean up after yourself," she finished. "Come to think of it, you could clean up yourself, too."

He glared at her. "Fine. Now for my rules. First—"

Mona shook her head. "Uh-uh. This is my place. The only rules that get made here are by me."

"That hardly seems fair."

"None of this is fair," she shot back. "Remember, nobody asked you to tag along after me."

"Nobody asked you to give me that money," he said and promptly disappeared.

"I hate it when you do that."

"Good," a disembodied voice replied.

Mona stared thoughtfully at the now-empty sofa cushions and found herself wondering what it would be like to be invisible, which got her thinking about all the ways one could be nonintrusive and still observe the world. After awhile, she got up and took down one of her old sketchbooks, flipping through it until she came to the notes she'd made when she'd first started planning her semi-autobiographical strip for *The Girl Zone*.

"My Life as a Bird"
Notes for chapter one:

(Mona and Hazel are sitting at the kitchen table in Mona's apartment having tea and muffins. Mona is watching Jamaica, asleep on the windowsill, only the tip of her tail twitching.)

MONA: Being invisible would be the coolest, but the next best thing would be, like, if you could be a bird or a cat—something that no one pays any attention to.

HAZEL: What kind of bird?

MONA: I don't know. A crow, all blue-black wings and shadowy. Or, no. Maybe something even less noticeable, like a pigeon or a sparrow.

(She gets a happy look on her face.)

MONA: Because you can tell. They pay attention to everything, but no one pays attention to them.

HAZEL: And the cat would be black, too, I suppose?

MONA: Mmm. Lean and slinky like Jamaica. Very Egyptian. But a bird would be better—more mobility—though I guess it wouldn't matter, really. The important thing is how you'd just be there, another piece of the landscape, but you'd be watching everything. You wouldn't miss a thing.

HAZEL: Bit of a voyeur, are we?

MONA: No, nothing like that. I'm not even interested in high drama, just the things that go on every day in our lives—the stuff most people don't pay attention to. That's the real magic.

HAZEL: Sounds boring.

MONA: No, it would be very Zen. Almost like meditating.

HAZEL: You've been drawing that comic of yours for too long.

The phone rang that evening while Mona was inking a new page for "Jupiter Jewel." The sudden sound startled her and a blob of ink fell from the end of her nib pen, right beside Cecil's head. At least it hadn't landed on his face.

I'll make that a shadow, she decided as she answered the phone.

"So do you still have an invisible friend?" Jilly asked.

Mona looked down the hall from the kitchen table where she was working. What she could see of the apartment appeared empty, but she didn't trust her eyesight when it came to her uninvited houseguest.

"I can't see him," she said, "but I have to assume he hasn't left."

"Well, I don't have any useful news. I've checked with all the usual sources and no one quite knows what to make of him."

"The usual sources being?"

"Christy. The professor. An old copy of *The Newford Examiner* with a special section on the fairy folk of Newford."

"You're kidding."

"I am," Jilly admitted. "But I did go to the library and had a wonderful time looking through all sorts of interesting books, from K.M. Briggs to *When the Desert Dreams* by Anne Bourke, neither of whom write about Newford, but I've always loved those fairy lore books Briggs compiled and Anne Bourke lived here, as I'm sure you knew, and I really liked the picture on the cover of her book. I know," she added, before Mona could break in. "Get to the point already."

"I'm serenely patient and would never have said such a thing," Mona told her.

"Humble, too. Anyway, apparently there are all sorts of tricksy fairy folk, from hobs to brownies. Some relatively nice, some decidedly nasty, but none of them quite fit the Nacky Wilde profile."

"You mean sarcastic, grubby and bad mannered, but potentially helpful?"

"In a nutshell."

Mona sighed. "So I'm stuck with him."

She realized that she'd been absently doodling on her art and set her pen aside before she completely ruined the page.

"It doesn't seem fair, does it?" she added. "I finally get the apartment to myself, but then some elfin squatter moves in."

"How are you doing?" Jilly asked. "I mean, aside from your invisible squatter?"

"I don't feel closure," Mona said. "I know how weird that sounds, considering what I told you yesterday. After all, Pete stomped out and then snuck back while I was with you last night to get his stuff—so I know it's over. And the more I think of it, I realize this had to work out the way it did. But I'm still stuck with all this emotional baggage, like trying to figure out why things ended up the way they did, and how come I never noticed."

"Would you take him back?"

"No."

"But you miss him?"

"I do," Mona said. "Weird, isn't it?"

"Perfectly normal, I'd say. Do you want a shoulder to commiserate on?"

"No, I need to get some work done. But thanks."

After she hung up, Mona stared down at the mess she'd made of the page she'd been working on. She supposed she could try to incorporate all the squiggles into the background, but it didn't seem worth the bother. Instead she picked up a bottle of white acrylic ink, gave it a shake and opened it. With a clean brush she began to paint over the doodles and the blob of ink she'd dropped by Cecil's head. It was obvious now that it wouldn't work as shadow, seeing how the light source was on the same side.

Waiting for the ink to dry, she wandered into the living room and looked around.

"Trouble with your love life?" a familiar, but still disembodied voice asked.

"If you're going to talk to me," she said, "at least show your face."

"Is this a new rule?"

Mona shook her head. "It's just disorienting to be talking into thin air—especially when the air answers back."

"Well, since you asked so politely...."

Nacky Wilde reappeared, slouching in the stuffed chair this time, a copy of one of Mona's comic books open on his lap.

"You're not actually reading that?" Mona said.

He looked down at the comic. "No, of course not. Dwarves can't read—their brains are much too small to learn such an obviously complex task."

"I didn't mean it that way."

"I know you didn't, but I can't help myself. I have a reputation to maintain."

"As a dwarf?" Mona asked. "Is that what you are?"

He shrugged and changed the subject. "I'm not surprised you and your boyfriend broke up."

"What's that supposed to mean?"

He stabbed the comic book with a short stubby finger. "The tension's so apparent—if this bird story holds any truth. One never gets the sense that any of the characters really like Pete."

Mona sat down on the sofa and swung her feet up onto the cushions. This was just what she needed—an uninvited, usually invisible squatter of a houseguest who was also a self-appointed analyst. Except, when she thought about it, he was right. "My Life as a Bird" was emotionally true, if not always a faithful account of actual events, and the Pete character in it had never been one of her favourites. Like the real Pete, there was an underlying tightness in his character; it was more noticeable in the strip because the rest of the cast was so Bohemian.

"He wasn't a bad person," she found herself saying.

"Of course not. Why would you let yourself be attracted to a bad person?"

Mona couldn't decide if he was being nice or sarcastic.

"They just wore him down," she said. "In the office. Won him over to their way of thinking, and there was no room for me in his life anymore."

"Or for him in yours," Nacky said.

Mona nodded. "It's weird, isn't it? Generosity of spirit seems to be so old-fashioned nowadays. We'd rather watch somebody trip on the sidewalk than help them climb the stairs to whatever it is they're reaching for."

"What is it you're reaching for?" Nacky asked.

"Oh, god." Mona laughed. "Who knows? Happiness, contentment. Some days all I want is for the lines to come together on the page and look like whatever it is that I'm trying to draw." She leaned back on the arm of the sofa and regarded the ceiling. "You know, that trick you do with invisibility is pretty cool." She turned her head to look at him. "Is it something that can be taught or do you have to be born magic?"

"Born to it, I'm afraid."

"I figured as much. But it's always been a fantasy of mine. That, or being able to change into something else."

"So I've gathered from reading this," Nacky said, giving the comic another tap with his finger. "Maybe you should try to be happy just being yourself. Look inside yourself for what you need—the way your character recommends in one of the earlier issues."

"You really have been reading it."

"That is why you write it, isn't it—to be read?"

She gave him a suspicious look. "Why are you being so nice all of a sudden?"

"Just setting you up for the big fall."

"Uh-huh."

"Thought of what I can do for you yet?" he asked.

She shook her head. "But I'm working on it."

"My Life as a Bird"

Notes for chapter seven:

(So after Mona meets Gregory, they go walking in Fitzhenry Park and sit on a bench from which they can see Wendy's Tree of Tales growing. Do I need to explain this, or can it just be something people who know will understand?)

GREGORY: Did you ever notice how we don't tell family stories anymore?

MONA: What do you mean?

GREGORY: Families used to be made up of stories—their history—and those stories were told down through the generations. It's where a family got its identity, the same way a neighbourhood or even a country did. Now the stories we share we get from television and the only thing we talk about is ourselves.

(Mona realizes this is true—maybe not for everybody, but it's true for her. Argh. How do I draw this???)

MONA: Maybe the family stories don't work anymore. Maybe they've lost their relevance.

GREGORY: They've lost nothing.

(He looks away from her, out across the park.)

GREGORY: But we have.

In the days that followed, Nacky Wilde alternated between the sarcastic grump Mona had first met and the surprisingly good company he could prove to be when he didn't, as she told him one night, "have a bee up his butt." Unfortunately, the good of the one didn't outweigh the frustration of having to put up with the other and there was no getting rid of him. When he was in one of his moods, she didn't know which was worse: having to look at his scowl and listen to his bad-tempered remarks, or telling him to vanish but know that he was still sulking around the apartment, invisible and watching her.

A week after Pete had moved out, Mona met up with Jilly at the Cyberbean Café. They were planing to attend the opening of Sophie's latest show at The Green Man Gallery and Mona had once again promised herself not to dump her problems on Jilly, but there was no one else she could talk to.

"It's so typical," she found herself saying. "Out of all the hundreds of magical beings that populate folk tales and legends, I had to get stuck with the one that has a multiple personality disorder. He's driving me crazy."

"Is he with us now?" Jilly asked.

"Who knows? Who cares?" Then Mona had to laugh. "God, listen to me. It's like I'm complaining about a bad relationship."

"Well, it is a bad relationship."

"I know. And isn't it pathetic?" Mona shook her head. "If this is what I rebounded to from Pete, I don't want to know what I'll end up with when I finally get this nasty little man out of my life. At least the sex was good with Pete."

Jilly's eyes went wide. "You're not…?"

"Oh, please. That'd be like sleeping with the eighth dwarf, Snotty—the one Disney kept out of his movie and with good reason."

Jilly had to laugh. "I'm sorry, but it's just so—"

Mona wagged a finger at her. "Don't say it. You wouldn't be laughing if it was happening to you." She looked at her watch. "We should get going."

Jilly took a last sip of her coffee. Wrapping what she hadn't finished of her cookie in a napkin, she stuck it in her pocket.

"What are you going to do?" she asked as they left the café.

"Well, I looked in The Yellow Pages, but none of the exterminators have cranky dwarves listed among the household pests they'll get rid of, so I guess I'm stuck with him for now. Though I haven't looked under exorcists yet."

"Is he Catholic?" Jilly asked.

"I didn't think it mattered. They just get rid of evil spirits, don't they?"

"Why not just ask him to leave? That's something no one else but he can do for you."

"I already thought of that," Mona told her.

"And?"

"Apparently it doesn't work that way."

"Maybe you should ask him what he can do for you."

Mona nodded thoughtfully. "You know, I never thought of that. I just assumed this whole business was one of those Rumpelstiltskin kind of things—that I had to come up with it on my own."

"What?" Nacky said later that night when Mona returned from the gallery and asked him to show himself. "You want me to list my services like on a menu? I'm not a restaurant."

"Or computer software," Mona agreed, "though it might be easier if you were either, because then at least I'd know what you can do without having to go through a song and dance to get the information out of you."

"No one's ever asked this kind of thing before."

"So what?" she asked. "Is it against the rules?"

Nacky scowled. "What makes you think there are rules?"

"There are always rules. So come on. Give."

"Fine," Nacky said. "We'll start with the most popular items." He began to count the items off on his fingers. "Potions, charms, spells, incantations—"

Mona held up a hand. "Hold on there. Let's back up a bit. What are these potions and charms and stuff."

"Well, take your ex-boyfriend," Nacky said.

Please do, Mona thought.

"I could put a spell on him so that every time he looked at a woman that he was attracted to, he'd break out in hives."

"You could do that?"

Nacky nodded. "Or it could just be a minor irritation—an itch that will never go away."

"How long would it last?"

"Your choice. For the rest of his life, if you want."

Wouldn't that serve Pete right, Mona thought. Talk about a serious payback for all those mean things he'd said about her and The Girl Zone.

"This is so tempting," she said.

"So what will it be?" Nacky asked, briskly rubbing his hands together. "Hives? An itch? Perhaps a nervous tic under his eye so that people will always think he's winking at them. Seems harmless, but it's good for any number of face slaps and more serious altercations."

"Hang on," Mona told him. "What's the big hurry?"

"I'm in no hurry. I thought you were. I thought the sooner you got rid of Snotty, the eighth dwarf, the happier you'd be."

So he had been in the café.

"Okay," Mona said. "But first I have to ask you. These charms and things of yours—do they only do negative stuff?"

Nacky shook his head. "No. They can teach you the language of birds, choose your dreams before you got to sleep, make you appear to not be somewhere when you really are—"

"Wait a sec'. You told me I had to be born magic to do that."

"No. You asked about, and I quote, 'the trick you do with invisibility,' the emphasis being mine. How I do it, you have to be born magic. An invisibility charm is something else."

"But it does the same thing?"

"For all intents and purposes."

God, but he could be infuriating.

"So why didn't you tell me that?"

Nacky smirked. "You didn't ask."

I will not get angry, she told herself. I am calmness incarnate.

"Okay," she said. "What else?"

He went back to counting the items on his fingers, starting again with a tap of his right index finger onto his left. "Potions to fall in love, to fall out of love. To make hair longer, or thicker. To make one taller, or shorter, or—" he gave her a wicked grin "—slimmer. To speak with the recent dead, to heal the sick—"

"Heal them of what?" Mona wanted to know.

"Whatever ails them," he said, then went on in a bored voice. "To turn kettles into foxes, and vice versa. To—"

Mona was beginning to suffer overload.

"Enough already," she said. "I get the point."

"But you—"

"Shh. Let me think."

She laid her head back in her chair and closed her eyes. Basically, what it boiled down to, was she could have whatever she wanted. She could have revenge on Pete—not for leaving her, but for being so mean-spirited about it. She could be invisible, or understand the language of bird and animals. And though he'd claimed not to have a pot of gold when they first met, she could probably have fame and fortune, too.

But she didn't really want revenge on Pete. And being invisible probably wasn't such a good idea since she already spent far too much time on her own as it was. What she should really do is get out more, meet more people, make more friends of her own, instead of all the people she knew through Pete. As for fame and fortune...corny as it might sound, she really did believe that the process was what was important, the journey her art and stories took her on, not the place where they all ended up.

She opened her eyes and looked at Nacky.

"Well?" he said.

She stood up and picked up her coat where she'd dropped it on the end of the sofa.

"Come on," she said as she put it on.

"Where are we going?"

"To hail a cab."

She had the taxi take them to the children's hospital. After paying the fare, she got out and stood on the lawn. Nacky, invisible in the vehicle, popped back into view. Leaves crackled underfoot as he joined her.

"There," Mona said, pointing at the long square block of a building. "I want you to heal all the kids in there."

There was a long moment of silence. When Mona turned to look at her companion, it was to find him regarding her with a thoughtful expression.

"I can't do that," he said.

Mona shook her head. "Like you couldn't make me invisible?"

"No semantics this time," he said. "I can't heal them all."

"But that's what I want."

Nacky sighed. "It's like asking for world peace. It's too big a task. But I could heal one of them."

"Just one?"

Nacky nodded.

Mona turned to look at the building again. "Then heal the sickest one."

She watched him cross the lawn. When he reached the front doors, his figure shimmered and he seemed to flow through the glass rather then step through the actual doors.

He was a gone a long time. When he finally returned, his pace was much slower and there was a haunted look in his eyes.

"There was a little girl with cancer," he said. "She would have died later tonight. Her name—"

"I don't want to know her name," Mona told him. "I just want to know, will she be all right?"

He nodded.

I could have had anything, she found herself thinking.

"Do you regret giving the gift away?" Nacky asked her.

She shook her head. "No. I only wish I had more of them." She eyed him for a long moment. "I don't suppose I could give freely give you another couple of dollars…?"

"No. It doesn't—"

"Work that way," she finished. "I kind of figured as much." She knelt down so that she wasn't towering over him. "So now what? Where will you go?"

"I have a question for you," he said.

"Shoot."

"If I asked, would you let me stay on with you?"

Mona laughed.

"I'm serious," he told her.

"And what? Things would be different now, or would you still be snarly more often than not?"

He shook his head. "No different."

"You know I can't afford to keep that apartment," she said. "I'm probably going to have to get a bachelor somewhere."

"I wouldn't mind."

Mona knew she'd be insane to agree. All she'd been doing for the past week was trying to get him out of her life. But then she thought of the look in his eyes when he'd come back from the hospital and knew that he wasn't all bad. Maybe he was a little magic man, but he was still stuck living on the street and how happy could that make a person? Could be, all he needed was what everybody needed—a fair break. Could be, if he was treated fairly, he wouldn't glower so much, or be so bad-tempered.

But could she put up with it?

"I can't believe I'm saying this," she told him, "but, yeah. You can come back with me."

She'd never seen him smile before, she realized. It transformed his features.

"You've broken the curse," he said.

"Say what?"

"You don't know how long I've had to wait to find someone both selfless and willing to take me in as I was."

"I don't know about the selfless—"

He leaned forward and kissed her.

"Thank you," he said.

And then he went whirling off across the lawn, spinning like a dervishing top. His squatness melted from him and he grew tall and lean, fluid as a willow sapling, dancing in the wind. From the far side of the lawn he waved at her. For a long moment, all she could do was stare, open-mouthed. When she finally lifted her hand to wave back, he winked out of existence, like a spark leaping from a fire, glowing brightly before it vanished into the darkness.

This time she knew he was gone for good.

"My Life as a Bird"

Mona's closing monologue from chapter eleven:

The weird thing is I actually miss him. Oh, not his crankiness, or his serious lack of personal hygiene. What I miss is the kindness that occasionally slipped through—the piece of him that survived the curse.

Jilly says that was why he was so bad-tempered and gross. He had to make himself unlikable, or it wouldn't have been so hard to find someone who would accept him for who he seemed to be. She says I stumbled into a fairy tale, which is pretty cool when you think about it, because how many people can say that?

Though I suppose if this really were a fairy tale, there'd be some kind of "happily ever after" wrap up, or I'd at least have come away with a fairy gift of one sort or another. That invisibility charm, say, or the ability to change into a bird or a cat.

But I don't really need anything like that.

I've got The *Girl Zone*. I can be anything I want in its pages. Rockit Grrl, saving the day. Jupiter, who can't seem to physically show up in her own life. Or just me.

I've got my dreams. I had a fun one last night. I was walking downtown and I was a birdwoman, spindly legs, beak where my nose should be, long wings hanging down from my shoulders like a ragged cloak. Or maybe I was just wearing a bird costume. Nobody recognized me, but they knew me all the same and thought it was way cool.

And I've touched a piece of real magic. Now, no matter how grey and bland and pointless the world might seem sometimes, I just have to remember that there really is more to everything than what we can see. Everything has a spirit that's so much bigger and brighter than you think it could hold.

Everything has one.

Me, too.

The Night Market

Holly Black

Holly Black is the bestselling author of contemporary fantasy novels for teens and children. She is perhaps best known for *The Spiderwick Chronicles*, created with illustrator Tony DiTerlizzi, which was adapted into a motion picture of the same name. She recently co-edited the anthology *Zombies vs. Unicorns* with Justine Larbalestier.

Much of this anthology uses Brothers Grimm or Hans Christian Andersen or another European-based fairytale as its base for storytelling. Holly Black takes us to the Philippines and exposes us to one of their favorite fairytales.

Tomasa walked down the road, balancing the basket of offerings on her head. Her mother would have been angry to see her carrying things like one of the maids. Even though it was night and there had been a heavy rain that day, the road was hot under Tomasa's sandaled feet. She tried to focus on the heat and not on the bottle of strong *lambanog* clinking against the dish of *paksiw na pata* or the smell of the rice cakes steamed in coconut. It would be very bad luck to eat the *parang* that was supposed to bribe an elf into lifting his curse.

Not that she'd ever seen an elf. She wasn't even sure if she believed the story that her sister, Eva, had told when she'd rushed in, clutching broken pieces of tamarind pod, hair streaming with water. Usually, the sisters walked home from school together. But today, when it started to rain, Eva had ducked under a tree and declared that she would wait out the storm. Tomasa had thought nothing of it—Eva hated to be dirty or wet or windblown.

She kicked a shard of coconut shell out into the road, scattering red ants. She shouldn't have left Eva. It all came down to that. Even though Eva was older, she had no sense. Especially around boys.

A car slowed as it passed. Tomasa kept her eyes on the road and after a moment it sped away. Girls didn't usually go walking the streets of Alaminos alone at night. The Philippines just wasn't safe—people got kidnapped or killed, even this far outside Manila. But with her father and the driver out in the provinces and her mother in Hong Kong for the week, there was only Tomasa and their maid, Rosa, left to decide who would bring the gift. Eva was too sick to do much of anything. Rosa said that was what happened when an *enkanto* fell in love—his beloved would sicken just as his heart sickened with desire.

Looking at Eva's pale face, Tomasa had said she would go. After all, no elf would fall in love with her. She touched her right cheek. She could trace the shape of her birthmark without even looking in a mirror—an irregular splash of red that covered one of her eyes and stopped just above her lips.

Tomasa kept walking, past the whitewashed church, the narrow line of shops at the edge of town, and the city's single McDonald's. Then the buildings began to thin. Spanish-style houses flanked the road, while rice fields spread out beyond them into the distance. Mosquitoes buzzed close, drawn by her sweat.

By the time Tomasa crossed the short bridge near her school, only the light of the moon let her see where to put her feet. She stepped carefully through thick plants and hopped over a ditch. The tamarind tree was unremarkable—a wide trunk clouded by thick, feathery leaves. She set her basket down among the roots.

At least the moon was only half-full. On full moon nights, Rosa said that witches and elves and other spirits met at a market in the graveyard where they traded things like people did during the day. Not that she thought it was true, but it was still frightening.

"*Tabi-tabi po*," she whispered to the darkness, just like Rosa had told her, warning him that she was there. "Please take these offerings and let my sister get better."

There was only silence and Tomasa felt even more foolish than before. She turned to go.

Something rustled in the branches above her.

Tomasa froze and the sound stopped. She wanted to believe it was the wind, but the night air was warm and stagnant.

She looked up into eyes the green of unripe bananas.

"Hello," she stammered, heart thundering in her chest.

The *enkanto* stepped out onto one of the large limbs of the tree. His skin was the same dark cinnamon as a tamarind pod and his feet were bare. His clothes surprised her—cut off jeans and a T-shirt with a cracked and faded logo on it. He might have been a boy from the rice fields if it wasn't for his too-bright eyes and the fact that the branch hadn't so much as dipped under his weight.

He smiled down at her and she could not help but notice that he was beautiful. "What if I don't make your sister well?" he asked.

Tomasa didn't know what to say. She had lost track of the conversation. She was still trying to decide if she was willing to believe in elves. "What?"

He jumped down from his perch and she took a quick step away from him.

The elf boy picked up the *lambanog* and twisted the cap free. His hair rustled like leaves. "The food—is it freely given?"

"I don't understand."

"Is it mine whether I make your sister better or not?"

She forced herself to concentrate on his question. Both answers seemed wrong. If she said that the food was payment, it wasn't a gift, was it? And if it wasn't a gift, then she wasn't really following Rosa's directions. "I suppose so," she said finally.

"Ah, good," the elf said and took a deep swallow of the liquor. His smile said that she'd given the wrong answer. She felt cold, despite the heat.

"You're not going to make her better," she said.

That only made his smile widen. "Let me give you something else in return—something better." He reached up into the foliage and snapped off a brown tamarind pod. Bringing it to his lips, he whispered a few words and then kissed it. "Whoever eats this will love you."

Tomasa's face flushed. "I don't want anyone to love me." She didn't need an elf to tell her that she was ugly. "I want my sister not to be sick."

"Take it," he said, putting the tamarind in her hand and closing her fingers over it. He tilted his head. "It is all you'll get from me tonight."

The elf was standing very close to her now, her hand clasped in both of his. His skin felt dry and slightly rough in a way that made her think of bark. Somehow, she had gotten tangled up in her thoughts and was no longer sure of what she ought to say.

He raised his eyebrows thoughtfully. His too-bright eyes reflected the moonlight like an animal's. Tomasa was filled with a sudden, nameless fear.

"I have to go," she said, pulling her hand free.

Over the bridge and down the familiar streets, past the closed shops, her feet finding their way by habit, Tomasa ran home. Her panic was amplified with each step, until she was racing the dark. Only when she got close to home did she slow, her shirt soaked with sweat and her muscles hurting, the pod still clasped in her hand.

Rosa was waiting on the veranda of their house, smoking one of the clove cigarettes that her brother sent by the carton from Indonesia. She got up when Tomasa walked through the gate.

"Did you see him?" Rosa asked. "Did he take the offering?"

"Yes and yes," Tomasa said, breathing hard. "But it doesn't matter."

Rosa frowned. "You really saw an *enkanto*? You're sure."

Tomasa had been a coward. Perspiration cooling on her neck, she thought of all the things she might have said. He'd caught her off guard. She hadn't expected him to have a soft smile, or to laugh, or even to exist in the first place. She looked at the tamarind shell in her hand and watched as her fingers crushed it. Bits of the pod stuck in the sticky brown fruit beneath. For all that she'd thought Eva was stupid around boys, she'd been the stupid one. "I'm sure," she said hollowly.

On her way up the stairs to bed, it occurred to Tomasa to wonder for the first time why an elf that could make a love spell with a few words would burn with thwarted desire. But then, in all of Rosa's stories the elves were wicked and strange—beings that cursed and blessed according to their whims. Maybe there was just no making sense of it.

The next day the priest came and said novenas. And after that, the *arbularyo* sprinkled the white sheets of Eva's bed with herbs. Then the doctor came and gave her some pills. But by nightfall, Eva was no better. Her skin, which had been as brown as polished mahogany, was pale and dusty as that of a snake ready to shed.

Tomasa called her father's cell phone and left a message, but she wasn't sure if he would get it. Out far enough in the provinces and getting a signal was chancy at best. Her mother's Hong Kong hotel was easier to reach. She left another message and went up to see her sister.

Eva's hair was damp with sweat and her eyes were fever-bright when Tomasa came to sit at the end of her bed. Candles and crucifixes littered the side table, along with a pot of strong and smelly herb tea.

Eva grabbed Tomasa's hand and clutched it hard enough to hurt.

"I heard what you did." Eva said with a cough. "Stay away from his goddamned tree."

Tomasa grinned. "You should drink more of the tea. It's supposed to help."

Eva grimaced and made no move toward her cup. Maybe it tasted as bad as it smelled. "Look, I'm serious," she said.

"Tell me again how he cursed you," Tomasa said. "I'm serious too."

Eva gave a weird little laugh. "I should have listened to Rosa's stories. Maybe if I'd read a couple less magazines…I don't know. I just thought he was a boy from the fields. I told him to mind his place and leave me alone."

"You didn't eat any of his fruit, right?" Tomasa asked suddenly.

"I had a little piece," Eva said, looking at the wall. "Before I knew he was there."

That was bad. Tomasa took a deep breath and tried to think of how to phase her next question. "Do you…um…do you think he might have made you fall in love with him?"

"Are you crazy?" Eva blew her nose in a tissue. "Love him? Like him? He's not even human."

Tomasa forced herself to smile, but in her heart, she worried.

Rosa was sitting at a plastic table in the kitchen chunking up cubes of ginger while garlicky chicken simmered on the stove. Tomasa liked the kitchen. Unlike the rest of the house, it was small and dark. The floor was poured concrete instead of gleaming wood. A few herbs grew in rusted coffee cans along the windowsill and there was a strong odor of sugar-cane vinegar. It was a kitchen to be useful in.

Tomasa sat down on a stool. "Tell me about elves."

Rosa looked up from her chopping, a cigarette dangling from her lips. She breathed smoke from her nose. "What do you want me to tell you?"

"Anything. Everything. Something that might help."

"They're fickle as cats and twice as cruel. You know the tales. They'll steal your heart if you let them and if you don't, they'll curse you for your good sense. They're night things—spirits—and don't care for the day. They don't like gold either. It reminds them of the sun."

"I know all that," Tomasa said. "Tell me something I don't know."

Rosa shook her head. "I'm no *mananambal*—I only know the stories. His love will fade; he will forget your sister and she will get well again."

Tomasa pressed her lips into a thin line. "What if she doesn't?"

"It has only been a two days. Be patient. Not even a cold would go away in that time."

Two days turned into three and then four. Their mother had changed her flight and was due home that Tuesday, but there was still no word from their father. By Sunday, Tomasa found that she couldn't wait anymore. She went to the shed and got a machete. She put her gold Santa Maria pendant on a chain and fastened it around her neck. Steeling herself, she walked to the tamarind tree, although her legs felt like lead and her stomach churned.

In the day, the tree looked frighteningly normal. Leafy green, sun-dappled and buzzing with flies.

She hefted the machete. "Make Eva well."

The leaves rustled with the wind, but no elf appeared.

She swung the knife at the trunk of the tree. It stuck in the wood, knocking off a piece of bark, but her hand slid forward on the blade and the sharp steel slit open her palm. She let go of the machete and watched the shallow cut well with blood.

"You'll have to do better than that," she said, wiping her hand against her jeans. She worked the blade free from the trunk and hefted it to swing again.

But somehow her grip must have been loose, because the machete tumbled from her hands before she could complete the arc. It flew off into the brush by the stream.

Tomasa stomped off in the direction of where it had fallen, but she found no trace of it in the thick weeds. "Fine," she shouted at the tree. "Fine!"

"Aren't you afraid of me?" a voice said and Eva whirled around. The elf was standing in the grass with the machete in his hand.

She found herself speechless again. If anything the daylight rendered him more alien looking. His eyes glittered and his hair seemed to move with a subtle wind as though he was underwater.

He took a step toward her, his feet keeping to the shadows. "I've heard it's very bad luck to cut down an *enkanto*'s tree."

Tomasa thought of the gold pendant around her neck and stepped into a patch of sunlight. "Good thing for me that it's only a little chipped then."

He snorted and for a moment, he looked like he was going to smile. "What if I told you that whatever you do to the tree, you do to the spirit?"

"You look fine," she said, edging back to the bridge. He did. She was the one that was bleeding.

"You're either brave or stupid." He turned the blade in his hand and held it out to her, hilt first. She would have to step closer to him, into the shadows, to take it.

"Well, I'd pick stupid," she said. "But not that stupid." She walked quickly over the bridge, leaving him still holding the machete.

Her heart beat like a drum in her chest as she made her way home.

That night, lying in bed, Tomasa heard distant music. When she turned toward the window, a full moon looked down on her. Quickly, she dressed in the dark, careful to clasp her gold chain around her neck. Holding her shoes in one hand, she crept down the stairs, bare feet making only a soft slap on the wood.

She would find a *mananambal* to remove the *enkanto*'s curse. She would go to the night market herself.

The graveyard was at the edge of town, where the electrical lines stopped running. The moonlight illuminated the distant rice fields where kerosene lamps flickered in Nipa huts. Cicadas called from the trees and beneath her feet, thorny touch-me-nots curled up with each step.

Close to the cemetery, the Japanese synth-pop was loud enough to recognize and she saw lights. Two men with machine guns slung over their shoulders stood near marble steps. A generator chugged away near the trees, long black cords connecting it to floodlights mounted on tombs. All across the graves a market had been set up, collapsible tables covered with cloth and wares, and people squatting among the stones.

From this distance, they didn't look like elves or witches or anything supernatural at all. Still, she didn't want to be rude. Unclasping the Santa Maria pendant from her neck, she put it in her mouth. She tasted the salt of her sweat and tried to find a place for it between her check and her tongue.

She wondered if the men with guns would stop her, but they let her pass without so much as a glance. A man on the edge of the tables played a little tune on a nose flute. He smiled at her and she tried to grin back, even though his teeth were unusually long and his smile seemed a touch too wide.

A few vendors squatting in front of baskets called to Tomasa as she passed. Piles of golden mangos and papaya paled in the moonlight. Foul smelling durians hung from a line. The eggplant and purple yams looked black and strange, while a heap of ginger root resembled misshapen dolls.

At another table, split carcasses of goats were spread out like blankets. Inside a loose cage of bamboo, frogs hopped frantically. Nearby was a collection of eggs, some of which seemed too slender and leathery for chickens.

"What is that?" Tomasa asked.

"Snake *balut*," said the old woman behind the table. She spit red into the dirt and Tomasa told herself that the woman was only chewing betel nut. Lots of people chewed betel nut. There was nothing strange about it.

"Snake's tasty," the vendor went on. "Better than crow, but I have that too."

Tomasa took two steps back from the table and then braced herself. She needed help and this woman was already speaking with her.

"I'm looking for a *mananambal* that can take an *enkanto*'s spell off my sister," she said.

The old woman grinned, showing crimson-stained teeth and pointed past the largest building. "Look for the man selling potions."

Tomasa set off in that direction. Outside of an open tomb, men argued over prices in front of tables spread with guns. A woman with teeth as white as coconut meat smiled at Tomasa, one arm draped around a man, and her upper body hovering in the air. She had no lower body. Wet innards flashed from beneath a beaded shirt as she moved.

Tomasa rolled the golden pendant on her tongue, her hands shaking. No one else seemed to notice.

A line of women dressed in tight clothing leaned against the outside wall of the tomb. One had skin that was far too pale, while another had feet that were turned backwards. Some of them looked like girls Tomasa knew from town, but they stared blankly at her as she passed. Tomasa shuddered and kept moving.

She passed vendors selling horns and powders, narcotics and charms. There were candles rubbed with thick salves and small clay figurines wound with bits of hair. One man sat behind a table with several iron pots smoking over a small grill.

Steam rose from them, making the hot night hotter. Bunches of herbs and flowers littered the table, along with several empty Johnny Walker and Jim Beam bottles and a chipped, ceramic funnel.

The man looked up from ladling a solution into one of the empties. His longish hair was streaked with gray and when he smiled at her, she saw that one of his teeth had been replaced with gold.

"This one has hundred herbs boiled in coconut oil," he said, pointing to one of the pots. "*Haplas*, will cure anything." He pointed to another. "And here, *gayuma*, for luck or love."

"*Lolo*," she said with a slight bob of her head. "I need something for my sister. An *enkanto* has fallen in love with her and she's sick."

"To break curses. *Sumpa*, an antidote." He indicated a third pot.

"How much?" Tomasa asked, reaching for her pockets.

His grin widened. "Wouldn't you like to assure yourself that I'm the real thing?"

Tomasa stopped, unsure of herself. What was the right answer?

"What's that in your mouth?" he asked.

"Just a pit. I bought a plum," she lied.

"You shouldn't eat the fruit here," he said, extending his hand. "Here. Spit it out. Let me see."

Tomasa shook her head.

"Come on." He smiled. "If you don't trust me a little, how can you trust me to cure your sister?"

Tomasa hesitated, but she thought of Eva, flushed and pale. She spat the golden pendant into his palm.

He cackled, the sound dry in his throat. "You're more clever than I thought."

She didn't know if she should be pleased or not.

One of the *mananambal*'s fingers darted out to dot her forehead with oil. She felt wobbly.

"What did you do?" she managed to ask. Her voice sounded thick and slow as smoke.

"You're a fine piece of flesh, even with that face. I'll get more than I could use in a thousand brews."

It sounded like nonsense to Tomasa. Her head had started to spin and all she wanted to do was sit down in the dirt and rest. But the gold-toothed man had her by the arm and was dragging her away from his table.

She stumbled along, knocking into a man in a wide straw hat who was running down the aisle of vendors. When he caught hold of her, she saw that his eyes were green as grass.

"You," she said, her voice syrup-slow. She stumbled and fell on her hands and knees. People were shouting at each other, but that wasn't so bad because at least no one was making her get up. Her necklace had fallen in the dirt beside her. She forced herself to close her hand over it.

The elf pushed the *mananambal*, saying something that she couldn't quite understand, because all the words seemed to slur together. The old man shoved back and then, grabbing the *enkanto*'s arm at the wrist, bit down with his golden tooth.

The elf gasped in pain and brought down his fist on the old man's head, knocking him backwards. The bitten arm hung limply from the elf's side.

Tomasa struggled to her feet, fighting off the thickness that threatened to overwhelm her. Something was wrong. The potion vendor had done this to her. She narrowed her eyes at him.

The *mananambal* grinned, his tooth glinting in the floodlights.

"Come on," he said, reaching for her.

"Leave me alone," she managed to say, stumbling back. The *enkanto* caught her before she fell, supporting her with his good arm.

"Let her alone," said the *enkanto*, "or I will curse you blind, lame and worse."

The old man laughed. "I'm a curse breaker, fool."

The elf grabbed one of the Jim Beam bottles from the table and slammed it down, so that he was holding a jagged glass neck. The elf smiled a very thin smile. "Then I won't bother with magic."

The old man went silent. Together, Tomasa and the elf stumbled out of the night market. Once the music had faded into the distance, they sank down beneath a balete tree.

"Why?" she asked, still a little light-headed.

He looked down and hesitated before he answered. "You're brave to go to the night market alone." He made a little laugh. "If something had happened to you, it would have been my fault."

"I thought I was just stupid," she said. She felt stupid. "Please, end this, let my sister get better."

"No," he said suddenly, standing up.

"If you really loved her, you would let her get better," said Tomasa.

"But I don't love her," the *enkanto* said.

Tomasa didn't know what to make of his words. "Then why do you torment her?"

"At first I wanted to punish her, but I don't care about that now. You visit me because she's sick," he said with a shy smile. "I want you to keep visiting me."

Tomasa felt those words like a blow. Shock mingled with anger and a horrible, dangerous pleasure that rendered her almost incapable of speech. "I won't come again," she shouted.

"You will," said the *enkanto*. He pulled himself up onto a branch of the tree, then hooked his foot in the back and climbed higher, to where the thick green leaves hid him from view.

"I will never forgive you." Tomasa meant to shout it, but it came out of her mouth in a whisper. There was no reply but the gentle night breeze and distant radio.

Her hands were shaking. She looked down at them and saw the loop of gold chain still dangling from her fingers.

And suddenly—just like that—she had a plan. An impossible, absurd plan. She made a fist around the gold pendant, feeling its edges dig into her palm. Her feet found their way over brush and vine as she darted through the town to the tamarind tree.

The elf was sitting on one of the boughs when she got there. His eyebrows rose slightly, but he smiled. She smiled back.

"I've been rude," she said, hoping that when he looked at her he would think the guilt in her eyes was for what she'd done, not for what she was about to do. "I'm sorry."

He jumped down, one arm touching the trunk to steady him. "I'm glad you came."

Tomasa walked closer. She put one hand where the old man had bitten him, hoping that he wouldn't notice her other hand was fisted. "How's your arm?"

"Fine," he said. "Weak. I can move it a little now."

Steeling herself, she looked up into his face and slid her hand higher on his arm, over his shoulder and to his neck. His green eyes narrowed.

"What are you doing?" he asked. "You're acting strange."

"Am I?" She searched for some passable explanation. "Maybe the potion hasn't really worn off."

He shook his head. His black hair rustled against her arm, making her shiver.

She slid her other hand to his throat, twining both around his back of his neck.

He didn't push her away, although his body went rigid.

Then, as quick as she could, she wrapped the chain around his neck like a golden garrote.

He choked once as she clasped the necklace. Then she stepped back, stumbling on the roots of the tamarind. His hands flew to his throat but stopped short of touching the gold.

"What have you done?" he demanded.

She crouched down in the dirt, scuttling back from him. "Release my sister from your curse." Her voice sounded cold, even to her. In truth, she didn't know what she'd done.

"It is my right! She insulted me." The elf swallowed hard around the collar.

Insulted him? Tomasa almost laughed. Only an elf would let one girl stab his tree, but curse another for being insulting. "I won't take the chain off your neck unless you make her well."

The *enkanto*'s eyes flashed with anger.

"Please," Tomasa asked.

He looked down. She could no longer read his expression. "She'll be better when you get home," he muttered.

She crept a little closer. "How do I know you're telling the truth?"

"Take it off me!" he demanded.

Tomasa wanted to say something else, but the words caught in her throat as she reached behind his neck and unhooked the chain. She knew she should run. She'd beaten him and if she stayed any longer, he would surely put a curse on her. But she didn't move.

He watched her for a moment, both of them silent. "That was…" he said finally.

"Definitely bad luck," she offered.

He laughed at that, a short soft laugh that made her cheeks grow warm. "You really wanted me to come and visit?"

"I *did*," he said with a snort.

She grinned shyly. Balling up the necklace in her hand, she tossed it in the direction of the stream.

"You know," he said, taking one of her wrists and placing it on his shoulder. "Before, when you had your hand right here, I thought that you were going to kiss me."

Her face felt hot. "Maybe I wish I had."

"It's not too late," he said.

His lips were sour, but his mouth was warm.

By the time that Tomasa got home, the sky was pink and birds were screeching from their trees. Eva was already awake, sitting at the breakfast table, eating a plate of eggs. She looked entirely recovered.

"Where were you?" Rosa asked, refilling Eva's teacup. "Where's your pendant?"

Tomasa shrugged. "I must have lost it."

"I can't believe you stayed out all night." Eva gave her a conspiratorial smile.

"*Mananambal*," Rosa whispered as she returned to the kitchen. Tomasa almost stopped her to ask what she meant, but the truth made even less sense than anyone's guesses.

Upstairs, Tomasa picked up the crushed tamarind pod from her dresser. His words were still clear in her mind from that first meeting. *Whoever eats this will love you.* She looked into the mirror, at her birthmark, bright as blood, at her kiss-stung lips, at the absurd smile stretching across her face.

Carefully separating out the crushed pieces of shell, she pulled the dried pulp free from its cage of veins. Piece by piece, she put the sweet brown fruit in her own mouth and swallowed it down.

The Rose in Twelve Petals

Theodora Goss

Theodora Goss' stories have been nominated for the Nebula Award and the World Fantasy Award. Hey story "The Singing of Mount Abora," from the anthology *Logorrhea*, won the World Fantasy Award for Best Short Fiction in 2008. Goss is currently pursuing her Ph.D. in English while also teaching full-time at Boston University.

Goss is one of my favorite writers that I discovered for myself over the past decade. Her writing style has a density and simplicity that I find very compelling. I only wish that there was more of it to read. This is the second version of Sleeping Beauty in this anthology, and as different as Karen Joy Fowler's take was on the fairytale, Goss' take is different yet again.

I. The Witch

This rose has twelve petals. Let the first one fall: Madeleine taps the glass bottle, and out tumbles a bit of pink silk that clinks on the table—a chip of tinted glass—no, look closer, a crystallized rose petal. She lifts it into a saucer and crushes it with the back of a spoon until it is reduced to lumpy powder and a puff of fragrance.

She looks at the book again. "Petal of one rose crushed, dung of small bat soaked in vinegar." Not enough light comes through the cottage's small-paned windows, and besides she is growing nearsighted, although she is only thirty-two. She leans closer to the page. He should have given her spectacles rather than pearls. She wrinkles her forehead to focus her eyes, which makes her look prematurely old, as in a few years she no doubt will be.

Bat dung has a dank, uncomfortable smell, like earth in caves that has never seen sunlight.

Can she trust it, this book? Two pounds ten shillings it cost her, including postage. She remembers the notice in *The Gentlewoman's Companion*: "Every lady her own magician. Confound your enemies, astonish your friends! As simple as a cookery manual." It looks magical enough, with *Compendium Magicarum* stamped on its spine and gilt pentagrams on its red leather cover. But the back pages advertise "a most miraculous lotion, that will make any lady's skin as smooth as an infant's bottom" and the collected works of Scott.

Not easy to spare ten shillings, not to mention two pounds, now that the King has cut off her income. Rather lucky, this cottage coming so cheap, although it has no proper plumbing, just a privy out back among the honeysuckle.

Madeleine crumbles a pair of dragonfly wings into the bowl, which is already half full: orris root; cat's bones found on the village dust heap; oak gall from a branch fallen into a fairy ring; madder, presumably for its color; crushed rose petal; bat dung.

And the magical words, are they quite correct? She knows a little Latin, learned from her brother. After her mother's death, when her father began spending days in his bedroom with a bottle of beer, she tended the shop, selling flour and printed cloth to the village women, scythes and tobacco to the men, sweets to children on their way to school. When her brother came home, he would sit at the counter beside her, saying his *amo, amas*. The silver cross he earned by taking a Hibernian bayonet in the throat is the only necklace she now wears.

She binds the mixture with water from a hollow stone and her own saliva. Not pleasant this, she was brought up not to spit, but she imagines she is spitting into the King's face, that first time when he came into the shop, and leaned on the counter, and smiled through his golden beard. "If I had known there was such a pretty shopkeeper in this village, I would have done my own shopping long ago."

She remembers: buttocks covered with golden hair among folds of white linen, like twin halves of a peach on a napkin. "Come here, Madeleine." The sounds of the palace, horses clopping, pageboys shouting to one another in the early morning air. "You'll never want for anything, haven't I told you that?" A string of pearls, each as large as her smallest fingernail, with a clasp of gold filigree. "Like it? That's Hibernian work, taken in the siege of London." Only later does she notice that between two pearls, the knotted silk is stained with blood.

She leaves the mixture under cheesecloth, to dry overnight.

Madeleine walks into the other room, the only other room of the cottage, and sits at the table that serves as her writing desk. She picks up a tin of throat lozenges. How it rattles. She knows, without opening it, that there are five pearls left, and that after next month's rent there will only be four.

Confound your enemies, she thinks, peering through the inadequate light, and the wrinkles on her forehead make her look prematurely old, as in a few years she certainly will be.

II. The Queen

Petals fall from the roses that hang over the stream, Empress Josephine and Gloire de Dijon, which dislike growing so close to the water. This corner of the garden has been planted to resemble a country landscape in miniature: artificial stream with ornamental fish, a pear tree that has never yet bloomed, bluebells that the gardener plants out every spring. This is the Queen's favorite part of the garden, although the roses dislike her as well, with her romantically diaphanous gowns, her lisping voice, her poetry.

Here she comes, reciting Tennyson.

She holds her arms out, allowing her sleeves to drift on the slight breeze, imagining she is Elaine the lovable, floating on a river down to Camelot. Hard, being a lily maid now her belly is swelling.

She remembers her belly reluctantly, not wanting to touch it, unwilling to acknowledge that it exists. Elaine the lily maid had no belly, surely, she thinks, forgetting that Galahad must have been born somehow. (Perhaps he rose out of the lake?) She imagines her belly as a sort of cavern, where something is growing in the darkness, something that is not hers, alien and unwelcome.

Only twelve months ago (fourteen, actually, but she is bad at numbers), she was Princess Elizabeth of Hibernia, dressed in pink satin, gossiping about the riding master with her friends, dancing with her brothers through the ruined arches of Westminster Cathedral, and eating too much cake at her seventeenth birthday party. Now, and she does not want to think about this so it remains at the edges of her mind, where unpleasant things, frogs and slugs, reside, she is a cavern with something growing inside her, something repugnant, something that is not hers, not the lily maid of Astolat's.

She reaches for a rose, an overblown Gloire de Dijon that, in a fit of temper, pierces her finger with its thorns. She cries out, sucks the blood from her finger, and flops down on the bank like a miserable child. The hem of her diaphanous dress begins to absorb the mud at the edge of the water.

III. The Magician

Wolfgang Magus places the rose he picked that morning in his buttonhole and looks at his reflection in the glass. He frowns, as his master Herr Doktor Ambrosius would have frowned, at the scarecrow in faded wool with a drooping gray mustache. A sad figure for a court magician.

"Gott in Himmel," he says to himself, a childhood habit he has kept from nostalgia, for Wolfgang Magus is a reluctant atheist. He knows it is not God's fault but the King's, who pays him so little. If the King were to pay him, say, another shilling per week—but no, that too he would send to his sister, dying of consumption at a spa in Berne. His mind turns, painfully, from the memory of her face, white and drained, which already haunts him like a ghost.

He picks up a volume of Goethe's poems that he has carefully tied with a bit of pink ribbon and sighs. What sort of present is this, for the Princess' christening?

He enters the chapel with shy, stooping movements. It is full, and noisy with court gossip. As he proceeds up the aisle, he is swept by a Duchess' train of peau de soie, poked by a Viscountess' aigrette. The sword of a Marquis smelling of Napoleon-water tangles in his legs, and he almost falls on a Baroness, who stares at him through her lorgnette. He sidles through the crush until he comes to a corner of the chapel wall, where he takes refuge.

The christening has begun, he supposes, for he can hear the Archbishop droning in bad Latin, although he can see nothing from his corner but taxidermed birds and heads slick with macassar oil. Ah, if the Archbishop could have learned from Herr Doktor Ambrosius! His mind wanders, as it often does, to a house in Berlin and a laboratory smelling of strong soap, filled with braziers and alembics, books whose covers have been half-eaten by moths, a stuffed basilisk. He remembers his bed in the attic, and his sister, who worked as the Herr Doktor's housemaid so he could learn to be a magician. He sees her face on her pillow at the spa in Berne and thinks of her expensive medications.

What has he missed? The crowd is moving forward, and presents are being given: a rocking horse with a red leather saddle, a silver tumbler, a cap embroidered by the nuns of Iona. He hides the volume of Goethe behind his back.

Suddenly, he sees a face he recognizes. One day she came and sat beside him in the garden, and asked him about his sister. Her brother had died, he remembers, not long before, and as he described his loneliness, her eyes glazed over with tears. Even he, who understands little about court politics, knew she was the King's mistress.

She disappears behind the scented Marquis, then appears again, close to the altar where the Queen, awkwardly holding a linen bundle, is receiving the Princess' presents. The King has seen her, and frowns through his golden beard. Wolfgang Magus, who knows nothing about the feelings of a king toward his former mistress, wonders why he is angry.

She lifts her hand in a gesture that reminds him of the Archbishop. What fragrance is this, so sweet, so dark, that makes the brain clear, that makes the nostrils water? He instinctively tabulates: orris-root, oak gall, rose petal, dung of bat with a hint of vinegar.

Conversations hush, until even the Baronets, clustered in a rustic clump at the back of the chapel, are silent.

She speaks: "This is the gift I give the Princess. On her seventeenth birthday she will prick her finger on the spindle of a spinning wheel and die."

Needless to describe the confusion that follows. Wolfgang Magus watches from its edge, chewing his mustache, worried, unhappy. How her eyes glazed, that day in the garden. Someone treads on his toes.

Then, unexpectedly, he is summoned. "Where is that blasted magician!" Gloved hands push him forward. He stands before the King, whose face has turned unattractively red. The Queen has fainted and a bottle of salts is waved under her nose. The Archbishop is holding the Princess, like a sack of barley he has accidentally caught.

"Is this magic, Magus, or just some bloody trick?"

Wolfgang Magus rubs his hands together. He has not stuttered since he was a child, but he answers, "Y-yes, your Majesty. Magic." Sweet, dark, utterly magic. He can smell its power.

"Then get rid of it. Un-magic it. Do whatever you bloody well have to. Make it not be!"

Wolfgang Magus already knows that he will not be able to do so, but he says, without realizing that he is chewing his mustache in front of the King, "O-of course, your Majesty."

IV. The King

What would you do, if you were James IV of Britannia, pacing across your council chamber floor before your councilors: the Count of Edinburgh, whose estates are larger than yours and include hillsides of uncut wood for which the French Emperor, who needs to refurbish his navy after the disastrous Indian campaign, would pay handsomely; the Earl of York, who can trace descent, albeit in the female line, from the Tudors; and the Archbishop, who has preached against marital infidelity in his cathedral at Aberdeen? The banner over your head, embroidered with the twelve-petaled rose of Britannia, reminds you that your claim to the throne rests tenuously on a former James' dalliance. Edinburgh's thinning hair, York's hanging jowl, the seams, edged with gold thread, where the Archbishop's robe has been let out, warn you, young as you are, with a beard that shines like a tangle of golden wires in the afternoon light, of your gouty future.

Britannia's economy depends on the wool trade, and spun wool sells for twice as much as unspun. Your income depends on the wool tax. The Queen, whom you seldom think of as Elizabeth, is young. You calculate: three months before she recovers from the birth, nine months before she can deliver another child. You might have an heir by next autumn.

"Well?" Edinburgh leans back in his chair, and you wish you could strangle his wrinkled neck.

You say, "I see no reason to destroy a thousand spinning wheels for one madwoman." Madeleine, her face puffed with sleep, her neck covered with a line of red spots where she lay on the pearl necklace you gave her the night before, one black hair tickling your ear. Clever of her, to choose a spinning wheel. "I rely entirely on

Wolfgang Magus," whom you believe is a fraud. "Gentlemen, your fairy tales will have taught you that magic must be met with magic. One cannot fight a spell by altering material conditions."

Guffaws from the Archbishop, who is amused to think that he once read fairy tales.

You are a selfish man, James IV, and this is essentially your fault, but you have spoken the truth. Which, I suppose, is why you are the King.

V. The Queen Dowager

What is the girl doing? Playing at tug-of-war, evidently, and far too close to the stream. She'll tear her dress on the rosebushes. Careless, these young people, thinks the Queen Dowager. And who is she playing with? Young Lord Harry, who will one day be Count of Edinburgh. The Queen Dowager is proud of her keen eyesight and will not wear spectacles, although she is almost sixty-three.

What a pity the girl is so plain. The Queen Dowager jabs her needle into a black velvet slipper. Eyes like boiled gooseberries that always seem to be staring at you, and no discipline. Now in her day, thinks the Queen Dowager, remembering backboards and nuns who rapped your fingers with canes, in her day girls had discipline. Just look at the Queen: no discipline. Two miscarriages in ten years, and dead before her thirtieth birthday. Of course linen is so much cheaper now that the kingdoms are united. But if only her Jims (which is how she thinks of the King) could have married that nice German princess.

She jabs the needle again, pulls it out, jabs, knots. She holds up the slipper and then its pair, comparing the roses embroidered on each toe in stitches so even they seem to have been made by a machine. Quite perfect for her Jims, to keep his feet warm on the drafty palace floors.

A tearing sound, and a splash. The girl, of course, as the Queen Dowager could have warned you. Just look at her, with her skirt ripped up one side and her petticoat muddy to the knees.

"I do apologize, Madam. I assure you it's entirely my fault," says Lord Harry, bowing with the superfluous grace of a dancing master.

"It *is* all your fault," says the girl, trying to kick him.

"Alice!" says the Queen Dowager. Imagine the Queen wanting to name the girl Elaine. What a name, for a Princess of Britannia.

"But he took my book of poems and said he was going to throw it into the stream!"

"I'm perfectly sure he did no such thing. Go to your room at once. This is the sort of behavior I would expect from a chimney sweep."

"Then tell him to give my book back!"

Lord Harry bows again and holds out the battered volume. "It was always yours for the asking, your Highness."

Alice turns away, and you see what the Queen Dowager cannot, despite her keen vision: Alice's eyes, slightly prominent, with irises that are indeed the color of gooseberries, have turned red at the corners, and her nose has begun to drip.

VI. The Spinning Wheel

It has never wanted to be an assassin. It remembers the cottage on the Isles where it was first made: the warmth of the hearth and the feel of its maker's hands, worn smooth from rubbing and lanolin.

It remembers the first words it heard: "And why are you carving roses on it, then?"

"This one's for a lady. Look how slender it is. It won't take your upland ram's wool. Yearling it'll have to be, for this one."

At night it heard the waves crashing on the rocks, and it listened as their sound mingled with the snoring of its maker and his wife. By day it heard the crying of the sea birds. But it remembered, as in a dream, the songs of inland birds and sunlight on a stone wall. Then the fishermen would come, and one would say, "What's that you're making there, Enoch? Is it for a midget, then?"

Its maker would stroke it with the tips of his fingers and answer, "Silent, lads. This one's for a lady. It'll spin yarn so fine that a shawl of it will slip through a wedding ring."

It has never wanted to be an assassin, and as it sits in a cottage to the south, listening as Madeleine mutters to herself, it remembers the sounds of seabirds and tries to forget that it was made, not to spin yarn so fine that a shawl of it will slip through a wedding ring, but to kill the King's daughter.

VII. The Princess

Alice climbs the tower stairs. She could avoid this perhaps, disguise herself as a peasant woman and beg her way to the Highlands, like a heroine in Scott's novels. But she does not want to avoid this, so she is climbing up the tower stairs on the morning of her seventeenth birthday, still in her nightgown and clutching a battered copy of Goethe's poems whose binding is so torn that the book is tied with pink ribbon to keep the pages together. Her feet are bare, because opening the shoe closet might have woken the Baroness, who has slept in her room since she was a child. Barefoot, she has walked silently past the sleeping guards, who are supposed to guard her today with particular care. She has walked past the Queen Dowager's drawing room thinking: if anyone hears me, I will be in disgrace. She has spent a larger portion of her life in disgrace than out of it, and she remembers that she once thought of it as an imaginary country, Disgrace, with its own rivers and towns and trade routes. Would it be different if her mother were alive? She remembers a face creased from the folds of the pillow, and pale lips whispering to her about the lily maid of Astolat. It would, she supposes, have made no difference. She trips on a step and almost drops the book.

She has no reason to suppose, of course, that the Witch will be there, so early in the morning. But somehow, Alice hopes she will be.

She is, sitting on a low stool with a spinning wheel in front of her.

"Were you waiting for me?" asks Alice. It sounds silly—who else would the Witch be waiting for? But she can think of nothing else to say.

"I was." The Witch's voice is low and cadenced, and although she has wrinkles at the corners of her mouth and her hair has turned gray, she is still rather beautiful. She is not, exactly, what Alice expected.

"How did you know I was coming so early?"

The Witch smiles. "I've gotten rather good at magic. I sell fortunes for my living, you see. It's not much, just enough to buy bread and butter, and to rent a small cottage. But it amuses me, knowing things about people—their lives and their future."

"Do you know anything—about me?" Alice looks down at the book. What idiotic questions to be asking. Surely a heroine from Scott's novels would think of better.

The Witch nods, and sunlight catches the silver cross suspended from a chain around her neck. She says, "I'm sorry."

Alice understands, and her face flushes. "You mean that you've been watching all along. That you've known what it's been like, being the cursed princess." She turns and walks to the tower window, so the Witch will not see how her hands are shaking. "You know the other girls wouldn't play with me or touch my toys, that the boys would spit over their shoulder, to break the curse they said. Even the chambermaids would make the sign of the cross when I wasn't looking." She can feel tears where they always begin, at the corners of her eyes, and she leans out the window to cool her face. Far below, a gardener is crossing the courtyard, carrying a pair of pruning shears. She says, "Why didn't you remove the curse, then?"

"Magic doesn't work that way." The Witch's voice is sad. Alice turns around and sees that her cheeks are wet with tears. Alice steps toward her, trips again, and drops the book, which falls under the spinning wheel.

The Witch picks it up and smiles as she examines the cover. "Of course, your Goethe. I always wondered what happened to Wolfgang Magus."

Alice thinks with relief: I'm not going to cry after all. "He went away, after his sister died. She had consumption, you know, for years and years. He was always sending her money for medicine. He wrote to me once after he left, from Berlin, to say that he had bought his old master's house. But I never heard from him again."

The Witch wipes her cheeks with the back of one hand. "I didn't know about his sister. I spoke to him once. He was a kind man."

Alice takes the book from her, then says, carefully, as though each word has to be placed in the correct order, "Do you think his spell will work? I mean, do you think I'll really sleep for a hundred years, rather than—you know?"

The Witch looks up, her cheeks still damp, but her face composed. "I can't answer that for you. You may simply be—preserved. In a pocket of time, as it were."

Alice tugs at the ribbon that binds the book together. "It doesn't matter, really. I don't think I care either way." She strokes the spinning wheel, which turns as she touches it. "How beautiful, as though it had been made just for me."

The Witch raises a hand, to stop her perhaps, or arrest time itself, but Alice places her finger on the spindle and presses until a drop of blood blossoms, as dark as the petal of a Cardinal de Richelieu, and runs into her palm.

Before she falls, she sees the Witch with her head bowed and her shoulders shaking. She thinks, for no reason she can remember, Elaine the fair, Elaine the lovable…

VIII. The Gardener

Long after, when the gardener has grown into an old man, he will tell his grandchildren about that day: skittish horses being harnessed by panicked grooms, nobles struggling with boxes while their valets carry armchairs and even bedsteads through the palace halls, the King in a pair of black velvet slippers shouting directions. The cooks leave the kettles whistling in the kitchen, the Queen Dowager leaves her jewels lying where she has dropped them while tripping over the hem of her nightgown. Everyone runs to escape the spreading lethargy that has already caught a canary in his cage, who makes soft noises as he settles into his feathers. The flowers are closing in the garden, and even the lobsters that the chef was planning to serve with melted butter for lunch have lain down in a corner of their tank.

In a few hours, the palace is left to the canary, and the lobsters, and the Princess lying on the floor of the tower.

He will say, "I was pruning a rosebush at the bottom of the tower that day. Look what I took away with me!" Then he will display a rose of the variety called Britannia, with its twelve petals half-open, still fresh and moist with dew. His granddaughter will say, "Oh, grandpa, you picked that in the garden just this morning!" His grandson, who is practical and wants to be an engineer, will say, "Grandpa, people can't sleep for a hundred years."

IX. The Tower

Let us get a historical perspective. When the tower was quite young, only a hovel really, a child knocked a stone out of its wall, and it gained an eye. With that eye it watched as the child's father, a chieftain, led his tribe against soldiers with metal breastplates and plumed helmets. Two lines met on the plain below: one regular, gleaming in the morning sun like the edge of a sword, the other ragged and blue like the crest of a wave. The wave washed over the sword, which splintered into a hundred pieces.

Time passed, and the tower gained a second story with a vertical eye as narrow as a staff. It watched a wooden structure grow beside it, in which men and cattle mingled indiscriminately. One morning it felt a prick, the point of an arrow. A bright flame blossomed from the beams of the wooden structure, men scattered, cattle screamed. One of its walls was singed, and it felt the wound as a distant heat. A castle rose, commanded by a man with eyebrows so blond that they were almost white, who caused the name Aelfric to be carved on the lintel of the tower. The castle's stone walls, pummelled with catapults, battered by rams, fell into fragments.

From the hilltop a man watched, whose nose had been broken in childhood and remained perpetually crooked. When a palace rose from the broken rock, he caused the name D'Arblay to be carved on the lintel of the tower, beside a boar rampant.

Time passed, and a woman on a white horse rode through the village that had grown around the palace walls, followed by a retinue that stretched behind her like a scarf. At the palace gates, a Darbley grown rich on tobacco plantations in the New World presented her with the palace, in honor of her marriage to the Earl of Essex. The lintel of the tower was carved with the name Elizabeth I, and it gained a third story with a lead-paned window, through which it saw in facets like a fly. One morning it watched the Queen's son, who had been playing ball in the courtyard, fall to the ground with blood dripping from his nostrils. The windows of the palace were draped in black velvet, the Queen and her consort rode away with their retinue, and the village was deserted.

Time passed. Leaves turned red or gold, snow fell and melted into rivulets, young hawks took their first flight from the battlements. A rosebush grew at the foot of the tower: a hybrid, half wild rose, half Cuisse de Nymphe, with twelve petals and briary canes. One morning men rode up to the tower on horses whose hides were mottled with sweat. In its first story, where the chieftain's son had played, they talked of James III. Troops were coming from France, and the password was Britannia. As they left the tower, one of them plucked a flower from the rosebush. "Let this be our symbol," he said in the self-conscious voice of a man who thinks that his words will be recorded in history books. The tower thought it would be alone again, but by the time the leaves had turned, a procession rode up to the palace gates, waving banners embroidered with a twelve-petaled rose. Furniture arrived from France, fruit trees were planted, and the village streets were paved so that the hooves of cattle clopped on the stones.

It has stood a long time, that tower, watching the life around it shift and alter, like eddies in a stream. It looks down once again on a deserted village—but no, not entirely deserted. A woman still lives in a cottage at its edge. Her hair has turned white, but she works every day in her garden, gathering tomatoes and cutting back the mint. When the day is particularly warm, she brings out a spinning wheel and sits in the garden, spinning yarn so fine that a shawl of it will slip through a wedding ring. If the breezes come from the west, the tower can hear her humming, just above the humming that the wheel makes as it spins. Time passes, and she sits out in the garden less often, until one day it realizes that it has not seen her for many days, or perhaps years.

Sometimes at night it thinks it can hear the Princess breathing in her sleep.

X. The Hound

In a hundred years, only one creature comes to the palace: a hound whose coat is matted with dust. Along his back the hair has come out in tufts, exposing a mass of sores. He lopes unevenly: on one of his forepaws, the inner toes have been crushed.

He has run from a city reduced to stone skeletons and drifting piles of ash, dodging tanks, mortar fire, the rifles of farmers desperate for food. For weeks now, he has been loping along the dusty roads. When rain comes, he has curled himself under a tree. Afterward, he has drunk from puddles, then loped along again with mud drying in the hollows of his paws. Sometimes he has left the road and tried to catch rabbits in the fields, but his damaged paw prevents him from running quickly enough. He has smelled them in their burrows beneath the summer grasses, beneath the poppies and cornflowers, tantalizing, inaccessible.

This morning he has smelled something different, pungent, like spoiled meat: the smell of enchantment. He has left the road and entered the forest, finding his way through a tangle of briars. He has come to the village, loped up its cobbled streets and through the gates of the palace. His claws click on its stone floor.

What does he smell? A fragrance, drifting, indistinct, remembered from when he was a pup: bacon. There, through that doorway. He lopes into the Great Hall, where breakfast waits in chafing dishes. The eggs are still firm, their yolks plump and yellow, their whites delicately fried. Sausages sit in their own grease. The toast is crisp.

He leaves a streak of egg yolk and sausage grease on the tablecloth, which has remained pristine for half a century, and falls asleep in the Queen Dowager's drawing room, in a square of sunlight that has not faded the baroque carpet.

He lives happily ever after. Someone has to. As summer passes, he wanders through the palace gardens, digging in the flower beds and trying to catch the sleeping fish that float in the ornamental pools. One day he urinates on the side of the tower, from which the dark smell emanates, to show his disapproval. When he is hungry he eats from the side of beef hanging in the larder, the sausage and eggs remaining on the breakfast table, or the mice sleeping beneath the harpsichord. In autumn, he chases the leaves falling red and yellow over the lawns and manages to pull a lobster from the kitchen tank, although his teeth can barely crack its hard shell. He never figures out how to extract the canary from its cage. When winter comes, the stone floor sends an ache through his damaged paw, and he sleeps in the King's bed, under velvet covers.

When summer comes again, he is too old to run about the garden. He lies in the Queen Dowager's drawing room and dreams of being a pup, of warm hands and a voice that whispered "What a beautiful dog," and that magical thing called a ball. He dies, his stomach still full with the last of the poached eggs. A proper fairy tale should, perhaps, end here.

XI. The Prince

Here comes the Prince on a bulldozer. What did you expect? Things change in a hundred years.

Harry pulls back the brake and wipes his forehead, which is glistening with sweat. He runs his fingers through blond hair that stands up like a shock of corn. It is just past noon, and the skin on his nose is already red and peeling.

Two acres, and he'll knock off for some beer and that liver and onion sandwich Madge made him this morning, whose grease, together with the juice of a large gherkin, is soaking its way through a brown paper wrapper and will soon stain the leather of his satchel. He leans back, looks at the tangle of briars that form the undergrowth in this part of the forest, and chews on the knuckle of his thumb.

Two acres in the middle of the forest, enough for some barley and a still. Hell of a good idea, he thinks, already imagining the bottles on their way to Amsterdam, already imagining his pals Mike and Steve watching football on a color telly. Linoleum on the kitchen floor, like Madge always wanted, and cigarettes from America. "Not that damn rationed stuff," he says out loud, then looks around startled. What kind of fool idiot talks to himself? He chews on the knuckle of his thumb again. Twenty pounds to make the Police Commissioner look the other way. Damn lucky Madge could lend them the money. The bulldozer starts up again with a roar and the smell of diesel.

You don't like where this is going. What sort of Prince is this, with his liver and onion sandwich, his gherkin and beer? Forgive me. I give you the only Prince I can find, a direct descendant of the Count of Edinburgh, himself descended from the Tudors, albeit in the female line. Of course, all such titles have been abolished. This is, after all, the Socialist Union of Britannia. If Harry knows he is a Prince, he certainly isn't telling Mike or Steve, who might sell him out for a pack of American cigarettes. Even Madge can't be trusted, though they've been sharing a flat in the commune's apartment building for three years. Hell, she made a big enough fuss about the distillery business.

The bulldozer's roar grows louder, then turns into a whine. The front wheel is stuck in a ditch. Harry climbs down and looks at the wheel. Damn, he'll have to get Mike and Steve. He kicks the wheel, kicks a tree trunk and almost gets his foot caught in a briar, kicks the wheel again.

Something flashes in the forest. Now what the hell is that? (You and I know it is sunlight flashing from the faceted upper window of the tower.) Harry opens his beer and swallows a mouthful of its warm bitterness. Some damn poacher, walking around on his land. (You and I remember that it belongs to the Socialist Union of Britannia.) He takes a bite of his liver and onion sandwich. Madge shouldn't frown so much, he thinks, remembering her in her housecoat, standing by the kitchen sink. She's getting wrinkles on her forehead. Should he fetch Mike and Steve? But the beer in his stomach, warm, bitter, tells him that he doesn't need Mike and Steve, because he can damn well handle any damn poacher himself. He bites into the gherkin.

Stay away, Prince Harry. Stay away from the forest full of briars. The Princess is not for you. You will never stumble up the tower stairs, smelling of beer; never leave a smear of mingled grease and sweat on her mouth; never take her away (thinking, Madge's rump is getting too damn broad) to fry your liver and onions and empty your ashtray of cigarette butts and iron your briefs.

At least, I hope not.

XII. The Rose

Let us go back to the beginning: petals fall. Unpruned for a hundred years, the rosebush has climbed to the top of the tower. A cane of it has found a chink in the tower window, and it has grown into the room where the Princess lies. It has formed a canopy over her, a network of canes now covered with blossoms, and their petals fall slowly in the still air. Her nightgown is covered with petals: this summer's, pink and fragrant, and those of summers past, like bits of torn parchment curling at the edges.

While everything in the palace has been suspended in a pool of time without ripples or eddies, it has responded to the seasons. Its roots go down to dark caverns which are the homes of moles and worms, and curl around a bronze helmet that is now little more than rust. More than two hundred years ago, it was rather carelessly chosen as the emblem of a nation. Almost a hundred years ago, Madeleine plucked a petal of it for her magic spell. Wolfgang Magus picked a blossom of it for his buttonhole, which fell in the chapel and was trampled under a succession of court heels and cavalry boots. A spindle was carved from its dead and hardened wood. Half a century ago, a dusty hound urinated on its roots. From its seeds, dispersed by birds who have eaten its orange hips, has grown the tangle of briars that surround the palace, which have already torn the Prince's work pants and left a gash on his right shoulder. If you listen, you can hear him cursing.

It can tell us how the story ends. Does the Prince emerge from the forest, his shirtsleeve stained with blood? The briars of the forest know. Does the Witch lie dead, or does she still sit by the small-paned window of her cottage, contemplating a solitary pearl that glows in the wrinkled palm of her hand like a miniature moon? The spinning wheel knows, and surely its wood will speak to the wood from which it was made. Is the Princess breathing? Perhaps she has been sleeping for a hundred years, and the petals that have settled under her nostrils flutter each time she exhales. Perhaps she has not been sleeping, perhaps she is an exquisitely preserved corpse, and the petals under her nostrils never quiver. The rose can tell us, but it will not. The wind sets its leaves stirring, and petals fall, and it whispers to us: you must find your own ending.

This is mine. The Prince trips over an oak log, falls into a fairy ring, and disappears. (He is forced to wash miniature clothes, and pinched when he complains.) Alice stretches and brushes the rose petals from her nightgown. She makes her way to the Great Hall and eats what is left in the breakfast dishes: porridge with brown sugar. She walks through the streets of the village, wondering at the silence, then hears a humming. Following it, she comes to a cottage at the village edge where Madeleine, her hair now completely white, sits and spins in her garden. Witches, you know, are extraordinarily long-lived. Alice says, "Good morning," and Madeleine asks, "Would you like some breakfast?" Alice says, "I've had some, thank you." Then the Witch spins while the Princess reads Goethe, and the spinning wheel produces yarn so fine that a shawl of it will slip through a wedding ring.

Will it come to pass? I do not know. I am waiting, like you, for the canary to lift its head from under its wing, for the Empress Josephine to open in the garden, for a sounds that will tell us someone, somewhere, is awake.

The Red Path

Jim C. Hines

For many years, Jim C. Hines focused on short fiction. His work has appeared in more than forty magazines and anthologies. During this time, he also picked up a Masters degree in English from Eastern Michigan University. His first published fantasy novel was *Goblin Quest*, a funny, popular tale about a nearsighted goblin runt named Jig. Thanks to the work of his wonderful agent, the book has since been translated into several other languages, and was picked up by DAW Books, along with sequels *Goblin Hero* and *Goblin War*. He's now working on a new series about a trio of butt-kicking princesses. *The Stepsister Scheme* came out in January of 2009, and DAW has contracted him for three more books in the series.

Hines takes Little Red Riding Hood and completely fleshes the story out. In many respects it was like hearing the fairytale all over again for the first time.

Roudette had sinned twice by the time she closed the door. Her first sin was theft. Father had been baking for the past three days in preparation for the Midsummer festival, when he and the other elders would ask God to renew his blessing upon the town for another year. Even though Roudette believed the church would have smiled upon her goal, she had still taken the muffins and cakes without permission.

Her second sin was disobedience. Though her parents hadn't explicitly forbidden her from visiting Grandmother this morning, Roudette knew what they would say if she asked. Respect for one's elders was a central tenant of the Savior's Path. She would be punished, and rightfully so, upon her return.

"Roudette?"

Perhaps punishment would come even sooner. She turned to see Mother standing in the doorway. Roudette's little brother Jaun peeked from behind brown-painted shutters and stuck out his tongue.

Roudette's fingers tightened around the handle of her basket as she planned a third sin. The instant her mother turned away, Jaun was getting a muffin right between the eyes.

"Inside. Now." Mother kept her voice low, to avoid drawing the neighbors' attention. Her gaze slipped past Roudette to the whitewashed homes on the opposite side of the road. Roudette's father was a Patriarch of the church, the highest office in which a human could serve. Even in a small town, it was a position of great respect. It wouldn't do for his daughter to be seen quarreling with his wife.

Roudette spoke softly, out of respect. "Grandmother has been back only a few days. Why can't I visit—"

"Your grandmother turned her back on us," Mother interrupted. "She left the Path. I won't allow you to follow her into temptation."

"But isn't devotion to family an important part of the Path?"

"So is obedience."

Roudette used one hand to pull her cloak tight. Her fingers brushed the gold symbols embroidered into the blood-red wool. Each symbol was said to represent one step of the Savior's path. Descended from Heaven with the rest of fairy-kind during the uprising, the Savior had sacrificed himself on the cross to protect humanity from God's wrath.

Her mother wore a similar cloak, though hers was blue. Roudette would receive her blue cloak when she turned thirteen at the end of the summer. Mother had embroidered hundreds of such cloaks over the years; her skill with the silver needle was unmatched by mortal hands.

"What if Grandmother hasn't truly strayed?" Roudette asked, trying a different tactic. "What if she's simply lost? Perhaps all she lacks is a guide to lead her back?"

Mother's hesitation was brief, barely noticeable to anyone who didn't know her. "Your grandmother has never shown any interest in guidance."

"Are you sure?" Roudette asked, pressing her advantage. "Do you know what's in her heart?"

It was an unfair question. Only magic could reveal one's thoughts, and human magic was forbidden by church law.

"I remember when she left us," Mother said. "My father tried to stop her. He told us later that she had done terrible things."

"Then isn't it even more important to guide her back?" Roudette asked. "So that she might find forgiveness and be reborn? Midsummer is a time for forgiveness, is it not? The Savior forgave even the human who drove the iron nails through his flesh."

Roudette bowed her head and waited. She knew scripture almost as well as her father. They both knew who would win this argument.

"You'll return by noon," Mother said at last. "And for trying to sneak away, you'll rise early tomorrow and scour the ovens."

"Yes, Mother," Roudette said.

"The lies of the fallen are seductive," Mother said. "Don't let her lead you astray."

"Thank you, Mother." Roudette pulled up her hood and walked away, stopping only when she heard the door close behind her. After making sure nobody else was watching, she opened her basket.

The muffin struck the left shutter, slamming it against the frame and making Jaun yelp. The Savior would frown on her actions, but he hadn't grown up with a little brother.

Roudette pulled a fairy cake from the basket and ate as she walked. Her father used a special brass brand to burn the sign of the cross onto the top of each cake. The jam inside was supposed to represent the blood of the sacrifice.

Until she was five years old, Roudette had believed the Savior tasted like strawberries.

She was finishing off the second cake when the cottage came into view. It stood alone in a small clearing atop a hill. Roudette stepped carefully onto a fallen tree which spanned the stream winding past the hill. She crossed the makeshift bridge quickly, as she had done many times over the years. There, looking up at her Grandmother's cottage, she hesitated.

Curiosity had always been Roudette's weakness, whether it was exploring the woods or reading the "adult" books her father kept locked away in the church. As far as she could tell, they were the same as the books she had studied when she was younger, only her father's versions had more begatting.

It was curiosity that had brought her back to Grandmother's abandoned cottage each year, trying to imagine where Grandmother had gone after she left. Grandmother's last visit had been shortly after Jaun's birth.

Then, three days ago, Roudette had discovered smoke rising from the chimney. When she peeked through a window, she had been stunned to find Grandmother butchering a pair of squirrels in the kitchen.

The sight had wiped all semblance of manners from Roudette's mind. She burst through the door, squealing like the child she had been when last she saw Grandmother.

To be fair, Grandmother had smiled to see Roudette's joy. They embraced, and then Grandmother had studied Roudette for a long time, until she began to feel uncomfortable. Finally, Grandmother had shooed Roudette away, saying, "Your parents would spit hellfire if they saw you here with me. Please go, and leave me in peace."

What peace could Grandmother have, alone and lost? Curiosity had led Roudette here, but it was duty that made her return today. Duty to family, to try to save a loved one who had strayed. Brushing crumbs from the front of her cloak, Roudette made her way to the door.

The air was still today, and the woods were silent, save for the faint trickling of the stream. The green door was open, though the windows were shuttered tight. Roudette stopped in the doorway. She blotted her forehead on the sleeve of her cloak.

"Grandmother?" There was no answer. Roudette rapped her knuckles on the doorframe as she stepped inside.

The kitchen was a mess. Flies swarmed over the remains of a rabbit on the floor. Roudette wrinkled her nose.

A low growl made her jump. The sound had come from the bedroom. Perhaps another animal had snuck into the cottage. A fox or a wolf, or even a wildcat. That must be what had killed the rabbit.

Roudette grabbed a knife from the counter, clutching the bone handle in sweat-slick fingers. A part of her longed to flee back to the safety of town, but what if the animal had attacked Grandmother? She couldn't leave.

"God protect me." She imagined she could feel her cloak grow warmer in response to her whispered prayer.

Smears of blood darkened the hard dirt floor leading into the bedroom. Holding the knife in front of her, Roudette peered through the doorway.

Stretched out on the cot was an enormous silver wolf. Blood matted its side, soaking into the blankets.

Roudette's hand shook. She nearly dropped the knife. But there was no sign of Grandmother. Holding her breath, she started to back away.

Though she made no sound, one of the wolf's big ears twitched. It turned toward Roudette, its huge eyes spearing her in place.

The wolf bared its teeth and growled again. Such enormous teeth, no doubt all the better for eating foolish girls who didn't listen to their mothers' advice.

Should she flee, or would that just encourage the wolf to chase her down? Wasn't that what such beasts did?

She looked the wolf in its eyes. Was that another mistake? She knew dogs would take a direct stare as a challenge or threat.

Such big eyes it had. Round and gentle, belying the terror of those teeth. They were pale gray, tinged with blue. A fleck of black marred the ring of the left eye.

Roudette swallowed, remembering her previous visit and the way Grandmother had stared at her. Grandmother's left eye was flecked in exactly the same way as the wolf.

"Grandmother?" Roudette whispered. Thoughts of demons and devils raced through her mind. Those who strayed from the Path were said to be vulnerable to such things. But the wolf had relaxed, and made no move to attack as Roudette took a slow step into the room.

"What's happened to you?" She moved closer, her attention drawn to the wound on the wolf's side. Blood continued to drip from the dark gash between the ribs.

The wolf sniffed the air and its— *her* lips drew back in a snarl.

"What is it?" Roudette asked.

The wolf sprang from the cot, moving too quickly for Roudette to react. The knife spun away as huge paws clubbed her chest. She slammed to the floor. Teeth snapped at her throat, locking around her cloak. The wolf dragged her into the bedroom.

Roudette tried to break free, but a sharp shake of the wolf's head left her stunned. The wolf yanked again, and the cloak tore free. The wolf backed away, taking the cloak with her. The gold embroidery was lit up like tiny flames. The material had caught in the wolf's teeth, and appeared to be causing her pain. She stumbled toward the doorway, pawing at the cloak.

There were no windows, and the wolf blocked the only escape. Roudette fled into the closet and yanked the door shut behind her. Peeking through the crack, she saw the wolf tearing the cloak apart. The fur around her jaws was blackened, as were her paws where she had touched the cloak. The light from the symbols flickered like candlelight, slowly dying as the wolf destroyed the cloak.

Roudette held her breath. Her basket lay spilled on the floor, crushed muffins and cakes scattered in the dirt. Blood dripped over torn scraps of red as the wolf limped to the cot, pausing only to growl at the closet.

Roudette's hands shook. The door was flimsy. No doubt the wolf could smash right through. But whatever magic had blossomed from Roudette's cloak had clearly weakened the wolf. Even as she climbed back into the cot, her rear legs collapsed, and she had to try twice more to pull herself onto the sagging mattress.

"What have you done?" The voice was male, the enunciation clear and perfect. Again the wolf snarled.

Roudette watched through the crack in the doorway as a tall man stepped into view. He wore hunter's garb, a vest of dark green leather over a loose black shirt. Green bracers circled his wrist, and a quiver of arrows was slung over his right shoulder. A golden crucifix hung from a chain round his neck.

Roudette silently made the sign of the cross. That symbol marked the hunter as a Bishop of the church. Roudette had never seen one of the fey so close. Surely he could counter whatever curse had taken her grandmother. She started to open the door.

The wolf lurched to her feet, yipping loudly. In response, the hunter drew a silver-bladed knife. "Don't play the vicious beast with me. I know what you are." He nudged the scraps of Roudette's cloak with his boot, then stooped to pick up one of the bloody pieces. "Feasting on your own kind? You're lucky the cloak didn't destroy you."

The hunter lunged forward, driving the knife into the wolf's chest. The wolf's yipe muffled Roudette's gasp.

"Or perhaps not so lucky." He yanked the blade down, then ripped the skin back with his free hand. His body concealed the gruesome details, but when he finished, he dropped a bloody wolf skin on the floor. Roudette's grandmother lay curled on the cot, naked save for a leather necklace. Her chest and side were bloody, though the hunter's blow hadn't been a deep one.

He kicked the skin away, then wiped his hands on his trousers. "Filthy, primitive magic."

Grandmother coughed. "Grand Bishop Bernas didn't think so."

Roudette started. Grand Bishop Bernas had been one of the founders of the church, more than a hundred years ago. He had died a martyr, fighting a demon to protect his followers.

The hunter raised his knife, then caught himself. "If you confess, I am authorized to be lenient. Who are you working with, human?"

Grandmother smiled. Her lips were burnt and blistered, her teeth stained with blood. "I work with God. Who do you serve, you fairy serpent?"

Roudette closed her eyes. Mother was right. Grandmother would never return to the Path. To speak to one of God's chosen in such a way....

"Are there other skins?"

"Why, Bishop Tomal, is that fear in your voice?"

Tomal's snarl was as frightening as the wolf's had been. "Very well. Then you shall feel the fires of damnation." Without another word, he spun and left.

As soon as the cottage door slammed behind him, Grandmother rolled onto her side. She groaned and clutched her side. "Roudette?"

Roudette pushed open the closet door. "Grandmother? I don't understand. What—"

"Hush, girl," Grandmother said. "Tomal will be outside, preparing his 'cleansing fire,' and I haven't much time." She lay back in the cot. "The fey poison their blades."

Roudette picked up one of the crushed fairy rolls that had spilled from her basket. The cross on top was mostly intact. "There's still time. If you repent before the poison takes you—"

Grandmother took the roll from Roudette's hand and crushed it. Jam ran between her thin fingers. Her smile was both warm and gruesome. "The church garbs you in curses," she said, glancing toward the scraps of Roudette's cloak. "Those symbols your mother copies so carefully? Enchantments that would burn you alive for attempting the simplest magic."

Roudette stared at the remains of her cloak. "Mother never said anything—"

"She doesn't know. It's one more way to keep us controlled."

"No," Roudette said. "It's because man is weak. Because magic tempts us from the Path, leading us to...to *this*." She pointed to the wolf skin. "Only God's chosen have the wisdom to use magic properly."

Grandmother coughed again, spitting blood. Roudette used a corner of the blanket to wipe her mouth.

"Thank you." Grandmother lay back. "I have been to lands where the Church of the Fey is looked upon with scorn and derision. I have seen magic wielded by men and women to heal the sick. I have met those who believe humans, not fairies, are God's true children."

Roudette shook her head. "Please stop," she said.

"I never should have returned. But the opportunity was too great."

Curiosity forced Roudette to ask, "What opportunity?"

"The Midsummer festival. They say the Grand Bishop himself plans to attend this year."

Despite her fear, Roudette's heart leapt at the thought. The Grand Bishop visited only one human town each year. That he would bestow such an honor on her father's town—

"I thought I could use the skin, as my great-grandfather used it to kill Bernas." Grandmother looked away, almost as though she were ashamed. "I was too eager. I allowed them to discover who I was. I never even noticed Tomas tracking me."

She touched the deep cut on her ribs. "His spear pierced my side before I realized he was there."

"But why would you want to hurt the Grand Bishop?" Roudette asked.

Burnt fingers stroked Roudette's hair. "Because I couldn't bear to see my grandchildren live as slaves." Her voice grew raspier. "You must go, child. The wolf has taken too many of his kind over the years. Now that he's found me, he'll seek out your family. He'll kill them all to protect his people."

Roudette backed away. "My family has never strayed from the Path. He wouldn't punish them for—"

"That's what I thought too." Her voice was distant. "The gift of magic is carried in the blood. Your mother. Your brother. Even if the flames took this skin, you have the power to create another. Tomas won't risk your survival."

Outside the cottage, Roudette could hear flames crackling to life. "Grandmother, let me help you." She reached out, but Grandmother pushed her away.

"I'm beyond saving," Grandmother said. "But your family needs you. Take the skin. Save them from Tomas."

"I can't—"

"Please, Roudette." Grandmother coughed again, spitting blood into her hand. "Isn't it the child's duty to honor the wishes of her elders, and to comfort those who are dying?"

"Of course," Roudette said automatically. "But—"

"Well I'm both. Take the skin."

Slowly, Roudette nodded.

"Thank you." Grandmother slumped. One hand closed around her necklace. The pendant was a simple cross made of three iron nails. Roudette had never seen the forbidden metal, but its blackened appearance matched the descriptions her father had read to her.

Grandmother began to mumble. She was *praying*, though the prayers were unfamiliar to Roudette. Her face was twisted from the pain, but her voice was serene. At peace. The kind of peace the church said was impossible for those who left the Path.

Smoke darkened the air. Roudette dropped to her knees, where it was easier to breathe. She touched the wolf skin, half-expecting it to burn her the way her cloak had burnt Grandmother. She thought of her parents, and of Jaun.

"Goodbye, Grandmother." Roudette picked up the skin and fled.

The wolf skin was heavier than Roudette had expected. The head and front paws dragged through the dirt as she fled the burning cottage.

Though the flames soon engulfed the thatched roof, the trees appeared untouched. Bishop Tomas was already gone. On his way to Roudette's home, if Grandmother was right.

As Roudette moved further from the fire, the breeze chilled the sweat on her skin, raising goosebumps along her arms.

Wood cracked, and a section of roof thundered down with an explosion of sparks. She had never imagined a fire could be so loud.

"Grandmother. . . ." Smoke and tears stung her eyes. She turned toward the sky, amazed to see the sun still hours from its peak. How had her life changed so much in so little time?

The wolf skin was stiff, like badly-tanned leather. Sweat and blood stained the inside. Roudette could see a gash on the side, presumably from Bishop Tomas' spear. Roudette looked more closely, finding older cuts, all carefully repaired with silver thread.

The skin smelled like Grandmother, full of autumn leaves, fresh-baked apple bread and stale ginger beer. Grandmother, who had died a sinner, whose soul was damned for all time. How many of God's chosen had she killed?

Mother couldn't have known. She never would have allowed Roudette to visit if she had suspected Grandmother of such evil. To murder the Grand Bishop during the festival. . . . "Evil is seductive," she whispered, quoting one of her father's favorite verses.

This was what Mother had warned her against. Not a villain luring her from the Path with promises of forbidden pleasure and lurid decadence, but a loved one begging for help.

"God help me." Bundling the skin under her arm, she hurried toward home.

Even from the road, Roudette could hear Bishop Tomas preaching to her family. Both Jaun and Mother were crying. Their voices came from the kitchen, at the back of the house.

Her fingers dug into the fur of the skin. Her grandmother's blood had begun to dry, stiffening the fur into bristled spikes that scratched her arms.

She circled through the alley between her house and the next. She nearly dropped the skin as she scaled the fence into their garden. The smell of crushed tomatoes wafted through the air as she hurried toward the storeroom window and climbed inside.

Roudette crossed through the storeroom, pressing her body against the stacked firewood as she peeked in at Tomas and her family.

Heat from the stone oven rippled the air. Her parents stood in front of the oven, with Jaun between them. Jaun's face was buried in Father's apron.

Bishop Tomas rested one hand on the hilt of his knife. In his other hand, he held a piece of Roudette's cloak.

"That's hers," Mother said, her voice faint. She reached toward the scrap, then drew back. "I made that cloak myself."

"I'm sorry," said the Bishop. "The old woman gave herself over to evil. To devour her own kin. . . ."

Jaun's cries grew louder. Father put a hand on his shoulder.

"I should have been stronger," said Mother. "I should have ordered her to stay away."

"Yes, you should have." Bishop Tomas stared at her for a long time, then asked, "How long have you known of your mother's sins?"

Mother bowed her head. "She strayed years ago, when I was very young. But I promise, I never knew what she had become. If I had—"

"You couldn't have stopped her," he said, not unkindly.

If not for Grandmother's words, Roudette probably wouldn't have noticed the way Tomas' hand never left his knife, or the way he studied her family. . .like a farmer trying to decide which animal to butcher.

"It's written that the sins of the parent live on in the child," Bishop Tomas continued.

Both of Roudette's parents stiffened. Father swallowed and wiped his hands on his apron. "My wife has never strayed."

"But she will," the Bishop said softly, drawing his knife. "Her blood is tainted by her mother's sins."

Or by her mother's magic? Grandmother had said magic was carried in the blood.

No! Grandmother had planned to murder a Grand Bishop. She had admitted so herself. To murder God's own tool in this world. . .Roudette set the skin atop the firewood and backed away. Her father was a Patriarch. She couldn't turn her back on him. She refused to follow Grandmother to damnation. But did that mean giving herself up to Tomas and his knife? Allowing him to kill Roudette and her family?

"What do I do?" she whispered. If this was truly God's will, who was she to fight it? Would God condemn her family for her Grandmother's sins?

She had lost her way. The revelation felled her. On her knees, she begged, "Please guide me, Lord. Lead me back."

"Please!" Father was almost shouting. "Her faith is as strong as any I've known."

"Then she will be rewarded."

The Bishop's thrust was quick and sure. Mother grunted and stumbled back. She made no further sound as she collapsed at the base of the oven.

Tomas used the bloody knife to make the sign of the cross. "Go with God, and be reborn into grace."

"Mommy!" Jaun broke away and ran to Mother. He touched her shoulder, gently at first. When she didn't respond, he began to shake her, yelling louder and louder as tears dripped from his cheeks.

Roudette didn't realize she was crying until one of her tears landed on her arm. She jerked back, unable to look away from Mother. . .from Mother's body.

There had been no sign. No divine guidance to tell her which was the right choice. She had waited, and now her mother was dead. Because of her.

"I'm sorry," said Tomas, stepping toward Jaun. Father started to move between them, then turned away, his shoulders shaking.

Roudette rose and grabbed the wolfskin. "Leave him alone." Her voice was still hoarse from the smoke at Grandmother's cottage.

Father spun. "Roudette!" For a moment, joy filled his face. Then he looked at Tomas, and his expression turned to despair.

Jaun ran to her, wrapping his arms around her waist. Roudette ran one hand through his hair, holding him close. With her other, she pulled the skin over one shoulder.

"No!" Tomas shouted. "Don that skin, and you join your grandmother in hell."

Roudette gently pried Jaun away, pushing him behind her. She drew the skin tight around her body.

"Roudette, please," said Father. "You mustn't turn away from the Path, not now. Not when—"

Tomas leapt at her. Roudette grabbed a log from the firewood and hurled it into his chest. Perhaps grief gave her strength, or maybe the skin's magic had already begun to take her. The log felt light as a twig, smashing Tomas backward.

She could feel the wolf's skin embracing her. Pain crushed her fingers and feet, pulling them into the wolf's paws. Her vision darkened momentarily as the head pressed down on her own. She blinked, her ears twitching to follow Tomas' footsteps as he came at her again.

Roudette bounded past him. She shook her head. Already her eyesight had returned, keener than before. She could see the sweat beading Tomas's forehead. She could smell his terror.

"The beast has taken your daughter," he said, brandishing his knife. "She will kill us all."

Father started toward her. Roudette growled, and he jumped back.

In that moment of distraction, Tomas attacked. But Roudette heard his footsteps and leapt easily away from his knife. Her claws gouged the bloody floor.

"Help me, damn you!" Tomas shouted.

Father didn't move. And Jaun was too afraid to act.

Baring her teeth, Roudette pounced.

Removing the skin was painfully difficult. Roudette's fangs pierced her own skin several times as she struggled to rip the seam back from her stomach. She pulled harder, cramping her neck and shoulder until she finally freed one arm from the wolf's skin. Once she had the use of her hand, she was able to peel the rest of the skin from her body.

Her clothes were little more than tattered rags. She lay on the floor, trying to adjust to the blurred vision, the abrupt loss of scent.

"Roudette?" Jaun stood in the doorway, looking from her to Father.

"What have you done?" whispered Father.

The Bishop lay crumpled on the floor, his throat a bloody mess. Roudette brushed her mouth with the back of her hand. Her lips were blistered, and her mouth felt as though she had bitten hot coals, seared by Tomas' magic. The taste of blood in her throat made her stomach convulse, and she fought to keep from vomiting.

"I've saved my brother," she said. If this had been the right choice, shouldn't her doubt be gone?

Father shook his head. "At the cost of your soul. Bishop Tomas was right. Your blood is cursed."

"No, Father." But there had been truth in Tomas' words. At the moment her teeth closed around his throat, Roudette had experienced a thrill like nothing she had ever known. An animal pleasure. Even now, a part of her longed to feel such freedom again. "Maybe," she admitted, bowing her head. "But he—"

"Don't." He knelt beside Mother. Without looking up, he whispered, "Get out."

Roudette's throat tightened. "What?"

"Your mother died to serve God. You turned your back on him. I'll not have you in my home."

"Mother died because. . . ." Because Roudette had hesitated, waiting for God to decide for her.

"She died because of your grandmother's evil. The same evil you now embrace."

Hearing the grief in his voice, Roudette realized it didn't matter what she said. Father was a Patriarch of the church. To turn away from the Path meant abandoning everything he believed. More importantly, it would mean Mother had died for nothing, and that he had stood by and watched as Tomas murdered his wife.

"I'm sorry," Roudette said. "I hope someday you can forgive me."

He didn't answer. Roudette rose, carrying the skin in one hand. With her other, she reached for Jaun.

"What are you doing?" Father asked. He started to rise.

Something in Roudette's eyes stopped him. "Taking Jaun somewhere he'll be safe." She hesitated. "You could come with us. Tomas died in your home. You'll be punished if—"

"Would you trade your mortal span for an eternity of suffering? If you lead Jaun from the Path, you damn him as well."

Roudette thought about the necklace Grandmother had worn, the reverence with which she had cradled the iron cross. She squeezed her brother's hand. He pressed close to her in response. "Perhaps God will help us find a different Path."

Blood & Water

Alethea Kontis

When Alethea Kontis told her parents that if writing didn't work out she could fall back on being an actress and they informed her that those weren't careers, those were hobbies. She replied that she intended to be a professional hobbyist. Since this did not go over well, Alethea mollified them by earning a degree in chemisty. Thankfully the pristine white walls of the lab drove her back into the loving arms of writing and publishing. She is the author of the *New York Times* bestselling book *AlphaOops: The Day Z Went First* and its sequel *AlphaOops: H is for Halloween*. She recently sold her novel *Sunday* to Houghton Mifflin.

This was the first story I acquired for the anthology; it came highly recommended to me by several people and they were right. If you're like me, many of the versions of these fairytales that I know are simplified for children. Kontis introduces much-needed maturity and depth to the Little Mermaid story. This is not a cleaned-up, cartoon version of this fairytale, this version is real and visceral.

Love.

Love is the reason for many a wonderful and horrible thing.

Love was the reason I lived, there in the Deep, in the warm embrace of the ocean where Mother Earth's loins spread and gave birth to the world. Her soul was my soul.

Love is the reason she came to me in the darkness, that brave sea maiden. I remember the taste of her bravery, the euphoric sweetness of her fear. It came to me on wisps of current past the scattered glows of the predators.

The other predators.

Her chest contracted and I felt the sound waves cross the water, heard them with an organ so long unused I had thought it dead.

Help me, she said. *I love him.*

The white stalks of the bloodworms curled about her tail. We had a common purpose, the worms and I. We were both barnacles seeking the same fix, clinging desperately to the soul of the world. Their crimson tips brushed her stomach, her breasts. They could feel it in her, feel her soul in the blood that coursed through her veins. I felt it too. I yearned for it. A quiet memory waved in the tide.

Patience.

My answer was slow, deliberate. *How much do you love him, little anemone?*

More than life itself, she answered.

She had said the words.

I had not asked her to bring the memories, the pain. There is no time in the Deep, only darkness. I could but guess at how much had passed since those words had been uttered this far down. Until that moment, I had never been sure if the magic would come to me. Those words were the catalyst, the spark that lit the flame.

Flame. Another ancient memory.

The empty vessel that was my body emptied even further. I held my hands out to her breast, and there was light.

I resisted the urge to shut my inner eyelids to it and reveled in the light's painful beauty. It shone beneath her flawless skin like a small sun, bringing me colors… perceptions I had never dared hope to experience again. Slivers of illumination escaped through her gills and glittered down the abalone-lustered scales of her fins. Her hair blossomed in a golden cloud around her perfect face. And her eyes…her eyes were the blue of a sky I had not seen for a very, very long time.

She tilted her head back in surrender and the ball of light floated out of her and into my fingers, thin, white and red-tipped, much as the worms themselves. I cupped her brilliant soul in my palms and felt its power gush through me. So long. So long I had waited for this escape. I had stopped wondering what answer I would give if I should ever hear the words again, ever summon the magic. When the vessel was full, when my dead heart beat again, would I remember? Would I feel remorse? Would I have the strength of will to save her, to turn her away?

You will see him, I told her.

She smiled at me over the pure flame of her soul.

I was a coward.

I pressed her soul into my breast. The moment the light filled me I became her. I could see my body through her eyes—translucent white skin marred by jagged gills, blood red hair tossed up by the smoky vents and tangling about the worms, black eyes wide, lips parted in ecstasy.

I could see him in the back of her mind, the object of her affection. He was tall and angular, with sealskin hair. There had been a storm and a wreck, and she had saved him. She had dragged him onto a beach and fallen in love with him as she waited for him to open his eyes. She had run her fingers through his hair, touched his face, traced the lines of the crest upon his clothes. He was handsome and different and beautiful. When he awoke, he took her hand in his and smiled with all his heart. And when he kissed her, she knew she would never be able to live a life without him in it.

In that small moment, as the glow of her soul dimmed into me, she told herself it was worth it.

Once the transformation began, the pain pushed all other thoughts out of her head. Water left her as suddenly as her soul had left her, her gills closing up after it. The pressure that filled her chest made her eyes want to pop out. She clamped her mouth shut, instinct telling her that she could no longer breathe her native water. She beat furiously with her tail, fleeing for the surface.

Halfway there, the other pain began. It started at the ends of her fin and spread upwards, like bathing in an oyster garden. The sharpness bit into her, skinning her, slicing her to her very core. Paralyzed, she let her momentum and the pressure in her chest pull her closer to the sky. Part of her hoped she could trust the magic enough to get her there. Part of her didn't care. It wanted to die, and knew it could not.

That price had already been paid.

Her head burst above the waves and she opened her mouth, letting the rest of the water in her escape. Her first full breath of the insubstantial air was like a lungful of jellyfish. She coughed, her upper half now as much in agony as her lower half, not wanting to take that next breath and knowing that she had to.

She lay there on the undulating bed that was once her home and let it heal her. She stared up at the sky until it didn't hurt so much to breathe, until her eyes adjusted, until rough hands plucked her out of the sea.

She was dragged across the deck of a ship much like the one from which she had rescued her lover, right before it had been crushed between the rocks and the sea. The man who had pulled her up clasped her tightly to him. He was covered in hair, more hair than she had ever seen in her life, and in the strangest places. It did not reach the top of his head, but spread down his face and neck and onto his chest. Perhaps it liked this upper world as little as she did and sought a safer, darker haven beneath his clothes. She reached out a hand to touch it, and he spoke to her. The sounds were too high, too light, too short, too loud. She did not understand them. His breath smelled of sardines. She ran a finger through the hair on his face, and he dropped her.

Misery shot through her and she collapsed on the deck. Her hair spilled around her…and her legs. She stared at her new skin. It looked so calm and innocent, but every nerve screamed beneath it. Another man stood before her now, wearing more clothes than the hairy man and shiny things on his ears and around his neck. His bellow was deeper than the first man's but still as coarse and profane, and still foreign to her. He crouched down before her and brushed her hair back from her face. He cooed at her. She touched the bright thing around his neck that twinkled the sun at her, and he grinned. His teeth were flat. She wasn't threatened. Braver now, she pulled at the necklace. He let her slide it over his head and put it around her own neck.

He picked her up and carried her to a place that hid her from the sky and set her somewhere softer than the deck. She liked this place and this man who now worshipped her. He had given her a gift, and now he would take care of her. If only there was a way she could tell him why she was there. She was sure he would help her. Perhaps he could see into her heart and just know.

The man removed his shirt, and she relaxed even more. He wanted to put her at ease. By looking like her, he would make her feel like she belonged. He took off the rest of his clothes and came up beside her. He patted her head, ran his hands down her hair. He touched her breasts, her belly and her legs. Still sensitive, she brushed his hand away. He put it back. She tried to push it away again, but he was stronger. She frowned. He smiled all those flat teeth at her once more. She wondered if she might have been mistaken. He moaned, parted her knees and entered her.

The misery she had felt before was nothing compared to this anguish. She inhaled the excruciating air and screamed a hoarse cry. She clawed at him, pushed at his weight on top of her, but she could not move him. Agony ripped her body apart again. A tingling sensation washed over her and the light in her eyes began to dim. Somewhere in that darkness, through the pain, she could feel his heartbeat. The emptiness in her cried out. He had something she needed.

She reached up, pulled him to her, and sunk her pointed teeth deep into the skin of his neck. She drank him down, consuming his soul, filling the barren places inside her. He collapsed on top of her and still she drank, until there was nothing left.

The door burst open and the hairy man entered. He pulled the naked man off of her. He could tell what the man had done from the blood between her legs. He could tell what she had done from the blood she now licked from her lips.

"Siren," he whispered.

She gasped. In her brain there was an avalanche.

Words flooded her, images and thoughts, smells and sounds. Knowledge. She cried out again and slapped her palms to her head. She had taken the man's soul, and his life right along with it. She watched as the shafts of her golden hair turned deep red, filled with the captain's blood.

The first mate had named her. He knew what she was. She was death, the shark, the thing to be afraid of. She lured men to their graves with her beauty.

In one swift motion he pulled the knife from his belt. She did not flinch as he approached her. There was nothing left to fear.

The knife swept down and split the captain's throat open, hiding the teethmarks in the cut. He stared deep into her eyes as he pulled a large ruby ring off the dead man's finger and put it on his own. The knife, streaked with what little crimson was left in the captain's body, he brandished at the crowd of men gathered at the door.

"Eddie Lawless, what's goin' on?" the man in front asked. The men behind him whispered low, words like "magic" and "evil" and "witch" catching in her ears.

"It's Lawson, Cooky," the hairy man responded. "Cap'n Lawson. An' don't ye forget it."

"Yessir," the men mumbled. "Yessir, Cap'n."

"Leave me," Lawson ordered.

"But sir, what about Cap'n—"

"*I* am the cap'n," he told them. "Ye can collect the carcass later. Leave me now." He slammed the door in their faces.

The mattress shifted under his weight as he sat down across from her. She did not want to look at him, concentrating instead on the ends of her new hair and the line across the dead man's throat.

Lawson shoved the body onto the floor. "Siren."

She looked up.

"So. Ye can understand me then."

She nodded once.

"Good." He pulled the sheet down and wiped his knife blade with it. "Understand this. I know what ye are, what ye need and what ye do. If ye do exactly as I tell ye, I won't kill ye."

If she had known how to laugh, she would have. It was unsettling. She knew what laughter was, what caused it and why someone did it, but she didn't have the slightest idea of how to make her body perform such a feat. It was the same with the words—she could understand them, but she couldn't get her tongue around them and speak back. She would have laughed at the thought of this man killing her, for she would have welcomed death. But she there was one task she meant to accomplish before that happened. She had to find her lover.

She nodded her head once more.

"Excellent." He left the bed and went to open a trunk on the other side of the room. He rummaged through it for a moment, and then tossed a bundle of burgundy material into her lap. She stared at it, marveling in the slight difference between it and the color of her hair. She reached out and stroked its softness, drawing patterns on it with her finger.

His chuckle brought her out of her state. "Ye 'ave no idea what to do with it, do ye?" He took her by the hand and gently eased her off the bed. "Come on, stand up."

She placed one foot flat on the floor, then the other. Then she pushed up with all her might, locking her knees and propelling herself forward into him.

He caught her before she hit the floor. "Woah. Easy. Ye 'ave to get yer sea legs." He helped her balance enough to stay upright. Surprisingly her feet held her without too much trouble.

"Now," he said, grabbing the bundle off the bed, "ye're lucky I 'ave a daughter an' I'm used to doin' this." He spun her around so that she faced the wall. "Six years ago I only knew 'ow to *un*dress a woman." He pulled her hands up above her head and eased the material down around her. He moved her hair to one side so he could button up the back.

"There." He turned her back around. "It's a bit large an' it'll probably be a tad warm. But it'll keep the sun off ye, and the…my…men away from temptation."

He looked her up and down. "Not that they'll need much warnin', mind. But ye get enough rum into a man…well…stranger things 'ave 'appened."

He looked down at the former captain's body. "Ye won't need to…eat…again for a while then?"

She shook her head.

"Right. Best if ye only do it when I tell ye." He shoved the knife back into his belt.

Her eyes widened.

"Oh, don't worry," he chuckled. "Ye're aboard a pirate ship, darlin'. If there's one thing we've always got more than our share of, it's blood."

He wasn't wrong.

They encountered a ship three days later. There were blasts from cannons spread amidst the cries of men. She lost her footing when the ship lurched sideways, hooks pulling the losing ship close enough so that men might cross over. She peeked through the windows at the smoke of the guns, swords clashing as the blood flew.

Lawson came back to her room when the battle had died down. He opened the door and threw a man down at her feet. His clothes were ripped and his face was a bloody mess. Gray eyes looked up at her from the red-stained face and filled with terror.

"No…oh, God, no." were the last words he spoke.

His fear was intoxicating.

She closed her eyes when she was finished and let the magic wash over her. It wasn't just the blood she craved; it was everything. She needed the senses and the feelings, the emotions and the pain, the good and the bad. She needed his life, his soul.

Rejuvenated, she tossed her hair back and peered up at Lawson. He cupped her cheek and wiped a spot of blood away from the corner of her mouth. "There's my girl." He threw open the door and kicked the man's body over the threshold. "There's yer cap'n, men," he bellowed. "Seems 'e got into a spot of trouble. Any of ye want the same trouble, just cross me."

Crews were mixed and booty was swapped, and then they were off in search of the next victim.

The second ship they burned. It was spectacular. She ran to the railing and held her hand out to the beautiful, live thing that danced on the sea as it consumed sails and timbers and bodies alike. She had seen candles and lamps, but this was a beast, wild and hot and bright as the sun. Hands grabbed at her clothes to keep her from falling over the rail, and they pinned her down when the magazine finally exploded, taking the rest of that ship's crew with it.

On the third one, she found him.

The battle this time was a long one, and by the time Lawson brought her the captain of the other ship, he was half dead. She drank him anyway. And somewhere in the memories of this man was the someone she had been looking for.

She gasped when his face came to her. She drew back, her teeth disengaging from her meal, blood running down her chin and staining her dress. This man knew her lover. Not well, but he knew him. She tried to make sense of the jumble of images that flowed through her, but nothing connected. She searched his body for a sign, a hint, something. She found it on the smallest ring he wore, a gold band stamped with the crest she had traced over and over on the beach that day.

When Lawson returned, she pointed at herself and then held up the ring. He smiled and patted her on the head. "O'course ye can keep it, darlin'. Ye can 'ave all the trinkets yer little 'eart desires."

He didn't understand. How would she make him understand? She slid the ring over her red-tipped thumb. She would save it until she thought of a way.

The fourth ship was a long time coming.

She spent most of that time at the bow of the ship. The crew didn't grumble much about having a woman on deck. Most of them apparently didn't consider her a woman. Lawson made it plain that he enjoyed having her there. Word was getting around about Bloody Captain Lawson and the Siren. They struck fear in the hearts of men and made quite a profit as a result, so if anyone had disagreements, no one made mention of them.

Lawson called her their figurehead. It was an apt description, based on what she had seen on the prows of other ships. She would lean against the rail, arms spread, red hair trailing behind her in the breeze. She liked letting the wind slip through her fingers. It reminded her of home. The currents of air were not that different from the currents of water. Men did not have the freedom of movement that her kind enjoyed, but the principles were the same. They walked among it, breathed it in, let it give them life. It brought sounds and smells to them. They did not see it or think to taste it, but it was always there in them, touching them, surrounding them.

She stood there, day after day, until the salt encrusted her lips and her hair was a burnished orange. What little red appeared in the tips of her fingers had been burned there by the sun. The men avoided her and prayed hard for another ship. They tread lightly around the captain. No one wanted to be the Siren's next meal.

Lawson finally bade her return to the stateroom, and she was too weak to disobey. The table was covered in maps and charts. She walked past them on the way to the bed and glanced down at the area Lawson was plotting. A symbol caught her eye, and she jumped back. She waved at Lawson. She pointed to herself, and to the ring around her thumb. She pointed to herself, and to the same symbol down on the map.

"There?" he asked her. "Ye want to go there? Why?"

She could not answer, so she just kept pointing to herself and the map.

"That's 'ome," Lawson told her. "Where Molly is. I promised never to go back until I 'ad a ship full o'riches. She deserves no less." He shook his head. "No, darlin', we can't go there. Not yet."

Frustrated, she closed her eyes. Disjointed thought flashes skipped through her mind. She tried to remember the man with the ring, tried to bring his soul to the surface. But it had been so long, and she was so weary…and there was a port…

Her eyes snapped open. She moved her finger on the map to an island just off the coast of the country bearing her lover's symbol. She pointed at Lawson, and then stamped her finger back down on the map.

"There? What's there?"

She threw her hands up in exasperation and scanned the room. She held up the medallion of her necklace to him.

"Gold?"

She nodded and kept searching. She found his knife on the table, picked it up, and then shook her head.

"Swords?"

She shook her head again.

"This?" He removed the pistol from his belt and held it out to her. She nodded emphatically.

He cocked his head and grinned. "Siren, if ye're right about this, I'll take ye anywhere in the world." He strode out of the room and hollered to his first mate. "Hard to port, matey!"

"Cap'n?" the first mate asked.

Lawson hooked his thumbs in his belt. "We're goin' 'ome."

The greatest tale of Bloody Lawson and the Siren is the Massacre at Windy Port. Legend has it that their ship, cloaked in dark magic, slipped by the watchmen unnoticed. Once docked the crew cut a gruesome swath through the town, led by Lawson and his Sea Witch. Lawson brandished a rapier in one hand, a pistol in the other. The Siren, dressed in fine burgundy velvet, marched through town before him, seducing men to their grisly deaths. Her eyes were as black and cold as a shark's, her hair a mass of ebony fire waving about her. They left none living in their wake, took what they wanted and stole back into the night as invisibly as they had arrived.

Like most legends, not a word of it was true.

They sailed into Windy Port under a royal flag they had appropriated from a previous hunt. They docked without incident, the crew scattering to the winds to pick up intelligence, hefty bar tabs, and the occasional whore.

The moment Lawson set her down on the dock, she fell. The hollowness inside her throbbed. She could not believe anything could have been so still as land. There was no life in it. The air was not strong enough to keep it fluid. It was rock. Still, empty, dead rock. She was but a shell, a humble reconstruction of the world upon which man walked every single day. How did they survive without a connection? She hugged her stomach, doubled up and gagged, only emptiness escaping her dry heaves.

"You okay, honey? Take it easy. It'll pass soon."

The words spoken to her had a cadence she had never heard before, and it surprised her so much she didn't understand them at first. The hands that pulled her hair back away from her face were small and delicate. The woman had on a black dress. Her hair was pinned up on her head and decorated with shiny black beads. She smelled…soft and nice. And she was gentle when she accepted the Siren's embrace.

"It's all right," the woman said as she patted her back. "Everything's going to be all right."

She didn't scream when pointed teeth pierced her flesh.

Everything was going to be just fine.

Suddenly conscious of her appearance, she pulled her dress over her head and began tearing at the woman's clothes. Lawson knelt beside her and motioned for his men to surround them so as not to draw attention to the scene. "Discovered vanity, 'ave we?" he chuckled as he helped her undress the woman's corpse. Once she had changed, the men weighted the body and rolled it into the ocean.

Lawson helped her stand. He tossed a dark cloak about her and covered her hair with its hood. She was glad he didn't force her to wear shoes—it was hard enough enduring this much separation from the water. She didn't know how much more she would be able to bear.

The inn they went to almost pushed her sanity over the edge from sensory overload. The room was filled with people of all shapes and sizes. There were smells from the food, the ale, the dogs in front of the fire, the fire itself. Men and women talked and shouted and joked and laughed. A scrawny youth crawled up beside the dogs at one point and sang for his supper. She was mesmerized. These were so different from the songs of the water, the flash of fish in the currents, the mating of whales in the deep. Some were slow and soft; some were fast and loud. And when the rest of the room joined in, she clapped her hands in merriment.

The crew dropped in one by one to report and consult with Lawson throughout the night. There were nods and low whispers. She watched as papers were signed and money changed hands. Thus Bloody Lawson conquered Windy Port, without ever leaving his seat. When the festivities ended he paid for his meal, tipped heavily and left, dragging his cloaked companion behind him. It was the sailors and merchants that returned to their vessels the next morning and found them empty or missing who took their anger out on the citizens of the port. Lawson and his crew were miles away before the massacre even began. Bloody Lawson and the Siren were never heard from again.

Several months later, Edward Malcolm opened a waterfront inn in the capitol city named The Sea Lass. He purchased the house next door as well. It had a master suite and a nursery and a very large kitchen that could be used to supplement the inn's in case of overflow. One of the rooms in the house had a door with seven locks. They were installed the day before Molly's return from school.

Molly's homecoming was a grand event. Lawson, now called Edward, had covered every flat surface in the house with sweets and cakes and flowers. He had hired a seamstress to take Molly's measurements for a whole new wardrobe, the only one that didn't seem overly preoccupied with the Prince's upcoming wedding. Paper-wrapped packages of all sized littered the largest of the tables. A doll and a rose waited on the chair for his princess.

The Siren sat on a stool in the corner, cut off from the sun and the earth, the water and wind. She waned as she watched the miniature cherub-faced human run through the door to embrace her father. Her mop of dark brown curls disappeared in her father's coat as she hugged him, right before he picked her up and twirled her around the room. There was something about this strange apparition, this child, and she could not decide what it was.

Molly giggled as she snuggled her doll. She reached out to the rose.

"Be careful," her father warned her.

"Yes, Papa," she said smartly. "I will watch for the pricklies and the thornies." She buried her nose in the crimson petals and took a deep breath. When she opened her eyes, Molly saw the Siren there in the shadows.

The child set her doll down carefully on the table. "Who is she, Papa?" Molly whispered.

"She's..." he started, twisting the ruby ring on his finger. "I saved 'er," he said finally.

"She's so pretty," Molly said. The child came around the table and held the flower out to her. "She's just like the flower."

"Yes," he said. "Just like the rose. She's got pricklies and thornies too, Molly. You have to be careful around her."

Molly took another step forward, still offering the flower. The Siren took it and grinned, being careful not to show any teeth. Before her father could stop her, Molly launched herself into the Siren's arms.

The child's skin was softer than the woman's at the pier. Her hair smelled of sugar and...something...indescribable. She took another deep breath. There was life within this little bundle, so much life she all but vibrated with it.

Edward wrenched her away. He took her by the arms and held her tightly. He sank down to his knees, so that he could address Molly eye to eye.

"Don't ye *ever* go near 'er again," he said sternly.

"But Papa, she's so sad," Molly cried.

"She is dangerous," he admonished. "Just be a good girl and do as yer papa says."

Molly bowed her head. "Yes, Papa."

"We'll even call 'er Rose, okay? So ye don't forget." Edward chucked her under the chin. "Now, what are ye gonna name yer dolly?"

Molly's eyes brightened again and she rushed back to the table for her doll.

The Siren sunk her nose into the flower and inhaled sugar and sweetness while she watched the child open the rest of her gifts.

That night as he escorted her to her room, he said to her, "Ye touch my daughter, I'll kill ye." Then he shut the door and turned seven keys in seven locks.

Each day after that was much the same. She was not allowed to leave the house, and the third time Edward caught her staring out the windows, he forbade her that too. Each night he would take her to her room and give her the same warning about his daughter before turning the seven keys of her prison.

She would sit on her bed and stare into the darkness, wondering what she had done wrong. Had she not given him the riches he desired? Had she not paved the way for him to return home to be with his daughter? She had made him happy—why should she suffer as a result?

She edged closer to the window and watched the moon move across the sky. Somewhere not far, the reflection of that same light was skipping across the waves. Somehow, she would escape from this prison. Someday, seven locks would not hold her.

Every few nights he would bring her someone, long after Molly was asleep. He would wake before the dawn and take the body away. She learned all she could from these poor souls, but it was never enough. They were whores or cheats or liars, people whose absence in some way benefited Edward and whose minds were such a jumble of unreliable information she could never discern anything that could help her.

She waited. She waited while he scolded her every night. She waited as he shoved each of the seven bolts home. She waited as he fed her, sparingly, enough to survive. She waited for him to get comfortable, to slip, to let something get by him.

Like the snitch.

Edward bent over and the unconscious man fell from over his shoulder and onto the bed before her. "Small, but 'e's all ye'll get, understand?"

She opened her mouth, throat contracting. "Yeth," she managed to say.

"Good. 'Cause if ye touch my daughter, I'll kill ye." He shut the door. She counted slowly to seven before pulling the man into her lap and feasting.

Her heart pounded with a foreign pulse.

He was there.

Her lover.

He was everywhere inside this man's head. He sat at the head of a table, talking sternly to a group of older men dressed in black. He sat in a large chair at the end of a hallway. He rode a horse down the path through the garden and along the beach. He rode in a carriage beside a beautiful, golden-haired maid and people threw flowers in the street before them.

He was the prince.

And he was getting married in a week.

Edward fell ill the next day. He did not come to let her out of her cell. The first two days of isolation weren't bad. The third day, the snitch's body began to smell. The fourth day, she tried to feed off it again and gagged. There had not been much in him to begin with, and whatever was left in him now was gelled and rancid. The fifth day, she began to shake. She pounded on the door and the walls and the window until the skin of her fists shed. The sixth day, she began to scream. It came out of her as a long, keening wail. It echoed her hunger, her desperation, her emptiness. Her voice gave out as the sun rose on the seventh day, his wedding day.

She spent the hours curled up against the door, hoping to hear something. Any sign of movement at all would have been welcome. She played with the ends of her faded hair, teasing them in and out between her toes. The shadows moved, lengthened, and eventually, the sun's light died. Her hopes went right along with it. She placed her palm flat on the door beside her head.

It was warm.

She closed her eyes and could feel the energy radiating from the other side. She could hear small, shallow breaths. She could taste sugar on the air.

Molly.

She knocked two times on the door.

"Rose?" the tiny voice called hesitantly.

She knocked two times again.

"Daddy's sick and he had to go away." Skirts rustled against the floorboards. "I'm lonely. Are you lonely?"

Two knocks.

"Do you want to play with my dolly?"

She spread her fingers against the door. "Yeth," she croaked.

The warmth faded, and there were sounds of a heavy chair being dragged across the floor. One, two, three, for, five, six, seven keys were all slowly turned in their locks. The chair was pushed aside, and the door opened.

Molly flew into her arms, the momentum pushing her back onto the bed in her weakened state. She cradled the frightened child in her arms, felt the porcelain head of her dolly poking into her side. She soaked up the child's energy, willing it into her empty body. She bent her head and smelled the sweetness of her. She nuzzled her nose in the softness of her, like burrowing into the petals of a newly-opened flower.

She shouldn't. She knew she shouldn't, but he had caused her so much pain, and she had nothing left to lose.

Molly screamed and fought, but every bit of her gave the Siren the strength to hold her down, to fill the abyss inside her with this soul of pure innocence. It was so beautiful. The sensations did not wait until she was finished. They exploded into her mind every second. There was fear, yes, sweet fear, but then came sadness and betrayal. There was happiness and laughter, anger and tears, but most importantly, she finally realized the *whys*. She knew why a person felt joy and why they felt pain. She learned the elation of seeing something for the very first time, and the despair in losing it.

Loss. She knew now what she had been dealing out all this time. There was no way she could have ever known the impact of death without knowing what it was like to live a life. The weight of all the souls she had consumed pressed heavily upon her. She learned consequences. She realized that the things she did affected people other than the person she was killing. She understood that all the pain she had felt before was nothing to the pain these people would feel for the rest of their lives. She felt regret, and love.

Love.

It spread through her. Unconditional love tickled her down to the red tips of her fingers and toes. Love was trust. Love was faith. Love was believing in the impossible. The rainbow of Molly's soul filled her with love until the last drop. She held Molly's limp body in her arms…and she laughed.

She laughed and laughed, her voice echoing through the dark, vacant house. She laughed until she cried, tears flowing unchecked down her cheeks. She cried for Molly, for all of them. She cried for all the things she had done. She cried for herself, for everything she had lost, for nothing.

Or was it nothing?

She had to hurry. She had to leave this place and never come back. She gently laid Molly's body out on the bed and curled her arm around her dolly. She smoothed back the dark curls and kissed her forehead. She covered herself in the black cloak and fled into the night.

She was glad again to be in the air and running over the earth, despite what little support they gave her. She followed her heart and the dim memories of the snitch up to the castle gates.

She strode up to the guards there and threw her hood back. Those that knew of her let her pass. Those that didn't know of her learned.

The myriad halls and stairs and rooms made the castle a giant labyrinth, but she knew where she was going. Up and up and up…to the balcony suites of the Prince's bedchamber. She did not stop until she was at the foot of his bed, staring down at his sleeping body. She wanted to shake him awake, wanted to explain everything to him, wanted to scream her love for him to the rafters.

But she couldn't.

If he awoke now, he would know what she had become. He would see the evil inside of her, the mark of it in her hair and on her skin. She had saved his life, true, but how many others had she taken on her path back to him? With love came regret. She knew what she had to do. She knew that the only thing she had to offer him now was her absence. If she could just touch him one more time…she reached out a hand to him and stopped herself.

No.

It would not stop at a touch, she knew that from what had happened with Molly. She could never be with him, truly be with him, because eventually she would consume him. His soul was not bright enough for her to survive alone outside it, nor was it strong enough to sustain him once she had consumed it. If she stayed beside him, it would mean his death.

She was a monster.

She forced her hand back to herself and placed it over her heart. She hoped that it spoke enough in the silence for him to hear it, to feel how much she loved him. If it had been water and not air between them, she knew he would have felt it.

He stirred and opened his eyes.

She gave herself one moment, one tiny, blessed moment of looking into his eyes before she turned and ran.

She tripped down the stairs and cut her feet on the stones. The cloak caught on something and she unfastened it. She was sure that soon they would come for her. They would hunt her like the beast she was. She tasted the tears that streamed down her face and knew there was only one refuge.

The cold beach sand kissed her feet like a prayer. The salty spray mixed with her tears, chasing them away. The first tiny wave reached up and licked her toes. Waves rumbled in a cadence she had almost forgotten how to translate.

Come, they pulled.

Home, they crashed.

She took small steps forward. The sand slipped out from beneath her if she stayed too long. The force of the waves pushed her backwards in opposition to the call she felt.

Come, they pulled.

She stumbled, and the tide ripped her sideways along the beach. Gasping, she managed to regain her footing and continue walking out to sea. The current grabbed at her clothes, and she tore them off. The tips of her hair mingled with the foam. Flotsam swirled around her waist.

Home, they crashed.

She walked until the undertow took her and dragged her out to sea.

I lost her sometime before that, back when the moon shone off her white skin and blood red hair. But I didn't have to live inside her anymore to know where she was headed.

She would grab the first sharp object she found—maybe a crab's claw or a clam's shell—and rip gills into herself so that the water could flow through her again. The first one might have been straight, but the rest would be ragged and flawed. She would make her way to the Deep, her body drawn to the neverending call of the soul of the world. She would make a home there among the bloodworms and the warm vents and the other predators.

She would take her love and regret with her. She would heal in the balm of the ocean, away from the complexities of mortal life. She would tell herself that if the day came, if the words were spoken and the magic came to her, she would turn them away. She would not let evil back into the world. The suffering would end with her. She would stew in the self-affliction until it became a dim memory, tucked away in the recesses of her mind like sight and sound, air and fire. Time would fade her lover's face, his name into nothing, and then time itself would melt into darkness. She would ebb and flow and never die.

And when that day did come, ages and ages from now, she would choose the light. She would choose the escape. She would let the evil out one last time just to feel it all again, to live.

As I had.

Strong arms wrapped around me, brushing my satin bedclothes against the small jagged scars on either side of my chest. I leaned back against him, feeling his heartbeat through his chest.

"I just had the strangest dream," he said. I felt his deep voice rumble through the skin of my back. "You came to me while I lay in bed, only your hair was red and your skin was different. You stared at me like you wanted to say something, and then you ran. You looked so…sad."

He turned me around to face him. "The day you saved me was the happiest day of my life. And this day should be the happiest day of yours. Don't be sad."

I smiled and shook my head.

"Good." He kissed me then, long and slow and deep. He hugged me tightly before pulling away. "Come back to bed?"

"Yeth," I whispered, the words still foreign to my tongue. He kissed me once more and left me. I looked out over the moonlit water once more and said my goodbyes before following him, my prince, my soulmate, my love.

Love.

It was the reason I lived.

Hansel's Eyes

Garth Nix

Garth Nix was born in 1963 in Melbourne, Australia. A full-time writer since 2001, he has worked as a literary agent, marketing consultant, book editor, book publicist, book sales representative, bookseller, and as a part-time soldier in the Australian Army Reserve. Garth's books include the award-winning fantasy novels *Sabriel*, *Lirael* and *Abhorsen*; and the cult favourite YA SF novel *Shade's Children*. His fantasy novels for children include *The Ragwitch*; the six books of *The Seventh Tower* sequence, and *The Keys to the Kingdom* series. More than five million copies of his books have been sold around the world, his books have appeared on the bestseller lists of *The New York Times*, *Publishers Weekly*, *The Guardian*, and *The Australian*, and his work has been translated into thirty-seven languages. He lives in a Sydney beach suburb with his wife and two children.

Hansel and Gretel are quite wicked children. Isn't that why the witch wants to eat them? Garth Nix shows you just how wicked they are.

Hansel was ten and his sister, Gretel, was eleven when their stepmother decided to get rid of them. They didn't catch on at first, because the Hagmom (their secret name for her) had always hated them. So leaving them behind at the supermarket or forgetting to pick them up after school was no big deal.

It was only when their father got in on the "disappearing the kids" act that they realized it was serious. Although he was a weak man, they thought he might still love them enough to stand up to the Hagmom.

They realized he didn't the day he took them out into the woods. Hansel wanted to do the whole Boy Scout thing and take a water bottle and a pile of other stuff, but their dad said they wouldn't need it. It'd only be a short walk.

Then he dumped them. They'd just gotten out of the car when he took off. They didn't try to chase him. They knew the signs. The Hagmom had hypnotized him again or whatever she did to make him do things.

"Guess she's going to get a nasty surprise when we get back," said Hansel, taking out the map he'd stuffed down the front of his shirt. Gretel silently handed him the compass she'd tucked into her sock.

It took them three hours to get home, first walking, then in a highway patrol cruiser, and finally in their dad's car. They were almost back when the Hagmom called on the cell phone. Hansel and Gretel could hear her screaming. But when they finally got home, she smiled and kissed the air near their cheeks.

"She's planning something," said Gretel. "Something bad."

Hansel agreed, and they both slept in their clothes, with some maps, the compass, and candy bars stuffed down their shirts.

Gretel dreamed a terrible dream. She saw the Hagmom creep into their room, quiet as a cat in her velvet slippers. She had a big yellow sponge in her hand, a sponge that smelled sweet, but too sweet to be anything but awful. She went to Hansel's bunk and pushed the sponge against his nose and face. His arms and legs thrashed for a second, then he fell back like he was dead.

Gretel tried and tried to wake from the dream, but when she finally opened her eyes, there was the yellow sponge and the Hagmom's smiling face and then the dream was gone and there was nothing but total, absolute darkness.

When Gretel did wake up, she wasn't at home. She was lying in an alley. Her head hurt, and she could hardly open her eyes because the sun seemed too bright.

"Chloroform," whispered Hansel. "The Hagmom drugged us and got Dad to dump us."

"I feel sick," said Gretel. She forced herself to stand and noticed that there was nothing tucked into her shirt, or Hansel's, either. The maps, candy bars, and compass were gone.

"This looks bad," said Hansel, shielding his eyes with his hand and taking in the piles of trash, the broken windows, and the lingering charcoal smell of past fires. "We're in the old part of the city that got fenced off after the riots."

"She must hope someone will kill us," said Gretel. She scowled and picked up a jagged piece of glass, winding an old rag around it so she could use it like a knife.

"Probably," agreed Hansel, who wasn't fooled. He knew Gretel was scared, and so was he.

"Let's look around," Gretel said. Doing something would be better than just standing still, letting the fear grow inside them.

They walked in silence, much closer together than usual, their elbows almost bumping. The alley opened into a wide street that wasn't any better. The only sign of life was a flock of pigeons.

But around the next corner, Hansel backed up so suddenly that Gretel's glass knife almost went into his side. She was so upset, she threw it away. The sound of shattering glass echoed through the empty streets and sent the pigeons flying.

"I almost stabbed you, you moron!" exclaimed Gretel. "Why did you stop?"

"There's a shop," said Hansel. "A brand-new one."

"Let me see," said Gretel. She looked around the corner for a long time, till Hansel got impatient and tugged at her collar, cutting off her breath.

"It is a shop," she said. "A Sony PlayStation shop. That's what's in the windows. Lots of games."

"Weird," said Hansel. "I mean, there's nothing here. No one to buy anything."

Gretel frowned. Somehow the shop frightened her, but the more she tried not to think of that, the more scared she got.

"Maybe it got left by accident," added Hansel. "You know, when they just fenced the whole area off after the fires."

"Maybe…" said Gretel.

"Let's check it out," said Hansel. He could sense Gretel's uneasiness, but to him the shop seemed like a good sign.

"I don't want to," said Gretel, shaking her head.

"Well, I'm going," said Hansel. After he'd gone six or seven steps, Gretel caught up with him.

Hansel smiled to himself.

Gretel could never stay behind.

The shop was strange. The windows were so clear that you could see all the way inside to the rows of PlayStations all set up ready to go, connected to really big television screens. There was even a Coke machine and a snack machine at the back.

Hansel touched the door with one finger, a bit hesitantly. Half of him wanted it to be locked, and half of him wanted it to give a little under his hand. But it did more than that. It slid open automatically, and a cool breeze of air-conditioned air blew across his face.

He stepped inside. Gretel reluctantly followed. The door shut behind them, and instantly all the screens came on and were running games. Then the Coke machine clunked out a couple of cans of Coke, and the snack machine whirred and hummed and a whole bunch of candy bars and chocolate piled up outside the slot.

"Excellent!" exclaimed Hansel happily, and he went over and picked up a Coke. Gretel put out her hand to stop him, but it was too late.

"Hansel, I don't like this," said Gretel, moving back to the door. There was something strange about all this—the flicker of the television screens reaching out to her, beckoning her to play, trying to draw them both in…

Hansel ignored her, as if she had ceased to exist. He swigged from the can and started playing a game. Gretel ran over and tugged at his arm, but his eyes never left the screen.

"Hansel!" Gretel screamed. "We have to get out of here!"

"Why?" asked a soft voice.

Gretel shivered. The voice sounded human enough, but it instantly gave her the mental picture of a spider, welcoming flies. Flies it meant to suck dry and hang like trophies in its web.

She turned around slowly, telling herself it couldn't really be a spider, trying to blank out the image of a hideous eight-legged, fat-bellied, fanged monstrosity.

When she saw it was only a woman, she didn't feel any better. A woman in her mid-forties, maybe, in a plain black dress, showing her bare arms. Long, sinewy arms that ended in narrow hands and long, grasping fingers. Gretel couldn't look directly at her face, just glimpsing bright-red lipstick, a hungry mouth, and the darkest of sunglasses.

"So you don't want to play the games like your brother, Hansel," said the woman. "But you can feel their power, can't you, Gretel?"

Gretel couldn't move. Her whole body was filled up with fear, because this woman was a spider, Gretel thought, a hunting spider in human shape, and she and Hansel were well and truly caught. Without thinking, she blurted out, "Spider!"

"A spider?" laughed the woman, her red mouth spreading wide, lips peeling back to reveal nicotine-stained teeth. "I'm not a spider, Gretel. I'm a shadow against the moon, a dark shape in the night doorway, a catch-as-catch-can…witch!"

"A witch," whispered Gretel. "What are you going to do with us?"

"I'm going to give you a choice that I have never given before," whispered the witch. "You have some smattering of power, Gretel. You dream true, and strong enough that my machines cannot catch you in their dreaming. The seed of a witch lies in your heart, and I will tend it and make it grow. You will be my apprentice and learn the secrets of my power, the secrets of the night and the moon, of the twilight and the dawn. Magic, Gretel, magic! Power and freedom and dominion over beasts and men!

"Or you can take the other path," she continued, leaning in close till her breath washed into Gretel's nose, foul breath that smelled of cigarettes and whiskey. "The path that ends in the end of Gretel. Pulled apart for your heart and lungs and liver and kidneys. Transplant organs are so in demand, particularly for sick little children with very rich parents! Strange—they never ask me where the organs come from."

"And Hansel?" whispered Gretel, without thinking of her own danger, or the seed in her heart that begged to be made a witch. "What about Hansel?"

"Ah, Hansel," cried the witch. She clicked her fingers, and Hansel walked over to them like a zombie, his fingers still twitching from the game.

"I have a particular plan for Hansel," crooned the witch. "Hansel with the beautiful, beautiful blue eyes."

She tilted Hansel's head back so his eyes caught the light, glimmering blue. Then she took off her sunglasses, and Gretel saw that the witch's own eyes were shriveled like raisins and thick with fat white lines like webs.

"Hansel's eyes go to a very special customer," whispered the witch. "And the rest of him? That depends on Gretel. If she's a good apprentice, the boy shall live. Better blind than dead, don't you think?" She snapped out her arm on the last word and grabbed Gretel, stopping her movement toward the door.

"You can't go without my leave, Gretel," said the witch. "Not when there's so much still for you to see. Ah, to see again, all crisp and clean, with eyes so blue and bright. Lazarus!"

An animal padded out from the rear of the shop and came up to the witch's hand. It was a cat, of sorts. It stood almost to the witch's waist, and it was multicolored, and terribly scarred, lines of bare skin running between patches of different-colored fur like a horrible jigsaw. Even its ears were different colors, and its tail seemed to be made of seven quite distinct rings of fur. Gretel felt sick as she realized it was a patchwork beast, sewn together from many different cats and given life by the witch's magic.

Then Gretel noticed that whenever the witch turned her head, so did Lazarus. If she looked up, the cat looked up. If she turned her head left, it turned left. Clearly, the witch saw the world through the cat's eyes.

With the cat at her side, the witch pushed Gretel ahead of her and whistled for Hansel to follow. They went through the back of the shop, then down a long stairway, deep into the earth. At the bottom, the witch unlocked the door with a key of polished bone.

Beyond the door was a huge cave, ill lit by seven soot-darkened lanterns. One side of the cave was lined with empty cages, each just big enough to house a standing child.

There was also an industrial cold room—a shed-size refrigerator that had a row of toothy icicles hanging from the gutters of its sloping roof—that dominated the other side of the cave. Next to the cold room was a slab of marble that served as a table. Behind it, hanging from hooks in the damp stone of the cave wall, were a dozen knives and cruel-looking instruments of steel.

"Into the cage, young Hansel," commanded the witch, and Hansel did as he was told, without a word. The patchwork cat slunk after him and shot the bolt home with a slap of its paw.

"Now, Gretel," said the witch. "Will you become a witch or be broken into bits?"

Gretel looked at Hansel in his cage, and then at the marble slab and the knives. There seemed to be no choice. At least if she chose the path of witchery, Hansel would only...only...lose his eyes. And perhaps they would get a chance to escape. "I will learn to be a witch," she said finally. "If you promise to take no more of Hansel than his eyes."

The witch laughed and took Gretel's hands in a bony grip, ignoring the girl's shudder. Then she started to dance, swinging Gretel around and around, with Lazarus leaping and screeching between them.

As she danced, the witch sang:

"Gretel's chosen the witch's way, And Hansel will be the one to pay. Sister sees more and brother less— Hansel and Gretel, what a mess!"

Then she suddenly stopped and let go. Gretel spun across the cave and crashed into the door of one of the cages.

"You'll live down here," said the witch. "There's food in the cold room, and a bathroom in the last cage. I will instruct you on your duties each morning. If you try to escape, you will be punished."

Gretel nodded, but she couldn't help looking across at the knives sparkling on the wall. The witch and Lazarus looked, too, and the witch laughed again. "No steel can cut me, or rod mark my back," she said. "But if you wish to test that, it is Hansel I will punish."

Then the witch left, with Lazarus padding alongside her.

Gretel immediately went to Hansel, but he was still in the grip of the PlayStation spell, eyes and fingers locked in some phantom game.

Next she tried the door, but sparks flew up and burned her when she stuck a knife in the lock.

The door to the cold room opened easily enough, though, frosted air and bright fluorescent light spilling out. It was much colder inside than a normal refrigerator. One side of the room was stacked high with chiller boxes, each labeled with a red cross and a bright sticker that said URGENT: HUMAN TRANSPLANT. Gretel tried not to look at them, or think about what they contained. The other side was stacked with all kinds of frozen food. Gretel took some spinach. She hated it, but spinach was the most opposite food to meat she could imagine. She didn't even want to think about eating meat.

The next day marked the first of many in the cave. The witch gave Gretel chores to do, mostly cleaning or packing up boxes from the cold room in special messenger bags the witch brought down. Then the witch would teach Gretel magic, such as the spell that would keep herself and Hansel warm.

Always, Gretel lived with the fear that the witch would choose that day to bring down another child to be cut up on the marble slab, or to take Hansel's eyes. But the witch always came alone, and merely looked at Hansel through Lazarus's eyes and muttered, "Not ready."

So Gretel worked and learned, fed Hansel and whispered to him. She constantly told him not to get better, to pretend that he was still under the spell. Either Hansel listened and pretended, even to her, or he really was still entranced.

Days went by, then weeks, and Gretel realized that she enjoyed learning magic too much.

She looked forward to her lessons, and sometimes she would forget about Hansel for hours, forget that he would soon lose his eyes.

When she realized that she might forget Hansel altogether, Gretel decided that she had to kill the witch. She told Hansel that night, whispering her fears to him and trying to think of a plan. But nothing came to her, for now Gretel had learned enough to know the witch really couldn't be cut by metal or struck down by a blow.

The next morning, Hansel spoke in his sleep while the witch was in the cave. Gretel cried out from where she was scrubbing the floor, to try and cover it up, but it was too late. The witch came over and glared through the bars.

"So you've been shamming," she said. "But now I shall take your left eye, for the spell to graft it to my own socket must be fueled by your fear. And your sister will help me."

"No, I won't!" cried Gretel. But the witch just laughed and blew on Gretel's chest.

The breath sank into her heart, and the ember of witchcraft that was there blazed up and grew, spreading through her body. Higher and higher it rose, till Gretel grew small inside her own head and could feel herself move around only at the witch's whim.

Then the witch took Hansel from the cage and bound him with red rope. She laid him on the marble slab, and Lazarus jumped up so she could see. Gretel brought her herbs, and the wand of ivory, the wand of jet, and the wand of horn. Finally, the witch chanted her spell. Gretel's mind went away completely then. When she came back to herself, Hansel was in his cage, one eye bandaged with a thick pad of cobwebs. He looked at Gretel through his other, tear-filled eye.

"She's going to take the other one tomorrow," he whispered.

"No," said Gretel, sobbing. "No."

"I know it isn't really you helping her," said Hansel. "But what can you do?"

"I don't know," said Gretel. "We have to kill her—but she'll punish you if we try and we fail."

"I wish it was a dream," said Hansel. "Dreams end, and you wake up. But I'm not asleep, am I? It's too cold, and my eye…it hurts."

Gretel opened the cage to hug him and cast the spell that would warm them. But she was thinking about cold—and the witch. "If we could trap the witch and Lazarus in the cold room somehow, they might freeze to death," she said slowly. "But we'd have to make it much colder, so she wouldn't have time to cast a spell."

They went to look at the cold room and found that it was set as cold as it would go. But Hansel found a barrel of liquid nitrogen at the back, and that gave him an idea.

An hour later, they'd rigged their instant witch-freezing trap. Using one of the knives, Hansel unscrewed the inside handle of the door so there was no way to get out. Then they balanced the barrel on top of a pile of boxes, just past the door. Finally, they poured water everywhere to completely ice up the floor.

Then they took turns sleeping, till Gretel heard the click of the witch's key in the door. She sprang up and went to the cold room. Leaving the door ajar, she carefully stood on the ice and took the lid off the liquid nitrogen. Then she stepped back outside, pinching her nose and gasping. "Something's wrong, Mistress!" she exclaimed. "Everything's gone rotten."

"What!" cried the witch, dashing across the cave, her one blue eye glittering. Lazarus ran at her heels from habit, though she no longer needed his sight.

Gretel stood aside as she ran past, then gave her a hefty push. The witch skidded on the ice, crashed into the boxes, and fell flat on her back just as the barrel toppled over. An instant later, her final scream was smothered in a cloud of freezing vapor.

But Lazarus, quicker than any normal cat, did a backflip in midair, even as Gretel slammed the door. Ancient stitches gave way, and the cat started coming apart, accompanied by an explosion of the magical silver dust that filled it and gave it life.

Gretel relaxed for an instant as the dust obscured the beast, then screamed as the front part of Lazarus jumped out at her, teeth snapping. She kicked at it, but the cat was too swift, its great jaws meeting around her ankle. Gretel screamed again, and then Hansel was there, shaking the strange dust out of the broken body as if he were emptying a vacuum cleaner. In a few seconds there was nothing left of Lazarus but its head and an empty skin. Even then it wouldn't let go, till Hansel forced its mouth open with a broomstick and pushed the snarling remnant across the floor and into one of the cages.

Gretel hopped across and watched it biting the bars, its green eyes still filled with magical life and hatred. "Hansel," she said, "your own eye is frozen with the witch. But I think I can remember the spell—and there is an eye for the taking here."

So it was that when they entered the cold room later to take the key of bone from the frozen, twisted body of the witch, Hansel saw the world through one eye of blue and one of green.

Later, when they found their way home, it was the sight of that green eye that gave the Hagmom a heart attack and made her die. But their father was still a weak man, and within a year he thought to marry another woman who had no love for his children. Only this time the new Hagmom faced a Gretel who was more than half a witch, and a Hansel who had gained strange powers from his magic cat's eye.

But that is all another story…

He Died That Day, In Thirty Years

Wil McCarthy

Wil McCarthy is a writer of science fiction and science fact, when he's not launching rockets, designing satellite constellations, or building robots for the aerospace industry. His goal in writing is to find the edge that balances action and depth, entertainment and enlightenment, science and fiction. He is particularly interested in stories which, however outlandish, could actually happen.

Alice in Wonderland is not a fairytale in a traditional sense, but it contains all sorts of fairytale elements. McCarthy modernizes the story, without losing any of its power or trippiness. If anything, McCarthy's version feels all the more plausible given modern technology than the original ever did, and I find that terrifying (in a good way).

Monday through Friday, Jeremy spent his daylight hours in a stuffy, windowless cubicle. Plenty of twilight hours, too—working "Chinese overtime" at seventy-five percent pay, crunching numbers and contemplating the raison d'etre of his servitude: the ownership of a house. Not a big one or a fancy one, just a simple tract home on the outskirts of Southampton, in a not-too-dingy neighborhood twenty miles from the ocean and fully seventy from his native London.

Just barely affordable, he'd told himself, but like a ship sailing through northern fogs, he'd espied mortgage payments peeking out above the waters of his finance, never guessing they might prove the merest tips of a single monstrous iceberg that held insurance, utilities, maintenance, repairs, lawn chemicals, and every other conceivable thing in its vast, frozen bulk. Never guessing that a hidden spur could tear his hull lengthwise at any moment, filling his holds with the chill waters of bankruptcy.

The alternative, of course, was to cut his losses and dash back to the flats that had previously housed him. Throwing away his blood and sweat, just handing it off, serflike, to some absentee landlord. And sharing walls, yes, like sharing the back side of his shirt with some sweaty stranger. Even buying an apartment wouldn't fix that, and anyway he was damned if he'd own a piece of real estate that didn't touch the ground. If the building burned down, he'd be left with, what? Deed to a volume of empty air?

No. Call it a character flaw, but he needed an actual house around him, owned and operated by him, so at night he could look up sleepily at the ceiling and know that it was his ceiling, held up by his walls and standing on his own little piece of the Earth. His kingdom. But as his mother would say, nothing worth having came any way but dear; for his double sins of greed and pride, he paid. Did he ever! These sins are exactly the thing that killed him.

His savings dwindled, his credit card bills swelled, and then his pipes gave out and there was nothing for it but to call in a plumber who charged, it seemed, by the millisecond. When finally it became clear that it might be his destiny to lose the house, and his credit rating along with it, he moped around a bit and then took a weekend job to bring in extra money.

Tending bar was, he found, just exactly like being at a party. Unfortunately, it was the sort of loud, smoky party attended by people who liked a drink first thing on Friday evening and then didn't draw a sober breath until Sunday at the earliest, and he was the one washing their glasses and wiping up their spills, and a captive audience for all the stupid stories that no one else wanted to hear, and he didn't get to go home with some pretty girl when he got tired of it. He didn't even get to go home alone, not until the hour had come, the place had cleared out and he'd scrubbed his sinks and counters down with cleansing solution and left it all to dry for the next day.

His lawn took on a rough, unshaven look, the hedges along it growing wild as mop heads, but fortunately it became a rare enough thing for him to see his home in daylight that the sight rarely intruded, and the irony of that certainly wasn't lost on him.

Then one Friday evening, a pretty girl did come down and sit by him, and she didn't drink herself stupid or tell him any stories about her week while he washed and stacked the glasses. Instead, she ordered a Coke, rooted around in her purse, filed her nails for a bit, and then turned and asked him if he was happy.

"I beg your pardon?" he replied, not really sure he'd understood the question.

"Are you happy," she repeated, giving him a sort of vague, half-knowing smile.

"It's just that I never see you here during the week, and you don't quite seem like the sort of person who tends bar. So I thought maybe it wasn't by choice."

Jeremy set down his rag, waved a hand through the coils of smoke hanging in the air. "By choice? Why, does anyone do this by choice?"

"Well of course. It's a position of respect, of dignity. You're trusted with significant sums of money, and with stock and equipment worth many times more than that. People come to you with their problems, and when somebody picks a fight and you tell them to break it up, they listen to you. It's like being a fire chief or an office manager or something."

"He's the office manager," Jeremy said, jerking a thumb at the door behind him. "And I've never broken up a fight in my life. Can I freshen that for you?"

"Thanks, yes."

He went back to washing glasses, until a gaggle of drinkers boiled up from the restaurant floor with fresh orders, and the pair at the end of the bar decided they needed another round, and that touched off another series that kept him jumping for a good ten minutes. But when he'd finished, the young woman was still there, jutting up like a rock in a river as patrons swirled about her, calling and laughing and singing along with the radio.

"It's nice to stay busy," she observed. "Makes the time go."

"Does it?" Jeremy asked shortly. But he felt a smile rising, felt it break the surface.

"There, now, that's not so bad, is it?" What her voice lacked in finish it made up for in sincerity. This was, he thought, a grocer's daughter, or perhaps even a barman's. Not a good girl, per se, judging by the short black skirt and less-than-missionary blouse she'd chosen to wear, but then again who dressed like a saint on Friday night? He'd dated his share of gentlemen's ladies, and there really wasn't much to remember them by.

"I'm Jeremy," he said, wiping a hand dry and then offering it to her.

"Alice," she said, taking it. And then she did a thing he'd heard about but never actually seen done: she raised their joined hands to her mouth, and gently nibbled the end of his middle finger. He had absolutely no idea what to say to that, and evidently neither did she—in another moment they were both laughing, alone together in a bubble, a pocket universe into which the barroom hubbub scarcely seemed able to penetrate.

This is what killed him.

Jeremy's business, by the way, was in the mathematics of fate. It worked like this: turbulent phenomena were fine and predictable over short spans of time, but ugly and messy and random in the long run. Even the most detailed weather simulations, for example, were useless past about five days, because you knew your starting conditions with only finite precision. Even the tiniest errors would grow over time, and if you twiddled your guesses one way the long-range forecast might be one thing, and if you twiddled them ever so slightly in the other way, it might yield something entirely different.

But from this sea of infinite possibility there arose a kind of meta-order, occasional reefs of near-certainty jutting up from the deeps. The weather would fluctuate, right enough, but winter would come along eventually, and spring after it, and sometimes you could say with 95% confidence that on an afternoon twenty-six days hence, it would be snowing hard in Bonn. So, far from banishing the concept of destiny, twenty-first century mathematics had enshrined and legitimized it—in a world of turbulence, there were still some things you could count on.

It mattered very little that Jeremy's training was in marine meteorology while his actual work was in finance. The numbers didn't care about abstractions like that. If only human society were so forgiving!

The woman's eyes, he noted, were brown.

"A Newcastle, please," someone said later, a moment or an hour, breaking the spell. The two of them shared a regretful look before the receding tide pulled Jeremy away. After that he was busy for the rest of the night, never sharing another word with her, but she watched him as he worked, cast little smiles and funny faces at him now and then, and somehow that was enough. Their acquaintanceship grew. When closing time came, he half expected her to come straight home with him, and was oddly pleased to receive instead nothing more than a business card and a peck on the cheek.

"Come 'round and see me tomorrow," she said, not sultrily or coquettishly but in a simple way that indicated her hope that he really would.

"Count on it," he told her, thinking maybe this weekend job thing wasn't so bad after all.

Watching the unself-conscious, high-heeled swivel of her buttocks as she walked away, he felt a stab of passion rather more intense and possessive and smugly self-satisfied than he had any right to. Jesus, Jer, it's not like you fucked her right there on the bar. The image that came to him then was sharp, vivid with sensory detail: soft pinkness against the wood, her breath coming out in grunts and gasps. And most of all, the taste of sweat. God, yes.

"Alice Frane, Designer," the card said in delicate letters. It gave an address, a telephone number, an email, and smelled faintly but distinctly of her.

He wandered home in a fog.

In the morning he awoke, having slept well and deeply, dreaming of nothing. He admired his calm as he downed morning stimulants, arranged breakfast, showered. Only when he'd begun to dress did he give up and have a wank, throwing himself back on the bed and imagining, once more, Alice's body writhing beneath his. Not on the bar, this time, but on the blasted, hellish surface of the planet Venus, the yellow air hot against their skins, bodies rising and sinking in puddles of molten lead. Stop! Don't! Save it! a part of him was screaming. We might need this! But the rest of him just laughed at the idea. Plenty more where that came from.

After he really did get dressed, he felt calmed enough to pick up the phone and dial the number on the card. Alice Frane, Designer.

"Hello?" a voice said after the second ring. Her voice? Maybe.

"Is Alice there?" he asked.

"Oh. Is this Jeremy?"

"Yes."

"She's at services right now. Can you come around at eleven?"

"Eleven? Well, yes. Of course. But…May I ask whom I'm speaking with?"

"This is her answering machine," the voice said.

Well, well. Software like that cost several times what Jeremy earned in a month. This "designing" must pay pretty well, assuming the voice didn't belong to a sister or roommate or even Alice herself, having him on.

"Is there a message?" the voice inquired patiently.

"No. Uh, yes. I mean, I'll be there. Can you give directions?"

"Uh huh. Where are you coming from?"

The directions that followed were clear and succinct, and he was even warned to avoid the construction on such-and-such street, and encouraged to take advantage of the much lighter traffic on so-and-so. It wasn't a sister, he decided. Or if it was, she had a taxi dispatcher's workstation bolted to her nightstand.

He thanked the voice and rang off.

When he arrived at the specified address, he thought at first that there must be some mistake. Too nice. Much too nice. Fancy answering machines were one thing, but nobody with the wherewithal to live here would be dropping into seedy little pubs to pick up on the barmen. The building's software seemed to be expecting him, though; the pedestrian gate was exceedingly polite.

Did he feel a stab of house envy? Not really, he decided. Four walls and a roof, that was the thing. If he did somehow own a place like this, he'd probably swap it for a place like his current, and set up the excess in a trust to pay the property taxes in perpetuity. But it would be nice, affording it.

Alice's front door was made of real wood, and he'd only knocked once before it opened wide to reveal…Well, Alice herself was the first thing he noticed—dressed now in a fine Sunday jumper, for all that today was Saturday. Floral print on white with a matching jacket over the top. Behind her was another surprise, though: the house, rather than being posh inside, appeared all but empty, one giant interior space whose vastness was broken only by some cluttered tables up against the far wall.

"Hello," Alice said, sounding pleased.

"Hi."

"Won't you come in?"

He smiled. "Dying to, actually."

Inside, he saw the space was not quite as barren as he'd thought. Off to one side was a kitchen; off to the other, a bedroom set, and in the distance an automobile, sitting before a large, automatic carport door. White floor, white ceiling…only the interior walls were lacking. But the central area, the livingroom if you will, looked more like an unusually spacious laboratory than anything else. He saw two computer-like devices, a rack of small, marked bottles, some standing glassware, other objects less identifiable.

"I've got a kettle on," she offered as she ushered him in, closing the door behind him.

"That'd be great, thanks."

She showed him to a seat at the kitchen table, busied herself with the clink of cups and saucers.

"Nice place you have here," he said. "Kind of, uh, surprising."

"People always say that." She smiled and handed him a cup, then picked up her own and sipped from it. He glanced at his own, sniffed it. Not tea but coffee, pale with added milk. Fiercely sweet when he sipped it.

"It was…a pleasure," he attempted, "meeting you last night. I'm glad you invited me over."

"Really, Jeremy?" She turned, faced him fully, her face suddenly earnest. "Did you feel it, too?"

"Feel it?"

"That sense, that destiny. Like we'd known each other already. Oh, listen to me, putting the cart before…I don't even know your last name."

"It's Hobb."

"Hobb." She sampled it, nodding. "Do you believe in love at first sight, Jeremy Hobb?"

His heart fluttered. Love? That was a big word. "First sight" too, for that matter. His first glimpse of her hadn't been anything all that remarkable. And yet…

Without warning, she dropped to her knees in front of him, placing a hand on each of his thighs. Her eyes sparkled. His heart fluttered again.

"Do you feel the chemistry?" she demanded, leaning forward, her face upturned, red-painted lips mere inches from his crotch. "Do you feel a particular longing, a particular hunger? To be with me? Not just to be with someone, not with me just because I'm conveniently here. Do. You. Want. Me?"

"Yes," Jeremy admitted. "You. Not just anyone. We made a…connection last night, and I wanted to know more. It's why I'm here."

"Not just for the hope of sex?"

Um…

"I'd be lying if I said that weren't part of it," he said truthfully.

"But not all?"

"No. Definitely not."

"Good," she said, relaxing visibly. Her hand dove into a jacket pocket, came back holding something. A pill, red. She held it out to him.

"Er," he commented.

"Trust me, Jeremy Hobb. If you feel what you say, take the pill for me."

"It's…"

"Not birth control," she said. "It's a psychoactive. Designed by me. I want you to have it."

"None for you?"

"No, no, that would ruin the effect."

Jeremy, being very much a creature of the times, did take drugs at parties, sometimes without asking what they were. This request was not so completely out of line. But usually there were lots of other people taking them as well—safety in numbers, as it were—so it wasn't all that much in line, either.

But then again, what did Alice Frane, Designer, stand to gain by poisoning him? His worldly riches? Hardly.

He took the pill, washing it down with a swallow of the too-sweet coffee, and wondered what, exactly, she had in mind. The pill seemed to dissolve in his throat, rising vaporlike into his sinuses.

This is not what killed him.

"How long until this takes effect?" he asked.

She smiled, rubbing her face against his inner thigh. "It should be nearly instantaneous. From the nasal and bronchial mucosa straight to the blood-brain barrier. It—"

"Stop that, please," he said, moving his leg.

She pulled away a bit. "Why? What's wrong?"

He pulled back, scooting his chair a bit. Feeling something a little off. Wondering, now, why he'd let her give him the pill. A desire to please? To be pleased, no matter what the cost? Not bright. She wasn't even all that pretty, not really.

"Jeremy, what's wrong?" she repeated.

He sighed, scooting his chair farther back, looking at her there on her knees, trying fumblingly to arouse him, to coax some promise of love out of him. Giving him drugs for it! Suddenly, he was glad things hadn't got any further than this. The thought of waking up in this woman's bed was, actually, not that pleasant. He'd probably come to his senses just in time.

"I...don't think this is a very good idea, you and I," he said, as gently as he could manage under the circumstances. "I mean, you're very nice, but I don't know that we're really one another's type, if you see what I mean."

"You don't love me, then?"

To her credit, she didn't betray any signs of deep hurt or embarassment. Well, good. Better that she salvage her dignity. Better that this be over with.

"No," he said, "I'm afraid I don't."

"No sense of connection? No special bond?"

He shook his head. "No, Alice. I'm sorry. I should have—"

"Do you even like me?"

His reflex was to answer yes, to spare her feelings, but it seemed he owed her something more than that. He couldn't blame her for getting the wrong idea, after all. Not after the way he'd come here, the way he'd spoken to her...Really, if her feelings got hurt it was largely his own fault. And that wasn't something he wanted.

"I have no dislike for you," he said honestly. "I think we could, for example, be friends. If that's what you want."

She lifted her head, smiling with a curious wickedness. "You have no idea," she said, "how happy I am to hear that."

"Excuse me?"

Rising to her feet, she dusted her knees off with a swipe and then held a hand out to him. "Alice Frane, Designer. What you've ingested is an oxytocin antagonist, a chemical designed to block the brain's response to...call it infatuation. The early stages of love."

He blinked. "What?"

"I've been working on it for months, and you have no idea how hard it is to find a suitable test subject in this town. The dosage is tiny, by the way. You should be fine in a minute."

Oxytocin antagonist? thought Jeremy. Test subject? What the hell was she talking about?

"I apologize for the deception," she said, holding her hand out closer to him and waving it slightly, a nonverbal demand that he shake it. "It's necessary that the subject's romantic interest be genuine. We can induce it chemically, but then the spatial distribution inside the brain is all wrong, which is another way of saying there are side effects. To get a proper test, we need all the variables constant, wouldn't you say?"

Jeremy took the hand, shook and released it, then wondered why he'd done it. Something very confused in his brain, in his feelings. Not so much the confusion of ambivalence or ignorance as that of a sharp blow to the head. Although he was feeling damned ignorant as well. And ambivalent.

"How're you doing?" Alice asked, now sounding genuinely, if slightly, concerned. "You look..."

"Confused," he said. "Angry. You tricked me."

"Yes," she admitted.

He rose unsteadily from the chair. "I'm getting out of here."

She shrugged. "I don't blame you, actually, but let me give you something for your trouble before you go. You don't imagine I'm quite that callous, do you?"

Well...Before he could answer, she'd turned, snatched something off the counter. A check register—the paper kind. She took up a pen, scribbled quickly. Tore off a sheet.

"Here. Please."

He took it from her, again before he'd really thought it through. The hell of it was, he did want to please her. To be liked by her. He looked: her writing, barely legible, had made the check out to him. For much more money than he'd been prepared to see, a sum slightly more than he made in a weekend at the pub.

"Not bad for a minute's work, eh?"

He stared at the check for a moment, then flipped it over. Found a notice to the effect that endorsement was required for deposit, and constituted a release of the payor from any further obligation, financial or otherwise, for services rendered.

"What is this?" he asked, his brain rising finally, turgidly, up out of the fog. "What kind of racket are you running?"

"No racket," she said, surprised, not quite defensive.

"You're a drug designer."

"Mood designer, yes. What did you think?"

What did he think? That she'd liked him, wanted him in some way? It had seemed a reasonable hypothesis at the time. Now he'd fallen in love with her in an evening, fallen out in ten seconds, and fallen...what, back in love again? Just as she was giving him this really, particularly good reason to despise her? It was too much, too many feelings at once. Contradictory feelings that, far from canceling one another out, seemed to crash together like incoming and outflowing waves, sending up towers of spray.

"It doesn't matter what I thought," he said with what struck him as a pathetic sort of dignity.

"Were there side effects?"

"Yes," he said. Then: "None of your business, actually. I think I'll take the hush money, and hush. Now if you'll excuse me…"

"It isn't hush money," she said, standing straighter, not quite barring his way. Cup and saucer clinking in her hands. "What I've done is perfectly ethical. This is a licensed pharmogenia, you came here voluntarily, took the enhancement voluntarily…You haven't been harmed in any way."

"You lied to me," he pointed out curtly.

"Did not either! When did I lie?"

He felt his face grow hot. Hotter, actually—he'd been blushing for quite some time, now. He spoke slowly: "You pretended to like me. To be romantically interested. On what planet is that considered ethical?"

She quirked her brows together, looking honestly puzzled. "Who said I wasn't interested? I needed a genuine attraction, somebody charming and witty and available, somebody with enough sense to see the same things in me. I was so happy to find you there last night, hopping around with that towel on your arm, playacting. More like a barman than any real one I've ever seen."

She stopped, examined her nails for a moment, met his eyes again.

"I do believe in love at first sight, Jeremy Hobb. The marriages ruined by it, the kingdoms toppled…What would the world give for a cure? Mood design is the art and science of liberation, the decoupling of human spirit from the engines of biological imperative."

He shook his head, perplexed, once more at a loss. "You want a world without love?"

"Oh," she said, "God, no." And she leaned forward and kissed him on the lips.

That was what killed him.

The rest of their conversation went like this: he had a perfect right to be angry—she certainly would be if their situations were reversed—but she hoped he would let her make it up to him. They could spend the day together. He didn't know about that. Well, how about this: she knew he needed the money. He virtually radiated debtor's anxiety. If he'd agree to sample two more substances for her, she would see him well compensated, and get to spend time with him besides. He really didn't know about that. What did she take him for? But she named a figure, shockingly high, and he crumpled.

"They're a bit more…experimental," she admitted. "We can't be completely sure of the effects. I need someone intelligent enough to articulate the experiences clearly."

That would be, a part of him insisted, a really exceptionally bad idea. Whether she liked him or not—and he wasn't at all convinced that she did, that she wasn't just leading him on for her own purposes—it was pretty obvious that his relative poverty, his double sins of greed and pride, had been a large part of what had drawn her to him. Intelligent, yes. Alone, yes. Ready to fall in love on a moment's notice, and vulnerable to...financial persuasion.

But the money, countered another part of him. Eleven point two house payments! Enough to really dig himself out, to quit the pub, quit the overtime, to stay dug out on a long-term basis. That was not a small thing, not a thing he could easily walk away from and live with himself afterward.

And a third part of him: God help the underdamped system. Chaos would have its way with any variable not sufficiently anchored by stabilizing influences. His work took fate for granted, a gift from the gods, but what, really, built up those islands of gellid near-certainty? Sinks and sources—features existing on a larger scale, mathematically speaking, than the perturbations that sought to disrupt them. What ocean liner was ever capsized by a three-foot wave? What nation drowned beneath the flood of a single minor river?

Base axiom of the financial fractanalyst: the occurrence of islands could not be controlled; the seizing and holding of them could.

Unhappily, he observed: "You know which buttons to push."

"Well, I hope so," Alice said. And then she smiled and dropped her eyes, suddenly shy.

Had he doubted her beauty? Had he really?

The first pill she gave him was blue, washed down with a hot sip of freshened coffee, fiercely sweet.

"How long for this to take effect?"

"I'm guessing about an hour."

"But you don't know?"

"Not really. Are there any immediate effects?"

He paused, sniffed, thought for a moment. "A slight dizziness. And...is that garlic I smell?"

"Garlic," she said, writing that down in a little paper notepad. "Interesting. I wanted an olfactory telltale, but interpretation can be so subjective. The smell—" she winked "—is in your head. How's the dizziness? Still there? Maybe you should sit."

They'd been leaning side-by-side against the kitchen counter, their hips almost touching.

"I think I will," he agreed, moving away and taking his seat. What was going on in his brain? What was she doing to him now? The light-headed feeling was slight, passing already, but the sense of foreboding persisted. As well it should: this was not a smart thing to be doing. Not something he could, for example, easily explain to his mother.

Alice, still standing, loomed over him. Inspecting. "How do you feel?"

"Unwise," he said.

She laughed. "Fair enough. The love snuffer should be just about dissipated by now, I think. Are you...repelled by me?"

Repelled? She tossed her hair, and he felt himself grow hard at the sight. She licked her lips and the erection became painful, straining against clothing, straining against the skin which contained it.

"That's not a word I would choose," he offered guardedly, wary that this might be some new trick. "Why, have you given me some sort of aphrodisiac?"

"No, something quite different. Whatever emotion you're feeling now comes directly from your own heart." She leaned closer, placed a finger on the edge of his jaw, traced downward. Touch of feathers: tingly, electric. "Is there a spark in your heart, Jeremy? A trace of desire?"

"Maybe," he allowed. But his voice betrayed him, trembling, cracking.

"Well, come on then," she said, and her hands moved to the closures of the jumper and pulled them apart, revealing white brassiere lace underneath. She found a hook and parted that as well. Her breasts, pushed together by taut fabric, seemed to grope for him, pink nipples like blind, soft eyes.

He could have resisted, he would later think. He could have walked away. He was not, after all, some mindless rutting machine. But even his hands were hungry for her, and who was he to refuse them?

In another moment she was in his lap, jacket discarded, floral-print jumper peeled to the waist. Brassiere still clinging to the shoulders, open and welcoming, framing the bob and swell of her. Light taste of sweat on her skin, nipples hardening beneath his tongue.

"Oh," she said.

He lifted her, carried her, legs wrapping around his waist. The bed wasn't far at all.

She resisted, at first, when he tried to relieve her of those last bits of clothing. No words exchanged, but reproach clear in her manner: please me and we'll see. He did his best, and minutes or hours later she was peeling the jumper off herself, rolling to the side, distentangling her legs. She kicked the fabric away, clad now only in pink cotton underpants. He kissed them, deep, wanting, pressing the heat of his breath through to her. Then he pulled them down off her and she said nothing, wordlessly approving. He traced the rise and fall of her knee, the sharp curve of ankle as he slipped them off and away.

Her pubic hair was soft and brown, exactly the color of her eyes. He went for his own shirt buttons, undid one, found her hands there stopping him. Reproachful: please me and we'll see. Dying to, actually. She tasted exactly as he imagined.

How many times did she shudder beneath his ministrations? Soon it was one continuous shudder, one steady, panting moan, until finally, wordlessly, she willed him to stop. Enough; he'd proven his sincerity, could take what he wanted of her. It was she, this time, who unfastened his buttons.

It was he who stopped her—the dizziness back again, the smell of garlic. Stronger this time.

"Something's happening," he said.

She sat up, suddenly alert. "Garlic?"

"Garlic," he agreed, "it's back."

Her smile was mischevous, almost cruel. "Unfortunate timing for you, I'm afraid. I'd better dress."

She took a moment to wipe his mouth with a clean corner of sheet.

Disappointed: "Stop it. Dress? Why?"

"You'll see."

He didn't much like the sound of that, but he rolled off the bed and stood, watching her reach for panties, bra, jumper. The act of dressing was itself maddeningly erotic. Soon she was on her feet, slipping back into her shoes and urging him into the kitchen. Her jacket lay where it had fallen; she retrieved it.

Unhappily, he took his seat. Dizziness and garlic stronger than ever, overpowering.

"What's happening to me?"

"We'll see," she said, handing him the cup and saucer again.

Something surged through the insides of his skull, not so much a pain as a pressure. Alarming. But then the garlic smell was fading, the nausea and dizziness shrinking away.

"How do you feel?" she asked.

"Better. What happened?"

She shrugged. "You tell me."

Shaking a little, he took a sip from his coffee. Stone cold. He dropped the cup, watched it spin, fall, shatter.

"How long before it takes effect?" he asked, his voice swimming out from between his lips with underwater slowness.

"You're just coming out of it now," she said. "What's the last thing you remember?"

"Taking the pill," he said, slowly but without hesitation. "And then a smell."

"Garlic?"

"That's right."

"And then a feeling of light-headedness?"

He thought about that. "Yes, I think. A little."

"And are there any unusual sensations right now?"

He thought again, taking quick stock of himself. "I'm sweaty," he said. "And my… testicles are a bit sore."

That certainly brought an un-clinical smile to her lips. "Normal," she assured him, "under the circumstances. Anything else?"

"Well, um…I seem to have broken my cup. Only I don't remember its happening."

"You've lost a little time."

He nodded unhappily. "I thought maybe I had. How awful. Is that the effect? Is that what's supposed to happen?"

"More or less," she said, nodding and smiling. "It's a memory drug, but the details are…complicated. You know, why don't you let me explain it to you over, say, a continental lunch?"

Hesitation. "I haven't brought much money."

"Oh, please," she said, flipping a hand at him, annoyed at the implied insult. "My treat. Believe me, you've earned an afternoon on the town."

The way she said this somehow struck him as nakedly erotic. God, but she was beautiful, and he couldn't shake the sense, somehow, that their relationship was already an intimate one. He even fancied he could taste, vividly, the musk of her on his lips.

The restaurant she took him to was quiet, dim, cool. Filled with discreet niches which seemed to swallow patrons whole, leaving no verbal or auditory trace of their presence.

The pill she gave him to ingest was green, translucent, tasteless. Slick going down, rising up again as vapor.

"What will this one do?"

She paused for a guilty moment, then seemed to decide he had a right to know. "Right frontal inhibitor, to suppress your filters, for heightened sensitivity. If I've got it tuned for the proper stimulus pathways, it should…enhance your dining experience. I call it 'Gourmand.'"

"That doesn't sound so bad," he said.

"No. But I may be skewing the results by providing an a priori description. Autohypnosis can be as powerful as any mood alteration I've ever cooked up. But what the hell, it's been a brilliantly successful day. Let's live a little."

"You make it sound almost like we're partners," he observed, taking a sip from his water. Frowning.

"You have no idea how much you've helped, and I do mean to make it up to you. I hope you're hungry."

"Famished, actually."

They studied menus, discussed them a little, closed them. A waiter appeared, as if from nowhere.

"Cassoulet, please," Alice said. "And a glass of red wine."

A vintage and year were suggested and agreed to. The waiter turned.

"And for sir?"

"Escargot," Jeremy instructed, "lightly sauteed. Green salad with buttermilk, hold tomato. Trout with almonds, medium well, slice of dark rye on the side. Glass of Coke, vodka chaser, and a fresh glass of water; this came out of the tap. If you haven't got anything bottled, at least put a lime in it to cover that awful mustiness."

"Very good, sir. Very perceptive. Cook will be pleased."

"No doubt."

The waiter retreated, amused.

"I don't know how you usually order," Alice observed.

Distractedly: "Neither do I. Not like that, I suppose. Same knowledge, different inclination."

"How are you feeling?"

"Hungry."

Their drinks arrived. The glass of water, its sides sweaty with condensation, sported a thin wheel of lime on its rim. Jeremy took the glass, raised it, sipped experimentally. Better, much better. Tasting more of water than of pipe. But he dropped the lime in anyway, for flavor. The Coke was better: biting, sharp, bubbles carrying the essence of it deeper into the tongue the way Coke bubbles always had. The vodka was excellent.

He realized Alice was speaking: "…more generalized inhibitor, but there'd have been too many alternate pathways for breakdown. The mood designer always strives for specificity of effect."

"That's nice," he said.

"About the memory drug you had this afternoon," she began.

He sipped the vodka again, savoring the deep, almost oily texture of it, the clean ethanol aroma, the taste like buttered steam.

"Yes?"

"I'm thinking of calling it 'Finals Week.' Once I get the dosage and decay times worked out, I'm shooting for a latency of about twelve hours per pill. Take you through the days you'd rather not experience."

He finished the vodka, let it dissipate a little before drinking from the Coke. Why wasn't there bread here? What kind of restaurant didn't bring bread?

"I'm not sure I understand," he said.

She smiled self-consciously. "Of course not, I'm sorry. What, exactly, was your experience of that enhancement?"

"The blue pill? Not much. I took it, and suddenly my cup was on the floor." Instant coffee, heavily sweetened and creamed. Bleah. Maybe he'd get a cup of the real thing after eating. Probably he would, yes.

"Your experiences of any particular moment form an electrochemical signature," she said, "which can be captured almost like a photograph can be captured."

"Okay."

His salad arrived. Lifting a fork, he stabbed a crisp leaf and raised it, dripping, to his lips. Eh. The dressing a bit sour, a bit salty for some reason. Adequate, but far from optimal.

"Memories from that point forward," Alice went on when the waiter had gone, "can be tagged. When the decay point arrives, the tags are deleted, along with all associated memory, and the original snapshot is restored. The world is full of amnesia narcotics, but usually they just interrupt the memory process on a continuous basis, which leads to confusion and erratic behavior. The subject can't remember things from one moment to the next, and while subjective chronology is disrupted as a result, there's still generally some sense of time having passed. And of course there are side effects like euphoria and suggestibility that distort the personality further.

"What I'm after is more like the 'Skip' button on a disc player, simply jumping ahead to a point in the future without any delay or confusion. The perfect cure for impatience! You say that was your experience?"

Around a mouthful of cress: "I guess so. Why 'Finals Week,' though?"

She shrugged. "Just a thought. I always hated times like that in school, all the work and the stress, and I don't know what I'd have paid for the chance to skip over it all. And colleges are a lucrative market."

He paused, stopped eating for a moment. "How much time did I lose this afternoon?"

"About an hour."

"An hour? God. And I was conscious during that time? What was I doing? In the kitchen the whole time?"

"Well, most of it," she said, coloring slightly in the candlelight.

"But aware? Talking? Behaving normally?"

"Well, yes. I mean, to within my ability to judge."

"Your invention is useless, then."

She blinked, her face drawing down. Not liking that. "Useless how?"

"Think about it," he said. "You take the pill, maybe wash it down with a nice woodruff-tinctured May wine. Sit back, wait for your exam or whatever it is to be over. But it isn't over. You're still there, living through it, and you say to yourself, 'What a gyp! What a robbery! I'm the unlucky one!'"

"Unlucky?" She was shaking her head, not quite grasping his point.

"Unlucky," he repeated. "For practical purposes, you've been split into two people: one who takes the final exam, and one who doesn't. And if you're still sitting there right after you take the pill, if you haven't skipped ahead, then you're the one who's stuck with the exam you were trying to avoid! And, you take another sip of your wine, savoring, mulling it over the tongue a bit, and contemplate the fact that for your trouble, for sitting down and taking the test like a good little girl, you get killed. Erased! And the other you, the lazy bitch who stuck you with the chores, skips off with the credit! Think about it: you take the pill, and suddenly you're saying 'oh, my God, I'm the one that gets erased!'"

He leaned closer, wiping a smudge of buttermilk dressing off his chin. "If somebody did that to me, I'd want to get back at them. Not take the exam at all, for starters. Maybe go off and have a little party, too, with the credit cards. Buy a decent meal, smoke a cherrywood pipe, then sit around drinking French roast until the axe falls. That's what I'd do."

"But that's ridiculous," Alice protested, partly amused and partly, he thought, irate that a putative employee should criticize her this way. "It's you who gave you the enhancement. You'd only be hurting yourself."

"I'd be hurting the bastard that killed me."

"Nobody killed you. You'd wake up with a little hole in your memory and a whole lot of consequences to pay."

"No, he'd have the consequences to pay. I'd just be a temporary storage file spooled off by his brain and then deleted. If identity is the continuity of memory, and if my memories will never reach him, then I'm not a part of him, and he has no right to command or abuse me. No more than a twin brother has."

"But there's only one of you," she said, as if correcting an obvious error. "One body, one brain, and in the end, one memory."

"In the end, yes. After the temporary is gone. Imagine that it's a physical copy, rather than a…mental ghost, if you will. Imagine that you've taken a *Star Trek* transporter beam and made a perfect duplicate of yourself. She has all your thoughts and memories, she's exactly like you in every way, except that she's programmed to turn to dust at the end of twelve hours. And you expect her to spend those twelve hours doing chores for you and then peacefully go off and die. How do you feel about the morality of that?"

"That would be wrong, obviously, but it's not the same thing."

"How would you feel if you were the duplicate? Would you do the chores?"

"Of course not. But it's not the same thing. Drugs don't create copies of you. At worst, they delete small pieces of the original. That's all."

"If I'm the piece that's going to be deleted, how is that different? In what way is that better for me?"

The waiter reappeared, setting a basket of dinner rolls down on the table. "Everything all right?" he asked, eyeing the two of them uncertainly.

"Fine," Jeremy told him. "Is there butter for these?"

"On your left, sir."

"Ah. Great."

Alice unfurled a hand partway, subtly inviting the waiter to remain a moment longer. "Garçon," she said, "if you'd ingested a drug which, in twelve hours' time, would erase your memory of those twelve hours, would you behave irresponsibly?"

The man twitched under her gaze, caught between the conflicting goals of pleasing the customer and remaining, as was his job, invisible. "Er," he replied, "well, no."

"If you had chores to do, would you do them?"

"Of course."

"Would you view yourself as any sort of temporary creature, doomed to die when the drug wore off?"

Uncertainty in his manner; would this conversation affect his tip? Would his supervisors approve if they overheard? "I…don't think so, miss. Should I?"

"No, of course not. Thank you."

"Will there be anything else?"

"No. Thanks."

"Thank you," he corrected, and slipped politely, if gratefully, back into the shadows.

"You see?" Alice said, turning, her smile vaguely triumphant.

Jeremy, tucking away the last of a bitter, sandy-tasting roll, snorted. After a rigorous proof like that, what was there to say? Alice wasn't so much a scientist, he realized, as an elaborate sort of dope pusher. He wondered about her training—what sort of school had she gone to, exactly?

A muffled voice drifted over from a nearby table, its owner unseen: "I'm with you, buddy. Nobody sets me up, deletes me and then gets away with it, even if it's me that does it. I'd maybe take that drug for something really bad, if I had to shoot my dog or something, but never for an exam. Now will you please lower your voices?"

Alice sighed and said, more quietly, "It takes all kinds, I supppose. This is useful information: people who think the way you do would never be interested. I doubt the percentage is all that high, though."

"Have you ever taken it yourself?" he asked.

She shook her head.

"Might think differently if you did. Take the pill, find you haven't skipped yet, find out you are the skip…"

There was nothing, it seemed, to say to that, and anyway the waiter returned a minute later with their food.

"The kitchen staff would all take the exam, miss," he said, a bit tentatively, as he moved the plates from tray to table. "I asked them for you."

"Really." Alice's eyes glittered at him. "That was very thoughtful."

"They also said, ah, that they wouldn't take the drug, miss. Not for that. Maybe for something more...dreadful."

"Really."

Oops. The waiter clearly knew right away that he'd overstepped himself, that he'd brought displeasure to the table. "I...may have asked the question wrong," he said. "Do enjoy your meals."

He took his tray and departed.

The aromas of the food drove all else from Jeremy's mind. He set to it with conviction, recoiled, set to it again.

"How is it?" Alice asked distantly, watching him eat but now only partly interested.

"The snails?" he grunted, making faces. "Like shit. Literally. Bird droppings in their food supply. The trout's not much better; he's overcooked the skin, undercooked the meat, and the non-stick coating must be wearing out in the bottom of his pan, because he's used that spray stuff on it. I can taste it from three feet away."

She flipped her hair and smiled at him peculiarly, the way a lover might, after a quarrel that had petered out unsatisfactorily. "Hyperacuity," she said, popping a spoonful of cassoulet into her mouth. "I'll remember to reduce the dosage a bit next time."

Back at Alice's house, back in what passed, more or less, for his right mind, Jeremy refused a third pill. "You said two," he explained carefully. "I'm entitled to another check. The big one, as we agreed."

"As we agreed," she said grumpily, taking up her check book and scribbling. "You can't tell me it's been such a horrific experience, though."

He held his hands up. "I never said it was. But I can really use this money, as I think you're aware, and I'm not interested in dancing for it any more than I have to. I've house payments to make. Why, what is it? The pill, I mean."

"Finals Week again," she said hopefully. "I thought I'd go for a longer gap this time."

"Ah, no," he said, emphatically but with, he thought, reasonably good humor. "I thought we went over that. I'd never have taken it the first time if I'd known what it was. I mean, really, you couldn't pay me enough."

A sly smile slid onto her face, clicking firmly into place. "You're still here, Jeremy. We're still talking. You are willing to be persuaded. You're asking to be persuaded."

"I'm not," he said.

"You are," she insisted, stepping forward. "You haven't walked out or told me to bugger off yet. You still want something. But it isn't money—we've already solved that problem. So what other problem is there, that you'd like me to solve for you?"

She cocked a hip, suggestively.

"No," he said. "Goodbye, Alice."

"Just a Sunday," she said. "An empty, do-nothing day. Your…duplicate…won't be stuck with some unpleasant chore, he'll be making love with me, all day long."

"And forgetting about it afterward? No thanks."

"I didn't say he'd be the only one," she said, her voice more confident now. "You get your share as well. Effective immediately."

Her hands moved to the closures of the jumper and pulled them apart, revealing white brassiere lace underneath. She found a hook and parted that as well. Her breasts, pushed together by taut fabric, seemed to reach for him, pink nipples looking out like blind, soft eyes.

He could have resisted, he would later think. He could have walked away. He was not, after all, some mindless rutting animal. But his eyes and hands and loins were hungry for her, and who was he, really, to refuse them?

Afterward she gave him a pill. Garlic, vertigo, then nothing. Every sensation perfectly normal. Was this, he thought, feasting his eyes on her unclothed-at-last body, what fate felt like? Going through the motions of life, seeking small pleasures where he could but knowing full well that his continuity, his chain of memory, his life, would end in less than a day?

He thought about hopping up, grabbing his credit card, running out and spending it to the limit. Punishing himself, his other self, for this slow execution. But what purpose would that serve? In what way would that improve his final hours? Better to stay here and rut.

He looked at her, face now peaceful in repose. She'd played him well, gotten just what she wanted out of him. Bought him off with beads and trinkets, cast a spell, something. The hell of it was, he was still glad he'd met her, still glad to be in her arms now. He would slay dragons for her, he realized. Battle armies, fulfill quests. How tragic for him.

"How are you?" she asked, watching him watch her.

"Brilliant," he muttered. "Everything is going just brilliantly."

"And are you still you?" A slight smile accompanied the question.

"I feel like me, yes, obviously," he said, piecing the words together slowly, trying to place in her mind the very obvious ideas looming in his. "But when this thing wears off, what I'm feeling now won't matter. At present, I'm the me that doesn't get to continue."

"And the…other you? The original, who you think you're a copy or a fragment of?"

Jeremy shrugged. "He's done me an injustice, yes. All right; if you prefer, I've done myself an injustice, but either way, the experience of this conversation will not be integrated into the person we both call Jeremy Hobb. So I fail to see how I, the person having the conversation, can be the same person he is. No matter how similar we are, no matter that we share the same body. Mathematically speaking, we're separate entities."

"Love," she chided, "you've got a split personality."

"I suppose I have, yes. Temporarily."

"Need something to take your mind off it?"

"Hmm."

"Wondering what my lips can accomplish that the rest of me hasn't?"

"Hmm. Maybe." She moved. "Probably." Moved again. He sighed. "Almost certainly, yes."

He spent the night with her, only belatedly realizing he'd forgotten to call the pub and quit. Bad form; they'd be angry, withold his pay. Well, let them.

In the morning she made him breakfast, made him a man several times, made him lunch. They listened to music through a lazy afternoon, and then finally ordered delivery of a Chinese dinner.

"Shouldn't I be forgetting about now?" he asked, finally, over moo goo gai pan growing cold in its container.

"I'd've thought so," she agreed. "Well before now. I'd like to take some measurements, if it's all right."

He sighed. "I've denied you nothing else, Alice. By all means, have your way."

She either missed or—more likely—chose to ignore the irony in his tone. A cap was fitted over his head, connected by wires to a thing like a computer. Blood and urine samples were collected. Colored lights were shined, one by one, into his eyes.

"That should be enough," she said finally. "I'll run some simulations, see if I can figure out what's happened. There's nothing much for you to do but go home and wait."

"Just like that?" he asked.

"Like what?"

"Kicking me out, sending me home. Already?"

She clucked, reproachful. "What did you think, love, that you could just move in? I didn't say I wouldn't call."

After I'm erased, he thought, and flashed her a grimace. "No, of course. You need your results."

"Partly," she said, "yes. But not entirely. I think you know I'm a bit sweet on you. Come on, it's probably safer if I drive you home."

Home. His home, standing on his own little piece of the planet. That for which he had sacrificed...what? Not the continuity of his life—that was sold even cheaper. It was hard to believe, he reflected, just how much damage the right woman could do. Better to have loved and lost your mind, then never to have lost your mind at all?

Well, no sense crying about it now. One trick he'd always been proud of was the ability to put himself to sleep, no matter what. He invoked that magic now, grimly determined, fully expecting not to wake up as himself.

But he did.

Morning stimulants, shower, breakfast, a quick peek at the newspaper, and then it was time for work. Work! Financial fractanalysis! The idea struck him as more than a little absurd: spending eight hours crunching numbers in a windowless cubicle, and him a dead man at any moment. A man who, at any moment, would have a doppelgänger beamed into his body straight from Saturday evening. Straight from Alice Frane's bed. What a shock.

God, what had he been thinking? Should he stay home? Call in sick? Anxious, wanting answers, he called Alice instead.

"Found anything?" he asked her, in the most offhand tone he could muster.

"Maybe," she said, guardedly, sounding not quite prepared to be speaking with him. "I…hope not. Are you home? Can I come over?"

"Um…Well, yes. Why, though?"

"We need to talk."

Oh. Need-to-talk news was never good. Why go to all the trouble of having her over? Telephones were perfect in that you could hang up whenever you'd heard enough. Which mightn't be long at all.

"Just tell me now," he said, the words like ash in his mouth.

"I may…" she began, then stalled.

"Go on."

"I need to know something about you. Whether you believe in an afterlife."

He tried a laugh. "That's not a very encouraging question, Alice."

"Do you?"

"Believe in heaven? No."

"Then you're in trouble. I may have miscalculated the gap. I mean, obviously I miscalculated, but…I'd assumed a more or less linear growth of decay time as a function of dosage, but it looks like it might actually be exponential. Meaning we're talking about a much longer latent period than what we thought."

Icy waves broke over him, chilled him, numbed him. "How much longer?"

"A lot."

Pounding his fist on the table. "Dammit, Alice, how much longer?"

"Three hundred years," she said.

Three. Hundred. Years. A nervous giggle escaped him. "What? Am I supposed to be worried? Three hundred years from now, secure in my grave, I'll forget everything?"

"Jeremy," she said, "there's more. Listen to me: the erasure can occur prematurely if the decay process is short-circuited."

"By?"

"By certain…irreversible chemical reactions in the brain. Reactions which occur during, um, death."

"Ah." A kind of calm settled over him.

"I can make this up to you, Jeremy, I really can."

"Really," he said. "Kiss cock until you're blue in the face, is that it? Buy me off with sex and dinners?"

A pause. "Something like that."

He felt his forehead: clammy, wet. Whence this fear? What had he lost? Alice's question was very perceptive; if he believed in heaven, he lost nothing. A moment's forgetfulness, and then paradise. But the atheist's heaven, nothing more than the realization of death, a quick moment to compose one's thoughts, to assess one's memories…That moment, that final reconciliation, would never come.

"I didn't have to tell you this," Alice said when his silence had gone on too long. "If I didn't care what happened to you, I could have just said everything was fine. Didn't work, okay, you won't be forgetting. You'd never have known to complain. Not until…"

"No, not until."

"I didn't have to tell you," she repeated.

"True," he said, conceding the point. "Your candor is appreciated. Really."

"I don't think there's anything legally actionable here," she added quickly. "Even if you could prove it, what would you be proving? Your life won't be shortened one second, and when the end comes it'll be like dying in your sleep, never knowing anything had happened."

"No," he said coldly, "it won't be like that at all."

And then, suddenly, the proverbial lighthouse beam winked on over his head, and he saw what it would be like. He began to laugh.

"Jeremy? Jeremy, are you all right?"

"I'm fine," he said, meaning it. "And you know what? I think you should come over. If you've a guilty conscience to assuage, who am I to leave you suffering?"

Her breath, huffing softly in the telephone mouthpiece, filled him with images: her mouth on him, his mouth on her, the involuntary grunt of her voice as they lay twined together, spinning out wave after wave of pleasure. But these sounds were different: the huffing of an animal, suddenly afraid, suddenly realizing it might be in danger. Preparing its fight or flight.

"If you work with me," she said carefully, "there's every chance we can find a solution. Induce you early."

Induce him early? What a laugh! Kill him early, she might as well say. If he—if the fragile memories that comprised him—had to be erased, why should it be one second, one instant earlier than necessary?

"I'm not angry," he said gently. "You're right, it's really not so bad. Not for me."

And she must have caught his meaning then, because the exhalation of her breathing slid aside into uneasy laughter. Not him who would suffer, no, but that other, very similar person who had sold him out for a roll in the hay. For that Jeremy Hobb it would be a warm cuddle, the popping of a pill, and then…what, the smell of garlic and then straight into the arms of the reaper? The thought was terrifying: to skip not a day, not a week, but every future moment except the last! What worse fate was there than to become, all at once, an old man gasping on his deathbed, all the intervening hours and days and years forgotten? With that moment of reckoning there, the awful realization that he'd traded himself away, the realization that life had burned away in an instant, that there would be no more?

But for this version, for the temporary person now inhabiting this flesh, there was nothing but an indefinite postponement of the erasure he dreaded, an opportunity to steal back the future he otherwise lacked. And what was so dreadful about that?

"Forget it, Alice," Jeremy Hobb said, laughing harder, the river of his joy slopping up over its banks to threaten the entire landscape. "You've cured my split personality. And you know? It serves the son of a bitch right."

And that, dear fiends, was what killed him.

Snow In Summer

Jane Yolen

Jane Yolen's books and stories have won the Caldecott Medal, two Nebula Awards, two Christopher Medals, the World Fantasy Award, three Mythopoeic Fantasy Awards, the Golden Kite Award, the Jewish Book Award, the World Fantasy Association's Lifetime Achievement Award, and the Association of Jewish Libraries Award among many others. She is also a poet, a teacher of writing and literature, and a reviewer of children's literature. She has been called the Hans Christian Andersen of America and the Aesop of the twentieth century.

If that didn't get you jumping to the story, you should. Yolen's take on Snow White is not to be missed.

They call that white flower that covers the lawn like a poplin carpet Snow in Summer. And because I was born in July with a white caul on my head, they called me that, too. Mama wanted me to answer to Summer, which is a warm, pretty name. But my Stepmama, who took me in hand just six months after Mama passed away, only spoke the single syllable of my name, and she didn't say it nicely.

"Snow!" It was a curse in her mouth. It was a cold, unfeeling thing. "Snow, where are you, girl? Snow, what have you done now?"

I didn't love her. I couldn't love her, though I tried. For Papa's sake I tried. She was a beautiful woman, everyone said. But as Miss Nancy down at the postal store opined, "Looks ain't nothing without a good heart." And she was staring right at my Stepmama when she said it. But then Miss Nancy had been Mama's closest friend ever since they'd been little ones, and it nigh killed her, too, when Mama was took by death.

But Papa was besot with my Stepmama. He thought she couldn't do no wrong. The day she moved into Cumberland he said she was the queen of love and beauty. That she was prettier than a summer night. He praised her so often, she took it ill any day he left off complimenting, even after they was hitched. She would have rather heard those soft nothings said about her than to talk of any of the things a husband needs to tell his wife: like when is dinner going to be ready or what bills are still to be paid.

I lived twelve years under that woman's hard hand, with only Miss Nancy to give me a kind word, a sweet pop, and a magic story when I was blue. Was it any wonder I always went to town with a happier countenance than when I had to stay at home.

And then one day Papa said something at the dinner table, his mouth greasy with the chicken I had cooked and his plate full with the taters I had boiled. And not a thing on that table that my Stepmama had made. Papa said, as if surprised by it, "Why, Rosemarie..." which was my Stepmama's Christian name, "why, Rosemarie, do look at what a beauty that child has become."

And for the first time my Stepmama looked—really looked—at me.

I do not think she liked what she saw.

Her green eyes got hard, like gems. A row of small lines raised up on her forehead. Her lips twisted around. "Beauty," she said. "Snow," she said. She did not say the two words together. They did not fit that way in her mouth.

I didn't think much of it at the time. If I thought of myself at all those days, it was as a lanky, gawky, coltish child. Beauty was for horses or grown women, Miss Nancy always said. So I just laughed.

"Papa, you are just fooling," I told him. A daddy has to say such things about his girl." Though in the thirteen years I had been alive, he had never said any such overmuch. None in fact that I could remember.

But then he added something that made things worse though I wasn't to know it that night. "She looks like her Mama. Just like her dear Mama."

My Stepmama only said, "Snow, clear the dishes."

So I did.

But the very next day my Stepmama went and joined the Holy Roller Mt. Hosea Church, which did snake handling on the fourth Sunday of each month and twice on Easter. Because of the Bible saying, "Those who love the Lord can take up vipers and they will not be killed," the Mt. Hosea folk proved the power of their faith by dragging out rattlers and copperheads from a box and carrying them about their shoulders like a slippery shawl. Kissing them, too, and letting the pizzen drip down on their cheeks.

Stepmama came home from church, her face all flushed and her eyes all bright, and said to me, "Snow, you will come with me next Sunday."

"But I love Webster Baptist," I cried. "And Reverend Bester. And the hymns." I didn't add that I loved sitting next to Miss Nancy and hearing the stories out of the Bible the way she told them to the children's class during the Reverend's long sermon. "Please, Papa, don't make me go."

For once my Papa listened. And I was glad he said no. I am feared of snakes, though I love the Lord mightily. But I wasn't sure any old Mt. Hosea rattler would know the depth of that love. Still, it wasn't the snakes Papa was worried about. It was, he said, those Mt. Hosea boys.

My Stepmama went to Mt. Hosea alone all that winter, coming home later and later in the afternoon from church, often escorted by young men who had scars on their cheeks where they'd been snakebit. One of them, a tall blond fellow who was almost handsome except for the meanness around his eyes, had a tattoo of a rattler on his bicep with the legend "Love Jesus Or Else" right under it.

My Papa was not amused.

"Rosemarie," he said, "you are displaying yourself. That is not a reason to go to church."

"I have not been doing this for myself," she replied. "I thought Snow should meet some young men now she's becoming a woman. A beautiful woman." It was not a compliment in her mouth. And it was not the truth, either, for she had never even introduced me to the young men nor told them my true name.

Still, Papa was satisfied with her answer, though Miss Nancy, when I told her about it later, said, "No sow I know ever turned a boar over to her litter without a fight."

However, the blond with the tattoo came calling one day and he didn't ask for my Stepmama. He asked for me. For Snow. My Stepmama smiled at his words, but it was a snake's smile, all teeth and no lips. She sent me out to walk with him, though I did not really want to go. It was the mean eyes and the scars and the rattler on his arm, some. But more than that, it was a feeling I had that my Stepmama wanted me to be with him. And that plumb frightened me.

When we were in the deep woods, he pulled me to him and tried to kiss me with an open mouth and I kicked him in the place Miss Nancy had told me about, and while he was screaming, I ran away. Instead of chasing me, he called after me in a voice filled with pain, "That's not even what your Stepmama wanted me to do to you." But I kept running, not wanting to hear any more.

I ran and ran even deeper into the woods, long past the places where the rhododendron grew wild. Into the dark places, the boggy places, where night came upon me and would not let me go. I was so tired from all that running, I fell asleep right on a tussock of grass. When I woke there was a passel of strangers staring down at me. They were small, humpbacked men, their skin blackened by coal dust, their eyes curious. They were ugly as an unspoken sin.

"Who are you?" I whispered, for a moment afraid they might be more of my Stepmama's crew.

They spoke together, as if their tongues had been tied in a knot at the back end. "Miners," they said. "On Keeperwood Mountain."

"I'm Snow in Summer," I said. "Like the flower."

"Summer," they said as one. But they said it with softness and a kind of dark grace. And they were somehow not so ugly anymore. "Summer."

So I followed them home.

And there I lived for seven years, one year for each of them. They were as good to me and as kind as if I was their own little sister. Each year, almost as if by magic, they got better to look at. Or maybe I just got used to their outsides and saw within. They taught me how to carve out jewels from the black cave stone. They showed me the secret paths around their mountain. They warned me about strangers finding their way to our little house.

I cooked for them and cleaned for them and told them Miss Nancy's magic stories at night. And we were happy as can be. Oh, I missed my Papa now and then, but my Stepmama not at all. At night I sometimes dreamed of the tall blond man with the rattler tattoo, but when I cried out, one of the miners would always comfort me and sing me back to sleep in a deep, gruff voice that sounded something like a father and something like a bear.

Each day my little men went off to their mine and I tidied and swept and made-up the dinner. Then I'd go outside to play. I had deer I knew by name, gray squirrels who came at my bidding, and the sweetest family of collared doves that ate cracked corn out of my hand. The garden was mine, and there I grew everything we needed. I did not mourn for what I did not have.

But one day a stranger came to the clearing in the woods. Though she strived to look like an old woman, with cross-eyes and a mouth full of black teeth, I knew her at once. It was my Stepmama in disguise. I pretended I did not know who she was, but when she inquired, I told my name straight out.

"Summer," I said.

I saw "Snow" on her lips.

I fed her a deep-dish apple pie, and while she bent over the table shoveling it into her mouth, I felled her with a single blow of the fry pan.

My little men helped me bury her out back.

Miss Nancy's stories had always ended happy-ever-after. But she used to add every time: "Make you own happiness, Summer dear."

And so I did. My happiness—and hers.

I went to the wedding when Papa and Miss Nancy tied the knot. I danced with some handsome young men from Webster and from Elkins and from Canaan. But

I went back home alone. To the clearing and the woods and the little house with the eight beds. My seven little fathers needed keeping. They needed my good stout meals. And they needed my stories of magic and mystery. To keep them alive.

To keep me alive, too.

THE ROSE GARDEN

Michelle West

Michelle writes as both Michelle Sagara and Michelle West; she is also published as Michelle Sagara West (although the Sundered books were originally published under the name Michelle Sagara). I first encountered West's fiction in the anthology *Zodiac Fantastic*, and I've been enjoying it ever since.

West is one of those authors whose name will make me pick a book off the shelf and take it home with me. The thing that always surprises me is how well she sets up the story to go one way and then changes direction part way through. I never see the shift coming, and at the same time, I'm never disappointed. West's version of Beauty and the Beast is no different. By the time I felt I had a handle on where the story was going West was taking me somewhere else.

Once upon a time doesn't cut it here. Fairies? Dragons? Evil wizards? Knights? Gone. Long gone. The vast forests in which men came of age are tame little gardens, fenced in by naturalists and big city environmentalists, with their placards, their slogans, their angry words.

He lived in one, once.

Was proud, in one. Arrogant. Even that word doesn't mean what it once did;

words are shades. They have no power. He's got some.

Because he's what's left. He and the dozens of dwindling demi-mortals, cursed by old power to linger. Forgotten, they're clearly not dead, and they certainly haven't been freed.

Not, at least, in the traditional sense. He left his forest at the turn of the century, when he realized the boundaries that kept him trapped there were withering like waterless flowers. Trees—normal trees, dwarfed and stunted and with only a hint of true grandeur—overgrew his cage of a ruined kingdom. If kingdom was a word that could describe the empty, small space that remained of his serfs, his peasants, the men and women who laboured in droves in the finery of his shadowed castle, shunning his presence, shunning all sight of his face. Even the form that he was chained to was forgotten; it drifted past as the cities grew across the landscape. As cars replaced coaches, and enlightenment replaced romance. He was here.

It's at least a century since he was forced from his forest home; since the prison bars were bent out of shape and the magic of containment fled. He didn't know what had killed the old witch that had cursed him, but he could guess: There's a steel here that knows no life and responds to no magic. Instead of swords, men have guns, and the guns are often too heavy for a single one of them to lift.

He never had that problem. He was doomed to be trapped in the form of a raging beast until the spell at last ended, and he joined the war. The men couldn't see him for what he was; the spell was *that* weak.

The war was fought in trenches. It was fought with gas, with guns, with the unfashionable bayonets given to the less valuable soldiers when armaments were in short supply.

He survived, but he knew he would. He made no friends, but at least he had comrades—people who trusted him to guard their backs. Trusted him to survive. He had ordered men to their deaths at his leisure as a noble, and once or twice, he'd made an entertainment of it.

The war was less entertaining. Perhaps because the men who died in it—boys, really—didn't deserve death. They hadn't thwarted his will. And they didn't complain about a man who looked as if he would have been more at home on a Viking war ship, although they did complain about his stench.

After the war—and the medals that were somehow significant in that diminished age, he drifted for a couple of decades. He had money, and he knew that money was of value because he had *always* had money. He used it wisely, and it grew.

He joined the second great war as well, and his ferocity and strength were again tested, as was the witch's curse. Both held true; he didn't die. But he lost most of the men assigned to him, on a beach somewhere in Europe; he walked among the carnage, thinking that monsters were no longer something to be feared. Not when men alone could do so much damage.

And again, for surviving—and killing—he was given medals and decorations, and he was paid. The money grew. The respect grew. He used both sparingly, because he had not yet left the forest entirely behind, and he knew what he was: The Beast.

But in time, the forest at last left him, and the captivity left as well: he was a free man. The witch, he thought, was certainly dead, and good riddance. He bought a house. And when he found the neighbours too persistently *friendly*, he sold that one and bought another.

The only thing of value he had left behind in the ruined kingdom of his forgotten youth was his garden. And as time passed, he missed it. In the city, with postage stamp backyards, there's not a lot of room for rose bushes. He began to grow them anyway, changing their colour and the folds of their leaves with time and patience; making them diminutive or giant when the whim took him. Other men took such flowers to hothouses across the continent and won prizes for their supposed mastery of their craft. He didn't want to share. He never had.

He was no longer the Beast. The name belonged to some muppet in a children's show that played drums. But even memory of that began to fade, with time and fashion. He lost dirt and hair. Everyone in the city he chose as his home showered at least once a day; sometimes more in the summer months. Far be it from him to stand out, although the transition was harder than the one that had given him an earned home: the guns and the noise and the screaming deaths were gone, and their echoes teased memory. He let them.

He remembered the day his hair fell out. It fell out in clumps. He looked more pathetic than chemo patients, because he was tall and his shoulders were linebacker broad. His teeth, praise whatever gods lived in the electronic age, didn't go the same route, but they blunted and shortened, losing edge and sharpness. They were still too yellow, but he disguised that fact by the simple expedient of smoking. Smoking fell out of fashion, though. He still indulged anyway. The confederacy of smokers was growing as small as the forests that once kept salvation at bay.

He had been a prince, in his kingdom. And he offended a powerful witch. He no longer remembered how; witches were easily offended, and they didn't usually bother to offer an explanation if it provided their victims any comfort. But the covenant between the cursed and the curser still bound her, and she was forced to tell him what the rules of his confinement were; forced as well to tell him the key that would set him free. It had something to do with roses and women. That's right. He had to earn the love of a woman while trapped in the form of the Beast, and he would be a man once again.

And on this particular day, he thought of that old curse with something approaching rage—a rage that had died with the death of Hitler, with V day, with the end of that war.

Something about the war had scarred him. He couldn't say what. Others did, and at leisure, over the decades. Psychologists. Veterans. The children of the men who had died, unknown, upon those distant fields. He hadn't. Maybe he suffered from survivor's guilt. He couldn't say. But for the first time in two wars, he *wanted* to.

So he started the roses again, and he began to look for a woman. Somehow they would cure him, and he could let go. Age would creep in, and death, but he'd seen death and youth, and he could *still* see it, whenever he closed his great, round, animal eyes. The senselessness of it. The range. Not even as the ruler of his beleaguered kingdom had he seen such carnage, and for the first time since he'd escaped his captivity, he regretted the loss of those old magics. There wouldn't have been war, that's for sure. A lot of useful curses, but no war.

But the witch was demonstrably gone, killed by lack of belief, by boredom, by technology. Her curse remained, and he set about lifting it with a vengeance.

He met his share of women. In the fifties, it was difficult. But later, in the decades to follow, things changed. In the seventies, and the eighties; in the nineties and even at the turn of the millennium. When the wars, and the fear of wars, were gone. The women weren't shy, they weren't often young, but they had a raw energy—a visceral bestiality—that he found attractive. They didn't simper. They didn't plead. They didn't get thrown out by their families if they happened to lose their virginity. That took him a while to get used to. The lack of weeping and wailing. The lack of fear.

But the thing is: they were all the same. They wanted sex, not love. They sometimes confused the two. Sometimes he confused them.

Still, sex brought him a certain sense of skin comfort, and he accepted the exchange of pleasure for moments without any memory other than scent and touch. He became content, to be the Beast, in this city. He changed his name. He changed his house. He mowed the lawn, and he found neighbours that wouldn't pry too closely into his private life.

He didn't choose a poor neighborhood to live in, and it sort of grew up around him, a forest of cement and wood and aluminium, of shale shingles, and asbestos, things neat and orderly in the hands of men. The advantage of living in an upper middle class neighbourhood was this: No one was home during the day. They worked long, long hours. They went to cottages or vacation condos on the weekends. Or skiing, when the season was right for it.

Raccoons became more of an enemy than the men with sharp swords used to be. They picked tiles off his roof. He could hear one of them now, tearing the vines off the garage that hemmed in his little green space to the North. They'd even chewed a hole in the siding on the remodelled back end of the house, which really annoyed him. Had he still had the teeth and the jaws of a beast, he would have eaten them with great satisfaction. But he tried, once, and he ended up getting rabies shots as a result. It wasn't pleasant, and it didn't keep the little bastards away.

He had a car. Not a little one; a little one didn't fit. He had as much food as an army of serfs could produce, two blocks away, in neat isles, stacks of tins and boxes, labelled with colour and content. He had no need to hunt or kill.

Perhaps the loss of the need for sustenance and survival caused the melancholy.

When he first left the forest, when he first made his home here, he looked like a hairy barbarian. Now he looked like a civilized man, just one side of his prime. The mirror didn't recognize the changes, but it didn't matter; no one else saw the Beast.

Which seemed, to the only man who could observe the *truth*, to mean that he could never actually be free of the curse itself.

Then again, what harm did it do these days? He was going to live forever. He would never age. He had everything a mortal man claimed to want in this age of youth and beauty.

And he was tired of it all. So he continued to grow his roses. He made a shrine of his tiny backyard. He watered them, fed them light, fed them nutrients. He tied their branches up in place while the bushes themselves matured, and he tended them whenever he could. Thinking of salvation.

He tended his roses in the day, and when the day was done, he dressed up and went out for the evening, looking for salvation. There were a lot of people who hit the bars looking for salvation, and he had as much reason as any of them did.

He never found it.

There was a time when he thought he would. In those days, relationships could last months. One even made it past the crest of a year before it fell apart, in tears and accusations. And the accusations—something to do with fidelity—were entirely true. He wasn't. It wasn't in his nature. It never had been.

He wasn't dishonest about that. Honesty was less costly than the stressful web of lies and deceit. *Everyone* lied, these days. It was the fashion. Sometimes the lies were big, and sometimes they were small. Sometimes they referred to wealth and money, sometimes they referred to age. Sometimes they referred to love, but usually in those instances, the lies were like double-edged, forgotten swords: they cut both ways.

They weren't for him.

Because he was no longer quite the Beast. Sure, he prowled. He prowled as much as the next guy. But he wasn't required, by his curse, to kill.

Which was a pity, at this particular moment, in this time. He didn't speak much. When he did, his voice was low, a growl of a voice. A bear's voice. A Beast's voice. It was the only thing that truly remained, and he hoarded it carefully.

Usually. But today? No. He couldn't contain his outrage, and he *roared.* The leaves in his garden trembled at the force of a sound they were never subjected to. He thought the roses might wilt, and that leant his fury strength, sustaining it. Hope wasn't much, but apparently when there was little of it, it was vastly more valued.

"How the hell did you get in here?"

The subject of his anger was as white as the whitest of his flowers—if you didn't count the dirt and the weather-beaten look of skin too long in the sun. Hair that made his early hair look *clean* by comparison grew round a gaunt expression like an oily, greasy, frame. Dirt was smeared like make-up across the face that met his, caught in the motionless O of surprise that was rapidly turning to fear.

He took a step forward, and the interloper took a step back, crying out when the roses caught the dirty sweater. A girl's voice. High and fluting, wordless.

"Answer my question!"

Which, of course, produced no response. Well, not no response. Her hands clutched the stem of the flower she'd snapped from the bush. And her teeth bit her lip, the way thorns bit her dirty skin. How *dare* she touch his flowers?

He pulled a cell phone from his jacket pocket and waved it in front of her, like a gun. "I want to know how you did it. I lock the damn garage, and you didn't come in through the house. My yard is a greenhouse; it's domed by expensive glass, and heated year round. There are no gates. The only way in is through the garage or the house. You didn't get in by the house."

She said nothing. Nothing at all. But blood seeped between her fingers, tracing lines around her small knuckles. Shaking hands. Foolish girl.

"I'm going to call the police."

The police were useful. They owed their allegiance to no king, no kingdom; they weren't soldiers. They had guns, yes, but their uniforms were meant to be trusted, and if you had money in a well-off neighbourhood, trust was easily invested.

"Oh. You don't want me to call the police? And why not? Look at you. Your jeans have holes in them. They're a size too large. No, two sizes too large. And they haven't been washed in two weeks. Your sweater is two size too small. You stink."

She swallowed. Her hands were red, and the blood made them seem white as ivory. Small hands. Too thin to be strong.

Her fear seemed to eat away at the edges of outrage. But it didn't still his voice.

"What did you come here to steal? You can *see through the damned glass*. You've got eyes. You're an ugly little urchin, you're probably three different kinds of addict. You might have aids. You think the police won't cart you off and stick you where you deserve to be?"

But it was clear that she thought they *would*. She should have run. Then again, the garden was all of fifteen feet long; there weren't many places to run *to*.

"And your hand is *bleeding*. Did you think roses don't grow without thorns, you stupid child?"

She spoke for the first time, her voice so soft he had to strain to catch it. "I know all about thorns," she said bitterly. "And bleeding. You want your damn flower back? Here!" She held it out. But it didn't roll down her open palm; the thorns went deep, and they anchored themselves to her dirty skin.

He might be able to save it. He might be able to graft it to another bush.

He took it from her, and she cried out; he wasn't particularly gentle. But he had to stow the phone away in a pocket to do it.

Yes, he thought, calming slowly. He *could* save the flower. The prize of his collection, black rose. Night blossom.

"Why this flower?" he said bitterly, the softness of his words a wolf's growl.

"I meant it as a gift," she replied, just as bitterly. "It's a flower. You've got so damn many, I didn't think you'd miss one."

"I'd miss this one," he snapped. In spite of himself, his nose wrinkled. The *stench* of the girl was overpowering.

He reached for the garden hose and turned it on her face. And then, when she gasped and floundered, he snorted in disgust and picked her up by the back of her neck. She wasn't very heavy. She kicked him. She scratched at his arm. But she didn't bite. Good thing, for her.

He dragged her, cursing and swearing, into his house and he dragged her up the stairs to the bathroom. There, he turned on the bath, and let the water run until it was hot. He shifted the switch, and rain poured down from metal casing. Into that manmade storm, he thrust the girl, handing her soap as he did.

"You can clean yourself," he said, "Or I can." It was a threat. It worked.

She slammed the glass door shut on him, and he watched her for a while.

"Take the clothes *off*," he growled.

"Not while you're here!"

He considered his options with growing disgust, and then snorted and walked out, slamming the door. From behind its closed surface, he said, "You do know how to *use* soap, right?"

And she swore a lot, the words muted by the fall of water.

But the time he lost in taking the girl to the shower was the rose's time, and when he returned in haste to the garden, he saw that the stem itself was too dry. His anger returned, and he brought the flower into the house, and set it in a vase. He added sugared water. The bud would blossom; he would have at least that much of it. But it was already dead. Like so many people, it simply didn't know it yet.

The water fell silent.

He touched, as delicately as he could, the rose's petals, and then he pushed himself up from the table and bounded up the stairs, three at a time.

The girl, dressed still in clothing that reeked of the streets, had sidled out of the bathroom, her bright hair dripping. It was a deep shade of brown, and it took him a moment before he understood why it seemed so familiar: it was the colour of his coat fur in bygone ages.

Her face was whiter than it had been, but her scent—the scent of soap—was lost to the unwashed clothing. His sense of smell was acute; she was overpowering.

"You-will-take-those-off," he said, wanting to kill her. Wanting very much to kill her.

"I don't have any others," she replied, taking a step back. She dripped water across his carpets. No fine halls these, but they were still *his*.

"You can wear mine."

Her brows rose. The difference in their size—he, widened and strengthened by fury—was apparent.

He said, "The doors are locked. If you attempt to leave before I return, I will kill you."

Just that, but the promise in the words was plain, and she swallowed and nodded, still nursing the hand that had clutched the rose's stem. He walked into his room and took an older shirt from his closet; this he threw at her as he entered the hall.

"Wear this," he said.

"But the pants—"

"It will look like a dress. You are not the first woman to spend time in this house. If I am lucky, you will spend *less* time than any other; you will certainly have no enjoyment from it."

She clutched the collar of his shirt, retreating to the bathroom; humid air escaped in a rush before she closed the door. He waited, listening, and after a moment, she returned. She looked younger, in a shirt that dwarfed her frame.

"Come," he said, as if he were still a ruling lord.

She followed, subdued. Afraid.

He led her to his kitchen, the brightest of the rooms in his house. There, the flower, bud closed, stood in the vase that would be its last home.

"Do you see?" He said, shaking.

She nodded, her eyes dark with fear. And wonder. "It was just one flower," she said, but weakly now. "I'm sorry."

A drunk driver might apologize to the family of his victim in just such a tone, and with just as much effect.

"You're *sorry*?" He roared.

She lifted thin hands to her ears. Tears welled in her eyes; he knew the look. He'd seen it so often on the faces of other women. But she did not shed them.

Instead, he leaned toward her, meaning to intimidate her with his size and bulk. He did. "Why did you take it?"

"I told you—for a friend."

"And how will you pay for what you have done, you stupid, stupid child?"

"I don't have much money," she said at last.

It was the wrong thing to say. He slapped her.

She fell. She fell back, travelling the length of the kitchen's gleaming floor.

"Don't speak to me of *money*," he roared again. "You have taken from me a flower, and I have done *nothing at all* to merit its destruction."

"It's just a—" The word fell away as she rubbed her jaw, rising slowly, risking that much.

"And to whom would you have taken it?"

She said nothing, and then, with a bitterness that her years could not possibly have earned, she said, "A dying friend."

Death had so much more meaning in this world than it had in the previous one. Although his anger and his resolve did not lessen, he gentled his voice. Which made it a growl. Her reaction indicated that it was not, in her mind, an improvement. He reached for his phone again, and held it front of her, like a threat.

"I'll work," she said quickly. "I can work. I'm good at it."

"You are *not* good at it. If you were, you wouldn't have come in that sorry state!"

Her head hung low; her hair, thin, was already drying. Her eyes were blue, a grey blue, when she lifted her face. And they were also reddened.

"What work?" He said.

"I can do you," she said at last, with a hint of unease. "For free."

"'Do me'?"

"You know. Do it. Here."

He laughed. It was harsh and unpleasant. "I assure you," he said coldly, "that I have no shortage of companionship, and I do not have to purchase it." His gaze made clear that she was in no way attractive to him. It must have made other things clear, because she straightened her shoulders, and although her cheeks were now red, she said, "Don't look down on *me*."

"You killed my rose," he said darkly.

And her brows rose in anger and confusion. "You care about that more than you care about people?"

"Much more."

"It must be nice."

He stopped.

"To have so many people in your life that you can be so careless. Look at this place. Look at this *kitchen*. It's probably worth a small *house*."

"If you had just stolen money," he told her with contempt, "I would have let you go."

"Money won't help," she told him, her voice quavering.

He almost slapped her again. But he had no control over his own strength, and he knew that killing the girl here would cause him trouble. With the police. With the neighbours.

But he could not just let her leave. She had to pay. "Where is this friend?" He said at last.

Her lips compressed. The line was thin and unpleasant.

"She is not the author of your misfortune. I will not hurt her for *your* crime." He held out a hand. In the bright light of the kitchen, it looked almost paw-like, the fingers short and stubby, the nails hard. A man's hand.

Her eyes rounded, but she understood there was no request in the gesture, and she put her own in his. It was dwarfed, insignificant. And it trembled. "Why do you want to see her?" She stopped. "And how do you know it's a she?"

"I have difficulty believing you'd steal my roses for a man."

"I wouldn't do anything for a man," she snapped. She made fists of her hand, and he saw that the one was still bleeding.

With no grace whatsoever, he led her to the kitchen cupboard in which he had placed bandages and ointment. "Give me the hand," he said coldly. "The injured one."

She did as she was ordered, and he brought out the tube, squeezing its cap off. With rough care, he tended her wounds. He'd done it before; no doubt he would do it again. When he finished, he bound it carefully.

She was staring up at his face. "I don't understand," she said at last.

"No, you don't."

"Why are you trying to help me?"

"I'm not. But I don't like the smell of blood. And I don't like the smell of old sweat and urine. I don't give a shit what you do with your life—it'll be short and messy, no doubt. But while you're in my presence, you will *smell* like a person."

"I can leave."

"No," he said, voice shading into danger. "You can't. Not without me. Take me," he added, dropping her hand, "to this friend."

If she was surprised at his car, she didn't show it. She was meek and quiet by his side.

She strapped herself in, fastening the seat belt; her whole hand was pressed against the window, slender fingers splayed wide.

"Where?"

"Casey House," she said quietly.

He wasn't surprised. He started the car and they drove.

But the traffic was bad, and they were forced to start and stop. Road repair did that to the city; it clogged the arteries, arresting movement.

"Where do you live?" He asked her.

"None of your business."

His hand brushed her shoulder and then settled there in a ferocious grip. "I don't live anywhere."

"Where *did* you live?"

She shook her head. "Doesn't matter," she told him, and her eyes were now entirely grey. "I'm not going back."

"You haven't been on the streets long."

"Long enough."

"You're what, eighteen? Nineteen?"

"Sixteen. Seventeen in four days."

"School?"

She shrugged. "Who the hell needs school? People with houses. People with cars. People with families."

"People who want to someday *have* those things," he growled.

"What are you, a parent?"

"No."

"Then spare me the lecture. I don't want any of those things."

"What *do* you want, besides the destruction of my roses?"

"To help a friend," she replied darkly. "The only friend I have left."

"They're not magic," he snapped.

She raised a dark brow. "Nothing is. Can I smoke?"

"No."

"Why not? You do."

"Because you're underage."

He could hear her grinding her teeth. He stopped speaking to her at all as the traffic began to move.

The woman in the bed was old. Old enough that he couldn't easily tell what her actual age was. She had hair, but it was patchy; her skin was covered in a rash, and it was clear she had bedsores. Her mouth, when she opened it, hid fungus, things that grew in damp places. She tried to smile when the girl walked into the room.

But frowned when he instantly followed, hand on the girl's wrist.

"Trina," the young girl said, trying unsuccessfully to free herself. She smiled gently, and it softened her angular face in a way that he couldn't describe.

"Apple. Who is that with you?"

"A man I met."

"Where?"

"In a rose garden."

Trina, if that was her name, shook her head. "A rose garden? Which one?"

"Not a public one," the Beast said coldly. But something about the pathos of this woman stilled anger in an unexpected way. "You like roses?"

The woman nodded quietly. "Before I ran away from home," she said, as if running away from home were a simple part of growing up, "I used to tend them. Our neighbors had them. The old woman there loved them. She loved the buds; she loved the blooms; she loved it when the petals fell. She'd gather them and soak them and boil them in her kitchen. Smell of roses," the woman added, in a sweet, cracked voice. She held out a shaky hand, and Cassie took it and pressed it between her palms, as if she were a book and the hand, a flower that she intended to preserve forever. "That was my real home," she told them both, her pupils widening. "With Mrs. Grayson. She loved roses. She taught me to love them." She turned toward the window. He thought she wanted a moment to gather her expression, but when she started to cough, he understood that she meant to spare Cassie the pain of her decay.

"What do you know of roses?"

She began to tell him. And listening, he understood that she had made a story of the growth of thorn and blossom; that she had made a legend of their names, the way they were grown, the amount of sun that they needed, the cruel emptiness of their branches in winter. He thought words had no power, but he was wrong: there was power in her cadence, and terrible desire. For comfort. For the things that she had lost.

He touched Cassie's shoulder.

"Why are you wearing that?" Trina asked, when she saw the gesture.

"My sweater fell apart," Cassie lied. "And he offered me a shirt—"

"You haven't started to—to work again?"

"No, Trina. I promised."

"Good. Don't end up like me."

Cassie shook herself free of his grip and bending, kissed the woman's brow. "We're in it together," she said, and her voice was as steady as rock.

"She gave me a place to stay," Cassie told him, staring out the window of the moving car. "The first time she found me. I'd been badly beaten," she added, as if she were speaking of a stubbed toe. "She took me to the hospital. And then she took me home. She took care of me."

He nodded, but absently.

"She's dying," the girl added dispassionately. "I can't stand to see it. But I have to go. She was there for me."

"And you don't have a place to live now."

She shrugged. "She lost her place when she couldn't work. But it doesn't matter. She's got one now, and she won't be leaving it until they find a box that'll fit her."

He said nothing.

"The black rose," she continued, looking at light through the veined hand across glass. "I wanted it for her. Because I've never seen one growing before. She would have liked it."

"She didn't grow roses?"

"Not in a small apartment, she didn't."

He nodded again. But he did not speak until they arrived in his garage and the door had slid shut on its rails.

"How did you know I grew roses?"

She shrugged. "I was casing the neigbourhood," she said at last. "People work a lot. They go out. It's easy enough to smash a pane of glass, run in, grab a few things. I can sell them."

"And not your body."

"I'd sell that too," she told him bitterly. "And more easily. I look like a kid. Men like that."

He didn't.

"But she wanted to work for the both of us. She made me go back to school." She swallowed air. "She made me promise that I wouldn't work. Not that way."

"You offered me—"

"That wasn't work. That was restitution."

"Big word."

"Fuck off."

He caught her chin and held it. "Never say that again."

Swallowed more air. She couldn't nod; not with his hand on her face. But after a minute he let her go, hoping he hadn't bruised her chin. Wondering why he cared.

They entered the rose garden. Passed through it while he eyed her suspiciously. At last, he said, "I will let you work here."

"I told you—I promised—"

"Not that work." He opened the back door of his house, and entered the kitchen. "You made a promise. You'll keep it."

"What kind of work?"

"The hardest kind," he told her. He took his phone out of his pocket. "But for now, you can clean the kitchen."

"It's already clean."

"Then practice."

She shrugged and entered after him. He closed the door on her, and stood in the garden, fingers against the rubber numbers of the keypad.

The ambulance arrived that evening.

"Do you know how to cook?"

"Some. I learned a bit. In school."

"You can cook."

"I told you—"

"For us."

"What do you mean, us?"

"You," he said severely, because she needed food. "Me. And Trina."

"What??"

The doorbell rang. He rose. "I'll get it."

"What did you mean, Trina?"

But he passed her by without a word, and answered the door. He followed the ambulance attendant out, and when he returned, he carried Trina in his arms, as if she were a child. "I'm not your Mrs. Grayson," he said quietly. She was coughing and shaking. "She was a nice old lady. I'm a mean old man."

But she didn't answer him, because he had brought her to the table. The bud's outer leaves were beginning to curl away from the rose's heart. She reached out in wonder—in obvious wonder—and her fluttering hands caused a petal to fall. He caught it carefully and placed it in her palm.

"Do you like the light?" He asked her gently, ignoring Cassie's open mouth.

Trina nodded.

"Good. I have a guest room. It has a large bay window, and the bed there is high; you'll be able to see the sun and the trees on the lawn."

She clutched the petal as if it were a talisman.

"But first," he continued gently, "I thought I would show you my garden. Cassie, open the door."

And Cassie, wordless, did exactly as he told her, her hands shaking as she pulled the door handle down. He carried Trina into his small garden, its glass dome distorting the pale face of the evening moon.

He showed her his roses. His arms did not tire beneath the woman's weight; she felt precious to him, although he could not say why. Perhaps because she understood roses. Perhaps because she found, in their growth, hope or comfort.

When Trina was at last asleep—and it didn't take long—he turned to Cassie. Cassie still held the old woman's hand in her own; those fingers were her petals. "Cassie," he said quietly.

Cassie raised tearing eyes, and she quietly set Trina's hands upon the coverlet before she rose and backed away. "Thank you," she said, meaning it. "When will the ambulance come back?"

"When she's dead."

"W-what?"

"It won't be long," he continued, almost enjoying the young girl's confusion. "She doesn't have long at all. But while she lives, she can spend some time in my garden."

"Why are you doing this?"

"Why am I doing what?"

"This. For her. Being nice."

"Honestly?"

She nodded, and her expression was bleak.

"Because she loves roses," he replied. And he studied the girl for a moment with careful eyes.

"But I killed the black one."

"Yes."

"And you hate me because of it."

"Yes."

"But—"

"I don't hate *her*. She didn't kill my flower." He looked down from a height. "While you were sitting with her, I laundered your clothing. The sweater—I'm sorry—shrunk. But the pants, unfortunately, didn't. Put the pants on, Cassie."

"Why?"

"We're going to the mall."

In the mall, surrounded by brand names as dense as any jungle, he found clothing for her. She didn't choose, and he made it absolutely clear that if she tried to five finger discount *anything*, he'd let the police throw her in jail. What there was left of her.

But she didn't protest when he pulled out a credit card, and she didn't protest when he signed the bill. He handed her the bags and said, "We'd better get home."

She clutched them to her chest a moment, and then said, "You want to, you know—"

"No. Never. Not with you."

"Why not?"

"I don't like children."

She shrugged. "I have a school girl uniform. I had one," she added, her face falling. "Some men like it."

"Cassie." He caught her arms more roughly than he intended.

But she met his face, and hers was a mixture of steel and fluff. A young face. "What?"

"I am not one of those men. I told you, I don't lack for companionship. And I don't think that anything I *pay* for is going to be worth what I pay *with*."

She nodded, and as they made their way to the parking lot, he added, "You'll go back to school."

Her lips thinned. "I won't."

"You will. It will help your friend."

Mutinous, she said nothing at all.

But she went. She looked clean, but the wariness in her eyes made her seem a hunted creature. It did not suit his nature. He wanted to hunt her, then. Instead, he practically threw her out of the car. "I'll be back," he told her roughly, "at three fifteen."

Trina woke several times during the five hours Cassie was gone, and he was aware of her each time she did. He carried her out to the garden, lifting her as if she were an infant, and cradling her, unconscious of the movement, to his broad chest. Because he took her to the roses, and let her talk and ask questions until her strength failed, she seemed to forget that he was one of those despised creatures: a man.

But when she wearied, and she also did this quickly, he returned her to her room.

"I don't know your name," she said, when he had rearranged the coverlet and pulled the curtains wide.

The phone rang before he could answer her. He answered it instead, with a momentary relief. But the voice at the other end of the line was just another one of his conquests, and he was brusque as he rid himself of the call.

"Does it matter?" He asked her, surprised to see that she was still awake.

"I don't want to call you Mrs. Grayson," she told him, with just the faint hint of wry smile. Thirty-five, he thought her. Or forty. But aged so badly by her life and her dying, that the truth of those numbers was buried.

"Don't call me anything."

"What were you called?"

"When I was in the war?"

"What war?"

He shrugged. She was drugged, and in pain, but still sharp. "The Beast," he said at last.

She laughed, coughing before the laugh could die a natural death. "Beast," she said. "It doesn't really suit you."

"You didn't see me in the war."

Cassie was waiting for him. She got in the car and he drove home, letting her out in front of the house. "Sit with Trina," he told her. "I'll go shopping."

Shopping for three—for two, if Trina's appetite were taken into consideration—was different. He realized as he pulled produce from its bins and tins from their shelves, that he was purchasing things almost blindly. That he hoped that they would like food that he didn't normally eat.

On the other hand, he decided that one night of Cassie's cooking was enough. He cooked.

She came downstairs while he was busy, and she watched him from the safety of a bar stool tucked under the breakfast counter. "I'm not doing much work," she said quietly.

"You are," he told her. "You're comforting the dying."

She hung her head. "I don't want her to die."

"No."

"Can you—do you think there's anything—"

"No." He turned the stove down and removed his apron. "But Cassie, I understand now why you killed my flower. I can almost forgive you."

She was silent; he looked up and saw that she was watching his broad back. "I don't understand you," she said at last.

"That makes two of us."

He wasn't much impressed with the marks she got on her first test, and he let her know it; he growled. She flinched.

"Cassie," he said, "you aren't a stupid girl. What is *this*?"

She shrugged. "Math."

"Look, your job here is to comfort a dying woman. Do you think that *this* is comforting?"

"I don't think she'll care."

"Then why don't we ask her? Come on; she's awake now. I can hear the television; it just went on." He held out a hand, and she swore at him in two different languages. This time, however, he didn't slap her.

"You told me that she sent you to school. You told me that she—"

"All right, you stupid, interfering bastard. Enough."

Trina lasted longer than he expected. Although she didn't improve, and her bedsores still lingered, she kept pace with the slow blossoming of the dark rose. He gathered petals for her, one at a time, and carried them to the room, placing them between the bowls of liquid that were the only food she could keep down.

"Beast," she said quietly, one afternoon.

"Trina?"

"Cassie told me."

"What? About the flower? I've already forgiven her."

"Not the flower. I wouldn't have seen her cut it," she added, with genuine regret. "But if she hadn't, we wouldn't be here."

"Then about what?"

"She told me that she offered to pay you."

Ah. That. He was cautious when he met Trina's sharp eyes.

"You didn't take her up on her offer."

"I took her to school."

"Why?"

Because Trina was not a child, and because he knew she was tiring rapidly, he gave up as gracefully as he knew how. "She has the body of an anorexic."

Trina frowned. Clearly this was not the answer she wanted.

"She's too young," he added. "And I don't find her at all attractive."

"Liar."

He raised a brow.

"Why didn't you take her up on that offer? You get around enough. I've heard the phone calls."

"I'm not lying. I don't find her attractive."

"You're lying about your reason."

He shrugged. After a moment, trusting death to keep his secrets, he said, "she killed my flower. I can have sex any time I want—it's meaningless. The flower wasn't."

"I know. I've seen you with your roses. They're the only thing you seem to care about."

"Oh?"

"You come alive when you talk about them."

He laughed. "So do you."

"I don't want to sleep with her either."

"Well then," he said, rising, his eye on the clock. "Let me go and pick her up."

She nodded, but as he reached the door, she said, "she can't repay you."

"No."

"What will you do with her?" *When I'm dead.*

He had no answer for her. None at all.

Cassie cooked. She *insisted* on cooking. The Beast took refuge in Trina's room, his face fixed in a scowl that was almost affectionate.

"Let her. It'll make her feel useful."

"I don't think she cares all that much about being useful."

Trina's sharp eyes narrowed. "It's all she does care about. But the type of use most find for her doesn't sustain her. It wouldn't sustain anyone."

"She'll ruin the meat."

"So?"

"You only say that because you can't actually *eat* any of it."

Trina smiled. It was a pain-filled smile. He thought about morphine; thought that it was almost time for it. But he said nothing. Because he thought the morphine would dull her wit and her tongue, and he found that he wanted to keep these for himself for as long as possible.

"You trying to be a knight in shining armor?"

"No. I never found a suit of armor that wouldn't crush me."

"Or a horse that you wouldn't break the back of?"

He laughed out loud. "I had one or two that were big enough," he said. "When I wasn't eating them."

She thought he was joking, and she laughed, and he let it be. He also forced himself to eat Cassie's meal, and found that it wasn't as hard as he'd thought it would be. When he finished, she started to clear the table, and he lifted a hand and gestured for her to sit. "You cooked," he told her firmly. "I'll clean up."

"But I—"

"Trina hasn't seen you all day. She wants your company. On the stairs, you'll find a bag; it's full of books. I wasn't certain what she would read, and what she would throw away. But you can find something there to read to her."

Cassie pushed her chair away from the table; it fell over as she left it. She was almost out of the kitchen at a run, and he knew why: beneath the hall light, her cheeks were glistening.

"She had a hard adolescence," Trina told him quietly.

"She's still an adolescent."

"She is that. But she's still had it hard."

"Harder than you?"

Trina shrugged. "Maybe. I was too old, when I found her. Too old to change. Already dying. I didn't know it, then."

He nodded. "And now?"

"She's all scarred. Scared because of it."

"Scared of what?"

"Of what happens when I die." There. She'd said it. And because she had, he couldn't ignore it.

"She's tough enough."

"She's not. That's the point. She's not. She isn't afraid you'll turn her out into the streets—she expects that. But she loves the books." The old woman's eyes narrowed. "Harry Potter? You told her you bought that for *me*?"

"You chose it."

"I thought she'd like it enough to keep reading it on her own."

"You were right." He reached out and gently lay petals across the erratic movement of her chest. Black petals all. "It's almost in full bloom," he told her gently. "And when it is, you'll see the color of its heart. I never thought it would last this long. And I never thought I'd be grateful just to share its beauty with someone that understands how much it means. She gave me that. It's a gift."

Trina coughed for a long time, her shaking hands scattering the petals. But she caught them at last and held them in a shaky cupped palm. "She's afraid of the end of this."

"Not your death?"

"That too. But no. She's . . . almost happy here. I've only ever seen her like this once."

"When?"

"When we first met."

He nodded.

"She won't tell you this because she can't—but she loves being able to clean. This room. The room you gave her. The kitchen. She's trying to learn how to cook. She wants to—" coughing destroyed the sentence; pain destroyed the thought.

He caught her hand in his, just as Cassie so often did. "She'll be home soon," he told her softly, rising.

He picked her up. "You should have a license," he told her quietly, as she got out of the car. She stopped a moment, her shoulders bunching together, her neck falling.

"I won't need it," she said at last, choosing defiance and anger with which to answer him. "I won't have a car for much longer." She ran into the house. He had stopped locking the door, which was foolish.

The next day, he brought her a key. He gave it to her, and she looked at it as if it were a magic wand. "I can't take this," she told him. "I don't live here."

"You are living here."

But her gaze fell to the blossoming rose that graced the empty table. The last of its petals were opening now, and the stem was drooping and wilting.

"Not for long," she told him, bitterly. "Look. It's almost done." As if she believed that Trina's life and this rose's were intertwined somehow.

Why shouldn't she? He believed it as well. He stared at the dying rose, and he shuddered at the passing of beauty. Then he lifted the vase with care and took it to Trina's room.

That night, he called a doctor, and the day after, the morphine drip was installed.

But with the cessation of pain, Trina didn't simply disappear in the soft folds of narcotic embrace. She sat up when he entered the room. And she pointed, almost wordless, to the flower: the last of the petals were open, and the heart's center at last laid bare. It was red.

He nodded. "Cassie didn't want to go to school today. Will you stay until she gets back?"

"I'll stay."

"And after?"

Trina shook her head. Her smile was pleasant, and it was calm, but it was also shorn of illusion. "Beast," she said quietly, "what will you do with my girl?"

I can't keep her here, he wanted to say. But he found that she, like the thorny roses that were his first hope, had grown round him. She cut him in ways that the roses had, when he had not yet learned to navigate their sharp points, their hidden edges.

"I'll never sleep with her," he said at last.

"Good."

He nodded.

She said, after a pause, "She'll never trust you again if you do."

And to his great surprise, as if knowledge were blossoming with the rose, he said, "I know. I knew it, the first day she offered."

"You still don't find her attractive?"

"I find her beautiful," he replied quietly.

This time, it was the right thing to say. "So do I."

⁂

That night, with Cassie reading by her side, Trina closed her eyes. She would never open them again.

He knew it; he caught the scent of death well before Cassie's cry dragged him up the stairs. He had been staring out the windows at his garden; he longed for the roses, but he also knew that if he were outside, he might miss Cassie's cry. And he was right. Because it started out so quietly, he could almost mistake it for intense conversation. He took the stairs at a run, and opened the door to Trina's room.

Cassie was on the ground by the bed's side, her hands clutched tight to Trina's. Trina's were slack and grey; her face, mottled by sores, was also grey. Her chest was still, but a blanket of petals adorned it. Black petals. Red heart stood in the window upon a drooping stem—all that remained of his flower.

He caught Cassie by the shoulders, as he so often did, and when she was still, he said, "her pain is ended, Cassie."

"She's *dead*!"

"Yes. But sometimes that's the only way that pain does end."

She turned and began to hit him, her flat open palms becoming fists. They were so light that they fell like heart beats on the outside of his skin, and he let them rain down, sharing, in them, some part of the loss he had never expected to feel.

He let her rage. He let her leave him for a moment to throw books across the room. He let her scream at Trina, and at him, in a rising alternating frenzy, until she was suddenly spent. And then he carried her to her room, and he tucked her into her bed. "In the morning," he said quietly, "we can decide on funeral arrangements."

⁂

But he had already made his decision.

And because he had, he almost lost Cassie for good. He was outside, digging up the part of the garden in which no roses grew. He didn't hear the door of Cassie's room swing open. He didn't hear the light tread of her footsteps. Didn't see her with her school satchel, stuffed with clothing, as she made her way to the front door.

But he saw her, because he looked up at the moment, and she was a shadow just beyond the bright glow of kitchen lights. He dropped his spade then, and he ran.

Caught her as the front door opened, his hand upon her arms. "What do you think you're doing?" He shouted, roaring as he had not done since had first laid eyes on her.

She was afraid; he saw that in an instant. It robbed him of his voice, and his voice was the last thing, beside the roses, that was left of his old self, his old life. But he saw more, besides: he saw that she was not afraid of his anger, not afraid of his question. She said, "The rose is gone," in a little girl voice. The only time he had heard that voice was while she read Harry Potter aloud.

"Trina is gone," he told her. "But I wanted to bury her here, beneath the garden. She'll he happy here. You can still come and read to her."

"She won't hear me." The little girl voice hardened; the street returned to the cadence of those harsh syllables.

"I will," he told her quietly. So quietly. All rumble gone from his voice, all growl.

"I don't care about your stupid roses. I only wanted them for *her*."

"I know."

She shook her head, and then she turned to face the kitchen that she had made half her own. Her face had grown less gaunt with food and shelter. She was not beautiful.

But she was. Oh, she was.

She said, flatly, "Let me go." More in the words than his hands could cause. He trembled as he removed them.

She opened the door. Stepped out.

"You have the key," he shouted after her retreating back. "I'm not about to change the locks."

She stared at him for a minute, and then she turned and ran. And he let her go.

Three days, he waited. He counted them, counted hours and minutes. Counted the times when he could not drive her to school, and the times when he could not retrieve her. He ate very little. Too little. The bulk seemed to vanish from his frame; he was shrinking in on himself, drooping as the black rose had, trapped in its slender vase.

He walked up to Trina's empty room, and he stood a moment in the door frame. The phone was ringing, but he ignored it; it was just another call, and he didn't feel like fending off a stranger whose body he happened to know.

On the fourth day, he slipped into Trina's bed. The smell of death was there, but it was faint; roses lingered instead, for he'd cut them and he'd placed them in the window whose light the old woman had loved. He closed his eyes and slid into delirium.

And woke to a familiar face, familiar small hands slapping him, a familiar high voice screaming, *screaming* in his ear.

"Don't you do it!" She shouted. "Don't you leave me too!"

It made no sense. He looked up at her, and thought that she had grown, or that he had diminished. "I wasn't the one who left," he said at last. No roar in his voice. Just the quiet of words.

She lifted a key in trembling hands. "I came back," she said at last. "And I'm making—I'm making dinner."

He closed his eyes as she left the room. His face was wet, and he raised a heavy hand to brush those tears away, never noticing that his fingers were longer, his palms smaller.

But when he didn't come down to join her, she made her way up with familiar bowls—soup bowls. Trina's bowls. She tended him, as he had done with Trina, all the while crying.

"I want to stay here," she told him, when she had control of her voice. "I want to live here. I want to read those books, in that garden. I want to—" And she cried again.

He reached up and brushed her tears away. "You have to go to school," he told her quietly. "Because Trina's still here. And you can't work," he added, "because you promised."

"She's *dead*."

"You aren't. And it was your promise."

She fed him soup, ignoring his words for a long time. And then she offered him a tentative, a terrified, smile. "You'll hate living with me," she told him. "I'm impossible. Even Trina said so."

"I have been living with you," he answered. "And I don't hate it."

"You don't want *me.*"

"I don't want something meaningless from you. I don't want sex with you. I want—"

She held her breath.

"I want to see you grow," he said. "Thorns and all, little Cassie. I want to see you blossom. I want to see—"

"I'm not a rose."

"But you are," he said. "More precious than the black rose. I know you're afraid of me. I would be. But I want you to stay. Will you stay?"

And she said, "Yes. Beast."

He felt the curse lifting as she said the words, and he almost laughed. Because she would never say it, and he would never say it, but they were bound by it anyway: she had learned to trust him, in a few short weeks. And she had learned to love him.

It was not what he had been searching for, in those crowded bars, in his isolated bedroom, in the lives of those countless women.

It was more.

The Little Magic Shop

Bruce Sterling

Bruce Sterling is one of the founders of the cyberpunk movement. He's also a founder of the Turkey City Writer's Workshop in Austin, TX. Sterling, purportedly a novelist by trade, actually spends most of his time aimlessly messing with computers, modems, and fax machines. He and his wife Nancy have a daughter Amy, born in 1987. They live in Austin, Texas.

While Sterling is closely identified with cyberpunk, this story is decidedly something else entirely. It doesn't cleave to any particular fairytale, but you can't deny its fairytale elements.

The early life of James Abernathy was rife with ominous portent.

His father, a New England customs inspector, had artistic ambitions; he filled his sketchbooks with mossy old Puritan tombstones and spanking new Nantucket whaling ships. By day, he graded bales of imported tea and calico; during evenings he took James to meetings of his intellectual friends, who would drink port, curse their wives and editors, and give James treacle candy.

James's father vanished while on a sketching expedition to the Great Stone Face of Vermont; nothing was ever found of him but his shoes.

James's mother, widowed with her young son, eventually married a large and hairy man who lived in a crumbling mansion in upstate New York.

At night the family often socialized in the nearby town of Albany.

There, James's stepfather would talk politics with his friends in the National Anti-Masonic Party; upstairs, his mother and the other women chatted with prominent dead personalities through spiritualist table rapping.

Eventually, James's stepfather grew more and more anxious over the plotting of the Masons. The family ceased to circulate in society. The curtains were drawn and the family ordered to maintain a close watch for strangers dressed in black. James's mother grew thin and pale, and often wore nothing but her houserobe for days on end.

One day, James's stepfather read them newspaper accounts of the angel Moroni, who had revealed locally buried tablets of gold that detailed the Biblical history of the Mound Builder Indians. By the time he reached the end of the article, the stepfather's voice shook and his eyes had grown quite wild. That night, muffled shrieks and frenzied hammerings were heard.

In the morning, young James found his stepfather downstairs by the hearth, still in his dressing gown, sipping teacup after teacup full of brandy and absently bending and straightening the fireside poker.

James offered morning greetings with his usual cordiality. The stepfather's eyes darted frantically under matted brows. James was informed that his mother was on a mission of mercy to a distant family stricken by scarlet fever. The conversation soon passed to a certain upstairs storeroom whose door was now nailed shut. James's stepfather strictly commanded him to avoid this forbidden portal.

Days passed. His mother's absence stretched to weeks. Despite repeated and increasingly strident warnings from his stepfather, James showed no interest whatsoever in the upstairs room. Eventually, deep within the older man's brain, a ticking artery burst from sheer frustration.

During his stepfather's funeral, the family home was struck by ball lightning and burned to the ground. The insurance money, and James's fate, passed into the hands of a distant relative, a muttering, trembling man who campaigned against liquor and drank several bottles of Dr. Rifkin's Laudanum Elixir each week.

James was sent to a boarding school run by a fanatical Calvinist deacon. James prospered there, thanks to close study of the scriptures and his equable, reasonable temperament. He grew to adulthood, becoming a tall, studious young man with a calm disposition and a solemn face utterly unmarked by doom.

Two days after his graduation, the deacon and his wife were both found hacked to bits, their half-naked bodies crammed into their one-horse shay. James stayed long enough to console the couple's spinster daughter, who sat dry-eyed in her rocking chair, methodically ripping a handkerchief to shreds.

James then took himself to New York City for higher education.

It was there that James Abernathy found the little shop that sold magic.

James stepped into this unmarked shop on impulse, driven inside by muffled screams of agony from the dentist's across the street.

The shop's dim interior smelled of burning whale-oil and hot lantern-brass. Deep wooden shelves, shrouded in cobwebs, lined the walls. Here and there, yellowing political broadsides requested military help for the rebel Texans. James set his divinity texts on an apothecary cabinet, where a band of stuffed, lacquered frogs brandished tiny trumpets and guitars. The proprietor appeared from behind a red curtain. "May I help the young master?" he said, rubbing his hands.

He was a small, spry Irishman. His ears rose to points lightly shrouded in hair; he wore bifocal spectacles and brass-buckled shoes.

"I rather fancy that fantod under the bell jar," said James, pointing.

"I'll wager we can do much better for a young man like yourself," said the proprietor with a leer. "So fresh, so full of life."

James puffed the thick dust of long neglect from the fantod jar.

"Is business all it might be, these days?"

"We have a rather specialized clientele," said the other, and he introduced himself. His name was Mr. O'Beronne, and he had recently fled his country's devastating potato famine. James shook Mr. O'Beronne's small papery hand.

"You'll be wanting a love-potion," said Mr. O'Beronne with a shrewd look. "Fellows of your age generally do."

James shrugged. "Not really, no."

"Is it budget troubles, then? I might interest you in an ever-filled purse." The old man skipped from behind the counter and hefted a large bearskin cape.

"Money?" said James with only distant interest.

"Fame then. We have magic brushes—or if you prefer newfangled scientific arts, we have a camera that once belonged to Montavarde himself."

"No, no," said James, looking restless. "Can you quote me a price on this fantod?" He studied the fantod critically. It was not in very good condition.

"We can restore youth," said Mr. O'Beronne in sudden desperation.

"Do tell," said James, straightening.

"We have a shipment of Dr. Heidegger's Patent Youthing Waters," said Mr. O'Beronne. He tugged a quagga hide from a nearby brassbound chest and dug out a square glass bottle. He uncorked it. The waters fizzed lightly, and the smell of May filled the room. "One bottle imbibed," said Mr. O'Beronne, "restores a condition of blushing youth to man or beast."

"Is that a fact," said James, his brows knitting in thought. "How many teaspoons per bottle?"

"I've no idea," Mr. O'Beronne admitted. "Never measured it by the spoon. Mind you, this is an old folks' item. Fellows of your age usually go for the love-potions."

"How much for a bottle?" said James.

"It is a bit steep," said Mr. O'Beronne grudgingly. "The price is everything you possess."

"Seems reasonable," said James. "How much for two bottles?"

Mr. O'Beronne stared. "Don't get ahead of yourself, young man." He recorked the bottle carefully. "You've yet to give me all you possess, mind."

"How do I know you'll still have the waters, when I need more?" James said.

Mr. O'Beronne's eyes shifted uneasily behind his bifocals. "You let me worry about that." He leered, but without the same conviction he had shown earlier. "I won't be shutting up this shop—not when there are people of your sort about."

"Fair enough," said James, and they shook hands on the bargain.

James returned two days later, having sold everything he owned. He handed over a small bag of gold specie and a bank draft conveying the slender remaining funds of his patrimony. He departed with the clothes on his back and the bottle.

Twenty years passed.

The United States suffered civil war. Hundreds of thousands of men were shot, blown up with mines or artillery, or perished miserably in septic army camps. In the streets of New York, hundreds of antidraft rioters were mown down with grapeshot, and the cobbled street before the little magic shop was strewn with reeking dead. At last, after stubborn resistance and untold agonies, the Confederacy was defeated.

The war became history.

James Abernathy returned.

"I've been in California," he announced to the astonished Mr. O'Beronne. James was healthily tanned and wore a velvet cloak, spurred boots, and a silver sombrero. He sported a large gold turnip-watch, and his fingers gleamed with gems.

"You struck it rich in the goldfields," Mr. O'Beronne surmised.

"Actually, no," said James. "I've been in the grocery business. In Sacramento. One can sell a dozen eggs there for almost their weight in gold dust, you know." He smiled and gestured at his elaborate clothes.

"I did pretty well, but I don't usually dress this extravagantly. You see, I'm wearing my entire worldly wealth. I thought it would make our transaction simpler." He produced the empty bottle.

"That's very farsighted of you," said Mr. O'Beronne. He examined James critically, as if looking for hairline psychic cracks or signs of moral corruption. "You don't seem to have aged a day."

"Oh, that's not quite so," said James. "I was twenty when I first came here; now I easily look twenty-one, even twenty-two." He put the bottle on the counter. "You'll be interested to know there were twenty teaspoons exactly."

"You didn't spill any?"

"Oh, no," said James, smiling at the thought. "I've only opened it once a year."

"It didn't occur to you to take two teaspoons, say? Or empty the bottle at a draught?"

"Now what would be the use of that?" said James. He began stripping off his rings and dropping them on the counter with light tinkling sounds. "You did keep the Youthing Waters in stock, I presume."

"A bargain's a bargain," said Mr. O'Beronne grudgingly. He produced another bottle. James left barefoot, wearing only shirt and pants, but carrying his bottle.

The 1870s passed and the nation celebrated its centennial.

Railroads stitched the continent. Gaslights were installed in the streets of New York. Buildings taller than any ever seen began to soar, though the magic shop's neighborhood remained obscure.

James Abernathy returned. He now looked at least twenty-four. He passed over the title deeds to several properties in Chicago and departed with another bottle.

Shortly after the turn of the century, James returned again, driving a steam automobile, whistling the theme of the St. Louis Exhibition and stroking his waxed mustache. He signed over the deed to the car, which was a fine one, but Mr. O'Beronne showed little enthusiasm. The old Irishman had shrunken with the years, and his tiny hands trembled as he conveyed his goods.

Within the following period, a great war of global empires took place, but America was mostly spared the devastation. The 1920s arrived, and James came laden with a valise crammed with rapidly appreciating stocks and bonds. "You always seem to do rather well for yourself," Mr. O'Beronne observed in a quavering voice.

"Moderation's the key," said James. "That, and a sunny disposition." He looked about the shop with a critical eye. The quality of the junk had declined. Old engine parts lay in reeking grease next to heaps of moldering popular magazines and spools of blackened telephone wire. The exotic hides, packets of spice and amber, ivory tusks hand-carved by cannibals, and so forth, had now entirely disappeared.

"I hope you don't mind these new bottles," croaked Mr. O'Beronne, handing him one. The bottle had curved sides and a machine-fitted cap of cork and tin.

"Any trouble with supply?" said James delicately. "You let me worry about that!" said Mr. O'Beronne, lifting his lip with a faint snarl of defiance.

James's next visit came after yet another war, this one of untold and almost unimaginable savagery. Mr. O'Beronne's shop was now crammed with military surplus goods. Bare electric bulbs hung over a realm of rotting khaki and rubber.

James now looked almost thirty. He was a little short by modern American standards, but this was scarcely noticeable. He wore high-waisted pants and a white linen suit with jutting shoulders.

"I don't suppose," muttered Mr. O'Beronne through his false teeth, "that it ever occurs to you to share this? What about wives, sweethearts, children?"

James shrugged. "What about them?"

"You're content to see them grow old and die?"

"I never see them grow all that old," James observed. "After all, every twenty years I have to return here and lose everything I own. It's simpler just to begin all over again."

"No human feelings," Mr. O'Beronne muttered bitterly.

"Oh, come now," said James. "After all, I don't see you distributing elixir to all and sundry, either."

"But I'm in the magic shop business," said Mr. O'Beronne, weakly. "There are certain unwritten rules."

"Oh?" said James, leaning on the counter with the easy patience of a youthful centenarian. "You never mentioned this before. Supernatural law—it must be an interesting field of study."

"Never you mind that," Mr. O'Beronne snapped. "You're a customer, and a human being. You mind your business and I'll mind mine."

"No need to be so touchy," James said. He hesitated. "You know, I have some hot leads in the new plastics industry. I imagine I could make a great deal more money than usual. That is, if you're interested in selling this place." He smiled. "They say an Irishman never forgets the Old Country. You could go back into your old line—pot o' gold, bowl of milk on the doorstep...."

"Take your bottle and go," O'Beronne shouted, thrusting it into his hands.

Another two decades passed. James drove up in a Mustang convertible and entered the shop. The place reeked of patchouli incense, and Day-Glo posters covered the walls. Racks of demented comic books loomed beside tables littered with hookahs and handmade clay pipes.

Mr. O'Beronne dragged himself from behind a hanging beaded curtain. "You again," he croaked.

"Right on," said James, looking around. "I like the way you've kept the place up to date, man. Groovy."

O'Beronne gave him a poisonous glare. "You're a hundred and forty years old. Hasn't the burden of unnatural life become insupportable?"

James looked at him, puzzled. "Are you kidding?"

"Haven't you learned a lesson about the blessings of mortality? About how it's better not to outlive your own predestined time?"

"Huh?" James said. He shrugged. "I did learn something about material possessions, though...Material things only tie a cat down. You can't have the car this time, it's rented." He dug a hand-stitched leather wallet from his bell-bottom jeans. "I have some fake ID and credit cards." He shook them out over the counter.

Mr. O'Beronne stared unbelieving at the meager loot. "Is this your idea of a joke?"

"Hey, it's all I possess," James said mildly. "I could have bought Xerox at fifteen, back in the '50s. But last time I talked to you, you didn't seem interested. I figured it was like, you know, not the bread that counts, but the spirit of the thing."

Mr. O'Beronne clutched his heart with a liver-spotted hand. "Is this never going to end? Why did I ever leave Europe? They know how to respect a tradition there...." He paused, gathering bile. "Look at this place! It's an insult! Call this a magic shop?" He snatched up a fat mushroom-shaped candle and flung it to the floor.

"You're overwrought," James said. "Look, you're the one who said a bargain's a bargain. There's no need for us to go on with this any longer. I can see your heart's not in it. Why not put me in touch with your wholesaler?"

"Never!" O'Beronne swore. "I won't be beaten by some coldblooded...bookkeeper."

"I never thought of this as a contest," James said with dignity. "Sorry to see you take it that way, man." He picked up his bottle and left.

The allotted time elapsed, and James repeated his pilgrimage to the magic shop. The neighborhood had declined. Women in spandex and net hose lurked on the pavement, watched from the corner by men in broad-brimmed hats and slick polished shoes. James carefully locked the doors of his BMW.

The magic shop's once-curtained windows had been painted over in black. A neon sign above the door read ADULT PEEP 25$.

Inside, the shop's cluttered floor space had been cleared. Shrink- wrapped magazines lined the walls, their fleshy covers glaring under the bluish corpse-light of overhead fluorescents. The old counter had been replaced by a long glass-fronted cabinet displaying knotted whips and flavored lubricants. The bare floor clung stickily to the soles of James's Gucci shoes.

A young man emerged from behind a curtain. He was tall and bony, with a small, neatly trimmed mustache. His smooth skin had a waxy subterranean look. He gestured fluidly. "Peeps in the back," he said in a high voice, not meeting James's eyes. "You gotta buy tokens. Three bucks."

"I beg your pardon?" James said.

"Three bucks, man!"

"Oh." James produced the money. The man handed over a dozen plastic tokens and vanished at once behind the curtains.

"Excuse me?" James said. No answer. "Hello?"

The peep machines waited in the back of the store, in a series of curtained booths. The vinyl cushions inside smelled of sweat and butyl nitrate. James inserted a token and watched.

He then moved to the other machines and examined them as well. He returned to the front of the shop. The shopkeeper sat on a stool, ripping the covers from unsold magazines and watching a small television under the counter.

"Those films," James said. "That was Charlie Chaplin. And Douglas Fairbanks. And Gloria Swanson...."

The man looked up, smoothing his hair. "Yeah, so? You don't like silent films?"

James paused. "I can't believe Charlie Chaplin did porn."

"I hate to spoil a magic trick," the shopkeeper said, yawning. "But they're genuine peeps, pal. You ever hear of Hearst Mansion? San Simeon? Old Hearst, he liked filming his Hollywood guests on the sly. All the bedrooms had spy holes."

"Oh," James said. "I see. Ah, is Mr. O'Beronne in?"

The man showed interest for the first time. "You know the old guy? I don't get many nowadays who knew the old guy. His clientele had pretty special tastes, I hear."

James nodded. "He should be holding a bottle for me."

"Well, I'll check in the back. Maybe he's awake."

The shopkeeper vanished again. He reappeared minutes later with a brownish vial. "Got some love-potion here."

James shook his head. "Sorry, that's not it."

"It's the real stuff, man! Works like you wouldn't believe!" The shopkeeper was puzzled. "You young guys are usually into love-potions. Well, I guess I'll have to rouse the old guy for you. Though I kind of hate to disturb him."

Long minutes passed, with distant rustling and squeaking. Finally the shopkeeper backed through the curtains, tugging a wheelchair. Mr. O'Beronne sat within it, wrapped in bandages, his wrinkled head shrouded in a dirty nightcap. "Oh," he said at last. "So it's you again."

"Yes, I've returned for my—"

"I know, I know." Mr. O'Beronne stirred fitfully on his cushions.

"I see you've met my...associate. Mr. Ferry."

"I kind of manage the place, these days," said Mr. Ferry. He winked at James, behind Mr. O'Beronne's back.

"I'm James Abernathy," James said. He offered his hand.

Ferry folded his arms warily. "Sorry, I never do that."

O'Beronne cackled feebly and broke into a fit of coughing. "Well, my boy," he said finally, "I was hoping I'd last long enough to see you one more time...Mr. Ferry! There's a crate, in the back, under those filthy movie posters of yours...."

"Sure, sure," Ferry said indulgently. He left.

"Let me look at you," said O'Beronne. His eyes, in their dry, leaden sockets, had grown quite lizardlike. "Well, what do you think of the place? Be frank."

"It's looked better," James said. "So have you."

"But so has the world, eh?" O'Beronne said. "He does bang-up business, young Ferry. You should see him manage the books...." He waved one hand, its tiny knuckles warped with arthritis. "It's such a blessing, not to have to care anymore."

Ferry reappeared, lugging a wooden crate, crammed with dusty six-packs of pop-top aluminum cans. He set it gently on the counter.

Every can held Youthing Water.

"Thanks," James said, his eyes widening. He lifted one pack reverently, and tugged at a can.

"Don't," O'Beronne said. "This is for you, all of it. Enjoy it, son. I hope you're satisfied."

James lowered the cans, slowly. "What about our arrangement?"

O'Beronne's eyes fell, in an ecstasy of humiliation. "I humbly apologize. But I simply can't keep up our bargain any longer. I don't have the strength, you see. So this is yours now. It's all I could find."

"Yeah, this must be pretty much the last of it," nodded Ferry, inspecting his nails. "It hasn't moved well for some time—I figure the bottling plant shut up shop."

"So many cans, though...."James said thoughtfully. He produced his wallet. "I brought a nice car for you, outside...."

"None of that matters now," said Mr. O'Beronne. "Keep all of it, just consider it my forfeit." His voice fell. "I never thought it would come to this, but you've beaten me, I admit it. I'm done in."

His head sagged limply.

Mr. Ferry took the wheelchair's handles. "He's tired now," he said soothingly. "I'll just wheel him back out of our way, here...." He held the curtains back and shoved the chair through with his foot. He turned to James. "You can take that case and let yourself out. Nice doing business—goodbye." He nodded briskly.

"Goodbye, sir!" James called. No answer.

James hauled the case outside to his car, and set it in the backseat. Then he sat in front for a while, drumming his fingers on the steering wheel.

Finally he went back in.

Mr. Ferry had pulled a telephone from beneath his cash register.

When he saw James he slammed the headset down. "Forget something, pal?"

"I'm troubled," James said. "I keep wondering...what about those unwritten rules?"

The shopkeeper looked at him, surprised. "Aw, the old guy always talked like that. Rules, standards, quality." Mr. Ferry gazed meditatively over his stock, then looked James in the eye. "What rules, man?"

There was a moment of silence.

"I was never quite sure," James said. "But I'd like to ask Mr. O'Beronne."

"You've badgered him enough," the shopkeeper said. "Can't you see he's a dying man? You got what you wanted, so scram, hit the road." He folded his arms. James refused to move.

The shopkeeper sighed. "Look, I'm not in this for my health. You want to hang around here, you gotta buy some more tokens."

"I've seen those already," James said. "What else do you sell?"

"Oh, machines not good enough for you, eh?" Mr. Ferry stroked his chin. "Well, it's not strictly in my line, but I might sneak you a gram or two of Senor Buendia's Colombian Real Magic Powder. First taste is free. No? You're a hard man to please, bub."

Ferry sat down, looking bored. "I don't see why I should change my stock, just because you're so picky. A smart operator like you, you ought to have bigger fish to fry than a little magic shop. Maybe you just don't belong here, pal."

"No, I always liked this place," James said. "I used to, anyway... I even wanted to own it myself."

Ferry tittered. "You? Gimme a break." His face hardened. "If you don't like the way I run things, take a hike."

"No, no, I'm sure I can find something here," James said quickly.

He pointed at random to a thick hardbound book, at the bottom of a stack, below the counter. "Let me try that."

Mr. Ferry shrugged with bad grace and fetched it out. "You'll like this," he said unconvincingly. "Marilyn Monroe and Jack Kennedy at a private beach house."

James leafed through the glossy pages. "How much?"

"You want it?" said the shopkeeper. He examined the binding and set it back down. "Okay, fifty bucks."

"Just cash?" James said, surprised. "Nothing magical?"

"Cash is magical, pal." The shopkeeper shrugged. "Okay, forty bucks and you have to kiss a dog on the lips."

"I'll pay the fifty," James said. He pulled out his wallet.

"Whoops!" He fumbled, and it dropped over the far side of the counter.

Mr. Ferry lunged for it. As he rose again, James slammed the heavy book into his head. The shopkeeper fell with a groan.

James vaulted over the counter and shoved the curtains aside. He grabbed the wheelchair and hauled it out. The wheels thumped twice over Ferry's outstretched legs. Jostled, O'Beronne woke with a screech.

James pulled him toward the blacked-out windows. "Old man," he panted. "How long has it been since you had some fresh air?" He kicked open the door.

"No!" O'Beronne yelped. He shielded his eyes with both hands. "I have to stay inside here! That's the rules!" James wheeled him out onto the pavement. As sunlight hit him, O'Beronne howled in fear and squirmed wildly. Gouts of dust puffed from his cushions, and his bandages flapped. James yanked open the car door, lifted O'Beronne bodily, and dropped him into the passenger seat.

"You can't do this!" O'Beronne screamed, his nightcap flying off.

"I belong behind walls, I can't go into the world…"

James slammed the door. He ran around and slid behind the wheel.

"It's dangerous out here," O'Beronne whimpered as the engine roared into life. "I was safe in there."

James stamped the accelerator. The car laid rubber. He glanced behind him in the rearview mirror and saw an audience of laughing whooping hookers. "Where are we going?" O'Beronne said meekly.

James floored it through a yellow light. He reached into the backseat one-handed and yanked a can from its six-pack. "Where was this bottling plant?"

O'Beronne blinked doubtfully. "It's been so long…Florida, I think…."

"Florida sounds good. Sunlight, fresh air…." James weaved deftly through traffic, cracking the pop-top with his thumb. He knocked back a swig, then gave O'Beronne the can. "Here, old man. Finish it off."

O'Beronne stared at it, licking dry lips. "But I can't. I'm an owner, not a customer. I'm simply not allowed to do this sort of thing. I own that magic shop, I tell you."

James shook his head and laughed.

O'Beronne trembled. He raised the can in both gnarled hands and began chugging thirstily. He paused once to belch, and kept drinking.

The smell of May filled the car.

O'Beronne wiped his mouth and crushed the empty can in his fist.

He tossed it over his shoulder.

"There's room back there for those bandages, too," James told him.

"Let's hit the highway."

BLACK FEATHER

K. Tempest Bradford

K. Tempest Bradford has had short fiction appear in such places as *Strange Horizons*, *Electric Velocipede*, *Sybil's Garage* and *Federations*. She is perhaps better known for her active online presence where she speaks out for racial and gender equality both within and outside the genre community.

What would happen if birds started talking to you? If a little old man wanted you to guess his name or he'd take your child? I've often wondered how the modern person would actually react if faced with fairytale. Bradford investigates how someone might deal with being the middle of the Seven Swans fairytale.

Exactly one year before she saw the raven, Brenna began to dream of flying. Sometimes she was in a plane, sometimes she was in a bird, sometimes she was just herself—surrounded by sky, clouds, and too-thin-to-breathe air. In the dark, in the light, over cities and oceans and fields, she flew. Every night for a year.

Then, on the twelfth day of the twelfth month, the dreams changed. They ended with a crash and fire and the feeling of falling. Most nights she almost didn't wake up in time.

Exactly one year from the night the dreams began, Brenna struggled out of sleep, the phantom smell of burning metal still in her nose. She reached out for Scott—he was not there. He was never there. He had never been there. She fell back onto her pillows and groaned. Another dream of flying, another reaching out for Scott; she wished she could stop doing both.

Brenna lived in Manhattan—a small, insignificant corner of it way at the very tip-top. On an island of concrete and glass and steel she had found the one place still mostly untouched. It had a lake and a forest and a hill she could climb without ever realizing how high she was at the top. From there everything seemed far away, not far down. Not like when you're in a building—or falling from the sky.

She had lived by this park, this forest, for two months now. The apartment, her new apartment, was paid up for the summer. A graduation gift from her mother.

That morning, while the sky was still pink and yellow, she went out and up the hill to the small meadow at the very top. She thought of it as *her* place.

It was there in that meadow, amongst the crumbling remains of benches and street lamps long abandoned to the regrowing wilderness, that Brenna first met the raven. She was meditating under a large oak tree when she heard a raven's cry. The sound didn't register at first, and might not have ever, if it hadn't been so persistent. The constant cawing didn't stop until she opened her eyes. There, on the fallen tree trunk in front of her, stood a black raven. It had been a long time since she'd seen one. Not since England, when she put aside her fear of flying to follow Scott across an ocean. A year ago.

"Did you follow me?" she joked.

The raven looked right at her and cawed. It came back to her then, a rush of emotion and memory, half hidden, half forgotten. A warm day by the sea, looking back over the ocean toward New York, a raven standing out on the rocks, her plea to him. *I want to fly. I want to fly and be free and go wherever and whenever…I want to fly!* She wanted it so badly that she felt her heart would break.

The feeling had overwhelmed her then and it overwhelmed her now. Here in the forest, an ocean between her and England, and she could still feel it. She found that she was crying. The raven's call echoed in her mind, but when she wiped the tears away he was gone without a sound—or had there been wings flapping? She turned to pick up her bag and saw a feather, long and shiny and black, lying on the rock by her side.

Brenna showed the feather to a friend. The psychic one.

"Feathers are powerful messages and special gifts," she said while shuffling a tarot

deck. "Draw a card."
Brenna drew the Hanged Man.
"Sacrifice."
"But of what?"

The next day Brenna saw the raven again. He was staring at her through the bedroom window—the one with the view of the hill. She thought he was the only one, but soon there were two, then three. One day she saw them all. Twelve ravens, high up in the oak tree, watching over her.

She showed the feather to another friend. The non-psychic one.
"Crow's feather, you mean," she said.
"It is? How can you tell?" Brenna asked.
"Because we don't have ravens in New York. We have crows."

They called to her in her dreams. She heard them but couldn't find them. Their feathers littered the floor: long and shiny and black. She dreamed of flying through a forest of black trees and shiny ebony leaves, always following the raven's song. She had six nights of this. Six nights of searching and never finding. Six nights of waking up sweaty with raven feathers in her hair.

On the seventh night the dream changed again. She found herself in a little wooden cabin, fire crackling in the hearth, twelve small beds along the wall. She stood in the middle wearing nothing but a man's white shirt.
The ravens called to her from outside, but she did not want to go. One by one they flew in through the open door. And in a moment, a blink, an instant, they were not ravens but young men. The youngest of all looked a lot like her.
"Who are you?" she asked.
"We are your brothers," one said.
"We died for you," said another.
The dream ended.

Brenna ran into Scott—accidentally on purpose—taking a cigarette break in front of the building where he taught his summer course. The only thing she regretted about graduating was not being able to take his classes anymore.

"So you live in Inwood now?" he asked as they walked toward his office.

"Yeah. Right by the hill."

"There are some interesting cave formations up there. Do you want to come explore them with me?"

"Sure, that'd be cool."

"Okay. Meet you by the baseball diamond at noon tomorrow."

He flicked his cigarette away and went back inside.

Brenna sighed. *Twenty-four hours. Yeah, I'll survive.*

On the eighth night she dreamed again. The cabin, again. This time the young men were already there.

"We're hungry," one said.

So she cooked them dinner.

They were each careful not to stain their white shirts.

The dream ended.

Scott took her up the hill to where the village Shorakapkok used to be at the base of a cliff—black rocks piled on one another, embedded in the soil, rising up and up and up farther than Brenna was willing to look.

"See up there?" Scott pointed. "The opening? It leads to a cave. Let's see if we can get in."

Scott hopped up on a boulder and started climbing like it was the easiest thing in the world. Brenna forgot that, though his hair was completely white, Scott was only in his forties. He played the old wise man but didn't move like one.

She was torn. Should she go up? Risk being that high? If she slipped she had no wings to spread, to catch the air, to glide higher.

If she slipped and stumbled and fell, she would die. She just knew it.

"Don't worry," he said. "I won't let you fall."

She carefully made her way to him, then went ahead, glancing back to make sure he was close.

He talked while they climbed. "This was an Algonquin village. You can still see some of their markings on the rocks."

She focused on climbing, taking her time—finding the footholds, the handholds, the way up.

"You're part Native American, aren't you?" he asked.

"Yeah, on my father's side."

She did not look down. She did not look up. She only climbed.

"And on your mother's?"

"Black and Irish."

They reached the shelf he'd pointed out. Brenna timidly peeked over the edge and down to the bottom. Though she'd always been afraid of heights, she loved high places. She'd discovered this two summers before while rock climbing in Arizona. She'd been trying to impress a guy then, too.

"Did they really live in these caves?" she asked. The opening seemed awfully small to her.

"No, they were used for different purposes." Scott pulled an aluminum flashlight from his pocket. "Initiation rituals. Remember the Glastonbury Druids I told you about in the England class? The Chalice Well and the caves under the Tor? Same concept here. Just a different place, different time."

He crawled in, obviously expecting her to follow.

Brenna poked her head into the opening—still dark, even with the faint glow of flashlight ahead. The cave, not much wider than she was, felt oppressive and smelled foreboding.

Scott's voice bounced back to her. "You really should see this. It's amazing."

She made some inarticulate reply, but could barely breathe. The walls were pressing against her. The darkness was pushing her out. *The flapping of wings. The call of ravens.* Panicked, she scrambled backwards, catching herself just before falling off the shelf.

A while later Scott slid out, head first, and smiled reassuringly at her.

"No initiation for you today, huh?"

She smiled back. "I guess I'm just not ready."

Later, in her apartment, Brenna showed the feather to Scott.

"It's not from a crow," he said.

"It's not?"

"No. Not a feather that big. That's definitely from a raven."

She stared at it.

"They're rarer than crows in New York, but not unheard of." He stared at her.

She invited him to stay longer. He declined.

On the ninth night, she dreamed again. The cabin again. The young men were asleep. She went outside, into the forest, but there was nothing to see. In the garden behind the cabin, twelve lilies grew. She picked one for each brother.

The sound of wings. She looked up. They were ravens again, flying away.

The dream ended.

"It's a symbol. You have to find the meaning," her psychic friend said.

"It's nothing. You're overtired," her non-psychic friend said.

"Ravens are messengers from the otherworld. Someone there wants your attention," her psychic friend said.

"You probably ate too many tacos before bed," her non-psychic friend said.

"Past life regression." Brenna's psychiatrist spoke with authority.

It sounded like something her psychic friend would suggest.

"I assure you, I am serious," he said to the look on her face. "I've done them before and they've helped my patients every time."

She said she would try anything once. And if it didn't work, at least she'd get some sleep.

She lay on the couch listening to his words. She went back and back and back. Back along her life's path, growing younger with each breath. Back through high school, middle school, her first kiss, her first pitch, her first word, until she came to a place, comfortable, warm, familiar, red, the place just before birth, her mother's womb. Her arms wrapped around another, protecting him. She knows that she must hold on tight and never let go. She cannot lose him. But she is going back and back and back and his eyes open and his heart beats along with hers and he looks at her (I am your brother—I died for you) then the sound of wings.

She did not know when she began to scream, but she knew it took a long time for her to stop.

As a child Brenna had desperately wanted a brother. She would try to adopt the neighborhood boys into her family. She would try to walk away with babies at the mall. Other girls her age had crushes and pretend boyfriends. Brenna had pretend big brothers.

When she was nine Brenna's mother told her that she was a twin. She had had a brother in the womb with her and on the ultrasound pictures she seemed to be hugging him. But in the eighth month only one of their hearts was beating. They were delivered by emergency C-section. Brenna held on to her brother until the end—he was born first, though born dead.

Her parents had named him Benjamin. When she was twelve, her mother finally took her to see his grave. Beloved Son and Brother. After that, the thought of a brother only made Brenna incredibly sad. She no longer wished for one. She pushed it out of her mind and forgot about it entirely. Until now.

She was reluctant to go to Scott. Lately he'd been more standoffish than usual. Brenna had hoped that once she was no longer his student he'd be more affectionate. On the contrary, he'd been more reticent than usual since they went to the park. But she was desperate.

"The shrink didn't know what he was doing," Scott said.

"And you do?" she replied.

"Yes."

She believed him.

"Don't worry," he said. "I won't let you fall."

Again she went back and back and back, this time one hand in the physical world, safely tucked in Scott's, his voice guiding her along the path of her life. She watched her life roll back like a movie on rewind, and when she came to the womb she was inside looking in, apart from the two small not-yet-people holding on to each other. The one that was not her opened his eyes (I am your brother—I love you) then the sound of wings.

Brenna flew through the air, faster and faster and faster, flew back through her lives, each one freezing at one moment, a picture in her soul. She flew through them all until she came to the last one, the first one, and she could fly no more.

She is just a baby. They carry her out into the courtyard while they watch. Each son is led to the block, the oldest first, to have his head chopped off. And as the oldest falls, the next one becomes the oldest. Then he falls, then another, then another, until the twelfth son, the youngest who is now the oldest, is led to the block. He looks at her, his baby sister (I love you—I died for you) and he falls, too. She cries and cries. Her mother coos and cuddles. But there is no end to her crying.

"She cries for them," her mother says.

"She could not possibly understand," her father says.

She understands.

That night Brenna didn't want to dream, didn't want to sleep. She lay in bed watching the constellations roll across the sky like hieroglyphs, and just as undecipherable. She looked over the pictures in her mind, the lives frozen. There had been twelve including this one, but not including the first. In each she saw a brother. In each he died.

Brenna took the feather, her gift from the raven, and placed it beside her pillow. Her eyes drooped, then closed. She slipped into sleep, then into dreams.

She is flying. Back and back and back through her lives, frozen in place, until she comes to the first one and she can fly no more. So she speaks instead.

"Why are there twelve white shirts in the wash, Mother?" she asks the queen.

"Because they are not clean, Daughter," the queen answers with sadness. She has always been sad, even when she is happy.

"What soils them, Mother?"

"Blood."

The dream ended.

The next night she flew back again.

She is in a garden.

"Why does this plot have twelve lilies and nothing else, Mother?"

"Because nothing else will grow there, Daughter."

"Why is that?"

"Because that is where your brothers are buried."

The dream ended.

The next night she flew back again.

"Why are all my brothers dead, Mother?"

"Your father had them killed, Daughter."

"Why did he do that?"

"So you could have all the wealth and kingdom for yourself."

(The Dream Ended)

Brenna asked Scott, "Are they dreams, or are they memories?"

"What's the difference?" was his enigmatic reply.

She was starting to get frustrated.

"Try asking your dream what it wants you to understand."

That was a thought.

That afternoon, Brenna lay in bed; too afraid to sleep, too depressed to rise. So you could have all the wealth and kingdom for yourself, the queen had said. How senseless.

A raven stared through her bedroom window. She mouthed to him, "I'm sorry."

That night she reluctantly slept again, dreamed again. This time she did not pick a destination, but still ended up flying back and back and back until she could fly no more. She was running away and into the woods. She had to stop herself. Stop and think and ask…ask what?

"You're a very inquisitive child, aren't you?" A voice from above. She looked up. From a tree hung a man with long white hair bound in a ponytail. He hung from one foot, upside down. He didn't seem at all affected by it. "Go ahead, ask me something. I know almost everything now."

"Why…"

"…is the sky blue? …do fools fall in love? …do birds suddenly appear? You'll have to be more specific, my dear."

She was supposed to ask him about…about…"How…"

"Yes…"

"How can I bring my brothers back?"

"Ah! Now that is the question of the day, is it not? I could tell you—"

"Please tell me!"

"Oh, there are so many ways," the Hanging Man said. "You could sit in this tree and not speak a word for seven years. Maybe a handsome king would come by and make you his bride, hmm? Or, you could sew twelve brother-sized shirts. Or, you could convince the stars to give you their key to the glass mountain. You could do all of that. And more. In fact, you already have."

"When?"

"Before."

"Before?"

"In another time. In another world.

"In a fairy tale. In a myth.

"In the stories your mothers would tell."

Once upon a time there was a princess *For a long time she didn't know that she had brothers* One day she overheard people talking *She was the one who had caused their misfortune* When night came she ran away and into the forest **I'm looking for my brothers** She went to the stars **I'll keep walking as far as the sky is blue to find them** They were kind and gave their key to the glass mountain *The way is hard, you won't be able to free us* You'd have to remain silent for seven years *Neither speak nor laugh* You'd have to sew twelve little shirts *The conditions are too hard* If you utter just a single word **If the key is lost** You cannot enter the glass mountain *Everything will be in vain* All your work would be for naught

The fragments danced in the corner of her mind's eye. But were they real memories, or the memories of dreams?

"What's the difference?" the Hanging Man asked.

The flapping of wings. Twelve ravens perched in the tree—looking at Brenna, watching over her.

"You say you want your brothers back? Here they are."

"They're birds," she said.

"They're ravens."

"Why?"

"Because they're dead."

The ravens began to call out to her. Calling and calling and calling. Brenna covered her ears and closed her eyes and willed herself awake. Struggled up and up and up out of sleep. But the calling continued outside her bedroom window. Twelve ravens on the fire escape—calling to her.

Fly with us! Fly, fly, fly!

"I can't!" Brenna yelled through the window. "I can't, it's too high!"

You're afraid, one said. Then the others. *You're afraid! You're afraid! You're afraid!*

Afraid to die!

The phone rang and she jerked awake. The room was silent. She looked out the window—nothing there but the night. The phone rang again and she quickly picked it up.

"What?" she barked.

A short silence. "I'm sorry I woke you. I thought you'd appreciate it." Scott.

"How…how did you know?" She wasn't sure if she wanted the answer.

Another silence. "What are you afraid of, Brenna? Truly afraid of?"

She swallowed. On the other side of the window it was just becoming morning. The dark outline of the hill with the dark outline of the apartments with the dark outline of the bridge against the less dark of the sky.

"Falling," she finally said.

"Flying is nothing more than controlled falling."

There was a long silence.

"Come find me later, we'll talk," he said, then hung up.

Brenna couldn't fall back to sleep. There was no sleep left in her, even in the cool light of dawn.

She slipped out of bed and got dressed in the semi-darkness. She went out the door, down the street, and into the forest. Halfway up the hill she came upon a little wooden cabin. It had never been there before. She went inside. On the table was a white shirt. She took it up and began to sew.

"There are many certainties in this world, Brenna," the Hanging Man said. He hung from nowhere, his head beside hers. His breath smelled of smoke. "One of them is that you always completed the tasks that I gave you. Without fail. No matter how hard or how many."

She could only regard him with a questioning gaze. She could not, must not, speak. This she knew.

"So what do you want now? Another twelve lives? Another twelve tries?"

She finished the sleeve, the shirt was complete.

The dream ended.

Brenna woke up in her bed. It was noon.

It was a dream…

She slipped out of bed and got dressed in the mid-day sun. She went out the door, down the street, and into the forest. She headed to her place, her favorite tree. She pulled herself up into the branches, stepped out onto a limb and looked down. She was surrounded by fire. She screamed.

"There are many certainties in this world, Brenna," the Hanging Man said. His white ponytail hung low, almost touching the flames. He didn't seem affected by it. "One of them is that your brothers will never let you die."

The flames shot higher.

"They will always choose to die for you."

"Why?"

"Because they love you. Because you are not ready."

"But I'm the reason they die!"

"No. You're the reason they live."

Ravens circled the tree, beating away flames with their wings.

"You completed the tasks a long time ago, so I granted your wish. Each brother lived a life equal to the one he would have had if not for you."

"Even Benjamin?"

"Even Benjamin."

"And if I wish again?"

"You will get the same. No more, no less."

The tips of their wings ignited—black feathers scorched blacker. The ravens flapped fire, succumbing to the flames one by one.

"No!"

"Death is inevitable. Whether you fear it or face it bravely."

The fire nearly consumed her.

The dream ended.

Brenna woke up in her bed. It was almost evening.

It was…

A raven stared at her through the window. A white shirt hung from the doorknob.

She slipped out of bed and pulled the shirt from the knob. Held it close to her as sunlight seeped slowly from the sky.

"Okay," she said to herself. Then to the raven, "Okay."

She put on the shirt, then took the feather from her bedside and put it in her hair. She went out the door, down the street, into the forest, up to the cliff. The glass mountain.

She began to climb. Taking her time—finding the footholds, the handholds, the way up. Higher and higher. The sun began to set. Higher and higher. The air began to mist. Higher and higher. She did not look down, she did not look up, she only climbed.

She reached the shelf, the mouth of the cave, took a deep breath and crawled inside. Deep into the darkness. The walls pressing in on her from every side. The darkness drawing her in, driving her forward, welcoming her to the end—the peak of the glass mountain.

Her brothers were there, waiting for her in their white shirts. She ran to them, held them tight, and danced with each in turn. Then, one by one, they took off their shirts, the shirts she had sewn, and became ravens again. Flying in circles. Calling to her.

Flying is nothing more than controlled falling.

She stepped to the edge of the mountain, faced the setting sun, and nodded.

"Yes. I'm ready."

She fell forward from the edge, fell into the air. Her white shirt came apart at the seams, falling away from her as she turned, arms spread, wings spread, black, shiny fingers-feathers catching the wind, lifting her up and up and up as she joined the ravens, her brothers, in the sky. Flying into the sun, into the west. Flying home.

Fifi's Tail

Alan Rodgers

Alan Rodgers' first story, "The Boy Who Came Back from the Dead," won a Stoker award and was nominated for a World Fantasy Award. Since then, he's written a dozen novels, and was the editor of *Night Cry*, a horror digest.

What starts out as a simple John Gardner-esque retelling of Little Red Riding Hood quickly becomes a delirious mash-up of all sorts of fairytales and modern contrivances. Every time you think you have a handle on what Rodgers is doing, he turns the story on its head again.

The wolf caught scent of the huntsman long before he heard the girl-child plead for mercy.

He *knew* that scent. *Knew* it. That was the huntsman who'd ambushed him just as he'd been about to devour the riding-hood girl—the wolf would have known his foul stink anywhere. He tracked it quietly through the brush, stalking, savoring . . . the huntsman would pay for his crimes. Hideously! He would pay for his crimes against the wolf, against *all* wolves; he would pay for all hunters for all time!

The forest opened out into a clearing. And there in the center of the clearing stood the huntsman—and the *girl.* The big oaf had a knife in hand, drawn and raised as if he were about to pierce the girl's *innocent* heart—and then the little witch began to weep!

"Oh dear huntsman," she said, "leave me my life. I will run away into the wild forest, and never come home again."

The wolf would have laughed if he could have. But wolves of his blood never laugh, for there is no mirth inside them.

"The queen will take my life," the huntsman said. "I dare not leave you live."

The girl gave him a look that could have melted stone.

"But I am so small and so weak! If I ever should survive this wood, how could I find my way back to the castle? The Queen need never know you spared my life!"

She looked downright pensive—and she ought to be, the wolf thought.

"All right," he growled. *"Enough of this."*

And leapt through the air to devour the huntsman in a single gulp.

The girl swore when she saw him.

"What took you so long!?" she shouted as the huntsman's left boot vanished down the wolf's vast maw. "He could have *killed* me!"

The wolf smiled at her hungrily.

"Would've," he said, licking his chops.

And then said nothing more.

The wolf had known the girl was trouble from the moment he first set eyes on her. He knew it when he first saw her—and every solitary thing she did confirmed it, bit by bit by bit.

White skin, red lips—hair shimmery and black as coal. The girl was trouble. Trouble!

He was still in the chain-link pen that had been his prison for three long weeks (since the pathetic business with the pigs) when he first saw her. He was in the pen, and she was in the corridor outside, strolling toward him with that hapless oaf of a dogcatcher. She approached him purposely, directly, staring at him as though she knew who and what he was and exactly where he'd be.

She caught his eye and *smiled* at him.

"That's the one I want," she said, kneeling close before the prison, *smiling* as she looked him in the eye. "Call me Snow White," she said to the wolf. "You won't need my other names."

She spoke her words sweetly, and carried herself like a princess of all things innocent and pure—but the wolf saw through that clearly as all canae see into the hearts of men and women: there was an evil in that child that was deeper than the blackness of the wolf's own heart.

If the wolf had had a choice, he would have turned tail and run from her.

He surely would.

But he had no choice.

He stood chained and imprisoned in that fateful place, utterly unable to object:

the dogcatcher didn't care about the wolf's feelings in the matter, and it wouldn't have mattered if he *had* cared, because that man was deaf to the language of wolves and dogs, and thought that the wolf's speech was nothing but the yipping of a cur.

How he would pay, the wolf swore!—But he'd sworn that a thousand times, now, in the three weeks since the dogcatcher had caught him unawares as he howled mournfully outside the bricked fortress that was the house of the great pig—the brick sanctuary of the three pigs, stronghold of the third. And no matter how he swore he would revenge himself for the dogcatcher's indignities, the dogcatcher persisted, blithe, dim, hapless, and unafraid.

"*This* dog? Big, ugly, bad-tempered Fido? You're sure?"

"Yes," the girl said. "I'm certain he's the dog I want."

"You're out of your mind, young lady!—What would a pretty girl like you want with a mutt like that?"

"I am not Fido!" the wolf shrieked. *"And my blood is the pure true blood of the great war-wolves of the Iron Mountains! Slander me and* die!"

The dogcatcher hardly took notice of this. He kicked the wolf's cage and threatened him with the prod—but he did not deign to take his leering eyes off the girl.

"I'm going to call him Fifi, not Fido," the girl said. "I think it suits him."

As the wolf screamed mournfully to Diana, Goddess of the Moon, who is the secret patron of all wolves.

She left his prayer unanswered.

"I hope you have a muzzle for him," the dogcatcher said. "That mutt is *loud.*"

The girl had neither muzzle, the way it happened, nor any interest in acquiring one. The dogcatcher had equipped her with a leash and a choke collar for the wolf before he'd let the girl take him from the pound, but even these she used reluctantly. When they were out of sight of the pound, she knelt before the wolf and removed the leash. Oh how he savored that! The hunger, the slavering, the promise of her dainty bones crushing in his jaws. . . ! She put her hand to his throat, unfastening the leash; in a moment the collar would go, too—

And then the child did the thing he should have anticipated, but did not: She pressed her fingers through the thick fur of his coat. Found his skin and pressed something small and sharp and cruel into his flesh.

And then she cast her spell upon him.

Bear me bind me obey me

she chanted,

Defy me at your peril,
monster from the night.

And the wolf's heart froze.

He wanted to scream in rage, frustration, and fear. He knew what was to come, for he'd been bound to necromancy more than once before.

"You will suffer for that, child," the wolf said. *"I promise you you will."*

The girl frowned.

"And I promise you I'll slap your nose with a newspaper if you threaten me again!" she said.

The wolf tried to lunge at her, but his muscles defied him—they could not move against the charm she'd put upon him.

"Why, girl-child, why? Why have you bound me? Why have you sought me out?"

The girl smiled hungrily. "My step mom's up to no good," she said. "You know, the Wicked Queen? I don't trust her. And *you* are going to be my ace in the hole."

The wolf howled mournfully, but his Goddess still did not answer.

Fifi licked his chops again. "So greasy!" he complained. "And smelly, too. Next time you make me eat something, make sure it takes a bath first!"

Snow White gave him a cross look.

"Mind your manners, Fifi, or it's back to the pound for you! Didn't you learn your lesson in that story with the three pigs?—Oh, never mind. If you didn't learn following that blond with the red hat, you aren't ever going to learn."

"Stop calling me Fifi!" the wolf demanded.

Snow White smiled ruefully. "The name suits you," she said.

The girl brushed the dust off her dress and started deeper into the woods.

"Shouldn't we be going back to the castle?"

Snow White rolled her eyes. "And let that old bat try to poison me or something? No thanks! We'll find someplace else to stay."

The wolf didn't care much for this, since he'd grown fond of the table scraps available from the castle's kitchen. But he had no more choice about following the girl into the woods than he'd had about following her from the pound.

And so the girl and Fifi wandered deeper and deeper into the woods, till now they came upon the ruins of a straw house.

The wolf growled resentfully at the sight of them, for the memory was still fresh in him, then, and it enraged him.

But it did not enrage him as much as the ruins just beyond the next hillock—for those were the ruins of the wood house, and the events that had befallen him in that place were even farther beneath his dignity.

The wolf shuddered with rage as they passed the wooden ruin.

"I always thought you had bad breath," Snow White said. "Now I know."

Beyond the bend was a brick house, intact and occupied. Inside it there were three well-dressed pigs, watching television contentedly.

As Fifi edged up toward the brick house, the rage and hunger began to overcome his best judgment—for he had an awful and unquenchable impulse to jump through the window and devour the pigs, and in a moment the impulse would consume him—

"Don't get any ideas," Snow White said. "Those pigs are armed and dangerous."

As the largest of the pigs opened the window and leaned out, leveling a shotgun at the wolf.

"You'd better put a leash on that thing, lady," the great pig said. It was a vast, hungry, feral-looking pig, a pig that even the wolf could fear.

Snow White snorted indignantly. "Don't you pick on my Fifi," she said.

The wolf slunk away with his tail between his legs, muttering.

As the afternoon wore on, the Wicked Queen grew anxious.

She had instructed the huntsman explicitly—he was to return to her directly with Snow White's heart and liver, so that she could cook and eat them. Not even the Wicked Queen herself was entirely sure why she wanted to eat the poor girl's heart out; it could be that she was hungry, and unwilling to waste a meal; it could also be that she was just plain mean, which she certainly was.

"Where's my huntsman?" she muttered. "He should have come back by now! He's got my heart and liver, and I'm hungry!"

At last she turned to the mirror which she kept in a compact in her purse.

"Mirror, mirror in my hand, who's the fairest in this land?"

An ugly and loathsome countenance appeared in the mirror—a face as hideously ugly as the Wicked Queen was beautiful; a face as ugly as the shadow of her heart.

"Snow White. Next question?"

"Where is she?" the Wicked Queen demanded. "And where's my huntsman!? Where're my heart and liver?"

"She's wandering around the enchanted woods, looking for a place to stay. A wolf ate your huntsman. And your heart and liver are inside you, where they've always been."

"Oh!!!" cried the Wicked Queen. "You just can't get good help these days. You want something done, you have to do it yourself."

"I could have told you that a long time ago, if you'd bothered to ask," the mirror said.

"Enough from you," the Wicked Queen said, closing her compact and secreting it in her purse.

And so she dressed up as a peasant woman, so that she could avoid public scrutiny, and stomped out into the enchanted woods.

That wasn't the smartest thing that the Wicked Queen ever did. By a lot! They didn't call the Enchanted Forest an enchanted forest for nothing, after all. No sooner had she stepped into the forest than she found herself utterly lost and alone, completely confused and unable to get her bearings.

At great length she came to a small house made of gingerbread. As she approached it an Anthropophagous Witch came out to greet her, more as a matter of professional courtesy than out of any personal affection.

"Have you seen my huntsman?" the Wicked Queen asked. "He was supposed to bring me back a heart and lungs. I just love those hearts!"

The Anthropophagous Witch frowned. Even if professional courtesy obliged her to greet the Wicked Queen politely, she didn't like to see competition working her territory.

"Haven't seen him," the Anthropophagous Witch said. "But I could offer you some gingerbread."

The Wicked Queen, who knew exactly what that gingerbread was for, scowled. "I don't think so, deary," she said, "I'm hungry, but not hungry enough to end up on the wrong end of the food chain."

"Darn," the Anthropophagous Witch said. "Some days I just can't win."

And with that the Wicked Queen turned and stomped off into the forest, leaving the Anthropophagous Witch to her just desserts.

"She could've stayed for tea. It isn't like I bite. Er. Hmm. Well, it isn't like I chew!—Oh. Well. Maybe *some*times. . . ."

As something loud and clumsy stumbled through the brush at the edge of the forest, and Hansel emerged from the woods, followed by his sister Gretel.

The Anthropophagous Witch's eyes grew wide and bright with anticipation and delight, and she chortled quietly. "There they are!" she said. "And right on time."

With that the Anthropophagous Witch hurriedly ducked into her house, hoping to remain unobserved.

"Oh Gretel," Hansel exclaimed. "Look, look, a gingerbread house the size of a cottage!"

"Hansel, I think it *is* a cottage. Look, there's somebody in there, by the window. Nobody lives in a real gingerbread house!"

But Hansel, hungry and impetuous young lad that he was, had already snapped off a shutter and begun to gnosh on it. And the shutter was indeed made of gingerbread!

"You ought to try some, Gretel," he said, stuffing his face with a wide lump of iced windowsill. "It's awfully tasty!"

"Mark my word, Hansel," Gretel said, "No good will come of this." But she was starving, just as Hansel was, so Gretel elbowed her brother aside and set to work eating her way through the cottage wall.

In no time at all the two children had managed to eat their way through the cottage's living room wall, and now they began to grow logy from having overeaten.

"I'm tired, Gretel," Hansel said, looking not entirely unlike the pop-n-fresh doughboy. "I want to take a nap."

"Me too, Hansel," Gretel replied.

In a moment the two were snoring noisily just outside the ruptured living room of the gingerbread house.

"I've got them now," the Anthropophagous Witch said, rubbing her hands as she emerged from her hiding place inside the living room closet. "I'll be eating roast peasant tonight!"

And, indeed, she would have eaten well that night if Snow White and her pet wolf Fifi had not chosen that exact moment to emerge from the woods themselves.

"Oh," the Anthropophagous Witch said, catching Snow White's eye, "visitors! I *love* visitors!"

Fifi gave the Anthropophagous Witch a wary glance.

"With gravy and dumplings," he muttered.

"We were looking for a place to stay," Snow White said. "Can you direct us to a hotel? We're travel-weary and very tired."

"Hotels," the Anthropophagous Witch said. "Hmmmm. Hotels, hotels. I don't know of any . . . say! I could put you up, you know!"

"In salt and vinegar, with your vegetable preserves," the wolf said, *sotto voce.*

The Anthropophagous Witch turned a deaf ear to Fifi's comments. Snow White heard them clearly enough, but before she could react the entire moment slipped from everyone's grasp—as Gretel stirred enough in her sleep to open her eyes and see the Anthropophagous Witch, the wolf, and Snow White.

"Hansel!" she screamed. "Hansel, wake up, it's a monster!"

"No!" the Anthropophagous Witch shouted. "No no no no!"

Hansel woke, tubby and sputtering. "An *Anthropophagous Witch* and a monster!" he shouted, grabbing his sister's hand and dragging her away into the woods.

In a moment Hansel and Gretel had vanished into the woods, and the Anthropophagous Witch began to weep in frustration.

"I'll always be hungry—again," she wept. *"Always!"*

"Your name isn't Scarlet, is it?" Snow White asked her.

The Anthropophagous Witch favored her with an indignant glance. "My name is Abigail," she said. "And don't you forget it."

Hansel and Gretel ran wildly through the woods for most of twenty minutes before they came across the Wicked Queen, who sat on a large rock near a small, noisy stream, looking exhausted and confused.

"Kids," the Wicked Queen said, "I hate 'em."

"Gee," Hansel said, wild-eyed and breathless, "we don't hate you."

The Wicked Queen regarded him suspiciously.

"That's what my stepdaughter always said. I gave her the best years of my life!—Well, her governess did, anyway. And what did the little witch give me in return? She tried to eclipse me! Made herself prettier and prettier, till she started turning heads all over the kingdom! I was *born* to be a Beautiful Queen, not second fiddle to some little starlet!"

Gretel, who'd only then caught up with her brother, looked querulously at the beautifully Wicked Queen. "Surely the girl has no control over how beautiful she is? I mean, beauty is as beauty does, or something like that. I'm sure she doesn't mean to be prettier than you."

The Wicked Queen shook her head woefully. "You could never be more wrong, child," she said at last. "That girl's taken the mail-order course from the Enchantress' Guild. She knows exactly what she's doing!"

"Oh," said Gretel.

Hansel pried a stone loose from the meadow dirt with the toe of his left shoe. "I'm sure she doesn't mean anything by it," he said. "I mean, it isn't like she's trying to kill *you* or anything."

The Wicked Queen sneered at him. "You really think so? Ha! That nasty husband of mine, her father the king, is a real piece of work. How do you think the girl's mother died? You really believe that died-in-childbirth story? Ha! Ha again! He likes 'em young and pretty. And when I'm no longer the fairest in the land, I'll have an *accident* too."

With that the Wicked Queen began to weep dolefully as self-pity consumed her.

Gretel crept up to the Wicked Queen and gave her a hug. "There, there," she said.

"Have you considered hiring a good divorce lawyer?" Hansel asked. "I hear that they can do amazing things with restraining orders nowadays."

As the Wicked Queen's piteous weeping suddenly metamorphosed into a piercing, keening wail, and she began to go to pieces.

The wolf began to grow inpatient with the conversation between the girl and the Anthropophagous Witch the third time it looped around to start where it'd begun. *Oh,* the girl would say, *you never told me where I might find an inn!* And the Anthropophagous Witch would dissemble and obfuscate till the subject wandered to something else entirely.

"She's leading you on," the wolf said at last. *"You might as well just leave."*

"Hush, Fifi!" the girl said. "One more interruption from you and I *will* swat your nose with that newspaper!"

The Anthropophagous Witch favored him with an especially cross look. "One more from you," the witch said in unaccented High Canae, "and I'll cook your carcass beside hers."

This was a terrible mistake on the part of the Anthropophagous Witch, for it assumed that the princess Snow White had no ear for doggerel. And that was far from the truth! The princess spoke the tongue of wolves and dogs, and understood it well.

"Now you wait just a second, Little Mrs. Cannibal!" she said. "I won't have my dog speaking to you rudely—but I'm not about to let you threaten either of us."

"Well," said the witch, "I never!" and then, after a moment's reflection, "And what exactly are you threatening to do to *me,* child?"

"Fifi!" Snow White shouted.

And Fifi lunged.

And swallowed the witch whole.

After a long while, the Wicked Queen's sobs began to ease, and now she wiped her tears into her kerchief and stopped crying.

"Oh dear me, children," she said. "You're so right! And here all this time I thought divorce was out of the question!"

Gretel shook her head. "Of course it isn't," she said. "You need a women's shelter, that's all."

"And a lawyer," Hansel chimed in.

"A *good* lawyer," the Wicked Queen insisted, for no matter how sad and bereaved she might be, she was also a practical woman with an eye toward the future.

And so Hansel, Gretel, and the Wicked Queen set out across the Enchanted Forest in search of a women's shelter and a telephone that the Wicked Queen could use to call her lawyer.

"Well," Snow White said, "Now that Little Mrs. Cannibal is out of the way, we might as well stay here."

The wolf growled.

"I don't like it," he said. *"This place stinks of her. It promises a trap."*

"Oh, don't be silly," Snow White said, "What can she do to us now? She's dead!"

The wolf had no argument for her, but he knew how wrong she was, all the same.

"As you wish," he said. *"But I have warned you."*

Snow White went to the larder of the gingerbread house, fixed herself a big and satisfying meal, and took a nap on the witch's couch. After a long while, the wolf fell asleep on the floor beside her.

And that was his undoing, just as it had been during the episode with the seven kids—just as it had been when he'd ingested the Riding Hood girl's grandmother.

For he had swallowed both the huntsman and the Anthropophagous Witch whole, and without chewing either of them properly.

Worse, and more to the point, the huntsman had been holding a knife when the wolf devoured him. And no sooner had the wolf drifted off to sleep than the huntsman set about cutting his way out of the wolf's belly!

It wasn't easy going, for Fifi had a cast-iron stomach, but soon enough the huntsman managed to open up an aperture large enough to crawl through.

The Anthropophagous Witch followed him out, and when she was clear seven large stones fell out behind her, which in the long run was no small relief to the wolf, since he'd carried those rocks in his gullet for three years and a day, since the episode with the seven kids.

"Ick!" said the Anthropophagous Witch. "So messy!"

The huntsman gave her a sidelong glance. "Just count yourself lucky that the wolf wasn't listening when his mother told him to chew all his food completely," he said.

"Lucky, schmucky," said the Anthropophagous Witch. "When I'm done with these two they won't have the time to wish they knew how to chew their food."

She said this in something of a voluble tone of voice, which was a terrible mistake, since it woke Snow White—who screamed, mostly because the huntsman and the Anthropophagous Witch looked absolutely disgusting, covered as they were in stomach juice and bits of chewed up grass and all the other odd and repellant things one is liable to find inside the stomach of a wolf.

Screamed, and screamed, and screamed again. And finally shouted, *"Fifi!"* which woke the wolf and sent him charging at the recently disgorged pair. He'd've eaten them again, in fact, if his small intestine hadn't slipped out through the hole in his gullet and gotten caught up in his hind legs, causing the wolf to trip all over himself.

As it were.

Being practical and sensible folks, the huntsman and the Anthropophagous Witch took the opportunity before them to run for their lives.

While they still could.

Hansel, Gretel, and the Wicked Queen wandered through the forest for hours, over sharp stones and through cruel thorns and worse things, too—not so much for want of decent clear paths to walk upon as because none of them had the woods-sense to stay on the path.

Finally, toward late afternoon, they came upon a little house in the deep woods that was surrounded by forest flowers and shady gardens. The house belonged to the seven dwarfs, who were at that hour still working in their mine on the far side of the Enchanted Forest—which is to say it was a nice little place, considering that it was a bachelor pad, and it was very empty.

"I bet there's a phone in there," Hansel said, jimmying the window.

"Hansel!" the Wicked Queen shouted, scolding him, for no matter how wicked she was she was also a law-abiding citizen.

But law abiding or not, she was also a woman in a terrible position, and when Hansel slipped in through the living room window and came back out to let her and Gretel in through the front door, she walked into the dwarfs' cottage.

Thereby reducing herself to a common burglar, or at least a burglar's apprentice, for the breaking and entering laws apply as much in the Enchanted Forest as they do in town.

They found no telephone in the cottage, but they did find lots of small but neat and orderly furniture.

There was a little table with seven little plates, seven little spoons, seven little knives and forks, seven little mugs, and against the wall there were seven little beds, all freshly made.

The Wicked Queen was hungry and thirsty, and so were Hansel and Gretel, so they ate a few vegetables and a little bread from each little plate, and from each little glass they drank a drop of wine.

Well, maybe more than a dollop.

After all that food and wine, the three were all exhausted, and none-too-eager to wander out into the sunset in search of a telephone.

"If we wait, the folks who live here will come home and tell us where we can find a phone," Gretel said.

"Sure," Hansel said, yawning. "I'll wait."

He sat down on one of the small beds, and tried to make himself comfortable.

"Why not?" said the Wicked Queen, plonking herself down on the bed beside Hansel's.

In a moment all three of them were asleep on the little dwarf-beds, snoring like a trio of chainsaws.

Three and a half hours later, the dwarfs came home late from work in the mine, overtired and more than a little grouchy. They lit their seven little candles, and saw that strangers had been in their house.

The first one said, "Who's been sitting in my chair?"

The second one said, "Who's been eating from my plate?"

The third one said, "Who ate my bread?"

The fourth one said, "They didn't finish my vegetables!"

The fifth one said, "They got something icky all over my fork!"

The sixth one said, "It's on my knife, too!"

The seventh one said, "And in my mug!"

"Ewwww!" they cried in unison.

Which prompted the first dwarf to examine his bed. "Who stepped on my bed?" he demanded.

The second one chimed in, "And someone has been lying in my bed."

And so on until the fifth one, who found Gretel snoring loudly away in his bed, fast asleep.

Beside her was the beautiful and Wicked Queen.

Beside the Queen was Hansel.

The seven dwarfs all came running, and they cried out with amazement. They fetched their seven candles and looked at trio of fellow travelers.

"My God! My God!" they cried. "Will you look at that! Three of them!"

None of them liked having strangers in their beds, but they weren't the sort to chase off guests—even uninvited guests like these. So they ate what was left of their dinners quietly, and when the Wicked (but beautiful) Queen woke they spoke to her politely and with great interest.

"I've got to call my lawyer," the Wicked Queen told the seven little men. "Can you direct us to a telephone?"

The senior dwarf (whose name, contrary to what you may have heard, was *not* Stinky, and if you doubt me I suggest you try calling him that name to his face) the senior dwarf scratched his head.

"Us dwarfs don't have much use for telephones," he said. "Some people say we're still living in the Middle Ages!—But I think I saw a pay phone down by the truck stop on the far side of the mine."

"We can take you there in the morning," said the dwarf whose name really *was* Greasy, and for good cause. "Would you like me to show you the way? Huh huh huh?"

"Uhm," the Wicked Queen said. "Can I get back to you on that?"

It took Snow White most of three whole hours to untangle Fifi's guts from his legs, and most of another two to sew everything back together again. The wolf, fortunately, was made of Tougher Stuff Than Most, and Not Afraid of a Little Dirt, so he survived it well enough. But he certainly didn't enjoy it!

"Ouch," the wolf said. "Ouch ouch ouch."

"Stop your bellyaching, Fifi," said Snow White. "You aren't making this any easier."

"Gee," said the wolf. "I thought my part was hard enough."

Snow White scowled. "Not as hard as it could be!" she said, deliberately jabbing him in the rear with her sewing needle.

"Yow!" cried the wolf.

"See, I told you!"

Meanwhile, the huntsman and the Anthropophagous Witch were running for their lives, and running in a very straight line. After a while the huntsman realized that they were getting near the castle, and shouted to the witch:

"Follow me!" he shouted. "I think I know a way to get us out of here."

Whereupon he led the Anthropophagous Witch out of the Enchanted Forest, into the capital of the kingdom.

Now, it'd been a long long time since the Anthropophagous Witch had got to town—she was the sort of cannibal who can't abide crowds, or, more exactly, can't wander through a crowd without feeling and acting like a kid in a candy store, and no one takes it well when you drool over them cannibalistically in public.

Well, almost nobody. And those few who do enjoy that sort of thing were all in therapy that year.

"O huntsman," the Anthropophagous Witch said, just barely controlling herself, "What on earth have you led me into?"

"This is just the town, Mrs., um, Abigail," he told her. "We'll go to the castle in a moment and seek an audience with the king."

"The king? Whatever for?"

"Why, to tell him our tale. And to make sure the Wicked Queen doesn't return and try to seek revenge on us."

The Anthropophagous Witch sneered. "I wouldn't worry about her, deary," she said. "But keep your eye on that little girl—*she* is dangerous."

When the dwarfs were in their cups, the one who wasn't Stinky had an idea that delighted him to no end. "You don't have to go to the women's shelter," he told the Wicked Queen. "After you come back from calling your lawyer, you can come back here. We can put you up as long as need be—if you keep the place tidy for us, you'll more than pull your own weight."

"Um," said the Wicked Queen, for she wasn't much on housework, and foresaw herself on the King's Alimony, continuing to live a life in the style to which she'd become accustomed.

"You'd have the place to yourself most of the time," not-Stinky said. "We come home in the evening, and supper must be ready by then, but we spend the days digging for gold in the mine. You will be alone then. Watch out for the King! Don't let anybody in when we aren't here!"

"Um again," the Queen said, looking furtively to Hansel and Gretel for support or half a clue.

But they were both still fast asleep.

The huntsman and the Anthropophagous Witch didn't manage to get an audience with the king until well after dinner—and even that they only managed because the huntsman promised the Royal Steward that he had seriously nasty gossip about the Queen.

"The Queen is trying to kill your beloved daughter, O King," the huntsman said when they stood at last before the throne.

The king favored the huntsman with a jaundiced look.

"My daughter is a dangerous little minx herself," he said. "She can handle herself, I wager."

"It's worse than that," the witch chimed in. "A little bird told me that she's calling her lawyer and plans to take you to the cleaners."

"What!?" cried the King, rising to his feet. "She's calling *who?*"

In the morning The Wicked Queen (who'd grown a good deal less wicked by then) traveled with the dwarfs to the Enchanted Forest Exit Truckstop. Hansel and Gretel went with her, hoping to use the same phone to call their dad to come pick them up.

The calls went well enough—for the Wicked Queen, anyway. She managed to contact the law offices of Dewey, Cheatam, and Howe, and engage the services of Dick Cheatam, the firm's most senior divorce specialist.

"Don't you worry, Queenie baby," said the Dick (as he was affectionately known throughout the kingdom). "We'll take His Highness right to the cleaners for you."

"Can you recommend a good women's shelter?" she asked.

The Dick considered this for a moment. "You'd be better off with friends," he said at last. "Every shelter in the Kingdom operates under the King's protection and his seal. In your particular case, that might not be much help."

"Hmm," said the Wicked Queen, uncomfortably considering the proposition that the dwarf who was not Stinky had made to her.

"Can you do it?"

"Well," she said, "I guess. . . ."

Hansel's call to his dad was another matter altogether. For it was his nasty stepmother who picked up the phone on the other end, and the last thing she was about to do was send his father half-way across the Kingdom to retrieve him.

"You mean to tell me you're *still* alive, you little wretch?" she fumed. "What's it going to take to kill you? Do I have to get out the axe and cut you up myself?"

"Gee," Hansel said. "That doesn't sound like fun."

The truth about Hansel was that he was a pretty dim bulb, when you get right down to it.

"That's strange," said his nasty stepmother, "it sounds like an *awful* lot of fun to me!"

And with that she gave an evil, bone-chilling cackling laugh, and slammed the phone into its cradle, hanging up on poor Hansel.

"I wonder if the dwarfs could use a couple of extra gardeners?" he said, stunned and altogether taken aback.

At sunrise the King called for his ministers.

"I'm calling a war party," he said, rising from his throne to pace the length of the throne room. "The Queen has left the castle and called the best divorce lawyers in the land. This outrage will not stand!"

The Minister of War was the first to make the mistake of raising his objections. "But sire," he began, "knights and foot soldiers are for taking hills, not, ahm, tracts of land—"

The King motioned to one of this guards. Drew a finger across his throat, and then pointed at the Minster of War. In a moment the Minister's head and shoulders had parted ways forever at the neckline—the guard advanced; the minister screamed. The guard drew his sword and the minister's head went flying across the room as his body tumbled to the floor.

"Do I have any other objections to answer?" the King asked. "I assure you all, I am eager to address them."

"Not a one, sire," said the Minister of Education.

"Great plan, chief," said the Minister of Welfare.

"You Da Man," said the Minister of Justice.

"Brilliant, sire," said the Minister of State.

And so the King called his vast war party into existence: every knight in the land, every soldier in the realm, every blackguard, barbarian, and sell-sword for hire gathered in the forecourt of the castle keep to march off and do battle with the lawyers of the enemy.

The king brought his own Justice, too, of course—including his entire personal and executive legal staff, seven consulting attorneys, three hanging judges and a pair of headsmen.

And when they'd all gathered in the keep, the King lead his war party into the

Enchanted Forest, intending to be done with the Queen once and for all.

Hansel, Gretel, and the Wicked Queen got back to the dwarf house a little after ten in the morning. They would have gotten back a lot earlier—not-Stinky had had them at the truck-stop right up against the Crack of Dawn, and maybe even inside it—they would have gotten back a lot earlier, but Hansel had gotten hold of the map not-Stinky had drawn for them, and read it at right angles (and even upside down!) till he had them lost, lost again, and now turned utterly around.

No great wonder this kid's step-mom was trying to murder him by getting him lost in a forest. The Wicked Queen had half a mind to murder him herself. And letting him navigate was as sure a recipe for devastation as any she could imagine.

In the end she'd lost patience, seized the map, and led them back to the cottage herself. It didn't take long, once she had the reins.

"I'm tired," Hansel said as they stumbled into the dwarf house.

"I'm hungry," Gretel added.

"I told you you should have eaten at the truck stop while you could," the Wicked Queen told them.

Gretel made a face. "Who could eat in *that* greasy spoon? Even the roaches in that place were sick with food poisoning!"

"Pshaw, young lady! I'll have you know that that is the single finest Enchanted Truck-Stop Dining Area in the entire kingdom!"

Hansel rolled his eyes. "It's the *only* Enchanted Truck-Stop Dining Area in the kingdom," he said. "Heck, it's the only truck-stop in the kingdom. We don't have many highways here in the Middle Ages."

"Well, yeah," said the Wicked Queen. "But you're confusing the truth with facts! You'll make a mess of things that way."

Hansel sputtered three times, and was about to reply almost as senselessly as the Queen had, when suddenly a bird—a wren, or maybe it was a sparrow, neither Hansel nor the Wicked Queen knew their ornithology—suddenly a bird appeared on the windowsill and began to speak to him.

"The King has gathered a vast army," the little bird said, "and is leading it through the Enchanted Forest to capture you."

"Goodness," Hansel said. "What'd we do this time?"

The bird squawked.

"Not *you,* you little fool! The Queen! The Queen! He's going to make her dance in shoes as hot as branding irons!"

"Oh no," the Wicked Queen said, looking quietly scared out of her mind. "I have to run," she said.

"There's no time to run," Gretel pointed out.

"Then we'll have to hide her," Hansel said.

And they spent most of ten long minutes looking around the dwarf house and the surrounding woods, but there was no hiding place in any of that fit to shelter anything larger than a dwarf.

And probably for cause.

At length Hansel made room for the Wicked Queen inside the dwarfs' closet—no mean task, since the closet was about as full of skeletons as you can imagine.

It was terribly uncomfortable in that closet—it was small and cramped, and the skeletons, bony as they were, poked her like a dozen dozen elbows. Worse, she'd've sworn there were *live* dwarfs in there with her, as if they hadn't heard that things were cool nowadays and *every*body was supposed to come out of the closet and make an appearance on the *Jerry Springer Show*, if appropriate.

When the little bird had spoken its peace to Hansel, Gretel, and the Wicked Queen, it flew off directly to royal assemblage, intent on telling its tale directly to the King.

"The Queen is in the closet," the bird said. "In the dwarf house? You know the place where all seven of those little guys live?—She's in there with all the other skeletons the little guys have in their closet."

"I knew it," the King said. "Living in a state of ill repute with seven men."

"I wouldn't call them men," the bird replied, but by then the King was no longer listening. He was off among his knights, shouting orders and demanding fealty.

"We're going to storm that hill," the King shouted. "And then we'll demolish the cottage on the far side of it."

"Demolish. . . ?" asked the Silver Knight. "I don't understand. We're going to war against a cottage?"

The King made the neck-and-pointing sign at the Silver Knight, and in a moment he was in pieces, scattered across the forest floor.

"Anyone else here have trouble following simple instructions?" he asked.

"Not me, sire!"

"No sir!"

"Not a bit. You point, we storm."

"You direct, we wreck!"

"You Da Man, Kingy Baby!"

As the king and his minions stormed the hill and descended on the cottage, shredding it. Walls, furniture, pots, pans, and, most especially, skeletons went flying everywhere—literally and figuratively.

Hansel, brave lad that he was, tried to warn them off. But he was only one brave lad, and anyway he wasn't armed; when he stood up to the charging knights and warned them away, they ignored him.

And kept ignoring him, as he told them to go pick on something that could fight back, instead of tearing up the poor dwarfs' house.

Not that the knights (or the King) listened. They reduced the dwarf house to so much litter and debris, and when they were done the Wicked Queen stood alone in the center of a great pile of skeletons, looking scared out of her mind.

"Men!" she cried. "Can't you all just go away and leave a poor woman alone?"

"That's enough from you, trollop," said the King, who grabbed his wife by the wrist and proceeded to lead her up onto the hilltop. "Light a bonfire," he commanded, "and warm up her iron dancing shoes!"

"Robert!" she shouted, "do you know what my lawyer is going to do with this? Can you say spousal abuse? I knew you could."

"Silence, Darla! I am Justice in this land! You will do as my court commands!"

"Just *wait* till my lawyer gets ahold of you, Robert. Just *wait!* You're going to be sooooo sorry, I promise you."

"Silence, woman!" the King demanded. He gestured at his knights. "Assemble the courtroom! Bring on the jury!"

"And the witnesses," a small voice said from somewhere a thousand times closer than anyone expected.

The Wicked Queen gasped.

"Snow White," she said, in a voice even smaller than the girl's. "You've come for your revenge."

The girl smiled.

"Maybe," she said. "Maybe not."

"Snow White," said the King, "What are you doing here, child? This court is no place for a beautiful young lady like you."

The girl bit her lip.

"Somebody's got to stop you, Daddy," she said. "It just isn't right, is all."

"You tell him!" shouted the Wicked Queen.

"What do you mean, child?" asked the King, looking genuinely wounded.

"I mean, she's just afraid, is all," said the girl. "And who wouldn't be, after you killed my mother when she got middle aged and dumpy and *pregnant!?*"

The Wicked Queen gasped. So did most of the knights in earshot.

The King had a look on his face like he'd been hit with a mallet.

"What an awful thing to say," the King said at last. "Your mother died in childbirth, child. I'd never have harmed a hair on her head."

"Yeah, right," Snow White said. "Just like you'd've said you'd never hurt *this* wife if I'd asked you a week ago. But look at you! Dragging her up the hill, manhandling her! And where did you get those branding shoes? They look *used,* Daddy. Who did you use those shoes on the last time? Huh?"

"You men are all the same," the Wicked Queen said.

"Through and through," the Anthropophagous Witch chimed in. "And I ought to know, tee hee, tee hee."

"Goodness," the King said. He looked genuinely hurt—mortified, in fact.

"Ahem," said the hanging judge, who'd taken his position before the court. "If the litigants are prepared, I believe we can proceed. . . ."

"We are indeed," said the Dick, who'd appeared out of nowhere (as greasy lawyers are wont to do) only moments before. "If your honor will examine my brief. . . ."

The King blinked twice, then clapped his hands. Three dozen of the Kingdom's finest lawyers—anthropomorphed sharks, every last one of them—appeared immediately at his side. He led them presently aside to huddle.

"What's all this about?" the King asked. "Who's this man with the briefs? I'd just as soon boxers, myself, but in his case I don't honestly want to know!"

The lead shark shook his head. "No, sire," he said. "He has a legal brief in hand. Methinks he means to take you to the cleaners."

The King let out an exasperated sigh. "We have our own cleaners in the palace," he said. "And when they fail to do their work we behead them—as often we must. I have no need for this lawyer's out-sourced cleansing."

The shark shook it great sandpapery head. "No, sire," he repeated. "I mean to say she wants to take you for every penny you've got."

The King sighed.

"I could have told you that," he said. "Women! They're all the same."

"What a thing to say!" said Snow White, his daughter, who'd somehow wormed her way into the legalistic conclave.

The King threw up his hands. "Not you, child! You're my *daughter*, for God's sake!"

"And a woman, too."

"I'd say that you were still a girl," the King allowed. "But even so I take your point. What's behind it? Do you have a case to make, or are you here simply to bedevil me in my moment of forensic extremis?"

The girl shook her head. "You aren't a bad man, Daddy. I love you very much. But your judgment isn't always what it should be—you don't belong in charge of things."

"Child!" the King said, "You wound me!"

"You wound a lot of people, daddy. Look at the sharks you have working for you!"

And the lawyers were indeed sharks, and sharks of the hungriest and most fearsome breeds.

"My legal team is the finest in the land," the King insisted. "There are none better."

"You need to retire, Daddy."

"Retire?"

"Abdicate, Daddy. Pass the crown on, take a nice comfy cottage in the woods, and enjoy the pleasures that the world affords."

The King gaped, and kept gaping; he stood stunned and silent for the longest time.

"But what about your stepmother, the Wicked Queen?" he said at last. "What of her?"

Snow White rolled her inky eyes.

"Offer her a decent settlement. She'll go away quietly."

And the Queen did indeed accept the King's settlement. She took her money, bought a nice little cottage a few blocks from the House of the Great Pig, and made a comfortable and happy retirement for herself.

Hansel and Gretel stayed with her for a few weeks before they tried to find their way home to their dad and evil step mom, but always got lost no matter how they tried. Eventually they found their way back to the Queen's cottage, and she took them on as servants. They're still there, tending the gardens, cooking, tidying up around the house; their mistress is quite fond of them.

The seven dwarfs were thoroughly insured. When they got home and found their home in tatters, they immediately called their State Forest insurance agent, and he got them a check before sunrise.

With the insurance money in hand, they rebuilt their homey little house, this time with All Modern Conveniences, including a sun roof and a dish washer and a garbage disposal.

The King did indeed abdicate his throne. But he didn't go quietly into retirement! Far from it. When last seen, he was in Monte Carlo, living it up and dating all the pretty girls. It's a natural fact that he's a happy man.

Snow White, who inherited the Kingdom? She rules well enough, but there are those who say she's a little overbearing.

The real winner in all of this, though, is Fifi.

Fifi the wolf is Top Dog in the castle, and eats whatever he pleases.

Mostly he likes pork: ribs, bacon, butt roasts. Country sausage! Pork chops! And he's very choosy about which pigs the butcher slaughters for him.

The Faery Handbag

Kelly Link

Kelly Link is the author of three collections of short stories, *Stranger Things Happen*, *Magic for Beginners*, and *Pretty Monsters*. Her short stories have won three Nebulas, a Hugo, and a World Fantasy Award. She was born in Miami, Florida, and once won a free trip around the world by answering the question "Why do you want to go around the world?" ("Because you can't go through it.")

Not a story about any particular fairytale, Link nonetheless infuses the story with all the petty maliciousness that seems to follow fairies around. They're nothing but trouble and you just think people would know better and leave fairies alone. But, as Link shows us, people just don't learn.

I used to go to thrift stores with my friends. We'd take the train into Boston, and go to The Garment District, which is this huge vintage clothing warehouse. Everything is arranged by color, and somehow that makes all of the clothes beautiful. It's kind of like if you went through the wardrobe in the Narnia books, only instead of finding Aslan and the White Witch and horrible Eustace, you found this magic clothing world—instead of talking animals, there were feather boas and wedding dresses and bowling shoes, and paisley shirts and Doc Martens and everything hung up on racks so that first you have black dresses, all together, like the world's largest indoor funeral, and then blue dresses—all the blues you can imagine—and then red dresses and so on. Pink reds and orangey reds and purple reds and exit-light reds and candy reds. Sometimes I would close my eyes and Natasha and Natalie and Jake would drag me over to a rack, and rub a dress against my hand. "Guess what color this is."

We had this theory that you could learn how to tell, just by feeling, what color something was. For example, if you're sitting on a lawn, you can tell what color green the grass is, with your eyes closed, depending on how silky-rubbery it feels. With clothing, stretchy velvet stuff always feels red when your eyes are closed, even if it's not red. Natasha was always best at guessing colors, but Natasha is also best at cheating at games and not getting caught.

One time we were looking through kids' T-shirts and we found a Muppets T-shirt that had belonged to Natalie in third grade. We knew it belonged to her, because it still had her name inside, where her mother had written it in permanent marker when Natalie went to summer camp. Jake bought it back for her, because he was the only one who had money that weekend. He was the only one who had a job.

Maybe you're wondering what a guy like Jake is doing in The Garment District with a bunch of girls. The thing about Jake is that he always has a good time, no matter what he's doing. He likes everything, and he likes everyone, but he likes me best of all. Wherever he is now, I bet he's having a great time and wondering when I'm going to show up. I'm always running late. But he knows that.

We had this theory that things have life cycles, the way that people do. The life cycle of wedding dresses and feather boas and T-shirts and shoes and handbags involves The Garment District. If clothes are good, or even if they're bad in an interesting way, The Garment District is where they go when they die. You can tell that they're dead, because of the way that they smell. When you buy them, and wash them, and start wearing them again, and they start to smell like you, that's when they reincarnate. But the point is, if you're looking for a particular thing, you just have to keep looking for it. You have to look hard.

Down in the basement at The Garment District they sell clothing and beat-up suitcases and teacups by the pound. You can get eight pounds' worth of prom dresses—a slinky black dress, a poufy lavender dress, a swirly pink dress, a silvery, starry lamé dress so fine you could pass it through a key ring—for eight dollars. I go there every week, hunting for Grandmother Zofia's faery handbag.

The faery handbag: It's huge and black and kind of hairy. Even when your eyes are closed, it feels black. As black as black ever gets, like if you touch it, your hand might get stuck in it, like tar or black quicksand or when you stretch out your hand at night, to turn on a light, but all you feel is darkness.

Fairies live inside it. I know what that sounds like, but it's true.

Grandmother Zofia said it was a family heirloom. She said that it was over two hundred years old. She said that when she died, I had to look after it. Be its guardian. She said that it would be my responsibility.

I said that it didn't look that old, and that they didn't have handbags two hundred years ago, but that just made her cross. She said, "So then tell me, Genevieve, darling, where do you think old ladies used to put their reading glasses and their heart medicine and their knitting needles?"

I know that no one is going to believe any of this. That's okay. If I thought you would, then I couldn't tell you. Promise me that you won't believe a word. That's what Zofia used to say to me when she told me stories. At the funeral, my mother said, half-laughing and half-crying, that her mother was the world's best liar. I think she thought maybe Zofia wasn't really dead. But I went up to Zofia's coffin, and I looked her right in the eyes. They were closed. The funeral parlor had made her up with blue eyeshadow, and blue eyeliner. She looked like she was going to be a news anchor on Fox television, instead of dead. It was creepy and it made me even sadder than I already was. But I didn't let that distract me.

"Okay, Zofia," I whispered. "I know you're dead, but this is important. You know exactly how important this is. Where's the handbag? What did you do with it? How do I find it? What am I supposed to do now?"

Of course, she didn't say a word. She just lay there, this little smile on her face, as if she thought the whole thing—death, blue eyeshadow, Jake, the handbag, faeries, Scrabble, Baldeziwurlekistan, all of it—was a joke. She always did have a weird sense of humor. That's why she and Jake got along so well.

I grew up in a house next door to the house where my mother lived when she was a little girl. Her mother, Zofia Swink, my grandmother, babysat me while my mother and father were at work.

Zofia never looked like a grandmother. She had long black hair, which she plaited up in spiky towers. She had large blue eyes. She was taller than my father. She looked like a spy or ballerina or a lady pirate or a rock star. She acted like one too. For example, she never drove anywhere. She rode a bike. It drove my mother crazy. "Why can't you act your age?" she'd say, and Zofia would just laugh.

Zofia and I played Scrabble all the time. Zofia always won, even though her English wasn't all that great, because we'd decided that she was allowed to use Baldeziwurleki vocabulary. Baldeziwurlekistan is where Zofia was born, over two hundred years ago. That's what Zofia said. (My grandmother claimed to be over two hundred years old. Or maybe even older. Sometimes she claimed that she'd even met Genghis Khan. He was much shorter than her. I probably don't have time to tell that story.) Baldeziwurlekistan is also an incredibly valuable word in Scrabble points, even though it doesn't exactly fit on the board. Zofia put it down the first time we played. I was feeling pretty good because I'd gotten forty-one points for *zippery* on my turn.

Zofia kept rearranging her letters on her tray. Then she looked over at me, as if daring me to stop her, and put down *eziwurlekistan,* after *bald.* She used *delicious, zippery, wishes, kismet,* and *needle,* and made *to* into *toe. Baldeziwurlekistan* went all the way across the board and then trailed off down the righthand side.

I started laughing.

"I used up all my letters," Zofia said. She licked her pencil and started adding up points.

"That's not a word," I said. "*Baldeziwurlekistan* is not a word. Besides, you can't do that. You can't put an eighteen-letter word on a board that's fifteen squares across."

"Why not? It's a country," Zofia said. "It's where I was born, little darling."

"Challenge," I said. I went and got the dictionary and looked it up. "There's no such place."

"Of course there isn't nowadays," Zofia said. "It wasn't a very big place, even when it was a place. But you've heard of Samarkand, and Uzbekistan and the Silk Road and Genghis Khan. Haven't I told you about meeting Genghis Khan?"

I looked up Samarkand. "Okay," I said. "Samarkand is a real place. A real word. But Baldeziwurlekistan isn't."

"They call it something else now," Zofia said. "But I think it's important to remember where we come from. I think it's only fair that I get to use Baldeziwurleki words. Your English is so much better than me. Promise me something, mouthful of dumpling, a small, small thing. You'll remember its real name. Baldeziwurlekistan. Now when I add it up, I get three hundred and sixty-eight points. Could that be right?"

If you called the faery handbag by its right name, it would be something like *orzipanikanikcz,* which means the "bag of skin where the world lives," only Zofia never spelled that word the same way twice. She said you had to spell it a little differently each time. You never wanted to spell it exactly the right way, because that would be dangerous.

I called it the faery handbag because I put *faery* down on the Scrabble board once. Zofia said that you spelled it with an *i,* not an *e.* She looked it up in the dictionary, and lost a turn.

Zofia said that in Baldeziwurlekistan they used a board and tiles for divination, prognostication, and sometimes even just for fun. She said it was a little like playing Scrabble. That's probably why she turned out to be so good at Scrabble. The Baldeziwurlekistanians used their tiles and board to communicate with the people who lived under the hill. The people who lived under the hill knew the future. The Baldeziwurlekistanians gave them fermented milk and honey, and the young women of the village used to go and lie out on the hill and sleep under the stars. Apparently the people under the hill were pretty cute. The important thing was that you never went down into the hill and spent the night there, no matter how cute the guy from under the hill was. If you did, even if you spent only a single night under the hill, when you came out again, a hundred years might have passed. "Remember that," Zofia said to me. "It doesn't matter how cute a guy is. If he wants you to come back to his place, it isn't a good idea. It's okay to fool around, but don't spend the night."

Every once in a while, a woman from under the hill would marry a man from the village, even though it never ended well. The problem was that the women under the hill were terrible cooks. They couldn't get used to the way time worked in the village, which meant that supper always got burnt, or else it wasn't cooked long enough. But they couldn't stand to be criticized. It hurt their feelings. If their village husband complained, or even if he looked like he wanted to complain, that was it. The woman from under the hill went back to her home, and even if her husband went and begged and pleaded and apologized, it might be three years or thirty years or a few generations before she came back out.

Even the best, happiest marriages between the Baldeziwurlekistanians and the people under the hill fell apart when the children got old enough to complain about dinner. But everyone in the village had some hill blood in them.

"It's in you," Zofia said, and kissed me on the nose. "Passed down from my grandmother and her mother. It's why we're so beautiful."

When Zofia was nineteen, the shaman-priestess in her village threw the tiles and discovered that something bad was going to happen. A raiding party was coming. There was no point in fighting them. They would burn down everyone's houses and take the young men and women for slaves. And it was even worse than that. There was going to be an earthquake as well, which was bad news because usually, when raiders showed up, the village went down under the hill for a night and when they came out again, the raiders would have been gone for months or decades or even a hundred years. But this earthquake was going to split the hill right open.

The people under the hill were in trouble. Their home would be destroyed, and they would be doomed to roam the face of the earth, weeping and lamenting their fate until the sun blew out and the sky cracked and the seas boiled and the people dried up and turned to dust and blew away. So the shaman-priestess went and divined some more, and the people under the hill told her to kill a black dog and skin it and use the skin to make a purse big enough to hold a chicken, an egg, and a cooking pot. So she did, and then the people under the hill made the inside of the purse big enough to hold all of the village and all of the people under the hill and mountains and forests and seas and rivers and lakes and orchards and a sky and stars and spirits and fabulous monsters and sirens and dragons and dryads and mermaids and beasties and all the little gods that the Baldeziwurlekistanians and the people under the hill worshipped.

"Your purse is made out of dog skin?" I said. "That's disgusting!"

"Little dear pet," Zofia said, looking wistful, "Dog is delicious. To Baldeziwurlekistanians, dog is a delicacy."

Before the raiding party arrived, the village packed up all of their belongings and moved into the handbag. The clasp was made out of bone. If you opened it one way, then it was just a purse big enough to hold a chicken and an egg and a clay cooking pot, or else a pair of reading glasses and a library book and a pillbox. If you opened the clasp another way, then you found yourself in a little boat floating at the mouth of a river. On either side of you was forest, where the Baldeziwurlekistanian villagers and the people under the hill made their new settlement.

If you opened the handbag the wrong way, though, you found yourself in a dark land that smelled like blood. That's where the guardian of the purse (the dog whose skin had been been sewn into a purse) lived. The guardian had no skin. Its howl made blood come out of your ears and nose. It tore apart anyone who turned the clasp in the opposite direction and opened the purse in the wrong way.

"Here is the wrong way to open the handbag," Zofia said. She twisted the clasp, showing me how she did it. She opened the mouth of the purse, but not very wide, and held it up to me. "Go ahead, darling, and listen for a second."

I put my head near the handbag, but not too near. I didn't hear anything. "I don't hear anything," I said.

"The poor dog is probably asleep," Zofia said. "Even nightmares have to sleep now and then."

After he got expelled, everybody at school called Jake Houdini instead of Jake. Everybody except for me. I'll explain why, but you have to be patient. It's hard work telling everything in the right order.

Jake is smarter and also taller than most of our teachers. Not quite as tall as me. We've known each other since third grade. Jake has always been in love with me. He says he was in love with me even before third grade, even before we ever met. It took me a while to fall in love with Jake.

In third grade, Jake knew everything already, except how to make friends. He used to follow me around all day long. It made me so mad that I kicked him in the knee. When that didn't work, I threw his backpack out the window of the school bus. That didn't work either, but the next year Jake took some tests and the school decided that he could skip fourth and fifth grade. Even I felt sorry for Jake then. Sixth grade didn't work out. When the sixth graders wouldn't stop flushing his head down the toilet, he went out and caught a skunk and set it loose in the boys' locker room.

The school was going to suspend him for the rest of the year, but instead Jake took two years off while his mother homeschooled him. He learned Latin and Hebrew and Greek, how to write sestinas, how to make sushi, how to play bridge, and even how to knit. He learned fencing and ballroom dancing. He worked in a soup kitchen and made a Super 8 movie about Civil War reenactors who play extreme croquet in full costume instead of firing off cannons. He started learning how to play guitar. He even wrote a novel. I've never read it—he says it was awful.

When he came back two years later, because his mother had cancer for the first time, the school put him back with our year, in seventh grade. He was still way too smart, but he was finally smart enough to figure out how to fit in. Plus he was good at soccer and he was yummy. Did I mention that he played guitar? Every girl in school had a crush on Jake, but he used to come home after school with me and play Scrabble with Zofia and ask her about Baldeziwurlekistan.

Jake's mom was named Cynthia. She collected ceramic frogs and knock-knock jokes. When we were in ninth grade, she had cancer again. When she died, Jake smashed all of her frogs. That was the first funeral I ever went to. A few months later, Jake's father asked Jake's fencing teacher out on a date. They got married right after the school expelled Jake for his AP project on Houdini. That was the first wedding I ever went to. Jake and I stole a bottle of wine and drank it, and I threw up in the swimming pool at the country club. Jake threw up all over my shoes.

So, anyway, the village and the people under the hill lived happily ever after for a few weeks in the handbag, which they had tied around a rock in a dry well that the people under the hill had determined would survive the earthquake. But some of the Baldeziwurlekistanians wanted to come out again and see what was going on in the world. Zofia was one of them. It had been summer when they went into the bag, but when they came out again, and climbed out of the well, snow was falling and their village was ruins and crumbly old rubble. They walked through the snow, Zofia carrying the handbag, until they came to another village, one that they'd never seen before. Everyone in that village was packing up their belongings and leaving, which gave Zofia and her friends a bad feeling. It seemed to be just the same as when they went into the handbag.

They followed the refugees, who seemed to know where they were going, and finally everyone came to a city. Zofia had never seen such a place. There were trains and electric lights and movie theaters, and there were people shooting each other. Bombs were falling. A war going on. Most of the villagers decided to climb right back inside the handbag, but Zofia volunteered to stay in the world and look after the handbag. She had fallen in love with movies and silk stockings and with a young man, a Russian deserter.

Zofia and the Russian deserter married and had many adventures and finally came to America, where my mother was born. Now and then Zofia would consult the tiles and talk to the people who lived in the handbag and they would tell her how best to avoid trouble and how she and her husband could make some money. Every now and then one of the Baldeziwurlekistanians or one of the people from under the hill came out of the handbag and wanted to go grocery shopping, or to a movie or an amusement park to ride on roller coasters, or to the library.

The more advice Zofia gave her husband, the more money they made. Her husband became curious about Zofia's handbag, because he could see that there was something odd about it, but Zofia told him to mind his own business. He began to spy on Zofia, and saw that strange men and women were coming in and out of the house. He became convinced that either Zofia was a spy for the Communists, or maybe that she was having affairs. They fought and he drank more and more, and finally he threw away her divination tiles. "Russians make bad husbands," Zofia told me. Finally, one night while Zofia was sleeping, her husband opened the bone clasp and climbed inside the handbag.

"I thought he'd left me," Zofia said. "For almost twenty years I thought he'd left me and your mother and taken off for California. Not that I minded. I was tired of being married and cooking dinners and cleaning house for someone else. It's better to cook what I want to eat, and clean up when I decide to clean up. It was harder on your mother, not having a father. That was the part that I minded most.

"Then it turned out that he hadn't run away after all. He spent one night in the handbag and came out again twenty years later, exactly as handsome as I remembered, and enough time had passed that I had forgiven him all the quarrels. We made up and it was all very romantic and then when we had another fight the next morning, he went and kissed your mother, who had slept right through his visit, on the cheek, and then he climbed right back inside the handbag. I didn't see him again for another twenty years. The last time he showed up, we went to see *Star Wars* and he liked it so much that he went back inside the handbag to tell everyone else about it. In a couple of years they'll all show up and want to see it on video and all of the sequels too."

"Tell them not to bother with the prequels," I said.

The thing about Zofia and libraries is that she's always losing library books. She says that she hasn't lost them, and in fact that they aren't even overdue, really. It's just that even one week inside the faery handbag is a lot longer in library-world time. So what is she supposed to do about it? The librarians all hate Zofia. She's banned from using any of the branches in our area. When I was eight, she got me to go to the library for her and check out biographies and science books and Georgette Heyer romance novels. My mother was livid when she found out, but it was too late. Zofia had already misplaced most of them.

It's really hard to write about somebody as if they're really dead. I still think Zofia must be sitting in her living room, in her house, watching some old horror movie, dropping popcorn into her handbag. She's waiting for me to come over and play Scrabble.

Nobody is ever going to return those library books now.

My mother used to come home from work and roll her eyes. "Have you been telling them your fairy stories?" she'd say. "Genevieve, your grandmother is a horrible liar."

Zofia would fold up the Scrabble board and shrug at me and Jake. "I'm a wonderful liar," she'd say. "I'm the best liar in the world. Promise me you won't believe a single word."

But she wouldn't tell the story of the faery handbag to Jake. Only the old Baldeziwurlekistanian folktales and fairy tales about the people under the hill. She told him about how she and her husband made it all the way across Europe, hiding in haystacks and in barns. What she told me was how once, when her husband went off to find food, a farmer found her hiding in his chicken coop and tried to rape her. But she opened up the faery handbag in the way she showed me, and the dog came out and ate the farmer and all his chickens too.

She was teaching Jake and me how to curse in Baldeziwurleki. I also know how to say *I love you,* but I'm not going to ever say it to anyone again, except to Jake, when I find him.

When I was eight, I believed everything Zofia told me. By the time I was thirteen, I didn't believe a single word. When I was fifteen, I saw a man come out of her house and get on Zofia's three-speed bicycle and ride down the street. He wore funny clothes. He was a lot younger than my mother and father, and even though I'd never seen him before, he was familiar. I followed him on my bike, all the way to the grocery store. I waited just past the checkout lanes while he bought peanut butter, Jack Daniel's, half a dozen instant cameras, and at least sixty packs of Reese's peanut butter cups, three bags of Hershey's Kisses, a handful of Milky Way bars and other stuff from the rack of checkout candy. While the checkout clerk was helping him bag up all of that chocolate, he looked up and saw me. "Genevieve?" he said. "That's your name, right?"

I turned and ran out of the store. He grabbed up the bags and ran after me. I don't even think he got his change back. I was still running away, and then one of the straps on my flip-flops popped out of the sole, the way they do, and that made me really angry so I just stopped. I turned around.

"Who are you?" I said.

But I already knew. He looked like he could have been my mom's younger brother. He was really cute. I could see why Zofia had fallen in love with him.

His name was Rustan. Zofia told my parents that he was an expert in Baldeziwurlekistanian folklore who would be staying with her for a few days. She brought him over for dinner. Jake was there too, and I could tell that Jake knew something was up. Everybody except my dad knew something was going on.

"You mean Baldeziwurlekistan is a real place?" my mother asked Rustan. "My mother is telling the truth?"

I could see that Rustan was having a hard time with that one. He obviously wanted to say that his wife was a horrible liar, but then where would he be? Then he couldn't be the person that he was supposed to be.

There were probably a lot of things that he wanted to say. What he said was, "This is really good pizza."

Rustan took a lot of pictures at dinner. The next day I went with him to get the pictures developed. He'd brought back some film with him, with pictures he'd taken inside the faery handbag, but those didn't come out well. Maybe the film was too old. We got doubles of the pictures from dinner so that I could have some too. There's a great picture of Jake, sitting outside on the porch. He's laughing, and he has his hand up to his mouth, like he's going to catch the laugh. I have that picture up on my computer, and also up on my wall over my bed.

I bought a Cadbury Creme Egg for Rustan. Then we shook hands and he kissed me once on each cheek. "Give one of those kisses to your mother," he said, and I thought about how the next time I saw him, I might be Zofia's age, and he would be only a few days older. The next time I saw him, Zofia would be dead. Jake and I might have kids. That was too weird.

I know Rustan tried to get Zofia to go back with him, to live in the handbag, but she wouldn't.

"It makes me dizzy in there," she used to tell me. "And they don't have movie theaters. And I have to look after your mother and you. Maybe when you're old enough to look after the handbag, I'll poke my head inside, just long enough for a little visit."

I didn't fall in love with Jake because he was smart. I'm pretty smart myself. I know that smart doesn't mean nice, or even mean that you have a lot of common sense. Look at all the trouble smart people get themselves into.

I didn't fall in love with Jake because he could make maki rolls and had a black belt in fencing, or whatever it is that you get if you're good in fencing. I didn't fall in love with Jake because he plays guitar. He's a better soccer player than he is a guitar player.

Those were the reasons why I went out on a date with Jake. That, and because he asked me. He asked if I wanted to go see a movie, and I asked if I could bring my grandmother and Natalie and Natasha. He said sure and so all five of us sat and watched *Bring It On* and every once in a while Zofia dropped a couple of Milk Duds or some popcorn into her purse. I don't know if she was feeding the dog, or if she'd opened the purse the right way, and was throwing food at her husband.

I fell in love with Jake because he told stupid knock-knock jokes to Natalie, and told Natasha that he liked her jeans. I fell in love with Jake when he took me and Zofia home. He walked her up to her front door and then he walked me up to mine. I fell in love with Jake when he didn't try to kiss me. The thing is, I was nervous about the whole kissing thing. Most guys think that they're better at it than they really are. Not that I think I'm a real genius at kissing either, but I don't think kissing should be a competitive sport. It isn't tennis.

Natalie and Natasha and I used to practice kissing with each other. Just for practice. We got pretty good at it. We could see why kissing was supposed to be fun.

But Jake didn't try to kiss me. Instead he just gave me this really big hug. He put his face in my hair and he sighed. We stood there like that, and then finally I said, "What are you doing?"

"I just wanted to smell your hair," he said.

"Oh," I said. That made me feel weird, but in a good way. I stuck my nose in his hair, which is brown and curly. I smelled it. We stood there and smelled each other's hair, and I felt so good. I felt so happy.

Jake said into my hair, "Do you know that actor John Cusack?"

I said, "Yeah. One of Zofia's favorite movies is *Better Off Dead.* We watch it all the time."

"So he likes to go up to women and smell their armpits."

"Gross!" I said. "That's such a lie! What are you doing now? That tickles."

"I'm smelling your ear," Jake said.

Jake's hair smelled like iced tea with honey in it, after all the ice has melted.

Kissing Jake is like kissing Natalie or Natasha, except that it isn't just for fun. It feels like something there isn't a word for in Scrabble.

The deal with Houdini is that Jake got interested in him during Advanced Placement American History. He and I were both put in tenth-grade history. We were doing biography projects. I was studying Joseph McCarthy. My grandmother had all sorts of stories about McCarthy. She hated him for what he did to Hollywood.

Jake didn't turn in his project—instead he told everyone in our AP class except for Mr. Streep (we call him Meryl) to meet him at the gym on Saturday. When we showed up, Jake reenacted one of Houdini's escapes with a laundry bag, handcuffs, a gym locker, bicycle chains, and the school's swimming pool. It took him three and a half minutes to get free, and this guy named Roger took a bunch of photos and then put the photos online. One of the photos ended up in the *Boston Globe,* and Jake got expelled. The really ironic thing was that while his mom was in the hospital, Jake had applied to M.I.T. He did it for his mom. He thought that way she'd have to stay alive. She was so excited about M.I.T. A couple of days after he'd been expelled, right after the wedding, while his dad and the fencing instructor were in Bermuda, he got an acceptance letter in the mail and a phone call from this guy in the admissions office who explained why they had to withdraw the acceptance.

My mother wanted to know why I let Jake wrap himself up in bicycle chains and then watched while Peter and Michael pushed him into the deep end of the school pool. I said that Jake had a backup plan. Ten more seconds and we were all going to jump into the pool and open the locker and get him out of there. I was crying when I said that. Even before he got in the locker, I knew how stupid Jake was being. Afterwards, he promised me that he'd never do anything like that again.

That was when I told him about Zofia's husband, Rustan, and about Zofia's handbag. How stupid am I?

So I guess you can figure out what happened next. The problem is that Jake believed me about the handbag. We spent a lot of time over at Zofia's, playing Scrabble. Zofia never let the faery handbag out of her sight. She even took it with her when she went to the bathroom. I think she even slept with it under her pillow.

I didn't tell her that I'd said anything to Jake. I wouldn't ever have told anybody else about it. Not Natasha. Not even Natalie, who is the most responsible person in all of the world. Now, of course, if the handbag turns up and Jake still hasn't come back, I'll have to tell Natalie. Somebody has to keep an eye on the stupid thing while I go find Jake.

What worries me is that maybe one of the Baldeziwurlekistanians or one of the people under the hill or maybe even Rustan popped out of the handbag to run an errand and got worried when Zofia wasn't there. Maybe they'll come looking for her and bring it back. Maybe they know I'm supposed to look after it now. Or maybe they took it and hid it somewhere. Maybe someone turned it in at the lost-and-found at the library and that stupid librarian called the FBI. Maybe scientists at the Pentagon are examining the handbag right now. Testing it. If Jake comes out, they'll think he's a spy or a superweapon or an alien or something. They're not going to just let him go.

Everyone thinks Jake ran away, except for my mother, who is convinced that he was trying out another Houdini escape and is probably lying at the bottom of a lake somewhere. She hasn't said that to me, but I can see her thinking it. She keeps making cookies for me.

What happened is that Jake said, "Can I see that for just a second?"

He said it so casually that I think he caught Zofia off guard. She was reaching into the purse for her wallet. We were standing in the lobby of the movie theater on a Monday morning. Jake was behind the snack counter. He'd gotten a job there. He was wearing this stupid red paper hat and some kind of apron bib thing. He was supposed to ask us if we wanted to supersize our drinks.

He reached over the counter and took Zofia's handbag right out of her hand. He closed it and then he opened it again. I think he opened it the right way. I don't think he ended up in the dark place. He said to me and Zofia, "I'll be right back." And then he wasn't there anymore. It was just me and Zofia and the handbag, lying there on the counter where he'd dropped it.

If I'd been fast enough, I think I could have followed him. But Zofia had been guardian of the faery handbag for a lot longer. She snatched the bag back and glared at me. "He's a very bad boy," she said. She was absolutely furious. "You're better off without him, Genevieve, I think."

"Give me the handbag," I said. "I have to go get him."

"It isn't a toy, Genevieve," she said. "It isn't a game. This isn't Scrabble. He comes back when he comes back. If he comes back."

"Give me the handbag," I said. "Or I'll take it from you."

She held the handbag up high over her head, so that I couldn't reach it. I hate people who are taller than me. "What are you going to do now?" Zofia said. "Are you going to knock me down? Are you going to steal the handbag? Are you going to go away and leave me here to explain to your parents where you've gone? Are you going to say good-bye to your friends? When you come out again, they will have gone to college. They'll have jobs and babies and houses and they won't even recognize you. Your mother will be an old woman and I will be dead."

"I don't care," I said. I sat down on the sticky red carpet in the lobby and started to cry. Someone wearing a little metal name tag came over and asked if we were okay. His name was missy. Or maybe he was wearing someone else's tag.

"We're fine," Zofia said. "My granddaughter has the flu."

She took my hand and pulled me up. She put her arm around me and we walked out of the theater. We never even got to see the stupid movie. We never even got to see another movie together. I don't ever want to go see another movie. The problem is, I don't want to see unhappy endings. And I don't know if I believe in the happy ones.

"I have a plan," Zofia said. "I will go find Jake. You will stay here and look after the handbag."

"You won't come back either," I said. I cried even harder. Or if you do, I'll be like a hundred years old and Jake will still be sixteen."

"Everything will be okay," Zofia said. I wish I could tell you how beautiful she looked right then. It didn't matter if she was lying or if she actually knew that everything was going to be okay. The important thing was how she looked when she said it. She said, with absolute certainty, or maybe with all the skill of a very skillful liar, "My plan will work. First we go to the library, though. One of the people under the hill just brought back an Agatha Christie mystery, and I need to return it."

"We're going to the library?" I said. "Why don't we just go home and play Scrabble for a while." You probably think I was just being sarcastic here, and I was being sarcastic. But Zofia gave me a sharp look. She knew that if I was being sarcastic that my brain was working again. She knew that I knew she was stalling for time. She knew that I was coming up with my own plan, which was a lot like Zofia's plan, except that I was the one who went into the handbag. *How* was the part I was working on.

"We could do that," she said. "Remember, when you don't know what to do, it never hurts to play Scrabble. It's like reading the I Ching or tea leaves."

"Can we please just hurry?" I said.

Zofia just looked at me. "Genevieve, we have plenty of time. If you're going to look after the handbag, you have to remember that. You have to be patient. Can you be patient?"

"I can try," I told her. I'm trying, Zofia. I'm trying really hard. But it isn't fair. Jake is off having adventures and talking to talking animals, and who knows, learning how to fly and some beautiful three-thousand-year-old girl from under the hill is teaching him how to speak fluent Baldeziwurleki. I bet she lives in a house that runs around on chicken legs, and she tells Jake that she'd love to hear him play something on the guitar. Maybe you'll kiss her, Jake, because she's put a spell on you. But whatever you do, don't go up into her house. Don't fall asleep in her bed. Come back soon, Jake, and bring the handbag with you.

I hate those movies, those books, where some guy gets to go off and have adventures and meanwhile the girl has to stay home and wait. I'm a feminist. I subscribe to *Bust* magazine, and I watch *Buffy* reruns. I don't believe in that kind of shit.

We hadn't been in the library for five minutes before Zofia picked up a biography of Carl Sagan and dropped it in her purse. She was definitely stalling for time. She was trying to come up with a plan that would counteract the plan that she knew I was planning. I wondered what she thought I was planning. It was probably much better than anything I'd come up with.

"Don't do that!" I said.

"Don't worry," Zofia said. "Nobody was watching."

"I don't care if nobody saw! What if Jake's sitting there in the boat, or what if he was coming back and you just dropped it on his head!"

"It doesn't work that way," Zofia said. Then she said, "It would serve him right, anyway."

That was when the librarian came up to us. She had a name tag on as well. I was so sick of people and their stupid name tags. I'm not even going to tell you what her name was. "I saw that," the librarian said.

"Saw what?" Zofia said. She smiled down at the librarian, like she was Queen of the Library, and the librarian was a petitioner.

The librarian stared hard at her. "I know you," she said, almost sounding awed, like she was a weekend bird-watcher who had just seen Bigfoot. "We have your picture on the office wall. You're Ms. Swink. You aren't allowed to check out books here."

"That's ridiculous," Zofia said. She was at least two feet taller than the librarian. I felt a bit sorry for the librarian. After all, Zofia had just stolen a seven-day book. She probably wouldn't return it for a hundred years. My mother has always made it clear that it's my job to protect other people from Zofia. I guess I was Zofia's guardian before I became the guardian of the handbag.

The librarian reached up and grabbed Zofia's handbag. She was small but she was strong. She jerked the handbag and Zofia stumbled and fell back against a work desk. I couldn't believe it. Everyone except for me was getting a look at Zofia's handbag. What kind of guardian was I going to be?

"Genevieve," Zofia said. She held my hand very tightly, and I looked at her. She looked wobbly and pale. She said, "I feel very bad about all of this. Tell your mother I said so."

Then she said one last thing, but I think it was in Baldeziwurleki.

The librarian said, "I saw you put a book in here. Right here." She opened the handbag and peered inside. Out of the handbag came a long, lonely, ferocious, utterly hopeless scream of rage. I don't ever want to hear that noise again. Everyone in the library looked up. The librarian made a choking noise and threw Zofia's handbag away from her. A little trickle of blood came out of her nose and a drop fell on the floor. What I thought at first was that it was just plain luck that the handbag was closed when it landed. Later on I was trying to figure out what Zofia said. My Baldeziwurleki isn't very good, but I think she was saying something like "Figures. Stupid librarian. I have to go take care of that damn dog." So maybe that's what happened. Maybe Zofia sent part of herself in there with the skinless dog. Maybe she fought it and won and closed the handbag. Maybe she made friends with it. I mean, she used to feed it popcorn at the movies. Maybe she's still in there.

What happened in the library was Zofia sighed a little and closed her eyes. I helped her sit down in a chair, but I don't think she was really there anymore. I rode with her in the ambulance, when the ambulance finally showed up, and I swear I didn't even think about the handbag until my mother showed up. I didn't say a word. I just left her there in the hospital with Zofia, who was on a respirator, and I ran all the way back to the library. But it was closed. So I ran all the way back again, to the hospital, but you already know what happened, right? Zofia died. I hate writing that. My tall, funny, beautiful, book-stealing, Scrabble-playing, storytelling grandmother died.

But you never met her. You're probably wondering about the handbag. What happened to it. I put up signs all over town, like Zofia's handbag was some kind of lost dog, but nobody ever called.

So that's the story so far. Not that I expect you to believe any of it. Last night Natalie and Natasha came over and we played Scrabble. They don't really like Scrabble, but they feel like it's their job to cheer me up. I won. After they went home, I flipped all the tiles upside-down and then I started picking them up in groups of seven. I tried to ask a question, but it was hard to pick just one. The words I got weren't so great either, so I decided that they weren't English words. They were Baldeziwurleki words.

Once I decided that, everything became perfectly clear. First I put down *kirif* which means "happy news", and then I got a *b,* an *o,* an *l,* an *e,* a *f,* another *i,* an *s,* and a *z.* So then I could make *kirif* into *bolekirifisz,* which could mean "the happy result of a combination of diligent effort and patience."

I would find the faery handbag. The tiles said so. I would work the clasp and go into the handbag and have my own adventures and would rescue Jake. Hardly any time would have gone by before we came back out of the handbag. Maybe I'd even make friends with that poor dog and get to say good-bye, for real, to Zofia. Rustan would show up again and be really sorry that he'd missed Zofia's funeral and this time he would be brave enough to tell my mother the whole story. He would tell her that he was her father. Not that she would believe him. Not that you should believe this story. Promise me that you won't believe a word.

ASHPUTTLE

Peter Straub

Peter Straub was called a national treasure by Lawrence Block. Straub began his career writing horror novels including *Julia* and *Ghost Story*. As Straub's career has progressed, he's moved into more complex and ambitious novels such as *The Hellfire Club* and *Mr. X*. He's co-authored the novels *The Talisman* and *Black House* with Stephen King. His fiction has won multiple World Fantasy, Stoker, and International Horror Guild awards. Straub has also worked as an editor, serving on the board as well as putting together an issue of the literary journal *Conjunctions*. He also edited several books for the Library of America including the two-volume set *American Fantastic Tales*.

Most readers will find Straub's take on Cinderella chilling and disturbing. Running underneath it all is Straub's wickedly dark humor. This is not your cartoon-variety version of Cinderella, this is the real deal.

People think that teaching little children has something to do with helping other people, something to do with service. People think that if you teach little children, you must love them. People get what they need from thoughts like this.

People think that if you happen to be very fat and are a person who acts happy and cheerful all the time, you are probably pretending to be that way in order to make them forget how fat you are, or cause them to forgive you for being so fat. They make this assumption, thinking you are so stupid that you imagine that you're getting away with this charade. From this assumption, they get confidence in the superiority of their intelligence over yours, and they get to pity you, too.

Those figments, those stepsisters, came to me and said *Don't you know that we want to help you?* They came to me and said *Can you tell us what your life is like?*

These moronic questions they asked over and over—*Are you all right? Is anything happening to you? Can you talk to us now, darling? Can you tell us about your life?*

I stared straight ahead, not looking at their pretty hair or pretty eyes or pretty mouths. I looked over their shoulders at the pattern on the wallpaper and tried not to blink until they stood up and went away.

What my *life* was like? What was *happening* to me?

Nothing was happening to me. I was *all right.*

They smiled briefly, like a twitch in their eyes and mouths, before they stood up and left me alone. I sat still on my chair and looked at the wallpaper while they talked to Zena.

The wallpaper was yellow, with white lines going up and down through it. The lines never touched—just when they were about to run into each other, they broke, and the fat thick yellow kept them apart.

I liked seeing the white lines hanging in the fat yellow, each one separate.

When the figments called me *darling*, ice and snow stormed into my mouth and went pushing down my throat into my stomach, freezing everything. They didn't know I was nothing, I would never be like them; they didn't know that the only part of me that was not nothing was a small hard stone right at the center of me.

That stone has a name. MOTHER.

If you are a female kindergarten teacher in her fifties who happens to be very fat, people imagine that you must be very dedicated to their children, because you cannot possibly have any sort of private life. If they are the parents of the children in your kindergarten class, they are almost grateful that you are so grotesque, because it means that you must really care about their children. After all, even though you couldn't possibly get any other sort of job, you can't be in it for the money, can you? Because what do people know about your salary? They know that garbagemen make more money than kindergarten teachers. So at least you didn't decide to take care of their delightful, wonderful, lovable little children just because you thought you'd get rich, no no.

Therefore, even though they disbelieve in all your smiles, all your pretty ways, even though they really do think of you with a mixture of pity and contempt, a little gratitude gets in there.

Sometimes when I meet with one of these parents, say a fluffy-haired young lawyer, say named Arnold Zoeller, Arnold and his wife Kathi, Kathi with an i, mind you, sometimes when I sit behind my desk and watch these two slim, handsome people struggle to keep the pity and contempt out of their well-cared-for faces, I catch that gratitude heating up behind their eyes.

Arnold and Kathi believe that a pathetic old lumpo like me must love their lovely little girl, a girl say named Tori, Tori with an i (for Victoria.) And I think I do rather love little Tori Zoeller, yes I think I do think I love that little girl. My mother would have loved her, too. And that's the God's truth

I can see myself in the world, in the middle of the world.

I see that I am the same as all nature.

In our minds exists an awareness of perfection, but nothing on earth, nothing in all of nature, is perfectly conceived. Every response comes straight out of the person who is responding.

I have no responsibility to stimulate or satisfy your needs. All that was taken care of a long time ago. Even if you happen to be some kind of supposedly exalted person, like a lawyer. Even if your name is Arnold Zoeller, for example.

Once, briefly, there existed a golden time. In my mind existed an awareness of perfection, and all of nature echoed and repeated the awareness of perfection in my mind. My parents lived, and with them, I too was alive in the golden time. Our name was Asch, and in fact I am known now as Mrs. Asch, the Mrs. being entirely honorific, no husband having ever been in evidence, nor ever likely to be. (To some sixth-graders, those whom I did not beguile and enchant as kindergarteners, those before whose parents I did not squeeze myself into my desk chair and pronounce their dull, their dreary treasures delightful, wonderful, lovable, above all *intelligent*, I am known as Mrs. Fat-Asch. Of this I pretend to be ignorant.) Mr. and Mrs. Asch did dwell together in the golden time, and both mightily did love their girl-child. And then, whoops, the girl-child's Mommy upped and died. The girl-child's Daddy buried her in the estate's churchyard, with the minister and everything, in the coffin and everything, with hymns and talking and crying and the animals standing around, and Zena, I remember, Zena was already there, even then. So that was how things were, right from the start.

The figments came because of what I did later. They came from a long way away—the city, I think. You don't have to be religious to have inspirations. We never saw city dresses like that, out where we lived. We never saw city hair like that, either. And one of those ladies had a veil!

One winter morning during my first year teaching kindergarten here, I got into my car—I *shoved myself* into my car, I should explain, this is different for me than for you, I *rammed myself* between the seat and the steering wheel, and I drove forty miles east, through three different suburbs, until I got to the city, and thereupon I drove through the city to the slummiest section, where dirty people sit in their cars and drink right in the middle of the day. I went to the department store nobody goes to unless they're on welfare and have five or six kids all with different last names. I just parked on the street and sailed in the door. People like that, they never hurt people like me.

Down in the basement was where they sold the wallpaper, so I huffed and puffed down the stairs, smiling cute as a button whenever anybody stopped to look at me, and shoved myself through the aisles until I got to the back wall, where the samples stood in big books like the fairy-tale book we used to have. I grabbed about four of those books off the wall and heaved them over onto a table there in that section and perched myself onto a little tiny chair and started flipping the pages.

A scared-looking black kid in a cheap suit mumbled something about helping me, so I gave him my happiest, most pathetic smile and said, well, I was here to get wallpaper, wasn't I? What color did I want, did I know? Well, I was thinking about yellow, I said. Uh huh, he says, what kinda yellow you got in mind? Yellow with white lines in it. Uh huh, says he, and starts helping me look through those books with all those samples in them. They have about the ugliest wallpaper in the world in this place, wallpaper like sores on the wall, wallpaper that looks like it got rained on before you get it home. Even the black kid knows this crap is ugly, but he's trying his damndest not to show it.

I bestow smiles everywhere. I'm smiling like a queen riding through her kingdom in a carriage, like a little girl who just got a gold-and-silver dress from a turtledove up in a magic tree. I'm smiling as if Arnold Zoeller himself and of course his lovely wife are looking across my desk at me while I drown, suffocate, stifle, bury their *lovely, intelligent* little Tori in golden words.

I think we got some more yellow in this book here, he says, and fetches down another big fairy-tale book and plunks it between us on the table. His dirty-looking hands turn those big stiff pages. And just as I thought, just as I knew would happen, could happen, would probably happen, but only here in this filthy corner of a filthy department store, this ignorant but helpful lad opens the book to my mother's wallpaper pattern.

I see that fat yellow and those white lines that never touch anything, and I can't help myself, sweat breaks out all over my body, and I groan so horribly that the kid actually backs away from me, lucky for him, because in the next second I'm bending over and throwing up interesting-looking reddish goo all over the floor of the wallpaper department. O God, the kid says, O lady. I groan, and all the rest of the goo comes jumping out of me and splatters down on the carpet. Some older black guy in a clip-on bow tie rushes up toward us but stops short with his mouth hanging open as soon as he sees the mess on the floor. I take my hankie out of my bag and wipe off my mouth. I try to smile at the kid, but my eyes are too blurry. No, I say, I'm fine, I want to buy this wallpaper for my kitchen, this one right here. I turn over the page to see the name of my mother's wallpaper—Zena's wallpaper, too—and discover that this kind of wallpaper is called "The Thinking Reed."

You don't have to be religious to have inspirations.

An adventurous state of mind is like a great dwelling place.

To be lived truly, life must be apprehended with an adventurous state of mind.

But no one on earth can explain the lure of adventure?

Zena's example gave me two tricks that work in my classroom, and the reason they work is that they are not actually tricks!

The first of these comes into play when a particular child is disobedient or inattentive, which, as you can imagine, often occurs in a room full of kindergarten-age children. I deal with these infractions in this fashion. I command the child to come to my desk. (Sometimes, I command two children to come to my desk.) I stare at the child until it begins to squirm. Sometimes it blushes or trembles. I await the physical signs of shame or discomfort. Then I pronounce the child's name. "Tori," I say, if the child is Tori. Its little eyes invariably fasten upon mine at this instant. "Tori," I say, "you know that what you did is wrong, don't you?" Ninety-nine times out of a hundred, the child nods its head. "And you will never do that wrong thing again, will you?" Most often the child can speak to say *No*. "Well, you'd better not," I say, and then I lean forward until the little child can see nothing except my enormous, inflamed face. Then in a guttural, lethal, rumble-whisper, I utter, "OR ELSE." When I say, "OR ELSE," I am very emphatic. I am so very emphatic that I feel my eyes change shape. I am thinking of Zena and the time she told me that weeping on my mother's grave wouldn't make a glorious wonderful tree grow there, it would just drown my mother in mud.

The attractiveness of teaching is that it is adventurous, as adventurous as life.

My mother did not drown in mud. She died some other way. She fell down in the middle of the downstairs parlor, the parlor where Zena sat on her visits. Zena was just another lady then, and on her visits, her "social calls," she sat on the best antique chair and held her hands in her lap like the most modest, innocent little lady ever born. She was half-Chinese, Zena, and I knew she was just like bright sharp metal inside of her, metal that could slice you but good. Zena was very adventurous, but not as adventurous as me. Zena never got out of that town. Of course all that happened to Zena was that she got old, and everybody left her all alone because she wasn't pretty anymore, she was just an old yellow widow-lady, and then I heard that she died pulling up weeds in her garden. I heard this from two different people. You could say that Zena got drowned in mud, which proves that everything spoken on this earth contains a truth not always apparent at the time.

The other trick I learned from Zena that is not a trick is how to handle a whole class that has decided to act up. To keep life under control you must maintain an adventurous state of mind. These children come from parents who, thinking they know everything, in fact know less than nothing. These children will never see a classical manner demonstrated at home. You must respond in such a way that demonstrates your awareness of perfection. You must respond in a way that will bring this awareness to the unruly children, so that they too will possess it.

It can begin in a thousand different ways. Say I am in conference with a single student—say I am delivering the great OR ELSE. Say that my attention has wandered off for a moment, and that I am contemplating the myriad things I contemplate when my attention is wandering free. My mother's grave, watered by my tears. The women with city hair who desired to give me help, but could not, so left to be replaced by others, who in turn were replaced by yet others. How it felt to stand naked and besmeared with my own feces in the front yard, moveless as a statue, the same as all nature, classical. The gradual disappearance of my father, like that of a figure in a cartoon who grows increasingly transparent until total transparency is reached. Zena facedown in her garden, snuffling dirt up into her nostrils. The resemblance of the city women to certain wicked stepsisters in old tales. Also their resemblance to handsome princes in the same tales.

She who hears the tale makes the tale.

Say therefore that I am no longer quite anchored within the classroom, but that I float upward into one, several, or all of these realms. People get what they need from their own minds. Certain places, you can get in there and rest. The classical was a cool period. I am floating within my cool realms. At that moment, one child pulls another's hair. A third child hurls a spitball at the window. Another falls to the floor, emitting pathetic and mechanical cries. Instantly, what was order is misrule. Then I summon up the image of my ferocious female angels and am on my feet before the little beasts even notice that I have left my desk. In a flash, I am beside the light switch. The Toris and Tiffanys, the Joshuas and Jeremys, riot on. I slap down the switch, and the room goes dark.

Result? Silence. Inspired action is destiny.

The children freeze. Their pulses race—veins beat in not a few little blue temples. I say four words. I say, "Think what this means." They know what it means. I grow to twice my size with the meaning of these words. I look over them, and darkness pours out of me. Then I switch the lights back on, and smile at them until they get what they need from my smiling face. These children will never call me Mrs. Fat-Asch, these children know that I am the same as all nature.

Once upon a time a dying queen sent for her daughter, and when her daughter came to her bedside the queen said, "I am leaving you, my darling. Say your prayers and be good to your father. Think of me always, and I will always be with you." Then she died. Every day the little girl watered her mother's grave with her tears. But her heart was dead. You cannot lie about a thing like this. Hatred is the inside part of love. And so her mother became a hard cold stone in her heart. And that was the meaning of the mother, for as long as the little girl lived.

Soon the king took another woman as his wife, and she was most beautiful, with skin the color of gold and eyes as black as jet. She was like a person pretending to be someone else inside another person pretending she couldn't pretend. She understood that reality was contextual. She understood about the condition of the observer.

One day when the king was going out to be among his people, he asked his wife, "What shall I bring you?"

"A diamond ring," said the queen. And the king could not tell who was speaking, the person inside pretending to be someone else, or the person outside who could not pretend.

"And you, my daughter," said the king, "what would you like?"

"A diamond ring," said the daughter.

The king smiled and shook his head.

"Then nothing," said the daughter. "Nothing at all."

When the king came home, he presented the queen with a diamond ring in a small blue box, and the queen opened the box and smiled at the ring and said, "It's a very small diamond, isn't it?" The king's daughter saw him stoop forward, his face whitening, as if he had just lost half his blood. "I like my small diamond," said the queen, and the king, straightened up, although he still looked white and shaken. He patted his daughter on the head on his way out of the room, but the girl merely looked forward and said nothing, in return for the nothing he had given her.

And that night, when the rest of the palace was asleep, the king's daughter crept to the kitchen and ate half of a loaf of bread and most of a quart of homemade peach ice cream. This was the most delicious food she had ever eaten in her whole entire life. The bread tasted like the sun on the wheatfields, and inside the taste of the sun was the taste of the bursting kernels of the wheat, even of the rich dark crumbly soil that surrounded the roots of the wheat, even of the lives of the bugs and animals that had scurried through the wheat, even of the droppings of those foxes, beetles, and mice. And the homemade peach ice cream tasted overwhelmingly of sugar, cream, and peaches, but also of the bark and meat of the peach tree and the pink feet of the birds that had landed on it, and the sharp, brittle voices of those birds, also of the effort of the hand crank, of the stained, whorly wood of its sides, and of the sweat of the man who had worked it so long. Every taste should be as complicated as possible, and every taste goes up and down at the same time: up past the turtledoves to the far reaches of the sky, so that one final taste in everything is *whiteness*, and down all the way to the mud at the bottom of graves, then to the mud beneath that mud, so that another final taste in everything, even in peach ice cream, is the taste of *blackness*.

From about this time, the king's daughter began to attract undue attention. From the night of the whiteness of turtledoves and the blackness of grave-mud to the final departure of the stepsisters was a period of something like six months. It was in this period, when nothing was happening to the king's daughter, when she was all right, that she learned what it was to live in the middle of the world and be the same as all nature.

I thought of myself as a work of art. I caused responses without being responsible for them. This is the great freedom of art.

They asked questions which enforced the terms of their own answers. *Don't you know we want to help you?* Such a question implies only two possible answers, 1: no, 2: yes. The stepsisters never understood the queen's daughter; therefore, the turtledoves pecked out their eyes, first on the one side, then on the other. The correct answer, 3: person to whom question is directed is not the one in need of help, cannot be given. Other correct answers, such as 4: help shall come from other sources, and 5: neither knowledge nor help mean what you imagine they mean, are also forbidden by the form of the question.

Assignment for tonight: make a list of proper but similarly forbidden answers to the question *What is happening to you*? Note: be sure to consider conditions imposed by use of word *happening*.

The stepsisters arrived from the city in grand state. They resembled peacocks. The stepsisters accepted Zena's tea, they admired the house, the paintings, the furniture, the entire estate, just as if admiring these things, which everybody admired, meant that they, too, should be admired. The stepsisters wished to remove the king's daughter from this setting, but their power was not so great. Zena would not permit it, nor would the ailing king. (At night, Zena placed her subtle mouth over his sleeping mouth and drew breath straight out of his body.) Zena said that the condition of the king's daughter would prove to be temporary. The child was eating well. She was loved. In time, she would return to herself.

When the figments asked, *What is happening to you?* I could have answered, Zena is happening to me. This answer would not have been understood. Neither would the answer, *My mother is happening to me.*

Undue attention came about in the following fashion. Zena knew all about my midnight feasts, but was indifferent to them. Zena knew that each person must acquire what she needs. This is as true for a king's daughter as for any ordinary commoner. But she was ignorant of what I did in the name of art. Misery and anger made me a great artist, though now I am a much greater artist. I think I was twelve. (The age of an artist is of no importance.) Both my mother and Zena were happening to me, and I was happening to them, too. Such is the world of women. My mother, deep in her mud-grave, hated Zena. Zena, second in the king's affections, hated my mother. Speaking from the center of the stone at the center of me, my mother frequently advised me of how to deal with Zena. Silently, speaking with her eyes, Zena advised me on how to deal with my mother. I, who had to deal with both of them, hated them both.

And I possessed an adventurous mind?

The main feature of adventure is that it goes forward into unknown country.

Adventure is filled with a nameless joy.

Alone in my room in the middle of Saturday, on later occasions after my return from school, I removed my clothes and placed them neatly on my bed. (My canopied bed.) I had no feelings, apart from a sense of urgency, concerning the actions I was about to perform. Perhaps I experienced a nameless joy at this point. Later on, at the culmination of my self-display, I experienced a nameless joy. And later yet, I experienced the same nameless joy at the conclusions of my various adventures in art. In each of these adventures as in the first, I created responses not traceable within the artwork, but which derived from the conditions, etc., of the audience. Alone and unclothed now in my room, ready to create responses, I squatted on my heels and squeezed out onto the carpet a long cylinder of fecal matter, the residue of, dinner not included, an entire loaf of seven-grain bread, half a box of raisins, a can of peanuts, and a quarter pound of cervelat sausage, all consumed when everyone else was in bed and Zena was presumably leaning over the face of my sleeping father, greedily inhaling his life. I picked up the warm cylinder and felt it melt into my hands. I hastened this process by squeezing my palms together. Then I rubbed my hands over my body. What remained of the stinking cylinder I smeared along the walls of the bedroom. Then I wiped my hands on the carpet. (The white carpet.) My preparations concluded, I moved regally through the corridors until I reached the front door and let myself out.

I have worked as a certified grade school teacher in three states. My record is spotless. I never left a school except by my own choice. When tragedies came to my charges or their parents, I invariably sent sympathetic notes, joined volunteer groups to search for bodies, attended funerals, etc., etc. Every teacher eventually becomes familiar with these unfortunate duties.

Outside, there was all the world, at least all of the estate, from which to choose. Certain lines from Edna St. Vincent Millay describing the manner in which the world, no wider than the blissful heart, stands out on either side, best express my state of mind at this moment. I well remember the much-admired figure of Dave Garroway quoting the poet's lovely words on his Sunday afternoon television program, and I pass along Miss Millay's beautiful sentiment to each fresh class of kindergarteners. They must start somewhere, and at other moments in their year with me they will have the opportunity to learn that nature never gives you a chance to rest. Every animal on earth is hungry.

Turning my back on the fields of grazing cows and sheep, ignoring the hills beyond, hills seething with coyotes, wildcats, and mountain lions, I moved with stately tread through the military rows of fruit trees and, with papery apple and peach blossoms adhering to my bare feet, passed into the expanse of the grass meadow where grew the great hazel tree. Had the meadow been recently mown, long green stalks the width of a caterpillar leapt up from the ground to festoon my legs. (I often stretched out full length and rolled in the freshly mown grass meadow.) And then, at the crest of the hill that marked the end of the meadow, I arrived at my destination. Below me lay the road to the unknown towns and cities in which I hoped one day to find my complicated destiny. Above me stood the hazel tree.

I have always known that I could save myself by looking into my own mind?

I stood above the road on the crest of the hill and raised my arms. When I looked into my mind I saw two distinct and necessary states, one that of the white line, the other that of the female angels, akin to the turtledoves. The white line existed in a calm rapture of separation, touching neither sky nor meadow but suspended in the space between.

The white line was silence, isolation, classicism. This state is one-half of what is necessary in order to achieve the freedom of art, and it is called "The Thinking Reed." The angels and turtledoves existed in a rapture of power, activity, and rage. They were absolute whiteness and absolute blackness, gratification and gratification's handmaiden, revenge.

The angels and turtledoves came streaming up out of my body and soared from the tips of my fingers into the sky, and when they returned they brought golden and silver dresses, diamond rings and emerald tiaras.

I saw the figments slicing off their own toes, sawing off their heels, and stepping into shoes already slippery with blood. The figments were trying to smile, they were trying to stand up straight. They were like children before an angry teacher, a teacher transported by a righteous anger. Girls like the figments much younger than my present age—never did understand that what they needed, they must get from their own minds. Lacking this understanding, they tottered along, pretending that they were not mutilated, pretending that blood did not pour from their shoes, back to their pretend houses and pretend princes. The nameless joy distinguished every part of this process?

Lately, within the past twenty-four hours, a child has been lost.

A lost child lies deep within the ashes, her hands and feet mutilated, her face destroyed by fire. She has partaken of the great adventure, and now she is the same as all nature.

At night, I see the handsome, distracted, still hopeful parents on our local news programs. Arnold and Kathi, he as handsome as a prince, she as lovely as one of the figments, still have no idea of what has actually happened to them—they lived their whole lives in utter abyssal ignorance—they think of hope as an essential component of the universe. They think that other people, the people paid to perform this function, will conspire to satisfy their needs.

A child has been lost. Now her photograph appears each day of the front page of our sturdy little tabloid-style newspaper, beaming out with luminous ignorance beside the columns of print describing a sudden disappearance after the weekly Sunday School class at St. Mary-in-the-Forest's Episcopal Church, the deepening fears of the concerned parents, the limitless charm of the girl herself, the searches of nearby video parlors and shopping malls, the draggings of two adjacent ponds, the slow, painstaking inspections of the neighboring woods, fields, farms, and outbuildings, the shock of the child's particularly well off and socially prominent relatives, godparents included.

A particular child has been lost. A certain combination of variously shaded blond hair and eyes the blue of early summer sky seen through a haze of stratocumulus clouds, of an endearingly puffy upper lip and a recurring smudge, like that left on Corras-able bond typing paper by an unclean eraser, on the left side of the mouth, of an unaffected shyness and an occasional brittle arrogance destined soon to overshadow more attractive traits, will never again be seen, not by parents, friends, teachers, or the passing strangers once given to spontaneous tributes to the child's beauty.

A child of her time has been lost. Of no interest to our local newspaper, unknown to the Sunday School classes at St. Mary's-in-the-Forest, were this moppet's obsession with dolls Exercise Barbie and Malibu Barbie, her fanatical attachment to My Pretty Ponies Glory and Applejacks, her insistence on introducing during classtime observations upon the cartoon family named Simpson, and her precocious fascination with the music television channel, especially the "videos" featuring the groups Kriss Kross and Boyz II Men. She was once observed holding hands with James Halliwell, a first-grade boy. Once, just before nap time, she turned upon a pudgy, unpopular girl of protosadistic tendencies named Deborah Monk and hissed, "Debbie, I hate to tell you this, but you *suck*."

A child of certain limitations has been lost. She could never learn to tie her cute but oddly blunt-looking size 1 running shoes, and eventually had to become resigned to the sort fastened with Velcro straps. When combing her multishaded blond hair with her fingers, she would invariably miss a cobwebby patch located two inches aft of her left ear. Her reading skills were somewhat, though not seriously, below average. She could recognize her name, when spelled out in separate capitals, with narcissistic glee; yet all other words, save and and the, turned beneath her impatient gaze into random, Sanskrit-like squiggles and uprights. (This would soon have corrected itself.) She could recite the alphabet all in a rush, by rote, but when questioned, was incapable of remembering if O came before or after S. I doubt that she would have been capable of mastering long division during the appropriate academic term.

Across the wide, filmy screen of her eyes would now and then cross a haze of indefinable confusion. In a child of more finely tuned sensibilities, this momentary slippage might have suggested a sudden sense of loss, even perhaps a premonition of the loss to come. In her case, I imagine the expression was due to the transition from the world of complete unconsciousness (Barbie and My Pretty Ponies) to a more fully socialized state (Kriss Kross). Introspection would have come only late in life, after long exposure to experiences of the kind from which her parents most wished to shelter her.

An irreplaceable child has been lost. What was once in the land of the Thinking Reed has been forever removed, like others before it, like all others in time, to turtledove territory. This fact is borne home on a daily basis. Should some informed anonymous observer report that the child is all right, that nothing is happening to her, the comforting message would be misunderstood as the prelude to a demand for ransom. The reason for this is that no human life can ever be truly substituted for another. The increasingly despairing parents cannot create or otherwise acquire a living replica, though they are certainly capable of reproducing again, should they stay married long enough to do so. The children in the lost one's class are reported to suffer nightmares and recurrent enuresis. In class, they exhibit lassitude, wariness, a new unwillingness to respond, like the unwillingness of the very old. At a school wide assembly where the little ones sat right up in front, nearly every one expressed the desire for the missing one to return. Letters and cards to the lost one now form two large, untidy stacks in the principal's office, and with parental appeals to the abductor or abductors broadcast every night, it is felt that the school will accumulate a third stack before these tributes are offered to the distraught parents?

Works of art generate responses not directly traceable to the work itself. Helplessness, grief, and sorrow may exist simultaneously alongside aggressiveness, hostility, anger, or even serenity and relief. The more profound and subtle the work, the more intense and long-lasting the responses it evokes?

Deep, deep in her muddy grave, the queen and mother felt the tears of her lost daughter. *All will pass.* In the form of a turtledove, she rose from grave darkness and ascended into the great arms of a hazel tree. *All will change.* From the topmost branch, the turtledove sang out her everlasting message. *All is hers, who will seek what is true.* "What is true?" cried the daughter, looking dazzled up. *All will pass, all will change, all is yours,* sang the turtledove?

In private conference with the principal, I recently announced my decision to move to another section of the country after the semester's end.

The principal is a kindhearted, limited man still loyal, one might say rigidly loyal, to the values he absorbed from popular music at the end of the 1960s, and he has never been able quite to conceal the unease I arouse within him. Yet he is aware of the respect I command within every quarter of his school, and he has seen former kindergarteners of mine, now freshmen in our tri-suburban high school, return to my classroom and inform the awed children seated before them that Mrs. Asch placed them on the right path, that Mrs. Asch's lessons would be responsible for seeing them successfully through high school and on to college.

Virtually unable to contain the conflict of feelings my announcement brought to birth within him, the principal assured me that he would that very night compose a letter of recommendation certain to gain me a post at any elementary school, public or private, of my choosing.

After thanking him, I replied, "I do not request this kindness of you, but neither will I refuse it."

The principal leaned back in his chair and gazed at me, not unkindly, through his granny glasses. His right hand rose like a turtledove to caress his greying beard, but ceased halfway in its flight, and returned to his lap. Then he lifted both hands to the surface of his desk and intertwined the fingers, still gazing quizzically at me.

"Are you all right?" he enquired.

"Define your terms," I said. "If you mean, am I in reasonable health, enjoying physical and mental stability, satisfied with my work, then the answer is yes, I am all right."

"You've done a wonderful job dealing with Tori's disappearance," he said. "But I can't help but wonder if all of that has played a part in your decision."

"My decisions make themselves," I said. "All will pass, all will change. I am a serene person." He promised to get the letter of recommendation to me by lunchtime the next day, and as I knew he would, he kept his promise. Despite my serious reservations about his methods, attitude, and ideology—despite my virtual certainty that he will be unceremoniously forced from his job within the next year—I cannot refrain from wishing the poor fellow well.

Author's Note: (Certain phrases and sentences here have been adapted from similar phrases and sentences in the writings of the painter Agnes Martin. There is no similarity at all between Mrs. Asch and Agnes Martin.

THE EMPEROR'S NEW (AND IMPROVED) CLOTHES

Leslie What

Leslie What is a Nebula Award-winning novelist and short story writer. Her most recent collection, *Crazy Love*, was a finalist for the Oregon Book Award. Her stories and essays have appeared in *The Macguffin*, *Calyx*, *Asimov's*, *Electric Velocipede*, *Parabola*, *Fugue*, *SciFi.com*, *Midstream*, and other places. New work appears in the anthology, *Is Anybody Out There?* and in *The Los Angeles Review*.

Many fairytales feature secondary characters that feel rather flat. What takes the two weavers/tailors from the Emperor's New Clothes and gives them proper motivations for tricking the Emperor and his people.

Stop me if you've heard this.

Once upon a time—in a central European palace as crumbly as blue cheese—there lived a rich and greedy Emperor.

Meanwhile, across pine-covered bills and turnip-infested dales, there lived two hooligan brothers (or *schmaltzovniks*, as they were called in their native land), current owners of the proverbial magical cloak. Times were hard, and these two schmaltzovniks were in a deep funk. Their country had suffered greatly during the postwar years; realism had replaced fantasy as the dominant literary form. To top things off, the Commies had seized power.

Jusef, the bully, practically *screamed* fashion statement, dressed, as always in the primary colors red and blue that subtly complemented his fair skin and Stalinblack hair. He was the Leonardo di Caprio of fairy-tale bullies. A) Children cheered him. B) Women loved him. C) Men feared him. D) All the above. He had it all, and don't think his slight but very shrewd younger brother, Shecky, didn't notice.

Shecky sat back in his rocker, cradling a home-study leather-bound legal text in his lap. Whereas Jusef had inherited the brawn, Shecky had been stuck with the brains, which had never done him much good.

Jusef stood in the center of the one-room luxury garden apartment, thinking up new ways to fleece and swindle the masses. He stomped one of his boot heels against the slate floor, then adjusted the massive filigree codpiece adorning his velvet pants.

"Brother," Jusef began in a deep baritone, "I hear of a greedy Emperor who's still got zlotys in his pants. What do you say we pay him a little call?"

Frankly, Shecky was a little conflicted. He wanted to get out of the business, but his long and relatively successful career as a fairy-tale swindler had ruined him for other types of work. Funny thing—the boys came from a good family: a virtuous mother, who had died young; a kindly but impotent dad, who had wasted no time before taking up with a lovely but extremely evil wife. Shecky knew that Jusef worried about him. He had always felt uncomfortable being a thug and to this day, he struggled with his inner nice guy.

Yet it was hard to argue with destiny. Here was his brother, suggesting a way out of his funk. So Shecky put aside all misgivings over Jusef's newest devious plan.

"Never say 'no' to adventure," Shecky said.

The late afternoon sun streamed through an open window, lighting the fine hairs of Shecky's beard to a mottled brown the color of potatoes (incidentally the national crop). A niggling suspicion took hold: that his brother was about to get the better of him. He decided to turn things around to his advantage. "Say, Jusef," Shecky said. "What do you suppose ever became of our old invisible cloak?"

Being a jock, Jusef was faster on his feet. He ran for the coat rack before Shecky could react.

"Out of sight, out of mind," Jusef said. He batted his arm through the air until he felt a soft web, transient and cool as drizzle. "Got it," Jusef said, "I think." When Jusef tugged the cloak free from its hook, his hand vanished beneath invisible fabric.

It was a cool effect, but eerie.

Shecky remained nonplussed. "No way, Jose," said Shecky.

"It's my turn to be invisible, remember? You used cloak last time, in that Grimm's fairy tale about the twelve dancing princesses."

Jusef's face warmed and he grinned broadly. "Yeah," he said, "that was one mighty fine adventure." He smacked his lips together as if still tasting the memory.

They had been away from the life far too long.

Shecky shrugged. "I want the cloak! It's my turn for a little fun. Gimme the garment!"

Jusef thought about being nice, but saw no reason to go against type. He pointed to Shecky's legal text and stuck out his tongue. "You're the one who's always saying 'possession is ninety percent of the law.' Tough luck, bro, 'cause I'm bagging the cloak. Ciao," he said, disappearing beneath the fabric.

The front door opened and Jusef's footsteps could be heard pattering across the cobblestones. He made his way through a quaint courtyard leading to stables that were converted into one-car garages back in the thirties. There was only one car in all the land, a station wagon that coincidentally belonged to the brothers.

Shecky shut his book and slid it into his valise. He closed the small-paned window and locked the front door, headed toward the station wagon, which waited ever prepacked in the event adventure called.

"Wait for me," Shecky screamed.

Jusef, who figured he could use some brains for this caper, did just that.

"You drive," Jusef said.

Shecky started up the engine. "Say, Jusef," he said. "Take a good look in the back seat and see if we still have that mysterious trunk." An experienced swindler went in prepared. One never knew just what might come in handy.

Okay, now let's talk Emperor.

This particular Emperor, Konstantin the Thirteenth, had stolen all the gold and fine jewels he could from his subjects, and now schemed to turn the scenic landscape into a coal-and-uranium-mine wasteland. He spent his waking hours kissing the Kremlin's kanakas to maintain his position of authority. These were the futile acts of a desperate man. Konstantin was about to be overthrown and replaced by a despot half his age, but he didn't know that.

Konstantin was richer than triple-cream Camembert, yet he remained unhappy and dissatisfied. See, he was the kind of character who always wanted more than what he had—really all it takes to be a villain, in case anyone was wondering.

Now, no villainous Emperor gets to be in a fairy tale without the requisite dead wife, bless her innocent soul, who forgot to bear him sons, and this guy, Konstantin, was no exception.

The poor dead Empress had been a beautiful though delicate woman, always in frail health. She had managed to produce the one daughter, Wilma, a few moments before the deadline (in the empress' case this was death by childbirth).

Modern readers familiar with fairy-tale literature can surmise that Wilma was a lovely and honest princess, clever as she was kind. The only flaw even worth mentioning, and I wouldn't bother mentioning this if it didn't figure prominently into the plot, was Wilma's annoying, tendency to faint unexpectedly.

As the schmaltzovniks schemed about extracting riches from the Emperor, Konstantin schemed of destructive methods to extract uranium from turnips.

Wilma, who had dated a guy from the Green Party until her father got wind of it, wanted to be both a loyal daughter *and* an environmentalist—an impossible situation for anyone. Emotionally, she was a wreck.

Too bad for the schmaltzovniks, their station wagon broke down in the *burbs* near Warsaw. The engine became a worthless paperweight the moment a fan belt popped; there wasn't a spare part to be had east of the Berlin Wall. The brothers would have been stranded still if not for Shecky's bright idea to trade a pack of Camels for a mule.

Jusef, the magic cloak now snugly hidden in his magnificent codpiece, insisted he be allowed to steer the rig, which left Shecky to clean up after the mule.

Shecky was not pleased.

They drove across the land and fmally arrived in the appropriately idyllic village.

Jusef pulled in the reins to park. He whipped out the magic cloak and disappeared beneath it. "Back in a flash," said he.

Shecky growled. Once again he had been left to manage the scutwork while his lazy brother gallivanted about. But being a practical man, Shecky immediately got down to business. In a matter of minutes, he talked a reticent yokel into leasing out an empty storefront apartment facing the town square.

Shecky carted in the brothers' luggage, folding chairs, mysterious trunk, sewing machines, garment racks, a small round table, and his valise. He switched on an overhead lamp and found his place in his law book, then read the entire chapter on family law before starting the one on tort reform.

The hypocrisy of the moment bore heavily upon him.

As if sensing the grunt work was finished, Jusef reappeared. He crumpled up the magic cloak to hide it where Shecky would never dare look for it, beneath his codpiece, and set to work hanging a sign outside the door that said "The Schmaltz Brothers' Emporium. Purveyors of Sartorial Expertise."

When Jusef had finished, Shecky asked, "How you want to do it this time?"

"Extortion?" suggested Jusef.

Shecky scratched his head. "I was thinking more like fraud, but we're arguing nits? I assume your Emperor is a rich-and-greedy type?"

"It goes without saying," said Jusef. "What I want to know is this: does he have a beautiful daughter?" He squatted close to the floor and began practicing his isometrics.

"Now, hold on a second," Shecky said. "I agreed to let you wear the cloak, but it's my turn to get the girl."

"I suppose that's only fair," said Jusef, "but then what's in it for me?"

Shecky snapped shut his book. "Trust me," he said.

"Like I would my own stepmother."

Both brothers laughed.

"All kidding aside, what is your plan?" Jusef asked.

"Take a letter," answered Shecky, nonplussed. "Inform said Emperor that if he's truly worthy, for a limited time only, we'll custom-fit his cummerbunds for free."

The next morning, the letter had arrived at the castle.

Konstantin and his lovely, honest, clever, and kind daughter, Wilma, grew excited upon hearing that not only had new purveyors of sartorial expertise come to town, but they were discounting cummerbunds.

The two immediately rushed right down to the square to take advantage of this limited-time offer. Konstantin and Wilma waltzed into the store and found both schmaltzovniks hard at work.

Shecky peeked out from behind a sewing machine and waved them away, thereby creating dramatic tension until the final inevitable moment. "Take a number," he said. He smoothed an invisible wrinkle from the invisible fabric, and marveled at its fine texture.

"Now, brother, settle down. How may we help you?" asked Jusef, who sat at the table, squinting at something unseen. He held a needle as if threading it with air. Highlights shimmered about his fingers like the glint of fire reflected through crystal.

"Perhaps we can interest you in some garments light as cobwebs?" Jusef said.

Try as he might, Konstantin could not fathom what it was the brothers were doing. He looked to Wilma for advice, but she seemed mesmerized by Jusef. Honestly, he thought, at times, bringing a princess along to shop was useless.

Jusef took advantage of Wilma's fixation. He stood and approached, reaching out to take her hand. You should already know, from your careful reading of Andersen's seminal work, what happened next.

Just in case you missed it, here's a recap: The virginal Wilma fainted from the shock of seeing Jusef's bulging codpiece, which led Jusef to assume that, for sure, he had won the girl.

Meanwhile, the greedy Emperor was wooed and wowed by the younger brother, who easily convinced him to order some dry goods from the rack.

But what that other competing fairy tale never explained was the science of how their scheme worked.

See, these schmaltzovniks ran their con by making full use of their advanced knowledge of color theory. They knew which colors made one beautiful; they knew which colors went with green eyes or splotchy skin.

In olden times, Shecky had studied with enchanted cave bats who had taught him how to make magic suits from infrared thread. This thread was invisible unless viewed through a special type of goggles.

The next thing you know, the schmaltzovniks had carted out their mysterious trunk and demanded that the Emperor and his now revived daughter each wear a set of goggles before being permitted to view the Brothers' fabulous designer line.

See, here's the gimmick: the real money wasn't in the clothes, it was in the goggles!

And Shecky and Jusef had managed to corner the goggles market worldwide. The invisible clothes were what was called, in retail, a loss leader. In fact, the suit the Emperor picked was on sale, sixty percent off!

Now we come to the parade part, always a favorite.

Picture the virginal Wilma, eyes averted so as not to see her father in the buff. At her side walked Shecky, who waved to the crowds.

Jusef trailed behind, pushing a wheelbarrow filled with infrared goggles.

Segue to that critical moment in the story when that obnoxious little boy jumped out from the bleachers to yell. "Look, Ma. The Emperor has no clothes!"

The crowds were scornful. The Emperor was humiliated.

Wilma fainted, but recovered with the help of some of Shecky's smelling salts, at which point she pleaded with her eyes.

"Help my evil father repent his ways, stop this senseless destruction of the environment, and in the process, cover up his keister, and you shall have my heart," was what Shecky took her pleading eyes to mean.

If you really must know, she was simply doing her princess best to keep from slobbering over Jusef's codpiece.

But love is blind, so Shecky believed his feelings for Wilma were reciprocated. "Of course I'll help," Shecky said. He pulled a set of goggles from his pocket and tossed them to that obnoxious little boy, who, thank God, got eaten by a hideous troll in the fairy tail coming up next.

"Wear these goggles," Shecky shouted to the boy, "and tell us what you see."

The spoiled brat did as he was commanded. A miraculous thing occurred! He gasped to see the Emperor. "Excellent! Magnificent!" he said. "And *so* thin! All hail!" The kid fell to his knees in supplication.

You'd have thought this would be enough, but the throngs continued to scoff, unable to confirn what the child had seen. This was one tough audience.

The Emperor shouted to his guards, "Grab those goggles at once and disperse them to the throngs!"

But before the guards could obey, Jusef pulled out the magic cloak from his magnificent codpiece, covered himself and the wheelbarrow, and utterly disappeared.

Pandemonium ensued.

The Emperor had never felt so exposed.

Wilma probably fainted maybe three or four times before finally getting it out of her system.

At which point, Shecky winked at her and rubbed his hands together, anticipating the reward that would soon be his.

"I bet you'd like an estimate on outfitting the masses," Jusef said to the Emperor.

The shamed Konstantin had no choice but to negotiate on the spot.

Shecky had the contract ready. "My brother can have the money, but I, as the older brother, am thereby entitled by law to marry first. The castle, I might point out, comes with the girl," Shecky said, thankful he had taken the time to study law.

The deal was struck. The goggles were passed out and the Emperor's keister covered.

The final finagling and tallying was left to the accountants and later, a widowed wedding consultant who took the train all the way down from Minsk.

For the most part, everybody lived happily ever after, but it being a fairy tale, there were some consequences.

The land was temporarily spared from environmental destruction, but when that got old, they held a nuclear meltdown in Chernobyl.

Konstantin and the marriage consultant fled to the east to elope. Konstantin got on as a doorman at KGB headquarters and eventually worked his way up to comptroller.

Shecky and Wilma married without haste and were soon blessed with twin sons, only a couple of months premature. One of the boys bore a strong resemblance to Jusef, causing quite a stir before all the newspapers were again taken over by the state.

Sadly, both little tykes suffered from astigmatism, flat feet, and dental caries—afflictions which, while not life-threatening, were severe enough to keep them out of the literature of the fantastic. When last anyone heard, the twins had been put in charge of janitorial at EuroDisney.

With the boys finally out of the house, Wilma discovered the works of Betty Friedan. She returned to school to study biology and destiny, and was awarded the Nobel Prize for her discovery of the princess gene. By the turn of the century, fainting became a relic of the past.

Alas, poor Jusef was left angry at being stuck with only a magic cloak, a magnificent codpiece, and an empty mysterious trunk to call his own. He now lives bitter and alone in a decrepit warehouse north of Newark, where he endlessly plots his revenge.

PINOCCHIO'S DIARY

Robert J. Howe

Robert J. Howe is a graduate of the Clarion writing program and has sold stories to *Analog Science Fiction and Fact*, *Salon.com*, *Electric Velocipede*, *Black Static*, and others.

This is the only original story in this volume, and it's a heartbreaking take on the life and hard times of a small boy named Pinocchio.

Of all the tools father uses to make me, the chisel is the cruelest. Long after he has had his Ciró and retired for the evening, I lie on my bed of shavings, my half-formed body criss-crossed with burning gouges. In the small hours I finally drift into a kind of stupor, my head full of the scent of resin that seeps from the cuts.

He does this because he loves me.

"It is growing pains," he tells me, "all boys have them."

And it is true that he otherwise touches me very gently, in a way that makes me feel loved indeed.

Other little boys have mothers, I know from the stories father tells me. But we just have each other, which makes us closer. So father says as he takes the rasp to my face. When I complain that it hurts, he says it is making me handsome.

Outside it is high summer. Dark brown buffalo move somnolently like bovine sleepwalkers against the brilliant green grass, and mingled scents of honeysuckle and sweet hay waft through the open window. Inside the cottage it is always the same: dim and stinking of lamp oil, overlaid with the tangy odor of fresh curls of wood carved from my body.

I want to be out there, I tell my father, who nods patiently as he wields the tool. I want to run in green meadows and splash in cold streams, like other boys. Without strings piercing my palms and feet; without the shadow of the *traversa* over my head. But then I think of my father's weathered hand, blunt fingers curled lightly around the cross, and the thought of running free makes me sad. To reject my father would break his heart—I can see that in his face, and feel it in the pressure of his fingers through the fine-grained sandpaper he uses to caress my features to smoothness.

Still I long to be finished. When I ask him when that will be, he just smiles absently, more intent on my body than my words. I wish he would talk to me—it makes the work easier to bear.

I try to concentrate on the sounds outside the window, imagining myself with the other children at play in the fields and vineyards. Even in my daydreams, however, I can't see myself as a normal boy. I see myself as the other boys would see me: stiff and expressionless. I don't know how I would be able to run and play without my father standing above me. For that alone they would not want me around.

Constable Gaffore in his dusty tan uniform comes to the house. "If he is a boy he must be in school," he tells my father with upraised hands. "I do not make the rules."

"Impossible!" my father says. "You don't know what you're saying. He has never been on his own. Who will hold his strings? Without me there…" he trails off with a look at me. Whatever he was going to say, he has stifled it to spare me. I can see the pain in his face.

Constable Gaffore, despite his protestations that his hands are tied, does not like my father. I can sense that much, though I don't understand why he should bear my father any enmity. They are of the same age, and are even distantly related, as are many people in Orsomarso.

My father continues to protest, and I want to cover my ears to block out the sound of his voice, simultaneously hostile and pleading. "Traduco's son is older than my boy. He does not go to school."

"I am not speaking with Traduco, I am speaking with you," the constable says, his eyes growing hard.

My father begins to speak, but Constable Gaffore cuts him off with a curt gesture. "*Basta!* He goes, Gepetto. That is all."

I am excited and apprehensive. I must hold my own strings—which is awkward and strange—the first time I have done anything without my father to guide me.

At first the teacher and the other children seem kind. I am assigned a seat and given a primer, other than my hand-sewn clothes, the first things I have ever had that belong to me.

But the stares turn from curious to contemptuous as my first day progresses. At recess I cannot follow my schoolmates in their games, as it takes all of my concentration merely to walk and sit and turn my head.

I envy them their fluid unselfconsciousness, me who must plan every move in advance. I feel their eyes on me as I make my halting way from the schoolhouse door to the bench beneath the old chestnut tree.

"You are old Gepetto's son," says Falco, one of the bigger boys in the class.

"Yes," I say. He and several friends stand around me in the shade of the tree.

"You don't belong in school. You're not a real boy," Falco says.

"I am a real boy!" I say it with as much conviction as I can, but the boys all laugh at me.

"He can't be a real boy," Falco says to his friends, "he doesn't even have a mother!"

"I have a mother," I say, and as soon as the words are out of my mouth, I feel something peculiar happening to my face.

The other boys are laughing at me.

"You don't have a mother," Falco says, his tone ugly. "You're a piece of wood that Gepetto stole from the carpenter's scrap pile."

"That's not true," I say. "My mother is very beautiful, she…"

The boys are staring at me now, but that isn't what chokes off my words. Not only can I feel something happening to my face, I can *see* my own nose getting longer.

"What's wrong with your nose?" Falco says. "You're a freak of nature. Gepetto's little bush!"

"I'm not a freak!" I say, but they are all laughing at me and don't hear.

"Tell us about your *mother*," Falco says, drawing out the word for effect. The others snigger behind him.

"Shut up," I say, though not very forcefully.

Falco shoves me, and I go down in a tangle of limbs and strings. This gets Signore Gioppolo's attention.

"Get up off the ground," he says brusquely to me. "No horseplay unless you want to stay inside during recess."

Behind his back the other boys can barely suppress their glee at my chastisement. When he walks away they are all laughing again.

By the time recess is over, I have a nickname: Pinocchio, "pine eye." It is an unkind play on my wooden limbs and a slang word for an anus, "knothole."

"It was the great navigator, Christopher Columbus, who proved to us the Earth is round," Teacher is saying. "His crew was fearful when he sailed to find the new world, afraid they would fall off the edge."

A smallish boy with ears that stick far out from his head, raises his hand. Teacher tries to ignore the hand.

"But the Captain knew better…"

"Signore Gioppolo."

"Yes, Pietro," Teacher says.

"Wouldn't the ancients have known the world was round?"

Signore Gioppolo hesitates. When he finally speaks, there is a weary tone to his voice. "And how would they know that?

"Did they not have ships, the Romans and the Greeks?" Pietro asks.

"Yes, but they never ventured far from the coasts—"

"Yes, but when a ship comes upon another ship at sea, or returns to the Bay of Napoli, for example," Pietro says, "would not the sailors have wondered why they would see only the tips of the masts at first, or the peak of Etna?"

Signore Gioppolo seems perplexed by the question for a long moment, then waves it away. "You see the top first because it is higher than the rest."

"Yes, but Signore, why…?" Pietro starts to ask, but Teacher cuts him off.

"What has this to do with the Captain?" he says. He looks at the other students as if inviting them to share a joke. "Are you saying he did not discover the New World? That it doesn't exist?"

Falco speaks without raising his hand. "Pietro has not discovered how to make water standing up," he says.

I'm shocked by the boldness of this, but Signore merely smiles benignly. My classmates snigger, once they see no rebuke is forthcoming, and Falco basks. He is clearly one of Signore's favorites.

The rest of the afternoon grinds slowly by as I try to keep my mind on the lessons. From the corner of my eye I catch mocking glances and mouthed taunts from my schoolmates who relieve their boredom when Signore Gioppolo is writing on the board.

My father is waiting in the schoolyard when we are dismissed, and I am so exhausted from the strain of the first day, and from working my own strings, that I barely care what the other children will think when he scoops me into his arms to take me home.

After his dinner, my father is seated by the fire with his glass. It is the best time to ask him questions.

"Why don't I have a mother?" I say.

He looks at me sadly over his vino. "Do I not love you enough?" he says.

"Yes, yes—I didn't mean that," I say. "I just wonder why I don't have a mother."

"Some boys do not," he says. "It makes no matter. We are poor, but we have each other."

I want to tell him about the boys in school, and about my nose—since shrunk back to its usual size—but I can't find the words in the face of his melancholy.

That evening the bite of the rasp is almost soothing in its familiarity. I lie on my pallet, buoyed upon the comforting scent of resin.

By the end of the first week, all of the children and even the schoolmaster are referring to me by my nickname. It is not even funny to them anymore, just a matter-of-fact acknowledgment of my inferiority to real boys.

And anyway, there are already uglier taunts sent my way, and physical cruelties. One of the boys takes to throwing fallen chestnuts at the back of my head, the hollow thump making his friends laugh. When I complain to Signore Gioppolo that another boy jerked my strings, causing me to drop my primer in a puddle, he tells me that I must learn to get along with the other children.

"No one likes a tattletale, Pinocchio," he says to me. It is clear he means that *he* does not like a tattletale. He does not like me.

When I finally tell my father, he says I will find my way among the other boys; I should just ignore their taunts. He tells me about his own boyhood, during which he had to put a bully in his place with fists more than once. When I protest that he was a real boy and I am not, my father has no response but a pained expression. After a while I can't bear to see the sadness in his eyes, and I stop talking about school altogether.

Another strange thing is the clothes. Before I started attending school, I only wore my one homemade suit on the infrequent occasions we had visitors. It seemed completely natural to go naked otherwise.

Now, more and more, I am uncomfortable without my clothes. When I say so to my father, he points out that I have only the one set, which I must save for school.

"Why can't I have another set?" I ask. "The other boys have different clothes every day."

"We are poor," my father says, looking stricken. "You know that. Why would you ask me such a thing?"

I am instantly ashamed for having hurt my father's feelings. I wish I were a real boy, so that I would not be so selfish and ungrateful.

On Friday something different happens. After recess, Signore Gioppolo leaves the room and is replaced by Sister Antoinetta. She is a nun who lives in the convent on Via Dolorosa, and she has come, as she does every week apparently, to teach us about Jesus.

I have seen nuns in the village, especially at the market on Saturdays, long black habits covering everything but their faces. But this is the first time I have been able to look at one up close. Sister is a little frightening: her voice isn't easy, like Signore Gioppolo's, and the other boys do not call out or make little jokes as they do with him.

She calls me by my right name, Tiberio, which causes the beginning of a titter to ripple through the room. The giggles are stifled instantly, however, by Sister's icy look.

Most of the talk about Jesus goes past me, but I cannot look away from Sister. Her directness is a little frightening. So much conversation in the village, even the most trifling, is elaborate circumlocution ("*How are your figs, Signore?*" "*Ah, the rain, you know—too much or too little.*").

I listen attentively, my eyes riveted to the ruddy oval of Sister's face framed by the veil and wimple. I am terrified she will call on me and that I will be shamed in front of my classmates, but though she sends several glances my way, she does not ask me any questions.

Despite my difficulty in following the lesson, the afternoon speeds by. When class is dismissed at three o'clock, Sister tells me to stay in my seat. The look in her eye is frank, as if she is deciding what to do with me.

"You're Gepetto's boy," she says after a moment.

I nod, wondering at the "boy" part.

"Do you like school?"

I shake my head.

"The others tease you." Not a question. "Have you learned anything this week?"

On the spot, I search for some tidbit to satisfy her, but nothing comes to me. Since that first day, all I have done is sit in my chair and worry.

Without me saying anything she seems to understand.

"Starting Monday you will come to the Convent after school," she says finally. "We will teach you."

As I tell my father what I think is the good news, it slowly dawns on me that he is not happy, that he is angry. At me.

"Impossible," he says, when my words finally trail off. "What right has that witch to involve herself in my business?"

"Papa, I thought…" I start to say, but he cuts me off.

"No! Idiot son!" he says. "Don't you see? She will turn you into one of their dandy boys that hang about the convent door. Is that what you want? To be one of the little sissies holding onto her habit?"

Even in my confusion and disappointment, I pick out in my father's voice the same note he sounded with the constable. His querulous tone hurts me worse than the insults.

"You will tell her no," he says. "Gepetto will not have his son turned into a little convent pet."

I quail at the thought of delivering *that* message to Sister, but say nothing to my father. That night he doesn't touch me. He starts his Ciró with dinner and continues diminishing the bottle long after I have gone to my pallet.

The next school week goes by in fog of worried tedium, punctuated from time to time with the needleprick of fear when my schoolmates' rough taunts turn physical. I spend a half day suspended by my strings from the old chestnut until Signore Gioppolo thinks to come looking for me.

"How do you let these things happen to yourself?" he asks me as he untangles me.

Father does not meet me at the school, as he did the first week, which means I sometimes have to run the gauntlet of my schoolmates when we're dismissed. Mostly I sit at my desk, simultaneously looking forward to Friday afternoon and dreading it, for I will get to see Sister again, but I will have to tell her I'm not allowed to come to the convent for instruction.

Of course she knows, since I did not present myself on Monday, or any other day, as she said I should. As soon as she dismisses the pupils after our religion class, she leans back against Signore Gioppolo's desk and crosses her arms over her chest.

"Your father said no."

I nod.

She shakes her head and sighs. I am afraid she is angry at me, but when she speaks again, her voice is softer than usual.

"It is my fault," she says. "I should have known. What a week you must have had."

When she says this I feel an unfamiliar tightness in my chest. I don't know where to look.

"Come," she says. "Let's go talk some reason into your father."

My father knew this was coming. I could see it from the obstinate look on he face when Sister and I arrive at the small vegetable patch behind the house.

"Signore Gepetto," she says, "I am Sister Antoinetta. I teach the Catechism at your son's school."

After a brief look he turns back to his plants.

"I have come about Tiberio," Sister says. "Could you take a moment from your cucumbers to talk with me?"

"I know who you are and I know why you are here," my father says, then spits in the dirt between them.

I am shocked by the rudeness of the gesture, and look to Sister, but she seems unfazed.

"If you knew why I was here you would know it is for your son's benefit," she says. "He is not learning anything in that school."

"That old fool Gaffore intends he should go to school," my father says, getting up from his plants, "not that he should learn anything. I myself learned everything I know from hard work. No one took me by the hand."

"And for him?" Sister says, resting her hand on my head. "How will he learn?"

Her hand on my head—I could feel its warmth—seemed to enrage my father.

"Not by being one of your little convent Maries," he says, snatching me away. "You can't tell me what to do with him," he calls over his shoulder as he propels me toward the house, none too gently. "Now go—go back to your convent and leave my son be!"

I risk a glance backward and see that Sister is looking at me, and that she looks sad and defeated. Then I am inside and my father had slammed the door with such violence that the plates dance in the cupboard.

"What did I tell you?" he rounds on me, still gripping my wrist tightly. "I told you to tell that woman no, did I not?"

"I told her," I say, "but she wanted to talk to you."

"The word 'no,' is that so hard for you to remember, '*no*?' That is all you have to say to her, do you understand? *No*."

I nod my head, not daring to look up at his angry face. After a moment he releases my wrist. "Go to your bed," he says. "I don't want to look at you right now."

Usually the sound of my father in sleep carries me through the night, but tonight the small sounds from his bed fall upon my ears like recriminations. I am a stupid boy.

At the best of times it is lonely, of course, to lie in the dark and wait. I sometimes wonder how it would be to close my eyes and sleep. Father says it is like going away, but I don't understand where he goes in the long hours between snuffing the candle and the rising of the sun.

Monday is a bright fall day with a few high white clouds in the sky. Just before lunch, one of the smaller boys asks Signore Gioppolo where the clouds come from.

"They are bruises in the sky where angels have passed," Signore Gioppolo says.

Even I know that clouds are made of water, and they are where rain comes from. I find myself saying so before I realize it.

"Ah, Professore Pinocchio," Signore Gioppolo says, making the class titter. "I did not realize we had such an expert on clouds in our class. Tell us, *Professòre*, how then the water is held in the clouds?"

"It sticks together, like glue," I say. It is the first thing that comes into my head. I feel the uncomfortable tingle in my nose.

The class roars at this.

"I see," the teacher says. "And how did you come by this information?"

"I read it in a book," I answer. Almost instantly I realize my mistake. My nose immediately starts to grow, as does the hilarity among my schoolmates.

"Ah a book," Signore Gioppolo says. "What book would that be?"

I shake my head, since any answer is now a potential trap.

"You don't have any books, do you, Professore Pinocchio?"

"Yes I do!" I say, and am instantly rewarded with a few more inches of nose.

"Are you lying to me?" he asks.

I don't say anything; I don't dare shake my head for fear of my nose sprouting further from my face.

Signore Gioppolo puts his face down directly in front of mine. "You will answer me, puppet boy," he grates out, even the pretense of jocularity now gone.

"No," I say.

"No what? Speak up!" he says, his face so close to mine I can feel his breath on my cheeks.

"No, I don't have any books."

"And the clouds, like glue?"

I swallow. He is drinking in my humiliation like wine.

"I made it up."

Signore Gioppolo straightens and addresses the now-silent class. "Professore Pinocchio made it up," he tells my schoolmates, just in case any hadn't heard me. I want so bad to be in my dark little cottage, in my bed of shavings, that it is like a physical pain.

He lets the silence go on for several long moments. Finally he says, "Will we have any more helpful intrusions from the learned Professore?"

I shake my head, but that is not sufficient.

"I hear a gourd rattling," Signore Gioppolo says. "Did you say something, Professore Pinocchio?"

"I will not interrupt," I say, almost choking on the words.

"Very good," he says finally. "Let us continue with our lesson then."

But for the rest of the day, Signore is kinder to me than before. He calls on me twice more and nods approvingly, even though I know one answer is clearly wrong. And as I file past him out the door with the other students, he gently pats my head.

An odd thing happens that week. I have forgotten my primer and get halfway home before I remember and go back. As I enter the schoolroom, Falco is leaving.

"Pinocchio," he sneers as we pass, and as usual, raps his knuckles against my head. As I'm wondering why Falco stayed behind—he is Signore's favorite and not likely to be disciplined—I realize that I smelled resin as he passed. I look at my hands and bare shins, but there a no new cuts, yet the smell of resin hangs heavy in the schoolroom. A mystery.

The other boys continue to tease me—often in front of Signore Gioppolo, who offers no rebuke. In private, however, he is conciliatory, even gentle, and tells me I am improving in my studies. When the other boys are not around he smiles more and sometimes puts his arm around my shoulders when he speaks to me.

At home father seems to go between rage and melancholy. He does not take a tool to me all week. All he says when I come home is "take off your clothes." I go from the taunts of the schoolhouse to the frigid silence at home, and I don't know which is worse.

Gioppolo smiles thinly at me on Friday when Sister fails to arrive at the usual hour. He seems to be speaking directly to me when he tells the class that she will not be returning.

Until that moment I don't realize how much I am waiting to see her again. I once put back in the pond a little perch my father caught, out of sympathy for its gasping struggles. My father chided me humorously for being too soft. I feel like that fish now.

Would I cry, as I have seen the smaller ones do, if I were a normal boy? As it is, I just stare stupidly at the front of the room and endure the rest of the afternoon in a wallow of disappointment.

The only one who does not treat me as a curiosity is Sister, to whom I am simply Tiberio. And in his more expansive moods, Signore Gioppolo. I can't say Sister is not kind to me, though her kindness is not soft the way Signore Gioppolo's is, *when* he is kind.

I watch him with the other boys and I am sometimes envious of their ease with him especially when he plays with their hair or roughhouses with them. Around him I always feel awkward, and somehow undeserving of the attention he gives the others. It seems especially unfair that my arch nemesis Falco seems the closest of all to Signore Gioppolo.

That evening my father seems like his old self. The warmth is back in his eyes, and after dinner he goes to work again on my naked legs with the rasp.

It isn't until the old oil lamp is extinguished and I'm lying on my pallet with burning limbs, that the source of my father's good humor becomes clear to me. He knows that Sister has somehow been banished from the school.

The gouges on my shins throb bitterly, but I don't seem any closer to being finished. Often it seems father goes over the same spot several times before he is satisfied. I am scared of getting smaller, or having more and more of myself cut away until there's nothing left.

I have had these fleeting feelings before, but always dismissed them easily enough, secure in my father's benevolence. Now, lying in the dark, crisscrossed with lines on pain, my fears start to take root.

Through the long night my thoughts are full of fire and the sound of steel cutting into wood.

Of course my schoolmates have gossiped about my nose, but no one pays attention to what children say or think. In this case it is a blessing.

Some of the adults in the village are kind. Cuneo the farrier sometimes asks me to hold the bridle of a horse and speak to it while he shoes the animal. He says I have a good way with animals.

He often talks while he works, usually about horses and their care. Today he asks me about my lessons. I tell him what I have learned about geography and the history of the Mezzogiorno.

"And your schoolmates, are they friendly?" he asks. It is an innocent question, but the answer sticks in my throat. My silence makes him look over the back of the horse at me. "Do they tease you much?"

"No, no…" I start to say, and that is all I get out before I feel my nose sprout from my face.

Cuneo stares at me and crosses himself. Though the gesture is no doubt unconscious, it makes me feel a shameful freak.

"Tiberio, are you all right?" he finally says.

The concern in his voice is the final straw. I drop the reins and bolt from the stable, acutely conscious of my enlarged nose all the way home.

There are a few more incidents like this: hastily given answers to difficult questions. Hoping to deflect shame, I bring on humiliation. It is soon all over Orsomarso: everyone knows that I am the wooden boy whose nose grows long when he tells a lie. Men lounging in the shade say "Come, tell us a lie, Master Pinocchio." The women look at me with a mix of humor and pity that is almost worse.

Never before has my father worked on me after he's had his Ciró. Today, as soon as I am in the door I see he is well in his cups. Before I can put my primer down, he gestures with his chin at the worktable.

"Get up," he says thickly.

I tremble at the first touch of the tools, and before long I am in agony. His cuts are deeper and less calculated, and the blows on the chisel so wild that twice the mallet glances off and strikes me.

I can take it no longer when the chisels slips a third time, and as he bends to retrieve the tool, I jump from the bench and dash out the door—pulling my clothes from the hook as I go.

The schoolroom is lit with bars of late afternoon light and shadow, the sun slanting through the wooden blinds. I notice nothing except my own turmoil as I pull my clothes over my sore body.

Naturally I smell of resin, but today the schoolroom seems suffused with the stink, and I'm glad none of my schoolmates are here to note it. Then I hear the sounds, at once familiar and distressing, coming from Signore's office.

My curiosity is stronger than my fear. The door is ajar, and what I see peering through the crack freezes me to the spot. Falco lies atop Gioppolo's desk, and Signore is bent over him, rasp in hand.

Everything about the scene is nauseating in its familiarity: the tension between pain and submission, telegraphed by Falco's body. The cut lines on his belly that weep resin (yet Falco is a real boy—why does he not bleed?). The avid look on

Gioppolo's face, and the misery on Falco's.

It is like looking in a mirror, and it is ugly. I don't want to see my father's greedy expression in Gioppolo's face, nor the way Falco's limbs tremble with the suppressed desire to leap from the table and escape the knife.

I make some noise that alerts them to my presence. Signore Gioppolo's face wears his accustomed look of peevish impatience. But Falco's expression is the one that roots me to the spot. When our eyes meet, his are full of fear.

"Come here," Signore says, looking at me over the tops of his spectacles. In any other circumstance I might have interpreted his tone as a friendly one.

I stand rooted by competing impulses to obey and to flee.

The clatter of Signore putting down the rasp breaks the spell. I flee, my only hesitation leaving chief tormentor Falco behind.

Down the slight rise I run, heedless of strings and cross. My feet know where to take me, even if my head is clouded with Signore's long look over his spectacles. A guilty, speculative expression I had seen my father wearing many a long evening as he bent over me at the workbench.

It works in my favor that the village is in its afternoon stupor: there is no one outside to see me hurrying down the lane toward the convent, primer under one arm and my strings and cross under the other.

A very young nun, almost a girl, opens the door as I am about to knock. She has a basket of washing under one arm, and gives a little start when she sees me standing on the threshold.

"I'm sorry," I say. "I didn't mean to surprise you. I'm looking for Sister Antoinetta."

She looks at me for a moment, then puts the basket down. "Wait here," she says, and disappears back inside.

After a moment she reappears. "Come, Little One," she says, "Sister is in the kitchen."

I have never been in a house with a separate room just for cooking, and this one is enormous—dominated by a long table in the center and an iron cookstove.

Sister Antoinetta is sitting at one end of the table with two other nuns, shelling beans. The sleeves of their habits are rolled to the elbow, and they seem at ease, snapping the beans out of their pods.

"Tiberio, what's wrong?" Sister says, as soon as she sees me.

I don't know what I expect her to do, but Sister is the only adult I know who might do anything. When I try to tell her, it comes out garbled. "I went into the schoolroom and Papa was cutting Falco with the rasp."

"Your father? In the schoolroom?" Sister asks, as if that is the part that surprises her.

"Yes, no, I mean Signore Gioppolo—he was carving Falco's legs!"

"He'll hurt the boy," says the novice who let me in.

"There was no blood," I say, not to refute her, but because it just occurs to me. "There was only sap."

"Sap?" Sister asks.

"Resin," I mumble. "As from wood. Papa calls it my sap."

Sister exchanges a look with one of the older nuns at the table. "So I said," the older one says, continuing to shell beans into the pot. "You should get the constable."

This makes me afraid of what I started. What Sister says next truly scares me. "No, the Magistrato."

I have seen Il Magistrato in the village only once, when he arrived for the trial of Gianno Pietro who strangled his eighty-one-year-old mother with a goat tether. Senora Sclafani, who used to live next to us before she died, pointed out a tall man with a bony, liver-colored skull and false teeth too big for his mouth on the village square.

The big man fixed me with dark eyes for a long minute without speaking, then looked away. I felt like a lucky young rabbit dropped by the hawk.

"What's wrong?" Sister asks, seeing my stricken expression.

"He scares me," I say.

Sister pokes me gently with a bony finger. "You are not very good yet at knowing whom you should be afraid of, Tiberio."

Il Magistrato is the most famous jurist in the Mezzogiorno. He does not come to our little village every month; we will have to wait for his arrival. Meanwhile, I will have go to school and face Signore every day. The thought of it makes my heart sink.

Walking down the lane behind our house, I'm lost in my own fears and the yellow dust smell that rises up from my steps.

My hand is on the knob when I realize I hear voices inside: my father's, unusually jolly, and another, male voice. I realize with an ugly start that it is Gioppolo's voice. He and my father are talking easily just on the other side of the window.

"...I try to look out for him, Gepetto, but you know he is a difficult boy," Gioppolo is saying. "And one can protect a weak boy too much: it causes his schoolmates to chafe; they already mock him because of that nose."

My father laughs at this—he *laughs*! "It's true he needs to learn to stand on his own two feet," my father says. "It will only make him soft, knowing you or I will run to his rescue."

Their easy banter cuts me more cruelly than the chisel. How could my father be so chummy with Gioppolo the Ass? I hear the clink of the wine bottle against glass, and even the sound enrages me.

"Where is he, anyway?" Gioppolo asks, his voice a little thick with drink. "It will be dark soon."

"Ah," my father says, and I can picture the familiar, dismissive hand gesture. "He runs to those church whores when he is upset. He thinks I don't know. I have already made Gaffore have words with them. He didn't like it, but he knows I am right. The boy is my boy, and they can't interfere."

My father says "my boy" without affection, the way he would say "my chair" or "my saw." This explains Sister's sad distance: Constable Gaffore's hands are bound by the law.

I cannot go in, not with Gioppolo in there, and not while I am so roiled by ugly thoughts. I keep seeing my father bent over me with the rasp, but he wears Gioppolo's face. In my mind Gioppolo speaks and my father's words come out.

I want to hide myself, not just from Gioppolo and my father, but from everyone in the village. I have the feeling, standing on my own doorstep, that I belong nowhere, and that I wear my alien status on my chest like a sign.

I'm grateful for the deepening gloom, and even for the rain, when it begins, that makes people pull in their shutters: less chance they will see me, and less chance I will catch a snippet of conversation from some happy family sitting down to their evening meal.

I walk away from the village along the old road, a track of yellow mud that meanders in the folds between hillside farms and dense copses of olive trees. Carrying my string cross over my shoulder, I cleave to the high side of the road, trying to avoid the worst of the mud. Slow going. It is becoming full dark, and I can no longer tell the road from the ditch, when I see weatherbeaten house and barn just off the road.

I slink around the barn in the dark for a long time, listening hard for voices or footsteps. Hearing none, I slip the latch, opening the door just widely enough to edge in, then pull it to behind me.

It is warmer out of the blowing rain, and the barn smells pleasantly of hay and old wood and animals. I grope blindly until I find a stall that by smell and touch I can tell has a pile of hay.

A strange feeling has overtaken me. My limbs are heavy and I'm having trouble thinking of what to do next. I sink down into the hay with a pleasant sense of relief, and I realize that it is not merely dark in the barn—I am having trouble keeping my eyes open.

I lost track of my thoughts for a time—maybe moments, I do not know—then snap back to alertness. It is a strange sensation, though not an unpleasant one.

Again I lost track of myself, then suddenly snap back.

I am falling asleep.

That has never happened to me before. I try to wonder what this new fact about myself might mean, but the pull of it is too strong.

Just as I am abandoning myself to the delicious sensation, a rough voice brays in my ear, "Who is that?"

I am on my feet again instantly with a small explosion of hay, then go down, hard, as I tangle myself in my strings.

I roll over on my back to face the direction I think the voice came from and I hear one soft, unmistakable *clop* of a hoof. My eyes, strained wide open with fright, can pick out deeper shadows in the gray. Some light from the house, it seems, is coming in from the open hayloft.

It is a long moment of staring before I realize I'm looking at the soft round nose of a donkey.

"Did you just speak to me?" I say, wondering if this is what my schoolmates call a nightmare.

"I did," the donkey replies, his breath warm on my face and smelling of cut grass. "Why are you in my barn?"

"I'm running away," I say, still in wonderment over talking to a donkey.

"Where are you running from?"

"Orsomarso," I say.

"You haven't gotten far."

"No."

"Where will you go?"

Until Donkey asks I didn't know myself. "To Mormanno, to see Il Magistrato."

He makes a chuckling sound. "That is far away for a little boy with short legs," he says. "How will you get there?"

"On my short legs," I say. I am feeling the beginnings of impatience with this impertinent donkey.

"I can take you there, unless you'd rather walk."

"Why would you take me there?" I don't like the edge of suspicion in my voice, but as I have lately discovered, there have been many things I should have questioned and didn't.

Despite the sharp tone, Donkey takes the question with equanimity. "Because I also need to run away."

"You? Why?"

"I am old, and soon the man with the hammer will be coming for me."

The man with the hammer is Popeo, whose offal cart is drawn always by the animal in his stable he judges furthest from death. Popeo's judgment in this is not perfect, and more than once I have passed his cart in the middle of the road, one dead animal in the back and another in the traces.

I stare at Donkey's outline in the gloom. "Okay," I say to him. "When shall we start?"

"It would be best to be away from the village before first light," he says. "My master is fat and lazy, but he might send one of his sons looking for me."

I nod, and settle back into the straw. Again, just as the delicious feeling of sleepiness steals over me, Donkey speaks.

"Who are you running away from?"

"I told you, Orsomarso," I say.

"That is a place, not a person. Are you running away from the whole town?"

"No," I say, hoping that will end the conversation.

"Then who?"

"What does it matter?"

"It will matter a great deal if they come looking for you," Donkey says.

"My father. He will not come looking for me," I answer, wondering if it's true, and if I want it to be true.

"Why, does he beat you?"

"No." In my mind's eye I see the avid look on my father's face as he bends over me with the chisel. Too much to explain to a donkey.

"Go to sleep," I say. "Since we will be on the road early."

Donkey makes a rude noise, but says nothing else. Judging from his long, even breaths, he is asleep long before I.

In the dawn Donkey's gray, fleshy nose presses me awake.

"We should be leaving," he says when I open my eyes.

It takes me a few minutes to disentangle wakefulness from my dreams, in which Donkey not only spoke, but flew. He stands patiently, looking at me with his soft brown eyes while I sort myself out.

As I'm shaking straw from the cross and strings, Donkey says, "Are you going to drag that all the way to Mormanno?"

"What else shall I do with it?"

He nods his big head. "Okay, open the barn door."

It is still before dawn, though the birds are beginning to wake in the olive grove across the road. At Donkey's direction I close the barn door before mounting him.

"My master stays abed late," he says. "Let's not give the neighbor a reason to wake him."

Donkey's pace is even and slow, but soon the farmhouse is far behind us. It takes no effort to stay on his back, and through one dusty turn after another, I allow my thoughts to wander.

I worry about what I will say to Il Magistrato, and whether my father is looking for me right now. Thinking of him is painful, and yet I can't stop. I wonder whether things would be different between us, had I been a real boy.

Unbidden, and unwelcome, Donkey's question about the cross and strings keeps coming back to mind. Each time I push it away, the question comes back with renewed force.

Am I going to carry the cross and strings all the way to see Il Magistrato? And to what purpose? I cannot remember a time without them, and since I have been attending school, it has been an irritant to have to manage them and my books while walking to and from the schoolhouse.

"How far are we from Mormanno?" I ask Donkey, as much to stop thinking about the strings and cross as to know.

"Huh, I thought you were asleep," he says over his shoulder. "At this pace we would arrive late into the night, but I cannot walk all day."

"What will we do?"

"I know this road," Donkey says. "Not too far ahead is an old farmstead. No one lives there anymore. We will rest in its shade during the heat of the day. Past that we will start to see other travelers on the road—it is best to do so in the late afternoon, when they are thinking of getting home to their suppers, and not about a solitary boy on a donkey."

All that remains of the farmhouse is a stone foundation and an orchard gone to seed surrounding it. It is cool under the trees, and the smell of dropped fruit is heavy. It sits at a quiet spot off the road, and the only sounds are from birds coming and going through the branches.

Donkey noses through the fallen fruit for a time, eating only the pears. After he sucks water noisily from the spring he finds a deep patch of shade and is soon dozing peacefully.

Despite the setting and the quiet, I find myself restless. I explore the old farmstead. Spiders hunt among its cool, moss-slicked stones, and I periodically have to brush them from my strings, which they seem to consider a novel kind of web.

At one end of the foundation is a deep bed of ash where the hearth once sat. Buried in the fluffy, gray bed is a rusty blade, the handle long since burned away. I pick it up and use it to idly stir the ashes.

The abandoned hearth makes me think of my own, and the snug little cottage where my father and I live. The stone foundation seems suddenly chill and dreary to me. I put the cross up under one arm, and with the knife in the other hand, I scramble up out of the pit.

I settle in a sunny patch in the leaves and take another look at the knife. Despite the rust, it still seems sharp. Almost without thinking, I test its rust-pitted edge against the string that exits the back of my left hand.

I am surprised when the string parts. I drop the knife and try to reattach the string by knotting it to the stub end, but it's too short to accomplish, even if I could use both hands.

What have I done?

As the realization sinks in, I try more and more frantically to fix it, until my hands are shaking.

At that moment I hear the shuffle of a hoof on dry leaves and realize Donkey is peering down at me.

"What are you looking at?" I shout.

Donkey blinks slowly. "You cut the string."

"It was an accident!"

"Of course."

"I can't fix it," I say.

"Why?"

"I need both hands, and the end of the string is too short!"

"Why fix it?" Donkey says.

"Shut up!" I say, suddenly furious at him.

"I only ask," he says. "What you do is up to you."

"Go away and leave me alone."

"We should be on the road soon," Donkey says, making no move to let me be.

I have a peculiar and unpleasant sensation in my middle. I am scared, I want to tell Donkey, but the words will not come, making me even more furious.

I hurl a clod of leaves and dirt which bursts harmlessly against his gray chest. He nods his great head up and down, but neither turns away nor says anything to me.

"Why won't you go away?"

"You are not angry at me," he says.

"Yes I am!"

The words are barely out when to my mortification and fury I feel my nose begin to stretch.

I have a strange, pricking feeling in my eyes, and when I speak, my voice is strange in my ears. "I don't know what I think."

"Maybe things will seem clearer once we are on the road again," Donkey said. His braying voice is incapable of softness, but this comes out almost gently.

Lacking a better idea, I get to my feet and brush the leaves from the seat of my short trousers. I scramble onto his back again, holding the knife in one hand while using the other to pull myself up. Under the other arm rests the cross, one string hanging loose, a broken-winged bird.

Donkey is right. The road is empty now, and his slow, steady tread eats up the miles. Once I settle into the rhythm of the road, my mind begins to wander backward. I wonder whether my father is looking for me, or if he sits in his chair, worried at my disappearance. Several times I want to tell Donkey to stop, to turn back, but two things keep me from saying so. The man with the hammer, and the memory of the cold sound of my father's amusement at Gioppolo's jests.

But what if Il Magistrato refuses to hear me out? What if he has already gotten word about the runaway boy? I miss my safe bed of wood shavings, if not the sear of the chisel, and I am afraid I will be punished for defying my elders.

Regret chases worry until I am worn into numbness. At some point the gentle sway of Donkey's back sends me down into a slumber. When I wake, the stars are coming out. The air is cool and bears a tang of woodsmoke, and of the wild basil that grows in little shrubby clusters at the roadside.

"Please stop," I say to Donkey.

"You're awake," he says. "Good. There's a little stream ahead that passes under the road in a culvert. It's close, I can smell it. We'll stop there and drink."

The water is shockingly cold on my fingers. When I say so, Donkey nods. "It was snow yesterday," he says.

"What do you mean?"

"The stream, it runs down from the mountains," he says. "The white snowcaps melt and make little streams."

I look at a small white peak, barely visible in the settling gloom. There is so much I don't know about the world.

"You should drink," Donkey says. "It has been a long day."

I am drawn to the water, but he doesn't know I have never drank. I have seen the other boys drink from the well dipper, and my father many times of course, though usually not water.

I lower my face to the silvery surface. The water feels alive against my lips, and pleasant despite the chill. I take in a long draught and immediately start choking and coughing.

Donkey looks up at me from the far side of he stream. When the fit has passed he says, "You can't breathe while you drink."

"What?" I say, my eyes streaming.

"You have to hold your breath while you drink."

I try again, this time swallowing a mouthful of the sweet, icy water. It is very satisfying and I take two more swallows. I accidentally inhale some of the second swallow and start coughing again.

This drinking will take some getting used to.

Donkey moves a little way from the stream, and I get to my feet.

"Are we going?"

"Not yet," he says. "I need a rest."

I am increasingly anxious to have the journey over with. "I don't want to miss Il Magistrato," I say.

Donkey brays—a laugh. "Don't worry, you will not miss him. You slept while I carried you, now I will sleep. We will start again when the moon is up."

With that he settles into his head-down sleeping position and his soon motionless, except for his flanks which expand in slow rhythm like a gray bellows.

Despite my anxiety at somehow missing Il Magistrato, it is pleasant to lie in the fragrant herbs on the uphill side of the road. In truth, I am not sure I want the journey to end—on the road with Donkey I realize I am for the first time away from the pull of adults; outside their sway.

The sensation of freedom is at once heady and frightening. I am both glad not to be at someone's beck and call, and unsure of what to do with myself.

I look at the *traversa*, worse for the wear of travel. The strings are frayed and its arms have developed a wobble where they join at the center.

It is an ugly thing. It has *always* been ugly, I realize.

The strings pop as I draw the blade across them, no hesitation this time, knowing exactly what I am doing. For a long time after I sit with the cross in my lap, contemplating what I have done. It is more final than running away, and thinking about it makes my heart race. It is a prelude to what must happen when I meet Il Magistrato. Because of course going against Gioppolo means also to go against my father. There can be no other way.

Donkey looks at the abandoned *traversa* and cut strings lying by the roadside—along with the abandoned knife—and nods in what I am beginning to understand is a gesture of approval. His years show most in climbing the small cut in the streambank. From his back I feel the muscles and tendons strain. We walk in silence through the small hours of the morning, coming upon Mormanno just as day begins to break.

I expect it to be grander than it is, but it looks much like Orsomarso, another dusty town like every other bit of the Mezzogiorno, though with a few more houses lining the road.

Now that I am here, I have no idea how I will find the house of Il Magistrato, or even what I will say when I do. This early in the morning the streets are empty, though off in the fields we can see some men already tending the olive groves.

Though the morning is warm, Donkey is shivering beneath me. When I climb down he does not turn around.

"Is something wrong?" I ask.

"It has been a long time since I walked so far," he says. "I am tired and could use some hay."

It occurs to me that I haven't seen Donkey have anything to eat since the abandoned orchard. There is grass at the side of the road, but it is sere and brown, and my companion's worn, old teeth are not up to the task.

Donkey is just standing in the road, as if waiting for directions. His sudden passivity makes me anxious. There are several houses with barns nearby, and I pick the closest.

"Come on, I imagine there's some sweet hay in that one," I say. Donkey plods behind me willingly, if silently.

The barn is occupied by a gelding who makes no objection to our entrance, but watches us with a gimlet eye. The other stalls are empty—of animals and hay—and I am trying to decide whether I can risk taking an armful from the gelding's box, when Donkey says, "Over here."

He is standing head-down in front of a bin that has some tack piled on its lid. When I remove the harnesses and open the bin, Donkey nods his head with some animation.

"Oats," he says, and buries his nose in the bin without further ado.

The watering trough sits on the north side of the barn, away from the road. After a long, noisy drink, Donkey is ready to press on. His eyes are bright again.

"Now let's find your judge," he says, "before the day becomes too hot."

"But where?" I say. My relief at Donkey's improved condition is balanced by the return of all my fears. What will happen to me, once I find Il Magistrato?

An old man is coming down a path from the hills, a shotgun over his shoulder and a freshly shot hare in hand.

"Ask him," Donkey says.

Nervously, I raise my hand to the old man.

"Signore."

He looks up, seeming to notice Donkey and me for the first time. His chin is covered in gray stubble, and he has no teeth, but his eyes are lively enough.

"Yes?" he says.

"Signore, excuse me, but I am looking for the house of Il Magistrato."

The man gives me a closer inspection. "What for?" he finally says, in the rough way country people have.

I cannot possibly answer that question, though it's one I have considered all the way to Mormanno. *What do I expect Il Magistrato to do?*

"My father sent me," I say without thinking. Half a second later I curse myself as the old man stares incredulously at my freakish nose, grown suddenly longer.

"Please," I say, before he can ask another question. "I just need to see him."

The man looks at me suspiciously for a moment longer, then shrugs.

"It's the house with the gate," he says with a sideways nod of the head. "On the plaza."

I thank him and head off, Donkey at my side, in the direction the old peasant indicated. I don't look back, but I feel his eyes on us until we are on the road again.

"Plaza" is too strong a word for the wide spot in the dusty road, but at its northern end is indeed a house with a low black iron fence and a gate. It is the only thing that sets the house apart from its neighbors.

We stop at the gate. It is still early, and the house is quiet. The sight of it makes me frightened all over again of the enormity of my actions.

"What should I do?" I ask Donkey.

"Knock at the door," he says.

"It's too early."

"Too early for what?" Donkey says. "You and I are awake."

"I'm afraid he'll send me back," I say.

"If he sends you back it won't be because you disturbed his rest," Donkey says. "Anyway, we look foolish, standing out here at his gate like timid beggars."

My hot retort is stifled when Il Magistrato himself walks around from behind the house.

He is even taller than I remembered, dressed in rough clothes and carrying an armload of kindling. He stops in his tracks when he spots us at the gate, and I feel myself withering under his baleful gaze.

After a frozen moment he approaches us and swings the gate open.

"Signore, I am here to see you about…" I start to say, but he shakes his bald head and holding the gate with one knee and gestures for us to enter. When Donkey hangs back Il Magistrato makes an impatient come-on with his free hand.

Once in the front yard, the man closes the gate and sets the armload of kindling on the portico. He puts a massive hand on my shoulder and guides me up the two small steps to the front door of the house. I look back toward Donkey for reassurance: until this moment it didn't occur to me that I would have to speak with Il Magistrato without him present.

Inside, the house smells of food and strong coffee and cigar smoke. The hand's owner guides me through an archway and into a large, sunny dining room where a fat man sits at his breakfast, a coffee cup in one hand and a roll in the other.

The lace tablecloth is almost completely hidden by newspapers, plates, a writing pad, books, pots of jam and honey and loose papers.

"Ho, who have we here, Marco? A breakfast guest?" the fat man says when he looks up.

I look at my guide, who nods and gestures rapidly with both hands—some manner of sign language. It takes me a moment to realize that he is a mute. Before I can make the next logical leap—that he cannot be Il Magistrato—the fat man chuckles and looks at me.

"So you are looking for the judge," he says to me, putting down his cup and roll and brushing a shower of crumbs from his hands. When he stands I see he is *tall*, taller than the silent Marco. "Raphael Guercio, at your service," he says, extending a pink, meaty hand.

"I am Tiberio Gepetto…of Orsomarso," I manage to get out, almost stuttering in my nervousness. I have never been in such a fine house, nor shaken hands with a gentleman, much less a judge.

He gives me a long look, which while not unfriendly, I feel penetrates all the way through me. I am afraid he is going to question me on the spot, but after a few moments he merely nods.

"Welcome, Signore Gepetto. You have already met Marco," he says, with a look toward the manservant. "Would you care to join me for breakfast? Have you eaten?"

Have I eaten? No one has ever asked me this before, and a flurry of conflicting answers rush through my head while this seemingly kind man looks on.

Even I know the *correct* answer is to say that I've eaten, or that I am not hungry, especially in the house of someone so far above my station (my father would have heard "*Signore* Gepetto" as a dig). The social lie is not for me, however: my nose will give away even a well-meaning falsehood. The truth, I realize, is that I have been hungry since watering Donkey in the barn, and ravenous since entering this house of rich food smells. But propriety aside, I fear attempting to eat for the first time in front of Il Magistrato, however gentle his demeanor. I remember the coughing fit the first time I drank water, and for that matter, how fast a kindly adult expression can grow cold.

Finally I settle for the bare truth. "No, Signore Guercio, I haven't eaten."

I'm settled into a chair in a flurry of plates, napkins and utensils. Besides my father, who eats using his knife and fingers, I have only seen a handful of schoolmates eating—usually some small treats or a piece of fruit—never with utensils. I sit with food in front of me—toasted bread and jam, links of sausage, slices of orange and a glass of milk—but I don't know what to do.

Il Magistrato, sitting across from me, appears not to notice my discomfort. He beams at me cheerfully for a moment, then gestures with a blunt finger, "Go ahead, young man, don't wait for me—eat."

I pick up one utensil—it is silver and heavy—then put it down and pick up another. I am at a loss as to how I am supposed to get food from the plate to my mouth using these things.

"Is something wrong?" Il Magistrato asks.

"I don't know how to do this." I feel defeated.

"Is it the utensils?" He waves a hand dismissively. "We don't stand on ceremony here. Some of the best meals I've taken, I have eaten with my fingers."

"Signore, it is not that that I haven't eaten today," I say, forcing the words out. "It is that I have *never* eaten."

Il Magistrato purses his lips and the good cheer goes out of his eyes. After a moment he reaches for his cigar smoldering in the ashtray.

"Perhaps you should tell me why you have come to Mormanno," he says.

On the road from Orsomarso I have thought much about what I would say to Il Magistrato, but when it is time to explain myself, the words come very slowly.

I begin with what I saw of Gioppolo and Falco in the schoolroom, and then, as I am telling of overhearing the teacher and my father through the window, Il Magistrato stops me.

"What do you mean, your father 'made' you?" he says.

The question confuses me—what I meant, and what I am, seem self evident. "I mean...with the chisel and saw and rasp, he made me from wood."

Il Magistrato frowns around his cigar. "You remember this?"

"Not from the very beginning, Signore. But he has been working on me as long as I can remember."

I show him my forearms. "You can see the rasp marks here, they are not sanded out yet."

He looks at my arms and frowns. "Your father put these marks on you?"

I am about to say I do, but in the moment he asks, I see what he sees: a boy's arms, skinny—and dirty to be sure—with some faint scars on them. Now I am less than sure. I say nothing, and after a long moment, he nods. "How did you get here from Orsomarso?"

"Donkey. I hid in a barn, that first night. That's where I found him."

Il Magistrato raises his eyebrows. "You took him from the barn?"

"He took me here. He wanted to leave there."

He looks at me intently. "How did you know this?"

"He told me, in so many words," I say. Truth or no, I feel foolish. I wait for Il Magistrato to ridicule me.

"Still," Il Magistrato says, "you found him in a barn—he must belong to someone."

"He belongs to himself," I say.

"A novel defense," he says brusquely. "All right, go on."

Il Magistrato doesn't stop me again until I describe drinking for the first time at the stream.

"You had never drunk before?" he asks.

"No."

"Tell me the truth: you are saying that you have never taken a drop before—not milk, not water, not from your mother's breast?"

"I don't have a mother, Signore," I tell him. "Before that day I had never taken a drink of anything."

"And you are telling the truth?"

"Yes, Signore."

"And your father knows this?"

"He does, Signore."

When I have finished my story, Il Magistrato looks at me for a long minute, then heaves himself to his feet. "There will have to be a hearing," he says to me, heading for the door. "Maybe you can eat while I am not in the room. You should try: it will be a long ride to Orsomarso, if we intend to convene tomorrow."

"Signore, excuse me…we are going to Orsomarso? What is a hearing?"

He pauses with one hand on the doorpost. "One of the few legal words that means what it sounds like," he says. "I will call everyone into the courtroom and I will hear what they have to say. Only after I have heard all sides can I decide what is the next step in your case."

I now have a case, though I am not sure what that means. I will ask Donkey if he knows. I turn my attention to the food in front of me. It smells good and I want to eat it. I close my eyes and call to mind the boys at school eating treats, and my father at the table.

I must chew, that is the thing. I remember Gioppolo berating a boy who choked on a piece of candy, "Were you raised in a barn, Signore Falaise? *Chew* your food, don't swallow it whole."

I break off a piece of the toasted bread and put it in my mouth. Its crumbly texture is a little strange, but the jam is sweet. I concentrate on chewing, then almost without realizing it I have swallowed. Is that all there is to it?

I break off a piece of the sausage, and it too is delicious, though very different than the toasted bread. Soon nothing is left but the orange. I have seen my father peel and orange and eat it in moon-shaped bits, but this orange is cut into wedges with the skin on them. I try to bite a little piece off, but it is tough and it tastes bitter.

I try again, this time taking a bite from the softer inside of the orange. The orange is sweet in my mouth, but then something hard at the back of my throat makes me cough and the juice burns my nose.

When the coughing is finished my throat is sore and my eyes are streaming. I cautiously sip from the glass of milk, which is cool and soothes the raw feeling. I am just deciding that I am done with oranges when Il Magistrato returns.

"Ah, I see you have discovered how to eat after all," he says. "Good. Marco has the carriage ready. Why don't you go to the well behind the house and wash yourself?"

Donkey is lying in the shade of the wellhouse when I go outside. Marco, Il Magistrato's hired man, notices him at the same time I do, and he tries to hold me back, but I already know the worst and pull away from him.

His flanks are still warm, and his nose is pushed a little into the soft soil. I lift his head and gently brush away the dirt. His nose is soft.

While I hold his head, some of the cruel things I said to him come back to me. He was a true friend, and I never said so. In death he seems smaller, and fragile. There are worn spots on his blunt nose, and stubbly white whiskers.

After a while I notice Il Magistrato and Marco standing over me, the latter signing.

"Marco says if it were up to him, he would go the same way," Il Magistrato translates, his voice a little husky. "All at once, happy and with a full belly."

"Why did he have to die?" I ask. "He ran away with me to escape the man with the hammer."

The two men exchange looks. Marco signs, but Il Magistrato shakes his head as if he doesn't like what Marco has to say.

"What?" I ask, "What is it?"

"Marco says the animal knew his time was coming," Il Magistrato says, a slightly sour expression on his face. "That it is why he left Orsomarso."

I brush a fly away from Donkey's face. "We should bury him," I say.

"Bury him?" Il Magistrato almost shouts. "Oh, no, no, no, my young man. We have a man who will come and…take him away. I am sorry that he had to die when you had such an attachment to the animal, but I will not ask Marco to spend the better part—"

Marco interrupts with signing.

"It's not a matter of *minding*," Il Magistrato replies to Marco. "It will delay our departure for accursed Orsomarso. Besides, where shall we dig such a great big grave?"

Marco signs, and Il Magistrato shakes his head. "No."

Marco continues to sign while his employer looks more and more unhappy. Finally Il Magistrato throws a hand up in the air. "*Basta!*" he says. "Do as you will—a day lost digging a hole for the poor beast."

I help as much as I can. For a large man, Marco has a gentle touch, and he shows me how to use the shovel. When the hole is too deep for me to toss out my shovelfuls of dirt, Marco lifts me up to the edge and pantomimes bringing him a bucket of water from the well.

As Il Magistrato predicted, the digging takes most of the day. Refilling the hole is quicker. Marco says a silent prayer over the hole and gestures for me to toss in the first shovelful of soil. The soft thump of it against Donkey's flanks makes my eyes prickle.

Il Magistrato's carriage makes the journey to Orsomarso much more quickly than I imagined. The second meal of my life is taken from a basket that Marco has packed, and I must eat very slowly and carefully in the jouncing carriage. We arrive very late in the evening and go directly to the town hall, where the mayor is roused from his bed to accommodate us in the guest rooms.

Mayor Lapino, a slight, nervous man with drooping mustaches, recognizes me and starts to call me Pinocchio before he remembers Il Magistrato is standing there. He is obviously curious about my disappearance and return, but Il Magistrato is brusque with him, and we are soon in a suite of rooms that are opulent for Orsomarso, but I realize would probably be unremarkable elsewhere.

Before allowing him to retire, Il Magistrato hands the mayor a list of names. "Make sure these are notified they are to be in the courtroom at the stroke of nine tomorrow," Il Magistrato says.

"*Now* Signore?" the mayor says, eying the list.

"Immediately," Il Magistrato says. "I want no excuses, from them or you."

"I'll have Constable Gaffore get right to it," the mayor mutters as he leaves.

Marco shows me to a room, which I will apparently have to myself. It has a bed, a nightstand with a basin of water, a chair and a chest of drawers with a mirror. The bed has soft blankets and a down pillow.

I take off my clothes, now much travel stained, and slide under the sheets. Now that I am alone, my mind races back and forth between fear of what will take place tomorrow and the novelty of the room. I still don't understand exactly what this hearing will do, and I look forward to seeing my father with a mixture of dread and anticipation. I do not look forward to seeing Gioppolo, nor any of the others on the list Il Magistrato compiled in the carriage, with the exception of Sister. I am wondering what she will say at this hearing when I finally drift off.

I wake with gray dawn pressing on the curtains. I lie still, wondering for a moment at my surroundings, when a light tap comes at the door. I realize there was a previous tap which woke me.

"Yes?" I say.

The door opens and Marco cranes his head around it. He motions for me to dress, then withdraws. I pull on my clothes thinking how strange it is to have someone ask my permission to enter a room.

The main room of the town hall is the meeting hall, the marriage hall and the hall where everything else official in Orsomarso takes place. Today it is the courtroom by virtue of a long desk framed by a pair of flags, and its front two rows of wooden chairs separated from the rest by a moth-eaten velvet rope.

I sit in the front row, in the last seat on the left, with Marco between me and the rest of the chairs. Now that we are right down to it, my stomach is jumping with nervousness. People begin filing in just after we are seated, and it is soon clear that everyone in the town will try to push themselves into this room. I am just wondering what will happen when I see my father when a murmur runs through the crowd, and I know it is him. I turn around and find myself staring into his face.

For a brief second there is an flare of anger: teeth bared in an ugly grimace and hard eyes. Then he remembers where he is, and his face becomes impassive, like wood. He doesn't so much as nod at me. Next to him is Gioppolo, who favors me with a lingering smirk.

I am so upset I barely notice when Il Magistrato comes into the room. Mayor Lapino is pressed into service as the court's clerk, and despite his wrinkled brown suit and hangdog expression, he is briskly efficient.

"All stand for the Honorable Raphael Guercio, chief magistrate of *il circondario quattro*," Signore Lapino says.

Already a large man, in his black robe and snowy white cravat, Il Magistrato is even more imposing—almost forbidding. He nods unsmiling as he takes his seat, then gestures to Mayor Clerk.

"You may be seated," Signore Lapino tells the crowd. "This hearing is now in session. There will be no talking unless directed by the court."

The last is unnecessary, as Il Magistrato's grave demeanor has silenced everyone in the room.

"Signore Mayor," Il Magistrato says, "please call the first witness."

"Tiberio Gepetto, come to the witness chair," Signore Lapino intones.

For a moment I am rooted to my seat. I don't know what I expected to happen, but not this. Marco gives me a gentle nudge and nods to the chair set facing sideways to Il Magistrato's desk.

My legs feel weak as I walk to the witness chair. Signore Lapino holds a heavy, leatherbound book in his left hand and tells me to place my right hand on it. When I do so he says, "Do you swear to tell the truth, as God is your witness?"

This prompts a few snickers from the audience, which makes me wither with shame.

"Enough," Il Magistrato says, his tone of voice quelling the crowd instantly.

The mayor repeats the question.

"Yes," I say, obviously not loudly enough.

"Speak up, young man," Il Magistrato says firmly. "They have to hear you all the way in the back of the room."

"Yes, Signore," I say again, and the mayor tells me to be seated.

For the next quarter-hour, as measured by the ornate grandfather clock at the back of the hall, Il Magistrato asks me a series of simple questions, the answers to which he already knows: what is my name, where do I live, who is my father (he looks away from me when I say his name), where do I go to school, and so forth.

"Now tell the court what you observed on the afternoon of two days ago," Il Magistrato says.

Though I knew this was where the questions must lead, it is still hard to say it out loud.

"I saw Signore Gioppolo carving Falco with a rasp in the schoolroom," I say.

This sets off a few gasps and much murmuring in the room, and Il Magistrato has to slap his hand on the table to silence the noise.

"Who is this Falco?" Il Magistrato asks.

"He—I don't know, Signore. I only know him as Falco; I don't know where he lives or who his family is."

Mayor Lapino, standing to my right, leans in toward Il Magistrato. "Falco Severino," he says. "His family is from the North, I believe."

"Is he here?" Il Magistrato asks.

The mayor scans the room. "No, Il Magistrato: I don't see him, nor his family."

"Direct the constable to find him," Il Magistrato says.

From the back of the room Gaffore nods officiously and exits without waiting for Mayor Lapino to repeat the order.

"Go on, young man," Il Magistrato says, returning his attention to me.

I describe the scene as best I can, remembered through a blur of fear and surprise. I tell the court about the smell of resin and the weeping cuts on Falco's body. About the fear in the boy's eyes, and the crafty, hungry look of Gioppolo, as he beckoned me closer.

Aside from muttering and some disapproving clucks, the room is silent. From brief glances out of the corner of my eye, I see my father sitting impassively with his hands in his lap, as if waiting for a train.

"Now tell the court about the relationship with your father," Il Magistrato says.

"Signore?" I ask.

"Would you say it is troubled," Il Magistrato says.

Words fail me. I feel as though Il Magistrato has snuck up behind me and hit me with a club.

Il Magistrato does little to hide his impatience. "Come now: tell the court at least how you came to be."

"My father…" I start to say, but Il Magistrato cuts me off.

"Again, speak up, young man."

I start again, my insides shaking. "My father made me," I say, "from wood, with his carving tools. Just like Gioppolo did to Falco."

This time there is a general hubbub. "That's right, that's right…" I hear a woman's voice say. "He made the boy a little puppet."

Il Magistrato actually shouts the audience into silence. When it is quiet again he turns to me.

"So you were made of wood," Il Magistrato says. His tone is neutral, but I feel like a hot stone has been pressed into the pit of my stomach. "Tell the court how that is."

I describe the tools my father used to fashion me, and the way they felt—the burning feeling they left behind. I describe the *traversa* and the strings, and how I left them at the side of the stream on the way to Mormanno.

Il Magistrato asks me if I traveled alone, and feeling smaller and smaller, I explained about Donkey, and our conversations. There are a few titters in the room, but not many.

By the time I finish speaking, the only kind face I see in the room is Marco's. Even Mayor Lapino seems to regard me with pity and contempt as he directs me back to my seat.

The brash, smirking Gioppolo is not in evidence as he takes his seat in the witness chair. He is attentive and respectful, and dressed in a clean jacket and tie, I wince at the comparison the court must make with me in my ill-fitting and dirty clothing.

"Signore Gioppolo, how long have you been teaching school?" Il Magistrato asks.

"Almost twenty years, Excellency," he says. "The last five here in Orsomarso."

"So you are experienced in dealing with children," Il Magistrato says.

"Oh yes, very," Gioppolo says dryly, drawing a ripple of laughter from the audience.

"And Master Gepetto? Is he a typical pupil?"

"I would not say typical, Excellency," Gioppolo says, putting on his most thoughtful expression. "Rather I would say he is a type I know well."

"And what type is that?"

"He is very fanciful: a teller of tall tales, I believe because he desires attention. I don't say that as a criticism," Gioppolo says, holding up his palms, "It is probably a natural result of the boy lacking a mother. Nonetheless, he brings trouble on himself because of his tendencies."

"What sort of trouble?" Il Magistrato asks.

"The usual sort. The other boys are sometimes rough with him—I have had to step in a number of times. He can be disruptive in class, as well, sometimes diverting us from the lessons with his fancies."

Il Magistrato nods. "And what of the day in question? The one to which the boy referred?"

Gioppolo shakes his head sadly. "Perhaps he thinks he saw what he said, but it was nothing more than me removing a splinter from a boy's foot. I had him up on the desk because the light is better there, and because it is easier on an old schoolteacher's back."

"So there was no rasp, no chisel with this boy Falco?"

"A complete fabrication," Gioppolo says. "And a rather mean-spirited one."

"Yet you went to the boy's house afterward?" Il Magistrato says.

"Naturally, I was concerned. As was Signore Gepetto," Gioppolo says, nodding at my father. "As you know, the boy never came home."

"I see. And what of this nickname, *Pinocchio*?" Il Magistrato says, an expression of distaste on his face.

"Something the other pupils hung on him. I confess," Gioppolo says with a sheepish expression, "I have slipped myself, once or twice, and called him by that name."

"That is hardly becoming," Il Magistrato says. "Not a good example for your students."

"No, I am afraid it isn't," Gioppolo says contritely. "I can only add in my defense that when it is the only name one hears him called by, day after day, it is easy to make a slip."

Il Magistrato grunts. "Very well. You are dismissed."

When my father takes the witness chair, I see him as Il Magistrato must: sturdy, if old—a workingman in clothes that are plain but neat. His brushy white mustache is neatly trimmed, and his hair combed.

Once the preliminaries are past, Il Magistrato asks my father if he heard my testimony.

"Yes, Excellency," he says.

"And, Signore Gepetto?"

My father shrugs. "He is a good boy, mostly. He feels the absence of a mother keenly, as Signore Gioppolo has said. I have to support us, and so cannot be both a father and mother to him."

"He claims you made him," Il Magistrato says. "From wood."

"Il Magistrato, I wish I knew what to tell you," my father says with the weary air of someone saddled with the burden of a disobedient child. "My son has too much of an imagination for his own good. You heard him: a talking ass. I am just a woodcarver—from where he conjures these fantasies I cannot tell you."

"And of the marks on his arms? They come from the chisel, he told me," Il Magistrato says.

"I…A chisel? No! Excellency, he is a boy, and his schoolmates play roughly with him. Are there the tools of my trade in the house? Of course! And the boy likes to play with them."

I know it is not my place to speak, but I want to shout out loud that my father is lying. What outrages me more than the lie of putting marks on me is that he would say I touched his tools. Never, not once, knowing if I did I would have been severely punished. The silence of my neighbors, all of whom know what my father did with me, sickens me, but that is not a novel sensation. It is the way of the village, to turn a blind eye to what happens under another man's roof.

Il Magistrato moves on in his questioning. "Your wife, she died?'

"In childbirth, Excellency," my father replies. "Tiberio is our only child."

"And when he ran away, were you concerned?"

"Naturally," my father says. "I called for Constable Gaffore when the boy didn't return from dinner. We tried to find him, of course, but we had no idea which way he had gone."

Il Magistrato nods. "Signore Gepetto, there is but one road in and out of Orsomarso—could it have been all that difficult?"

"But who knew whether the boy struck out across the hills?" my father says, a querulous note creeping into his voice. "He is a willful boy, and that is just the kind of thing he would do."

"Yet you don't seem particularly glad to see him," Il Magistrato says. "I mean for all your worry."

"We are plain people, Excellency," my father says. "Working people. We don't wear our hearts on our lapels. I am glad to have him back home."

I had sat through Gioppolo's and my father's questioning in a kind of suspended state, listening to Il Magistrato's questions and their replies without thinking of the outcome, but my father's final words puncture my equilibrium. I will be sent back to my father's house, and to school, to who knows what end.

Sunk in the fear of what will happen to me, I don't notice my father being dismissed from the witness chair, nor the next witness being called.

I look up only when I hear Sister Antoinetta's voice saying the oath.

Sister sits in the witness chair calmly, without fidgeting. After taking the oath, Il Magistrato leads her through our meeting in the schoolroom and subsequent relations.

I look back over my shoulder. My father looks away, faced flushed with what emotion I'm not sure, when Sister describes her conversation with him outside the house.

"Signore Gepetto, you failed to mention this meeting. Do you have anything to add to the sister's recollections?" Il Magistrato asks.

From the audience, my father makes an irritated shake of the head, chin held high: a familiar gesture. "She was told to keep away from him," he says. Not once has my name passed his lips since we have been in this room. "Is the law one thing for me, and another for her?"

"That is one of the things we will settle today, isn't it?" Il Magistrato says. He turns to Sister. "Did Constable Gaffore warn you not to meddle in Signore Gepetto's family affairs?"

I expect Sister to say that she did nothing wrong: that it was I who came unbidden to the convent after seeing Gioppolo and Falco in the schoolhouse, but her answer surprises me.

"Obedience to the law is a good thing, up to a point," she says, "but sometimes the law demands unjust things."

"Oh, now she takes the law into her own hands!" my father blurts out. "She is above us all, Sister Too-Holy."

"Please!" Il Magistrato says sharply, one hand raised. "I will ask when I need your opinion."

He turns back to Sister. "Signore Gepetto raises an important question in his crude way: are we all to be free to follow our own hearts, despite the law?"

"Free?" Sister smiles. Her tone is not disrespectful, but neither is it fawning, like that of the other witnesses. "Excellency, I am not *free* in the sense you mean. Indeed, I am bound by tighter strictures than Signore Gaffore could imagine, much less have the wherewithal to enforce."

"Sister Antoinetta, it is not Constable Gaffore who sits in the judge's seat today," Il Magistrato says. His tone is even, but it sends chills down my back. For a moment I am more concerned what will happen to Sister than to myself.

"I respect you, Excellency, and I respect the law," Sister says, "but I am more afraid of seeing violence done to that little boy's body and soul than I am afraid of whatever sentence you could impose.

"I believe one day I will judged by One Whose laws I tremble to disobey."

Il Magistrato steeples his fingers in front of his chin for a moment before he speaks. "Pride," he says finally. "Beneath your humble words I detect a hard backbone of pride. You know what is better for the boy. *You*, not a semi-literate old woodcarver, should be the one to decide for Tiberio."

I hold my breath. In the audience, my father nods his head vigorously in agreement, despite the insult.

Sister looks down at her hands folded in her lap.

"Yes," she says quietly, "I admit that I have a low opinion of Signore Gepetto. It *is* my pride that I could do so much better for him than his know-nothing father; and I have contempt for the schoolmaster, who is worse in his way, turning his back on what he *knows* in favor of what he *wants*.

"I admit to all of that," Sister says, speaking slowly as if choosing every word deliberately. "I am ashamed for it. That I can have base motives is true, but it can also be true that I am right—that Tiberio would be better served anywhere but in his father's house. Or Signore Gioppolo's schoolroom."

"But how do you know?" Il Magistrato says. "How do you know you are right?"

"I pray. I ask for discernment. I struggle for the right answer," she says, looking Il Magistrato directly in the eye. "I try to set my own passions aside and put myself in the shoes of a little boy. I am willing to be wrong, but I am not willing to do nothing."

"And his father does not have the boy's best interests at heart?" Il Magistrato waves away the answer before it comes. "Never mind. What of the boy's so-called 'tall tales'? Let us speak plainly here, since much rests upon it: is the boy dishonest?"

So shamed am I by the hesitation in Sister's face that I want to disappear into my shoes.

"No more than most," she says, finally. "The donkey that speaks to him is hard to credit, I know. Sometimes, Excellency, we need to see things in a certain way to live with our circumstances. How much more is that so for a little boy?"

Il Magistrato looks grave. "I don't doubt that, Sister," he says. "You are dismissed."

He looks down at his list, then at the audience. Sometime during Sister's testimony, Constable Gaffore has slipped back into the room.

"The Falco boy?" Il Magistrato asks.

"Gone, Excellency," Gaffore says nervously. "His family has taken him back to Padova, apparently."

"Then there are no more witnesses," Il Magistrato says. "I will now render my opinion." The look of unhappiness in his face scares me.

"The law is about the truth, not what we might wish to be the truth," he says.

"There are the needs of the boy to consider, but also the rights of his father. Likewise, there are the reputations of Signore Gepetto and Signore Gioppolo to consider."

Any restiveness in the audience is gone. We all sit like stone waiting for Il Magistrato to deliver his judgment. Marco's large hand rests upon my shoulder.

"That Signore Gepetto is the most loving father is not at issue here, nor is Signore Gioppolo's expertise in the classroom," Il Magistrato says. "That the one has raised, clothed and fed him, and the other tried to educate him, is all that the law demands.

"Sister Antoinetta, though a warm advocate for the boy, said it herself: his stories are hard to credit. So unlikely were Master Gepetto's tales, in fact, that only the seriousness of his charges persuaded me to convene this hearing.

"In the end I am sure the charges are baseless," he says. "I release Tiberio Gepetto into his father's custody. This hearing is closed."

I hardly hear the confusion of voices in the room. When Il Magistrato began his speech I knew where it must end. While the din swirls around me, I resolve to run away as soon as I can—tonight, if possible—and this time to not place my fate in anyone else's hands, no matter how fair seeming nor august of reputation they may be.

Marco's hand is suddenly removed from my shoulder, and my father stands in front of me, unable to conceal his dark pleasure at my discomfiture. His hand on my wrist is not gentle.

"Come boy, I have wasted enough time on this," he says.

"Just a minute," Il Magistrato says, still standing behind the table. "I want to address the boy."

The room quiets when he speaks, everyone looking at him expectantly.

"Do I have your word that you will obey your father, and that you will not run away again?" he asks.

"Yes, Il Magistrato," I say without thinking. Of course my nose immediately erupts from my face, giving my plans away and filling me with humiliated fury.

The crowd reacts with loud amusement: *There goes Pinocchio's nose again!*

"Silence!" Il Magistrato shouts, not taking his eyes away from me.

"What just happened?" he asked me in a quiet, dangerous tone.

"My nose…" I can't go on.

"Your nose *what*, Master Gepetto?" Il Magistrato asks.

"When I lie, it grows," I mutter, provoking another round of titters from the audience.

"Only when you lie?"

"Yes, Il Magistrato."

"For how long has it done this?"

I think back. "I noticed it just this year, when I started going to school," I say.

"And is it absolutely reliable, this nose of yours?" he asks.

"As far as I can tell, Excellency, yes," I say miserably.

"Is what the boy says true?" he asks my father.

"Sometimes it does that, who knows why," my father says dismissively. "Did you not hear he is a peculiar boy?"

Il Magistrato looks around the room and fixes on Sister Antoinetta. "What do you know about this, Sister?" he asks.

"Excellency," Sister's voice carries over the amused murmur of the crowd, "I didn't mention it to spare Tiberio further humiliation, and because I have never seen it myself."

"And him being made from wood?" Il Magistrato says. "What of that?"

"I saw only a scared boy," she replies, "but it is commonly said that his father carved him from a stolen block, and that the boy's nose grows when he tells a lie."

"Said by *whom*?" Il Magistrato asks coldly.

Sister seems unafraid. "By everyone," she replies calmly, gesturing at the crowd around her. "This is a small village, Excellency. Word passes from mouth to mouth very quickly."

"I have heard it myself," says an old man in rather dirty overalls.

"And who are you?" Il Magistrato asks.

"Giovanni Penza, Your Lordship," the man says. "I have a small farm on the north side of the village. It was my ass the boy took to Mormanno."

"I'm not a lord," Il Magistrato says with an irritated wave. "You don't seem upset. Why did you not see fit to speak up sooner?"

"Well, he's an old ass," the farmer, no youngster himself, replies. "He can't work anymore, so it's fine with me if someone else feeds him."

"No one will be feeding him now," Il Magistrato says. "He died under my eaves."

"Huh," the old farmer grunts. "What did you do with the carcass?"

"My man buried him," Il Magistrato says, seeming a little ill at ease.

"You *buried* an ass?" the farmer cackles, drawing a laugh from the crowd. "I would have liked to see that! It must have been some hole!"

"Yes, yes," Il Magistrato says, dismissing the levity with a wave. "The boy was very distraught. He insisted."

Il Magistrato considered the old farmer for a moment, then the crowd. "Mayor Lapino, bring the court to order again," he finally says, "and have Signore Penza take the oath."

"Did you ever hear the ass speak?" Il Magistrato asks the farmer as soon as he is seated in the witness chair.

"No, Your Lordship, but if one ever did speak it would have been him: he was a smart devil."

Il Magistrato rolls his eyes at the honorific, but doesn't correct the old man again. "But you never heard him speak?"

"No, he understood when you talked, though," the farmer says. "More than once I'd tell my wife, God rest her soul, that I was getting ready to take something or other to market, and he'd overhear and take off in the opposite direction. I learned not to say anything where he could hear it."

This gets a laugh from the crowd.

"All right," Il Magistrato says. "Enough about that. You said you've heard the boy's nose grows when he tells a lie. You've never seen it?"

"No, Your Highness, I never met the boy before today, but everyone knows it."

"Who, specifically?" Il Magistrato asks.

Though everyone in Orsomarso knows of my shameful nose, only a few have seen it. As morning wears on, and the courtroom becomes hot and full of the smell of sweating bodies, Il Magistrato doggedly narrows the list to those who have actually caught me in a lie. It is at once tedious and humiliating.

The first witness is Guiseppe, a crony of Falco's.

After Guiseppe swears on the Bible, Il Magistrato asks him what he saw.

When my classmate starts to look toward the spot where Gioppolo sits in the courtroom, Il Magistrato almost shouts "Stop!"

Leaning over the desk, Il Magistrato catches Guiseppe's gaze. "Do not look anywhere but at me, young man," he says. "Now, did you see Master Gepetto's nose grow?"

"Yes, Signore," Guiseppe says, almost whispering. He can be heard only because the courtroom is deadly silent, as if the audience is holding its breath.

"When did this happen?"

"It was in September," Guiseppe says.

"No, I mean what happened just before his nose grew?"

"He said he had a mother, a pretty one."

Gasps from a few in the crowd.

"Anything else?" Il Magistrato asks.

"That he read something in a book—I forget what," Guiseppe says, almost stammering in his nervousness. "And that he had books in his house."

This brings a nervous titter from the audience. Anyone who knows my father knows that it is as likely he has a camel in our little house as a book.

"And what of him being carved from wood?"

Guiseppe looks as if he wants to disappear. "Yes, Excellency. He is made of wood, or he was—I don't know how to say it. But that's why we called him by the name."

"*Pinocchio*." Il Magistrato says.

"Yes."

Several more of my schoolmates tell substantially the same story, causing Gioppolo to roll his eyes extravagantly and mutter about schoolboy imaginations.

Gioppolo's muttering stops when Cuneo the farrier takes the witness chair. Moreso than with the others, I relive the painful sensation of being caught—visibly—in a lie as Cuneo lays out his story in a calm, deliberate way.

"And you knew he was lying?" Il Magistrato asks.

"Of course. Everyone in this room, save *Professore* Gioppolo, and possibly the boy's father, would acknowledge seeing Tiberio taunted by his schoolmates at one time or another."

Gioppolo's face colors at the sarcastic title, and he avoids looking at the farrier.

Il Magistrato asks a few more questions, then dismisses Cuneo. Il Magistrato's voice is hard when he has Gioppolo called back to the witness chair.

"You are under oath, Signore Gioppolo."

"I understand, Excellency," Gioppolo says. His composure has worn thin, judging from the tightness of his voice.

"Tell the court again what Master Gepetto witnessed in the schoolhouse on the day he saw you with this boy Falco."

"As I said, the boy had a cut I was tending to," Gioppolo said. "That was why Tiberio saw blood perhaps."

"A cut? It was a splinter in your last telling," Il Magistrato says.

"A cut, a splinter—the boy had injured himself somehow at play, that's all. I was tending to him."

"With woodworking tools?" Il Magistrato asks.

"There were no woodworking tools!" Gioppolo says, raising his voice. "You take the word of an addled boy, a proven fabricator, over mine?"

"There are no proven fabricators, yet, Signore Gioppolo," Il Magistrato tells him. "Though there are certainly some suspects. Let us turn to the question of the boy's nose. Why do you think it doesn't grow when he tells us what he saw of you in the schoolroom?"

"I couldn't possibly say why his accursed nose grows or doesn't grow!" Gioppolo says angrily. "The boy is prone to fantasies—maybe he believes he saw something, who can say?"

If the crowd had been treating the hearing as an entertainment for most of the morning, the mood has certainly changed in the last quarter hour. There was some grumbling during Cuneo's testimony ("That's right, the poor wooden boy—everybody knows his schoolmates made him the goat..."), but now the crowd is becoming plainly hostile to Gioppolo.

"How many other boys had *splinters* to be removed?" someone in the crowd shouts.

Il Magistrato admonishes the audience, but when he speaks to Gioppolo, it is through clenched teeth. "For a schoolmaster you are woefully short of answers, and courtesy, Signore Gioppolo," Il Magistrato grates out. "Your denials are becoming less and less believable. Can you tell me why you should not be barred from the schoolhouse?"

"It is my profession, Excellency," Gioppolo says in a wounded tone. "I have never been accused of anything untoward until this troublesome *boy*" (he glares at me) "entered my class."

Some in the crowd hiss at the schoolmaster.

"Again, your answer is deficient," Il Magistrato says. "Do you have anything to add?"

Gioppolo opens his mouth, looking as if he is about to speak, then shakes his head. "No, Excellency."

"A wise choice."

My father, never an expressive man, is himself like a wood carving on his second trip to the witness chair.

"Do you have anything to add, Signore Gepetto?"

My father's face wears its obdurate peasant scowl. "What has changed? The boy's nose is yet another embarrassment!"

"An embarrassment for whom?" Il Magistrato asks. "Tiberio told the court you *made* him with woodworking tools; which would be a spectacular untruth, no? Yet his nose grows not an inch.

"But when I ask him if he will not run away again from your house, it sprouts like a bush," Il Magistrato says. "Why do you think that is so?"

"He's a disobedient boy," my father snaps. "Of course he intends to run away again. Anything to cause more trouble and embarrassment for his elderly father!"

"I see," Il Magistrato says.

Whether my father sees the same thing is hard to tell: his face is a mask, and in it I can't find a trace of the kindly expression he would often wear with me in the workshop.

It seems, thinking back, that the only time his expression was soft was when he was cutting or sanding or gouging me. To make me a real boy. Most of the rest of the time I might have not existed.

Il Magistrato says nothing further to my father, but releases him from the witness chair with a curt nod.

"We will adjourn for lunch," he announces to the courtroom. "I will announce my judgment at two p.m."

Mayor Lapino jumps to his feet just ahead of Il Magistrato. "All Rise," he calls unnecessarily. Everyone is already on their feet and anxious to get out of the hot courtroom.

"Enough!" my father calls petulantly from behind his chair. "What more is there to judge? Either the boy is a liar or not." He makes a dismissive wave. "To be honest, it makes no difference to me whether he returns to school, or to my house!"

Gasps from the audience, and hisses.

My father rounds on his neighbors. "And who of you would take him in, this difficult boy?"

He turns back to Il Magistrato, who stares coldly at my father. "Speak the boy's fate now, and let us go back to our homes and work," my father says.

"The boy's fate I've already decided," Il Magistrato says slowly. "It is yours, and *Professore* Gioppolo's, fates that I wish not to decide too hastily."

Il Magistrato's words cause a flutter of excitement in the audience, and they wash out of the room in an excited tide. In a few moments, all that are left behind are the mayor, Sister, myself and Marco.

Sister starts to speak to Il Magistrato, but he forestalls her with a raised hand. "I know what you mean to say," he tells her. "You will have your chance."

He turns to the mayor. "Signore Lapino, please escort Sister out. I want to have some private words with Master Gepetto."

When it is just myself and Marco in the room with Il Magistrato, he tugs off his cravat, now damp with perspiration, and sits heavily back behind the desk.

"What would you have me do with you, Tiberio, if I don't return you to your father's house?" he asks.

"I don't know, Excellency," I say truthfully. I am almost equally afraid of being sent back to my father's house, or being consigned to some unknown future among strangers.

"Sister Antoinetta will offer to take you in at the convent," he says. "Do you think you would like that?"

I almost smile at the memory of the nuns' gentleness, and of the young Sister calling me "little one." But staying at the convent would still mean being here in Orsomarso. It is a small village—too small, I fear, for me, my father and Gioppolo.

Il Magistrato is waiting for an answer. A truthful one.

"I'm not sure, Excellency," I say. "May I have some time by myself to think about it?" I half expect my nose to erupt.

He looks at me for a long moment. "Yes, but do not wander far," he says. "We will start promptly at two."

The streets of Orsomarso are deserted in the hot sun. Everyone is either enjoying the afternoon meal or the afternoon nap. I walk east, because it is downhill and because it puts the glaring sun at my back.

I miss Donkey suddenly, and am seized with sadness that I will never speak to him again. He was wiser, in his way, than Il Magistrato. What would he have said at the hearing?

What will I say to Il Magistrato? It seems unlikely, though still possible, that he would return me to my father's house. What then? The convent? The sisters would be kind to me, no doubt, in the way they would be kind to a pet.

Donkey was the only one who ever treated me like I belonged to myself. Even Il Magistrato, for all his sympathy, thinks I must be someone's charge. It comes as a small surprise to me that someone can be well meaning, and even wise, but wrong.

I walk and walk, turning the problem over in my mind. Probably I can go live in the convent. That will not stop the teasing of the other boys, nor the rude stares of the adults. While I am in Orsomarso I will not know whether I am a real boy or just my father's wooden puppet.

My heart, and my feet, have made a decision before my head realizes it. My shadow extends far in front of me: it is long past two o'clock. At the crest of a small rise a breeze comes up, and on it, a slight salt tang. Down below me, far in the distance, is the blue Mediterranean. It is too far to reach before sunset, and anyway they will soon be looking for me, this time in earnest. I can imagine Il Magistrato driving the searchers relentlessly.

Soon I will leave the path and go to ground. When the moon is up I will resume my walk to the sea. I have heard that sturdy boys can easily find work on the ships that sail from Menestalla, out to the shores of Africa and beyond. If the life is hard, well, I am used to that.

The more I think of it, the more the idea takes root. I think I would prefer the cool, blue sea to the dusty Mezzogiorno. A ship will carry me beyond the reach of my father and Gioppolo, and even that of Il Magistrato. Despite his dignified demeanor and black robes, he is just a provincial official, the blue boundary of whose jurisdiction I can already see down below me.

If I'm not sure what it will be like, on the ships, at least I will have chosen it.

Little Red

Wendy Wheeler

Wendy Wheeler is an Austin-based writer of science fiction, fantasy, horror and mainstream fiction as well as a screenwriter, graphic artist, game designer, and teacher of writerly craft. Her work has appeared in *Analog*, *Gorezone*, *Aboriginal SF* and other periodicals and online at www.RevolutionSF.com. She's also placed updated fairytales and modern myth-based stories in the anthology series that never dies, *Snow White, Blood Red* (editors: Datlow/Windling), which has now been translated into French.

At its heart, most fairytales carry a chilling undercurrent. They are meant to teach us a lesson after all, to make us stop doing something "bad" by baldly calling out some baseness in us and calling it evil. These days, so many fairytales are remade into children's fare, and this wickedness is pruned out of the tale and we're left with a half story, a toothless monster under our bed. Wheeler restores the teeth to Little Red Riding Hood with a vengeance.

I think it began with the hat.

Helen had seen it in a shop on the way to our third rendezvous. Back then, we were still meeting in hotel rooms. She unbuttoned her shirtwaist dress as she told me about the hat and how it would look on her daughter, becoming all tittering and giddy, her pale face colored with something more than just anticipation of our lovemaking.

At this stage in my adventures, I enjoy making the grand gesture. "We'll go back together and buy it for your little girl," I'd said. "Afterwards." I remember how dark my hand looked on her white shoulder. My swarthiness usually pains me; I have even plucked the black hair from the back of my hands. But during these moments of *passion*, I find contrast only whets my appetite.

Helen had nodded, fingers to her lips, shivering from gratitude—or anticipation. The fresh smell of her was like an intoxicant. She didn't smoke or marcel her hair like some of the other women of my acquaintance. The planes of neck and collarbone above the bodice of her white slip had seemed achingly fragile. White slips have always excited me.

Later, after we drove in my new black Studebaker over to the store in one of the older sections of Chicago, I could understand her enthusiasm for the hat. When the shop girl lifted it out of the window, I took it from her myself before Helen could even reach out a hand. I caught my breath at the texture and plushness of the yarn.

"And such a darling color, too," breathed Helen. "That crimson will look just stunning on Regina."

It was a beret sort of style, hand-knit in Italy according to the tag. The wool had a clean, animal scent. I turned it around in my hand and saw the thing that was to fire my imagination.

On the side, a tiny red bud, so cunningly crocheted it almost looked alive. A flower as red as the hat itself, but with a slim green stem and two diminutive green leaves. Those tightly curled petals held an almost unbearable promise.

"How old did you say your daughter was?" I asked.

"She'll be fourteen in two weeks," said Helen, taking off one of her white cotton gloves to stroke the beret. Her nails were plain and unvarnished. She usually didn't even wear lipstick unless I asked her to. "This will make a wonderful gift."

I handed it to her. "With my compliments, then."

Helen blushed and shot a look at the shop girl. "Oh, I can't let her know it comes from you. But thank you, Josef. I will accept it on her behalf. You—you're very generous."

As the shop girl wrapped it up, I saw her unobtrusively stroke the tiny red bud. That caught my attention and made me look more closely at her, at the olive complexion free of makeup, the plain black dress, the dark hair pinned severely back. But there was a hint of fullness to her bottom lip, a certain set to her eyes. I fought the appetite that flared in me, tried to become totally the cultured man I truly am.

Still, I found a way to let my hand linger in hers as she returned my change.

Soon after, Helen and I began to meet at her mother's two-story brownstone on Bois d'Arc Street. Helen had inherited it upon her mother's death almost half a year earlier, but was unwilling or unable to do anything more with it than air it out every few weeks. Every piece of wax fruit, every antimacassar, every ceramic cat was left just as it had been when her mother died. I hated the dusty, old-woman smell, but stifled my discomfort to save the cost of hotel rooms.

It was here I saw my first photograph of Regina.

The picture sat with two others arranged on an ecru doily atop the Victorola. The pristine condition of the ornate frame told me this was one thing in the house that still received regular attention.

The girl in the photograph wore an antebellum costume with yards of lace and ruffles around a sweetheart neckline. Her back was arched and one hand toyed with her dark ringlets. And the face, the face was so…knowing. Dark eyes and brows (painted for the photograph in some middle-America version of stage makeup), a full lipsticked mouth, even a dimple in one cheek. This girl was born to wear the red hat.

"She's lovely," I had murmured. That tiny bud so tightly closed.

Helen was flitting around the room like a bird frantically beating its wings against a glass pane. It is the gentleness in women that speaks to me most. I missed that quality when Helen got so agitated.

What had attracted me to Helen that morning half-a-year ago was her hands. She'd come into my jewelry shop to resize her wedding ring, but the sight of her hands on the glass countertop, small and white and gentle, pious palms together and fingers laced as if in supplication, caused me to look again. When we began meeting at her mother's house, to calm her a little, I took to bringing a bottle of wine each time we met—that and cake. Helen loved *Gateau Robert*.

Now she paused in front of the photograph. "Yes, yes, she is. Boys just look at her and fall in love." Her smile was one of victory. "That was taken last year at the All-City Pageant. She won second place in that dress. I made it myself."

I knew about Helen's husband, The Right Reverend Henry Hunter of the Malletown Diocese, a pillar of the Episcopalian church. I had even seen them together, him in his clerical garb and she kneeling on the benches before him. How had they managed to engender such a charmer? "You only have the one child?" I asked.

"Just Regina." The words were said with pride. "I was the oldest of four." Helen began her flitting again. "The only daughter. I had responsibilities at an early age. My mother kept me at one task after another. None of that for Regina. I'm raising her differently; she's a perfect beauty."

The records in the Victorola cabinet, I noticed, were all ballroom tunes and German *leider*. My own taste runs to Verdi and Puccini, the Great Masters.

When I moved my fedora from the overstuffed couch and sat down, eddies of dust puffed up from the thick green carpet. I had to clean my shoes with my silk handkerchief. Helen's words irritated me a little. She should complain, I thought. Precious little my mother had done for me. "Yet your mother left you this house."

"Yes, the house." Helen almost spit the words. "My brothers would have friends over, lots of boys, and not all younger than me. They'd laugh and play their music, then they'd go off, leaving me on the front porch with my chores. I was invisible to them. *Invisible*." She tugged at a brown damask drapery as if she wanted to tear it down. "I *hate* this house."

I knew my cue. "You invisible, *ma cherie*? You're much too beautiful." I stood behind her and put my hands on her shoulders. Her agitation had warmed her, making her perspire with a scent that excited me. In her dark gray dress, no jewelry, no lipstick on her mouth, she was like a shadow in my hands. Another man would have passed her by, would have considered her too plain, too timid. I knew better. I can see the fire even when it's banked deep within.

I pulled the pin from her hat and tugged at the coil of pale brown hair beneath. "Show me the bed we'll use," I breathed in her ear. Though it was only two in the afternoon, my beard was already heavy enough to scratch her. It gave me a moment of chagrin to see the red abrasions on her skin, then I decided I liked leaving my mark on her, and nuzzled her again.

Helen's pulse leapt in her neck. Later, later I would kiss her there, open my mouth and feel her heartbeat against my teeth.

After I saw the photograph, I turned conversations with Helen more and more toward Regina. Helen had had her schooled in dance. She enrolled her in theatre classes. Regina had taken charm courses since the age of five. They were considering voice lessons. Her mother was insisting Regina wear lipstick now that she had turned fourteen.

And Regina had loved the hat I bought her.

"The little minx almost never takes it off," said Helen. "Why she'd wear nothing but that hat if I let her!"

I think it was this mental picture that set events on their course.

We were lying side-by-side on her mother's cherrywood four-poster bed. Helen was stroking the hair on my chest—my pelt, she called it. After some weeks, her distress at trysting in her mother's house had turned into something else. Now she seemed to relish having a lover in her mother's very bedroom. I was counting myself lucky to have found a woman like Helen, so proper outside this room and so wanton inside it.

I was still smarting from a discussion I'd had earlier that day with Madeline, the manager of my jewelry store. She'd raised her pencilled eyebrows, blown cigarette smoke from the corner of her mouth and asked in a loud tone, "Where are you off to now, Josef?"

Madeline is a hard woman, some would call her a harpy, although she does have excellent business sense. But her hands! Large, veined and muscled, with blood-red nails. I almost shudder when she touches my sleeve. "An appointment with a special customer, Madeline. Shouldn't be more than a few hours." I always smile when I talk to her; it's the best way to deal with strong women.

Madeline had all but thrown some diamond brooches back into their case. "You have too many 'special customers,' Josef. I suggest you pay more attention to the clientele that comes into your store." She took another drag on her cigarette and watched me through narrowed eyes. I wouldn't know, but I'm sure Madeline is the type of woman to take many lovers. She has that brittle quality.

I'd shrugged, at a loss for propitiating words, but then the salesboy Peter had called out from the back of the store with a question, and I was able to slip away. The whole drive to Bois d'Arc Street, however, I remained outraged.

I do take pride in my store. It is a small place, but in a very good location, and I carry only the highest quality merchandise. My business is the confirmation that I can deal successfully with the wealthy, the cultured. I've spent most of my life perfecting the knowledge. Yes, I have *petites amors*, but they are the perogative of a sophisticated man. As long as you don't allow your appetites to rule you, these small adventures add piquancy to life.

Helen's pliant nature I found delicious. I could lead her whatever direction I pleased. "What does your husband think of Regina?" I asked her now. "Does he know what a lucky man he is? Doubly lucky."

She sighed. "Henry listens to the Words of the Lord, Josef. With such competition, neither Regina nor I can much attract his notice." She put both arms around my neck. "But then, I'm a wicked, wicked woman."

To her thinking, she probably was, though I had courted her almost half a year before I'd won her. How these quiet ones love being pursued! I bent to kiss her. "You're not wicked," I said. "Just not appreciated. Neither you nor Regina."

When I asked her later to meet me Wednesdays and Saturdays as well as Tuesdays and Fridays, she hesitated only a moment before agreeing. I would have to cut back time with my other women, perhaps drop one or two. I was not too concerned about their reactions. Part of the adventure, after all, is that grand dramatic scene at the end.

And I'd already decided that Helen and her little family deserved my special attention.

Helen was surprised when I met them on the street in front of Regina's school; in her eyes I was still her illicit lover. She stopped dead still in the sticky Chicago air. But I had decided it was time to see Regina for myself. Enough of just imagining those knowing eyes beneath the red hat.

I knew the school, I knew the street, as I knew most things about Regina. I stood leaning on my Studebaker as they stood at the top of the steps, Regina and her mother, hand-in-hand.

Regina was indeed a tender young thing. Her black hair, unlike the ringlets in the photograph, was naturally wavy. She wore a green cardigan over an embroidered blouse, green plaid skirt and saddle oxfords. Perched at a captivating angle atop her head was the red hat. With only lipstick for makeup, her face seemed younger, but that didn't fool me. I knew utterly what type of creature she was.

I doffed my black fedora. Helen's cheeks were blazing. She moved forward again, but Regina had already noticed something amiss. Her dark eyes looked around until she saw me. As her glance swept over me, over my black pinstripe suit and red tie, my white silk shirt, my polished shoes, I felt an unarguable crackle of electricity.

"Come along, Regina," said Helen, as they descended the steps. "Head up." She tucked the girl's arm closer to her. "And walk decently."

"But, Mama, this is the man you meet at Grandma's," said Regina in a charming clear voice. "Aren't you even going to stop and say hello?"

Helen was speechless at that, but I recovered the situation for her. "Hello, Regina. May I call you Regina? I'm Mr. Volker. Yes, I've been consulting with your mother on her property, boring grown-up stuff. How was school today?"

Regina stopped. She put her head to the side and gave me a practiced smile, her dimple winking in and out. Yes, this was one knowing little female. "Just fine, thank you for asking."

Helen had finally recovered. "I—I'm surprised you know about our meetings, Regina. They're really nothing, nothing at all."

Regina patted her mother's hand. "I got curious when you brought me cake every day. And wondered why you always had sherry on your breath. Do you like horses, Mr. Volker?"

"Regina!" said her mother.

I ignored her. "Why, yes. Yes I do, very much. Do you like horses, Regina?"

"Oh, yes! I would much rather take horse-riding lessons than go to silly old ballet class. Mama says we can't consider it, though. It makes me so sad." Regina rolled her dark eyes and sighed.

"Regina is a very gifted dancer," said her mother through clenched teeth. "In her lovely costumes, all the boys adore her. Please stop this nonsense, Regina."

Regina thrust out her bottom lip. "Those costumes are silly, Mother. I wish you would buy me riding boots and dungarees. I could get those all muddy and no one would say a thing."

I opened my car door. "Well, I have no horse for you to mount, but I do have this black steed. Helen, may I offer you two a ride home?"

Helen shook her head, but Regina was already stepping inside. "What a lovely car! Thank you, Mr. Volker." I caught a flash of calf and thigh in the swirl of green plaid skirt. Pale skin, like her mother. Tender, young, untouched skin.

"We'll drive the long way," I said to Helen, ushering her to the car door. "Through the park to see the beautiful flowers."

Before she climbed in, Helen looked in my face as though something in my smile disturbed her. "I've never noticed before what white teeth you have, Josef," she murmured. "So large and white."

The flower beds at Littleton Park were so lush we decided to park the car and walk around. I was as charming to Helen as I could be, which mollified her quite a bit. As we strolled across the grass, Regina ran ahead of us, her sweater flying behind her.

"Regina, stop that!" called her mother. "Act like a young lady or we're getting back in the car." She rolled her eyes at me. "She has five young men calling her every day. She's a real heart-breaker, but then that's not her fault. I've told her be polite but don't let them get fresh."

"Gonna pick some flowers, Momma," called Regina, already tripping from bed to bed.

"Where's her lipstick?" said Helen, hand shading her eyes. "Is she wearing her lipstick?" She finally shrugged and sighed. "You gave me a terrible shock, Josef."

I took Helen's arm and led her to a bench. "I just had to show you how cozy we could all be together," I said. "I didn't mean to distress you. I would never hurt you and Little Red."

Regina had returned with an armful of gladiolus and day lilies. Her cheeks were pink and her hair wild as a hoyden's. It was difficult accepting this girl as the alluring creature in the photograph. But I see beneath the surface. "These are for you and Mr. Volker, Mother," she said. "Because you are so special. Who's Little Red?"

I brushed my fingers against the crocheted bud on her hat. "You," I said.

"I worship you and Little Red," I said to Helen. "You don't belong with him, that desiccated old crow. You deserve passion in your life. You didn't even know what passion was until you met me, did you?"

Helen lay spent across me. In my nose was the acrid scent of our cooling sweat. Her naked shoulders were pink with love bites. I could tell she was weakening. I'd been at her for almost a month to leave Reverend Hunter. She was in love with me, I could tell.

"But Regina..." she said, avoiding my eyes.

Regina was at the forefront of my mind. Regina and I spent several afternoons a week together, always in her mother's company, of course. Regina never took off the hat, and I would find myself sometimes almost hypnotized staring at that bud.

"I couldn't separate a child from her mother," I said, encouraged that it wasn't a flat no. "Little Red must live with us. She adores me, too, Helen, surely you can see that. I'll take care of you both, I promise."

Helen smiled. "She likes your name for her." She rolled away. "Oh, I don't know, I don't know. I was such a good wife, such a good mother. I took pride in my home, I was a tireless worker for the church. What am I now?"

"A woman," I whispered in her ear. "A passionate, beautiful woman. Your mother tried to keep you from it, your husband wouldn't acknowledge it. But that's what you are. I know that. I see that. Say yes, Helen. Say yes."

She curled on her side for all the world like a kitten or a dressed hare. How delicious she seemed. "Maybe," she said.

Taking a wife was something I'd planned for someday further in the future. I'd achieved most of my other goals: my own business with a select clientele, hand-made suits, an apartment (true, a tiny one) in the most exclusive high-rise in Chicago. Having a wife would limit my adventures, but surely it would make it easier to keep my passions at a more cultured level.

My breeding, or lack of it, is something I've overcome. It's more than just shaving my beard twice a day or having the stray hairs in my eyebrows tweezed. I've read the complete works of Shakespeare, I'm a self-taught student of philosophy, I attend the opera and know all the words to *La Donna e Mobile*. Some might call my predilection for adventures a weakness, but to that I say what better pastime for a man of taste?

And Helen would never be the kind of wife my mother was, though my mother had been a devout woman, too, in her own way. Her only half-way sober times had been Sunday mornings and confession. I could still see her sitting at our kitchen table wearing one of the white slips that had been her daily costume for most of my childhood. With each year, with each bottle, her pale skin had grown puffier, her red hair frowsier. She was always shrieking, always reaching out those big Irish hands of hers to grab at you, turn your head so you had to kiss her or, worse, pull you into her lap so she could pinch and maul you. All you could do was smile and duck away as fast as you could.

Six babies she'd had; me last. One right after the other, like some dog with a litter of pups. Disgusting. I could picture her lying on her side, six flat dugs on her chest to suckle us all at the same time.

I'd spent my life putting that all behind me.

Helen didn't say yes, however, until I asked her in Regina's presence. We were discussing whether or not to have lunch at a certain cafe where French dancers in berets and striped pullovers performed those semi-violent *apache* dances. Helen was curious I could tell, but worried about Regina.

Regina was all anticipation. "I want to see them. I've heard about those men and women, Mother; it's not so terrible. Maybe they're in love and that's why they dance like that."

"I'm in love," I said quickly, my hand on Helen's back. I felt her stiffen.

"With who?" asked Regina. Again, she was wearing the red hat.

"Helen, please," I whispered in her ear. "I love you and want you to marry me. I can't go on like this."

"Oh," she moaned. Her eyes were closed.

"You love my mother?" said Regina. She moved close to us; I could smell her floral perfume. "This is so romantic, isn't it, Mother? My father almost never spends time with us. Would you be like that, Josef? Would I live with you too?"

I drew Regina closer to us. "I want you both. What do you say, Helen?"

She opened her eyes and looked at my hand, so darkly hirsute against Regina's skin. I barely heard her breathe a "yes."

I know I can offer Helen and Regina a life of richness and culture. And they will start me on a new road of respectability and propriety. I will conquer my appetites and be the man I've always known I could be. Unfortunately, my apartment is a tiny place, too small for three people. We've had to begin our life together by moving into Helen's mother's house.

Regina seems to have taken all the changes with grace. I know she loves her father, all girls do, but I have faith that I can replace him in her heart. My optimism is fed by how at ease she seems to feel with me. Her curiosity today, for example.

After a few hours of moving various boxes and bags, I bathed and came out of the bath dressed in my black silk robe, and sat down to read the paper. Helen was out, buying supplies of whatever one runs out of in a closed-up house. I put the paper down to find Regina sitting on the ottoman at my feet. She was staring at my legs.

"You have much more hair than my father does," she said. "But I notice you have more muscles, too."

"Thank you," I said. Then daringly added, "and what do you have under *your* dress?"

She stroked her bodice, but said with an innocent look, "Just my chemise. Your face looks so dark this morning."

Embarrassment flamed, then I leaned forward and took her hand. "You're right; I still need to shave. Feel." I put her small hand on my jaw, then laughed as she shivered at the roughness of it.

"Do you love my mother very much, Josef? Do you kiss her a lot?"

I nodded, and kissed Regina's palm.

"You will take care of me, won't you?" she said, looking into my eyes. "Now that I'm your little girl, you will take care of me?"

Oh, yes, I thought. Oh, yes, my darling little bud. I know what you want of me. I will take care of you.

Helen came through the door then, arms loaded with packages. She saw us sitting close, Regina's hand on my cheek, then turned back to shut the door. "Lots of yummies for my family," she said. "Come help me put these up, please, Regina."

Tonight I left the bedroom door open. Helen didn't notice; the change in her circumstances has distracted her beyond belief, but she'll be fine once we start her divorce proceedings. She crept into our bed fairly shaking with tension. I cooed to her, and held her, convincing her to drink another glass of sherry from the carafe we now kept on the nightstand. It was important we make love on this, our first night as a family.

I calmed Helen, then, with stroking, began to excite her. Helen cried out, as did I. The sounds created curiosity down the hall, as I knew they would. I was certain I heard footsteps outside the door. First lesson, I thought. Big eyes watched us from the doorway; big ears listened to everything.

It made me even more ardent. I kissed and nibbled, plunged and reared. I could almost smell the blood beneath Helen's skin. Delicious, so delicious.

When we finally lay quiescent, a patter of feet retreated back down the hall. Helen started awake. "What's that? Mother?"

"No, no, nothing." I calmed her. "Just the settling of this old house. Go to sleep now. Go to sleep." She dropped off in no time, thank God.

I can finally slip out of bed, my hunger only whetted. This is the reward for my role soon to come, husband and father. It's what I deserve.

I've been reading the looks. I know when she talks what the words really mean. I can see the fires banked deep within.

The black silk robe drops around my shoulders like a caress. The door swings open without a creak. Beneath my feet, the old hall carpet feels like the grass of some deep wood. I touch her bedroom door; I see the white hand in the moonlight beckoning me so gently. I hear her breath.

I'm all appetite.

THE TROLL BRIDGE

Neil Gaiman

Neil Gaiman is an author of science fiction and fantasy short stories and novels, comic books and graphic novels, audio theatre, and films. His notable works include the comic book series *The Sandman* and novels *Stardust*, *American Gods*, *Coraline*, and *The Graveyard Book*. Gaiman's writing has won numerous awards, including the Hugo, Nebula, and Bram Stoker awards. His writing has also received the 2009 Newbery Medal and 2010 Carnegie Medal in Literature. He is the first author to win both the Newbery and the Carnegie medals for the same work.

This is the story that made me want to put this anthology together. I've never forgotten this story from the first time I've read it. I hadn't seen someone do things with words like Gaiman did in this story. Despite all the reading I had done to that point, there was something else going on in Gaiman's work that opened a door in my mind that's never been shut again.

They pulled up most of the railway tracks in the early sixties, when I was three or four. They slashed the train services to ribbons. This meant that there was nowhere to go but London, and the little town where I lived became the end of the line.

My earliest reliable memory: eighteen months old, my mother away in hospital having my sister, and my grandmother walking with me down to a bridge, and lifting me up to watch the train below, panting and steaming like a black iron dragon.

Over the next few years they lost the last of the steam trains, and with them went the network of railways that joined village to village, town to town.

I didn't know that the trains were going. By the time I was seven they were a thing of the past.

We lived in an old house on the outskirts of the town. The fields opposite were empty and fallow. I used to climb the fence and lie in the shade of a small bulrush patch, and read; or if I were feeling more adventurous I'd explore the grounds of the empty manor beyond the fields. It had a weed-clogged ornamental pond, with a low wooden bridge over it. I never saw any groundsmen or caretakers in my forays through the gardens and woods, and I never attempted to enter the manor. That would have been courting disaster, and besides, it was a matter of faith for me that all empty old houses were haunted.

It is not that I was credulous, simply that I believed in all things dark and dangerous. It was part of my young creed that the night was full of ghosts and witches, hungry and flapping and dressed completely in black.

The converse held reassuringly true: daylight was safe. Daylight was always safe.

A ritual: on the last day of the summer school term, walking home from school, I would remove my shoes and socks and, carrying them in my hands, walk down the stony flinty lane on pink and tender feet. During the summer holiday I would put shoes on only under duress. I would revel in my freedom from footwear until the school term began once more in September.

When I was seven I discovered the path through the wood. It was summer, hot and bright, and I wandered a long way from home that day.

I was exploring. I went past the manor, its windows boarded up and blind, across the grounds, and through some unfamiliar woods. I scrambled down a steep bank, and I found myself on a shady path that was new to me and overgrown with trees; the light that penetrated the leaves was stained green and gold, and I thought I was in fairyland.

A little stream trickled down the side of the path, teeming with tiny, transparent shrimps. I picked them up and watched them jerk and spin on my fingertips. Then I put them back.

I wandered down the path. It was perfectly straight, and overgrown with short grass. From time to time I would find these really terrific rocks: bubbly, melted things, brown and purple and black. If you held them up to the light you could see every colour of the rainbow. I was convinced that they had to be extremely valuable, and stuffed my pockets with them.

I walked and walked down the quiet golden-green corridor, and saw nobody.

I wasn't hungry or thirsty. I just wondered where the path was going. It travelled in a straight line, and was perfectly flat. The path never changed, but the countryside around it did. At first I was walking along the bottom of a ravine, grassy banks climbing steeply on each side of me. Later, the path was above everything, and as

I walked I could look down at the treetops below me, and the roofs of occasional distant houses. My path was always flat and straight, and I walked along it through valleys and plateaus, valleys and plateaus. And eventually, in one of the valleys, I came to the bridge.

It was built of clean red brick, a huge curving arch over the path. At the side of the bridge were stone steps cut into the embankment, and, at the top of the steps, a little wooden gate.

I was surprised to see any token of the existence of humanity on my path, which I was by now convinced was a natural formation, like a volcano. And, with a sense more of curiosity than anything else (I had, after all, walked hundreds of miles, or so I was convinced, and might be *anywhere*), I climbed the stone steps, and went through the gate.

I was nowhere.

The top of the bridge was paved with mud. On each side of it was a meadow. The meadow on my side was a wheatfield; the other field was just grass. There were the caked imprints of huge tractor wheels in the dried mud. I walked across the bridge to be sure: no trip-trap, my bare feet were soundless.

Nothing for miles; just fields and wheat and trees.

I picked an ear of wheat, and pulled out the sweet grains, peeling them between my fingers, chewing them meditatively.

I realised then that I was getting hungry, and went back down the steps to the abandoned railway track. It was time to go home. I was not lost; all I needed to do was follow my path home once more.

There was a troll waiting for me, under the bridge.

"I'm a troll," he said. Then he paused, and added, more or less as an afterthought, "Fol rol de ol rol."

He was huge: his head brushed the top of the brick arch. He was more or less translucent: I could see the bricks and trees behind him, dimmed but not lost. He was all my nightmares given flesh. He had huge strong teeth, and rending claws, and strong, hairy hands. His hair was long, like one of my sister's little plastic gonks, and his eyes bulged. He was naked, and his penis hung from the bush of gonk hair between his legs.

"I heard you, Jack," he whispered in a voice like the wind. "I heard you trip-trapping over my bridge. And now I'm going to eat your life."

I was only seven, but it was daylight, and I do not remember being scared. It is good for children to find themselves facing the elements of a fairy tale—they are well equipped to deal with these.

"Don't eat me," I said to the troll. I was wearing a stripy brown T-shirt, and brown corduroy trousers. My hair also was brown, and I was missing a front tooth. I was learning to whistle between my teeth, but wasn't there yet.

"I'm going to eat your life, Jack," said the troll.

I stared the troll in the face. "My big sister is going to be coming down the path soon," I lied, "and she's far tastier than me. Eat her instead."

The troll sniffed the air, and smiled. "You're all alone," he said. "There's nothing else on the path. Nothing at all." Then he leaned down, and ran his fingers over me: it felt like butterflies were brushing my face—like the touch of a blind person. Then he snuffled his fingers, and shook his huge head. "You don't have a big sister. You've only a younger sister, and she's at her friend's today."

"Can you tell all that from smell?" I asked, amazed.

"Trolls can smell the rainbows, trolls can smell the stars," it whispered sadly. "Trolls can smell the dreams you dreamed before you were ever born. Come close to me and I'll eat your life."

"I've got precious stones in my pocket," I told the troll. "Take them, not me. Look." I showed him the lava jewel rocks I had found earlier.

"Clinker," said the troll. "The discarded refuse of steam trains. Of no value to me."

He opened his mouth wide. Sharp teeth. Breath that smelled of leaf mould and the underneaths of things. "Eat. Now."

He became more and more solid to me, more and more real; and the world outside became flatter, began to fade.

"Wait." I dug my feet into the damp earth beneath the bridge, wiggled my toes, held on tightly to the real world. I stared into his big eyes. "You don't want to eat my life. Not yet. I—I'm only seven. I haven't *lived* at all yet. There are books I haven't read yet. I've never been on an airplane. I can't whistle yet—not really. Why don't you let me go? When I'm older and bigger and more of a meal I'll come back to you."

The troll stared at me with eyes like headlamps.

Then it nodded.

"When you come back, then," it said. And it smiled.

I turned around and walked back down the silent straight path where the railway lines had once been.

After a while I began to run.

I pounded down the track in the green light, puffing and blowing, until I felt a stabbing ache beneath my ribcage, the pain of stitch; and, clutching my side, I stumbled home.

The fields started to go, as I grew older. One by one, row by row, houses sprang up with roads named after wildflowers and respectable authors. Our home—an aging, tattered Victorian house—was sold, and torn down; new houses covered the garden.

They built houses everywhere.

I once got lost in the new housing estate that covered two meadows I had once known every inch of. I didn't mind too much that the fields were going, though. The old manor house was bought by a multinational, and the grounds became more houses.

It was eight years before I returned to the old railway line, and when I did, I was not alone.

I was fifteen; I'd changed schools twice in that time. Her name was Louise, and she was my first love.

I loved her grey eyes, and her fine light brown hair, and her gawky way of walking (like a fawn just learning to walk which sounds really dumb, for which I apologize): I saw her chewing gum, when I was thirteen, and I fell for her like a suicide from a bridge.

The main trouble with being in love with Louise was that we were best friends, and we were both going out with other people.

I'd never told her I loved her, or even that I fancied her. We were buddies.

I'd been at her house that evening: we sat in her room and played *Rattus Norvegicus*, the first Stranglers LP. It was the beginning of punk, and everything seemed so exciting: the possibilities, in music as in everything else, were endless. Eventually it was time for me to go home, and she decided to accompany me. We held hands, innocently, just pals, and we strolled the ten-minute walk to my house.

The moon was bright, and the world was visible and colourless, and the night was warm.

We got to my house. Saw the lights inside, and stood in the driveway, and talked about the band I was starting. We didn't go in.

Then it was decided that I'd walk *her* home. So we walked back to her house.

She told me about the battles she was having with her younger sister, who was stealing her makeup and perfume. Louise suspected that her sister was having sex with boys. Louise was a virgin. We both were.

We stood in the road outside her house, under the sodium yellow streetlight, and we stared at each other's black lips and pale yellow faces.

We grinned at each other.

Then we just walked, picking quiet roads and empty paths. In one of the new housing estates, a path led us into the woodland, and we followed it.

The path was straight and dark, but the lights of distant houses shone like stars on the ground, and the moon gave us enough light to see. Once we were scared, when something snuffled and snorted in front of us. We pressed close, saw it was a badger, laughed and hugged and kept on walking.

We talked quiet nonsense about what we dreamed and wanted and thought.

And all the time I wanted to kiss her and feel her breasts, and maybe put my hand between her legs.

Finally I saw my chance. There was an old brick bridge over the path, and we stopped beneath it. I pressed up against her. Her mouth opened against mine.

Then she went cold and stiff, and stopped moving.

"Hello," said the troll.

I let go of Louise. It was dark beneath the bridge, but the shape of the troll filled the darkness.

"I froze her," said the troll, "so we can talk. Now: I'm going to eat your life."

My heart pounded, and I could feel myself trembling.

"No."

"You said you'd come back to me. And you have. Did you learn to whistle?"

"Yes."

"That's good. I never could whistle." It sniffed, and nodded. "I am pleased. You have grown in life and experience. More to eat. More for me."

I grabbed Louise, a taut zombie, and pushed her forward. "Don't take me. I don't want to die. Take her. I bet she's much tastier than me. And she's two months older than I am. Why don't you take her?"

The troll was silent.

It sniffed Louise from toe to head, snuffling at her feet and crotch and breasts and hair.

Then it looked at me.

"She's an innocent," it said. "You're not. I don't want her. I want you."

I walked to the opening of the bridge and stared up at the stars in the night.

"But there's so much I've never done," I said, partly to myself. "I mean, I've never. Well, I've never had sex. And I've never been to America. I haven't…" I paused. "I haven't *done* anything. Not yet."

The troll said nothing.

"I could come back to you. When I'm older."

The troll said nothing.

"I *will* come back. Honest I will."

"Come back to me?" said Louise. "Why? Where are you going?"

I turned around. The troll had gone, and the girl I had thought I loved was standing in the shadows beneath the bridge.

"We're going home," I told her. "Come on."

We walked back and never said anything.

She went out with the drummer in the punk band I started, and, much later, married someone else. We met once, on a train, after she was married, and she asked me if I remembered that night.

I said I did.

"I really liked you, that night, Jack," she told me. "I thought you were going to kiss me. I thought you were going to ask me out. I would have said yes. If you had."

"But I didn't."

"No," she said. "You didn't." Her hair was cut very short. It didn't suit her.

I never saw her again. The trim woman with the taut smile was not the girl I had loved, and talking to her made me feel uncomfortable.

I moved to London, and then, some years later, I moved back again, but the town I returned to was not the town I remembered: there were no fields, no farms, no little flint lanes; and I moved away as soon as I could, to a tiny village ten miles down the road.

I moved with my family—I was married by now, with a toddler—into an old house that had once, many years before, been a railway station. The tracks had been dug up, and the old couple who lived opposite us used it to grow vegetables.

I was getting older. One day I found a grey hair; on another, I heard a recording of myself talking, and I realised I sounded just like my father.

I was working in London, doing A&R for one of the major record companies. I was commuting into London by train most days, coming back some evenings.

I had to keep a small flat in London; it's hard to commute when the bands you're checking out don't even stagger onto the stage until midnight. It also meant that it was fairly easy to get laid, if I wanted to, which I did.

I thought that Eleanora—that was my wife's name; I should have mentioned that before, I suppose—didn't know about the other women; but I got back from a two-week jaunt to New York one winter's day, and when I arrived at the house it was empty and cold.

She had left a letter, not a note. Fifteen pages, neatly typed, and every word of it was true. Including the PS, which read: *You really don't love me. And you never did.*

I put on a heavy coat, and I left the house and just walked, stunned and slightly numb.

There was no snow on the ground, but there was a hard frost, and the leaves crunched under my feet as I walked. The trees were skeletal black against the harsh grey winter sky.

I walked down the side of the road. Cars passed me, travelling to and from London. Once I tripped on a branch, half-hidden in a heap of brown leaves, ripping my trousers, cutting my leg.

I reached the next village. There was a river at right angles to the road, and a path I'd never seen before beside it, and I walked down the path, and stared at the partly frozen river. It gurgled and plashed and sang.

The path led off through fields; it was straight and grassy.

I found a rock, half-buried, on one side of the path. I picked it up, brushed off the mud. It was a melted lump of purplish stuff, with a strange rainbow sheen to it. I put it into the pocket of my coat and held it in my hand as I walked, its presence warm and reassuring.

The river meandered away across the fields, and I walked on in silence.

I had walked for an hour before I saw houses—new and small and square—on the embankment above me.

And then I saw the bridge, and I knew where I was: I was on the old railway path, and I'd been coming down it from the other direction.

There were graffiti painted on the side of the bridge: *Fuck* and *Barry Loves Susan* and the omnipresent *NF* of the National Front.

I stood beneath the bridge in the red brick arch, stood among the ice cream wrappers, and the crisp packets and the single, sad, used condom, and watched my breath steam in the cold afternoon air.

The blood had dried into my trousers.

Cars passed over the bridge above me; I could hear a radio playing loudly in one of them.

"Hello?" I said, quietly, feeling embarrassed, feeling foolish. "Hello?"

There was no answer. The wind rustled the crisp packets and the leaves.

"I came back. I said I would. And I did. Hello?"

Silence.

I began to cry then, stupidly silently, sobbing under the bridge.

A hand touched my face, and I looked up.

"I didn't think you'd come back," said the troll.

He was my height now, but otherwise unchanged. His long gonk hair was unkempt and had leaves in it, and his eyes were wide and lonely.

I shrugged, then wiped my face with the sleeve of my coat. "I came back."

Three kids passed above us on the bridge, shouting and running.

"I'm a troll," whispered the troll, in a small, scared voice. "Fol rol de ol rol."

He was trembling.

I held out my hand and took his huge clawed paw in mine. I smiled at him. "It's okay," I told him. "Honestly. It's okay."

The troll nodded.

He pushed me to the ground, onto the leaves and the wrappers and the condom, and lowered himself on top of me. Then he raised his head, and opened his mouth, and ate my life with his strong sharp teeth.

When he was finished, the troll stood up and brushed himself down. He put his hand into the pocket of his coat and pulled out a bubbly, burnt lump of clinker rock.

He held it out to me.

"This is yours," said the troll.

I looked at him: wearing my life comfortably, easily, as if he'd been wearing it for years. I took the clinker from his hand, and sniffed it. I could smell the train from which it had fallen, so long ago. I gripped it tightly in my hairy hand.

"Thank you," I said.

"Good luck," said the troll.

"Yeah. Well. You too."

The troll grinned with my face.

It turned its back on me and began to walk back the way I had come, toward the village, back to the empty house I had left that morning; and it whistled as it walked.

I've been here ever since. Hiding. Waiting. Part of the bridge.

I watch from the shadows as the people pass: walking their dogs, or talking, or doing the things that people do. Sometimes people pause beneath my bridge, to stand, or piss, or make love. And I watch them, but say nothing; and they never see me.

Fol rol de ol rol.

I'm just going to stay here, in the darkness under the arch. I can hear you all out there, trip-trapping, trip-trapping over my bridge.

Oh yes, I can hear you.

But I'm not coming out.

The Price

Patricia Briggs

Patricia Briggs is the author of the best-selling Mercy Thompson urban fantasy series, which includes the novels *Moon Called* and *Blood Bound*. She lives in Montana with her husband, children, and six horses.

Like me, Briggs finds the narrative of fairytales is often contrived and specious. If you brought in a fairytale for a class or workshop, your instructor would be asking questions like "Why would these characters talk to each other?" Briggs sometimes asks these questions herself and given the chance to "fix" problems in Rumpelstitlskin, she did.

Molly couldn't remember the first time she'd seen him. Certainly she'd never noticed him before this summer.

She did know that it wasn't until the fourth market of the season that she'd begun to watch for him. It was then that the market steadied to a trickling flow of people rather than the flood that came initially. She had time, sitting at her booth, to observe things that on busier days escaped her notice.

He would wait until she was occupied with a customer before coming to her small booth and touching the weaving on the tables. If she stopped to talk to him, he turned away and melted into the crowd as if he were uninterested.

Her first thought was that he was a thief, but nothing was ever missing. The next explanation that occurred to her was that he was too abashed by her looks to approach her. She knew that many men, even ones she'd known in childhood, were intimidated by her looks.

Being beautiful was better than being ugly, she supposed, but it caused quite as many problems as it solved. For instance, it cost her several weeks before the idea that he was worried that *she* would find *him* frightening crossed her mind.

It wasn't that he was ugly, not exactly, but he didn't look like anyone she'd ever seen either. Small and slight—he moved oddly, as if his joints didn't work quite the way hers did. He reminded her of the stories of the fauns that ran though the hills with human torsos on goats' feet. She'd even stolen a quick glance at his feet once, when he thought she was haggling with a customer—but his soft leather boots flexed just as hers did.

If she'd been certain that he was frightened of her, she would have let him choose his own time to approach her. But she had watched him closely last market day, and it didn't seem to her as if he were the sort to be easily intimidated. So she brought her small loom with her, the one she used for linen napkins, though usually she preferred to work with wool since caught her dyes better. The small loom made her appear to be busy when there were no customers about—and so hoped to lure him to her booth when she could talk to him.

He wandered over casually, and she pretended not to notice him. She waited until he became engrossed in a particularly bright orange-patterned blanket before she spoke.

"It's my own dye," she said, without looking up. "There's a plant in the swamp that a marsher collects for me each spring, I've never seen a color that can match it—rumpelstiltskin, they call it."

He laughed; it sounded rusty and surprised, as if he didn't do it often. She wasn't certain what the joke was, but she liked the sound of his laughter so she smiled into her weaving.

"I know it," he said, finally, when she thought that he'd decided to leave. "A wretched looking plant to be responsible for such beauty."

She looked at him then, seeing his face clearly for the first time. His features were normal enough, though his nose was a bit long for the almost delicate mouth and eyes. His skin mottled and roughened, as though someone had carved him from old oak and forgotten to sand the wood smooth. The effect was odd and unsettling.

He stood still under her regard, waiting for her judgment. She smiled, turning her attention back to her weaving. "Beauty is as beauty does, sir. A blanket will keep you warm whether it is orange or dust colored."

"But you made it beautiful."

She nodded, "That I did, for I must sell it, and most people look for pretty things. My face calls more people to my booth than might otherwise come here, and I am glad of it. But the blanket I sleep with is plain brown, because I find that it suits me so. Your face, sir, would not cause me to cross the street to look at you, but the way you touch my weavings led me to tease you into this conversation."

He laughed again. "Plain-spoken miss, eh?"

She nodded, then inquired mildly, "You are a weaver as well, sir?"

"And you are a witch?" His voice imitated hers.

It was her turn to laugh as she showed him the callouses on her fingers. "Your hands have the same marks as mine."

He looked at her hands, then at his own. "Yes," he said. "I am a weaver."

They talked for some time, until he relaxed with her. He knew far more than she about weaving in general, but he knew hardly anything about dying. When she asked him about it, he shrugged and said that his teacher hadn't used many colors. Then he made some excuse and left.

She wondered what it was that had bothered him so as she packed the merchandise that hadn't sold in the back of the pony cart with the tables she used to display her goods.

"Patches," she said to the patient little pony as he started back to the mill, "he never even told me his name."

On the next market day, a week later, she brought some of her dyes with her in a basket, making certain that she brought some of the orange he had admired so much. She left it out in the open, and it wasn't long until he approached.

She kept her gaze turned to the loom on her lap as she spoke. "I brought some dyes for you to try. If you like any of them, I'll tell you how to make them."

"A gift?" he said. He knelt in front of the little basket and touched a covered pot gently. "Thank you."

There was something in his voice that caused her to look at his face. When she saw his expression she turned her attention back to her weaving before he knew that she had seen: there were some things not meant for public viewing. When she looked up again, he was gone.

She didn't see him at all the next time she set up her booth, but when she started to set her weavings in the back of the cart there was already something in it. She pushed her things aside and unfolded the piece he'd left for her.

Her fingers told her it was wool, but her eyes would have called it linen, for the yarn was so finely spun. The pattern was done in natural colors of wool, ivory, white, and rich brown. It was obviously meant for a table cloth, but it was finer than any she'd ever seen. Her breath caught in her chest at the skill necessary to weave such a cloth.

Slowly she refolded it and set it gently among her own things then sent Patches off toward home.

The cloth was worth a small fortune, more than her weavings would bring her in a year—obviously a courting gift. To accept such a thing from a stranger was unthinkable…but he didn't seem like a stranger.

She thought about his odd appearance, but could find no revulsion in her heart—perhaps only someone who was very ugly or very beautiful could understand how little beauty mattered. The man who had created the table cover had beauty in his soul. She thought of the clever fingers caressing her weaving when he thought she wasn't looking, of the man who had been so afraid to frighten her, of the man who had bared his ugliness so that she would not be deceived into thinking he was something other than what he was. She thought of the man who gave her a courting gift and the gift of time to go with it. Molly smiled.

The path she took approached the old mill from behind, where the pony's field was. With an ease that was half skill and half habit for both of them, Molly backed the pony until the cart was sheltered by an overhang. She unharnessed him and turned him loose to graze in his paddock. She covered the wagon with a canvas that fastened down tightly enough to protect her goods until next market day, from rain or mice. She left his gift there until she knew what to do about it—but she was still smiling as she walked through the narrow way between the mill and the cottage where she lived with her father.

The mill pond's rushing water was so loud that she had no warning of the crowd that was assembled in front of the mill. Half a dozen young nobles gathered laughing and joking with each other while her father stood still among them with an expression on his face she hadn't seen since the day her mother died.

Fear knotted her stomach, and she took a step back, intending to go for help. Two things brought her to an abrupt stop. The first was that she finally recognized the colors that one of the young men was wearing—royal purple. There was no help to be had against the king. The second was that one of the young men had seen her and was even now tugging on the king's shirt.

She'd never seen him herself, though he had a hunting cottage nearby, for he seldom bothered to approach the village, generally bringing his own amusements with him. She'd heard that he was beautiful, and he was. She thought that the taut fit of his clothing showed both the cost of his tailor and the obsession with hunting that kept him fit. His hair was the shade of deepest honey and his eyes were limpid pools of chocolate. Despite the warm color, she thought his eyes were the coldest that she had ever seen.

"Ah," he announced. "Here she is, the fair damsel for whom we have waited. But she starts like a frightened doe. I weary of speech, Kemlin, I pray you, remind us of why we are here."

Molly saw the boy for the first time. A page, she thought, though she really knew nothing of court rankings. He looked frightened, but he spoke clearly enough.

"Sire, you asked me to wander about the town and tell you something amusing. So I walked the street from the time the cock crew until the sunset and returned to your lodge."

"And what did you report?" asked the king.

"I saw a spotted dog run off with a chicken from—"

The king held up a hand, smiling sweetly, "About the miller's daughter, I pray you." The rebuke was mild enough, but the boy flinched.

"I am sorry, sire. I came upon three men eating bread near the fountain at the center of town. Each apparently had a daughter who was passing fair. Each father tried to outdo the other as he spoke of his daughter until at last the miller—"

"How did you know it was the miller?" The king's voice was soft, but the titters of the other aristocrats told her that he was baiting the poor boy.

"I knew him because you sent me to the mill last week to find some fresh flour to powder my hair with, sire."

"Ah, yes. Continue."

"The miller, sire, stood and said that not only was his daughter the most beautiful woman in the kingdom, but that she was such a weaver as might spin flax into silk, wool into silver fit to bedeck a queen's neck, nay she might even spin straw into gold if she so chose."

Molly couldn't help glancing at her father who stood so silently in the courtyard. His gaze when it met hers was full of sorrow. She smiled at him, a small smile, just to tell him that she knew that it was not his fault that the bored nobles had decided to prey on something other than deer.

"After you told me your story this morning, what was it I said?" asked the king in a faintly puzzling tone, as if he couldn't quite recall.

"Sire, you said that if the paragon of maidenly virtues existed so fair, and so skilled: that she must be your bride." The boy looked at her now, with a wealth of guilt in his eyes.

Poor baited lamb, she thought, so tormented himself, but still able to feel compassion for another victim.

When the laughter died down, the king turned to her. "Fair maiden, I see that the first claim was not exaggerated. You have hair the color of mink and eyes like the sky." He paused, but she did not respond so he continued. "Therefore, you and your father will come to my lodge as my guests. Tonight, after we dine you will be shown a room full of flax that you may spin into fine silk thread. If you do not… what was it I said, Kemlin?"

Molly knew, and she was certain the boy did, too, that the king knew perfectly well what it was he had said.

"Sire," said the page reluctantly, "you said that if she did not, you would have the mill torn to the ground, her father's tongue put out for lying, and the girl herself beheaded in the town square."

The king smiled, revealing a pair of dimples. "Yes. I remember now. You will come with us now."

Though the king offered her a seat pillion behind one of his nobles, Molly asked to walk with her father. The king seemed ill inclined to press the matter, so she clasped her father's hand in hers and he returned her grasp until her hand hurt—though nothing of his torment showed on his face.

The king's hunting cottage was a castle in its own right, filled with assorted young men and women. Molly and her father sat together at the dining table, two ducks in a room of swans. Swans, for all their beauty, are vicious animals.

After the meal, she was taken to a room as big as her father's cottage filled waist-high with flax with a small spinning wheel set in the corner. She was given a small, closed lantern to light the chamber. She nodded goodbye to her father and waited until the door shut then allowed her shoulders to droop.

The flax was high quality, and there was more of it than she would ever be able to afford if she saved for the rest of her life. But it was flax, and no matter how good the yarn she spun it would make fine linen cloth, but not silk. Even if fine linen thread would have been acceptable, she would never be able to spin so much in a single night.

Despair clogged her throat and misted her eyes and she kicked a pile of flax and watched it drift to the top of another pile. Wiping her arm across her eyes she waded through flax to the spinning wheel and sat down to spin. Hours passed, and weariness slowed her quick fingers.

"Miss?"

She cried out with surprise.

The man from the marketplace shrank back as if to fade back to wherever it was he'd come from.

"No," she said quickly, reaching out to him. She didn't know how he could have entered this room, but it was good to see a friendly face. "Please don't go. I was only startled, how did you get in here?"

"I heard—" he said hesitantly, watching her as if he expected her to scream again, "— that you were here and why. It sounded as if you might need help."

She laughed; it sounded forlorn so she stopped.

Shaking her head she said, "There is only one wheel here—and even if you can spin faster than I, you cannot spin flax into silk."

"You might be surprised," he said, pulling back his hood, revealing funny tufts of red hair. "Let me tell you a story. Once upon a time there was a boy, not a bad boy, but not particularly good either. In a mountain near his village were caves that all of the village children had been warned against, but, as he wasn't as smart as he thought himself, the boy decided to go exploring in the caves. He got lost, of course, and spent a long time wandering through the caves until his candle burned to nothing. He tried to continue and fell down a hole, breaking any number of bones."

Molly thought about the odd way that he moved and winced in sympathy. "How did you survive?"

"Ah," he said, "that is the crux of this story. I was saved by a dwarf, an outcast from his own people, who was very lonely indeed to want the company of a human. He used magic to save me, to let me walk and speak normally and to repair my addled wits. He taught me how to weave, an odd talent for a dwarf, I know, but he was quite good at it. I stayed with him until he died, several years ago—of old age, I should add, in case you suspect me of any foul deeds."

She hadn't, but it was nice to know.

The man was quiet for a moment, then he said, "He taught me magic as well, if you like I can spin your flax into silk, but magic always has a price. The price for my life was to live it as you see, something not quite human, but clearly nothing else."

"What would be the price of spinning all of this to silk?"

"Something you value," he replied.

She bowed her head in thought and removed a copper ring from her finger. "This belonged to a young man that I loved, who loved me in return. He was called to fight in the king's army. Last year his brother brought back his body. Will this do?"

"Ah, miss," said the strange little man, a wealth of sorrow in his tone. "It will do very well—but I'm not certain I'm doing you any favors by my magic."

"Well," she said with a smile, though it wobbled a bit, "I would rather lose the ring than see my father without his living or his tongue; and dead, I would value the ring not at all."

The little man nodded and rolled the ring between his hands, spat on it once and muttered to himself. He opened his hands and the ring was gone.

Without speaking another word he gestured for her to give up her place at the spinning wheel and set to work. His fingers flew far more swiftly than hers, and she wasn't able to see exactly when the flax turned to silk. She watched for a long while, but finally she slept, her head pillowed upon a pile of silken thread. She didn't feel the gentle touch of his clever hands against her cheek, nor did she hear him leave.

She awoke to the sound of a key turning the lock. She looked swiftly to the spinning wheel, but there was no one there.

The king was the first to enter the room. He had been laughing, but as he stepped through the door and saw the silk his face went blank with astonishment.

Molly came to her feet and curtseyed. "Sire."

"It seems," said the king slowly, "that your father was not overly hasty in his words—I will leave him his mill. Tonight we shall see if he keeps his tongue. Come, you will break your fast with my court."

Breakfast was not as bad as dinner had been, maybe because Molly was so tired she was able to ignore everything but her plate and her father, who was once more seated beside her. They didn't speak, though he held her hand tightly, under the table where no one would see.

That night the king took her to the same room, but this time it was filled waist-deep with fine-combed wool.

"Tomorrow," the king said, "if you have not spun this wool into silver, your father shall have his tongue removed."

Molly raised her chin, fatigue silencing her normal caution. "I will have your word before the court that if the wool is spun to silver tomorrow morning, you will leave my father alone from that moment forward."

The king's eyebrows rose at her speech, "Of course, my dear, you have my word."

"And I will witness to it, " said a woman's voice.

"Mother!" said the king, astonished.

Molly looked at the woman who had approached. She didn't look old enough to have sired the king, only the slightest touch of grey sparkled in her golden hair. Her hand rested gently on the shoulder of the young page Molly recognized from the day yesterday.

The queen smiled at her son, though her eyes were shrewd. "Sir Thomas sent a message to me, telling me what you were up to. When I heard that there was a child here who was credited with such marvels I had to come and see. Kemlin tells me that she has already spun flax into silk."

"Why did Sir Thomas go whining to you?" asked the king in a dangerously soft voice.

The queen shook her head, "My dear, it's harvest time and you have the mill closed down because of some fantastic story you heard, of course he was upset. He had no way of knowing that the girl would be able to accomplish such a feat—she has no reputation for magic."

"I see," said the king in a voice that boded ill for Sir Thomas.

"Sir Thomas," said the queen in a soft voice, "is a particular friend of mine. I would be very upset if anything were to happen to him." She smiled. "Now shall we let this child get to work?"

Molly stepped into the room with her lantern and waited until the door shut behind her, then took the narrow path cleared through the wool to the spinning wheel in the far corner of the room. The wool that she walked past was of far higher quality than she'd ever worked with, as if someone had combed through all the fleeces in the land and chosen the very best. She thought that it would be far more beautiful spun and woven into cloth than it would be changed to cold silver.

She wondered if he would come back tonight, and if he did, whether he would be able to help her. She didn't know anything about magic, but she thought that there would be a significant difference between changing flax into silk and changing wool into silver: wool and silver are not very much alike.

"Miss," he said, from the other side of the spinning wheel, though he hadn't been there just a moment ago.

This time she didn't jump or start at all, just smiled. "Good evening to you, sir. I'm very glad to see you, though I could wish it were under different circumstances."

He nodded, glancing around the room. "It seems a shame to waste this, he could have chosen lesser wool."

"Shall we leave it then?" she said softly. "I would like to see how you are able to spin it into fine yarn for weaving."

He looked at her, light blue eyes dimmed by the shadows in the room. "You will die, if it is not spun to silver."

"And my father will lose his tongue." She took off her necklace. It was a cheap thing, made of beads and copper wire.

"Here," she said, "this was given to my grandmother by a traveling wiseman upon her marriage. Mother told me that it held a simple charm, just the blessing of the old man who made it, but she wore it from her marriage to her death even as her mother had."

He took it from her, weighing it in his hand. "It has magic still. Some from the maker, but more from the warmth of the women who have worn it—this will do nicely."

He cupped the necklace in his hands and blew on it gently. Then he set his lips to his hands, whispering words she couldn't quite make out, though they sounded soft and sweet. When he opened his hands the necklace was gone. Without a word he sat on the stool and began to spin.

She watched for a while as silver chain grew on his spindle, then she lay down in the soft wool to sleep. When she awoke he was gone and there was not a wisp of unwoven wool in the room, instead silver chain, as finely wrought as Ian Silvermaker had ever worked, sat in a pile that was taller than she was.

She realized that her head was resting on something soft and lifted it hurriedly, expecting to find a mound of wool. Instead she found his cloak. Even as she caressed it with her fingers it faded until it was no more.

"I know," she said to the empty room. "He must not know you've been here."

When the king entered the room there was expectation on his face. Molly watched as the courtiers filed in to finger the silver, and looked up to meet the old queen's speculative eyes.

That morning, at her majesty's request, Molly ate beside the queen.

The older woman fingered the soft woven brown and cream wool of her shawl and said softly, "I know a man who might be able to spin wool to silver."

Molly looked at the shawl and knew who had woven it. She'd only seen such weaving once before. She nodded her head. "I know a man who might weave wool into a shawl that fine."

"It was a gift from my son."

Neither smiled, but they understood each other well. The queen would not tell her son who was responsible for the magical transformations, but her first duty was to her son.

Molly's father was sent home without his daughter. He kissed her forehead before he left, and she held that kiss in her heart.

That night she was led to a different room, twice as large as the previous one. Inside was enough straw to bed down a large dairy herd every day for a year.

"If you can spin this into gold by morning," said the king with as much passion as she'd ever heard him use, "I will marry you before nightfall. If you do not, you will die, this I swear on my father's bones."

She nodded at him and stepped into the room, pulling the door shut behind her. As she heard the key turn in the lock, the little weaver emerged from one of the stacks, dusting off his shoulders.

"How do you know the queen?" she asked.

He smiled, "She knew my master, he did a little magic for her and some weaving as well. Since his death she's commissioned a number of tapestries and such from me. She's an honorable woman, one who would make a staunch friend."

Molly shook her head, and shrugged. Then struggled to make her decision plain without sounding plaintive. It was harder to tell him than she had thought it would be. "It doesn't matter what the queen is like. I have nothing more to give you to work your magic."

He looked so upset she stepped near him and touched his shoulder. "It's all right, you know. You kept my father safe, sir. I cannot tell you how grateful I am."

Silence fell between them, but she left her hand where it was.

"What did you think," he said finally, "of the table cloth I sent you?"

She was surprised at his choice of topic, but grateful that he wasn't arguing with her. "I thought it was the most remarkable piece I have ever seen."

"It might do. There was a little magic in its making—something so that you would not miss the intent of the gift." He looked away. "If you tell me where it is, I will get it for you."

"No." She would not sacrifice his gift so that she could marry the king. Especially since she wasn't certain that death would not be preferable to the life of a miller's daughter married to the king.

"It was just a table cloth," he said, though his eyes glittered with suspicious brightness.

She raised her chin, not letting tears fall for what might have been. "I will not sacrifice your work for his benefit—I would sooner sacrifice my first born child."

There was a long pause, while he measured her words, then he gave an abrupt nod. "Accepted."

"What?" she gasped, but he was already speaking the words of his spelling.

This night she stayed awake, watching the golden straw give way to mounds of gold. As she watched the realization came to her that he would not let her die, even though it meant she marry the king. She also realized that she would rather this odd man raise her child than have it raised in the court with the king as its father.

When the last bit of straw was gone, she got stiffly to her feet and walked to him where he stood beside the spinning wheel. He'd pulled the hood of his cloak over his face and she pushed it down, kissing his cheek.

"Take care of my child for me," she whispered.

He started to say something, but the sound of a group of people approaching the door interrupted him. He took two steps back and vanished.

Molly said nothing when the king entered the room; she said nothing when he married her, nor did she speak a word that night.

In the morning, the king asked her to spin more straw into gold.

She shook her head, "I was given three gifts of magic, I have no more."

He slapped her face and stormed out of the lodge, leaving his retinue to follow. The queen visited her later and gave her a cold, wet cloth to hold against her face.

"I have reminded my son—" she said, "—that his word was given based on your past deeds, and that the gold you brought was more than the amount most of the heiresses in the kingdom could have amassed. He's leaving for the castle, and I doubt he'll be back. Can you read?"

Molly nodded.

"Good. I will send you letters once a week and you will reply. I'll see you set up comfortably here—Sir Thomas's wife will be here shortly. She's a sensible soul and can give you advice if you need it. I've arranged for several of the servants to stay here in addition to the normal staff. Your father may visit you, if you wish, but you are not to set foot outside the hunting lodge unless my son or I summon you to court."

Molly nodded again, as there didn't seem to be anything else to do.

The queen left, and Molly was alone.

The child was born nine months later with his father's dimples and his mother's warm smile. Molly named him Paderick after her father. She sent no word to the court, but the queen arrived the evening after the baby did.

"I have persuaded my son to leave the baby here until he is weaned," she said. "After that I will see that he is well brought up."

"Like your son?" said Molly raising her eyebrow, for sometimes she forgot she was only a miller's daughter.

The queen flushed. "I am sorry for what his carelessness did to you. But I am not sorry to have a grandson. I doubt that my son would ever have married if he hadn't tricked himself into it." She took a closer look at the blanket that the baby was wrapped in. "Is that a table cloth?"

Molly smiled serenely and kissed her son's cheek. "It was a gift."

Months passed, and Molly forgot that she had ever been lonely. Her father came to the lodge every evening to play with his grandson, and the servants all joined in. When Paderick cried, which was seldom, there were fifteen pairs of arms to hold him. The page, Kemlin, one of the servants the queen had left behind, would play nonsense games that left the baby crowing for more.

A year passed, and Paderick was weaned. None of the servants had the heart to send word to the queen—Molly certainly would not. If it had not been for knowledge that the king would insist that her baby be sent to court and raised by servants, Molly would not have been able to give Paderick up to anyone, not even her strange little weaver. As it was, she worried that he had forgotten.

The queen came at last, with an army of nursemaids—but Molly's servants kept them away from the baby. So it was that only the queen was sitting with Molly when the weaver came at last.

"It is time," he said softly.

Molly nodded and gathered her son up from his bed.

"What is this?" asked the queen.

Molly cuddled Paderick against her shoulder, soothing him back to sleep. "Magic has its price, lady. This is the price of my dowry gold—the price of the king's whim."

"My grandson?" asked the queen. Molly noticed that she asked no other questions, and she wondered what magic the queen had asked for, and what its price had been.

The queen turned to the little weaver. "Is there nothing that could be done?"

The weaver looked at Molly's hands as they cradled her child. "I know of a way that you may keep the child." He spoke to Molly. "When I lost myself in the caverns, I lost my name as well. I was given one by my master—if you can tell me what it was, I will give you back the child and pay the price of the magic myself. You have three nights to do this—an hour each night."

"Heinrich," said the queen quickly. "Adam, Theodore."

"Molly must do the naming," he said. "But no, no and no."

Molly stepped toward him. "Leonard, Thomas, David." She knew that it would be none of those.

He shook his head.

She continued until the hour was up. The clock in the corner chimed the hour, and he looked sad as he shook his head for the last time. He bowed to Molly, took two steps back, and vanished.

The dowager queen spent the next day gathering names from books in the library, writing great long lists for Molly to read. Molly spent her day in her suite, playing blocks with Paderick and Kemlin.

"It doesn't matter, does it?" said Kemlin. "If the little man doesn't take him away, the old queen will."

Molly nodded.

"I would rather," said Kemlin seriously, "go live with a weaver, than return to court."

Molly read through the list the dowager had given her, then in the old queen's presence she read it again to the weaver. He shook his head at each of them.

The next day the old queen questioned the servants and sent them looking for odd names from nearby villages. Molly played with her son.

That afternoon a messenger came from the court with an urgent letter for the queen. She read it once, and turned as pale as milk. Molly took the letter from her.

After she had read it, she looked at the curious faces of the servants and said, "The king has suffered a fatal accident while hunting."

She left Paderick with his grieving grandmother, and went to her study. Alone, she set herself in front of her loom and began to weave while she thought.

Without the king, she could raise her son, could teach him kindness as she'd hoped the weaver could do. There was no reason to lose him now, if she could solve the riddle.

She knew that the little weaver didn't intend to take her child. He had given her a question that he thought she could answer.

It was a name given to him by his master who was a weaver and an outcast dwarf. It was a name that he, himself was not fond of—perhaps even embarrassed about, for he hadn't told her what it was. Although the queen had done business with both him and his master, she hadn't the faintest idea of his name.

It was not his own name, he said, his master had named him: as she might name a stray cat. She thought of the pets that she had—the pony, Patches; the mutt that had kept her company while she worked—Scruffy.

"He was named for his looks," she said out-loud in a tone of revelation. "His master was a weaver and named him after something he looked like." She stared at the orange yarn on her loom, remembering the funny laugh he'd given when she told him how she made it. She thought of the twisted orange and brown plant the dye came from—a plant any trained weaver would know if he had not been trained by a dwarf who lived in a cave. Brilliant colors, she thought, would be useless in a cave.

"Rumpelstiltskin," she said, very quietly.

That night, the little weaver looked at Molly, urging her silently to think.

"Drusselbart," she said, finishing the list the old queen had given her. "Rippenbeist, or Hammelswade?"

"No," he said, exasperated.

"If I name you," she said softly, "you will pay the price of the magic and I keep my son."

He nodded.

She wrapped the sleeping baby in the tablecloth that had been his first gift. She set Paderick into the weaver's arms, ignoring the queen's frightened questioning.

"I have no name for you," she said, leaning to kiss his soft lips. She would not have him pay a price for her rescue, magic had already cost him too much. "No name, sir, but love."

The wood in the fireplace burst into flames, and the lodge shook. In the hall, the servants who had been listening at the door cried out. The old queen screamed, either in fright or fury.

In the weaver's arms, Paderick giggled and shook his fists.

When the lodge settled once more upon its foundation, the room quieted. Not even the servants breathed a sound.

"Oh Molly," breathed the little weaver, though he now was taller than she by several inches. "Such a gift you have given me. Do you know what you have wrought?"

The hood fell back and she saw that the odd marks on his face were gone. Without them—well he wasn't as handsome as the king—but joy is very beautiful to behold whatever face it wears. His hair was still red, but it covered his head in thick waves. When he moved forward, he moved as any man did, his stride straight and strong. He kissed her.

"Love—" he said, pulling away only slightly, "— can pay any price and never show the cost. Will you come with me?"

As he spoke the hall clock chimed the end of the hour for naming.

"Oh Rumpelstiltskin," she laughed, for it did sound odd. "Oh my love, yes."

The weaver shifted Paderick until he held him with one hand while his other held the miller's daughter. Smiling he took two steps back and left the dowager queen alone in the room.

Search though she might, the old queen never found the miller's daughter or Paderick again. The throne passed in due time to a cousin who was a much better king than the last one. The old miller disappeared that night as well, leaving an empty mill behind.

When Kemlin told the story to his own children, he would smile and end it saying, "and they traveled to a place that the weaver knew of, where no one might bother them again. There they lived happily from that day until this."

Ailoura

Paul Di Fillippo

Paul Di Filippo is the author of hundreds of short stories, some of which have been collected in these widely-praised collections: *The Steampunk Trilogy*, *Ribofunk*, *Fractal Paisleys*, *Lost Pages*, *Little Doors*, *Strange Trades*, *Babylon Sisters*, and his multiple-award-nominated novella, *A Year in the Linear City*.

One of the few science fiction retellings in the anthology, Di Fillippo takes Puss in Boots into entirely new areas.

The small aircraft swiftly bisected the cloudless chartreuse sky. Invisible encrypted transmissions raced ahead of it. Clearance returned immediately from the distant, turreted manse—Stoessl House, looming in the otherwise empty riven landscape like some precipice-perching raptor. The ever-unsleeping family marchwarden obligingly shut down the manse's defenses, allowing an approach and landing. Within minutes, Geisen Stoessl had docked his small deltoid zipflyte on one of the tenth-floor platforms of Stoessl House, cantilevered over the flood-sculpted, candy-colored arroyos of the Subliminal Desert.

Geisen unseamed the canopy and leaped easily out onto the broad sintered terrace, unpeopled at this tragic, necessary, hopeful moment. Still clad in his dusty expeditionary clothes, goggles slung around his neck, Geisen resembled a living marble version of some young roughneck godling. Slim, wiry, and alert, with his laughter-creased, soil-powdered face now set in solemn lines absurdly counterpointed by a mask of clean skin around his recently shielded green eyes, Geisen paused a moment to brush from his protective suit the heaviest evidence of his recent wildcat digging in the Lustrous Wastes. Satisfied that he had made some small improvement in his appearance upon this weighty occasion, he advanced toward the portal leading inside. But before he could actuate the door, it opened from within.

Framed in the door stood a lanky, robe-draped bestient: Vicuna, his mother's most valued servant. Set squarely in Vicuna's wedge-shaped hirsute face, the haughty maid's broad velveteen nose wrinkled imperiously in disgust at Geisen's appearance, but the moreauvian refrained from voicing her disapproval of that matter in favor of other upbraidings.

"You arrive barely in time, Gep Stoessl. Your father approaches the limits of artificial maintenance, and is due to be reborn any minute. Your mother and brothers already anxiously occupy the Natal Chambers."

Following the inhumanly articulated servant into Stoessl House, Geisen answered, "I'm aware of all that, Vicuna. But traveling halfway around Chalk can't be accomplished in an instant."

"It was your choice to absent yourself during this crucial time."

"Why crucial? This will be Vomacht's third reincarnation. Presumably this one will go as smoothly as the first two."

"So one would hope."

Geisen tried to puzzle out the subtext of Vicuna's ambiguous comment, but could emerge with no clue regarding the current state of the generally complicated affairs within Stoessl House. He had obviously been away too long—too busy enjoying his own lonely but satisfying prospecting trips on behalf of the family enterprise—to be able to grasp the daily political machinations of his relatives.

Vicuna conducted Geisen to the nearest squeezer, and they promptly dropped down fifteen stories, far below the bedrock in which Stoessl House was rooted. On this secure level, the monitoring marchwarden hunkered down in its cozy low-Kelvin isolation, meaningful matrices of B-E condensates. Here also were the family's Natal Chambers. At these doors blazoned with sacred icons Vicuna left Geisen with a humid snort signifying that her distasteful attendence on the latecomer was complete.

Taking a fortifying breath, Geisen entered the rooms.

Roseate illumination symbolic of new creation softened all within: the complicated apparatus of rebirth as well as the sharp features of his mother, Woda, and the doughy countenances of his two brothers, Gitten and Grafton. Nearly invisible in the background, various bestient bodyguards hulked, inconspicuous yet vigilant.

Woda spoke first. "Well, how very generous of the prodigal to honor us with his unfortunately mandated presence."

Gitten snickered, and Grafton chimed in, pompously ironical: "Exquisitely gracious behavior, and so very typical of our little sibling, I'm sure."

Tethered to various life-support devices, Vomacht Stoessl— unconscious, naked and recumbent on a padded pallet alongside his mindless new body—said nothing. Both he and his clone had their heads wrapped in organic warty sheets of modified Stroonian brain parasite, an organism long-ago co-opted for mankind's ambitious and ceaselessly searching program of life extension. Linked via a thick living inter-parasitical tendril to its younger doppelganger, the withered form of the current Vomacht, having reached the limits of rejuvenation, contrasted strongly with the virginal, soulless vessel.

During Vomacht Stoessl's first lifetime, from 239 to 357 PS, he had sired no children. His second span of existence (357 to 495 PS) saw the birth of Gitten and Grafton, separated by some sixty years and both sired on Woda. Toward the end of his third, current lifetime (495 to 675 PS), a mere thirty years ago, he had fathered Geisen upon a mystery woman whom Geisen had never known. Vanished and unwedded, his mother—or some other over-solicitous guardian—had denied Geisen her name or image. Still, Vomacht had generously attended to all the legalities granting Geisen full parity with his half-brothers. Needless to say, little cordiality existed between the older members of the family and the young interloper.

Geisen made the proper obeisances at several altars before responding to the taunts of his stepmother and stepbrothers. "I did not dictate the terms governing Gep Stoessl's latest reincarnation. They came directly from him. If any of you objected, you should have made your grievances known to him face to face. I myself am honored that he chose me to initiate the transferance of his mind and soul. I regret only that I was not able to attend him during his final moments of awareness in this old body."

Gitten, the middle brother, tittered, and said, "The hand that cradles the rocks will now rock the cradle."

Geisen looked down at his dirty hands, hopelessly engrained with the soils and stonedusts of Chalk. He resisted an impulse to hide them in his pockets. "There is nothing shameful about my fondness for fieldwork. Lolling about in luxury does not suit me. And I did not hear any of you complaining when the Eventyr Lode which I discovered came online and began to swell the family coffers."

Woda intervened with her traditional maternal acerbity. "Enough bickering. Let us acknowledge that no possible arrangement of this day's events would have pleased everyone. The quicker we perform this vital ritual, the quicker we can all return to our duties and pleasures, and the sooner Vomacht's firm hand will regrasp the controls of our business. Geisen, I believe you know what to do."

"I studied the proper Books of Phowa enroute."

Grafton said, "Always the grind. Whenever do you enjoy yourself, little brother?"

Geisen advanced confidently to the mechanisms that reared at the head of the pallets. "In the proper time and place, Grafton. But I realize that to you, such words imply every minute of your life." The young man turned his attention to the controls before him, forestalling further tart banter.

The tethered and trained Stroonian lifeforms had been previously starved to near hibernation, in preparation for their sacred duty. A clear cylinder of pink nutrient fluid laced with instructive protein sequences hung from an ornate tripod. The fluid would flow through twin IV lines, once the parasites were hooked up, enlivening their quiescent metabolisms and directing their proper functioning.

Murmuring the requisite holy phrases, Geisen plugged an IV line into each enshrouding creature. He tapped the proper dosage rate into the separate flow-pumps. Then, solemnly capturing the eyes of the onlookers, he activated the pumps.

Almost immediately the parasites began to flex and labor, humping and contorting as they drove an infinity of fractally miniscule auto-anesthetizing tendrils into both full and vacant brains in preparation for the transfer of the vital engrams that comprised a human soul.

But within minutes, it was plain to the observers that something was very wrong. The original Vomacht Stoessl began to writhe in evident pain, ripping away from his life-supports.

The all-observant marchwarden triggered alarms. Human and bestient technicians burst into the room. Grafton and Gitten and Woda rushed to the pumps to stop the process. But they were too late. In an instant, both membrane-wrapped skulls collapsed to degenerate chunky slush that plopped to the floor from beneath the suddenly destructive cauls.

The room fell silent. Grafton tilted one of the pumps at an angle so that all the witnesses could see the glowing red numerals.

"He quadrupled the proper volume of nutrient, driving the Stroonians hyperactive. This is murder!"

"Secure him from any escape!" Woda commanded.

Instantly Geisen's arms were pinioned by two burly bestient guards. He opened his mouth to protest, but the sight of his headless father choked off all words.

Gep Vomacht Stoessl's large private study was decorated with ancient relics of his birthworld, Lucerno: the empty, age-brittle coral armature of a deceased personal exoskeleton; a row of printed books bound in sloth-hide; a corroded auroch-flaying knife large as a canoe paddle. In the wake of their owner's death, the talismans seemed drained of mana.

Geisen sighed, and slumped down hopelessly in the comfortable chair positioned on the far side of the antique desk that had originated on the Crafters' planet, Hulbrouck V. On the far side of the nacreous expanse sat his complacently smirking half-brother, Grafton. Just days ago, Geisen knew, his father had hauled himself out of his sickbed for one last appearance at this favorite desk, where he had dictated the terms of his third reincarnation to the recording marchwarden. Geisen had played the affecting scene several times enroute from the Lustrous Wastes, noting how, despite his enervated condition, his father spoke with his wonted authority, specifically requesting that Geisen administer the paternal rebirthing procedure.

And now that unique individual—distant and enigmatic as he had been to Geisen throughout the latter's relatively short life—the man who had founded Stoessl House and its fortunes, the man to whom they all owed their luxurious independent lifestyles, was irretrievably gone from this plane of existence.

The human soul could exist only in organic substrates. Intelligent as they might be, condensate-dwelling entities such as the marchwarden exhibited a lesser existential complexity. Impossible to make any kind of static "backup" copy of the human essence, even in the proverbial bottled brain, since Stroonian transcription was fatal to the original. No, if destructive failure occured during a rebirth, that individual was no more forever.

Grafton interpreted Geisen's sigh as indicative of a need to unburden himself of some secret. "Speak freely, little brother. Ease your soul of guilt. We are completely alone. Not even the marchwarden is listening."

Geisen sat up alertly. "How have you accomplished such a thing? The marchwarden is deemed to be incorruptible, and its duties include constant surveillance of the interior of our home."

Somewhat flustered, Grafton tried to dissemble. "Oh, no, you're quite mistaken. It was always possible to disable the marchwarden selectively. A standard menu option—"

Geisen leaped to his feet, causing Grafton to rear back. "I see it all now! This whole murder, and my seeming complicity, was planned from the start! My father's last testament—faked! The flow codes to the pumps—overriden! My role—stooge and dupe!"

Recovering himself, Grafton managed with soothing motions and noises to induce a fuming Geisen to be seated again. The older man came around to perch on a corner of the desk. He leaned over closer to Geisen and, in a smooth voice, made his own shockingly unrepentant confession.

"Very astute. Too bad for you that you did not see the trap early enough to avoid it. Yes, Vomacht's permanent death and your hand in it were all neatly arranged—by mother, Gitten and myself. It had to be. You see, Vomacht had become irrationally surly and obnoxious toward us, his true and loving first family. He threatened to remove all our stipends and entitlements and authority, once he occupied his strong new body. But those demented codicils were edited from the version of his speech that you saw, as was his insane proclamation naming you sole factotum of the family business. All of Stoessl Strangelet Mining and its affiliates was to be made your fiefdom. Imagine! A young desert rat at the helm of our venerable corporation!"

Geisen strove to digest all this sudden information. Practical considerations warred with his emotions. Finally he could only ask, "What of Vomacht's desire for me to initiate his soul-transfer?"

"Ah, that was authentic. And it served as the perfect bait to draw you back, as well as the peg on which we could hang a murder plot and charge."

Geisen drew himself up proudly. "You realize that these accusations of deliberate homicide against me will not stand up a minute in court. With what you've told me, I'll certainly be able to dig up plenty of evidence to the contrary."

Smiling like a carrion lizard from the Cerise Ergstrand, Grafton countered, "Oh, will you, now? From your jail cell, without any outside help? Accused murderers cannot profit from the results of their actions. You will have no access to family funds other than your small personal accounts while incarcerated, nor any real partisans, due to your stubbornly asocial existence of many years. The might of the family, including testimony from the grieving widow, will be ranked against you. How do you rate your chances for exculpation under those circumstances?"

Reduced to grim silence, Geisen bunched his muscles prior to launching himself in a futile attack on his brother. But Grafton held up a warning hand first.

"There is an agreeable alternative. We really do not care to bring this matter to court. There is, after all, still a chance of one percent or less that you might win the case. And legal matters are so tedious and time-consuming, interferring with more pleasurable pursuits. In fact, notice of Gep Stoessl's death has not yet been released to either the news media or to Chalk's authorities. And if we secure your cooperation, the aftermath of this tragic 'accident' will take a very different form than criminal charges. Upon getting your binding assent to a certain trivial document, you will be free to pursue your own life unencumbered by any obligations to Stoessl House or its residents."

Grafton handed his brother a hardcopy of several pages. Geisen perused it swiftly and intently, then looked up at Grafton with high astonishment.

"This document strips me of all my share of the family fortunes, and binds me from any future role in the estate. Basically, I am utterly disenfranchised and disinherited, cast out penniless."

"A fair enough summation. Oh, we might give you a small grubstake when you leave. Say—your zipflyte, a few hundred esscues, and a bestient servant or two. Just enough to pursue the kind of itinerant lifestyle you so evidently prefer."

Geisen pondered but a moment. "All attempts to brand me a patricide will be dropped?"

Grafton shrugged. "What would be the point of whipping a helpless, poverty-stricken nonentity?"

Geisen stood up. "Reactivate the marchwarden. I am ready to comply with your terms."

Gep Bloedwyn Vermeule, of Vermeule House, today wore her long blonde braids arranged in a recomplicated nest, piled high atop her charming young head and sown with delicate fairylights that blinked in time with various of her body-rhythms. Entering the formal reception hall of Stoessl House, she marched confidently down the tiles between ranks of silent bestient guards, the long train dependent from her form-fitting scarlet sandworm-fabric gown held an inch above the floor by tiny enwoven agravitic units. She came to a stop some meters away from the man who awaited her with a nervously expectant smile on his rugged face.

Geisen's voice quaked at first, despite his best resolve. "Bloedwyn, my sweetling, you look more alluring than an oasis to a parched man."

The pinlights in the girl's hair raced in chaotic patterns for a moment, then settled down to a stable configurations that somehow radiated a frostiness belied by her neutral facial expression. Her voice, chorded suggestively low and husky by fashionable implants, quavered not at all.

"Gep Stoessl, I hardly know how to approach you. So much has changed since we last trysted."

Throwing decorum to the wind, Geisen closed the gap between them and swept his betrothed up in his arms. The sensation Geisen enjoyed was rather like that derived from hugging a wooden effigy. Nonetheless, he persisted in his attempts to restore their old relations.

"Only superficial matters have changed, my dear! True, as you have no doubt heard by now, I am no longer a scion of Stoessl House. But my heart, mind and soul remain devoted to you! Can I not assume the same constancy applies to your inner being?"

Bloedwyn slipped out of Geisen's embrace. "How could you assume anything, since I myself do not know how I feel? All these developments have been so sudden and mysterious! Your father's cruelly permanent death, your own capricious and senseless abandonment of your share of his estate— How can I make sense of any of it? What of all our wonderful dreams?"

Geisen gripped Bloedwyn's supple hide-mailed upper arms with perhaps too much fervor, judging from her wince. He released her, then spoke. "All our bright plans for the future will come to pass! Just give me some time to regain my footing in the world. One day I will be at liberty to explain everything to you. But until then, I ask your trust and faith. Surely you must share my confidence in my character, in my undiminished capabilities?"

Bloedwyn averted her tranquil blue-eyed gaze from Geisen's imploring green eyes, and he slumped in despair, knowing himself lost. She stepped back a few paces and, with voice steeled, made a formal declaration she had evidently rehearsed prior to this moment.

"The Vermuele marchwarden has already communicated the abrogation of our pending matrimonial agreement to your house's governor. I think such an impartial yet decisive move is all for the best, Geisen. We are both young, with many lives before us. It would be senseless to found such a potentially interminable relationship on such shaky footing. Let us both go ahead—separately—into the days to come, with our extinct love a fond memory."

Again, as at the moment of his father's death, Geisen found himself rendered speechless at a crucial juncture, unable to plead his case any further. He watched in stunned disbelief as Bloedwyn turned gracefully around and walked out of his life, her fluttering scaly train visible some seconds after the rest of her had vanished.

The cluttered, steamy, noisy kitchens of Stoessl House exhibited an orderly chaos proportionate to the magnitude of the preparations underway. The planned rebirth dinner for the paterfamilias had been hastily converted to a memorial banquet, once the proper, little-used protocols had been found in a metaphorically dusty lobe of the marchwarden's memory. Now scores of miscegenous bestients under the supervision of the lone human chef, Stine Pursiful, scraped, sliced, chopped, diced, cored, deveined, scrubbed, layered, basted, glazed, microwaved and pressure-treated various foodstuffs, assembling the imported luxury ingredients into the elaborate fare that would furnish out the solemn buffet for family and friends and business connections of the deceased.

Geisen entered the aromatic atmosphere of the kitchens with a scowl on his face and a bitterness in his throat and heart. Pursiful spotted the young man and, with a fair share of courtesy and deference, considering the circumstances, stepped forward to inquire of his needs. But Geisen rudely brushed the slim punctilious chef aside, and stalked toward the shelves that held various MREs. With blunt motions, he began to shovel the nutri-packets into a dusty shoulderbag that had plainly seen many an expedition into Chalk's treasure-filled deserts.

A small timid bestient belonging to one of the muskrat-hyrax clades hopped over to the shelves where Geisen fiercely rummaged. Nearsighted, the be-aproned moreauvian strained on tiptoe to identify something on a higher shelf.

With one heavy boot, Geisen kicked the servant out of his way, sending the creature squeaking and sliding across the slops-strewn floor. But before the man could return to his rough provisioning, he was stopped by a voice familiar as his skin.

"I raised you to show more respect to all the Implicate's creatures than you just exhibited, Gep Stoessl. Or if I did not, then I deserve immediately to visit the Unborn's Lowest Abbatoir for my criminal negligence."

Geisen turned, the bile in his craw and soul melting to a habitual affection tinged with many memories of juvenile guilt.

Brindled arms folded across her queerly configured chest, Ailoura the bestient stood a head shorter than Geisen, compact and well-muscled. Her heritage mingled from a thousand feline and quasi-feline strains from a dozen planets, she resembled no single cat species morphed to human status, but rather all cats everywhere, blended and thus ennobled. Rounded ears perched high atop her densely pelted skull. Vertically slitted eyes and patch of wet leathery nose contrasted with a more-human-seeming mouth and chin. Now anger and disappointment molded her face into a mask almost frightening, her fierce expression magnifed by a glint of sharp tooth peeking from beneath a curled lip.

Geisen noted instantly, with a small shock, the newest touches of gray in Ailoura's tortoiseshell fur. These tokens of aging softened his heart even further. He made the second-most-serious conciliatory bow from the Dakini Rituals toward his old nurse. Straightening, Geisen watched with relief as the anger flowed out of her face and stance, to be replaced by concern and solicitude.

"Now," Ailoura demanded, in the same tone with which she had often demanded that little Geisen brush his teeth or do his schoolwork, "what is all this nonsense I hear about your voluntary disinheritance and departure?"

Geisen motioned Ailoura into a secluded corner of the kitchens and revealed everything to her. His account prompted low growls from the bestient that escaped despite her angrily compressed lips. Geisen finished resignedly by saying, "And so, helpless to contest this injustice, I leave now to seek my fortune elsewhere, perhaps even on another world."

Ailoura pondered a moment. "You say that your brother offered you a servant from our house?"

"Yes. But I don't intend to take him up on that promise. Having another mouth to feed would just hinder me."

Placing one mitteny yet deft hand on his chest, Ailoura said, "Take me, Gep Stoessl."

Geisen experienced a moment of confusion. "But Ailoura—your job of raising me is long past. I am very grateful for the loving care you gave unstintingly to a motherless lad, the guidance and direction you imparted, the indulgent playtimes we enjoyed. Your teachings left me with a wise set of principles, an admirable will and optimism, and a firm moral center—despite the evidence of my thoughtless transgression a moment ago. But your guardian duties lie in the past. And besides, why would you want to leave the comforts and security of Stoessl House?"

"Look at me closely, Gep Stoessl. I wear now the tabards of the scullery crew. My luck in finding you here is due only to this very demotion. And from here the slide to utter inutility is swift and short—despite my remaining vigor and craft. Will you leave me here to face my sorry fate? Or will you allow me to cast my fate with that of the boy I raised from kittenhood?"

Geisen thought a moment. "Some companionship would indeed be welcome. And I don't suppose I could find a more intimate ally."

Ailoura grinned. "Or a slyer one."

"Very well. You may accompany me. But on one condition."

"Yes, Gep Stoessl?"

"Cease calling me 'Gep.' Such formalities were once unknown between us."

Ailoura smiled. "Agreed, little Gei-gei."

The man winced. "No need to retrogress quite that far. Now, let us return to raiding my family's larder."

"Be sure to take some of that fine fish, if you please, Geisen."

No one knew the origin of the tame strangelets that seeded Chalk's strata. But everyone knew of the immense wealth these cloistered anomalies conferred.

Normal matter was composed of quarks in only two flavors: up and down. But strange-flavor quarks also existed, and the exotic substances formed by these strange quarks in combination with the more domestic flavors were, unconfined, as deadly as the more familiar antimatter. Bringing normal matter into contact with a naked strangelet resulted in the conversion of the feedstock into energy. Owning a strangelet was akin to owning a pet black hole, and just as useful for various purposes, such as powering star cruisers.

Humanity could create strangelets, but only at immense costs per unit. And naked strangelets had to be confined in electromagnetic or gravitic bottles during active use. They could also be quarantined for semi-permanent storage in stasis fields. Such was the case with the buried strangelets of Chalk.

Small spherical mirrored nodules—"marbles," in the jargon of Chalk's prospectors—could be found in various recent sedimentary layers of the planet's crust, distributed according to no rational plan. Discovery of the marbles had inaugurated the reign of the various Houses on Chalk.

An early scientific expedition from Preceptimax University to the Shulamith Wadi stumbled upon the strangelets initially. Preceptor Fairservis, the curious discoverer of the first marble, had realized he was dealing with a stasis-bound object and had unluckily managed to open it. The quantum genie inside had promptly eaten the hapless fellow who freed it, along with nine-tenths of the expedition, before beginning a sure but slow descent toward the core of Chalk. Luckily an emergency response team swiftly dispatched by the planetary authorities had managed to activate a new entrapping marble big as a small city, its lower hemisphere underground, thus trapping the rogue.

After this incident, the formerly disdained deserts of Chalk had experienced a landrush unparalleled in the galaxy. Soon the entire planet was divided into domains—many consisting of noncontiguous properties—each owned by one House or another. Prospecting began in earnest then. But the practice remained more an art than a science, as the marbles remained stealthy to conventional detectors. Intuition, geological knowledge of strata and sheer luck proved the determining factors in the individual fortunes of the Houses.

How the strangelets—plainly artifactual—came to be buried beneath Chalk's soils and hardpan remained a mystery. No evidence of native intelligent inhabitants existed on the planet prior to the arrival of humanity. Had a cloud of strangelets been swept up out of space as Chalk made her eternal orbits? Perhaps. Or had alien visitors planted the strangelets for obscure reasons of their own? An equally plausible theory.

Whatever the obscure history of the strangelets, their current utility was beyond argument.

They made many people rich.

And some people murderous.

In the shadow of the Tasso Escarpments, adjacent to the Glabrous Drifts, Carrabas House sat desolate and melancholy, tenanted only by glass-tailed lizards and stilt-crabs, its poverty-overtaken heirs dispersed anonymously across the galaxy after a series of unwise investments, followed by the unpredictable yet inevitable exhaustion of their marble-bearing properties—a day against which Vomacht Stoessl had more providently hedged his own family's fortunes.

Geisen's zipflyte crunched to a landing on one of the manse's grit-blown terraces, beside a gaping portico. The craft's doors swung open and pilot and passenger emerged. Ailoura now wore a set of utilitarian roughneck's clothing, tailored for her bestient physique and matching the outfit worn by her former charge, right down to their boots. Strapped to her waist was an antique yet lovingly maintained variable sword, its terminal bead currently dull and inactive.

"No one will trouble us here," Geisen said with confidence. "And we'll have a roof of sorts over our head while we plot our next steps. As I recall from a visit some years ago, the west wing was the least damaged."

As Geisen began to haul supplies—a heater-cum-stove, sleeping bags and pads, water-condensers—from their craft, Ailoura inhaled deeply the dry tangy air, her nose wrinkling expressively, then exhaled with zest. "Ah, freedom after so many years! It tastes brave, young Geisen!" Her claws slipped from their sheaths as she flexed her pads. She unclipped her sword and flicked it on, the seemingly untethered bead floating outward from the pommel a meter or so.

"You finish the monkey work. I'll clear the rats from our quarters," promised Ailoura, then bounded off before Geisen could stop her. Watching her unfettered tail disappear down a hall and around a corner, Geisen smiled, recalling childhood games of strength and skill where she had allowed him what he now realized were easy triumphs.

After no small time, Ailoura returned, licking her greasy lips.

"All ready for our habitation, Geisen-kitten."

"Very good. If the bold warrior will deign to lend a paw…?"

Soon the pair had established housekeeping in a spacious, weatherproof ground floor room (with several handy exits), where a single leering windowframe was easily covered by sheet of translucent plastic. After distributing their goods and sweeping the floor clean of loess drifts, Geisen and Ailoura took a meal as their reward, the first of many such rude campfire repasts to come.

As they relaxed afterward, Geisen making notes with his stylus in a small pocket diary and Ailoura dragging her left paw continually over one ear, a querulous voice sounded from thin air.

"Who disturbs my weary peace?"

Instantly on their feet, standing back to back, the newcomers looked warily about. Ailoura snarled until Geisen hushed her. Seeing no one, Geisen at last inquired, "Who speaks?"

"I am the Carrabas marchwarden."

The man and bestient relaxed a trifle. "Impossible," said Geisen. "How do you derive your energy after all these years of abandonment and desuetude?"

The marchwarden chuckled with a trace of pride. "Long ago, without any human consent or prompting, while Carrabas House still flourished, I sunk a thermal tap downward hundreds of kilometers. The backup energy thus supplied is not much, compared with my old capacities, but has proven enough for sheer survival, albeit with much dormancy."

Ailoura hung her quiet sword back on her belt. "How have you kept sane since then, marchwarden?"

"Who says I have?"

Coming to terms with the semi-deranged Carrabas marchwarden required delicate negotiations. The protective majordomo simultaneously resented the trespassers—who did not share the honored Carrabas family lineage—yet on some different level welcomed their company and the satisfying chance to perform some of its programmed functions for them. Alternating ogreish threats with embarassingly humble supplications, the marchwarden needed to hear just the right mix of defiance and thanks from the squatters to fully come over as their ally. Luckily, Ailoura, employing diplomatic wiles honed by decades of bestient subservience, perfectly supplemented Geisen's rather gruff and patronizing attitude. Eventually, the ghost of Carrabas House accepted them.

"I am afraid I can contribute little enough to your comfort, Gep Carrabas." During the negotiations, the marchwarden had somehow self-deludingly concluded that Geisen was indeed part of the lost lineage. "Some water, certainly, from my active conduits. But no other necessities such as heat or food, or any luxuries either. Alas, the days of my glory are long gone!"

"Are you still in touch with your peers?" asked Ailoura.

"Why, yes. The other Houses have not forgotten me. Many are sympathetic, though a few are haughty and indifferent."

Geisen shook his head in bemusement. "First I learn that the protective omniscience of the marchwardens may be circumvented. Next, that they keep up a private traffic and society. I begin to wonder who is the master and who is the servant in our global system?"

"Leave these conundrums to the preceptors, Geisen. This unexpected mode of contact might come in handy for us some day."

The marchwarden's voice sounded ennervated. "Will you require any more of me? I have overtaxed my energies, and need to shut down for a time."

"Please restore yourself fully."

Left alone, Geisen and Ailoura simultaneously realized how late the hour was and how tired they were. They bedded down in warm bodyquilts, and Geisen swiftly drifted off to sleep to the old tune of Ailoura's drowsy purring.

In the chilly viridian morning, over fish and kava, cat and man held a war council.

Geisen led with a bold assertion that nonetheless concealed a note of despair and resignation.

"Given your evident hunting prowess, Ailoura, and my knowledge of the land, I estimate that we can take half a dozen sandworms from those unclaimed public territories proven empty of stranglets, during the course of as many months. We'll peddle the skins for enough to get us both off-planet. I understand that lush homesteads are going begging on Nibbriglung. All that the extensive water meadows there require is a thorough de-snailing before they're producing golden rice by the bushel—"

Ailoura's green eyes, so like Geisen's own, flashed with cool fire. "Insipidity! Toothlessness!" she hissed. "Turn farmer? Grub among the waterweeds like some *platypus?* Run away from those who killed your sire and cheated you out of your inheritance? I didn't raise such an unimaginative, unambitious coward, did I?"

Geisen sipped his drink to avoid making a hasty affronted rejoinder, then calmly said, "What do you recommend then? I gave my legally binding promise not to contest any of the unfair terms laid down by my family, in return for freedom from prosecution. What choices does such a renunciation leave me? Shall you and I go live in the shabby slums that slump at the feet of the Houses? Or turn thief and raider and prey upon lonely mining encampments? Or shall we become freelance prospectors? I'd be good at the latter job, true, but bargaining with the Houses concerning hard-won information about their own properties is humiliating, and promises only slim returns. They hold all the high cards, and the supplicant offers only a mere savings of time."

"You're onto a true scent with this last idea. But not quite the paltry scheme you envision. What I propose is that we swindle those who swindled you. We won't gain back your whole patrimony, but you'll surely acquire greater sustaining riches than you would by flensing worms or flailing rice."

"Speak on."

"The first step involves a theft. But after that, only chicanery. To begin, we'll need a small lot of strangelets, enough to salt a claim everyone thought exhausted."

Geisen considered, buffing his raspy chin with his knuckles. "The morality is dubious. Still—I found a smallish deposit of marbles on Stoessl property during my aborted trip, and never managed to report it. They were in a floodplain hard by the Nakhoda Range, newly exposed and ripe for the plucking without any large-scale mining activity that would attract satellite surveillance."

"Perfect! We'll use their own goods to con the ratlings! But once we have this grubstake, we'll need a proxy to deal with the Houses. Your own face and reputation must remain concealed until all deals are sealed airtight. Do you have knowledge of any such suitable foil?"

Geisen began to laugh. "Do I? Only the perfect rogue for the job!"

Ailoura came cleanly to her feet, although she could not repress a small grunt at an arthritic twinge provoked by a night on the hard floor. "Let us collect the strangelets first, and then enlist his help. With luck, we'll be sleeping on feathers and dining off golden plates in a few short weeks."

The sad and spectral voice of the abandoned marchwarden sounded. "Good morning, Gep Carrabas. I regret keenly my own serious incapacities as a host. But I have managed to heat up several liters of water for a bath, if such a service appeals."

The eccentric caravan of Marco Bozzarias and his mistress Pigafetta had emerged from its minting pools as a top-of-the-line Baba Yar model of the year 650 PS. Capacious and agile, larded with amenities, the moderately intelligent stilt-walking cabin had been designed to protect its inhabitants from climactic extremes in unswaying comfort while carrying them sure-footedly over the roughest terrain. But plainly, for one reason or another (most likely poverty) Bozzarias had neglected the caravan's maintenance over the twenty-five years of its working life.

Raised now for privacy above the sands where Geisen's zipflyte rested, the vehicle-cum-residence canted several degrees, imparting a funhouse quality to its interior. Swellings at its many knee joints indicated a lack of proper nutrients. Additionally, the cabin itself had been miscegenously patched with so many different materials—plastic, sandworm hide, canvas, chitin—that it more closely resembled a heap of debris than a deliberately designed domicile.

The caravan's owner, contrastingly, boasted an immaculate and stylish appearance. To judge by his handsome, mustachioed looks, the middle-aged Bozzarias was more stagedoor idler than cactus hugger, displaying his trim figure proudly beneath crimson ripstop trews and utility vest over bare hirsute chest. Despite this urban promenader's facade, Bozzarias held a respectable record as a freelance prospector, having pinpointed for their owners several strangelet lodes of note, including the fabled Gosnold Pocket. For these services, he had been recompensed by the tight-fisted landowners only a nearly invisible percentage of the eventual wealth claimed from the finds. Despite his current friendly grin, it would be impossible for Bozzarias not to harbor decades-worth of spite and jealousy.

Pigafetta, Bozzarias's bestient paramour, was a voluptuous, pink-skinned geisha clad in blue and green silks. Carrying perhaps a tad too much weight—hardly surprising, given her particular gattaca—Pigafetta radiated a slack and greasy carnality utterly at odds with Ailoura's crisp and dry efficiency. When the visitors had entered the cabin, before either of the humans could intervene, Geisen and Bozzarias had been treated to an instant but decisive bloodless catfight that had settled the pecking order between the moreauvians.

Now, while Pigafetta sulked winsomely in a canted corner amid her cushions, the furry female victor consulted with the two men around a small table across which lay spilled the stolen strangelets, corralled from rolling by a line of empty liquor bottles.

Bozzarias poked at one of the deceptive marbles with seeming disinterest, while his dark eyes glittered with avarice. "Let me recapitulate. We represent to various buyers that these quantum baubles are merely the camel's nose showing beneath the tent of unconsidered wealth. A newly discovered lode on the Carrabas properties, of which you, Gep Carrabas"—Bozzarias leered at Geisen—"are the rightful heir. We rook the fools for all we can get, then hie ourselves elsewhere, beyond their injured squawks and retributions. Am I correct in all particulars?"

Ailoura spoke first. "Yes, substantially."

"And what would my share of the take be? To depart forever my cherished Chalk would require a huge stake—"

"Don't try to make your life here sound glamorous or even tolerable, Marco," Geisen said. "Everyone knows you're in debt up to your nose, and haven't had a strike in over a year. It's about time for you to change venues anyway. The days of the freelancer on Chalk are nearly over."

Bozzarias sighed dramatically, picking up a reflective marble and admiring himself in it. "I suppose you speak the truth—as it is commonly perceived. But a man of my talents can carve himself a niche anywhere. And Pigafetta *has* been begging me of late to launch her on a virtual career—"

"In other words," Ailoura interrupted, "you intend to pimp her as a porn star. Well, you'll need to relocate to a mediapoietic world then for sure. May we assume you'll become part of our scheme?"

Bozzarias set the marble down and said, "My pay?"

"Two strangelets from this very stock."

With the speed of a glass-tailed lizard Bozzarias scooped up and pocketed two spheres before the generous offer could be rescinded. "Done! Now, if you two will excuse me, I'll need to rehearse my role before we begin this deception."

Ailoura smiled, a disconcerting sight to those unfamiliar with her tender side. "Not quite so fast, Gep Bozzarias. If you'll just submit a moment—"

Before Bozzarias could protest, Ailoura had sprayed him about the head and shoulders with the contents of a pressurized can conjured from her pack.

"What! Pixy dust! This is a gross insult!"

Geisen adjusted the controls of his pocket diary. On the small screen appeared a jumbled, jittering image of the caravan's interior. As the self-assembling pixy dust cohered around Bozzarias's eyes and ears, the image stabilized to reflect the prospector's visual point-of-view. Echoes of their speech emerged from the diary's speaker.

"As you well know," Ailoura advised, "the pixy dust is ineradicable and self-repairing. Only the ciphers we hold can deactivate it. Until then, all you see and hear will be shared with us. We intend to monitor you around the clock. And the diary's input is being shared with the Carrabas marchwarden, who has been told to watch for any traitorous actions on your part. That entity, by the way, is a little deranged, and might leap to conclusions about any actions that even verge on treachery. Oh, you'll also find that your left ear hosts a channel for our remote, ah, verbal advice. It would behoove you to follow our directions, since the dust is quite capable of liquefying your eyeballs upon command."

Seemingly inclined to protest further, Bozzarias suddenly thought better of dissenting. With a disspirited wave and nod, he signalled his acquiesence in their plans, becoming quietly businesslike.

"And to what Houses shall I offer this putative wealth?"

Geisen smiled. "To every House at first—except Stoessl."

"I see. Quite clever."

After Bozzarias had caused his caravan to kneel to the earth, he bade his new partners a desultory goodbye. But at the last minute, as Ailoura was stepping into the zipflyte, Bozzarias snagged Geisen by the sleeve and whispered in his ear.

"I'd trade that rude servant in for a mindless pleasure model, my friend, were I you. She's much too tricky for comfort."

"But Marco—that's exactly why I cherish her."

Three weeks after first employing the wily Bozzarias in their scam, Geisen and Ailoura sat in their primitive quarters at Carrabas House, huddled nervously around Geisen's diary, awaiting transmission of the meeting they had long anticipated. The diary's screen revealed the familiar landscape around Stoessl House as seen from the windows of the speeding zipflyte carrying their agent to his appointment with Woda, Gitten and Grafton.

During the past weeks, Ailoura's plot had matured, succeeding beyond their highest expectations.

Representing himself as the agent for a mysteriously returned heir of the long-abandoned Carrabas estate—a fellow who prefered anonymity for the moment—Bozzarias had visited all the biggest and most influential Houses—excluding the Stoessls—with his sample strangelets. A major new find had been described, with its coordinates freely given and inspections invited. The visiting teams of geologists reported what appeared to be a rich new lode, deceived by Geisen's expert saltings. And no single house dared attempt a midnight raid on the unprotected new strike, given the vigilance of all the others.

The cooperation and willing playacting of the Carrabas marchwarden had been essential. First, once its existence was revealed, the discarded entity's very survival became a seven-day wonder, compelling a willing suspension of disbelief in all the lies that followed. Confirming the mystery man as a true Carrabas, the marchwarden also added its jiggered testimony to verify the discovery.

Bozzarias had informed the greedily gaping families that the returned Carrabas scion had no desire to play an active role in mining and selling his strangelets. The whole estate—with many more potential strangelet nodes—would be sold to the highest bidder.

Offers began to pour in, steadily escalating. These included feverish bids from the Stoessls, which were rejected without comment. Finally, after such highhanded treatment, the offended clan demanded to know why they were being excluded from the auction. Bozzarias responded that he would convey that information only in a private meeting.

To this climactic interrogation the wily rogue now flew.

Geisen turned away from the monotonous video on his diary and asked Ailoura a question he had long contemplated but always foreborne from voicing.

"Ailoura, what can you tell me of my mother?"

The cat-woman assumed a reflective expression that cloaked more emotions than it revealed. Her whiskers twitched. "Why do you ask such an irrelevant question at this crucial juncture, Gei-gei?"

"I don't know. I've often pondered the matter. Maybe I'm fearful that if our plan explodes in our faces, this might be my final opportunity to learn anything."

Ailoura paused a long while before answering. "I was intimately familiar with the one who bore you. I think her intentions were honorable. I know she loved you dearly. She always wanted to make herself known to you, but circumstances beyond her control did not permit such an honest relationship."

Geisen contemplated this information. Something told him he would get no more from the close-mouthed bestient.

To disrupt the solemn mood, Ailoura reached over to ruffle Geisen's hair. "Enough of the useless past. Didn't anyone ever tell you that curiosity killed the cat? Now, pay attention! Our Judas goat has landed—"

Ursine yet doughy, unctuous yet fleering, Grafton clapped Bozzarias's shoulder heartily and ushered the foppish man to a seat in Vomacht's study. Behind the dead padrone's desk sat his widow, Woda, all motile maquillage and mimicked mourning. Her teeth sported a fashionable gilt. Gitten lounged on the arm of a sofa, plainly bored and resentful, toying with a handheld hologame like some sullen adolescent.

After offering drinks—Bozzarias requested and received the finest vintage of sparkling wine available on Chalk—Grafton drove straight to the heart of the matter.

"Gep Bozzarias, I demand to know why Stoessl House has been denied a chance to bid on the Carrabas estate."

Bozzarias drained his glass and dabbed at his lips with his jabot before replying. "The reason is simple, Gep Stoessl, yet of such delicacy that you would not have cared to have me state it before your peers. Thus this private encounter."

"Go on."

"My employer, Timor Carrabas, you must learn, is a man of punctilio and politesse. Having abandoned Chalk many generations ago, Carrabas House still honors and maintains the old ways prevalent during that golden age. They have not fallen into the lax and immoral fashions of the present, and absolutely contemn such behavior."

Grafton stiffened. "To what do you refer? Stoessl House is guilty of no such infringements on custom."

"That is not how my employer perceives affairs. After all, what is the very first thing he hears upon returning to his ancestral homeworld? Disturbing rumors of patricide, fraternal infighting and excommunication, all of which emanate from Stoessl House and Stoessl House alone. Leery of stepping beneath the shadow of such a cloud, he could not ethically undertake any dealings with your clan."

Fuming, Grafton started to rebut these charges, but Woda intervened. "Gep Bozzarias, all mandated investigations into the death of my beloved Vomacht resulted in one uncontested conclusion: pump failure produced a kind of alien hyperglycemia that drove the Stroonians insane. No human culpability or intent to harm was ever established."

Bozzarias held his glass up for a refill and obtained one. "Why, then, were all the bestient witnesses to the incident terminally disposed of? What motivated the abdication of your youngest scion? Giger, I believe he was named?"

Trying to be helpful, Gitten jumped into the conversation. "Oh, we use up bestients at a frightful rate! If they're not dying from floggings, they're collapsing from overuse in the mines and brothels. Such a flawed product line, these moreauvians. Why, if they were robots, they'd never pass consumer-lab testing. As for Geisen—that's the boy's name—well, he simply got fed up with our civilized lifestyle. He always did prefer the barbaric outback existence. No doubt he's enjoying himself right now, wallowing in some muddy oasis with a sandworm concubine."

Grafton cut off his brother's tittering with a savage glance. "Gep Bozzarias, I'm certain that if your employer were to meet us, he'd find we are worthy of making an offer on his properties. In fact, he could avoid all the fuss and bother of a full-fledged auction, since I'm prepared right now to trump the highest bid he's yet received. Will you convey to him my invitation to enjoy the hospitality of Stoessl House?"

Bozzarias closed his eyes ruminatively, as if harkening to some inner voice of conscience, then answered, "Yes, I can do that much. And with some small encouragement, I would exert all my powers of persuasiveness—"

Woda spoke. "Why, where did this small but heavy bag of Tancredi moonstones come from? It certainly doesn't belong to us. Gep Bozzarias—would you do me the immense favor of tracking down the rightful owner of these misplaced gems?"

Bozzaris stood and bowed, then accepted the bribe. "My pleasure, madame. I can practically guarantee that Stoessl House will soon receive its just reward."

"Sandworm concubine!" Geisen appeared ready to hurl his eavesdropping device to the hard floor, but restrained himself. "How I'd like to smash their lying mouths in!"

Ailoura grinned. "You must show more restraint than that, Geisen, especially when you come face to face with the scoundrels. Take consolation from the fact that mere physical retribution would hurt them far less than the loss of money and face we will inflict."

"Still, there's a certain satisifaction in feeling the impact of fist on flesh."

"My kind calls it 'the joy when teeth meet bone,' so I fully comprehend. Just not this time. Understood?"

Geisen impulsively hugged the old cat. "Still teaching me, Ailoura?"

"Until I die, I suppose."

"You are appallingly obese, Geisen. Your form recalls nothing of the slim blade who cut such wide swaths among the girls of the various Houses before his engagement."

"And your polecat coloration, fair Ailoura, along with those tinted lenses and tooth-caps, speak not of a bold mouser, but of a scavenger through garbage tips."

Regarding each other with satisfaction, Ailoura and Geisen thus approved of their disguises.

With the aid of Bozzarias, who had purchased for them various sophisticated, semi-living prosthetics, dyes and offworld clothing, the man and his servant—Timor Carrabas and Hepzibah—resembled no one ever seen before on Chalk. His pasty face rouged, Geisen wobbled as he waddled, breathing stertorously, while the limping Ailoura diffused a moderately repulsive scent calculated to keep the curious at a certain remove.

The Carrabas marchwarden now spoke, a touch of excitement in its artificial voice. "I have just notified my Stoessl House counterpart that you are departing within the hour. You will be expected in time for essences and banquet, with a half-hour allotted to freshen up and settle into your guest rooms."

"Very good. Rehearse the rest of the plan to me."

"Once the funds are transferred from Stoessl House to me, I will in turn upload them to the Bourse on Feuilles Mortes under the name of Geisen Stoessl, where they will be immune from attachment. I will then retreat to my soul-canister, readying it for removal by your agent, Bozzarias, who will bring it to the spacefield—specifically the terminal hosting Gravkosmos Interstellar. Beyond that point, I cannot be of service until I am haptically enabled once more."

"You have the scheme perfectly. Now we thank you, and leave with the promise that we shall talk again in the near future, in a more pleasant place."

"Goodbye, Gep Carrabas, and good luck."

Within a short time the hired zipflyte arrived. (It would hardly do for the eminent Timor Carrabas to appear in Geisen's battered craft, which had, in point of fact, already been sold to raise additional funds to aid their subterfuge.) After clambering clumsily onboard, the schemers settled themselves in the spacious rear seat while the chauffeur—a neat-plumaged and discreet raptor-derived bestient—lifted off and flew at a swift clip toward Stoessl House.

Ailoura's comment about Geisen's attractiveness to his female peers had set an unhealed sore spot within him aching. "Do you imagine, Hepzibah, that other local luminaries might attend this evening's dinner party? I had in mind a certain Gep Bloedwyn Vermeule."

"I suspect she will. The Stoessls and the Vermeules have bonds and alliances dating back centuries."

Geisen mused dreamily. "I wonder if she will be as beautiful and sensitive and angelic as I have heard tell she is."

Ailoura began to hack from deep in her throat. Recovering, she apologized, "Excuse me, Gep Carrabas. Something unpleasant in my throat. No doubt a simple hairball."

Geisen did not look amused. "You cannot deny reports of the lady's beauty, Hepzibah."

"Beauty is as beauty does, master."

The largest ballroom in Stoessl House had been extravagantly bedecked for the arrival of Timor Carrabas. Living luminescent lianas in dozens of neon tones festooned the heavy-beamed rafters. Decorator dust migrated invisibly about the chamber, cohering at random into wallscreens showing various entertaining videos from the mediapoietic worlds. Responsive carpets the texture of moss crept warily along the tesselated floor, consuming any spilled food and drink wasted from the large collation spread out across a servitor-staffed table long as a playing field. (House chef Stine Pursiful oversaw all with a meticulous eye, his upraised ladle serving as baton of command. After some argument among the family members and chef, a buffet had been chosen over a sit-down meal, as being more informal, relaxed and conducive to easy dealings.) The floor space was thronged with over a hundred gaily caparisoned representatives of the Houses most closely allied to the Stoessls, some dancing in stately pavanes to the music from the throats of the octet of avian bestients perched on their multi-branched stand. But despite the many diversions of music, food, drink and chatter, all eyes had strayed ineluctably to the form of the mysterious Timor Carrabas when he entered, and from time to time thereafter.

Beneath his prosthetics, Geisen now sweated copiously, both from nervousness and the heat. Luckily, his disguising adjuncts quite capably metabolized this betraying moisture before it ever reached his clothing.

The initial meeting with his brothers and stepmother had gone well. Hands were shaken all around without anyone suspecting that the flabby hand of Timor Carrabas concealed a slimmer one that ached to deliver vengeful blows.

Geisen could see immediately that since Vomacht's death, Grafton had easily assumed the role of head of household, with Woda patently the power behind the throne and Gitten content to act the wastrel princeling.

"So, Gep Carrabas," Grafton oleaginously purred, "now you finally perceive with your own eyes that we Stoessls are no monsters. It's never wise to give gossip any credence."

Gitten said, "But gossip is the only kind of talk that makes life worth liv—oof!"

Woda took a second step forward, relieving the painful pressure she had inflicted on her younger son's foot. "Excuse my clumsiness, Gep Carrabas, in my eagerness to enhance my proximity to a living reminder of the fine old ways of Chalk. I'm sure you can teach us much about how our forefathers lived. Despite personal longevity, we have lost the institutional rigor your clan has reputedly preserved."

In his device-modulated, rather fulsome voice, Geisen answered, "I am always happy to share my treasures with others, be they spiritual or material."

Grafton brightened. "This expansiveness bodes well for our later negotiations, Gep Carrabas. I must say that your attitude is not exactly as your servant Bozzarias conveyed."

Geisen made a dismissive wave. "Simply a local hireling who was not truly privy to my thoughts. But he has the virtue of following my bidding without the need to know any of my ulterior motivations." Geisen felt relieved to have planted that line to protect Bozzarias in the nasty wake of the successful conclusion of their thimblerigging. "Here is my real counselor. Hepzibah, step forward."

Ailoura moved within the circle of speakers, her unnaturally flared and pungent striped musteline tail waving perilously close to the humans. "At your service, Gep."

The Stoessls involuntarily cringed away from the unpleasant odor wafting from Ailoura, then restrained their impolite reaction.

"Ah, quite an, ah, impressive moreauvian. Positively, um, redolent of the ribosartor's art. Perhaps your, erm, advisor would care to dine with others of her kind."

"Hepzibah, you are dismissed until I need you."

"As you wish."

Soon Geisen was swept up in a round of introductions to people he had known all his life. Eventually he reached the food, and fell to eating rather too greedily. After weeks spent subsisting on MREs alone, he could hardly restrain himself. And his glutton's disguise allowed all excess. Let the other guests gape at his immoderate behavior. They were constrained by their own greed for his putative fortune from saying a word.

After satisfying his hunger, Geisen finally looked up from his empty plate.

There stood Bloedwyn Vermeule.

Geisen's ex-fiancee had never shone more alluringly. Threaded with invisible flexing pseudo-myofibrils, her long unfettered hair waved in continual delicate movement, as if she were a mermaid underwater. She wore a gown tonight loomed from golden spidersilk. Her lips were verdigris, matched by her nails and eye-shadow.

Geisen hastily dabbed at his own lips with his napkin, and was mortified to see the clean cloth come away with enough stains to represent a child's immoderate battle with an entire chocolate cake.

"Oh, Gep Carrabas, I hope I am not interrupting your gustatory pleasures."

"Nuh—no, young lady, not at all. I am fully sated. And you are?"

"Gep Bloedwyn Vermeule. You may call me by my first name, if you grant me the same privilege."

"But naturally."

"May I offer an alternative pleasure, Timor, in the form of a dance? Assuming your satiation does not extend to *all* recreations."

"Certainly. If you'll make allowances in advance for my clumsiness."

Bloedwyn allowed the tip of her tongue delicately to traverse her patina'd lips. "As the Dompatta says, 'An earnest rider compensates for a balky steed.'"

This bit of familiar gospel had never sounded so lascivious. Geisen was shocked at this unexpected temptress behavior from his ex-fiancee. But before he could react with real or mock indignation, Bloedwyn had whirled him out onto the floor.

They essayed several complicated dances before Geisen, pleading fatigue, could convince his partner to call a halt to the activity.

"Let us recover ourselves in solitude on the terrace," Bloedwyn said, and conducted Geisen by the arm through a pressure curtain and onto an unlit open-air patio. Alone in the shadows, they took up positions braced against a balustrade. The view of the moon-drenched arroyos below occupied them in silence for a time. Then Bloedwyn spoke huskily.

"You exude a foreign, experienced sensuality, Timor, to which I find myself vulnerable. Perhaps you would indulge my weakness with an assignation tonight, in a private chamber of Stoessl House known to me? After any important business dealing are successfully concluded, of course."

Geisen seethed inwardly, but managed to control his voice. "I am flattered that you find a seasoned fellow of my girth so attractive, Bloedwyn. But I do not wish to cause any intermural incidents. Surely you are affianced to someone, a young lad both bold and wiry, jealous and strong."

"Pah! I do not care for young men, they are all chowderheads! Pawing, puling, insensitive, shallow and vain, to a man! I was betrothed to one such, but luckily he revealed his true colors and I was able to cast him aside like the churl he proved to be."

Now Geisen felt only miserable self-pity. He could summon no words, and Bloedwyn took his silence for assent. She planted a kiss on his cheek, then whispered directly into his ear. "Here's a map to the boudoir where I'll be waiting. Simply take the east squeezer down three levels, then follow the hot dust." She pressed a slip of paper into his hand, supplementing her message with extra pressure in his palm, then sashayed away like a tainted sylph.

Geisen spent half-an-hour with his mind roiling before he regained the confidence to return to the party.

Before too long, Grafton corralled him.

"Are you enjoying yourself, Timor? The food agrees? The essences elevate? The ladies are pliant? Haw! But perhaps we should turn our mind to business now, before we both grow too muzzy-headed. After conducting our dull commerce, we can cut loose."

"I am ready. Let me summon my aide."

"That skun— That is, if you absolutely insist. But surely our marchwarden can offer any support services you need. Notarization, citation of past deeds, and so forth."

"No. I rely on Hepzibah implicitly."

Grafton partially suppressed a frown. "Very well then."

Once Ailoura arrived from the servants' table, the trio headed toward Vomacht's old study. Geisen had to remind himself not to turn down any "unknown" corridor before Grafton himself did.

Seated in the very room where he had been fleeced of his patrimony and threatened with false charges of murder, Geisen listened with half an ear while Grafton outlined the terms of the prospective sale: all the Carrabas properties and whatever wealth of strangelets they contained, in exchange for a sum greater than the Gross Planetary Product of many smaller worlds.

Ailoura attended more carefully to the contract, even pointing out to Geisen a buried clause that would have made payment contingent on the first month's production from the new fields. After some arguing, the conspirators succeeded in having the objectionable codicil removed. The transfer of funds would be complete and instantaneous.

When Grafton had finally finished explaining the conditions, Geisen roused himself. He found it easy to sound bored with the whole deal, since his elaborate scam, at its moment of triumph, afforded him surprisingly little vengeful pleasure.

"All the details seem perfectly managed, Gep Stoessl, with that one small change of ours included. I have but one question. How do I know that the black sheep of your House, Geisen, will not contest our agreement? He seems a contrary sort, from what I've heard, and I would hate to be involved in judicial proceedings, should he get a whim in his head."

Grafton settled back in his chair with a broad smile. "Fear not, Timor! That wild hair will get up no one's arse! Geisen has been effectively rendered powerless. As was only proper and correct, I assure you, for he was not a true Stoessl at all."

Geisen's heart skipped a cycle. "Oh? How so?"

"The lad was a chimera! A product of the ribosartors! Old Vomacht was unsatisfied with the vagaries of honest mating that had produced Gitten and myself from the noble stock of our mother. Traditional methods of reproduction had not delivered him a suitable toady. So he resolved to craft a better heir. He used most of his own germ plasm as foundation, but supplemented his nucleotides with dozens of other snippets. Why, that hybrid boy even carried bestient genes. Rat and weasel, I'm willing to bet! Haw! No, Geisen had no place in our family."

"And his mother?"

"Once the egg was crafted and fertilized, Vomacht implanted it in a host bitch. One of our own bestients. I misapprehend her name now, after all these years. Amorica, Orella, something of that nature. I never really paid attention to her fate after she delivered her human whelp. I have more important properties to look after. No doubt she ended up on the offal heap, like all the rest of her kind."

A red curtain drifting across Geisen's vision failed to occlude the shape of the massive auroch-flaying blade hanging on the wall. One swift leap and it would be in his hands. Then Grafton would know sweet murderous pain, and Geisen's bitter heart would applaud—

Standing beside Geisen, Ailoura let slip the quietest cough.

Geisen looked into her face.

A lone tear crept from the corner of one feline eye.

Geisen gathered himself and stood up, unspeaking.

Grafton grew a trifle alarmed. "Is there anything the matter, Gep Carrabas?"

"No, Gep Stoessl, not at all. Merely that old hurts pain me, and I would fain relieve them. Let us close our deal. I am content."

The starliner carrying Geisen, Ailoura and the stasis-bound Carrabas marchwarden to a new life sped through the interstices of the cosmos, powered perhaps by a strangelet mined from Stoessl lands. In one of the lounges, the man and his cat nursed drinks and snacks, admiring the exotic variety of their fellow passengers and reveling in their hard-won liberty and security.

"Where from here—son?" asked Ailoura with a hint of unwonted shyness.

Geisen smiled. "Why, wherever we wish, mother dear."

"Rowr! A world with plenty of fish then, for me!"

THE FARMER'S CAT

Jeff VanderMeer

Widely regarded as one of the world's best fantasists, Jeff VanderMeer grew up in the Fiji Islands and spent six months traveling through Asia, Africa, and Europe before returning to the United States. These travels have deeply influenced his fiction. He is the recipient of an NEA-funded Florida Individual Artist Fellowship for excellence in fiction and a Florida Artist Enhancement Grant. VanderMeer's book-length fiction has been translated into fifteen languages, while his short fiction has appeared in several year's best anthologies and short-listed for *Best American Short Stories*.

There's something about VanderMeer's story that reminds me of Verna Aardema's children's book *Why Mosquitoes Buzz in People's Ears* (I just learned that the Dillons illustrated this book, small world, eh?). Now before you go off and read Aadrema's wonderful book, take the time to read VanderMeer's tale of a farmer's cat that is not what it appears.

A long time ago, in Norway, a farmer found he had a big problem with trolls. Every winter, the trolls would smash down the door to his house and make themselves at home for a month. Short or tall, fat or thin, hairy or hairless, it didn't matter—every last one of these trolls was a disaster for the farmer. They ate all of his food, drank all of the water from his well, guzzled down all of his milk (often right from the cow!), broke his furniture, and farted whenever they felt like it.

The farmer could do nothing about this—there were too many trolls. Besides, the leader of the trolls, who went by the name of Mobhead, was a big brute of a troll with enormous claws who emitted a foul smell from all of the creatures he'd eaten raw over the years. Mobhead had a huge, gnarled head that seemed green in one kind of light and purple in another. Next to his head, his body looked shrunken and thin, but despite the way they looked his legs were strong as steel; they had to be or his head would have long since fallen off of his neck.

"Don't you think you'd be more comfortable somewhere else?" the farmer asked Mobhead during the second winter. His wife and children had left him for less troll-infested climes. He had lost a lot of his hair from stress.

"Oh, I don't think so," Mobhead said, cleaning his fangs with a toothpick made from a sharpened chair leg. The chair in question had been made by the farmer's father many years before.

"No," Mobhead said. "We like it here just fine." And farted to punctuate his point.

Behind him, one of the other trolls devoured the family cat, and belched.

The farmer sighed. It was getting hard to keep help, even in the summers, when the trolls kept to their lairs and caves far to the north. The farm's reputation had begun to suffer. A few more years of this and he would have to sell the farm, if any of it was left to sell.

Behind him, one of the trolls attacked a smaller troll. There was a splatter of blood against the far wall, a smell oddly like violets, and then the severed head of the smaller troll rolled to a stop at the farmer's feet. The look on the dead troll's face revealed no hint of surprise.

Nor was there a look of surprise on the farmer's face.

All spring and summer, the farmer thought about what he should do. Whether fairly or unfairly, he was known in those parts for thinking his way out of every problem that had arisen during twenty years of running the farm. But he couldn't fight off the trolls by himself. He couldn't bribe them to leave. It worried him almost as much as the lack of rain in July.

Then, in late summer, a traveling merchant came by the farm. He stopped by twice a year, once with pots, pans, and dried goods and once with livestock and pets. This time, he brought a big, lurching wooden wagon full of animals, pulled by ten of the biggest, strongest horses the farmer had ever seen.

Usually, the farmer bought chickens from the tall, mute merchant, and maybe a goat or two. But this time, the merchant pointed to a cage that held seven squirming, chirping balls of fur. The farmer looked at them for a second, looked away, then looked again, more closely, raising his eyebrows.

"Do you mean to say..." the farmer said, looking at the tall, mute merchant. "Are you telling me..."

The mute man nodded. The frown of his mouth became, for a moment, a mischievous smile.

The farmer smiled. "I'll take one. One should be enough."

The mute man's smile grew wide and deep.

That winter, the trolls came again, in strength—rowdy, smelly, raucous, and looking for trouble. They pulled out a barrel of his best beer and drank it all down in a matter of minutes. They set fire to his attic and snuffed it only when Mobhead bawled them out for "crapping where you eat, you idiots!"

They noticed the little ball of fur curled up in a basket about an hour after they had smashed down the front door.

"Ere now," said one of the trolls, a foreign troll from England, "Wot's this, wot?"

One of the other trolls—a deformed troll, with a third eye protruding like a tube from its forehead—prodded the ball of fur with one of its big clawed toes. "It's a cat, I think. Just like the last one. Another juicy, lovely cat."

A third troll said, "Save it for later. We've got plenty of time."

The farmer, who had been watching all of this, said to the trolls, "Yes, this is our new cat. But I'd ask that you not eat him. I need him around to catch mice in the summer or when you come back next time, I won't have any grain, and no grain means no beer. It also means lots of other things won't be around for you to eat, like that homemade bread you seem to enjoy so much. In fact, I might not even be around, then, for without grain this farm cannot survive."

The misshapen troll sneered. "A pretty speech, farmer. But don't worry about the mice. We'll eat them all before we leave."

So the farmer went to Mobhead and made Mobhead promise that he and his trolls would leave the cat alone.

"Remember what you said to the trolls who tried to set my attic on fire, O Mighty Mobhead," the farmer said, in the best tradition of flatterers everywhere.

Mobhead thought about it for a second, then said, "Hmmm. I must admit I've grown fond of you, farmer, in the way a wolf is fond of a lamb. And I do want our winter resort to be in good order next time we come charging down out of the frozen north. Therefore, although I have this nagging feeling I might regret this, I will let you keep the cat. But everything else we're going to eat, drink, ruin, or fart on. I just want to make that clear."

The farmer said, "That's fine, so long as I get to keep the cat."

Mobhead said he promised on his dead mothers' eyeteeth, and then he called the other trolls around and told them that the cat was off limits. "You are not to eat the cat. You are not to taunt the cat. You must leave the cat alone."

The farmer smiled a deep and mysterious smile. It was the first smile for him in quite some time. A troll who swore on the eyeteeth of his mothers could never break that promise, no matter what.

And so the farmer got to keep his cat. The next year, when the trolls came barging in, they were well into their rampage before they even saw the cat. When they did, they were a little surprised at how big it had grown. Why, it was almost as big as a dog. And it had such big teeth, too.

"It's one of those Northern cats," the farmer told them. "They grow them big up there. You must know that, since you come from up there. Surely you know that much?"

"Yes, yes," Mobhead said, nodding absent-mindedly, "we know that, farmer," and promptly dove face-first into a large bucket of offal.

But the farmer noticed that the cat made the other trolls nervous. For one thing, it met their gaze and held it, almost as if it weren't an animal, or thought itself their equal. And it didn't really look like a cat, even a Northern cat, to them. Still, the farmer could tell that the other trolls didn't want to say anything to their leader. Mobhead liked to eat the smaller trolls because they were, under all the hair, so succulent, and none of them wanted to give him an excuse for a hasty dinner.

Another year went by. Spring gave on to the long days of summer, and the farmer found some solace in the growth of not only his crops but also his cat. The farmer and his cat would take long walks through the fields, the farmer teaching the cat as much about the farm as possible. And he believed that the cat even appreciated some of it.

Once more, too, fall froze into winter, and once more the trolls came tumbling into the farmer's house, led by Mobhead. Once again, they trashed the place as thoroughly as if they were roadies for some drunken band of Scandanavian lute players.

They had begun their second trashing of the house, pulling down the cabinets, splintering the chairs, when suddenly they heard a growl that turned their blood to ice and set them to gibbering, and at their rear there came the sound of bones being crunched, and as they turned to look and see what was happening, they were met by the sight of some of their friends being hurled at them with great force.

The farmer just stood off to the side, smoking his pipe and chuckling from time to time as his cat took care of the trolls. Sharp were his fangs! Long were his claws! Huge was his frame!

Finally, Mobhead walked up alongside the farmer. He was so shaken, he could hardly hold up his enormous head.

"I could eat you right now, farmer," Mobhead snarled. "That is the largest cat I have ever seen—and it is trying to kill my trolls! Only *I* get to kill my trolls!"

"Nonsense," the farmer said. "My cat only eats mice. Your trolls aren't mice, are they?"

"I eat farmers sometimes," Mobhead said. "How would you like that?"

The farmer took the pipe out of his mouth and frowned. "It really isn't up to me. I don't think Mob-Eater would like that, though."

"Mob-Eater?"

"Yes—that's my name for my cat."

As much as a hairy troll can blanch, Mobhead blanched exactly that much and no more.

"Very well, I won't eat you. But I *will* eat your hideous cat," Mobhead said, although not in a very convincing tone.

The farmer smiled. "Remember your promise."

Mobhead scowled. The farmer knew the creature was thinking about breaking his promise. But if he did, Mobhead would be tormented by nightmares in which his mothers tortured him with words and with deeds. He would lose all taste for food. He would starve. Even his mighty head would shrivel up. Within a month, Mobhead would be dead…

Mobhead snarled in frustration. "We'll be back when your cat is gone, farmer," he said. "And then you'll pay!"

If he'd had a cape instead of a dirty pelt of fur-hair, Mobhead would have whirled it around him as he left, trailing the remains of his thoroughly beaten and half-digested trolls behind him.

"You haven't heard the last of me!" Mobhead yowled as he disappeared into the snow, now red with the pearling of troll blood.

The next winter, Mobhead and his troll band stopped a few feet from the farmer's front door.

"Hey, farmer, are you there?!" Mobhead shouted.

After a moment, the door opened wide and there stood the farmer, a smile on his face.

"Why, Mobhead. How nice to see you. What can I do for you?"

"You can tell me if you still have that damn cat. I've been looking forward to our winter get-away."

The farmer smiled even more, and behind him rose a huge shadow with large yellow eyes and rippling muscles under a thick brown pelt. The claws on the shadow were big as carving knives, and the fangs almost as large.

"Why, yes," the farmer said, "as it so happens I still have Mob-Eater. He's a very good mouser."

Mobhead's shoulders slumped.

It would be a long hard slog back to the frozen north, and only troll to eat along the way. As he turned to go, he kicked a small troll out of his way.

"We'll be back next year," he said over his shoulder. "We'll be back every year until that damn cat is gone."

"Suit yourself," the farmer said, and closed the door.

Once inside, the farmer and the bear laughed.

"Thanks, Mob-Eater," the farmer said. "You looked really fierce."

The bear huffed a deep bear belly laugh, sitting back on its haunches in a huge comfy chair the farmer had made for him.

"I am really fierce, father," the bear said. "But you should have let me chase them. I don't like the taste of troll all that much, but, oh, I do love to chase them."

"Maybe next year," the farmer said. "Maybe next year. But for now, we have chores to do. I need to teach you to milk the cows, for one thing."

"But I hate to milk the cows," the bear said. "You know that."

"Yes, but you still need to know how to do it, son."

"Very well. If you say so."

They waited for a few minutes until the trolls were out of sight, and then they went outside and started doing the farm chores for the day.

Soon, the farmer thought, his wife and children would come home, and everything would be as it was before. Except that now they had a huge talking bear living in their house.

Sometimes folktales didn't end quite the way you thought they would. But they *did* end.

The Root of the Matter

Gregory Frost

Gregory Frost is an American author of science fiction and fantasy, and directs a fiction writing workshop at Swarthmore College in Swarthmore, Pennsylvania. He received his Bachelor's degree from the University of Iowa. A graduate of the iconic Clarion Workshop, he has been invited back as instructor several times, including the first session following its move to the University of California at San Diego in 2007. He is also active in the Interstitial Arts Foundation. His most recent novels include *Shadowbridge* and its sequel *Lord Tophet*.

Rapunzel is a fairytale full of awful, frightening imagery. Frost is not afraid to tackle this imagery head on and in ways that would make the Brothers Grimm proud. I've always found the idea of a young man finding a beautiful young woman alone in a tower shouldn't be chaste and Frost certainly obliges me.

1. Obloquy & Sortilege

I wanted a child, you see. You.

The rest I'd sacrificed long ago and, really, I didn't miss it much, except maybe on holidays. I'd grown up on holidays, to be with my family and smell the old smells, relive my childhood a little bit. For most children, I suppose it was something to look forward to. That being at the core of the wretched life I'd abandoned, it didn't make much sense that I'd ever go back again. Nice, liver-spotted daddy seated on the far side of the cranberry sauce that's lumped in its bowl like somebody's heart, is the same daddy who hoisted my slick pink bottom out of the bathtub bubbles and spread me with his thumbs and tore out the childhood in me. Childhood couldn't fit in beside his blunted cock, so childhood packed its bag and fled the same night; I had to wait another two years for a chance to follow it.

Now when I reflect back, I start to tell myself, "Gothel, there were plenty of alternatives to running away," but it isn't true. He was The Daddy. The God, the Almighty to whom the family were obedient. The "Don't Cry, Baby, Daddy's Here" savior. The Fucker. Besides, I didn't have any powers then, so I couldn't have dealt with him.

Some women, they just go find some other daddy, an adoptive daddy, a sweet sugar daddy. Not me, and not you—I've seen to us both.

I tried to remain in the city at first, but found I couldn't endure seeing the men. In the city, they were everywhere, with their little girls holding their hands. I'd see their eyes glittering like the cold eyes of birds, like his had done, and I'd know there was a stiffness in their pants and an ugliness like a tumor in their thoughts. I couldn't just sit by and watch the conspiracy take shape around some other poor wretch. That's what finally drove me from the city, into the wilderness—the conspiracy whereby fathers rape their daughters.

I was younger than you—I hadn't even been faced with my first . . . with the curse of bleeding. I'd no idea then what I would find in dark, redolent forests.

By the time I arrived at the place the Others called "The Rift", I hadn't eaten in days, I smelled dirty, and everything I had on itched. Little girls, running away from home, pack stuffed-animals and jammies. They don't understand the first thing about what they'll need in order to survive in the soulless world.

I stopped where I stopped because there was a stream. I dangled a hand in it, found it uncommonly warm. I waded in and lay down in the middle. And it was like a big, downy bed with bedding of water. I'd never felt anything so soothing and safe in my life. I must have—I did—fall asleep there in the water. I dreamt of sailing along, down to a river, past a quay and out into the sea.

The next I knew, people had come to the banks of the stream on both sides of me. The Others. Firefly people, I thought of them, because they burned, incandescent. I remember that I wasn't afraid but thought I should be. When I sat up, they reached and helped me out of the stream. Where they stepped, white light swirled in the water. They led me into the woods somewhere near, although I'm none too clear if it was the same woods as when I'd arrived. In any case, by morning, when they flitted away, I'd discovered my power. It had been there in me all along, dormant, needing cause or awareness for its release. I believe it sleeps in you, too, my love, and in all women. The Others taught me that, you see.

You're always asking for tricks, as if this is some kind of parlor game, this power, but there's a conservation of energy to sorcery, which means you don't produce it for free. It costs. To make magic is to burn off some of your own life. Like hurtful words, you can't take it back once it's done. If I performed right now every simple trick you've wanted in your fifteen sweet years, I'd turn five hundred years old myself in a blink and look twice that much. Silly girl.

Yes, I suppose they were fairies, the Others. A race, a people both strange and familiar, as though they lurked inside a forgotten dream somewhere. They were hermaphroditic, have I said? That means they had what you have as well as a tiny, useless, deflated cock. I know it's bewildering that I didn't react violently at seeing their maleness. Maybe because the display was so innocent, sexless—hairless bodies, and with little breasts, oh, much smaller than yours, my darling. More like castrated little children than men.

I worked to learn from them how to express my newfound sorceries. Afterward, I snuck back into the city.

There was a house there that my daddy had spoken of a few times to my mother, that took me in. Only women lived in it. I made a bargain with she who owned it, once I'd demonstrated for her how I could manipulate her clientele. I had to use one of the other girls. Only a single other time have I ever directed my power upon a woman. But we'll come to that event soon enough.

I preyed upon men. Only upon men. I made them do humiliating things, ugly things, you'd think; they cowered, and crawled like insects, like worms, but they obeyed every foul request. And when they'd had their fill of debasement, they offered me more power. Money, property, jewels. I decided that I wanted the piece of wilderness where the Others dwelled, and I lured the man who held title and got it deeded to me. By then I had a reputation in certain circles, and he arrived at the house thinking to conquer me with his maleness. They all tried in their way to best me. I was a challenge no male ego could resist: the little girl who drains men dry without so much as letting them touch her. Each one had his sweaty fantasy of turning the tables on me; none of them ever did. You remember the story I told you about the witch named Circe? She lived on an island alone, but men wandered there all the time, pretending to be blown off course. She turned every one of them into pigs, but they kept coming. Just to nibble at her painted toes awhile before the slaughter. Well, turning men into pigs is no particular feat. The real exercise is getting pigs to write checks.

Once I had the land, I made other men clear it and build me a house with a big wall around it, so that the stream would run through the property. Then I sent them away with no memory of where they'd been, and I was finally freed and wealthy and alone at the age of seventeen. I never needed to see another of them again.

What happened next was, I began dreaming about you, my love. I didn't anticipate you. For years I lived contentedly with only the Others for company. Maybe my dreams of you were an expression of the power they'd unleashed in me. The ache grew in me like a child itself. Like a hot wind, it would sweep over me as I lay in bed, and those nights I drove myself to pleasure, hoping to find peace in the aftermath of orgasm, but all I could think of still was the child who is you. I probably would have gone frustrated to my grave if civilization hadn't caught up with me.

I had never considered that if I could set down on a parcel of wilderness land so could anyone else. One morning, I woke up and there, right outside my wall, were men hammering together a frame, two stories, much higher than my wall. Men. Naked to the waist and covered with hair, bellowing and rude, exposing themselves and pissing into the wind—I thought I'd done with them and here they were like maggots crawling over the bones of a giant. I was so startled, so appalled, that I could only look on in horror as the roof was tarred and shingled, and leaded glass placed in the windows, and the bricks mortared in place. In no time, as if the materials leaped into place with every blink of my eye, it was done. The house, casting my house in its shadow, filled the eastern sky.

I crept down to the stream and peered over the wall, only to find that other tracts had been cleared behind me as well. Machines had destroyed it all. My forest had gone and I could see, through the distant haze, the gleam of a city skyline. The water emerging under my wall was already befouled. The Others had seen it coming much sooner. They'd departed, closing the Rift forever. I would have gone with them—they'd taught me so much. I suppose they thought of me me as part of this world, whatever else I meant to them. And I wouldn't have known you.

The first indication I had of the new occupants was the laughter of their children. You can imagine how that tore at me, ravenous as I was for you by then. Before long, there were lights at night. Bodies moved about, silhouettes in the windows—the man, a skinny little puppet thing; the woman, though, was titanic. An ungoverned earth-mother ripe as can be. I counted three children and here she was, pregnant with a fourth. As I hid in my shadowy hut, I heard her raise her squawking voice in anger, I heard a slap against the face of a disobedient babe. My cheek burned as if she'd slapped me. My resolve hardened into stone.

I used my power the same night, twice. First, I looked inside the ill–tempered cow and saw you, my tiny girl, the object of my dreams. I knew in an instant I'd found my destiny. Second, I set into motion an obsession. It was simple, because pregnant women are already poised on the brink of obsession; I had but to point a direction, give desire its goal, give the fat woman a push.

I had a garden that she could see from her high window. In it grew three rows of harebell—lovely big blue flowers that would catch her eye. She didn't call it harebell; where she came from the plant had a different name, which is your sweet name. You see, the magic was with the plant. I named you after it because you are part of that magic.

I made her crave the harebell root the way I craved the contents of her belly. She could not sleep because of it. She lost the energy to slap her children, though she raised her voice and railed when they dislocated her desire with their presence. Her mouth watered and she smacked her lips all the time, trying to find the missing flavor in every memory of food.

That was the second time I used magic on a woman, but she was so unkempt and irascible, I had no misgivings. Rejoice that you never knew her and never felt her hand across your cheek.

Bloated as she was, the woman couldn't possibly climb the wall to steal the plant. Naturally, she sent *him*. The husband.

I let him steal the roots the first time. That was part of the magic. He slithered back over the wall, and their house fell silent for the first time in a long time. I could imagine her devouring a sweet salad of root, her eyes rolling back in her head at the luscious pleasure squeezed out of each bite. No doubt for a while she squatted with oily fingers and drool upon her chin. Then the shouting, the wailing began. If I hadn't known he was in my garden before, I'd have known all about it from the cow screaming at the top of her lungs for him to "go get more rapunzel."

It was when he attempted to return that I barred his way. Caught him red-handed, with a half-dozen slender, fleshy roots dangling from his fist. He began to cry. He fell to his knees, begging my forgiveness. He accounted for himself by describing how his wife had become mad for the roots because of her pregnancy. He offered to pay for them. I laughed at him, poor, pathetic creature that he was. As if I needed his few coins.

Finally, I pretended sympathy and agreed to let him go. I told him that I understood his wife's ailment better than he. Of course, he assumed I meant I'd borne children of my own. My offer of recompense took him utterly by surprise.

I demanded you. I would keep the woman subdued, sated, absolutely sodden with rapunzel throughout the remaining five months of her pregnancy, at the end of which he would give me the baby.

Oh, no, he cried. Anything but that. It was all sham, his struggle with ethics.

He probably would have fought longer, except that the obese shrew began bellowing like a foghorn for him to get back there with her rapunzel. He positively squirmed, which was worth the years I was using up in working my magic on her. It was my offer of a holiday from that monster which ultimately turned him around. "All right," said he, "I have three already, don't I?" He wasn't really asking, he was justifying it, setting it right in his mind the way men do easily when they need to accept a break with decency. I'm sure my daddy had cleared my rapes with himself by calling it something morally proper that I deserved.

I let the man pass, brushing the roots as he did with a soporific dust. He went home and the bellow of the beast ceased that night. His children came to laugh freely again, and I even heard him joining in now and again. The sound of children laughing made my blood race as I bided my time.

When the night of delivery came, I waited at the window, listening for your first cries. No sweeter music have I ever heard, except your singing nowadays.

I saw him at the window—he made the agreed sign. I flew over the wall and sailed through his house like a ghost, past his sleeping children, right into the room where the exhausted woman slept. He was pacing the floor there, wringing his hands, the nails still black with my dirt.

The imminent act had driven him half-mad. I could see that he might recant at any second. I told him not to worry, that you would be well looked after. I promised to raise you right. Whatever he considered "right" to be, he didn't pursue it. After all, he hadn't carried you, kicking inside his belly; he hadn't been tied to you, feeding you all the time you were growing, he didn't know any bond like so close. You were a thing outside him, as all women are to all men. Now you see how that is true for you right from birth. And now you see how a man can steal anything from a woman, even a part of her own flesh; but you, my dearest, were fortunate, in that you were passed to me. Finally, he handed you over, then turned his back and told me to get out.

I never saw either of them again. What he told her, or if he told her anything, I have neither idea nor care. They didn't want you enough to fight for you even a little bit, to protect you as I have done so many years.

The rest you've been party to as you've grown. The forest where we lived, until you began your monthly cycle—and I've explained already that I removed you here to protect you from those men who began to come around, inevitably sniffing out your woman-scent. I knew they were there in the forest, watching, creeping closer every day. They would have had us both if we'd lingered longer.

No man will ever lay a hand upon you. Only I, because I know how to touch your heart, as you touch mine, my beautiful girl. I know what pleases you best because it pleases me the same. Never to strike you, to harm you, as that horrid creature that bore you would have done. As men would have done. If I spoil you silly with everything you want or need, well, who do I harm? And I always shall. I adore you, don't you see, my Rapunzel, my little blue-eyed bellflower. I adore you so very much.

2. Penetration

Dear Diary,

Mother Gothel had her sherry again and told me the story of how I got here, which I've heard maybe a hundred times already. It gets bigger every time she tells it, and the facts get changed. I mean, *I* never saw men creeping in the forest. Mother Gothel goes on about them constantly—how she rescued me from terrors I can't even imagine, about all these other things she's saved me from. The filth of the city; my cruel family. And the men. Touching me, sticking me with their weird pricking things; the way she describes cocks, it's like big pronged knives grow out of their bodies. When I was little, I used to cry when she described them. I had nightmares and everything. Now, I'm not so sure. The story looks threadbare to me. How did my mother have me, if she had to get cored by this thorny potato peeler of a cock first? She'd be dead I'm sure.

When we came to the lighthouse from the forest, I was twelve. That was only three years ago, but when she's in her cups, Mother Gothel behaves as if I don't remember the order of events, or recall that I never saw any men, or that she used her power to keep me unconscious the whole way here. In truth, I've no idea where "here" is. Near an ocean is all.

Her transformation and mine definitely began the night of my period. I woke up with something warm between my legs. I'd been feeling cranky and bloated for a week, and all of a sudden there I was, bleeding to death. I started screaming for my life. God, I was *dying*, I was just certain of it.

She cursed me and cursed me when she saw the blood; she stomped around the bed, slapped the mattress, called me a bitch, a slut, a cunt—I don't even know what that means. It's the nearest she's ever come to hitting me. I thought it was *my fault* what had happened. I kept crying, "I'm sorry, I'm sorry," even though I didn't know what for. Then, after she'd exhausted us both, she finally announced that she'd been expecting this. "It's a curse all women share but I'd prayed God it would skip over you." That moment I began to doubt everything she'd ever told me. It was *my* fault, was it? She was blaming *me*, but at the same time she'd known it would happen because it happens to all women? I couldn't wrestle sense from that, and I hated her for twisting me up in her perjury.

No more than two days after that, she began asking had I noticed anyone lurking about. Anyone like naked men hiding behind the trees. There was no one, of course, I hadn't seen a soul; I mean *ever*.

In my whole insular life I'd never met anyone on a path, in the stream, climbing a tree. We might have been the only two people in the whole world if she hadn't rattled on about these "men" who pursued us. And thereafter it was me—they smelled *me*, they hunted *me*. I'd like to see one, just to know that they're really down there somewhere.

Next she came in agitated and told me she'd spotted these men lurking near the garden, waiting to pounce on her if she went to gather her vegetables. For days she wouldn't let me go out, or even get close to a window. Finally, she locked me in and disappeared for a week herself. When she returned, she worked an enchantment on me. I slept there and awoke here.

We live on three floors at the top of the lighthouse; the rest is bricked up. For companionship now I have screeing gulls and a wide plain of ocean that glistens day and night. Sometimes objects float by, far away. They never come close. Never.

I'm the only means available for coming or going in this tower. I have a feeling she planned it that way all along. We were going to move to this tower from the day I was born.

She has never cut my hair. I think she thinks it would be the equivalent of beating me. My earliest memory is of being brushed at bedtime. Every night she takes out her brushes and unravels my braids. They lie near the glass door, coiled up like big ropes fastened to my head. Sometimes I imagine I'm a machine that runs on steam, and the braids are the hoses that connect me to the engine so I don't run down.

Whenever she wants to go out, Mother Gothel touches me and says into my ear, "Rapunzel, let down your hair now." Together, we carry the coils out onto the walkway girdling the turret. The railing has big hooks attached to it that I can wrap each braid around for support before dropping it over the side. My hair nearly touches the ground.

There's a small ladder of five rungs, an opening in the rail. Mother Gothel climbs onto it, takes hold of both braids and slides down the side of the tower as though she were a girl no older than me. I've never seen her do any sorcery, not really *real* sorcery—she complains that it wears her out—but I know she has secret powers, otherwise how could she move on the strands of my hair so easily? I hardly even feel her weight.

I can never leave. I am the ladder, how can I climb me?

Dear Diary,

Today is the strangest of all days ever.

It began simply enough. I was lying on my bed, with my earphones on, listening to something baroque. Mother Gothel only brings me baroque music. I've asked for something else, a variety, but she claims the other tapes are too expensive.

The morning had heated up early and was humid from yesterday's rain. I had chores to do but could not make myself stir. Mother Gothel came up beside me and gently stroked my braid where it joins my head. I dragged one phone from my ear. "Rapunzel, you lazy girl," she cooed, "get up. I have to go shopping."

I raised my head and looked at her. I was pretending to be a turtle. I blinked at her and tried to draw back into my shell.

She didn't like that. "The morning's half gone," she said sharply. "You haven't even dressed." That was true. I was lying naked on the bed. But just thinking about the effort of putting on petticoats and skirts in that heat exhausted me. I thought, the sooner I get rid of her the better.

I got up and wrapped the sheet around me and marched out to the balcony. If she saw that I was mad at having to get up, I didn't care. She ignored me, the way she always does when she's preparing to leave. She's always counting things in her mind, rummaging.

I don't even exist for her, not really. She keeps this image of me in her head, of what I am. When she speaks to me the way she does when she reminisces, she's talking to the illusion. Whenever I do something awful—like setting her birds free from their cages, making her capture them again— she sighs and says, "The child will be willful from time to time." What is that supposed to mean? The false-me can't get into trouble, no matter what I do. But then I'll have my monthly flow and she'll start screeching at me as if I did it to vex her. The image again—the image doesn't bleed. It's always twelve years old. I wish it would pop out from inside her head so I could grab it and throw it over the balcony. Then she would have to deal with me.

Before she climbed down, she gave me a peck on the cheek. "I'll be back at dusk," she said. "Have dinner ready, won't you?" I nodded, to let her know I'd heard, to avoid an argument. So many of them lately. I surprise myself these days with how readily I pursue arguments. I'm not certain I understand this any more than Mother Gothel does.

I watched her walk away from the tower as I hoisted the braids back up. She entered the hawthorn maze ringing the hilltop. Her magic grew that dark barrier. She claims the way through it is treacherous—between the thorns and all the dead ends—an added layer of protection against whatever's out there. *She* threads it easily enough.

When I'd piled the hair up, I slumped down beside it. The boards were warm beneath my face and smelled of brine. There came into my head the notion swimming out to one of the ships on the horizon. I needed a miracle right then, although I couldn't say what shape it should take. I think it was a premonition of the change about to occur.

I hadn't yet unlooped the braids from the hooks when I heard the soft call, "Rapunzel, Rapunzel, let down your hair." What, I wondered, was she doing back already? What had she forgotten? I didn't care, but I did hesitate to respond right away. When I thought she'd been frustrated enough, I pushed the hair off the side. A seagull had landed on the rail, and he flapped up, shrieking, at my movement. I watched him sail out in a great arc, catching an updraft and sailing higher than the lighthouse roof. I was dreaming about flying beside him, and the next thing I knew, there were footsteps on the ladder, and I turned my head, and I found a stranger staring at me.

I jumped up. The sheet caught in the board. I had to undo it and pull it, and of course it tore. I rewrapped myself, backed into the doorway—or tried to, anyway. But I remained hooked to the railing and couldn't retreat. I stopped, unable to decide what I should do.

The stranger stood motionless at the rail, holding the two strands of my hair together in front of him. His wide, dark eyes had the power to touch. Each glance brushed over me like fingers, almost like the caress of Mother Gothel's hands in the bath. All the while my heart was beating as wildly as in the bath. It was practically in my throat. The sun wheeled in the sky, and still we didn't move, either of us. I can't imagine what my own expression must have been. After all, he'd seen a girl before. But he was my first man.

He wore odd, torn clothing. I couldn't help from darting fearful glances at the spot where his legs met, but there was no treacherous blade visible.

All of a sudden, and the more shocking because I wasn't prepared for it, he spoke my name. His voice was soft, but deeper than Gothel's or mine, as his hair and skin were darker. The sound of my name plucked a string inside me, set me all to vibrating.

Without my asking, he undid the braids and drew them up, coiling them as if he had been doing it his whole life. I hadn't yet said a word, and I was free then to run, but I stayed. I waited. I wanted to know.

He came and sat down beside my hair. He began talking to me. "I spent the night inside your hawthorn trap. It's very clever. Looks like normal growth from without. You'd never know until you're in it how tricky it is to navigate." He had come upon Mother Gothel in her garden and followed her. Our tower, he said, hadn't been used since his grandfather's time, when great ships with huge sails as tall as the tower itself came rounding the point of land. He gestured out at the blue sea as he spoke. His words produced a warmth inside me, and all at once I blushed, thinking I'd begun my flow; but a quick look at the sheet told me I was wrong. Still, I was wet there.

He said, "I had to spend the night inside the maze. Last night I heard singing. A lullaby. It was the most wonderful voice I've ever heard. I lay back in there, a rabbit trapped in a snare, and just listened to the song. By the time it ended, I couldn't live without its sound. If it was a drink, I wanted to be intoxicated. It was water for my thirst, food for my hunger. And I know that the singer was you."

"Yes," I admitted. I could feel myself blushing, because of course I *had* been singing last night. He had heard me. He said he'd fallen in love with *me*. An emotional upheaval nearly drowned me. The realization came all at once, like lightning: I was no longer by myself. There was someone else. As he spoke, as he described how he'd set off from home and wandered through the country to seek the unknown of his future, I came to sense that he was in many ways more like me than Mother Gothel was.

Initially, I tried to deny this, falling back behind the security of her warnings about men's treacherous lies. But his were no lies. He was simply telling me his story, not trying to beguile me, flatter or cajole me. Mother Gothel warned me about the shape of the words of men, but she'd neglected to tell me how I would feel in the presence of one. Did all of them have hypnotic charms? If I entered a room full of them, would I become butter, melting away?

He spoke of faraway places, of markets, and trains, of his family—he had both brothers and sisters. I tried to imagine what such a family must be like.

All at once I started. The sun was setting behind him. I'd sat down to listen but I jumped up now and told him he had to leave. He looked on dumbly. He didn't understand.

"Mother Gothel will be returning," I told him. "She has powers, fierce powers. She'll destroy you. You have to go before she returns."

He considered. "All right," he said. "But I have to come back, now I know the way." He looked down over the rail, studying the maze, its pattern open to him. "What a jewel she guards."

I lowered my eyes when he said that. This was the sort of talk Mother Gothel had warned me about—calling us "jewels" or "goddesses". I'd enjoyed his company so much that I didn't want to think he was capable of it.

"Go," I urged. He looked forlorn, as if he'd been hoping for something else. He grabbed at me playfully, to make me come and kiss him, but I slapped his hand aside. "Don't be stupid," I said, "go." He sullenly climbed back over the edge, took hold of the braids and disappeared over the side.

He had barely let go when I saw Mother Gothel approaching from outside the ring of thorns. He must have hidden somewhere round the other side of the tower, because she did not see him. But when she climbed up, she began right away to shout at me. "Never let down your hair until I call to you! Ever."

I protested that I had done it as a courtesy. This seemed to work pretty well. At least, she stopped squawking about that and began complaining instead that I'd spent the whole day on nothing at all. I hadn't gotten dressed. I hadn't fixed a meal. And look how I'd torn a perfectly good bedsheet.

I had to turn away then, because I almost started to laugh, and if I'd done that, then she would have known. I couldn't have hidden the pleasure overtaking me.

Before I came in here tonight, I sat on the balcony and sang again. This time I knew he could hear, and I sang for him alone, wherever he hides in the woods. My heart races when I picture him listening.

He will come back. I will see him again. I wonder if I'll dream about him tonight, if in my dream I'll give him a name.

Dear Diary,

It has happened. I think now it was inevitable from the moment he arrived; or maybe it was when he confessed his love for my song.

Jon (for that's his name) climbed up again as soon as she was gone. He had new clothes this time, not torn by the maze. He didn't press for a kiss this time either, so I invited him into the tower, gave him a tour of all three floors.

He was most curious about the disused apparatus that had once signaled the ships. It's a lamp of some kind, with two large rods in the center. Even though he had never seen it before, he understood its workings, and showed me where the rods had melted in the middle. That was where the light was produced. "An arc," he said, when the two rods were brought close together. The light had reflected off large mirrors, but the remaining one lay now disassembled on the floor. It was curved like a shallow bowl and distorted our faces as we peered into it. He prattled on about its power to cast light far out to sea in a great sweeping beam that ships even over the horizon would see. He was showing off, but I didn't pay much attention. I couldn't help looking at the two of us in the mirror. What I did next surprised us both.

Jon didn't notice, so caught up was he in the fantasy of sailors and lights that guided them through their darkness. He wasn't watching me, I know, because I'd taken off everything and settled into the mirror before he turned and saw me, and whatever he was about to say was lost forever. His mouth hung open, shaping a word.

"This mirror is cold," I said.

He replied, "It's glass." He swallowed.

I leaned forward and stared at myself upside down looking up at me over my breasts. "I'm divided in two," I said. I was teasing him now, beginning to explore my power over him, which was proving substantial. Is this how Mother Gothel feels towards me?

"What should I do?" he asked, barely able to look my way.

I had but to open my arms for him to understand me. He turned his back to undress. Unlike him, I watched boldly as more and more of him was unveiled. His body had a hardness to it that neither I nor Mother Gothel shared. His muscles seemed chiseled in his sides, his legs. His stomach, when he turned, had ridges over it.

His cock was nothing like I'd expected. It bore no resemblance to the razor-edged and barbed weapons Mother Gothel had described. It seemed both rigid and flexible, and the tip sparkled with a drop of liquid. I could see how we were supposed to close together. She'd never discussed this except in ways to make me dread it, and jittery things did flutter in my stomach, but it wasn't dread, it was something else.

For all of his posturing the day before, he came to me shyly, clearly at a loss as to what we must do. I lay back and drew him up beside me. His cock slid along my thigh. We became arms and legs for a moment, an uncoordinated heap of limbs trying to establish mutual comfort and support. He propped himself on one elbow. His touch arrived light as a feather, and I twitched with pleasure. Each of us wanted to explore the same regions of the other, and it took us no time at all to excite ourselves. The knowledge must have been inside me all the time. If my monthly flow is woman's ancient curse, then maybe this comprehension of union is the ancient blessing accompanying it to balance the equation. I couldn't wait for him to decide. I took hold of him and urged him to fit himself between my wetted thighs.

In one respect Mother Gothel had foretold honestly—there was pain. It lasted an instant, a flash of fire, a brief scorch. But, then …then followed a consuming warmth like hot water poured through me. The tip of his cock touched somewhere deep inside, and stars seemed to burst round my eyes. I arched my back. I think I cried out. All that warmth filling me blasted down and out of me. Jon had his head up, the muscles rigid in his neck. He looked wild, feral as a demon, but almost as if he were in agony, as if he were dying. Abruptly, he collapsed on top of me. He twitched a few times, then let out a deep sigh and kissed me once more. It was that last, lingering kiss which told me he hadn't lied. Mother Gothel had so many times described how, the instant men were finished with you, they got up and left you to your pain and emptiness. "You mean nothing to them, the pretty words are all lies. They discard you." Jon did not behave like that. He clung to me as I to him. In the bowl of the mirror, with the voices of the seagulls like a chorus in the sky, we might have been at sea ourselves, rocking gently to and fro, a thought that prompted me to begin singing softly the lullaby he'd heard the first night. A great, drowsy smile spread over his face. His eyes so black gave me back my own face. "I love you, Rapunzel," he murmured. He closed his eyes and I sang him to sleep. I don't know if he knew I was crying.

I was reluctant to send him away again after that, but I had to. I had to. If she found him, who knows what she would do?

Diary,

I find her touch almost unbearable. Last evening, as we do regularly, we went down to the bath on the lower level. Mother Gothel lathered me as she has done since I was a child. She spends a great deal of time washing between my legs, and I've always let her. It felt so rapturous. Now, though the sensation's the same, I've no desire to let her enjoy me—that is what she does, why pretend otherwise? *She* is the one who takes her pleasure from me and walks away. She's the one for whom I'm a possession, an object. Why else am I kept here? If there are men, then let me deal with them. They're not half so fearsome as she believes. Jon says yes, there exist extraordinarily cruel men, evil men. But he admits the possibility (and proves it by existing) that there are good and fair men as well. Mother Gothel allows for no such thing. All are one color, one way. I cannot accept that. As Jon says, if it were all as she claimed, there'd be no people left.

Diary,

I've decided to run away.

It will be simple if I'm careful. Each time he comes now, he brings me a silk scarf to match the blue one I have already. I have eight of them, and I've begun knotting them together to create a ladder down which I can climb. Gothel will come after us I know, but Jon swears his family has power enough to bar her access once we've reached his home.

Today she never left, which was just as well, because I was sick the better part of the day. I don't want to be sick for him. When he arrives, he immediately wants to make love, and I want to make him happy. We've so little time together.

Diary,

My sickness returns almost daily. I can't even look at an onion now without my stomach twisting. Worse, even though I'm keeping less food in, I'm bloating up. When I wake up in the morning sometimes, my fingers are swollen. Sometimes my feet. Whatever this is, I'm scared. I've tried to hide the worst of it from both of them. Jon, I think, remains unaware, he's so much in love. I hide my discomfort and let him mount me, and afterward he's too drowsy to notice anything. But Mother Gothel has begun eyeing me suspiciously. She makes excuses not to leave on her usual rounds. I can't imagine how Jon endures day after day of living in the forest, waiting for her descent. My hair is all that binds us, binds us all.

Gods and saints, help me. She knows!

She ran my bath and I got in under the suds before she came in. But then she lathered my breasts and I could not help crying out. Her rough hands chafed my nipples. She asked what was wrong, her voice so sly.

"I'm not well," I said. "My breasts are tender, like it's my time of the month."

"What is it?" she asked.

"Flu," I told her. "It doesn't go away. And my clothes all feel uncomfortable. Mother Gothel, my dress is so tight now in the waist."

She withdrew her hands then, and stood up, staring in horror at my belly. I tried to be brave, but what could I do, knowing nothing of my own condition or what I had revealed?

"You monster," she snarled, "right under my nose. After all my warnings, all my declarations."

"I don't understand," I tried to say, but she interrupted me.

"Don't you dare try to pretend this is some immaculate miracle. No god climbed in here and fucked you, filthy whore." Then she cut loose with all of her sharp names for me. The litany of syllables that I don't have to define to understand. "Where is he? Are you hiding him here?" She pulled open a cabinet, tore out the shelves, threw linens every which way until the space inside lay empty. She stamped her foot on the sealed trap to the floor below.

"No," I said, but she dismissed me. She was clinging to that image of me again. The sweet girl hadn't done this. A beast had come in, a thing built of a dozen dirty names. She stormed out. I climbed from the bath and dried off quickly.

By the time I reached the top, she'd destroyed most of my room. The tapes she'd bought like candies for me lay strewn about, stepped on, crushed and unreeled. I thought of all the music lost to me forever, and my heart became stone. I struck out the only way I knew how. "He isn't here, he's gone," I said.

"Gone, I see." She looked right through me. I'd made the final blunder by admitting what she suspected. There could be no retreat from confession.

"He won't come while *you're* here," I told her.

"Of course he won't. He can't steal your soul with me around."

"He's not like that."

"They're *all* like that. Hasn't he promised to run away with you? To give you a life of luxury?" She began shout. "Didn't you listen to me? I've told you time and again what they'll do to you."

"No," I replied, but her portrayal had gone to ice in my heart. Jon had made all the promises she said. Still I defended him. "*You* lied to me, Mother Gothel. A million times."

That brought her up. "I never lied. Who is it, hiding men's swollen pricks inside her? Who is it that's got a baby growing in her belly?"

The next I knew, I'd dropped down on the bed. I didn't know what to say to that revelation. This, too, she had kept from me all along. I would have a baby now. My baby. Not hers. I stared at her and saw her at last without the rosy glass of kindness between us. I saw a sour old woman with her watery eyes shining a hateful madness; she who'd already stolen one woman's child. She'd done nothing but set limits for me, telling me only what she wanted me to know, maintaining my ignorance as the ultimate power over me.

She went out and returned. "He's never going to have you," she swore. She drew a carving knife from behind her.

So, I thought, she means to kill me. She's going to cut the child from me. I had nowhere to run in that tiny room. I sat on the bed and watched her approach, ready to die. She yanked one of my braids and slashed down with the knife. The hair tore out of my head. She sawed through the braid and threw it aside. Then she cut away the other. The braids belonged to the daughter Mother Gothel kept inside her mind, and I was no longer attached in any way to that image. She'd released me, a fairy princess from an evil queen's spell.

She kicked the braids out of the room and slammed the door. "You'll not climb down to him, either. No, my corrupt beauty, you're leaving us, but not like that." Again I thought she meant to kill me, but she went out. I heard the key scrape in the lock. I ran and tried to tear the door open, too late.

Now, as I sit here on the bed, there's a rising wind outside. The sky splits open with flashes of lightning but without thunder. The light is barely an arm's length beyond my window. Her voice rattles the door with chants in a foreign tongue. This is her sorcery that she would never let me see. How can I combat this? Jon, do you know? Can you see what's happening? Fly, my love, run far from here, go home to your protective family. Be the liar she says you are, and abandon me while you can. Find another singer whose song offers you pleasure. Maybe in her voice you'll find enough of me to satisfy you.

I do sense something like an electricity on the air, constricting in a band around me, enclosing me tighter with each blink of the eye. The tower's swaying like it's alive. I think I'm falling, falling. Mother Got

3. Rates of Exchange

From where I sat in the wood at dawn, I couldn't see a thing. A fog had moved in after that storm.

Because of Rapunzel's condition, the old woman went out less and less, and I didn't want to miss her because of the fog. I would like to say I was worried for Rapunzel, that my desire to get into the tower again was in order to look after her. The shameful truth is that I only wanted to fuck again. My body wanted her, and its desire completely overrode what ought to have been my real concern. Fortunately, as the sun rose, the fog thinned out until I could clearly see the tower.

Soon enough, the golden hair came unfurling down the side, followed by the bulky spider-shape of Gothel. She descended out of sight behind the hawthorns, but I held my place until she'd emerged and vanished over the hill before I got up and raced into the ring. The treacherous path led me all round and round the tower. Running, I kept trying for a glimpse of her on the balcony.

I climbed the lighthouse faster than I ever had, leaped over the rail like a gymnast. In my eagerness I was already tugging my shirt loose.

The balcony lay empty, washed in a sense of doom. Some of the planks had been ripped up. One of the large panes of glass had shattered inward. For a minute, taking in the obvious destruction, I didn't see what had happened. It was too enormous, too impossible. The severed braids hung right beside me, dangling from their hooks like bloody stumps. All at once I understood. I turned to escape—and there stood Gothel, the ogress, at the rail.

You've never seen anyone mad the way she was, and I hope you never will. Her face had twisted up till every fold and crease etched her with malice. Her eyes contained so much hatred of me, they couldn't blink.

"You interloper," she called me. "Invader. You freely bathed in my poor girl's innocence till it was all used up, poisoned by your pricking as if you were a thorn from the maze." She lifted a braid to her breasts. "You taught her how to cheat on me. All my precautions, all my barriers, and one of your kind still got through. Damn you, boy."

"I want—" I hesitated, choosing words more carefully in the face of her madness. "Madame Gothel, I *wish* to marry Rapunzel." In truth I hadn't considered it with anything but the lightest heart, but I was seeking to represent myself with more fairness than she gave me. But she knew me better than that.

"Fine enough to say," she answered, "yet we both of us know it's a lie of convenience to extricate yourself from a situation you'd rather not be in. Don't we? You lie and you lay her, it's all so casual." I could not meet her gaze. "The same as she—soiled in a way that no scrubbing can ever clean."

"All right," I said petulantly, "then I guess you won't mind if we two base creatures take our leave of you. Where is she?"

She became sly. "Oh, you'd like to know that, I'll bet. Transgressor, thief, plunderer. You'd like to, all right, but you won't."

"Rapunzel!" I called.

"Go on, look. In every cupboard and corner. Better check the bath to be sure I didn't drown her in it." She fingered the braid.

I believed she'd murdered her in the bath and was daring me to look. I ran down the spiral stairs, finding the room empty and in chaos. I went from room to shattered room. Each time I failed to find anything, the fear grew inside my head, till I nearly tore out my own hair from the pressure. I begged God forgive me. I confessed how I *had* taken Rapunzel for granted, and myself, and what we were doing. Let the punishment be mine, I asked, not hers.

Gothel waited at the rail. I had to come back to her, what else could I do? Where else could I go? She looked up at my approach as if I'd startled her, as if she'd forgotten I was there.

"Where?" I cried. "Where is she?"

"Far. I've sent her to a place made from all the hells in the world. You'll never reach her. You'll never slide on top of her again. You'll never ever see her." Her triumph dwindled, her expression weakened. "Neither of us will." She had done something irreversible and, admitting it, she began to wail. Black tears ran from her eyes. "Gone!" she shrieked.

I screamed, too, at least I think so. Maybe it was hers hammering at me. None of us knows what we're capable of in moments like that. I could've killed Gothel, that might have been my response, but I chose instead to kill me.

Shoving her aside, I launched myself in despair over the rail. I've a vague recollection of Gothel reaching out, but everything is jumbled from that moment. I know that I'd inadvertently looped a braid around my ankle, that as the ground shot toward my face, the braid snapped taut and dropped me. I spun dizzily, not to my death, but into the dry hawthorns. The interwoven branches broke my fall while a thousand thorns as long as my finger tore the skin off me. Two of them pierced my eyes like spikes. A flash of red paint burst inside my head. I struck the ground an instant later.

I lay in amongst the branches I've no idea how long. When I tried to crawl out, I screamed at the first movement. I thought I'd broken all my bones; thorns snagged me or stabbed into my palms. I thought it was night but of course it wasn't. I was blind. But so complete was my agony that the lack of sight seemed trivial. By instinct alone, I made my way out of the maze and crawled off toward where my camp must be. Before each pull forward, I patted the ground, certain that I was actually crawling toward an unseen cliff.

Eventually, I found myself on a carpet of leaves. Then my hand touched cloth. It was a shirt of mine. I could smell my own smell upon it. With a little effort, I located my canteen and drank deeply. Farther back, where it would be hidden, I had pitched a tent. Taking the canteen, I dragged myself there, where I collapsed.

I knew I'd been punished for playing with her affections. Gothel's accusations, like the thorns I pulled out with my swollen fingers, had pinned my guilt to me. All I'd ever thought about was the pleasure of thrusting into the old woman's daughter. I'd let obligation to my family hang—I was long overdue to write them and now they might never hear from me again. I had no hope for forgiveness because the one I'd wronged was gone forever. The old woman had banished her.

I deserved to die. Yet, I didn't die.

I healed up well enough to walk—the soles of my feet were about the only place the thorns hadn't penetrated. My sight was gone for good, though, and I couldn't wait there in the woods any longer: Gothel might come after me and finish the job I'd failed to do, but more than that, I couldn't stop hoping I might still find some trace of Rapunzel, some trail that I could follow. I packed as well as I was able, and set off using my walking stick as a cane on what I thought was the path that had brought me there. Instead, I wandered far afield. For days on end I stumbled about. No doubt I crossed the real path a hundred times and never knew it.

When I came across streams, I would wash and drink and refill my canteen. I had food enough for a few weeks, but I came to a town before that.

It was a small town, but I had to be guided through it. I might easily have been run down, or robbed—certainly I was easy picking—but I had the good fortune to befriend an honest man. He led me to a tavern, what's called an alehouse, where most of what you get is a variety of beer. I asked if they'd seen Rapunzel. They in turn asked me who she might be, and I told them. The whole story from my first step setting out from home. To them, to strangers I couldn't even see, I admitted my guilt. As if I were standing before a jury in a courtroom, I confessed to them, seeking their condemnation.

By the time I finished, the room had gone still.

Someone cleared his throat. A coin dropped on the table, then another and another. No condemnation—to my incomprehension I was being rewarded. My guide said, "You've a talent in you, storyteller. You can do well round here with tales of that sort." *Moral fables*, he called them.

That's how I survived, telling my tale till I also began to see the moral center of it. My guide stayed with me for a time. He may have been skimming money from our take, but I don't begrudge him. May it make him rich. Wherever we went, I asked for Rapunzel and, when no one knew of her, told my story. They all thought it a fiction, although my guide admitted, before he left, that he had come to believe most of it on account of I never changed or added anything.

Alone, I ventured out into new territory. Soon I could smell the tang of the ocean but did not reach it for another two days. There was a town there, a port with a seawall and a quay at the mouth of a river. By now, I'd come to believe that Rapunzel was nowhere in the lands I knew. I intended to search elsewhere.

I set out for the docks, smelling a storm in the air, being slapped by cold winds. But as I reached the quay, the storm collapsed, and I felt the warmth of sunlight on my face. For whatever reason, the sailors greeted me as I shuffled along the riverside. They'd decided I had driven off the storm, and therefore I was hailed as good luck. Booking passage on one of their ships was made easier as a result. I found a tramp freighter going where I wanted. If Rapunzel was in a land knitted from all the hells, then I would go to the most hellish lands on Earth.

Somewhere out at sea, one of the crew came and whispered to me that he knew I was under the protection of an angel but that he would keep my secret safe if I blessed him. I heard him dumbly, barely half aware of what he was suggesting, I'd become so preoccupied with Rapunzel. So many times had I relived the events, so often had I placed her face, her body, her sweet voice in my mind's eye, that she now rose up every few moments like a ghost inside me, blinding me finally even to my own thoughts.

In this state of mind I cast about for four years, first upon the sea. At port after port I asked about her, and told my story till it seemed to have happened to someone else separate from me. I felt as if I were sitting there, listening with them. Finally, the ship was to return home. I disembarked into the unknown again.

The land where I went had been scorched daily for millennia. The winters hardly existed, and far more people endured them without homes or possessions. I became one among an endless sea of beggars. Their language took me months to learn. It might have taken me years, but my survival depended upon it.

I began thinking about my family. By now they would be certain I'd died. What other explanation would suffice? My guilt increased as I thought of the anguish I'd inadvertently caused them all in undertaking my fruitless quest. I asked myself, why hadn't I died? Why, when I was ever more certain that *she* was dead, didn't I join her? Compulsion is my only explanation—I would sift every inch of the Earth before I conceded defeat.

Leaving the cities and most of the hapless nomads behind, I entered more arid regions. The store of food I'd saved dwindled to nothing. Nothing seemed to grow wherever I cast about for food—even lizards were faster than the skinny, sun-baked blind man I'd become. No one met me on the road.

When the last of the food and water ran out, I quickly became delirious. A horrible vision of Rapunzel burned alive confronted me, and I defeated it only by remembering that I had no eyes and therefore couldn't be seeing anything real at all.

By then, however, I didn't know where I was. I'd fallen into a patch of shade beneath some rocks, where I passed in and out of consciousness. I awoke at some point to the sound of flapping great wings—vultures settling down nearby. I swung my stick and shouted, and the birds angrily flew off.

On trembling legs, I got up and started walking again. You'll say I was guided, maybe by the angel that I never saw.

After awhile a distant refrain came to me. A lilting music. I thought I must be hallucinating again. The song refused to go away. It continued to grow. Like a beacon, it brought me across the cracked desert until I was running to embrace it.

All of a sudden, the song stopped. I stopped. Wheezing, I stumbled in a circle, straining to hear it again above my own ragged breaths.

I licked my cracked lips. Then, hoarsely, I called out that name I'd kept inside me too long. "Rapunzel!"

I heard footsteps. Quick and light. They came right up to me. A hand touched my brow. Her voice said, "Jon?"

"It is you, isn't it?" I asked. "I'm not mad, you're there?" I pressed my fingers to her face, her shoulders. She was unknown to me. Her body had become lean and hard. The voice, the song, belonged to no one else. She replied brokenly, "Yes, it's me." She hugged me close. So weak was I that I collapsed at her feet. She sank down beside me, drew me to her and placed my head in her lap. We said nothing. What could we say, who'd believed each other dead for so long?

Her tears dripped onto my face, ran down my cheeks. They splashed into my ruined eyes. I blinked, and made to rub the tears away, but stopped. With each blink, there seemed to come a flash of light. A flash of pain. I sat up. "Wait," I said, turning to her. "Wait." A milky image swam before me. I blinked again and it came clearer.

The face was lined and weathered, the hair a golden tangle around it. The years had worn her, weathered her, but not destroyed her. "I can see you," I said. "Rapunzel."

I kissed her then, softly against my pain. She had magic in her the same as Gothel; what one had taken away, the other had the power to restore. She was the angel.

Behind her lay a hut and a pathetic field of weedy crops. Two naked, bony children stood there, big-eyed and uncertain of this ragged stranger in their mother's arms. Do you remember? The girl was gypsy-dark, the boy as golden as his mother.

I remember that you led me inside the hut together, that your small hands took hold of mine. I can't recall the meal at all.

She and I had become very different people. I think the people we became were far better ones than who we'd been; I know I am. I think no longer of me, of my pleasure, but of her and of you. In that miserable desert, when your mother and I vowed our love finally, we knew its range, its depths, its endurance.

I love her past the point encompassed by the words. And I love both of you, my children.

Oddest of all is finding myself indebted to Gothel, your grandmother, whom you can't expect to meet in this life. Her tower, when we finally returned to it, had collapsed into a heap of broken stone and glass and dust.

Like a Red, Red Rose

Susan Wade

Susan Wade is a native of Austin, TX with a thing for fairy tales and red shoes. Her short fiction has appeared in *The Magazine of Fantasy & Science Fiction*, *Amazing Stories*, and several of Ellen Datlow's and Terri Windling's anthologies. Her first novel was an Edgar and Anthony finalist, and won the Barry.

Wade gives us something more like a brand-new story than a retelling of an old story. But there are elements from many well-known fairytales that are woven together in this story. The story does the wonderful job of feeling new and exciting and old and familiar at the same time.

At a time not so long ago, in a land much like our own, there was a cottage at the edge of a dark, haunted forest. In that cottage lived a woman and her daughter, and it was said by those in the villages and landholdings nearby that the woman was a witch.

Martine and her daughter lived in solitude, tending their animals and their garden, gathering herbs in the forest where none other dared go. The cottage was plain, perhaps a bit larger than most, but the only thing to set it apart was the magnificence of its garden. Luxuriant growths of every succulent fruit and vegetable known to that land (and some unknown) graced the garden: lush figs and grapes and pomegranates and perfect almonds and pears and beans and a myriad of other bounty. Even the stream that fed the garden was lined with watercress and mint. Among the villagers, it was whispered that the witch's magic was so powerful that, in her garden, a discarded rose would take root and flourish.

And if, of a dark night, people slipped away to visit the cottage by the wood—young girls in search of a love philter by which they might marry, or young men in search of a potion by which they might gain love without benefit of clergy—such things remained unspoken in the town.

So it was that little Blanche, for that was the name of the witch's daughter, lived with her mother, never knowing what it was to play with other children: no May games or ring-a-rosy or catch-as-can. Her games were fashioned for one: rose petals floated on the surface of the small garden stream, or pine cones stacked to form a castle in which tiny flowers bloomed, visited by princely bees. It may have been that Blanche was lonely, but having never known company other than her mother's, she did not notice it.

She was called Blanche (we must assume) because of her milky-fair skin, as pure and fine and fragrant as a petal from the great white rose tree which grew at the boundary between the cottage and the wood. Her hair was richly brown, as if carved from the polished wood of that same tree; her eyes as deep and true a green as its leaves. And each day, as soon as she had risen from her narrow bed, her mother would say to her, "It is morning, Blanche. Fetch me a rose from your tree, my child, that I may see how my daughter grows."

Blanche would scamper to the rose tree to pluck a newly-awakened blossom (and her mother must have been a witch indeed, for even in the depths of winter there would always be at least one glowing white bloom).

And bringing that blossom to her mother, Blanche would always hear, "Ah, I see my child is like a white rose, as pure and sweet as the morning." And her mother would catch Blanche up in her arms, and Blanche would place the rose in her mother's auburn hair where the flower would remain all that day.

As Blanche grew older, her life continued its solitary course; the only differences were in the nature of her games and the fact that her mother could no longer lift Blanche in her arms. But each morning, she still asked Blanche to bring her a rose from the tree, which she would wear in her hair for the day.

One day, as Blanche and her mother returned from gathering herbs and roots in the wood, Martine collapsed.

Her face was pale and lined, her breathing labored. Blanche raised her mother's head and gave her a sip from the bottle they always carried with them, filled from the spring that fed their garden.

Martine's color became more its usual shade, rosier than Blanche's fair skin ever was. Even so, Blanche thought her mother looked ill and far older than she had that morning. Blanche quickly crushed the amaranth flowers they had collected for one of the potions, a healing salve, and fed them to Martine. The deep purple-red of the blossoms stained her fingers, and she scrubbed them on the grass.

Her mother's breathing became easier and she laughed a little. Blanche was reassured. "The peasants call it 'Purple-Heart' or 'Love-Lies-Bleeding.'" Her voice still sounded strained. "Shall we go now?"

Blanche decided that it was too soon for them to continue; they would wait until Martine seemed more herself. So she merely looked at the dark stain on her fingers and said, "You never told me that."

"I prefer its true name," her mother said. "Amaranth."

Martine sat up then, determined to go home. She needed help to reach the cottage, but once there seemed to revive.

"Mother?" Blanche asked, once Martine had recovered. "What is wrong? Are you ill?"

"It is nothing," said her mother. "Only that I am no longer young."

Blanche found this difficult to credit, seeing her mother's face, its lovely color restored. With her smooth skin and rich auburn curls, Martine seemed unchanged from Blanche's earliest memories of her. "You must tell me if you are unwell," she said. "You must rest."

Martine sighed. "Perhaps it would be better if you went alone to collect the herbs. You know as well as I what is needed."

And so Blanche became chief gatherer, while her mother remained at the cottage to prepare and blend her potions, and life flowed much as it always had for the two of them.

Until the son of the largest landholder in the area, arriving early of an evening, caught a glimpse of the witch's lovely daughter (for she was quite lovely, as you have no doubt surmised). He had come for a consultation during which he would purchase a certain potion he found useful; the witch kept such sundries in a cupboard near her front gate, as she was reluctant to allow local folk to enter the cottage.

He himself was a comely youth, with a lavish tangle of black curls and eyes like midnight. His name was Allain, and he was well known among the women of the village, a fact which pleased him.

Yet, clever as he was in the arts of love, his expertise deserted him when he first saw Blanche. He abandoned his conversation with an abruptness few would have dared, and demanded of the witch the name of the irresistable creature who had appeared beside the stream.

"She is my daughter," Blanche's mother said, speaking with an awful emphasis which even a smitten lover could not misapprehend. "Do not trouble your heart with her. She will never marry."

And so taken was Allain that he never considered that it was not ordinarily marriage which he sought from his *inamorata.* At least his experience of women did not desert him with Blanche's mother; at her angry words, he bowed swiftly and said, "Ah, it is clear then whence came her beauty." And concluding his business with great charm and greater dispatch, he spoke not again of the vision glimpsed beside the stream: of a girl with hair like polished wood and skin as fair as a pearl.

All his way home, that brief scene was reenacted in his imagination: the lovely apparition, as of a nymph from the forest, with gleaming hair and brilliant eyes that glanced toward him and swiftly away. He recalled she had carried a basket woven of peeled willow branches, overflowing with greenery. It was not difficult to deduce that she had come from gathering herbs in the forest.

And with that deduction, a simple solution to Allain's dilemma was found: he would seek the witch's daughter in the wood, which, whatever its reputation, was far less intimidating than the witch herself. He knew from personal experience how effective Martine's magic could be.

So it came about that on a day soon after (as soon as he had learned the name of the witch's beautiful daughter, in fact), Allain entered the wood. He kept to its nearer boundaries, despite his reputation for daring. But the forest growth was of such density as to be nearly impenetrable, so he was well hid from the witch's view even as he passed by the cottage. And he was well rewarded for entering that dark place, for not much of the day had passed before he came upon Blanche, seated on a fallen pine in a small glade as she investigated a promising growth of bit-moss.

A more striking pose could not have been found had she studied for one: with a beam of sunlight touching her hair to reveal strands of gold hidden among rich brown, and her back a graceful curve which led the eye naturally to the even more graceful curve of her waist. And her skin! So pure and milky-fair was she that, for an instant, Allain wondered whether her mother had magicked the girl from a lily.

But then she turned, and saw him, and started; as shy as a dove. Any thoughts of her sorcerous nature faded from his mind.

"Blanche," he whispered.

Appearing even more startled, she looked up at him again, and he saw fully the glow of her eyes, so brilliant that they put the emerald shade of the forest to shame.

He came nearer, and when she would have gathered up her basket and fled, stayed her with a soft, "Ah, no, please!" And when she paused, he said, "I've come such a long way to speak with you, you couldn't be so cruel as to run away."

She turned to him at that, all her wondering curiosity in her eyes, and asked, "You've come to speak to me?"

"Why, yes," he answered. "Did you not know I would, after our souls met in the garden? I could not but come," he added, and possessed himself of her hand.

Blanche turned as if she would escape, and a hint of delicate color came into her cheeks.

The flesh of her hand, just of her hand! was so softly sweet and firm that Allain longed to test it with his teeth, trace it with his tongue; to consume that flesh with all the passion of which he was capable. But she was clearly innocent. Allain contented himself with a chaste kiss.

And saw, as his mouth caressed the tender curve of her palm, her lips part and her eyes become darker and lose their focus.

For Allain, these delicate signs of awakened passion were more inflaming than the intricate tricks of a seasoned courtesan.

His heart was lost from that moment.

For Blanche, the brief encounter in the forest filled a need she had never before recognized, never named. A need born of loneliness, perhaps, or simply a longing for companionship both more complex and less demanding than that of her mother. And with the satiation of that unspoken need, there came an awareness of an entire enchanted dimension beyond companionship.

Blanche turned in her narrow bed to see dawn light streaming through the high, small window. Had she slept at all? Or had it been simply a reliving of that waking dream of him? He had touched her, his mouth against her palm. She twisted her face against the bed linens to cool her skin.

She heard her mother stir in the single bedroom of the cottage, then footsteps as she came into the main room, where Blanche's small bed occupied a corner.

"It is morning, Blanche," her mother said, as she did each day. "Fetch me a rose from your tree, my dear, that I may see how my daughter does."

Blanche smiled at the familiar request. She rose and stretched, then pulled her gown over the simple shift that served her as nightwear.

In her bare feet, because it was summer (though, in truth, the garden was always in summer), she ran to pluck a rose from her tree. But when she reached it, she stopped, stunned.

In place of the snowy blossoms that had graced the tree all her life were creamy buds with a dusky goldenpink tinging the edge of each petal.

What could it mean? She reached a trembling hand to touch a blossom, then drew back. The roses were lovely, with a scent richer and more enticing than she remembered. And yet, and yet…they were not *her* roses, not the roses that were Blanche. Yet she knew she could not have mistaken the great rose tree, queen of all the garden, there on the verge of the wood.

"Blanche!" her mother called from the cottage. "Do not be dallying in the garden or your porridge will be done without you."

Blanche plucked a bloom then. It came to her hand no differently than the white rose had come the day before. Her mother would explain this to her; her mother's magic may have caused this to happen, Blanche turned and went to the cottage with hurried steps.

But the instant her mother saw the altered rose, her face grew terrible. She snatched the flower away and grasped Blanche's shoulder with a harsh hand. "Where did you see him?"

Shock tore the strength from Blanche's legs, and she nearly fell. Her mother had never spoken to her so, never looked at her so.

Her mother dropped the rose and shook Blanche. "Where?" she cried.

"In the forest," Blanche said.

At that, her mother released her and turned to pace a few steps. Then Martine turned back. "You are no longer pure, no longer the white rose. But it may not yet be too late to prevent the thing I fear most." She came close again to Blanche, her dark gaze holding the girl prisoner. "You know nothing of your own nature, nothing of what the world holds for such as we are. But you are my daughter and I will see that you do not live with the grief that I have borne. I will see you to a new life, whatever it costs."

Blanche trembled. The things Martine was saying made no sense, and her intensity was frightening; the more so because it was unaccustomed.

"We must take the love potions and the amaranth salve I use to heal wounds. As large a quantity as we can manage. They will support us until we have the opportunity to establish ourselves elsewhere," her mother went on. "As for clothing and household goods, very little will be necessary. Some food and water is all. Perhaps we can sell the chickens and the goat in the village."

Blanche stared at her mother. "We are to leave? Where will we go?"

Martine said distractedly, "That is to be seen, but, yes, we will leave. Tomorrow."

"But why?" Blanche asked. "I was born here. Why must we leave?"

"It is the only escape, I tell you. I will not let you suffer as I have."

"My only escape from what? If my life is to be changed, I must know why."

Martine hesitated for only an instant. Then she looked down at the creamy rose petals scattered on the floor, each limned in dusky color. "We leave so you will not lose all that you love. Now gather your things. We must be gone by first light."

The next morning saw them on the road leading south to the nearest village. Blanche's heart was heavy at leaving her home, its garden never more lovely than it was at that dawn: a glittering array of nature's jewels, all scent and color and light. Blanche was curious as well as frightened; her only experience of the world outside her mother's garden had been to wander in the forest, which seemed more an extension of the garden than a separate place.

The road was of dun earth, dull and gritty. Blanche was footsore before they had traveled far; keeping the goat and chickens to the road was a worrisome task, and the barrow she helped her mother push was heavy.

It was yet early morning when they reached the village. Blanche looked to her mother for guidance, but Martine was pale and listless and merely stood with her head low.

Blanche glanced around, curious at what the town would hold. A group of men stood by the village well, watching the two women. One of them moved forward at a difficult pace. His few strands of white hair did not conceal the brown marks of age on his skull. When he came within a few steps of them, she noticed that the whites of his eyes had yellowed, a condition for which her mother often prescribed an infusion of vervain. He cleared his throat and spat at Martine's feet.

"Witch!" he said. His voice cracked. "There is nothing here for you. Go back to your devil's garden."

Martine raised her head for the first time when he spoke the word "garden." She did not answer the old man, but only gazed at him. The other villagers crowded around. Blanche waited, certain her mother would wither this rude man with only a look.

He spat again. "Go back," he repeated. "None here will have you." Then he swung around and glared at Blanche. She saw that his yellow eyes were crazed with red lines. They looked as if they might crack open and spill blood in the dust, he stared so hard at her. "Nor her neither," the old man said, pointing at Blanche, "for all she is so fair. There's those here old enough to remember what your kind is. Go back."

Martine spoke then, in a voice so faint it was as if only the wind answered. "We won't trouble you. We only wish to sell the stock before we go on." She paused, then added as if in afterthought, "I will not even drink from your well."

The old man cackled. "That you won't," he said. "Nor any here take your stock. Raised on the devil's flesh, they was, and we know it. There's nothing for you outside that plot sown with devil seed. Go back and reap what you have planted, witch." The other villagers crossed themselves and made signs against the evil eye.

Martine said quietly to Blanche, "Leave them, then, the animals. You must take the barrow now, for I cannot any longer." Blanche had never known her mother to betray weakness. What was wrong?

Then Martine tossed her head back in her imperious manner. Blanche, seeing the moisture bead on her mother's brow, wondered what even that small gesture had cost.

"Yes, Mother," she said.

Martine walked past the villagers, then paused. "Perhaps those with more sense will take these animals and care for them," she said to Blanche. Her voice was pitched to carry, "Not all the people here disdain the fruits of my garden."

Several of the townsfolk moved back at Martine's words, glancing aside when Blanche looked at them. Now she recognized a face or two, those who had come to her mother for remedies.

Blanche singled out a kindly-faced matron from among them, one whose youngest child had been healed of a fever by Martine's magic. "Will you see the animals are cared for?" Blanche asked her. "They are not accustomed to feeding themselves."

The woman turned away.

Martine had stopped a little beyond the town and now looked back to summon Blanche with a gesture. The chickens had scattered to peck at grit beside the well, and the goat was nibbling at a coil of rope that hung nearby. Blanche sighed and lifted the handles of the barrow to follow her mother.

The road seemed very long, stretching before them without any known destination at its end. Blanche was worried about her mother, whose skin now looked waxen and damp. Martine walked stiffly and seemed barely aware of moving.

It was quite still on the road; even the dust barely stirred under their feet. As their distance from the forest increased, the trees lining the road became more widely spaced. The rays of the mid-morning sun stung Blanche's skin. "Mother?" she said. "Could we stop for a moment and rest in the shade?" Since they had no particular place to go, there was no reason to hurry their arrival. And it was very hot.

Blanche released the barrow's handles and blew on her blistered palms. Martine continued as if unaware her daughter had spoken.

"Mother?" Blanche left the barrow and hurried to catch Martine.

She did not stop until Blanche touched her arm, and then the cessation of motion seemed to overwhelm her, so that she swayed on her feet.

Blanche put an arm around her and led her to a small grove of trees which offered some shade. "Sit here and rest," she said. She went back onto the road to get the barrow. After only a moment in the shade, the sun's heat seemed too fierce to be borne.

When Blanche returned, her mother was asleep. Deeply worried, Blanche searched for one of the jugs of spring water Martine had insisted they bring.

She splashed the water into a small cup and knelt to hold it to her mother's lips. With the water's kiss, Martine's eyes opened and a bit of color returned to her cheeks.

"Are you ill?" Blanche asked. "You seem very tired, Mother."

Martine lifted a trembling hand to take the cup from her daughter. Blanche had to steady it as her mother drank. "If I am, there is nothing to be done for it," Martine said. Her voice shook as much as her hand. "We must go on."

"But it is the heat of the day," Blanche protested, "and you seem so tired. Perhaps we could rest here until it grows cooler."

Martine's eyes closed again. "Very well. Just for a short time, then," she mumbled. Then she opened her eyes and looked at Blanche. "Promise me," she said sharply, "that you will not return to the garden. Promise me, Blanche."

"Yes, Mother, I promise," Blanche said. "We will go to make a new life for ourselves, as you said we should. We will go together." Yet, as she spoke, she thought of Allain, of love left behind.

Martine's lips curved in a faint smile and her eyelids dropped. "Perhaps," was all she said before she slept again.

Blanche watched over her mother. As the afternoon wore on, Martine's breathing grew shallower, her skin more colorless. She could barely be roused to drink and did not speak. By late afternoon, Blanche was certain her mother was gravely ill.

It was not long after that Martine spoke again. "Remember your promise," she said to Blanche. "You must not go back." Her wax-white skin had shrunk against the bones, so that her face looked as bleached and spare as a naked skull.

"No, Mother," Blanche assured her.

Martine sighed then, a long, deep exhalation that shook her entire body. It was not followed by another breath.

It was thus that Allain found Blanche, bowed weeping over the body of her mother.

So grateful was he to have found his love that even the looming prospect of nightfall in the company of a dead witch did not daunt him. He called Blanche's name as he dismounted from his horse.

Blanche looked up at him, her drowning eyes such a clear and powerful green that, for an instant, Allain felt himself engulfed in forest shade. Then she came to him, flinging herself into his embrace. And his world became defined by the sensation of her body pressed to his: the velvet plush of her skin, the satin flow of her hair against his hands, the gentle stir of her sobbing breaths against his throat.

"Blanche," he whispered, caught by a desire more intense than he had known physical desire could be.

He stroked her hair, and her sobs quietened. She sighed and asked, "What shall I do?" Allain felt the brush of her lips against his throat and he trembled.

"Why, you will marry me," he said. "For you are my own true love. And lovers wed, do they not?"

She drew away and looked up at him, trouble burnishing the fairness of her face to an aching beauty. "I am to go away. I promised my mother." She choked and turned her head a little, toward where the still body lay. "Her dying wish."

Seeing her tremor, her anguish, Allain could no more resist her than he could resist breathing the air. He kissed her.

And as he took her lips, tasting of honey and mint and the sweetest of green grasses, and felt her mouth tremble in response to his touch, he knew that he must soon have her or die of it.

"Marry me," he whispered, and kissed her again: her lips, the silken splendor of her neck, the delicate arch of her ear.

"Marry me," he cajoled, stroking her throat, kissing her lids, bringing her hands to his face for yet more kisses.

"Say yes," he murmured.

"Yes," she said.

Out of concern for Blanche's weariness, Allain decided they should rest until moonrise. Sitting in the deep shadows of the trees, Blanche might have been a shadow herself, so quiet and withdrawn was she. Allain supposed that her mother's death weighed heavily. Martine had been Blanche's only relation; more, her only friend.

When the moon rose to pour its light over the world like silver syrup, Allain set to work. Cautiously, his respect only partly that a man shows for the mother of his betrothed, Allain swathed the body in his cloak and placed it over the withers of his horse. The beast shied and snorted until its eyes showed white, but when Blanche came forward to lead it (at Allain's instruction), the animal calmed.

Allain took the handles of the barrow and started back toward the village.

Blanche hesitated.

"Come along, my love," he coaxed. "I know you are weary, but we must see your mother safe home."

"I—cannot," she said then. "I must not return home. It was my final promise to her."

"Very well," he responded gently. "We shall take her to my father's priest, then, so she may be buried properly. And you will come to my home, to meet my family, as is suitable for my betrothed."

Still she hesitated.

"Please, love," he said. "It is only right that my parents comfort and sustain you at such a sad time. You would not want them to believe you disdain their hospitality, I know."

Blanche said, "It—the villagers would not take our animals. They called us 'devil's spawn.'"

Allain met her gaze steadily. "And were you surprised, love? The villagers fear what they do not understand."

"Yes, but. . . Your father…will he not feel as the villagers do? That I am of the devil? He may not wish such a wife for his son."

Allain came to her then, to lift her hand to his lips. "Ah, but my father is not a villager, sweet Blanche. He will be pleased that I have found such a beautiful bride."

She looked up at him then, her face as lovely as a budding rose. "Do you truly believe so?"

Allain pressed her palm to his chest, and said, "With all my heart."

It was nearing midnight when the two reached the village. Fearful of the townsfolk, Blanche was grateful to find it dark and still, the square deserted.

Allain was inclined to insist on lodgings at one of the cottages, so that Blanche might pass what remained of the night in comfort. But she was reluctant to face the villagers again, and preferred to continue. The road they must use wound past her home, and it may have been that Allain had hoped to spare her the painful reminder of her life there with Martine. But her tears persuaded him to complete their journey that night.

As they neared the witch's cottage, Blanche's steps grew more eager. It was not that she would ever disregard her mother's wish, she told herself, only that she longed to look once more on the place where her mother's memory dwelt. Mindful of her promise, she kept to the far verge of the road and did not slow her steps as they approached.

But when the garden came into sight, flooded with the silver moonlight, Blanche stopped in her tracks. Gone was the lush abundance, the boughs so burdened with fruit, they groaned, the profusion of flowers that had graced the plot of land for as long as Blanche could remember.

The garden was withered, sere. Dead branches carried only the dried husks of their former bounty. A few shriveled petals were all that remained of the thousand blossoms Blanche had left behind.

Except, at the far side of the garden, glimmering in the moonlight, she saw the great rose tree, still abloom. Only now the roses blushed, their petals a rich, true pink.

Blanche cried out and would have run to the garden, though she knew she could not restore it; but Allain caught her in his arms and held her back.

"Your promise," he said then. "Your mother must have known her magic was ended, and thought to spare you this. You must not let her last wish go unbidden, love."

She wept then, for her mother and for her mother's garden, both lost now forever. And perhaps, a bit, for herself, for she felt very lost, too. But Allain was there to comfort her and eventually, to lead her beyond the boundaries of the witch's property, so that she might reach safety and shelter that night.

It seemed an omen, like a promise of dawn, when at last they rounded a bend to see the portal of Allain's home aglow with torchlight.

"See?" he said to his betrothed. "Already my family welcomes you." And all his curiosity at the lighted torches dissolved with her answering sigh of pleasure.

Allain left the barrow then, and tied the horse behind it. "Come, my love," he said, and took her arm to lead her to his home. "Father?" he called out. "What's to do?"

The door opened then, and a great dark-haired bear of a man emerged, a-thunder with aggravation. "Allain! Is that you?" he shouted, his voice a growling rumble. Torchlight gleamed on the richly oiled curls of his black beard.

Several of the household came running at the sound of his shouting.

"Where have you been all the day and half the night? The villeins are nigh dead with exhaustion from searching for you," Allain's father said as he moved forward. He stopped abruptly when Allain stepped into the circle of the torchlight with Blanche on his arm. "We had word from the village," Alliain's father said then, and his voice was lower, more ominous, "that you had gone after the witch and her spawn, but I knew they lied."

Allain stiffened and raised his head. "Did you, now? And why would you be so sure of that, Father?"

The older man descended from the doorway with a speed that belied his size. "Because you are my son and not a fool."

Allain drew Blanche closer to him. "And is it foolishness to give my heart to one so lovely as this? Am I a fool to take this fairest of flowers to wife?"

His father looked at Blanche, and his eyes were hard and cruel; like tiny black pebbles set in his head. "A fool, indeed, to marry a witch," he said. "Priest!" he yelled then. "Fetch my priest!"

Blanche shrank back, because his anger frightened her. The servants began to whisper among themselves.

Then the gossiping servants were jostled aside, making way for a slight man wearing vestments. "I am here, sir. I came as soon as I heard shouting, thinking I might be needed. Has there been an accident?"

"An accident of nature, perhaps," said the lord. "Look at her," he flung a hand toward Blanche, "and tell me if she is a demon."

Allain started forward in fury, his fist raised to his father. The big man captured and held his son's hand as easily as he might a butterfly. "Nay," he said. "You'll stay and hear what the priest says of her, before there's any talk of marriage."

Allain's eyes flashed, and he turned back to Blanche. She shook her head at him, knowing that nothing good would come of defying his father. But perhaps if the holy man reassured him…

The priest stepped toward Blanche, who stood shivering, half in moonlight, half in torchlight. "Mmmph," he muttered. "I see no obvious mark of magic on her, though she is extraordinarily fair. Are you baptized, girl?"

Blanche shook her head and struggled to speak well, for Allain's sake and for her own. "My mother said the visiting priest refused to do it, because we lived so close to the forest, which he believed was haunted."

The priest snorted and nodded knowingly. "Some of these village priests are woefully ignorant."

Heartened, Blanche went on, "I am called Blanche, and I would be baptized so, if you are willing, sir."

The priest ruffled himself up like a pigeon and said, "Good, good." He looked at Allain's father and added, "Her name is Blanche, in praise of Our White Lady. I am willing to baptize her."

Allain still stood beside his father, but when he looked at Blanche, his eyes shone. "Why that seems quite satisfactory, don't you agree, Father?" he said.

His father looked at Blanche, and she saw his black eyes narrow. She fancied she caught a glimpse of some secret malice there. But all he said was, "Perhaps. We shall see how she seems once she is sprinkled with holy water."

The priest cleared his throat, then said to Blanche, "You wish to be baptized, here and now?"

She nodded, then remembering what Allain had spoken of earlier, said, "We came also to ask you to see my mother buried." Her voice shook as she said, "She was taken ill and—and—"

"Ah!" said Allain's father, and his face lightened. "Dead, is she?"

Blanche looked down, unable to speak. It was Allain who answered, talking so softly to his father that Blanche could not hear his words.

Then Allain's father nodded at the priest, who fidgeted briefly before saying, "Very well, have the body brought—"

"Not in the chapel," Allain's father said. "Do it here."

"It is most irregular—" the priest began.

"Here," said Allain's father, and his voice held a note of finality.

"Yes, well, bring the body to the steps here," said the priest. "And you—boy," he indicated one of the servants, "run fetch my stole from the vestry."

The boy ran off as commanded, but none among the servants moved toward the dark bundle on Allain's horse.

After a moment, Allain laughed. "I will bring her to you, priest, as I have brought her this far." He walked to the horse, which waited patiently beside the barrow, and untied the reins to lead it forward. When he reached the torchlight again, he handed the beast's reins to Blanche with a smile.

"Soon over, my love," he whispered to her, before he lifted her mother's body from the horse.

He laid the body on the steps as the priest had instructed, then lifted away the shrouding cloak.

Blanche saw his face go pale and rushed to his side.

Her mother's body was gone.

All that lay within the folds of the cloak was a bundle of shriveled rose canes, dried and black. At its root clung a clump of dark earth. At its crown clustered a few faded rose petals., which had once been red.

A cry of horror rose from the servants, and Blanche clutched Allain's hand.

As they watched, a wind stirred, and the earth that clung to the roots was swept upward. It became a whirling dark cloud, which hovered near Blanche for a moment, then spun off into the night. For an instant all was still.

Then Allain's father screamed, "Kill the witch! Stone her!" Blanche gasped and turned to see him pointing at her. "Loose the dogs!"

Most of the servants crossed themselves and huddled together, but two men dressed in leathers raced off toward the mews.

"Stone her!" Allain's father commanded again. One of the servants stooped to grope for a stone.

Allain jerked the reins from Blanche's numb fingers. Before she knew what he did, she was astride the horse, with Allain swinging up behind her.

And then the two of them were fleeing into the moonlit night, as the baying of the hounds echoed behind them.

Allain meant to make it a desperate race, there under the waning moon. But his horse was already spent, and the hounds were fresh. The sound of their baying grew ever louder over the faltering hoofbeats of the weary horse.

They came to a place on the road Blanche recognized, and she reached for the reins and tried to pull them back. "Stop," she said.

Allain yanked them free and slapped the horse's withers, but the lathered beast stumbled to a stop anyway, too exhausted to run further. "We cannot stop, love," Allain said. "The hounds are too close."

She turned then, as much as she could, so that she might look at him. "You must go back alone," she said. "Your father will not blame you, he will say you were bewitched. I cannot bring you death as a betrothal gift."

"No," he said. "Though it may be that I am bewitched, because the thought of leaving you is more horrible than that of dying in your arms. We will go on together."

Blanche grasped his arm. "No!"

He laughed then, a bright and vibrant sound, there on the empty, moon-soaked road. "But yes," he said. "Although I confess I would prefer to lie in your arms and *not* die."

The hounds gave voice then, in a rising howl that made Blanche shiver.

Allain said, "Sadly, it seems unlikely, for they are very near. Give me a kiss, my love, before we run."

Their kiss was sweet, a fatal sweetness born of danger and sparking passion. After a breathless moment when it seemed to Blanche that the stars wheeled overhead, Allain wrenched away.

"We will give them a run they will long remember," he said.

But Blanche laid an urgent hand on his. "Wait—the forest. The hounds never hunt there. And I know it well. We could hide there."

Allain hesitated. "The dogs are running on our scent now. It may be they will follow anyway."

"This poor horse is too tired to run anymore, and," Blanche smiled at him, "I would prefer to live through the night, too."

He looked at her, and perhaps it was her smile which swayed him. Or perhaps it was the belling of the hounds, almost upon them, "Very well." He swung off the horse and lifted Blanche down. "Quickly then." He pulled the reins so they hung loosely around the pommel of the saddle, then slapped the horse's rump. The startled beast broke into a shambling trot, and Allain took Blanche's hand. "Now you must lead," he said.

They ran to the edge of the road, and Blanche drew him into a narrow space between two trees. The undergrowth was thick and seemed to grasp at them. Every muscle, every nerve demanded urgent speed. It was not possible.

And then the clamoring voices of the hounds were there, very close, and Allain pulled Blanche to him. When she would have spoken, he pressed a finger to her lips. "Stillness will serve us best," he breathed in her ear, and she nodded, knowing they were yet too close to the road for safety.

The dogs were near enough that Blanche could hear their panting breaths whistle over their fangs. They snarled, and the sound seemed to stir round the two lovers. One of the dogs began to bark excitedly, and a rough male voice shouted. Blanche was certain they were discovered.

And then, farther up the road, several dogs howled in a distinctive note of discovery.

The pack swept on, past the section of wood where Blanche and Allain waited. Allain flinched when he heard his horse's screams.

They waited, hearts thundering, until it was clear the pack would not return, then worked their way deeper into the forest.

Blanche had said she knew the forest well, and she did. But now, masked by the night's darkness and her own exhaustion, the trees did not assume their familiar shapes. It was not long before she knew they were lost.

"Never mind," Allain said. "In the morning we will find our way again. For now, I am grateful we are alive and together."

They came to a small stream and drank thirstily. The cold water was like a tonic to Blanche, seeming almost to sparkle as it touched her tongue. She splashed her face and throat and felt revived.

"It is almost dawn," Allain said. "Hear the stillness? You should rest."

They were sitting beside the stream. Blanche touched his face. "If you will hold me, so I know we are together, then I shall rest. Otherwise, I will not sleep for fear I should wake and find you gone."

And so they lay together, on the mossy bank of the running stream, and found that they were not as weary as might have been expected.

For to find themselves safe and in each other's arms was a restorative. They spoke softly of things that lovers speak of, and touched and kissed and touched again.

The feelings Allain's touch aroused in Blanche were frightening. And yet it was such a small fear compared to that she had just overcome. His hands were gentle, each caress an experience in texture and fire and sensation, until she no longer needed gentleness; her own urgent hands showed him that.

They became lovers in truth, there on a moss-covered bank in the dimness of false dawn. And there was a wildness to the act, perhaps emanating from the forest itself, or perhaps merely stirring in Blanche's blood that which had been part of her always. It was an elixir that made her passionate and fierce and stronger than she had ever been. And so, when the pain came, and with it her virgin's blood spilled to the forest floor, that too was part of the wildness, and so the joy.

And when the joy grew unbearable, and her mind dimmed with it, then there was sleep, safe in the circle of Allain's arms.

The sun was long risen when Blanche awoke, bathing the glade where they rested in green-filtered light.

Allain lay on his stomach beside her, having turned during the night to sleep with one arm beneath his head; the other still curved over her hip. She sat up, and gently lifted his arm away. To see him sleeping so soundly made her smile.

A bubbling, contented happiness filled her; a feeling she could not recall ever experiencing before. It was as though she had been filled with sunshine; she thought her body might radiate light.

She stretched and looked around. And was shocked to see that the stream they had slept beside was the very same that ran below her mother's garden. They lay in the forest at the very edge of her own home.

Or what had been her home, until her mother's magic faded. And yet, it seemed the fearful moonlight of the previous night had been deceptive.

The garden was not withered, not completely. No, not at all.

For she could see blossoms swelling from their stems, with not a single bloom a moment past its prime. And even as she watched, bare boughs began to put forth fruit and budding leaves. Her mother's magic was *not* ended. The garden was restoring itself.

Delightedly—for however uncertain their future, they would at least break their fast in a familiar place—Blanche turned to waken Allain.

"Love," she whispered in his ear, and shyly kissed him. But he slept on, so she gave him a playful shake.

Still he did not stir.

Blanche cupped a handful of spring water and sprinkled it over his bare back.

And then fear grasped her in icy claws, because he stirred not at all, not even to draw breath; and she took his shoulders and pulled him around to her, though he lay so heavily she could scarcely move him.

And saw the enormous thorn that pierced his heart, its jagged edge as wide as her thumb.

And saw, in the earth beneath him, the deep-soaking stain of his heart's blood.

And could not weep, nor cry out, nor even speak his name, as she gazed beyond the spilled rivulet of her true love's blood. That bitter stain ran straight to the root of the queenly rose tree that spread its tangled canes above them.

Every branch bore a pale pink rose.

But, before her eyes, the blushing petals suffused with darker color, until each perfect bloom was blood-red.

She cut the treacherous rose tree off at the root and burned its thorny branches. Then she buried Allain at the boundary between the forest and her garden, near where they had lain together. And for some time, it mattered not at all to her whether the villagers or the servants of Allain's father would soon come to kill her.

But then she found that she was with child, and knew that indeed it did matter whether she lived or died, for her child's sake. And before fear could cause her to leave that place, an impenetrable thicket of thornbushes grew to surround her garden. She knew none of the townsfolk would dare breach its sorcerous guard.

So she ate of the garden's fruits and drank of its spring, and though she often wept knowing Allain would never share these things with her, it was enough that his child soon would.

And when her time was upon her, she labored alone to bring their babe into the world.

It was a long and difficult labor, but as soon as she was physically able, she swaddled the newborn babe and took it to where Allain lay.

To find an enormous rose tree thriving there, its root buried deep in her dead lover's heart. Its every bloom was purest white.

She named her daughter Amaranth.

Chasing America

Josh Rountree

Josh Rountree's fiction has appeared in tons of cool markets, some of the most recent being *Polyphony 6*, *Realms of Fantasy* and *Lone Star Stories*. Wheatland Press published a collection of Rountree's short fiction called *Can't Buy Me Faded Love* in 2008. If you haven't read this work yet, you're in for a treat.

In America, we call fairytales folktales. This is mostly due to a decided lack of fairies or other traditionally supernatural beasties. Rountree tackles an American classic, Paul Bunyan, and gives us a refreshing new take on it.

1. Go West, Young Giant—1837

It took longer than expected, crossing the Atlantic on clouds. Paul wished for a storm front to stretch out like a rumbling gray road beneath his feet, a pathway straight through to the New World. But he was accustomed to trials, and was content to pick his way from cloud to cloud, searching for the perfect westward drift, hoping one wouldn't dissipate before he found another. And driven by innate stubbornness and fear of the world he left behind, Paul found his new home.

After a period of careful searching, he determined that beanstalks were hard to come by in the New World. But he found a forest of tree-tops piercing a low-hung blanket of stratus, and decided one method of descent was as good as another.

A short climb later and Paul stood in America.

The forest surrounding him was quite unlike the ones he'd played in as a boy. The woods of Albion were shadow-drenched places of bent oak, wych elm and boxwood, so choked with history that you couldn't help but search the undergrowth for boggarts and goblin teeth, enchanted jewels and the bones of ancient barbarian kings. Every hidden grove gave solace to witches and whistling thieves, wolves with unsure motives and broken men who'd murder a child for the touch of copper against their palms.

But this American forest was unspoiled. Pines rose straight and stout, and they seemed to hold up the sky itself. Grasslands rolled away from the tree line, spilled into a busy valley that teemed with life. Horses pulled huge felled timbers, coaxed on by men in checkered shirts and woolen caps. Laughter and smoke poured from scattered wooden buildings. A white-capped river cut a path through the camp before disappearing beyond the valley's edge, and Paul imagined its continued progress. Beyond the valley stood a seemingly endless stretch of majestic forest, and beyond that, mountain peaks topped with snow, bathed in sunlight that chewed away the clouds.

There was room to live here. How easy to get lost in such a land, and easier still to evade the Jacks. They'd never find him.

Paul stepped boldly into the valley, drawing stares from the workers. A bent man with a drawn face and patchy beard approached and turned a bemused gaze upward. "Where the hell did you come from?"

"Albion," Paul said, as if that explained everything.

"Big fella, ain't you?"

Paul shrugged. "Big as I need to be, I guess."

"Can you handle an axe? Or a saw?" The man offered Paul an axe but the giant waved him off. He wrapped his arms around a skinny pine and pulled it from the soil with a few sharp tugs.

"Name's Charlie Blade," the man said, watching Paul lower the tree to the ground with a mixture of fear and admiration in his rheumy eyes. "I'm the foreman around here. You looking for work?"

Paul wasn't looking for work, but he *was* looking for a new home. The men here seemed content. And there would be plenty of time to get lost in the endless world beyond the mountains if the need arose.

He shook the foreman's hand, and the legend of Paul Bunyan was born.

Paul might have lived in the logging camp forever if Charlie Blade hadn't been crushed by a log spill. Paul loved the camaraderie a rough day's work fostered in the souls of working men, and he never grew tired of the quiet evenings, the sounds of work calls and blades on wood banished to the morning, when endless night crossed the world like the shadow of God. This was a land where all men were giants. And true giants like Paul? Well, they were something *more*.

In Albion, giants were accused of hoarding gold, stealing women and stomping houses beneath booted feet—a ridiculous notion. Paul was small for a giant, but the largest of his kind stood no taller than a ship's mast. Those stories were the product of fear and insecurity. The Americans wove their tales from the twin threads of admiration and respect, spreading wide a blanket of belief that anything was possible in a world so new and fine. There were no limits to what men could do, and Paul understood their need to express this. When they shared tales of how his footsteps created lakes or how he kept a giant blue ox for a pet, he'd simply smile, shrug and return to his labors. These men worked hard and they deserved their indulgences.

On the night before his death, Charlie Blade crowded the cook stove, rubbing his bony hands together to stave off the brutal cold. "So damn cold out tonight, the lantern light's liable to freeze solid."

Paul chuckled, rattling the bunkhouse and causing a few of the snoring loggers to stir beneath their blankets. "If it did, I'm sure they'd find a way to give me credit for it. Zeb Walton asked me this morning if it was true I punched a hole through the mountains to clear a path for the railroad."

"Well, you're stronger than a grizzly bear, but I doubt you have that kind of might." Charlie gave Paul a thoughtful look. "You're good to go along with all that. They ain't just teasing you, you know. They think highly of you."

"I know."

"This is a hard life and men need to know great things are possible. Just a little hope, you understand?"

Paul nodded. Hope was the reason he'd crossed the ocean.

There was no peace left for giants in Albion. The Jacks saw to it that they were always on the move, afraid even to rest easy in the ancient cloud cities for fear that the Jacks might one day organize and topple their entire existence. When Paul first came to the camp, he'd asked Charlie if there were any loggers named Jack. There'd been only one, a stone-faced, unhappy man named Jack Pierre and Paul had kept a close watch on him from day one. There was no fool-proof way to tell if Pierre had murderous intentions, for not all men named Jack were giant killers. But all giant killers *were* named Jack, and as a result, Paul had long since given up the luxury of sleep.

"You look tired, Charlie."

"Long day. Gonna be a longer day tomorrow. Got to get them logs ready for the river." Charlie went to bed and Paul left the bunkhouse, eliciting a chorus of shouts when the howling north wind carried into the room. Paul shut the door behind him and took a seat near the river's edge. The temperature had no effect on him; the cold night smelled like ice and pine needles, and the wind whispered forgotten stories of the forest, tales left behind for those who would hear them of a time before men walked the woods.

It was the most perfect place on earth, the only place Paul had ever found peace, and he wanted to absorb every second of the experience.

He remained by the river until light blossomed in the east and bunkhouse doors creaked wearily open, once again releasing men into the world with their coughs and laughter, banging pans, axes on whetstones. The misty air carried the logging camp smells of fried ham and morning urine, unwashed bodies and bitter black coffee. And within minutes they were hard at work again—Paul with them—whipping horses into action, bucking logs, working them toward the dump. Spring had come, and soon the river hogs would ride the shipment downriver.

Paul was helping some men choke a log when the ruckus started—panicked shouts, a low rumble, then a terrified scream truncated by horrible silence. Paul released the choke cable in his hands and leapt away from the rumbling logs. By the time he regained his feet, men were already lifting away the massive lengths of pine that had scattered like spilled matches. Paul heaved the logs away, one after another, no doubt giving birth to a hundred more stories. But it didn't matter, there were men trapped beneath.

They found seven dead in all, including Charlie Blade. Paul cried when he saw the old man's grizzled face, and he pulled the limp body from the timbers. But his sadness turned to a fear when he saw Jack Pierre standing just beyond the edge of the insanity, watching Paul with his smoky eyes, smiling. He held a cant-hook at his side like a medieval pike, and his breath came in malignant white clouds. There was no mistaking the man's cool malice.

Paul would have taken revenge on a normal man. But not a Jack, no matter how much he wanted to.

Paul was no fool.

He didn't wait for Charlie Blade's burial. That night, he chose the largest log and rode it downriver. And so it was that Paul began his life on the road.

2. A Giant Keeps His Back to the Wall—1876

Paul tossed back another nickel whisky and studied the cards in his hands. A pair of sevens to go with a mixed bag of nothing. Luck was not on his side.

The man seated across from him, however, was the luckiest son of a bitch he'd ever met. He'd introduced himself as Bill Hickok, and Paul recognized that name from the newspapers. He couldn't reign in all the details but Paul knew one thing for sure. The man took his gambling seriously.

"So you came here for the gold?" Bill tossed a couple of poker chips into the center of the table, then glanced back toward the door. He'd done this often enough during the course of the afternoon that Paul assumed he was waiting for someone. The saloon was filled with raucous men who smelled of earth and sweat; heavy drinkers, card players, and those who simply had nothing better to do. Women in nightclothes and stockings wandered from table to table, laughing and planting lipstick kisses on dirty foreheads, drumming up business for Swearengen's brothel. Bill and Paul had claimed the last unused table, far in the back of the room where they were mostly ignored by a bored-looking bartender who waged a losing battle for a clean countertop with a whisky-soaked rag.

"No. Had enough of that madness back in California." Paul matched Bill's ante. "I don't like watching what gold does to people."

"Then why in the hell did you come? Ain't nothing here *but* gold." Bill leveled a curious stare at Paul, and the giant met his gaze. The gambler's eyes looked to have soaked up every ounce of virgin wildness the West had to offer, and they provided a frank glimpse into Hickok's soul. This man had stared down the barrel of a Peacemaker rifle at a doomed Sioux chief, bested the famed John Wesley Hardin in Kansas, and followed Buffalo Bill around the country in his Wild West show. Hickok was the weaving, wandering spirit of America and Paul realized they were very much alike.

"I like to wander," Paul said. "Deadwood is just another place on the map. I spent time in a logging camp over in Minnesota, got tired there and headed out for Oregon. You ever been there? Trees big around as houses. I've been all through the Rockies, I lived a while in Texas, and I already told you about California. It was a lovely place to be until the prospectors came."

"Forgive me for saying, but you don't look old enough to remember California before the gold rush." A slanted smile broke beneath Bill's bushy moustache, the kind a man might use to humor a harmless drunk.

"I'm older than I look," Paul said. If Bill knew how old he really was, the gambler might choke on his whisky. Paul was aware he was sharing too much of himself, but he'd never held his alchohol well. Normally, he was very circumspect about his heritage, and especially his comings and goings. With the Jacks always on his trail, it was simple common sense. But Paul felt a kinship for the man they called "Wild" Bill; they were kindred spirits.

"You'd have to be a damn sight older."

Paul didn't reply. He folded another losing hand and waited for Bill to shuffle the cards.

Bill raked in a mound of chips. "In my experience, most men who say they're wandering are on the run from something. That the case with you?"

"Yes it is."

"What did you do? Kill someone?"

"No, nothing like that."

"Then why are you running."

"Because I'm a giant."

Bill dealt the cards, chuckling at Paul's revelation. "You damn sure are. I wasn't going to say anything, but as long as you brought it up, how tall are you? Ten foot easy, I reckon."

Paul shrugged. "I never measured."

"So what about being a giant caused you to be on the run? You escape from a circus?"

Paul let the unkind comment slide. "No, it's just the way giants are. We're restless. It comes from looking over your shoulder your whole life."

Bill glanced at the door again. "Speaking of that, you mind if we switch seats? I never like to sit with my back to the door. I got a lot of people in this world that don't like me. Keeping my back to the wall has kept me breathing a lot of years."

"Sorry. I have the same policy."

Bill nodded, looking only mildly put-out. "I understand. It's just that sitting this way irks the hell out of me."

"I'll watch your back."

"Guess that'll have to do."

They played for a time in silence. Bill won most hands, but occasionally Paul managed to get some of his money back. When it was Paul's turn to deal again, Bill poured another shot of whisky, slid it to Paul, then fixed another for himself. "I gotta know. What's so scary it keeps a giant on the run?"

"The Jacks." Paul drank the whisky and held out the glass for a refill. The drink was steering the conversation into dangerous waters, but he didn't care. His adopted homeland was wide and untamed, more far-reaching that he'd ever imagined. But it was also lonely. Paul sensed that Wild Bill was a man who understood that.

"Who're the Jacks?"

"Giant killers."

Bill laughed, then cut it short when he realized Paul was serious. "My grandma used to tell stories about a kid named Jack who went around killing giants, stealing their gold. Stuff like that."

"They aren't just stories."

"You're telling me there's a bunch of kids running around trying to cut off your head?"

"They're not kids. The old stories have been twisted. They're regular men, but they've got something in their blood that makes them hunt us."

"Something in their blood? Like it's carried down from father to son."

Paul shook his head. "More like a disease. You can't tell who they are by their family or how they're raised. The only thing they all have in common is they're named Jack. It's an ancient struggle, creatures of magic versus those who would banish us from the earth. And I've never found a reason for what they do beyond simple blind hatred."

"Men don't always need a good reason to kill." Bill skipped the shot glass and drank straight from the bottle. "Damn. I must have drank more than I figured. I actually believe what you're saying."

"I'm just telling the truth." Paul dealt the cards. The noise and smoke were giving him a headache but he wasn't ready to leave the game. It was rare to find a man like Hickok with whom he could share his troubles.

"Seems strange to me you'd run from these Jacks if they're just regular men. You're big enough. Why not just whip their asses?"

"Quite a few giants have tried. But it's never ended well. The Jacks are lucky. I'd say fate was on their side, but what does that say about my kind?"

"Fate pisses on everybody with the same stream. You just got to learn to keep out of the way." Bill discarded a single card and grinned. "I'll take one."

Paul was about to lose some more money. He slid a card across the tabletop, hoping it wasn't the one his companion was looking for. When he pulled back to study his own cards, he noticed the man standing a few feet behind Hickok and the .45 revolver he had aimed at the table. Paul's eyes widened and Bill was savvy enough to react. He was on his feet, gun in hand and beginning to turn when the assassin's bullet tore into the back of his head. Another bullet followed and Bill dropped his gun. He fell back into the chair and collided with the table edge. A pair of aces and a pair of eights slipped from the dead man's hand.

A group of men tackled the shooter and wrestled away his gun, but not before Paul recognized him. Jack McCall—a buffalo hunter he'd crossed paths with a few years back in Wyoming. He struggled against his captors, shouting about murder and giants, but his ravings meant nothing to the clientele of Saloon #10. Everyone in the room had seen him kill Wild Bill Hickok, and that was the only fact that mattered. Only Paul understood those bullets were meant for him; Bill's lightning-fast reflexes had propelled him into the path of the gunfire, and into frontier legend.

Paul didn't wait for the trial.

He left Deadwood before sunset.

3. This Land is Jack Land—1937

A roiling cloud of brown dust chased the battered flatbed Ford truck through the panhandle. Paul had a firm grip on the truck's bed, knees pulled up to his chest to keep his legs from dangling over the edge. The truck lurched at every pit and pothole, but Paul managed to hang on. Sand stung his eyes and settled as a fine layer of grit between his teeth. It rode the wind, a voracious brown cloud that chewed away sunshine and distance, swallowed families and dreams, feasted on jobs and land and lives. Paul huddled in the belly of the beast, desperate to be anywhere but Oklahoma, and he prayed the sand wouldn't follow them forever.

It wasn't the only truck leaving Oklahoma. For months Paul had seen them hurtling down the highways, ferrying dirty, beaten people away from wind and misery, and if the rumors were to be believed, toward a rich bounty waiting in California. Paul knew California wasn't the answer, but it suited him far better than waiting around to be buried in dirt. Besides, he'd stayed in one place long enough.

Two other men shared the truck bed with him. The first was a rangy man with nothing but a guitar case and a paper bag full of sandwiches who'd introduced himself as Woody. He seemed unconcerned that they might fly off the back of the truck any moment. One hand rested on his guitar, the other on his sandwich bag, and he watched the world recede with a weary smile, like he'd never seen anything at once so glorious and so heartbreaking.

The second man was gray with middle age and much less calm. His clothes were patched and a size too small, and he kept inching closer to the middle of the bed, shifting and groaning with every bump in the road. He hadn't volunteered his name yet, but in his mind, Paul had nicknamed him Jumpy.

"You comfortable yet?" Woody asked, flicking a cigarette butt over Jumpy's head and into to brown void.

"No I'm not," Jumpy said, missing the sarcasm. "Do you think he's going to drive this fast all the way to California?"

"Hope he does. The quicker we get there the better."

"Assuming we get there alive."

"If we don't, that's just one less thing to worry about." The truck lurched and Woody put a hand on his floppy hat to keep it in place. Jumpy endured a second of terror before settling down again.

"So, what's your story?" Woody asked. He shot Paul a quizzical look, as if he'd just noticed the giant was sitting next to him.

"What do you mean?"

"How'd you end up here? You don't exactly look like a native Oklahoman."

Paul considered the question and found no answer he was willing to share. Woody stared at him with probing eyes, but it didn't make Paul uncomfortable. From a normal person, he'd shun such close inspection, but he could tell Woody was studying him the way all great artists do. Soaking in the detail, saving it for a book, a song, a painting. Woody's connection to the realm of music was as visible to Paul as the man's weather-creased hat or the thin trails of dirt on his palms. The Music whirled about him like a shower of gold dust caught up in a tornado, and Paul knew this was no ordinary guitar picker. He was bound for something more. Woody scrutinized him for several more heartbeats, then nodded his head, unconsciously storing away everything he could remember about his giant traveling companion. Paul knew the man would write a song about what he'd seen some day. It wouldn't be a song about Paul Bunyan, roving frontier giant, but a song about everything he loved and feared. The vast majesty of America; man's desire for freedom and wide-open spaces; the pain of watching the last, lonesome places between the oceans shrink beneath cities, highways, fences, factories.

In short, the way the Jacks were ruining the country.

"I just left home and this is where I ended up," Paul said, answering Woody's question and yet offering no real insight.

"Well, you ended up in the wrong place. Smart you're getting out."

"You think life in California will be better?"

"Can't be worse," Woody said, munching on a sandwich. "Supposed to be plenty of farming jobs for those willing to work. And I am. Plus I figure somebody might want to pay me to play guitar. Better chance of that happening there than here."

"So you're a professional musician?"

"No," Woody grinned. "But I will be."

And Paul knew that was undoubtedly the case.

"Why are *you* headed to California?" Paul asked, inviting Jumpy into the conversation.

"I'm not really *headed* anywhere," he said. "I just like to keep on the move."

"How come?" Woody gave Jumpy the same stare-down he'd given Paul.

"Because if I stay too long in one place, the Germans will get me." Jumpy cast a searching look out into the dust storm as if his enemies might be lurking by the side of the road, waiting to take him out with a canister of mustard gas. Paul got the disctinct impression that the man was crazy, though he knew people would draw the same conclusions about him if he went around saying an ancient order of giant killers was hell bent on his destruction and willing to wrinkle the very fabric of America to get to him.

"And how come the Germans are after you?" Woody asked.

"Do you remember that pilot they had back in the Great War? Richthofen? The one they called the Red Baron."

"Course I do," Woody said, indignantly. He seemed insulted someone would think he didn't know who the Red Baron was. "What's he have to do with you?"

"I'm the one who killed him. The damn Germans have been out for my head ever since."

There were a quiet few seconds when all that could be heard was the hum of tires on the highway and the enraged howl of the relentless wind. Then Woody began to chuckle. It grew into a hearty laugh and Paul couldn't help but crack a smile. Jumpy didn't seem upset that he was being mocked. Instead, he just nodded his head as if he'd been expecting this reaction all along.

"See? That's why they'll get me some day. Because no one will ever believe me."

Paul's grin vanished and a sudden chill stole its way up his spine.

"You know some Canadian flyer shot down the Baron, right? They say it was either that or some Aussie ground gunner. Which one are you?" Woody tore one of his sandwiches apart and gave some to everyone. Paul could tell he was feeling guilty for making fun of Jumpy, but it was just too hard to resist.

"Neither," Jumpy said, taking the offered sandwich and sniffing it like it might be poisoned. "I'm a born and raised American, and I'm the one that killed him. No matter what the papers say. Why else would the Germans be after me?" As if this circular logic verified his every claim, Jumpy shoved the sandwich in his mouth and began chewing.

Paul and Woody exchanged amused glances, then Woody offered his hand to their traveling companion. "Well, I guess you did the free world a service then. What's your name?"

"I prefer to keep that confidential, he said, shaking Woody's hand. "You understand."

"Sure, sure. Best not to make it too easy for them." Woody winked at Paul. "You can tell me *your* name, can't you?"

"It's Paul."

"Not Paul Bunyan?" Jumpy's eyes grew wide and bits of sandwich flew from his mouth.

Paul was disturbed that this stranger knew his name, but he nodded. No sense lying. If Jumpy was a Jack, he already knew the truth. "How'd you know that?"

"You being a giant sort of gave it away. I mean, everyone knows who you are. My mother used to read me a book when I was a kid that told all about you. Shit, you're really *the* Paul Bunyan?"

"I suppose so." Paul hadn't known someone had written a book about him and it distressed him mightily.

"Did you really put out a forest fire by pissing on it?"

Woody choked with laughter. Jumpy's eager eyes stared at Paul and he could tell the man wanted the story to be true, even if it wasn't. It was no different than his obviously fabricated tale of killing the Red Baron. And Jumpy was no different than the loggers Paul had known nearly a century ago. For the first time in years, he thought of Charlie Blade, and he remembered the man saying that sometimes men just need to know great things are possible. Paul watched Jumpy squirm in his rag clothing, caked with grime and beaten flat by the world, making up stories to give his life some color. If ever a man needed hope, it was Jumpy.

"Yes I did," Paul said, and Jumpy hooted like a kid who'd just stumbled across Santa Claus filling his stocking with candy. "Good thing I drank a couple of lakes that morning or I'd have never been able to douse it all."

"Paul Bunyan! Can you believe that? I'm riding to California with a real live legend."

Woody's knowing smile was so wide it looked like his face would split in half. "Well, hell. I didn't know you was a celebrity too. Tell us what else you done, Paul."

"Yeah! And tell us about Babe!"

And so Paul did. He spent the next hour recalling every fantastic thing he'd supposedly done, allowing Jumpy to steer him toward the stories he'd forgotten. He spiced up the narrative with a few new twists that drew sparkling smiles from Woody and childlike laughter from Jumpy. He spoke of the water palaces that used to hang in the skies of Albion and how the sun drew golden sigils on the wings of visiting angels. He described the peculiar scent of memory, and spun tales of the faerie lands, destroyed centuries before by the absence of true belief. He even told them about his constant flight from the Jacks and the way they had started to organize in hopes of rooting out the last known giant in America. Pulling together to trample on the world he loved just because they could.

His companions didn't know the lies from the tall tales. Jumpy swallowed it all and Woody didn't believe a word of it. Yet they both seemed immensely satisfied when Paul's narrative drew to a close.

"See, this land was made for anyone who wants it. And I'll be damned if I let those bastards take it from me." Paul ended his speech with a bow of his head, and his companions broke into applause.

When night came, loneliness settled back into Paul's soul and he knew all his talk of fighting back against the Jacks was empty bravado. They seemed to have their hand in every aspect of the world—he wouldn't have been surprised to find they'd caused the dust storms just to flush him out of his comfortable life on the plains. They'd come so close to killing him on so many occasions, he found himself sometimes wondering if it would just be better to give up. But always there was a new horizon. And with it hope. He just wasn't sure that would be the case much longer.

"Nice stories," Woody whispered. Jumpy lay asleep on his back, hands folded across his chest like a dead man.

"Not all of them were stories," Paul said.

"Near enough, I guess," Woody said. "Not that it matters anyway. "It's hard to tell the truth from the lies sometimes."

Paul simply nodded. Woody's statement encapsulated his entire existence. The giant closed his eyes and kept them that way, not wishing to dwell on the dying frontier that he'd once found so ripe with possibility.

When he opened them again, he saw California stars.

4. The Spirit of the West—1950

Paul sat in the corner of a rumbling boxcar, trying to remember what magic was like. The memory of it lined his throat like the aftertaste of cheap beer and lingered in the air like the mostly forgotten scents of childhood. How long since he'd seen the brilliant threads of light that connected this land to the land of magic? How long since he'd heard the conversations of ghosts?

The Jacks had done their job well, squeezing it out with industry and urban sprawl, keeping Paul forever on the road, running, trying to cling to the last embers of enchantment that still flickered in the hidden wild places.

A plain-faced man dangled his feet out the boxcar's open door, watching nighttime rise above an endless stretch of unspoiled farmland. Unshaven and ripe with the stench of travel, the man spoke to himself in a persistent, frantic whisper like air leaking from a car tire. His hands were in constant motion and sweat poured down the back of his neck despite the cold temperature.

Paul watched him nervously. The guy probably wasn't a Jack, and he certainly wasn't *the* Jack who'd been on his tail in recent years. But paranoia kept Paul alive.

The man suddenly climbed to his feet, like he'd just remembered something he'd forgotten to do. He whirled to face Paul, focusing his bloodshot eyes on the giant for the first time since he'd hopped the train in Wyoming. One hand rubbed absently at his belly, the other pointed at Paul like the accusatory hand of God. "You like the lonely places, don't you?"

Paul found the stranger's statement to be both the most random and most trenchant observation anyone had ever made regarding his character. He watched the man sway back and forth in anticipation, then answered. "Yes."

"Yes, yes! I knew it! I could tell it by your eyes. Point 'em out the door and take a look. That's the last of it we'll see in our lifetime. The last dying hunk of the old lonely West, turning belly up right before our eyes. People like me and you, we appreciate that. Nobody else gives a shit this country's beat. But you understand, don't you?

"This used to be land of possibilities. Ideas! Oh, man I got ideas popping in my head. Can't even keep up with all of them. I don't care if she's dying, I want to see every inch of this bitch before they bury her. You dig that don't you? Yes! Yes! Aw, shit. Even if I could live forever I couldn't do it though. She ain't got that many days left."

Paul would have jumped into the one-sided conversation, but he might have drowned in the stream of consciousness.

"One thing she's still got is *magic*. See it out there?" The man crossed to the door and pointed out across a field of tilled earth, and beyond that to the snowcapped peaks that surrounded Denver. "Gorgeous, man. You can taste that shit." The stranger plopped down and dangled his legs again. His dialog had seemingly run its course, but his head still bobbed constantly like he was listening to music the rest of the world couldn't hear.

Paul remembered the days when he could hear that kind of music, and he wondered if the man really was tuned in. Several of the old stories told about mortals who'd found various ways to connect with the magic of creation, and it never ended well for them. For a time it was wonderful—seeing colors freshly escaped from the dreams of the gods, feeling the core of your soul touch every spot in the universe at once, and best of all, the music. The sound of every living thing striking a single endless chord, whispering and howling, crying and whistling through branch and flesh and stone. But the human mind could only cope with that type of glory for a short time. The magic would overcome them, twist their thoughts into obsessions, color their sight with unknowable visions and turn the sweet symphony of life into the shrill, painful wail of burgeoning insanity. Paul had never seen a mortal who'd stumbled upon the magic. But the wild-eyed man in his suit of rags might be the first.

It was as if he'd reached into Paul's mind and yanked out his thoughts—possible, perhaps, if they both shared a connection to the magic. Yet Paul's connection had dwindled over the years; the absence of magic haunted him like a missing limb. But if this man still felt it, then maybe it was still alive. Attainable. Maybe Paul could find it again.

He sat down next to the stranger in the boxcar's open doorway. His legs should have touched the rapidly passing ground, but he noticed they were hardly longer than the stranger's. In fact, he was only a foot taller than the man; he'd been shrinking right along with the rest of the country.

"What makes you think there's magic out there?"

"Man, how couldn't there be? Aw, it's not any of that fairy tale stuff; this is homegrown American magic. The stuff of freedom. Yes! Yes it is. That old kind is gone and this kind is fading fast, but you can still see it if you stare out at the mountains long enough. Look out there, Paul! Take a whiff of your own history."

"How'd you know my name?" Paul asked, but he was pretty sure he already knew the answer. No doubt, this guy was hooked up to the other plane, and his straight-through connection to Paul's mind meant the giant hadn't entirely lost touch with the land of creation.

"American magic! Best goddamned stuff there is! Aw hell, and I know you're worried about it, worried the Jacks are going to tear all of it away and leave the country naked and broken. Shit, man, that's their job! Of course that's what they're going to do. So quit worrying about it. Take a peek from another direction.

"You *are* magic. They can't kill it all as long as you're still on the move, one step ahead, fighting hard and pissing on their plans. You're a living breathing tall tale. A creature of the West. I got a friend who says the West just takes you over. And then you become it. That's you, man. You're the spirit of the goddamned West. That's me too. That's everybody that ever watched Kansas pass by from a train car or stood out in a summer thunderstorm with his thumb in the air hoping to hell somebody would pluck him up off that deserted road and *talk* to him for a while. That magic reaches farther than you think. There's a little of it in all of us. But you? You're the wellspring. The Jacks keep draining the creek and you keep filling it back up."

Paul stared in amazement at this boxcar prophet. Paul could feel him digging around in his head, working his brain like a lump of clay, trying to reshape it into something that resembled hope. He'd always felt like a coward, running from the Jacks but never actually doing anything to stop them. But if what Neal (the name popped into his head of it the prophet had left it there for him to find) said was true, the mere act of staying alive stoked the embers of the American fire.

"Neal? Do you travel a lot?"

Neal nodded vigorously. "Yes, yes. I know what you're wondering. Do I know the fellow keeps following you from place to place, from one end of the country to the other? Guy named Jack? You figure he's on the hunt."

"Isn't he?" Paul's heart thundered in his chest. The way Neal could pick up his thoughts was spooky, and it was more frightening still that he knew the man who'd been chasing him. Paul had almost written it off as paranoia. But here was the proof.

Neal smiled. "Guy's name is Kerouac. Sometimes he calls himself Sal for no god-damned reason. Beatest cat I ever saw, but he's a friend of mine. He ain't one of the one's on your tail; he's just another restless soul like you and me. We all have the spirit in us. As long as we keep moving, it keeps on pumping through the country's veins like fresh clean blood. Once we slow down then entropy sets in. America starts to wind down. It's plain to see that there ain't too many movers left in the world."

Neal patted his shirt pocket, sweat pouring down his face, life popping like fire-crackers in his wide eyes. "Say, you got any tea? I'm fresh out."

Paul shook his head. "Sorry."

"Ain't no problem. Once we get to Denver I know a guy who grows it in his garden. He's got a place near downtown not too far from the train station. Oh man, just wait till you see the bop cats they got in Denver. Yes, yes! Places open all night and if they don't have something to make you jump we'll commission a car and head out to Frisco. That's the real shit out there! You're getting off in Denver ain't you?"

"Actually, I think I'm going to keep moving."

Neal nodded sagely. "Yes. You do that. I think you understand it now. I'm getting off in Denver."

Paul would miss this frantic, enigmatic citizen of the road like he missed all the other transitory people in his life, but he was used to being alone.

"Freedom's a lonely road," Neal said.

Paul didn't answer.

5. The Giant and the Knoll—1963

Paul leaned against the back of the picket fence, trying to be as inconspicuous as possible. He kept his rifle hidden under a heavy wool trench coat—hot as hell for Texas, even in November, but it served its purpose. Beyond the fence, green grass tumbled toward Elm Street, and a number of excited onlookers buzzed like honey bees in the crisp fall sunshine.

By now, that crazy loon Oswald would be setting up shop in the School Book Depository, relishing the task at hand. The man approached murder with a failed military mind and a misplaced sense of patriotism. Paul wished for the hundredth time that he'd never met Oswald, never fallen in with the Cubans. They knew exactly what to promise. His dreams, served up on a platter for that taking. And yet, he was starting to think the price was too high.

Paul looked at his watch and pressed his transistor radio to his ear. The motorcade was crawling down Main, and they were about to turn onto Houston. Paul had a very serious decision to make in the next thirty seconds.

Paul had taken Oswald for a kindred spirit. The guy was always on the move—Russia, Mexico, Dallas, New Orleans. Paul couldn't help but accept the invitation to Florida. It was one of the few places in America he'd never visited. But he hadn't been expecting the meeting with the Cubans, and he damn sure hadn't been expecting them to know all about the Jacks.

Paul looked over his shoulder to make sure nobody was around before loading his rifle. Through a clutch of low-hanging tree branches that still held their leaves, Paul saw a convertible Lincoln Continental turn onto Houston Street. The crowd below cheered. Parents raised kids up on their shoulders, a couple of cops clapped; one man followed the car's progress with an 8mm camera.

Was he being used? The president had the right name, but how could he know the man was really a Jack? The Cubans had their own reasons for wanting the man dead, but they'd done a good job of building Paul up to the task. They'd spoken of magic and the fey folk—los niños de la tierra. They knew about Paul's connection to the source. And they knew the Jacks wouldn't rest until they'd killed every giant, paved over every enchanted glen with concrete and severed every string between this world and the other. How could they have known these things if they weren't telling the truth?

And yet, Paul couldn't help but feel he was nothing more than a disposable weapon. Oswald might relish that role, but he did not.

The motorcade turned right onto Elm Street and drew closer to the kill spot. Paul raised his rifle, pressed the stock against his shoulder and notched the barrel in a crook between two pickets. The Lincoln crawled closer. The president and first lady waved at the onlookers from the back row of seats. He wore a polished smile; she wore a pink dress and a pillbox hat. Another couple occupied the next row of seats—presumably the governor and his wife—and a pair of secret service agents sat in front.

Paul stared down the rifle's scope and found the president's head. The man he was supposed to kill. Paul's hands trembled; the crosshairs leapt from the president to his wife, then back again. If Paul decided to pull the trigger, the target had less than three breaths left. No more saber rattling at the Russians, no more space initiative, no more hobnobbing with Marilyn and Frank. Just a lifeless body that may or may not have belonged to an immensely powerful Jack. Tears welled in Paul's eyes.

When the sudden bark of gunfire broke the peace, he was just as shocked as everyone else.

Paul met Oswald at the Texas Theater in south Dallas. He slouched in his seat, staring blankly at the Audie Murphy flick that played to a nearly empty room. Oswald leaned toward him, reeking of sweat.

"I'm surprised you came," he said.

"Why? We agreed to meet here afterward."

"Yeah, but you chickened out. I figured you'd already be in Mexico by now."

Paul bristled. "I didn't chicken out. I changed my mind."

"Same damn thing. Why the hell didn't you shoot?"

"The more I thought about it, the more I figured those Cubans were just using us."

"Of course they were. You're just figuring that out." Oswald shook his head and snorted. "Hell, I knew all along they were using us. But what does it matter if everybody wants the same thing. They wanted him killed, we wanted him killed. What's the problem?"

"I'm not sure I wanted him killed."

A look of frustration crossed Oswald's gaunt face. "It's a little late for that."

Paul closed his eyes and listened to the projector clatter behind him. "I'm not even sure he's a Jack."

"Of course he is. You told me what they're trying to do. Look at all he's responsible for and tell me he ain't a Jack."

"That's just it. He hasn't really done anything."

"Aw, he's done plenty. He just doesn't let the media get wind of it. It's all under the table stuff, see? That man was running this country into the ground."

Paul wasn't convinced, but he nodded to shut the guy up. What had he been thinking? Even if the president was a Jack, he knew better than to try to kill him. That sort of thing never ended in a giant's favor. And if he was innocent, then killing him would make Paul no better than his enemies. Either way, the man was dead and Paul was glad he hadn't been the one to pull the trigger. A minor consolation, but it couldn't assuage his guilt.

"If he was a Jack, they're going to be hunting you."

Oswald laughed. "They won't have to look far. I'll be in jail. Speaking of, you better get moving. You don't want to be seen with me. I think I killed a cop."

"I'm serious," Paul said, rising to his feet. "Watch your back. The Jacks won't forget something like this."

"Sure thing," Oswald said, grinning. Paul knew he'd never believed any of the tales about Jacks and magic. He wondered what line the Cubans had used to snare *him*.

Paul left the theater and stood for a few seconds in the blinding sunlight, wondering where to go next. Unsure what else to do, he started down the sidewalk, hands stuffed in his trench coat pockets. Police sirens wailed in the distance, and a minute later, two cruisers sped past, lights flashing. People stopped to watch and speculate about where the cars were headed. Paul kept his head down until he reached the bus station, then he bought a ticket for the next one leaving town.

Paul spent the next few hours watching America speed past his window, listening to news of Oswald's arrest on his radio and wondering what would happen to the man. He kept expecting to hear himself named as an accomplice, but it never happened. As the sun began to set, Paul clicked off his radio and pressed his head back against the bus seat. He fell asleep wondering if he'd ever really know the truth about Jack Kennedy.

The next day, Jack Ruby answered his question.

6. A Jack by any Other Name—2007

Paul waited in the terminal, one hand clutching his boarding pass. The plane to Heathrow was scheduled to board any minute and he looked forward to his departure with a mixture of resignation and nostalgia.

When he'd first crossed the clouds from Albion, he could never have imagined going back. But the American Jacks had proven even more horrible than their old world counterparts, and Paul was ready to admit defeat. There was nothing left of the untamed nation he'd grown to love nearly two centuries ago, and his foes had taken on new identities.

The Jacks weren't always named Jack anymore.

This startling revelation had occurred to Paul after nearly a decade without encountering one of his ancient enemies. Yet a Jack by any other name—Microsoft, Enron, Halliburton—could still slay giants. Giants like Paul and giants like America. No more boundaries existed to slow their ambition, no magic to allow the wide-open spaces to flourish. No memory of better days when the world was large enough to get lost in. That sort of freedom had been driven from the country years ago.

A lady with a faux British accent informed the swarm of passengers it was time to board. Paul took his place in line, mobbed by the incessant chatter, the harsh ringing of cell phones, the droning newscaster on the CNN monitor, the coma-inducing Muzak. The greasy odor of fast food and bath-deprived humanity assaulted his nose and he fought the urge to run screaming from the terminal in hopes of escaping the throng. He kept his composure, and ten minutes later, Paul was in his seat.

He buckled his seatbelt—a perfect fit. Paul had shrunk along with the rest of the world and he doubted he'd ever regain his former stature. America, however, might still have a chance. Paul whispered an apology to his adopted country as the plane taxied down the runway. What might she have become if he'd stayed in Albion? If he hadn't led the Jacks across the ocean?

Leaving this place might give the Jacks reason to leave it too. It could be they no longer cared enough about giants to follow him, but his presence had fueled their destruction for far too long. His departure might be too late to change anything, but it was the only avenue of hope left to walk. Great things might still be possible.

Paul wouldn't linger long in Albion—she had her own share of Jack troubles—but he would continue on until he found some untouched land, a place where Jack boots had not yet soiled the earth. If the Jacks followed, then America would be allowed to thrive. And if they didn't, at least Paul would have a new home in which to wander.

The plane left the ground with a lurch and hurtled skyward. Paul gave a gasp when it punched through the clouds and emerged into a world of pure sunshine. It had been so long since he'd seen the land of his fathers that tears formed in his eyes and trailed down his bristly cheeks.

The plane leveled out and turned toward Albion.

And so it was The Spirit of the West left America for good.

Stalking Beans

Nancy Kress

Nancy Kress is the author of twenty-six books: sixteen science fiction novels, three fantasy novels, four short story collections, and three books on writing. She writes often about genetic engineering, as in her most widely known novel, *Beggars in Spain*. Nancy's most recent book is *Steal Across the Sky* (Tor, 2009), an SF novel about a crime committed by aliens against humanity 10,000 years ago—for which they would now like to atone. Her writing has won multiple Nebula and Hugo awards.

Jack and the Beanstalk is a lovely fairytale. But Kress looks at it and sees something different. She wants to explore the motivations of Jack. Are they as egalitarian as they seem, or is Jack motivated by the same base desires that drive most men?

Sometimes I try to make my wife angry. I clump in from the dairy in boots fouled by cow dung; I let the hearth fire die; I spill greasy mutton on the fresh cloth Annie insists on laying each night as if we were still gentry and not the peasants we have become. I wipe my nose with the back of my hand, in imitation of our neighbors. I get drunk at the alehouse. I stay away all night.

It's like fighting a pillow. All give, and feathers everywhere. Annie's pretty face flutters into wispy dismay, followed by wispy forgiveness. "Oh, Jack, I understand!" she cries and falls on my neck, her curls—that but for me would be bound in a fashionable coif—filling my mouth. "I know how hard our fall in the world is for you!" Never a word about how hard it is for her. Never a word of anger. Never the accusation, *You are to blame.* Always, she invites me to sink into her understanding, to lie muffled in it as in the soft beds we once owned, to be soundlessly absorbed. Sometimes it takes every fiber of my muscles not to hit her.

Only when, drunk, I traded our best cow to a dwarf for a sack of beans did Annie show a flash of the anger she should feel by right. "You...did...what?" she said, very deliberately. Her pale eyes sparkled and her thin, tense body relaxed for one glorious moment into anger. I took a step toward her and Annie, misunderstanding, cried, "Keep away from me!" She looked wildly around, and her eye fell on the shelf with our one remaining book, bound in red leather and edged with gold. She seized it and threw it at me. She missed. It fell into the fire, and the dry pages blazed with energy. But she couldn't make it last. A second later her shoulders drooped and she stared at the fire with stricken eyes. "Oh, Jack—I'm sorry! The book was worth more than the cow!" Then she was on my neck, sobbing. "Oh, Jack, I understand, I *do,* I know your pride has been so badly injured by all this, I want to be a good wife to you and understand..." Her hair settled into my mouth, over my nose.

Desperate, I said, "I cast away the beans in the forest, and vomited over them!" "Oh, Jack, I understand! It's not your fault! You couldn't help what happened!" What kind of man can never help what happens to him?

I can't bring myself to touch her body, even by chance. When one of us rolls toward the center of the sagging mattress, I jerk away, as if touched by rot. In the darkest part of the night, when the fire has gone out, I hear her sobbing, muffled by the thin pillow that is the best, thanks to my stupidity, we can now afford. I get out of bed and stumble, torchless, into the woods. There is no moon, no stars. The trees loom around me like unseen giants, breathing in the blackness. It doesn't matter. My feet don't fail me. I know exactly where I'm going.

She is taller than I am by perhaps a foot, and outweighs me by thirty pounds. Her shoes are held together with gummy string, not because she doesn't have better—the closet is filled with gold slippers, fine calfskin boots, red-heeled shoes with silver bows—but because this pair is comfortable, and damn how they look. There is a food stain on her robe, which is knotted loosely around her waist. Her thick blond hair is a snarl. She yawns in my face.

"Damn, Jack, I didn't expect you tonight."

"Is he here?"

She makes a mocking face and laughs. "No. And now that *you're* here, you may as well come in as not. What did you do, tumble down the beanstalk? You look like a dirty urchin." She gazes at me, amused. I always amuse her. Her amusement wakes her a little more, and then her gaze sharpens. She slides one hand inside her robe. "Since he's not here..." She reaches for me.

It's always like this. She is greedy in bed, frank, and direct. I am an instrument of her pleasure, as she is of mine, and beyond that she asks nothing. Her huge breasts move beneath my hands, and she moans in that open pleasure that never loses its edge of mockery. I ease into her and, to prolong the moment, say, "What would you do if I never climbed the beanstalk again?" She says promptly, "Hire another wretched dwarf to stalk another drunken bull." She laughs. "Do you think you're irreplaceable, Jack?"

"No," I say, smiling, and thrust into her hard enough to please us both. She laughs again, her attention completely on her own sensations. Afterwards, she'll fall asleep, not knowing or caring when I leave. I'll wrestle open the enormous bolted door, bang it shut, clump across the terrace to the clouds. It won't matter how much noise I make; she never wakes.

The morning air this high up is cool and delicious. The bean leaves rustle against my face. A bird wheels by, its wings outstretched in a lazy glide, its black eyes bright with successful hunting, free of the pull of the earth.

Annie is crying in the bedroom of our cottage. I'm not supposed to know this, since she thinks I'm still at market with this week's eggs and honey. I poke at the fire, adding up weeks in my head. They make the right sum. Annie must have her monthly flow again, our hopes for a child once more bleeding out between her legs.

I creep quietly out of the cottage to the dairy and sit heavily on a churning cask. I should go to her. I should take her in my arms and reassure her, tell her that maybe next month…But I can't go to her like this. The edge of my own disappointment is too sharp; it would cut us both. I sit on the churning cask until the two remaining cows low plaintively outside their byre. Inside the cottage Annie has lit the candles. She flies around the dingy room, smiling brightly. "Stew tonight, Jack! Your favorite!" She starts to sing, her voice straining on the high notes, her eyes shining determinedly, her thin shoulders rigid as glass.

The tax collector stands in my dairy, cleaning his fingernails with a jeweled dagger. I recognize the dagger. It once belonged to my father. Lord Randall must have given it to this bloated cock's comb for a gift, in return for his useful services. The tax collector looks around my cottage.

"Where is that book you used to have on that wooden shelf, Jack?"

Once he would never have dared address me so. Once he would have said "Master John." Once. "Gone," I say shortly. "One less thing for you to tax."

He laughs. "You've still luxury enough here, compared to your neighbors. The land tax has gone up again, Jack. You owe three gold pieces instead of two. Such is the burden of the yeomanry."

I don't answer. He finishes with his nails and sheathes the dagger. In his fat face his eyes are as shiny as a bird of prey. "By Thursday next, Jack. Just bring it to the castle." He smiles. "You know where it is."

Annie has appeared in the doorway behind us. If he says to her, as he did last time, "Farewell, pretty Nan," I will strike him. But he bustles out silently, and Annie pulls aside her faded skirts to let him pass. The skirts wouldn't soil his stolen finery; Annie has washed and turned and mended the coarse material until her arms ache with exhaustion and her skin bleeds with needle pricks. She turns to watch the tax collector go, and for one heart-stopping moment her body dips and I think she's going to drop him a mocking, insolent curtsy. But instead she straightens and turns to me. "It's all right, Jack! It wasn't your fault! I understand!" Her arms are around my neck, her hair muffling my breath.

Her name is Maria. Seven times I have climbed the beanstalk, and I've only just learned it. "Why did you need to know it before?" Maria said lazily. "You're not exactly carrying my favor into battle." She laughs her mocking laugh, the low chuckle that says, *This is not important, but it's amusing nonetheless.* I love her laugh.

"If I know your name is Maria," I argue lightheartedly, "I can call you that when I demand something. I could say, to give an instance, 'Maria, rub my back.' 'Maria, take off your shift."

"And do you wish me to take off my shift?"

"It's already off," I say, and she laughs and rolls over on her stomach, her enormous breasts falling forward onto the rumpled sheets. For once she hasn't fallen asleep. On the bedside table is a half-eaten orange, the skin dried and wrinkled as if it had been there several days. Maria yawns mockingly.

"Shall I put my shift back on so you can take it off again?"

"Do you want to?"

"I don't mind" she says, which is her answer to almost anything. She puts a hand on me, and a shudder of pleasure pierces from groin to brain. Maria laughs. "What an amorous poppet you are."

"And how good you are to be amorous with, *lux vitae,* Maria," I tell her. But even then she doesn't ask me my other name, just as she has never asked my circumstances. Does it strike her as odd that a man dressed like a peasant can flatter her in Latin?

She reaches for her shift, puts it on, and then proceeds to take it off so slowly, so teasingly, lifting a corner over one thigh and lowering a strap off one shoulder, bunching the cloth between her legs, mocking me from under lowered lashes, that I can barely keep my hands off her until she's ready. Not even when I was who I was, before, not even then had I ever known a woman so skilled in those arts of the body that are really the arts of the mind. When at long last we are sated again, and she is drifting off to sleep, I impulsively say to her, "You are extraordinary in bed. I wish I could take you back down with me."

Immediately a cold paralysis runs over my spine. Now I've done it. Now will come the start of feminine hope, the fumblingly hidden gleam of possession, the earnest, whispered half-promise designed to elicit promises from me: *Oh, do you think someday we actually might be together...*

I should know better. Instead, Maria gives me her mocking smile, rich with satisfaction. "Ah, but that would spoil everything. One always does most stylishly the things one cares nothing about. Don't you even know that, you ignorant boy?"

In another moment she's asleep. I get out of her bed and start for the door. But in the corridor I stop.

I have never explored the rest of the castle. What I wanted—the careless mocking smile, the voluptuous body, the instant dismissive sleep—were in this room, the room I stumbled into on my first journey. But now I walk down the stone passageway and open a second door.

And am staggered.

He must be gargantuan, different from Maria not just in degree but in kind, as she is not from me. The bed stretches the length of my father's tiltyard. An oaken chest could serve for my cow byre. How can Maria, lying in that enormous bed, be large enough to…I don't want to know. Whatever they do, it certainly hasn't soured her for bedding. I have already turned to leave when I catch the glint of gold beneath the bed.

There is a pile of coins—not on his scale, but on mine. Human coins. They look small there, unimportant, and maybe that is why I only take three. Or maybe it's from shame, having already taken from him so much else that he doesn't know about. Or maybe it's neither of these things, but only my sense of justice: I only need three to pay the tax collector. Justice is one of those things that separate me from such as Lord Randall. I am still an honorable man.

As I leave the room, I hear a harp begin to play, light and mocking as Maria's laugh.

Annie is in the yard beside her washpot, stirring hard. Steam rises in smelly clouds. All over the bushes and lines and the rough-hewn wooden bench I made for her are clothes I don't recognize: tunics and leggings and shifts too fine for our neighbors but not fine enough for Lord Randall and his thieving sons. Annie looks up, pushes her damp hair off her forehead, and smiles through exhaustion.

"What are you doing? Who do these tilings belong to?" I thunder at her.

Her smile disappears. 'To the servants at the castle. I took them to wash. If I can do eight pots every day I can earn—"

"You'll earn nothing!" I shout. "Do you think I want my wife to be a washer-woman! *You,* who should have been Lady Anne? How much do you think you can make me bear?"

Annie starts to cry. I hurl the three gold coins at her feet, and my arm remembers casting away the beans in the forest, which only increases my rage. "Here's the tax money! Why did you once again—*once again,* Annie—assume that I'm not man enough to get it? That only *you* possess will enough to save us?"

I don't think she hears me; she's crying too loud. But then Annie stoops and picks up the coins. She bites down on one, and her tears stop. She looks at me, smiles tremulously, and takes a step forward. "Oh, Jack, you earned the money for us—you're so *good!"* Her face glows with light. She understands with her whole tense, determined body how good a man I am. Annie returns the clothing to its owners. Before she does, I rub the unwashed ones with dirt. I don't want anybody paying her anything, she who should be issuing orders to them. Annie watches me ferociously scrubbing dirt over a pair of breeches and says nothing. I don't look at her face.

The next time I go up the beanstalk, Maria is asleep when I arrive. It's hard to wake her. The smell of sex lies heavy on her ripe body. I pause a moment, but then the very fragrance makes me try even harder to wake her; I have no right to be repulsed by being second with her. In fact, it seems to me that I owe him that. To leave now would be to insult him further by refusing to accept second place.

I finally wake her by sucking on the wide, sweet aureoles of her breasts, first one and then the other, alternating until she stirs drowsily and reaches for me. Afterward, she falls asleep again, and I creep down the stone passageway.

The pile of gold coins under the bed is gone. Instead, the room is full of giant chickens.

I stand in the doorway, astonished. All the chickens turn their heads to look at me, and they start such a cheeping and squawking that I might be a puny fox. I back out and slam shut the door, but not before one of the watch-chickens—what else could they be?—has darted past me into the passageway. The stupid creature is shrieking to wake the dead. I punch it; it's like punching a mattress. Even Maria, sated with sex, must hear it squawking.

I grab the chicken and run from the castle. Halfway down the beanstalk it gets its claws loose from against my jacket and rips open my left forearm. I scream and drop it. The chicken plunges to the ground, far below. When I reach the forest floor, the dead chicken is staring at me with reproachful eyes. Its rump, on which it landed, has been reduced to pulp. Among the oozing meat and dingy, scattered feathers is a golden egg, slimed with blood.

I stay in bed for two days, waiting, but nothing happens. Annie brings me hot ale and broth and a porridge she says is nourishing. She says very little else, but she smiles brightly, and hums with so much determination that it is painful to hear.

Maria's voice mocks me: *One always does most stylishly the things one cares nothing about.* By evening of the second day I decide that nothing is going to happen after all. The room was full of chickens; probably he didn't even know how many he had. Probably one was not even missed.

I get out of bed, wash, dress in what is left of my finery, and kiss Annie good-bye. I tell her I'll be gone for many days. She smiles brightly and clings to me too long. For many miles I feel her arms clenched on my neck.

In the city I put up at the Swan and Rose, pose as a traveling merchant set upon by robbers, and set about selling my one remaining piece of stock, a golden egg fashioned for a foreign princess who died before it could be completed. I get a good price. I pay my inn reckoning, buy a good horse, and travel home with dress material for Annie, a new leather Bible to replace the one she cast into the fire, and sixteen gold pieces.

Halfway home, sleeping in the best room of yet another inn, I have a dream of Maria's body. The dream is so powerful that my body shakes and shudders in ecstasy. In the dream, Maria and I were not in her bed but in *his,* while birds swoop around us unfettered as the wind. At home, Annie fingers the dress goods. For once she doesn't hum, or smile, or sing. She looks at me quietly, her pretty face pale. "Don't go out again tonight, Jack. You just arrived home. Please..."

But it seems that somewhere I can hear a harp play. "You took a hen," Maria says, later, in bed. I freeze. She had said nothing, hinted at nothing, seemed the same as always...I'd thought nothing had been noticed.

At the sight of my face, Maria laughs. "Do you think I care, little one? What's one hen more or less?" She reaches for her shift, a single lazy motion of bare arms, and leans back against her pillows.

"The hen .. . did *he* notice..."

"Of course he noticed," she says, amused. "He always knows what is his." She follows this chilling remark with a malicious smile. "But not always what is not."

"I don't understand you," I say stiffly, the stiffness because instead of falling asleep she has become more bright eyed, more alert. This is not the pattern. "I have a harp," Maria says. "Small—you would like it, little one—and very pretty. He had it ensorcelled. You see, he very much wants a child, and very much wants to keep accounts on everything he owns or does not own. From the moment he owns it. So the harp sings when I am with child. Listen."

I heard it then, a high sweet tune, very faint. "I shut it in a cupboard," she says. Her eyes are as shiny as a bird's. "After all, one can't listen to a damn harp all the time, can one? Even if it knows the exact moment one is to double its keeper's chattels?" The exact moment. I remember the smell of sex on her that day, and it seems I can feel all over again the sharp claws of the hen ripping my skin.

"It could…he and I both…it could .. ."

"Oh, it could indeed," Maria says, and laughs. "He won't know which of you it is for months yet. Not even the cursed harp will know for months yet." Her face changes, the first time I have ever seen on it anything but amused pleasure. She says in a low, quick rush, "And he thinks he can *own* me. *Me.*" I climb, naked, off her bed. My legs buckle at the knees. Before I can speak, a door slams and the whole room rumbles.

"Oh!" Maria cries, and stuffs her hand in her mouth. Looking at her, I know that her amused indifference, which pulled me like a lodestone, has finally run out. She did not expect him home so soon. Her eyes dart around the room; the skin on her neck pulls taut; her mouth rakes down in fear. She looks ugly. There is no stylishness to her now. She cares about being caught.

I turn my back on her.

The door opens. A huge voice shouts, "Where is he? I smell blood…I smell *human* blood!" I dive under the bed. The floor shakes, and a boot as tall as my cow byre looms into view. On hands and knees, I scuttle backward under the bed, until I can slip out the far side and run toward the door. I cross the open floor, but to my surprise, the giant doesn't follow. He doesn't seem to see me. I realize that he is blind. *"I smell him!"* he bellows, and the great head turns and peers, contorted with anger. But smell is not sight. He cannot tell from which direction it comes. I run out the open door, my bare feet soundless on the stone. In the passageway, I hear the sound of a cupboard door yanked open. A harp sings a melody I don't recognize. A bellow rips the air, followed by Maria's scream. Then there are footsteps behind me, shaking the world. I scramble down the beanstalk, expecting at any moment to be yanked back upward into the murderous sky. Birds circle me, crying with excitement, and one of them flies so close its talon creases my neck. On the ground, I cut down the beanstalk, working feverishly. It crumples to the earth not like a tree but like a rope, falling in stringy loops, its leaves whispering softly. It falls a long time, unnerving in its breathy quiet. But at the end there is a sudden noise: wood splintering and the sharp discordant sound of strings snapping, as the harp knotted into the top tendrils hits a pile of curling vines and shatters. Naked, I stumble home through the forest—where else should I go? Annie is not there. She has not even taken her new dress goods.

Once more it is deep summer. The hay is thick and yellow in the fields of the manor house. Summer flowers, looseweed and bouncing bet and wild roses, scent the warm nights. I sit outside my cottage and play the harp, which I have mended. The music is not very good; the harp was badly damaged in its fall, and I am no musician. Or maybe it's not that at all. The best music, the kind made by careless laughing musicians at the yearly Harvest Fair, is made by a light hand. One touch on each string, barely there. And the next day the musician moves jauntily on to another town, another fair, whistling down the road he may never see again.

I know where Annie is. But she will not see me, not talk to me. I have tried.

I know, too, that my child has been born. I heard it in the heavy music of the harp, lugubrious with exile. There are many things to hear in mended music of such as my harp.

Last night I went to the inn. A dwarf in the taproom had beans he was trying to peddle. Magic, he said. The start of an adventure. He winked, one dirty eyelid sliding lewdly up and down, the other eye still. But even without him and his greasy beans, I would have known that Maria was alive, and stalking again, and unchanged. Except to me.

Or maybe it's I that have changed.

I work my one field in all weathers. I milk, and plant, and mend, and weed. The sweat runs down my neck *and* under my collar, and birds follow me quietly in the furrows, nibbling on grubs overturned by my hoe. As I work, I try to plan, but all my plans have the rhythms, the tinkling inadequacy, of mended music.

I could buy the beans from the dwarf. I could grow the beanstalk, mount it until I found Maria asleep and *him* away. But what then? An infant is not a coin, nor a hen, nor even a harp. It might wake and cry. If it squalled too loud, I would have to drop it and run, or put my hands around its neck until it was quiet again, or let it fall down the beanstalk to make good my own escape. And I couldn't do that. Even though only a child will bring Annie back, I couldn't do that. Even though I have spent every spare moment carving a cradle with swooping birds on the wooden hood, I couldn't do that. I would botch the job, strain too hard and so ensure that the situation itself cracked.

I would, finally, care too much.

I don't know what to do. By the firelight within my cottage the empty cradle swings, and the one book sits upon its shelf, and the stolen harp sings.

Big Hair

Esther Friesner

Esther Friesner has published dozens of short stories mostly in magazines like *Asimov's Science Fiction* and *The Magazine of Fantasy & Science Fiction*. In addition to short stories, she has published a number of novels and is a prolific editor of anthologies. Among her recent books are *Nobody's Princess*, which takes the Greek legend of Helen of Sparta and gives it a new beginning, and its sequel, *Nobody's Prize*.

Friesner takes the Rapunzel concept and modernizes it into a perfect modern setting: the beauty contest. There are parts of this story that made me cringe, parts that made me smile, and parts that made me actually laugh out loud.

Mama took her to all the pageants, Mama kept the boys away. No one got near Ruby except the judges and the newspaper folks and the TV people unless Mama said. Even then, not too many of those got through. Mama told Ruby that a woman's greatest attraction was staying just out of reach and she was there to see to it that Ruby learned that lesson even if she had to keep her locked up in her hotel room the whole time to make sure she did.

Ruby disagreed, especially about the reporters. "What's wrong with a little extra publicity?" she asked Mama that night as they drove down the mountain, headed for Richmond and the next competition.

Mama's skinny fingers knotted tight on the wheel. She didn't answer Ruby's question, not directly, not at all. "Who you been talking to?" she wanted to know.

Ruby mumbled something under her breath, tucking her sweet, round little chin down into the collar of the buttoned-up trenchcoat Mama always made her wear, hot or cold, rain or shine. Mama pulled the car over to the side of the road and killed the engine and the headlights too, even though there was a storm following them down out of the mountains, roaring and grumbling at their backs like a hungry bear.

"What did you say?" Mama demanded.

"Other girls." Ruby still mumbled, but she got the words out loud enough to be heard this time.

"I thought so." Mama sat back stiff and tall against the driver's seat, making the old plastic covers creak and groan. There weren't any lights on this stretch of road except what the car carried with it, and those were out, but there were little licks of lightning playing through the cracks in the sky. One of them dashed across heaven to outline Mama's face with silver, knife bright, her chin like a shovel blade, her nose like a sailing ship's prow.

"Now you listen to me, little girl," Mama said out of the pitch black that always followed mountain lightning. "Anything those other girls tell you is a lie. Don't matter if it's got two bushel baskets full of facts behind it, don't matter if they say the sun rises up in the east or that air's the only thing fit to breathe, it's still a lie, lie, *lie*. And why? Because it came out of *their* mouths, God damn 'em to hell. Which is the place I'll toss your raw and bloody bones if I ever again hear you mouth one word those 'other girls' say. Is that clear?"

"Yes, Mama."

"'Yes, Mama.'" Mama mocked the soft, mechanical way that Ruby spoke. "Don't you even want to know the proof behind what I'm telling you?"

"No, Mama. You told me. That's good enough."

Mama reached over and jabbed her finger into Ruby's hip, a place where the bruise wouldn't show even in the bathing suit part of the competition, not even if the suit was one of those near-indecent high-cut styles. That place was already pretty mushed over with blues and greens and yellows, generations of hard, deep finger-pokes done by an expert hand. Mama knew her merchandise.

"You lie," she said. "You want a reason. You always do, these days, whether you come right out and say so, like an honest soul, or whether you follow your blood and lie. Ever since you grew titties, you've changed. Used to be you'd take my word and all, no questions, no doubts, but not now. You're getting to be more like your mother every day, so I know what's coming, if I let it come."

Ruby didn't say anything. Ruby didn't know quite what to say. Whenever Mama talked about Ruby's mother, it was like she was daring Ruby to find the breath to speak. Ruby couldn't, though. It was like cold wax was clogging up her throat, coating the roof of her mouth with its crackling shell. Sometimes the silence was enough to make Mama let go and give Ruby back her breath.

Sometimes it was enough, but not now.

"Your mother." Mama said the words like a curse woven out of dead things and dark places. "All her pretty promises about how we'd be more of a family with a child to raise, and the hell with what folks'd say. No more sneaking, no more lies about two old maids keeping house together to save on costs like we'd been saying. Even said how she'd be the willing one, glad to make the sacrifice of lying under as many men as it took to stick you in her belly. And when you rooted and grew, what didn't I do for her when she was carrying you? Anything she asked for, any whim that tickled that bubble she called a brain, I broke my back to fetch it. I gave up all the sweetness of the woods and the brightness of the stars for a set of overpriced rooms in a city I hated, just so she could stay in walking distance of fancy restaurants, movies, stores. The night her pains came on, who was it drove her to the hospital? I held her hand, made her breathe, caught your slime-streaked body, cut the birth cord. When she looked at you that first time, all wrinkly red, and turned her head away because you weren't pretty enough to suit her, I held you close and felt you nuzzle into my chest looking for what she wouldn't give you, and I wept because I would've given it to you if I could."

In the dark, Ruby heard Mama's voice catch on a dry, half-swallowed sob. Tears were smearing her own face, but she never made a sound. This was the longest Mama'd ever gone on about Ruby's mother. Usually all she harped on was the night that woman had run off, never to return, leaving the two of them behind. Mama was saying some things Ruby knew, but there was fresh knowledge jutting itself up out of the dark like a sprouting hedge of thorns. Each new revelation drew a drop of blood from somewhere that would never show, not even during the part of the contest where the judges asked you things. Ruby let the tears flow down. It wasn't like they'd hurt her makeup; she never wore any between pageants. Mama said not to. Ruby sat tight and bruised and bleeding, waiting in silence for Mama to be done.

"There is one decent road out of these mountains and I've put your feet on it," Mama said. She wasn't talking over tears any more. She was in charge of everything and heaven. "One road that won't lead you into treachery or shame, like the one *she* chose, the whore. All the things you want, all you hope to own, all waiting for you to call them in just like magic, once you've won your proper place in this world. Beauty's place, with no limits to it. People pay attention to looks. People give up the earth for beauty."

"Yes, Mama," said Ruby, small. Mama didn't even hear. Mama was too taken up treading the word-web of her own weaving.

"God knows you could get by with less, but I'd be lying if I told you I believed that'd content you," Mama said. "I know you too well. I've known you from the womb. You're a hungry one, greedy like she was, only difference being now I know how deep the greed runs in your guts. I'm not losing you too, girl. She took too much from me. You're mine, now 'til it's over and beyond. I'm too old and homely to find someone new, and I'm damned if I'm dying alone. I'll feed your hungers until you haven't a one left and then you'll stay. You'll have to. What'd there be left to lure you off if you got everything?"

"I ain't going anywhere, Mama," Ruby said, soft and pleading, the way she'd learned the judges liked to hear a girl speak.

The key turned in the ignition, the car stuttered to life. "So you say." Mama's face flashed grim in a shot of lightning, but then it vanished as the dark clapped down.

They drove out of the mountains and into the city, right up to the door of the big hotel where all the contestants were supposed to stay. Mama made Ruby sit in the car in the garage under the hotel until after she got them registered and had the key to the room in her hand. Then she went down to the car and had Ruby ride up in the service elevator so no one'd get to see her.

That's how she always did it. That's how it'd always worked before.

This time he was watching and Mama, who always seemed to know everything, never even knew.

He'd heard about Ruby, seen the tapes of all the other pageants. At first he told himself he was just doing it for the story— "Secrets of Mystery Glamour Queen Revealed!"—but the splinter of his soul that still believed he was a real writer told him another story.

He'd seen the tapes: The judges, almost evenly divided between the ones who looked ready to let their next yawn send them all the way off to dreamland and the ones who devoured the girls with their eyes; the audience, papered over with politic-perfect neutral smiles, playing no favorites, putting their own faces on the runway bodies or else imagining those bodies in their own beds; the girls themselves, shining, bouncing, gleaming for their lives. And her.

No hope, once she took the stage, no hope for anyone at all to take it back again. She'd always come in wearing whatever it was the contest demanded—bathing suit or business suit, evening gown or kitschy cowgirl outfit, furs, sequins, fringes, fluff, leather, lotion, vinyl, sweat—it didn't matter. She wore them all, always with that one accessory that didn't belong but that she could no more forget to wear than her bright blood-red lipstick.

All it was was a scarf. Just a wispy chiffon scarf the color of a summer garden's heart, a scarf she wore wrapped tightly around her head like a turban.

Not for long. He'd seen the tapes. She'd make her first appearance in the pageant with the scarf tied around her head, go one-two-three across the stage to deadliest center, reach up, give the tag end of it the merest twitch, the slightest tug and then. . .

BAM! Hair. Roils and curls and seething clouds of hair erupting anywhere you'd think it could be and a whole lot of places you never imagined. Down it came, all the waves of it, the golden spilling wonder of it, the flash flood of thick, endless, unbound tresses that drenched her from head to toes in impossible glory, bright as a polished sword. Hair that mantled her in the ripples of a sunkissed sea, remaking her in the image of a new Venus, born from the heart of the foam. Hair that boiled down to hide the swell of her breasts, the jut of her ass, and every tantalizing curve of her besides just enough to say *It's here, baby, but you can't have it, and oh my, yes, I know that only makes you want it more.*

Hair that was the sudden curtain rung down over the beauty of her body, a sudden, sharp HANDS OFF sign that made the half-slumbering judges wake up to the realization that they'd missed out, made the ravenous ones howl for the feast that had been snatched away from their eyes. And while they all gasped and murmured and scribbled their thwarted hearts out on the clipboards in their hands, she did a quick swivel-turn, flicked her trailing mane neatly, gracefully aside, out from under spikeheeled foot, and made her exit, clipping a staccato one-two-three from the stage boards, each jounce of her hair-swathed hips nothing more than a whisper, a promise, a deliciously wicked little secret peeping out from under the glimmering veil.

Sometimes the other contestants raised a fuss, but what could they do? Nothing in the rules against a girl wearing a scarf in, on, or over her hair; let them wear their own if they wanted.

As if that'd give them more than a butterfly's prayer in hell! *He* knew. He'd seen the tapes and once—just once, by the sort of accident that slams a man's legs out from under him and smashes a fist through his heart—he'd seen her. A reporter's supposed to cover police calls, but when it's a false alarm about a stick-up at the box office of the auditorium where the pageant's happening, well, what's a man to do? Toss it all up and go home when there's something else worth seeing? Of course he stayed to see her. He'd seen the tapes, but this was something else again.

And how. Seeing her pull that stunt with the scarf in person burned all the tapes to ash in his memory. He stood there, at the back of the auditorium, and felt the air conditioner dry his tongue as he gaped, blast-frozen in a impact of hair and hair and *hair*. Down it came, every strand taking its own tumbling path through spotlight-starred air, even the tiniest tendril of it lashing itself tight around his heart.

That night he dreamed about her and woke up in a tangle of love-soiled sheets. That morning he went in to see his editor and asked to leave the crime beat for just the shortest while to dog a different sort of story.

He pitched it hard and he pitched it pro. Human interest, yeah, that's the ticket! Everyone knew about this girl but nobody really knew a goddam thing. Shame if the state's next Miss America shoo-in got to hold onto her secrets. There were no secrets anyone could hold onto once she headed for the big time, the biggest pageant of them all, and wouldn't it be a shame if the honest citizens of this great state got left with egg on their faces in case this girl's secrets were of the sort that smeared the camera lens with slime?

His editor bought it and bit down hard. He set his hook and ran before second thoughts could intrude. That was how he'd come to be down there, waiting in the shadows of the hotel's underside, standing watch over the elevators in a borrowed busboy uniform, pretending to fix the cranky wheel of a food service cart. He'd done his homework, he'd checked out all the talk about how no one ever saw her before the pageant. He knew she had to get into the hotel somehow, that you couldn't just pluck that much woman out of thin air. Simple, really, the way it was done. He didn't waste much time thinking over why it was done at all.

Her Mama never even noticed him when she came down in the service elevator to fetch Ruby from the garage. He was the "help," invisible to her until called for. Women of a certain age would sooner give a nod of recognition to a potted plant than to the man he was pretending to be. When the two women came out of the garage and he managed the supposed miracle of fixing the food service cart just in time to share a ride up with them, he saw the old bitch's mouth go a tad tight, but she never so much as acknowledged his presence in the elevator.

He punched the button for five, she punched twelve. "Oops." He grinned and punched fifteen. That prune pit mouth hardened even more, but that was as far as the hag would go to admitting his existence. A fat lot he cared!

He'd seen what he'd come to see. . .nearly.

Braids. God damn it all to hell, she was wearing braids.

Mama hung up the phone and snorted, mad. "Of all the nerve."

"What is it, Mama?" Ruby came out of the bathroom, dewy and glowing from a hot shower, her wet hair trailing down her back, a golden serpent sinking into the sea.

"Can you believe the gall of those petty-minded creatures?"

"Who?" Mama was so upset she didn't even bother yelling at Ruby to put a towel around her nakedness.

"The judges. They want to know why you can't room with one of the other contestants."

Ruby's big blue eyes opened wide and melting-sweet with hope. She looked just like a dog that sees a house door left just a crack ajar and all the wide world beckoning sunlit beyond. "Room with—? Oh! That a part of the official rules, Mama? I wouldn't mind doing it, if that's so. I wouldn't want to get disqualified just for—"

"I know what you wouldn't mind." Mama was a thin slice of steel, edged, flying down straight to cut off all foolish notions. "I've made it my business to study the contest rules. There is no such a one. Most likely one of the judges has a favorite—some little chippy who's not too particular about who she does to win what's *your* rightful crown. Only thing is, the judge must've seen your past wins, he *knows* his pet whore hasn't got a prayer going up against you honestly, how she can't begin to compete with what you've got to show. So he wants the two of you shoved together so she can check out your weak spots."

"Do I have any weak spots, Mama?"

"None that show with your mouth shut." Mama had a look that could shoot cold needles right through Ruby's put-on innocence. "But then, what's to stop the bitch from making you some? Accidents happen. Hair doesn't bleed."

Ruby's mouth opened, red and wet, but she could hardly breathe. "You mean—?" She hugged her damp hair to her breasts, a mother cradling her babe out of sight while the monster passes by. "Oh! You mean one of them would actually— actually—" She couldn't say it. She could only make scissors of her fingers and tremble as they snipped the air.

Mama nodded. "Now you're getting smart." She headed for the door. "Don't worry, child. I'll soon set them right. Could be all they're fretted up about is me sharing this room for free. Stingy old badgers. I'll pay my share, if that's what it takes, but I'll never leave you to anyone's keeping but mine." She touched the door. "And put on a robe!" Then she was gone.

Ruby was still alone in her room when he knocked on the door. "Room service!"

She hadn't ordered anything, but she figured maybe Mama'd done it while she'd still been in the shower.

Sitting on the edge of the bed, the TV on to *Seinfeld*, Ruby didn't know what to do. Mama always told her not to open the door for anyone or anything. The knock came again, and the voice. She stole across the room to peer out through the peephole. Such a good-looking young man!

Ruby told herself that if Mama came back and didn't find her room service order laid out and waiting for her, she'd be mad. Mama'd been mad enough all the long drive here, mad over the message from the judges, no sense in riling her more. Ruby reasoned that a bite of food would be just what Mama'd need when she came back from setting those judges straight, but all the little angels blushed to know that Ruby only conjured up those kindly reasons for letting that young man inside well *after* she'd opened the door.

He almost died when he saw her. His hands clenched tight to the handle of the room service wagon he was pushing, his face abruptly hot with more than just the steam rising from the two steak dinners he'd brought up with him to complete his disguise. She was wearing the old-lady-style nightie and robe set Mama'd bought her for her birthday—plain blue cotton the color of a prisoner's sky—but she owned the power to turn such stuff indecent just by slipping it on. He saw her and his breath turned to broken glass in his throat and suddenly he knew he wasn't here for just the story.

Things moved fast after that. So long alone, so long instructed in her own unworthiness to be anything but Mama's beautiful, dutiful daughter, Ruby had never dreamed she'd ever hear another human being tell her she was all things lovesome. First thing he did was beg her pardon for having sent her mama off on a wild goose chase—the judges didn't give two shits about how Ruby roomed; he'd been the one to make the call that cleared the way in here for all his desires, known and unknown both. Almost in the same breath that he confessed his subterfuge, he turned it from a journalist's ruse to a masquerade of the heart.

"I saw you and I fell in love." It was too simply said for someone like her to do anything but believe it.

"I think. . ." she began. "I think I kind of love you too, I guess."

He didn't seem to care about how many qualifiers she tacked on to her declaration. He had her in his arms and time was flying faster than the hands he plunged into the damp warmth of her hair.

She let him. All her life she'd lived walled up behind a thousand small permissions. For once it felt so good, so very good to strike out against them all, sweep them away, deny they'd ever had any power to keep her in. He asked, she gave, and giving split her high stone tower wide open to the sun. And if the swiftness of it all seemed to smack of once-upon-a-time implausibility, the fact that it *did* happen just that fast wasn't anything a rational body could deny. He was handsome and in love, she was beautiful and alone, and neither one of them knew when her Mama might return. Things that happened that fast fell out the way they did because what other choice did they have? Anyhow, it takes longer to make lunch than to make love.

He didn't leave it at her hair, but he was skilled and gentle and she was flying way too high to feel the pain when he broke her somewhere that the judges wouldn't see the blood but the chambermaids would. He laughed, then he moaned over her, falling away still tangled in her hair. That was the only time he hurt her, when he yanked it like that, never meaning to, too caught up in his own sweet joy to pay anything else any mind.

Maybe that was how Mama managed to come in on them like that, with neither one of them able to hear the click of the door opening or see her standing over them, the lightning flash from the mountain storm frozen across her face.

They heard her scream all right, though. It gurgled up out of her from deeper than her throat and smashed itself shrill against the ceiling. Then it wound itself up into a banshee's howl that went on so long they neither one of them had the power left to notice that she'd got one of the steak knives in her hand.

Down it came, sharp and clean, slicing across the hand he held up to fend it off. His cry wasn't much more than a yelp from a kicked dog, and she did kick him, hard and where he'd remember it. She had to jab him off the bed, off Ruby, to do it, but it was a lesson to see how easy an old woman could herd a young man where she'd have him go as long as she held a knife. She only let him stand beside the bed a second before she jerked her foot up sharp between his legs and laid him down.

He was curled up on the floor at her feet, holding himself tight, blood from his hand striping him, belly and balls, when she went after Ruby. Ruby's screams brought folks, but by that time it was much too late. By the time anyone came from the other rooms on that floor or from the front desk or from the pageant authorities, Mama'd got her forearm wrapped with as much of Ruby's hair as she could twist 'round it, until it looked like she'd grown herself a shining gold coccoon from elbow to wrist. Then she sawed down with the blade.

It was thick hair but easy cutting, almost like such a mane was spun of dreams and had only been allowed to exist in the real world on the sufferance of someone with a witch's power over impossible things. It cut right off clean at the touch of the steak knife and it trailed down limp from Mama's arm while she stood there panting and the newspaper man lay there groaning and Ruby sobbed and sobbed into the stained sheets of her bed.

They were asked to leave the hotel right after that, all three, no surprise. Mama didn't even raise a peep of protest. She was satisfied. As soon as they told her to get out, she just started packing up her stuff, smug, and snapped at Ruby to do the same. Hotel security came to urge the newspaper man back into his clothes and down to the nearest police station to answer charges. Ruby was so taken up in too many different colors of grief that it was an hour at least before she found the strength to look after packing her things. The room door was closed but she could still hear the elated whispers of the other girls out in the hall, their giggles of delight. Even if she'd been able to deafen her ears to those sounds, there was still Mama.

"Happy?" the old witch hissed in her ear, and oh, her breath was cold on the back of Ruby's naked neck! "Was it worth it, what you did, what you threw away? Don't tell me your answer now, little girl; not just yet. We're going home. You can wait to tell me then, after you've taken any job you can find, waiting tables at the diner, standing on your feet all day at the Wal-Mart, packing boxes full of car parts at the factory. Or maybe what you'll have to do is spread your legs again and land a man who'll stuff you full of his brats and slap you around when you won't mind him just the way he wants. And you can all come visit dear old Granny at Christmastime. Oh yes, that'll do for me if you wait 'til then to tell was it worth it tonight."

And she kept on like that at Ruby until. . .

In all the fuss that had followed, in all the screaming and running and calling for the police to come, no one thought to call Room Service back and have them take away the cart. There were two steaks on that cart, two steak knives. Ruby didn't have any trouble laying her hands to the second one when Mama turned her back on her and had herself a good, long laugh.

That, too, happened fast.

Ruby's man got himself all bailed out in time to hear the story come in to Police HQ; he stuck around to see them bring her in. He was waiting for her there, threw himself into her arms so quick that the arresting officers couldn't shoulder him off before he whispered urgently in her ear for her to shut up, say nothing, hold on until his paper scared her up a lawyer. Crime of passion, that's what it was, and they played up that angle big at the trial. Provocation more than any human soul could bear. All it took was one look into those big, teary eyes of hers, one glance at the sawed-off ruin of her hair and the jury was at her feet. It didn't hurt any that she still knew how to work a crowd.

They let her off with a light sentence and she married her man before she went through the prison doors. It wasn't the kind of prison a mama'd fear to let her daughter go in, not that Ruby had anything like that to worry about any more. She got her high scool diploma while she was inside and she got an agent to book her on all the right talk shows when she got out and her husband got a book out of it and her hair grew back—maybe not as long or thick, but still pretty as you please. She thought it was pretty enough, anyhow.

When it was halfway down to her ass again she went back on the pageant circuit, took the Mrs. America crown like it'd been waiting for her in a bus station locker all that time. Then she retired, sold Mary Kay, had kids—Bobby, Jim, and Angel—lived happily ever after even if her man sometimes did stare at her hair and say how it's too bad it never did grow back *all* the way to how it was. Ruby was kind of sad that she couldn't please her man as much as she'd done that first time. Mama never did think she was too smart, but Ruby knew that if she put her mind to it, she'd think of something.

Angel's got her mama's hair; Angel's three. Angel goes to all the pageants, Daddy keeps the boys away. Ruby runs a brush through Angel's hair and tells her daughter that if she's beautiful, everything will be just fine.

The Return of the Dark Children

Robert Coover

Robert Coover is an avant-garde novelist, critic and playwright lauded for experimental forms and techniques that mix reality and illusion, frequently creating otherworldly or surreal situations and effects. A leading proponent of hypertext fiction and metafiction, Mr. Coover is known as a true revolutionary in contemporary American literature and language. Mr. Coover's first novel, *The Origin of the Brunists*, won the William Faulkner Award in 1966. He is also the recipient of the Brandeis University, American Academy of Arts and Letters, National Endowment of the Arts, Rhode Island Governor's Arts, Pell, and Clifton Fadiman Awards, as well as Rockefeller, Guggenheim, Lannan Foundation, and DAAD fellowships.

I wouldn't have found this story without Jeffrey Ford, and I feel the anthology would have been the lesser for it. There have been other takes on the Pied Piper in fiction before, but Coover's version is one of the few that focuses on how the parents dealt with losing their children. Deeply disturbing, but beautifully written, Coover's story will haunt you.

When the first black rats reappeared, scurrying shadowily along the river's edge and through the back alleyways, many thought the missing children would soon follow. Some believed the rats might *be* the children under a spell, so they were not at first killed, but were fed and pampered, not so much out of parental affection, as out of fear. For, many legends had grown up around the lost generation of children, siphoned from the town by the piper so many years ago. Some thought that the children had, like the rats, been drowned by the piper, and that they now returned from time to time to haunt the town that would not, for parsimony, pay their ransom. Others believed that the children had been bewitched, transformed into elves or werewolves or a kind of living dead. When the wife of one of the town councilors hanged herself, it was rumored it was because she'd been made pregnant by her own small son, appearing to her one night in her sleep as a toothless hollow-eyed incubus. Indeed, all deaths, even those by the most natural of causes, were treated by the citizenry with suspicion, for what could be a more likely cause of heart failure or malfunction of the inner organs than an encounter with one's child as a member of the living dead?

At first, such sinister speculations were rare, heard only among the resentful childless. When the itinerant rat-killer seduced the youngsters away that day with his demonic flute, all the other townsfolk could think about was rescue and revenge. Mothers wept and cried out the names of their children, calling them back, while fathers and grandfathers armed themselves and rushed off into the hills, chasing trills and the echoes of trills. But nothing more substantial was ever found, not even a scrap of clothing or a dropped toy, it was as though they had never been, and as the weeks became months and the months years, hope faded and turned to resentment—so much love misspent!—and then eventually to dread. New children meanwhile were born, replacing the old, it was indeed a time of great fertility for there was a vacuum to be filled, and as these new children grew, a soberer generation than that which preceded it, there was no longer any place, in homes or hearts, for the old ones, nor for their lightsome ways. The new children were, like their predecessors and their elders, plump and happy, much loved, well fed, and overly indulged in all things, but they were more closely watched and there was no singing or dancing. The piper had instilled in the townsfolk a terror of all music, and it was banned forever by decree. All musical instruments had been destroyed. Humming a tune in public was an imprisonable offense and children, rarely spanked, were spanked for it. Always, it was associated with the children who had left and the chilling ungrateful manner of their leaving: they did not even look back. But it was as though they had not really quite gone away after all, for as the new children came along the old ones seemed to return as omnipresent shadows of the new ones, clouding the nursery and playground, stifling laughter and spoiling play, and they became known then, the lost ones, the shadowy ones, as the dark children.

In time, all ills were blamed on them. If an animal sickened and died, if milk soured or a house burned, if a child woke screaming from a nightmare, if the river overflowed its banks, if money went missing from the till or the beer went flat or one's appetite fell off, it was always the curse of the dark children. The new children were warned: be good or the dark children will get you! They were not always good, and sometimes, as it seemed, the dark children did get them. And now the newest menace: the return of the rats. The diffident pampering of these rapacious creatures soon ceased. As they multiplied, disease broke out, as it had so many years before. The promenade alongside the river that ran through the town, once so popular, now was utterly forsaken except for the infestation of rats, the flower gardens lining the promenade trampled by their little feet and left filthy and untended, for those who loitered there ran the risk of being eaten alive, as happened to the occasional pet gone astray. Their little pellets were everywhere and in everything. Even in one's shoes and bed and tobacco tin. Once again the city fathers gathered in emergency council and declared their determination to exterminate the rats, whether they were bewitched dark children or not; and once again the rats proved too much for them. They were hunted down with guns and poisons and burned in mountainous heaps, their sour ashes blanketing the town, graying the laundry and spoiling the sauces, but their numbers seemed not to diminish. If anything, there were more of them than ever seen before, and they just kept coming. But when one rash councilor joked that it was maybe time to pay the piper, he was beaten and hounded out of town.

For, if the dark children were a curse upon the town, they were still their own, whereas that sorcerer who had lured them away had been like a mysterious force from another world, a diabolical intruder who had forever disturbed the peace of the little community. He was not something to laugh about. The piper, lean and swarthy, had been dressed patchily in too many colors, wore chains and bracelets and earrings, painted his bony face with ghoulish designs, smiled too much and too wickedly and with teeth too white. His language, not of this town, was blunt and uncivil and seemed to come, not from his throat, but from some hollow place inside. Some seemed to remember that he had no eyes, others that he did have eyes but the pupils were golden. He ate sparely, if at all (some claimed to have seen him nibbling at the rats), and, most telling of all, he was never seen to relieve himself. All this in retrospect, of course, for at the time, the townsfolk, vastly comforted by the swift and entertaining eradication of the rats, saw him as merely an amusing street musician to be tolerated and, if not paid all that he impertinently demanded (there had been nothing illegal about this, no contracts had been signed), at least applauded—the elders, like the children, in short, fatally beguiled by the fiend. No, should he return, he would be attacked by all means available, and if possible torn apart, limb from limb, his flute rammed down his throat, the plague of rats be damned. He who placed himself beyond the law would be spared by none.

Left to their own resources, however, the townsfolk were no match for the rats. For all their heroic dedication, the vermin continued to multiply, the disease spread and grew more virulent, and the sky darkened with the sickening ash, now no longer of rats only, but sometimes of one's neighbors as well, and now and then a child or two. Having lost one generation of children, the citizenry were determined not to lose another, and did all they could to protect the children, their own and others, not only from the rats but also from the rumored dark children, for there had been reported sightings of late, mostly by night, of strange naked creatures with piebald flesh moving on all fours through the hills around. They had the form of children, those who claimed to have seen them said, but they were not children. Some said they had gray fleshy wings and could hover and fly with the darting speed of a dragonfly. Parents now boiled their children's food and sterilized their drink, policed their bedrooms and bathrooms and classrooms, never let them for a single minute be alone. Even so, now and then, one of them would disappear, spreading fear and consternation throughout the town. But now, when a child vanished, no search parties went out looking for it as they'd done the first time, for the child was known to be gone as were the dead gone, all children gone or perished spoken of, not as dead, but taken.

The city elders, meeting in continuous emergency session, debated the building of an impregnable wall around the town to keep the dark children out and hopefully to dam the tide of invading rats as well. This had a certain popular appeal, especially among the parents, but objections were raised. If every able-bodied person in town worked day and night at this task, it was argued, it would still take so long, that the children might all be gone before it could be finished: then, they'd just be walling themselves in with the rats. And who knew what made a wall impregnable to the likes of the dark children? Weren't they, if they really existed, more like phantoms than real creatures for whom brick and stone were no obstruction? Moreover, the building of such a wall would drain the town of all its energy and resources and close it off to trade, it would be the end of the era of prosperity, if what they were suffering now could still be prosperity, and not only the children could be lost but also the battle against the rats which was already proving very taxing for the community. But what else can we do? We must be more vigilant!

And so special volunteer units were created to maintain a twenty-four-hour watch on all children. The playgrounds were walled off and sealed with double locks, a compromise with the proponents of the wall-building, and all the children's spaces were kept brightly lit to chase away the shadows, even as they slept at night. Shadows that seemed to move by themselves were shot at. Some observed that whenever a child disappeared a pipe could be heard, faintly, just before. Whether this was true or not, all rumors of such flaunting of the music laws were pursued with full vigor, and after many false alarms one piper was at last chased down: a little boy of six, one of the new children, blowing on a wooden recorder. He was a charming and dutiful boy, much loved by all, but he had to be treated as the demon he now was, and so, like any diseased animal, he and his pipe were destroyed. His distraught parents admitted to having hidden away the childish recorder as a souvenir at the time of outlawing musical instruments, and the child somehow, inexplicably, found it. The judges did not think it was inexplicable. There were calls for the death penalty, but the city fathers were not cruel or vindictive and understood that the parents had been severely punished by the loss of their child, so they were given lengthy prison sentences instead. No one protested. The prison itself was so rat-infested that even short sentences amounted to the death penalty anyway.

The dark children now were everywhere, or seemed to be. If the reports of the frightened citizenry were to be believed, the hills about now swarmed with the little batlike phantoms and there was daily evidence of their presence in the town itself. Pantries were raided, flour spilled, eggs broken, there was salt in the sugar, urine in the teapot, obscene scribblings on the school chalkboard and on the doors of closed shops whose owners had taken ill or died. Weary parents returned from work and rat-hunting to find all the pictures on their walls tipped at odd angles, bird cages opened, door handles missing. That these sometimes turned out to be pranks by their own mischievous children was not reassuring for one had to assume they'd fallen under the spell of the dark children, something they could not even tell anyone about for fear of losing their children to the severity of the laws of vigilance now in place. Whenever they attempted to punish them, their children would cry out: It's not my fault! The dark children made me do it! All right, all right, but shush now, no talk of that!

There were terrible accidents which were not accidents. A man, socializing with friends, left the bar one night to return home and made a wrong turning, stumbled instead into the ruined gardens along the promenade. One who had seen him passing by said it was as if his arm were being tugged by someone or something unseen, and he looked stricken with terror. His raw carcass was found the next morning at the edge of the river. One rat-hunter vanished as though consumed entirely. Another was shot dead by a fellow hunter, and in two different cases, rat poison, though kept under lock and key, turned up in food; in both instances, a spouse died, but the partners were miraculously spared. When asked if the killing was an accident, the hunter who had shot his companion said it certainly was not, a mysterious force had gripped his rifle barrel and moved it just as he was firing it. And things didn't seem to be where they once were any more. Especially at night. Furniture slid about and knocked one over, walls seemed to swing out and strike one, stairsteps dropped away halfway down. Of course, people were drinking a lot more than usual, reports may have been exaggerated, but once-reliable certainties were dissolving.

The dark children remained largely invisible for all that the town felt itself swarming with them, though some people claimed to have seen them running with the rats, swinging on the belfry rope, squatting behind chimney pots on rooftops. With each reported sighting, they acquired new features. They were said to be child-sized but adult in proportions, with long arms they sometimes used while running; they could scramble up walls and hug the ground and disappear right into it. They were gaudily colored and often had luminous eyes. Wings were frequently mentioned, and occasionally tails. Sometimes these were short and furry, other times more long and ratlike. Money from the town treasury disappeared and one of the councilors as well, and his wife, though hysterical with grief and terror, was able to describe in startling detail the bizarre horned and winged creatures who came to rob the town and carry him off. Ah! We didn't know they had horns. Oh yes! With little rings on the tips! Or bells! They were glittery all over as if dressed in jewels! She said she was certain that one of them was her own missing son, stolen away by the piper all those many years ago. I looked into his eyes and pleaded with him not to take his poor father away, she wept, but his eyes had no pupils only tiny flickering flames where the pupils should be! They asked her to write out a complete profile of the dark children, but then she disappeared, too. When one of the volunteer guards watching children was charged with fondling a little five-year-old girl, he insisted that, no, she was being sexually assaulted by one of the dark children and he was only doing all he could to get the hellish creature off her. The child was confused but seemed to agree with this. But what happened to the dark child? I don't know. The little girl screamed, a crowd came running, the dark child faded away in my grasp. All I managed to hold on to was this, he said, holding up a small gold earring. A common ornament. Most children wear them and lose them daily. I tore it out of his nose, he said. He was found innocent but removed from the unit and put on probation. In his affidavit, he also mentioned horns, and was able to provide a rough sketch of the dark child's genitalia, which resembled those of a goat.

The new children pretended not to see the dark children, or perhaps in their innocence, they didn't see them, yet overheard conversations among them suggested they knew more than they were telling, and when they were silent, they sometimes seemed to be listening intently, smiling faintly. The dark children turned up in their rope-skipping rhymes and childish riddles (When is water not wet? When a dark child's shadow makes it…), and when they chose up sides for games of ball or tag, they tended always to call one of their teams the dark children. The other was usually the hunters. The small children cried if they couldn't be on the dark children's team. When a child was taken, his or her name was whispered among the children like a kind of incantation, which they said was for good luck. The church organist, unemployed since the piper went through and reduced to gravetending, a task that had somewhat maddened him, retained enough presence of mind to notice that the familiar racket of the children's playground games, though still composed of the usual running feet and high-pitched squealing, was beginning to evolve into a peculiar musical pattern, reminiscent of the piper's songs. He transcribed some of this onto paper, which was studied in private chambers by the city council, where, for the first time in many years, surreptitious humming was heard. And at home, in their rooms, when the children played with their dolls and soldiers and toy castles, the dark children with their mysterious ways now always played a part in their little dramas. One could hear them talking to the dark children, the dark children speaking back in funny squeaky voices that quavered like a ghost's. Even if it was entirely invented, an imaginary world made out of scraps overheard from parents and teachers, it was the world they chose to live in now, rather than the one provided by their loving families, which was, their parents often felt, a kind of betrayal, lack of gratitude, lost trust. And, well, just not fair.

One day, one of the rat-hunters, leaning on his rifle after a long day's work and smoking his old black pipe, peered down into the infested river and allowed that it seemed to him that whenever a child vanished or died, the rat population decreased. Those with him stared down into that same river and wondered: Was this possible? A rat census was out of the question, but certain patterns in their movements could be monitored. There was a wooden footbridge, for example, which the rats used for crossing back and forth or just for cavorting on, and one could at any moment make a rough count of the rats on it. At the urging of the hunters, these tabulations were taken by the town clerk at dawn, midday, and twilight for several days, and the figures were found to be quite similar from day to day, no matter how many were killed. Then, a little girl failed to return from a game of hide-and-seek (the law banning this game or any game having to do with concealment was passing through the chambers that very day), and the next day the rat numbers were found to have dropped. Not substantially perhaps, one would not have noticed the change at a glance, but it was enough to make the bridge count mandatory by law. A child, chasing a runaway puppy, fell into the turbulent river and was taken and the numbers dropped again, then or about then. Likewise when another child disappeared (he left a note, saying he was going where the dark children were to ask if they could all be friends) and a fourth died from the diseases brought by the rats.

Another emergency session of the council was called which all adult members of the community were invited to attend. No one stayed away. The choice before them was stark but, being all but unthinkable, was not at first enunciated. The parents, everyone knew, were adamant in not wanting it spoken aloud at all. There were lengthy prolegomena, outlining the history of the troubles from the time of the piper's visit to the present, including reports from the health and hospital services, captains of the rat-hunting teams, the business community, the volunteer vigilance units, school and toilet monitors, the town clerk, and artists who provided composite sketches of the dark children based on reported sightings. They did not look all that much like children of any kind, but that was to be expected. A mathematician was brought in to explain in precise technical detail the ratio between the disappearance or death of children and the decrease in the rat population. He was convincing, though not well understood. Someone suggested a break for tea, but this was voted down. There was a brief flurry of heated discussion when a few parents expressed their doubts as to the dark children's actual existence, suggesting they might merely be the fantasy of an understandably hysterical community. This argument rose and faded quickly, as it had few adherents. Finally, there was nothing to do but confront it: their choice was between letting the children go, or living—and dying—with the rats.

Of course it was unconscionable that the children should be sacrificed to save their elders, or even one another. That was the opinion vehemently expressed by parents, teachers, clergy, and many of the other ordinary townsfolk. This was not a decision one could make for others, and the children were not yet of an age to make it for themselves. The elders nodded solemnly. All had to acknowledge the rightness of this view. Furthermore, the outcome, based on speculative projections from these preliminary observations, was just too uncertain, the admirable mathematics notwithstanding, for measures so merciless and irreversible. A more thorough study was required. As for the bridge counts themselves, seasonal weather changes were proposed as a more likely explanation of the decline in the rat population—if in fact there had been such a decline. The numbers themselves were disputed, and alternative, unofficial, less decisive tabulations made by others, worried parents mostly, were presented to the assembly and duly considered. And even if the official counts were true, a teacher at the school argued, the vermin population was probably decreasing normally, for all such plagues have their tides and ebbs. With patience, it will all be over.

The data, however, did not support this view. Even those sympathetic with them understood that the parents and teachers were not trying to engage in a reasoned search for truth, but were desperately seeking to persuade. The simple facts were that the town was slowly dying from its infestation of rats, and whenever a child was taken the infestation diminished; everyone knew this, even the parents. The data was admittedly sketchy, but time was short. A prolonged study might be a fatal misjudgment. A doctor described in uncompromising detail the current crisis in the hospitals, their staffs disease-riddled, patients sleeping on the floors, medications depleted, the buildings themselves aswarm with rats, and the hunters reminded the assembly that their own untiring efforts had not been enough alone to get the upper hand against the beasts, though many of them were parents, too, and clearly ambivalent about their testimony. Those who had lost family members to the sickness and risked losing more, their own lives included, spoke bluntly: If the children stay, they will all die of the plague like the rest of us, so it's not as though we would be sacrificing them to a fate worse than they'd suffer here. But if they go, some of us might be saved. A compromise was proposed: Lots could be drawn and the children could be released one by one until the rats disappeared. That way, some might be spared. But that would not be fair, others argued, for why should some parents be deprived of their children when others were not? Wouldn't that divide the community irreparably forever? Anyway, the question might be purely academic. Everyone had noticed during the mathematician's presentation the disconcerting relationship between the rate of decrease of the rat population and the number of children remaining in the town. They want the children, shouted a fierce old man from the back of the hall, so let them have them! We can always make more!

Pandemonium broke out. Shouts and accusations. You think it's so easy! cried one. Where are your own? It's not the making, cried others, it's the raising! They were shouted down and they shouted back. People were called murderers and cowards and egoists, ghouls and nihilists. Parents screamed that if their children had to die they would die with them, and their neighbors yelled: Good riddance! Through it all, there was the steady pounding of the gavel, and finally, when order was restored, the oldest member of the council who was also judged to be the wisest, silent until now, was asked to give his opinion. His chair was wheeled to the illumined center of the little platform at the front of the hall whereon, behind him, the elders sat. He gazed out upon the muttering crowd, his old hands trembling, but his expression calm and benign. Slowly, a hush descended.

There is nothing we can do, he said at last in his feeble old voice. It is the revenge of the dark children. Years ago, we committed a terrible wrong against them and this is their justified reply. He paused, sitting motionlessly in the pale light. We thought that we could simply replace them, he said. But we were wrong. He seemed to be dribbling slightly and he raised one trembling hand to wipe his mouth. I do not know if the dark children really exist, he went on. I myself have never seen them. But, even if they do not, it is the revenge of the dark children just the same. He paused again as if wanting his words to be thoroughly understood before proceeding, or perhaps because his thoughts came slowly to him. I have, however, seen the rats, and even with my failing eyesight, I know that they are real. I also know that the counting of them is real, whether accurate or not, and that your responses to this counting, while contradictory, are also real. Perhaps they are the most real thing of all. He seemed to go adrift for a moment, his head nodding slightly, before continuing: It may be that the diminishing number of rats is due to the day-by-day loss of our children or it may be due to nature's rhythms or to the weather or the success at last of our hunters. It may even be that the numbers are not diminishing, that we are mistaken. It does not matter. The children must go. There was a soft gasp throughout the hall. Because, he said as the gasp died away, we are who we are. The old man gazed out at them for a short time, and each felt singled out, though it was unlikely he could see past the edge of the platform. The children will not go one by one, he went on. They will go all at once and immediately. That is both fair and practical. And, I might add, inevitable. He nodded his head as though agreeing with himself, or perhaps for emphasis. They themselves will be happier together than alone. And if we who remain cannot avoid grief, we can at least share it and comfort one another. Even now, if our humble suggestions are being followed, the children are being gathered together and told to put on their favorite clothes and bring their favorite toys and they are then being brought to the town square outside this building. As parents, turning pale, rose slowly from their seats, he again wiped his mouth with the back of his hand and his expression took on a more sorrowful aspect. I foresee a rather sad future for our town, he said. The rats will finally disappear, for whatever reason, though others of us will yet perish of their loathsome diseases, and our promenade will reopen and trade will resume. Even should we repeal the music laws, however, there will still be little if any singing or dancing here, for there will be no children, only the memory of children. It has not been easy for the town's mothers and fathers to suffer so, twice over, and I feel sorry for them, as I am sure we all do. We must not ask them to go through all that again. He cocked his old head slightly. Ah. I can hear the children outside now. They are being told they are going off to play with the dark children. They will leave happily. You will all have an opportunity to wave goodbye, but they will probably not even look back. Nor of course will they ever return. In the shocked pause before the rush to the exits, he added, speaking up slightly: And now will we at last be free of the dark children? He sighed and, as his head dipped to his chest, raised one trembling finger, wagging it slowly as though in solemn admonishment. No. No. No, my friends. We will not.

ACKNOWLEDGMENTS

This anthology would not exist without the assistance of a large group of people: Jason Williams, Jeremy Lassen, and Ross Lockhart of Night Shade Books for publishing this book; Kristopher O'Higgins of the Scribe Agency; Jeremy Welvaert for going above and beyond the call of duty; Chris Roberson for helping me get in touch with Bill Willingham; Bill Willingham for writing such a great introduction; my family for putting up with the late nights and the hair pulling; and Mark Teppo, Darin Bradley, and William Shunn for being unwitting mentors through this process. I have to single out John Joseph Adams as being a singular source of aid and information. This book would never have come together without John's willingness to answer questions and provide guidance.

There is also an obvious acknowledgment that needs to be paid to Ellen Datlow and Terri Windling for their amazing series of anthologies of retellings of fairy tales stories from which many of the stories in this anthology were taken. Not only did I discover these remarkable stories (and many more!) and a whole world of writers to investigate, the series lead me to people like Katherine Briggs, who has written a number of incredibly fascinating books about fairies and folktales, and Heidi Anne Heiner and her remarkable SurLaLune website of information about fairy tales and folklore. If you enjoy the stories in this anthology and you've never heard of Briggs or Heiner you do yourself a disservice by not going right now to learn more about them and their work.

And finally, there's a big thank you to all the people who recommended stories to me for the anthology: William Alexander, Megan Arkenberg, Jerrod Balzer, Lauren Beukes, Steve Berman, Brenta Blevins, Richard Bowes, Stephanie Burgis, Allison Campbell-Wise, F. Brett Cox, Jennifer Dawson, Simon Drax, Willow Fagan, Jeffrey Ford, Gary Gibson, Jed Hartman, Sumana Harihareswara, Merrie Haskell, Alex Irvine, Emily Jane, Michael Jasper, N. K. Jemisin, Kelly Jensen, Paul Jessup, Olga Karengina, Anna Kashina, Matt Kressel, Geoffrey A. Landis, Michele Lee, Marissa Lingen, Alex Dally MacFarlane, the late F. Gwynplaine MacIntyre (to whom this book is dedicated), Michelle Muenzler, Kate Nepveu, Mari Ness, Sarah Prineas, Mark A. Rayner, Lawrence Schimel, Ekaterina Sedia, Fraser Sherman, Ana Silva, Brad Sinor, David Sklar, Tesria, C.D. Thomas, Sarah Trowbridge, Panteli Vassiliki, Cynthia Ward, Ian Watson, Jonathan Wood, and Anne Zanoni. If I missed anyone, I apologize. Your contribution meant a lot to the compilation of this book.

// Acknowledgment Is Made for Permission to Print the Following Material:

"The Night Market" by Holly Black. © 2004. Originally published in *The Faery Reel: Tales from the Twilight Realm*, 2004. Reprinted by permission of the author.
"Black Feather" by K. Tempest Bradford. © 2007 K. Tempest Bradford. Originally published in *Interfictions*, 2007. Reprinted by permission of the author.
"The Price" by Patricia Briggs. © 1999. Originally published in *Silver Birch, Blood Moon*, 1999. Reprinted by permission of the author and her agent Linn Prentis.
"Bear It Away" by Michael Cadnum. © 2000 Michael Cadnum. Originally published in *Black Heart, Ivory Bones*, 2000. Reprinted by permission of the author.
"Mr. Simonelli or the Fairy Widower" by Susanna Clarke. © 2000. Originally published in *Black Heart, Ivory Bones*, 2000 and later in *The Ladies of Grace Adieu*, 2006. Reproduced by permission of Bloomsbury Publishing Plc.
"The Return of the Dark Children" by Robert Coover. Copyright © 2002 by Robert Coover. Published 2005 by McSweeney's Books. First printed in the *Harvard Review*, 2002. Reprinted by permission of Georges Borchardt, Inc., for the author.
"My Life As a Bird" by Charles de Lint. © 2000 Charles de Lint. Originally published in *Black Heart, Ivory Bones*, 2000. Reprinted by permission of the author.
"Ailoura" by Paul Di Fillippo. © 2002 Paul Di Fillippo. Originally published in *Once Upon a Galaxy*, 2002. Reprinted by permission of the author.
"The Black Fairy's Curse" by Karen Joy Fowler. © 1998. Originally published in *Black Swan, White Raven*, 1998. Reprinted by permission of the author.
"Big Hair" by Esther Friesner. © 2000 Esther Friesner. Originally published in *Black Heart, Ivory Bones*, 2000. Reprinted by permission of the author.
"The Root of the Matter" by Gregory Frost. © 1993 Gregory Frost. Originally published in *Snow White, Blood Red*, 1993. Reprinted by permission of the author.
The Troll Bridge" by Neil Gaiman. © 1993 Neil Gaiman. Originally published in *Snow White, Blood Red*, 1993. Reprinted by permission of the author.
"The Rose in Twelve Petals" by Theodora Goss. © 2002. Originally published in *Realms of Fantasy* April, 2002. Reprinted by permission of the author.
"The Red Path" by Jim C. Hines. © 2009 Jim C. Hines. Originally published in *Terribly Twisted Tales*, 2009. Reprinted by permission of the author.
"Pinocchio's Diary" by Robert J. Howe. © 2011 Robert J. Howe. Original to this volume. Printed by permission of the author.

"Blood and Water" by Alethea Kontis. © 2008. Originally published in *Orson Scott Card's Intergalactic Medicine Show*, Issue 9, July 2008. Reprinted by permission of the author.

"Stalking Beans" by Nancy Kress. © 1993. Originally published in *Snow White, Blood Red*, 1993. Reprinted by permission of the author.

"The Faery Handbag" by Kelly Link. © 2004. Originally published in *The Faery Reel: Tales from the Twilight Realm*, 2004. Reprinted by permission of the author.

"The Seven Stage a Comeback" by Gregory Maguire. © 2000. Originally published in *A Wolf at the Door*, 2000. Revised for the stage 2010. Reprinted by permission of the author.

"He Died that Day, in Thirty Years" by Wil McCarthy. © 2002 Wil McCarthy. Originally published in *Once Upon a Galaxy*, 2002. Reprinted by permission of the author.

"Hansel's Eyes" by Garth Nix. © 2000. Originally published in *A Wolf at the Door and Other Retold Fairy Tales*, 2000. Reprinted by permission of the author.

"Fifi's Tail" by Alan Rodgers. © 1999 Alan Rodgers. Originally published in *Twice Upon a Time*, 1999. Reprinted by permission of the author.

"Chasing America" by Josh Rountree. © 2006. Originally published in *Polyphony 6*, 2006. Reprinted by permission of the author.

"The Little Magic Shop" by Bruce Sterling. © 1987 Bruce Sterling. Originally published in *Isaac Asimov's Science Fiction Magazine* October 1987. Reprinted by permission of the author.

"Ashputtle" by Peter Straub. © 1994. Originally published in *Black Thorn, White Rose*, 1994. Reprinted by permission of the author.

"And in Their Glad Rags" by Genevieve Valentine. © 2009 Genevieve Valentine. Originally published in *Straying from the Path*, 2009. Reprinted by permission of the author.

"The Farmer's Cat" by Jeff VanderMeer. © 2005. Originally published in *Polyphony 5*, 2005. Reprinted by permission of the author.

"Like a Red, Red Rose" by Susan Wade. © 1993 Susan Wade. Originally published in *Snow White, Blood Red*, 1993. Reprinted by permission of the author.

"The Sawing Boys" by Howard Waldrop. © 1994. Originally published in *Black Thorn, White Rose*, 1994. Reprinted by permission of the author.

"The Rose Garden" by Michelle West. © 2004 Michelle Sagara. Originally published in *Little Red Riding Hood in the Big Bad City*, 2004. Reprinted by permission of the author.

"The Emperor's New (and Improved) Clothes" by Leslie What. © 1999 Leslie What. Originally published in *Twice Upon a Time*, 1999. Reprinted by permission of the author.

"Little Red" by Wendy Wheeler. © 1995 Wendy Wheeler. Originally published in *Snow White, Blood Red*, 1995. Reprinted by permission of the author.

"Introduction" © 2011 by Bill Willingham.

"Snow in Summer" by Jane Yolen. © 2000. Originally published in *Black Hearts, Ivory Bones*, 2000. Reprinted by permission of Curtis Brown, Ltd.

Night Shade Books Is an Independent Publisher of Quality Science-Fiction, Fantasy and Horror

ISBN 978-1-59780-220-8 $14.99 www.nightshadebooks.com

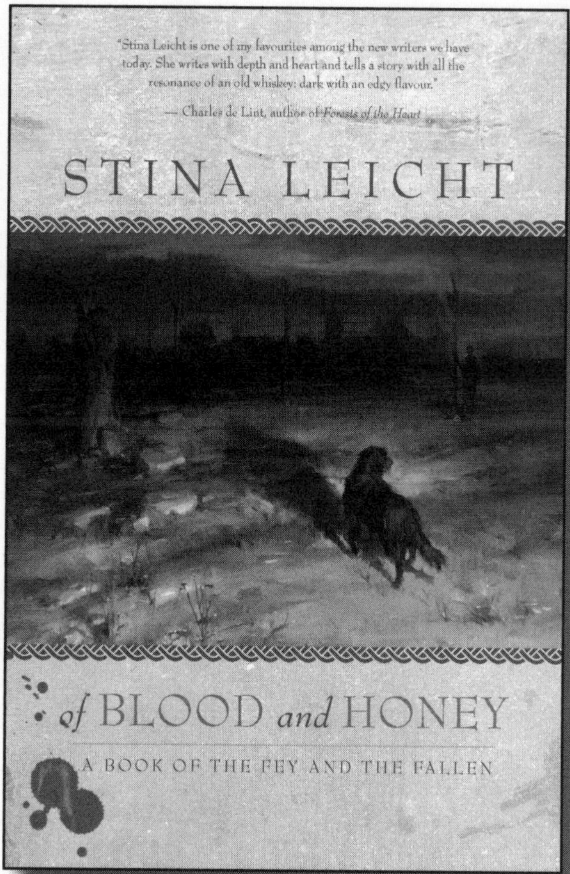

Fallen angels and the fey clash against the backdrop of Irish/British conflicts of the 1970s in this stunning debut novel by Stina Leicht.

Liam never knew who his father was. The town of Derry had always assumed that he was the bastard of a protestant—His mother never spoke of him, and Liam assumed he was dead.

But when the war between the fallen and the fey begins to heat up, Liam and his family are pulled into a conflict that they didn't know existed. A centuries old conflict between supernatural forces seems to mirror the political divisions in 1970s era Ireland, and Liam is thrown headlong into both conflicts.

Only the direct intervention of Liam's real father, and a secret catholic order dedicated to fighting "The Fallen" can save Liam... from the mundane and supernatural forces around him, and from the darkness that lurks within him.

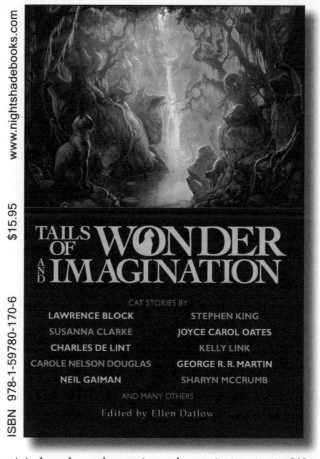

John Klima previously worked at *Asimov's, Analog,* and Tor Books before returning to school to earn his Master's in Library and Information Science. He now works full-time as a librarian. When he is not conquering the world of indexing, John edits and publishes the Hugo Award-winning genre zine *Electric Velocipede*. As of 2010, the magazine had been nominated for the World Fantasy Award four years in a row. In 2007 Klima edited an anthology of science fiction and fantasy stories based on spelling-bee winning words called *Logorrhea: Good Words Make Good Stories*. He and his family live in the Midwest.